LEONIDAS OF SPARTA

A PEERLESS PEER

LEONIDAS OF SPARTA

A PEERLESS PEER

Leonidas of Sparta: A Peerless Peer

Published by Wheatmark®
610 East Delano Street, Suite 104
Tucson, Arizona 85705 U.S.A.
www.wheatmark.com

International Standard Book Number: 978-1-60494-602-4
Library of Congress Control Number: 2011926396

rev201601

CONTENTS

INTRODUCTION AND ACKNOWLEDGEMENTS

LEONIDAS IS ARGUABLY THE MOST FAMOUS of all Spartans. Numerous works of art depict him. He was the hero of two Hollywood films. There is even a line of chocolate confectionery named after him. But no serious biography has ever been written, and what is most often portrayed is his death. Leonidas is remembered for commanding the Greek forces that defended the pass at Thermopylae against an invading Persian army. He is revered for refusing to surrender despite betrayal that made defeat absolutely certain. Thus Leonidas came to symbolize the noblest form of military courage and self-sacrifice. The events leading up to the three-day battle and the death of Leonidas with three hundred other Spartans and seven hundred Thespians at Thermopylae have been the focus of historians, writers, and artists from Herodotus onward.

But Leonidas was not a young man at the historic battle where he gave his life. He had lived close to half a century (if not more) and reigned for ten years before he took command of the Greek alliance defying Persia. It was those years preceding the final confrontation with Persia that made him the man he would be at Thermopylae. To the extent that we admire his defiant stand, learning more about his early life and tracing the development of his character is important.

Yet so very little is actually known about his early life that historians have been discouraged from attempting a biography.

Novelists, fortunately, enjoy more freedom, and what we do know about Leonidas' early life is enticing. In the first novel in this trilogy, *A Boy of the Agoge*, I built upon known facts about his birth and family situation and Sparta's unique educational system to construct a plausible picture of Leonidas' boyhood. In the second book of the trilogy (which can also be considered in its entirety as a three-part biographical novel), I focus on the next stage of his life, the years when he was a common citizen before he became a king. This is the period in which he married his niece Gorgo and gained experience in battle and politics. Building on the few known facts, listening to the sayings attributed to Leonidas and Gorgo, and knowing how Leonidas met his destiny at Thermopylae, I have written this novel. While based on all the known facts about Leonidas, Gorgo, and the society in which they lived, the novel goes beyond the bare bones of the historical record. It interpolates from these facts a reasonable hypothesis of what Leonidas and Gorgo might have been like and what they might have done, thought, and felt.

The characters that emerge are greater than the historical input. Leonidas is consciously portrayed as the quintessential archaic Spartan, because that is what he has become in legend. Gorgo, likewise, epitomizes that which set Spartan women apart from their contemporaries, without robbing her of individual traits and personality. The two principals are surrounded by a large cast of secondary, largely fictional characters, each of which is unique and complex. In short, this novel is quite candidly fiction.

This book, like its predecessor, contains a number of Greek terms that are specific to Leonidas' time and culture. Some of these terms are explained in context; all are defined in the glossary at the end of this book. Appendixes also outline the presumed organization of the Spartan army of the time and explain a number of other aspects of Spartan society.

I wish to thank Paul Bardunias for reading the manuscript with an eye to historical detail and accuracy that added an additional layer of authenticity to the manuscript. He meticulously pointed out even the slightest anachronism in phrase, image, or deed, and this manuscript has benefited immensely from his knowledge and insight. I also wish to thank my editor, Christina Dickson, for patiently correcting all my persistent spelling errors and inconsistencies in form and usage. Without their hard work, this book would not have been finished. I look forward to working with them on the last book in the trilogy, *Leonidas of Sparta: A Heroic King*.

LEONIDAS OF SPARTA

A PEERLESS PEER

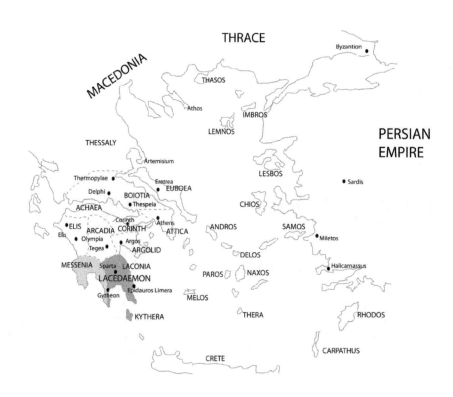

THRACE

MACEDONIA

Byzantion

THASOS

Athos

IMBROS

LEMNOS

PERSIAN
EMPIRE

THESSALY

Artemisium

LESBOS

Sardis

Thermopylae

Eretrea

Delphi

EUBOEA

BOIOTIA

CHIOS

Thespeia

ACHAEA

Corinth

Athens

ELIS

ARCADIA

CORINTH

ATTICA

ANDROS

SAMOS

Elis

Olympia

Argos

Miletos

Tegea

ARGOLID

DELOS

MESSENIA

Sparta

LACONIA

Halicarnassus

LACEDAEMON

PAROS

NAXOS

Gytheon

Epidauros Limera

MELOS

KYTHERA

THERA

RHODOS

CARPATHUS

CRETE

PROLOGUE

HOW DO YOU CHOOSE MEN FOR sacrifice? The question seemed to hang in the stagnant summer air, thick with the dust kicked up by the herds of sacrificial beasts driven into the city for the start of the Karneia. Leonidas had looked into the eyes of the passing steers, and they had looked back at him with recognition and understanding. "We are part of the same fraternity," the four-legged sacrifices seemed to say as they nodded their heads and moved on, flicking their tails at flies.

But Leonidas had come to terms with that. He had been selected by the Gods. He was a descendant of Herakles. He had taken up the burden of kingship with the conscious intention of leading Sparta to a better future. At the time, he had pictured different challenges, but he knew now this was his destiny. He would not fail.

But what about the others?

Leonidas looked about the empty streets. At this time of day on a holiday, the city seemed abandoned. School was closed and the children had been sent home to their families. The soldiers of Sparta's army were furloughed. The stalls in the market and the workshops of craftsmen were boarded up. The racecourses, palaestra, and gymnasia were deserted. Only on the edges of town and along the backstreets, behind the shuttered windows and closed doors of the houses, families rested in the noonday heat, gathering their strength for the athletic and choral competitions scheduled for later in the day and week.

Pleistarchos would be taking part in the sporting contests for the first time, and Agiatis had been selected to perform in one of the dances. Leonidas wanted to be there for them, cheering and applauding—but not if the price was that the next time they performed it would be as slaves for a Persian master!

The Persians were advancing faster than expected. Sparta could not wait until the end of the Karneia to deploy the army. By then it might be too late—particularly with half of Hellas in Olympia sticking their heads in the sand!

For a moment, the anger flared up in his chest. Two-thirds of the Gerousia and two of the ephors were as stupid as all the other Greeks, who thought Persia would respect the Olympic peace. They refused to see that this struggle was like none that had gone before. They refused to understand that Sparta and her allies could not wait for a convenient time to respond. They had to march *now*. If they didn't, they would come too late—as they had at Marathon.

The argument in the Council still echoed inside his aching head. The ghostly voices of his counterparts and the even more ghostly whispers of what he *should* have said had kept him from his sleep throughout the night. Leonidas felt acutely his failure to prevail in Council. He had mustered all the intelligence they had on Persian strength in men, ships, and horses. He had described in detail the terrain between the Persian host and Lacedaemon, underlining the advantages of a defense at Thermopylae. He had reminded them in gruesome detail of the costs of failure. And he had stressed until his throat was raw that too little, too late, could be fatal for all they held dear.

At length the Council agreed that Thermopylae, although far north of Sparta's sphere of influence and beyond the usual range of operation for her army, was the ideal place to make a stand. They agreed further to ask the Assembly to call up five classes of reserves, increasing the strength of the active army to three thousand men, and they agreed this force must deploy "as soon as possible." But the Council stubbornly insisted there could be neither an Assembly nor a deployment until the Karneia was over. To do either would be an insult to the Gods.

That was when Leonidas had taken a desperate gamble. Since a king could take the Guard anywhere he ordered, Leonidas had made a last attempt to force the Council's hand by announcing that if they would not give him the army at once, he would march north immediately with the Guard alone. To his dismay, they had agreed.

Three hundred men against a million!

Well, three hundred Spartiates and maybe twenty times that number of allies against the million.

A stray cat trotted purposefully but with lowered head along the side of the nearest barracks, disappearing into the next alley. A mouse hung limply from either side of her mouth. It was still twitching and left a trail of blood on the cobbles. Yet even a mouse, Leonidas thought, when cornered will stand and fight. They would fight.

Still, since he was allowed only three hundred Spartiates to hold Thermopylae until the army arrived after the Karneia, he couldn't take the Guard. They were all young men, the majority unmarried, all but a handful childless. Casualties were inevitable while waiting for the promised three-thousand-strong army to arrive. Leonidas did not want to have the extinction of any family on his conscience. So he had asked permission to substitute Guardsmen with volunteers from among the citizens with living sons. The ephors had agreed.

Leonidas expected about a thousand volunteers. He calculated that if he had a thousand men to choose from, he would be able to put together the balanced force he needed. He needed both canny veterans and enthusiastic youths. He needed men good at dogged defense, but also men capable of a quick sortie or a night raid. He needed men who cared more about the freedom of their families than their own lives, and that meant men who *loved* their families. He needed men who were prepared to die—but only after taking a heavy toll on the enemy first.

Oh, yes, he knew what he needed in principle, but how was he to select the men in fact? How was he supposed to walk down a line of men he'd known from childhood—men who'd sweated and bled beside him in the Argolid, youths he'd mentored as eirenes, men whose daughters sang and danced with his own, and men whose sons went to school with Pleistarchos—and decide who he was going to throw in front of the Persian host like bait?

Eventually, they would all fight. They would all take blood for blood when the time came. And every one of them—no matter whom he chose—was a trained soldier.

But because he'd failed to prevail in Council, only three hundred would be squinting into the sunlight to watch for the darkening that indicated a new volley of arrows. Only three hundred would stand in the murderous sun, shield to shield, while sweat poured from their straining bodies until their feet were churning mud rather than the dust of summer-baked earth. Only three hundred would be splattered with blood amid the screaming and the groaning of the dying—risking their limbs, their eyes, and their lives while the others remained with their wives and children, singing paeans and cheering the grape-runners and feasting in the nine ceremonial tents of the Karneia...

Was he supposed to pick the three hundred men like the helots chose a sacrificial lamb? For the beauty of their bodies? Was he supposed to select the best Sparta had to offer? Or should he do the opposite, and take with him those that Sparta could best afford to lose?

Leonidas realized he was not prepared to risk the latter. If he took the worst and they failed when it mattered most, Gorgo and Agiatis, no less than all the other women and children of Sparta, would pay the price. No, he had to take the best, to ensure they could hold Thermopylae until the full army reinforced them.

He picked up the pace and turned the corner to enter Tyrtaios Square, where he had requested the volunteers to muster. Instantly he was taken aback by the glare of sun reflected from bronze. The volunteers had drawn up across the square in full panoply. Although they stood at ease, with hoplons resting on their knees and helmets shoved back to expose their faces, they wore bronze fighting armor and red cloaks. The stiff black horsehair crests bristled proudly from their helmets.

Magnificent as they appeared, however, they were a mere handful—far fewer than the one thousand men Leonidas expected. Making a quick count of the ranks and files, he realized that exactly three hundred men awaited him. That could be no coincidence. Someone had made the selection for him. He frowned. He did not intend to let whoever it was get away with that! He would demand to see the complete list of volunteers.

He had been spotted. A voice called the men to attention. With remarkable unison for an ad hoc unit, the shields came to the ready. But Leonidas was now close enough to distinguish the faces under the helmets of the front rank. He halted abruptly, unable to move a step closer.

Dienekes stepped forward smartly. "Sir. May I present the three hundred volunteers of your Advance Guard, all fathers of living sons."

"And all my friends. Is not one of my enemies willing to defend Greece?"

"On the contrary, sir. Even your brother Brotus and your nephew Pausanias volunteered, but we turned them away."

"Just how many volunteers were there?" Leonidas looked at him suspiciously.

"1,359—not counting these men."

"You sent 1,359 men away?"

"That's right, sir."

"That was not what I told you to do," Leonidas told him in a low, ominous voice. "I told you to muster the volunteers—not to usurp my prerogative of selecting the Advance Guard." Leonidas was beginning to get angry, and his voice carried to the front rank.

"Leo." Alkander broke ranks to come up beside Dienekes. "It was our decision," he said softly.

"Who do you mean by that?" Leonidas snapped back. He did not want Alkander to come north with him. The risk was too great. He wanted him here in Sparta so he could be with Gorgo, Pleistarchos, and Agiatis when the news came that he was dead. He wanted Alkander to be the father Agiatis would need when she was old enough to marry. He was counting on Alkander standing by Gorgo and Pleistarchos in the years to come, when Pleistarchos would be a boy king with too few friends and too many enemies. And even after he was a man, Pleistarchos would need the advice of the utterly loyal and profoundly trustworthy Alkander.

"The men in the front rank," Alkander answered.

Leonidas glanced at them again. The others were still standing at attention, eyes fixed straight ahead. They were each in their way the best Sparta had to offer—even battered Prokles.

Alkander continued. "We chased Brotus away with insults and mocked Pausanias. A couple hundred others left with them to protest our rudeness. Then we put our case to the remaining men. We said they would all have the chance to show their courage soon enough. After all, the main body of troops—three thousand strong—is due to march out at the end of the Karneia; that's only ten days away. We pointed out that this Advance Guard was in effect your personal guard, and that it was only right that the men closest to you be allowed to serve in it."

"Why?" Leonidas asked. "Do you think I want to drag all of you down to Hades with me?"

"No. But nor will we let you face your death alone."

"I'll hardly be alone among three hundred Spartiates—not to mention the perioikoi and allies!" His distress made his deep voice rough; to the rankers at the back, who could not catch his words, it sounded like the growl of an angry lion.

Alkander did not answer directly; he just shook his head. "You may have made the decision to die on your own, but you have no right to tell us we cannot be beside you when it happens."

"Damn it! I am your king! I'll choose my own damn bodyguard!" Leonidas growled more loudly still.

"For the better part of your life you have been one of us—and proud of it," Alkander countered calmly. He had foreseen this reaction and was prepared with his arguments. "As Brotus has never forgotten or forgiven, you are king because we made you king. No matter how much of Herakles' blood runs in your veins, or how important it is to you that your son becomes the next Agiad king, you are *still* one of us. We turned away men who wanted to serve their *king*—in order to retain those who wanted to serve *you*. We will go with you, Leonidas, and die with you if need be, not as your subjects—but as your peers."

It took a moment for Leonidas to get sufficient control of his emotions to be sure he could speak. Then he nodded, took a deep breath, and managed to say: "You are right. The best part of my life I was no more and no less than a Spartan Peer."

CHAPTER 1

THE BOAR SLAYER

"But it would be exciting to go to war!" Chambias admitted to his friend Lychos with a grin, as he let his stallion stretch out his neck.

The two Corinthian youths, sons of leading families, were returning from Acrocorinth, where they had been trying to get a glimpse of the Spartan army. The Spartans had invoked the defensive treaty with Corinth and her other allies that required the allies to follow wherever Sparta led. For days now, allied contingents had been pouring into Corinth in response to the Spartan summons. Punctually at the start of the full moon, the Spartans themselves arrived.

As the sons of wealthy men on the brink of manhood, Chambias and Lychos were enrolled as ephebes in the Corinthian cavalry, and they took a keen interest in the impending war. They were particularly curious about the Spartans, because they flattered themselves that they understood "a thing or two" about things military, and the reputation of the Spartan army was unmatched anywhere in Hellas. They wanted to see it for themselves.

And so, taking their flashiest, most high-strung horses and carrying their javelins to underline their status as combatants, the two young men had set out to inspect the Spartan camp. They dressed in bright, patterned chitons to show off their status and wore their short cavalry capes, called chlamys, which fluttered straight out when they galloped. They also wore broad-brimmed leather hats and boots that laced halfway up their shins—all of the best quality.

They were soon disappointed. Unlike the troops of the other Peloponnesian allies, the Spartans set up a camp outside the fortress and then put up sentries that prohibited entry to the camp. Lychos and Chambias had been turned away.

The day being young and the weather good, however, they elected to ride around the back of the camp into the surrounding countryside to get away from the bustle, dust, and stink of the overcrowded city. They galloped a bit to wear off some of their frustration and energy, but now they let the horses walk on a long rein so they could talk.

Lychos didn't share Chambias' enthusiasm for the impending war because his father, the chief polemarch of Corinth, had returned from a symposium the previous night fuming that the Spartans wanted to invade Attica and bring down Athens' democratic government. Lychos eagerly explained to his friend what he had learned from his outraged father. "The only reason for this war is King Cleomenes' injured pride—or his loins. My father says there are rumors that Cleomenes has his eyes on the wife of the Athenian leader, Isagoras."

"I thought Cleomenes was married to the most beautiful woman in Sparta! Didn't people talk of a second Helen?" Chambias countered.

"That was years ago! She's had several children and is probably fat and sagging now," Lychos retorted with the wisdom of his nineteen years, his views reflecting the sum of his experience with women—his mother, grandmothers, and aunts.

Chambias nodded agreement, his experience being no different.

Lychos had inherited an interest in politics from his father, however, and he continued intensely, "What I don't understand is why the Spartans have kings at all—much less two!"

"That's because they are so pious," Chambias answered, echoing his father, chief priest of Apollo. "The Spartan kings are descendent from Herakles, after all, and to cast them out would be an insult to the Gods."

"But how can you have two men in command of an army? That would be like having two captains on a ship!" In addition to being the chief polemarch of Corinth, Lychos' father owned a trading empire that depended on a fleet of over a hundred ships. Lychos had sailed with his father often enough to understand command at sea. "What if the two kings disagree?" Lychos asked rhetorically, adding: "My father says the present Spartan kings hate each other. Demaratus is very jealous of Cleomenes, who he thinks is vain and takes too much credit for everything."

"Which one was which?" Chambias asked. "They all looked the same to me." Chambias was thinking of the ranks of Spartan soldiers, all wearing red chitons under their bronze armor and red cloaks. Even the shields were identical, all bearing the lambda of Lacedaemon— except for those of the officers, who had individual shields and whose crests, rather than black, were white or striped.

"The two kings wear cross-crested helmets," Lychos explained. "Crests that go from ear to ear. They rode ahead of the Guard. Cleomenes was on the right."

"On the white stallion?" Chambias could picture him now.

"Yes, exactly."

Chambias nodded thoughtfully. As the sons of aristocrats, they were both cavalrymen and connoisseurs of horseflesh. There was no denying that the Spartan kings had been exceptionally well mounted: something that surprised Chambias, who had always thought of the Spartans as infantrymen.

Lychos continued showing off his knowledge. "Cleomenes was on the flashier horse, but Demaratus won in the four-horse at the last Pythian Games, driving himself. My father predicts he will win again at Olympia."

"They weren't at all as I expected them to be," Chambias admitted, looking over at Lychos uncertainly. Lychos was a fair youth with even features over a lithe body, toned to perfection in the gymnasium. Chambias was plumper, poorer, and not so sure of himself. Chambias had only had one love affair, with a senior priest, and it had been rather short and vaguely humiliating. Lychos, in contrast, had attracted a very rich, witty Athenian, the kind of lover who drew attention and could be politically useful in the future. Chambias felt a touch of jealousy. Lychos had everything: he was the heir to one of the greatest fortunes in a rich city, he was attractive, he was healthy and bright, and his father adored him. Chambias had spent most of his life trying to keep up with Lychos and always coming up short.

"What do you mean?" Lychos asked.

Chambias shrugged uncomfortably. He didn't like Spartans. He didn't like men who were so disciplined and unimaginative, men who did everything in groups, men who were arrogant and sure of themselves. But until the day before yesterday, he had never actually seen one. "Well, you know, they're supposed to be taciturn and dour, but they were laughing and singing even as they marched. And today they flooded the bathhouses just like everyone else. They don't even—"

Chambias did not get a chance to finish his thought. Without warning his horse leaped sideways, reared up, and then spun around on its haunches, dumping Chambias on the ground. The youth landed on his knee with an audible crack and blinding pain shot upward, but he had no time for it. A massive boar with coarse black hair and gigantic tusks was charging at him with such force that the earth shook under his hooves.

Chambias saw his death in the malicious eyes of the black beast.

Lychos flung himself off his horse, grabbing his cavalry javelin from his back. He landed between the boar and his friend and hurled the javelin with all his strength. It was a gallant but futile gesture. The cavalry javelin was not designed to penetrate the tough hide of a boar.

The javelin glanced off the boar's shoulder without even slowing him down. An instant later, the boar rammed his tusks into Lychos' belly, and the youth crumpled forward.

The boar lifted his head with Lychos draped across his now bloody tusks and shook his head from side to side, with slow deliberate shakes. The beautiful gored youth screamed in agony as his guts were ravaged by each jerk.

Chambias staggered to his feet, screaming. He tore his chlamys off his back and tried waving it at the boar in a frenzied attempt to distract him. His friend's blood was splattering everywhere as he waved his arms and legs helplessly and screamed in agony from where he lay across the tusks of the boar.

Chambias could barely stand because of his shattered knee. His own two javelins had spilled onto the ground when he fell, and they now lay out of reach. He had no other weapon on him but his knife—a weapon far too short to damage a boar of this size, even if he could have thrown it with accuracy. He knew he had no chance of saving his friend or himself.

Out of nowhere, two men appeared on the run. They paused only long enough to grasp what was happening, and then reversed their spears from an underhand to an overhand grip and started to advance on the still-raging boar with a deliberation that made Chambias scream at them. "Hurry! He can't last much longer! Hurry!"

The two men ignored him. His friend was dying with each shake of the boar's massive head, yet the two men approached only with wary deliberation. Then, with a single exchanged glance, they raised their spears in a double-handed grip. The sun glinted briefly on the tips of the spearheads, and they brought their arms crashing down in almost perfect unison.

The boar saw the danger too late. He managed to toss the limp body of Lychos into the nearest gorse bush and turn toward his attakkers, but by then they had already struck. The boar crumpled onto his right haunch, but he was far from dead. Grunting his outrage, the boar shook his bloody tusks and flailed wildly with his forelegs, trying to regain his footing.

From out of the underbrush, the Spartans were suddenly joined by a hound. She threw herself into the fray without a second of hesitation. While the men impaled the boar, pinning it to the earth with the weight of their bodies, the dog leaped onto the boar's back and tried to bite down on the spine just behind the boar's head. Yet the wild animal was not subdued.

It was now evident to Chambias that his rescuers had not come prepared for boar hunting. They had attacked with ordinary war spears. These did not have a cross guard and were thinner, less sturdy. Chambias groaned in horror as he heard the unmistakable crack of a spear breaking.

"Hold him!" the man with the broken spear shouted urgently to his companion. The latter flung his weight forward onto his own spear a second time, while his friend stepped back, reversed his spear, and used the butt end—the "lizard sticker"—to gore the boar a second time.

This, too, failed to kill the boar, who with an abrupt, twisting motion sent the dog catapulting through the air. The man with the long spear gave a shout of alarm, realizing he could not hold the boar alone much longer, and instantly the man with the broken spear abandoned it to draw his sword.

With alarm Chambias registered that the sword was ridiculously short; yet that did not deter the swordsman. The man lunged forward and sideways—not, as Chambias expected, for the jugular, but to thrust the sword deep into the chest cavity of the boar from behind the right elbow. He ran the sword in all the way to the hilt. The boar thrashed violently with his forelegs one more time; but then the life went out of his eyes, and he sank down on the ground with an audible thud.

The two strangers were breathing very hard and dripping sweat, as they stared at the massive beast they had only with difficulty managed to dispatch between them. Their red chitons and himations identified them as Spartans, but Chambias could think only of his friend. "Lychos! Lychos!" He staggered forward, dragging his injured leg.

His cries and sobs of pain drew the attention of his rescuers, and they went over to where Lychos had been flung. Together they retrieved the bloody body from the bushes and stretched it out in the small clearing. The hound, having recovered from her toss into the bushes, ran frantically around them, panting in evident agitation.

"Is he alive?" Chambias asked, hobbling over painfully.

"Yes," came the succinct answer; and then as Chambias got nearer, he could hear and see for himself that his friend moaned and writhed, trying to stanch the bleeding and pain in his abdomen. The two Spartans, meanwhile, had opened Lychos' belt and sliced through the Egyptian linen of his bright yellow chiton to get a look at the wound. Chambias tasted his lunch in his mouth as his friend's innards slithered out of the gaping wound. The Spartan who had dispatched the boar deftly shoved the innards back inside the wound and held it firmly closed in a grip that made his knuckles go white under the blood of boar and man mixed together. Meanwhile, the other set about tearing one of their red cloaks into bandage strips and winding these firmly around Lychos' torso. Lychos screamed in pain as they worked, but they ignored him for his own good. When they finished, a broad band of scarlet held the wound closed and slowed the hemorrhaging. The second man then yanked off his himation and covered Lychos with it, tucking it in all around him and even winding it around his head so that he looked like a corpse, with only his face exposed.

"Will he live?" Chambias asked.

The Spartans looked over their shoulders and up at Chambias. To Chambias' astonishment, the two men looked hardly older than himself. One possessed the kind of classical features that the sculptors liked to put on statues of Apollo. He had short, curly blond hair, bright blue eyes, and gentle lips. Chambias couldn't help thinking he must have had lovers fighting over his favors as a boy. The other was less beautiful, with light-brown, coarse hair and green-gold eyes; but he was taller and broader than his companion, and he was the one who had thrust his short sword deep enough into the boar to kill it. It was also this young man who now replied. Without answering Chambias' question, he stated, "You'd better sit down and let us tend to your knee." He nodded toward Chambias' leg, already discolored and swelling.

Chambias didn't have the strength to protest. He hobbled toward a large boulder where, with an involuntary gasp, he eased himself down. The Spartans followed, the blond already working deftly to rip up what was left of his cloak.. When he started bandaging Chambias' knee, however, the pain was so intense that Chambias had to bite down hard to keep from crying out. Everyone knew the Spartans scorned anyone who couldn't endure pain with equanimity, and Chambias did not want to disgrace himself or his city. Despite what he wanted, however, he was trembling all over, and he could not hide that. He stammered an apology, "I don't know what's the matter with me. I'm not usually like this."

While the blond Spartan continued with the bandaging, the other tossed Chambias a smile and remarked, "Hopefully, you don't regularly get yourself nearly killed! Don't worry about it."

Chambias felt guilty for his earlier hostility to the Spartans. "Thank you. We would both be dead if you hadn't happened along."

The Spartan's expression grew serious again. "Your friend needs a surgeon. Are you from around here?"

Chambias nodded and then, remembering his manners, added, "I'm Chambias, son of Pytheas; and that is Lychos, son of Archilochos."

The Spartans flinched—as if they recognized the name—but made no comment. The spokesman merely asked, "Will your horses run home and alert someone about the accident, or should we chase after them?"

"Mine will probably run home. Lychos' mare is better about staying."

"I'll see if Beggar and I can catch her," the darker Spartan said to his companion; and whistling to his hunting dog, he set off. She was one of the big Kastorian hounds bred in Lacedaemon and admired around the world for their acute sense of smell, tenacity, and intelligence. This one had an ugly white patch on her face that would have made a wealthy Corinthian scorn her, Chambias noted; but she had certainly attacked the boar fearlessly. Now she bounded after her master with an eagerness and agility that was both beautiful and touching.

Chambias watched man and hound disappear behind the stunted trees and then turned awkwardly to the remaining Spartan. He found it disconcerting that because Spartans all wore identical red chitons and cloaks, he could not tell if this young man was rich or poor, the son of someone powerful or powerless. All his life up to now he had been able to tell at a glance whether he was dealing with someone of consequence. Now he could not.

The strange young man drew a goatskin off his back and offered it to Chambias, who accepted gratefully, only now conscious of how thirsty he was.

"Are you with the Corinthian army?" the Spartan asked.

"Not yet; we're both ephebes—in the cavalry," Chambias added proudly. "And you?"

"Peers," the Spartan answered simply—and inadequately from Chambias' point of view—but the yapping of a dog distracted them and they turned in the direction of the noise. A few moments later the other Spartan reappeared, leading Lychos' black mare. "If you can climb up on that rock," he suggested to Chambias, "you should be able to mount despite your leg."

Chambias looked at the indicated rock, at his friend's sweating and clearly nervous mare, and then down at his knee. The mere thought of trying to mount and ride with this knee made him nauseous. If the horse spooked and he was thrown a second time, it would be unbearable. He shook his head. "Can't either of you ride for help? I can direct you to my father's house. It is directly behind the Temple to Apollo; he is the chief priest." Chambias felt it was important that these Spartans realize that even though he was not as rich and important as Lychos, he was not a nobody.

The Spartans glanced at one another, and for a moment Chambias feared that neither of these ordinary Spartans was capable of riding; most Corinthian foot soldiers had little skill with horses. But then the darker of the two decided, "You had better go, Alkander. Beggar and I have a better chance of fighting off any predators."

The Spartan addressed as Alkander, the Apollo-like blond, frowned and seemed inclined to contradict, but the other Spartan shook his head once and the blond accepted the decision. Wordlessly and effortlessly he vaulted onto the mare before turning to Chambias for more instructions. These given, he trotted away, leaving Chambias with the other Spartan.

The latter went at once to check on Lychos, but quickly turned back to Chambias. "Could you lend your friend your chlamys? He is dangerously cold."

"Of course." Chambias was ashamed he had not noticed himself. The Spartans had, after all, already shredded one of their cloaks for bandages and wrapped Lychos in the second. Chambias pulled his short cape off his back and the Spartan came and took it from him. The Spartan seemed to hesitate as he noticed that the garment was of the finest wool, dyed a costly turquoise blue with an elaborate border. It was obviously very expensive. "It's all right," Chambias insisted. The Spartan returned to Lychos and, kneeling on one knee beside him, carefully tucked the chlamys around him.

Now that he was without a cloak, Chambias noted that the sun was behind the western mountains and it was getting chilly. He looked again at Lychos, who was rolling his head back and forth in evident pain. Chambias registered for the first time that it could take hours for someone to get here with a stretcher or litter. By then Lychos might be dead. Even if the bleeding had slowed, only the Gods knew what damage had been done to his insides. It would also soon be dark and, as the Spartan had already hinted, there were other wild beasts that might be drawn by the smell of blood.

The Spartan seemed to sense what was going through Chambias' head, because he abruptly broke in on his thoughts. "Alkander is a good rider, and we visited the Temple to Apollo this morning. He will find your father's house without trouble. Meanwhile, it's a fine night. The only thing I'm worried about is that the carcass of the boar may draw scavengers." He pointed to the wheeling vultures overhead. Finishing his thought, he added, "I'll build a fire to warm your friend, keep the wild animals away, and help Alkander find us again. Do you have bears or wildcats here?"

"No bears; but the cats, although small, are very vicious. And there are wolves, of course."

The Spartan nodded and started to collect dried wood, of which there was plenty. As he worked, Chambias noticed that he was holding his left arm cradled at his waist and worked only with his right hand.

"Are you hurt?" Chambias asked as the Spartan went down on one knee to build the fire, still cradling his left arm.

"The boar broke my left forearm as I went in for the kill. That's why I sent Alkander for help."

Chambias was ashamed to think that they were both suffering from broken bones and the other was doing all the work. "Can I help?" he asked.

"If you could strike the flint it would be a big help," the Spartan admitted with a smile.

Chambias looked blank.

"It's here. In my hip pouch." The Spartan indicated the leather pouch that hung from the right-hand side of his belt.

Chambias hobbled over, reached inside, and withdrew the flint; but the Spartan had to explain how to use it, and it took Chambias several tries before he managed to strike a spark. It took many more tries before he ignited the pile of dry leaves and twigs the Spartan had so carefully prepared. "I've never done this before," Chambias said, defensively excusing his obvious incompetence. "We have slaves to light our fires."

The Spartan nodded ambiguously, blowing gently to stoke the fire and then feeding it from the pile of kindling he had collected. Only after it was going solidly did he again turn his attention to the Corinthian, suggesting, "We might as well eat some of that boar."

This was going too far. It wasn't just that Chambias hadn't the faintest idea of how to go about flaying a carcass; he also did not think it a proper task for a youth of his station. No priest sullied his hands with the meat of the sacrificial beasts. His father employed no less than three professional butchers to flay and filet the sacrificial animals. They were skilled men, but all were slaves or former slaves.

The Spartan apparently understood his look of outrage and shrugged. "If you aren't hungry, we don't need to bother. I can go without." He then settled down to feed the fire.

"Have you spent the night out in the open before?" Chambias asked, glancing nervously at the darkening sky.

"Many times; haven't you?"

Chambias shook his head. It had never occurred to him that spending the night out in the open might be something desirable. In his experience only beggars, vagabonds, and shepherds slept out at night. It was a mark of status that he had never done so—but somehow this Spartan had managed to turn things on their head and make it sound like a deficit of some kind.

So they sat in silence, the Spartan feeding wood to the fire with one hand while his bitch gnawed happily at the carcass, and Chambias miserably listening to his best friend die.

———

"Master! Master! A catastrophe!" The slave burst into the symposium, at which his master was hosting a dozen important guests. "A horrible accident!" the slave gasped out.

Archilochos' symposia were famous for the quality of the food, entertainment, and conversation. Wealthy, well-traveled, and active in politics, Archilochos prided himself on employing the best cook and serving the most coveted wines in all Corinth, because he found both useful bait to pull men into his circle. He was, at the moment, exceedingly pleased to have snared one of the Spartan kings, Demaratus.

King Demaratus was not a handsome man. He was short and bowlegged and had a very large nose. Aware of this, he was not vain about his person, and he dressed in the practical clothes of a common ranker in the Spartan army, without any hint of his royal status. He braided his hair from the roots, as was custom, and bound the tips with tarred twine like marines did.

Despite the superficial differences between Demaratus and the elegant and cultured Archilochos, they found common ground in their opposition to the other Spartan king's plans to make war on Athens. They met tonight to discuss ways of putting an end to the ill-advised adventure; and Archilochos deplored the unprecedented interruption by a slave, who had no business in the symposium for any reason.

"Stop babbling!" Archilochos snapped.

But the old slave was Lychos' tutor, the man who had watched over him when he was growing up, and he was far too distressed to calm down. "Lychos has been gored by a wild boar. They say he was tossed around in the air, speared on the tusks of the boar, and his guts were spilling out of him!"

"Who says? What are you talking about?" Archilochos started to focus on what the man was saying.

"Master Lychos is bleeding to death! He—"

"Calm down and give me a coherent report!" Archilochos ordered, alarm rather than outraged propriety lending his voice an edge now.

Except for Demaratus, Archilochos' guests were all Corinthian aristocrats who knew their host's son personally; they exchanged horrified glances. Even Demaratus knew that his host had lost one son at sea, and guessed that this youth was Archilochos' heir.

"He was riding beyond Acrocorinth when his horse shied at the sight of a boar, and he was thrown to the ground, and the boar gored him!" The slave was trying desperately to get his master to do more than stare at him in horror.

"Where is he?" Archilochos demanded.

"In the forest on the far side of Acrocorinth!"

"*He's still out there?* But how did you hear of this?" Archilochos demanded, rearing up from his couch.

"A Spartan! A Spartan found him and killed the boar, but he could not bring him back. He only just managed to capture his horse and ride to Pytheas for help."

"Pytheas?"

"Of course!" The slave was impatient with his master's slowness.

"Lychos was riding out with Chambias, and Chambias gave instructions to his own house."

"Why didn't he come himself?" Archilochos demanded in terrified outrage, his anger an expression of his unfathomable fear. He could not lose this son, too!

"Chambias broke his knee falling from his horse. Lychos—"

"They left him out there? Bleeding to death?" Archilochos was grabbing for his himation, fumbling for his sandals.

Demaratus had never seen a grown man look so lost and helpless.

"The other Spartan and Chambias stayed with him, but we must get help to him! Master, we must get the surgeon!"

"Don't give me orders, slave!" Archilochos snarled back, and only then remembered his guests. He turned to them, unseeing, muttered "excuse me," and was gone, the old slave in his wake.

The other men collected their himations and slipped their feet into their sandals. The owner of the flute girls shooed them away while they chattered excitedly like a flock of chickens. Demaratus, however, took his time. While the other guests departed, he tied his own sandals and deliberately wrapped his thick red himation around him. Then he set his cross-crested helmet on the back of his head, the nosepiece on his forehead, and followed the others out.

Just as he had expected, he found his host in the outer courtyard. By now Archilochos had sent for a surgeon and ordered his horse tacked up, while a crowd of slaves collected in the courtyard carrying stretchers and torches. Demaratus moved calmly into the maelstrom of activity swirling around Archilochos.

Archilochos scowled in annoyance at the Spartan king. "Forgive me, but this must take precedence—"

Demaratus waved him silent. "Of course. I merely wanted to reassure you. If two Spartiates were at the scene of the accident, then you can be sure they did all that could be done to save your son."

"You don't even know who they were! How can you be so sure? Ordinary soldiers are no surgeons!"

"Spartiates have gone through the agoge, and they are huntsmen. They know how to treat wounds caused by sword and spear, claws, teeth, and tusks, as well as how to handle other common injuries from sprains to broken bones. They will have done all that is possible for your son until a surgeon can see him."

Archilochos was in no mood to listen, so Demaratus stepped back and let him go, but he called for his own horse. His helot attendant came forward at once. Having anticipated the order, he had already tacked both their horses. Demaratus swung himself easily onto the animal's back and followed in the wake of Archilochos' noisy party with their many torches.

They did not have far to ride. Just behind the huge Doric temple to Apollo, they stopped beside a house ablaze with torchlight. All the neighbors had lit torches, too, and slaves filled the street; the women crowded the balconies, shrouded in their shawls so that only their eyes showed.

Archilochos was met at the door by a man with long white hair and a flowing beard, who assured Archilochos that his own rescue party had set out a quarter of an hour earlier. Archilochos, however, was not calmed, and insisted on following them. Proceeding at a jogging pace along the long avenue leading out of the city to the west, they overtook the priest's rescue party before it had passed out of the city walls.

Demaratus tagged along, unseen by the others, until he suddenly cantered past the rest of the party to the young man who was leading them. He drew up sharply, his horse's hooves skidding on the paving stones. "Alkander! You? You killed this boar?"

"It was Leonidas who killed him. I merely pinned him down."

They gazed at one another while the Corinthians came to a halt in confusion.

"What is this? We must hurry!" Archilochos demanded, riding up beside Demaratus.

"Indeed. And so we shall. Let me introduce my wife's brother, Alkander." Demaratus hesitated, but then he decided it would eventually come to light anyway. "And you need not fear that your son's rescuers were 'ordinary soldiers.' The young man who killed the boar is none other than Leonidas, son of Anaxandridas and brother to King Cleomenes."

———

King Cleomenes was happy that Demaratus had accepted the invitation to dine with the Corinthian polemarch. As a result, he was the only king present in the royal mess. This gave him undivided precedence in everything, and enabled him to dictate what wine was poured and in what proportion it was mixed with water, to choose what songs (if any) were sung, and to dominate the conversation.

Cleomenes was thirty-three. Like his co-monarch, he was not a handsome man, though it was harder to say why. Cleomenes was tall, with no obvious blemish, and yet neither his features nor his limbs seemed to fit together gracefully. His forehead was too high, his chin too short, his shoulders too narrow, and his arms too long. He had huge knees over weak calves. But the worst of his features was the way his eyes wandered, never settling on anything for long and rarely looking another man in the eye—as if he wanted to avoid the disapproval, shock, or anger he so often saw reflected back at him in the faces of others.

Tonight was no exception. He either did not notice, or did not care, that the faces of the men around him were grim or disapproving as he drank more and more. Before too long the others had ceased drinking altogether, and shortly thereafter the five regimental commanders, the lochagoi, excused themselves one after the other.

This left only two priests. Yet even as Cleomenes addressed Asteropus, the younger of the two priests, Cleomenes did not actually look at him. Instead he gazed at the tent wall over his head. "So what's this I hear about the Corinthians having an omen foretelling *Corinthian* triumph?"

Asteropus had a long, acne-scarred face, and he stroked his short beard as he considered his king. Truth to tell, he did not like Cleomenes. He thought the king impious, arrogant, and excessively temperamental—although there was no doubt about his raw intelligence or his high level of education. Cleomenes could cut through superfluous discourse like a knife through butter, and he hated illogical argument. Asteropus had learned to admire that, because he was an ambitious young man and Cleomenes had offered him a rare opportunity—to be the Agiad representative to Delphi.

Asteropus had snatched at the opportunity not only because it was a fascinating job, but because he had not had many successes in his short life. He had been one of those boys and youths who, no matter how hard he tried, inevitably lost at contests of strength and speed and dexterity. He was short-sighted and had spent most of his years in the agoge slogging miserably behind the leaders. It had not helped that he could not sing or dance, either, as those were skills the Spartans admired at least as much as skill at sports. Only his wits had sometimes won him praise and respect; but once he had joined the army at age twenty-one, even that no longer mattered so much. In the army, skill at arms and physical courage eclipsed all other virtues. Asteropus hated army life.

Cleomenes had rescued him from it. He had reached out his bountiful hand and appointed Asteropus his representative to Apollo, and from that day forward Asteropus was exempt from military service.

Asteropus knew he had attracted the king's attention because, despite his mere twenty-five years of age, he had demonstrated an uncanny ability to read the omens of the Gods—as if his physical short-sightedness had been replaced with divine insight. When still in the agoge, for example, he had predicted a disastrous thunderstorm that killed five boys during the Phouxir. And just this spring he had foretold the disaster that would strike Cleomenes' half-brother, Dorieus. The latter in particular brought him Cleomenes' favor, because the Agiad king hated his brother Dorieus—even more than he hated his co-regent King Demaratus.

Dorieus had been born to Cleomenes' father, King Anaxandridas, by his first wife—but only *after* the ephors had made Anaxandridas take Cleomenes' mother, Chilonis, as his second wife. Although Cleomenes had been born a year before Dorieus, Dorieus had been such a paragon of manly virtue while growing up that there had been a faction that supported his claim to the throne, saying he had precedence since he was son to the first (and implicitly only legal) wife of their father. At Anaxandridas' death, the ephors and Council had ruled in Cleomenes' favor and the Assembly had ratified the decision—albeit by a small (and some said dubious) majority. Outraged by the slight, Dorieus left Sparta in a rage, unwilling to accept Cleomenes as his king. He first tried to set up a colony in Africa, but was expelled by the Carthaginians. The oracle at Delphi then advised him to go to Sicily and found a city in honor of Herakles, promising him success if he did so. With only a handful of Spartiates but many perioikoi, he departed. Cleomenes had been glad to see him go; but he also feared that Dorieus, if successful abroad, might return to challenge Cleomenes at home—this time with an army at his back.

Cleomenes' worries increased incrementally as news of Dorieus' successes filtered back to Sparta. Dorieus appeared to be growing richer and more powerful by the month. Soon alarming news arrived: Dorieus' Spartan colony was considered so powerful that he had been asked to assist in local wars—just as Sparta did at home. Cleomenes could picture the fleet that would land on the western shore of the Peloponnese and sweep through Messenia, rallying his subjects to revolt against him. His nightmares became so dreadful that Cleomenes consulted Sparta's senior seer, Hekataios, but the answer was ambiguous and unsatisfying. He had then, almost as an insult to the older man, asked Hekataios' barely mature son, Asteropus, what he thought Dorieus would do next.

In a flash of inspiration from his "second sight," Asteropus had replied without hesitation. "You have nothing to fear from Dorieus, for he will pay for transgressing the instructions of the oracle. He will leave his body on the field of honor and be in Hades as soon as he tries to use his arms for a purpose other than that assigned him by Apollo." Within just two months a ship from Sicily put in with the news that Dorieus was indeed dead, and Asteropus had secured the job of Cleomenes' personal representative at Delphi.

Unfortunately, he had no flash of inspiration now. The Gods were fickle, after all, and he did not have an answer that would calm Cleomenes' unease.

"Well?" the king prodded impatiently, reaching again for his wine. "What is all this nonsense about? Our allies share our victories and defeats. The Corinthians cannot win a victory without us. Surely they can see that?"

"Undoubtedly—if only the signs we had were not so adverse."

"So why are they adverse?" Cleomenes demanded.

Asteropus was relieved by the arrival of a helot messenger. The man entered the tent and respectfully came to a halt before Cleomenes, his eyes down and his hands by his side.

"What is it?" Cleomenes demanded irritably.

"The surgeon sent me to inform you that your brother has been injured by a wild boar, sir."

"Which brother?" Cleomenes wanted to know. Even with Dorieus dead, he still had two younger half brothers, likewise sons of his father's first wife, and so from Cleomenes' point of view untrustworthy.

"Leonidas," the helot answered.

"Oh. Will he live?"

The helot glanced up, startled. "He has only a broken arm, sir."

"So why the fuss?"

The helot treated the question as rhetorical, and withdrew.

"Fool!" Cleomenes commented to Asteropus with contempt. "He shouldn't be out hunting boar if he doesn't know how to keep out of their way." Cleomenes reached again for his wine.

But in that moment Asteropus had one of his flashes of inspiration, and he warned Cleomenes, "Do not underestimate Leonidas. He may prove far more dangerous to you than Dorieus ever was."

"Little Leo? Nonsense. Cleombrotus is the one to watch. He covets my throne. Leonidas is as docile as a lamb. Lambonidas would be a better name for him!" Cleomenes liked his own joke and laughed at it.

Asteropus let it go. He did not feel it was his job to contradict the king. He had done his duty by warning him.

———

Cleombrotus was Leonidas' twin brother. The news that Leonidas had killed a wild boar reached him in his tent, where he was dicing with his seven mess-mates. Hearing that Leonidas had broken an arm in the encounter, Cleombrotus snorted and remarked contemptuously, "Lucky someone was around to rescue him from worse harm!"

When they were little, Cleombrotus had been significantly bigger and stronger than Leonidas and had used both advantages to bully his brother. In the agoge they had been separated and rarely met; but Cleombrotus continued to excel, particularly at boxing, eventually winning in the youth competitions at Olympia. He had won the honors at the Feast of Artemis Orthia as well, and he carried that title and trophy for life. Throughout these early years he had looked down on his smaller twin, sneering at him for failing to be elected herd leader and for failing to win honors or Olympic laurels. But last year everything had turned upside down and bitter, when both youths were twenty-year-old instructors at the agoge, called eirenes. Cleombrotus lost his command after a case of unprecedented insubordination by his unit, resulting in its being turned over to his twin brother.

"That's not what Alkander is saying," noted the man who had brought Brotus the news.

"Alkander? That trembler! He p-p-probably shit at the sight of the b-b-boar and didn't notice what was g-g-going on." Cleombrotus imitated the stutter that Alkander had had as a boy, to the amusement of his companions.

When they stopped laughing, however, the messenger put him right. "You'd better come see the carcass first, Brotus. It's huge! It took four men to carry it, and the tusks are at least two feet long. Alkander held it down with his spear while Leonidas stabbed it with his sword. They weren't hunting and didn't have a proper boar spear with teeth—just their standard-issue war spears, which were still in it when Demaratus got there."

"Demaratus? What the hell was Leonidas doing hunting with the Eurypontids?" Cleombrotus made it sound like treason.

No one bothered to answer, because everyone knew that Leonidas and Alkander had been friends since boyhood, long before Alkander's sister married Demaratus. "Come and see for yourself," Brotus' comrade suggested sensibly, and they all scrambled out of the tent to take a look.

Torches were forbidden in a Spartan camp, no less than in the city of Sparta, but they didn't have much trouble finding the source of commotion. It was, after all, not yet late, and most men had not gone to sleep. The arrival of Demaratus with this immense trophy had brought many men out of their tents, and word had rapidly spread that Leonidas had killed it.

Despite himself, Cleombrotus was impressed. The boar was the largest specimen he had ever seen. Nor could he comfort himself that the beast was old, decrepit, or lame. Not a hair was gray, and there was not one other injury on its body besides the ones sticky with fresh blood. The boar was muscular, with bristling black hair and eyes that—even in death—were full of power and contempt for lesser creatures. How could Little Leo have vanquished such a beast? For the first time in his life, it occurred to Brotus that Leonidas might have qualities he had failed to notice up to now. Leonidas, he registered, might be more than he appeared to be.

CHAPTER 2

SPARTA AND HER ALLIES

LEONIDAS WAS NOT COMFORTABLE WITH THE attention he suddenly received. All his life he had lived in the shadow of his more prominent elder brothers. Cleomenes had been king since Leonidas was a child of eight, and kings were—whether one liked them or not—representatives of the Gods. Dorieus, on the other hand, had been exalted not by his position—he had been sent through the agoge just like an ordinary citizen's son—but by his innate superiority. Dorieus had simply been the best at everything. Even Brotus, until the incident when they were eirenes, had drawn more praise than Leonidas. Brotus was a Victor of Artemis Orthia, and he had taken the wreath in youth boxing at Olympia. But suddenly everyone, even strangers, stopped Leonidas to congratulate him for slaying the boar.

Leonidas didn't know how to react. He had not given much thought to what he was doing when he'd gone in for the kill. It had seemed the only way to resolve the situation positively. He certainly had not known the identity of the youths he was rescuing, and did not feel he should take credit —as one of the lochagoi had put it—for "single-handedly making the Corinthian chief polemarch indebted to Spartan arms." Mostly he was distressed because his company commander, Diodoros, had ordered him to pack his things and return to Sparta at once; until his injured arm healed, he was not fit for active service in the Spartan army.

Leonidas tried to argue. "It's just a fracture, sir," he pointed out, flapping the bandaged and splinted arm to show he didn't mind moving it. "I'm sure it will heal rapidly."

"Certainly, in six to ten weeks," Diodoros agreed; "but not before we march out tomorrow. You return to Lacedaemon today."

Leonidas snapped for air like a fish out of water. This was the first time the Spartan army had deployed since he'd come of age. He couldn't bear the humiliation of being sent home. "But, sir—"

Diodoros raised his eyebrows. It was not common for junior rankers, men barely out of the agoge, to question the orders of someone as exalted as a company commander. Nor did Diodoros know Leonidas well; there was a section leader and enomotarch between Leonidas and Diodoros, so their contact had been minimal up to now. Still, Diodoros did not cut Leonidas short: after all, he was a citizen, an equal, a Spartan Peer. He had an equal voice in the Assembly along with every other Spartan Peer, from ranker to lochagos. He had a right to state his mind.

"Even if I can't hold a hoplon, there must be some way I could be of use. I can still ride, for example, and could do reconnaissance?" Leonidas suggested hopefully.

Diodoros nodded once. "Maybe, but I don't command the light cavalry. All reconnaissance is conducted by the perioikoi. If you wish to assist, you'll have to ask your brother or Demaratus. Only the kings have command authority over the perioikoi."

Leonidas did not like that answer. As an Agiad, it would be humiliating for him to ask a favor of the rival royal house, the Eurypontids. As the son of his father's first wife, however, he had been raised to look down on Cleomenes—and Cleomenes returned the compliment. The brothers were not friendly. But these were his problems, and since there was nothing more he could say to or expect from Diodoros, he nodded and left the company command tent.

Outside he stood for a moment, debating what to do next. He had to seek out one of the kings or go home. With his broken arm he knew he couldn't stand in the line of battle, and so would have no opportunity to test either his skills or his courage whether he stayed with the army or not. But the Spartan army was about to cross the Isthmus of Corinth, and Leonidas had never been north of the Isthmus. He had been looking forward to seeing something beyond

the Peloponnese, and was particularly fascinated by the prospect of
seeing Athens.

Athens was the largest city in Greece. It had a population roughly
five times that of Sparta and twice that of Corinth. It was wealthy,
audacious, and increasingly aggressive. It dominated the slave and
olive-oil trade and was challenging Corinth's primacy in pottery. Most
intriguing to Leonidas, however, was that it had recently revised its
constitution again, reducing the influence of the landed aristocracy
still further, while increasing the franchise and giving more power to
the poor, often illiterate, classes. These changes had provoked lively
debate in the Spartan messes.

Leonidas, like all his fellow citizens, had learned about Solon's
constitution for Athens while still in school. In school the boys
were expected to understand and expound upon the differences
between the laws Lycurgus had given Sparta fifty Olympiads ago and
Solon's laws, which were half as old. Lycurgus, they had learned, had
addressed the injustice of great disparities in wealth by introducing a
land reform that guaranteed each Spartan citizen an estate, or kleros,
large enough to support him and his family. Thus, while disparities
of wealth remained, every citizen was by definition a landowner; and
Lycurgus' laws discouraged displays of wealth, so that even those
who had it did not flaunt it. Furthermore, Lycurgus' reforms ensured
that every Spartan enjoyed the same high standard of education:
fourteen years in the public school, or agoge, run by the state. Finally,
on gaining citizenship, Spartans did not pursue diverse trades and
personal economic interests, but were first and foremost hoplites, all
in the service of Lacedaemon.

In Athens, in contrast, Solon's reforms aimed not at equal-
izing wealth but just at removing the worst abuses, such as the then
common practice of reducing indebted citizens to slaves. He had not
attempted to make the citizens of Athens equals, nor ensured that all
enjoyed the same education. On the contrary, Leonidas had heard,
wealthy Athenian boys and youths had private tutors and trainers,
while the sons of poorer citizens received no education at all and
were consequently illiterate. Last but not least, Athenian citizens were
not professional soldiers, but were free to pursue any profession they
liked. The poorest were craftsmen—potters, tanners, cobblers, and

smiths; the rich did nothing at all except accumulate, display, and consume their wealth. The wealthy bought this freedom—or rather, reduced the risk of uprisings on the part of the poor—by supporting public projects such as temples, festivals, and plays, and by (and this was the key feature of Solon's reforms) giving poor citizens, even those with no land and no literacy, a say in government.

All this Leonidas knew from his years in the agoge, but the reforms to the Athenian constitution under Kleisthenes had occurred too recently for inclusion in the agoge curriculum. Leonidas, like his fellows, knew about these latest reforms only from the incomplete and sometimes incoherent reports of strangers who had come through Sparta after visiting Athens. There was something about the creation of seven new tribes that were then represented in the Areopagos, but also much talk about country bumpkins having a say in Assembly; about offices rotating among people based on the calendar rather than on merit; and courts in which the idle poor, rather than educated magistrates, passed judgment. These features sounded very peculiar, and Leonidas had been looking forward to seeing the effects of them himself.

Since Leonidas did not want to go home without seeing more of the world, he was going to have to try his luck with one of the kings. If he went to Demaratus, however, the Eurypontid would only look astonished and ask what his brother had said; so Leonidas resigned himself to talking to his brother. He drew a deep breath and directed his steps to his brother's tent.

Two members of the king's personal bodyguard stood watch in front of Cleomenes' tent, and they made no move to stop Leonidas from entering. Any Spartan citizen had the right to seek an audience with either of his kings, let alone the king's younger half brother.

A Spartan king was a commander, a high priest, and a very, very wealthy man. These facts were reflected in the larger size of the tent, the bloody altar near the door, and the murals painted on the surface of the canvas depicting the deeds of Herakles and scenes from the *Iliad*. But ever since the Spartans had accepted the Lycurgan constitution fifty Olympiads ago, conspicuous consumption and the ostentatious display of wealth was scorned—even by the kings. Thus the tent in which his brother resided on campaign was simply furnished.

There were woven straw mats on the floor, four identical reed beds for the king and his immediate entourage, and some folding stools and wooden chests for clothes and utensils. That was all. Leonidas stopped just inside the open flap and waited respectfully for his brother to notice him.

Cleomenes was reading a wax tablet. He did not interrupt himself. When finished, he set the tablet down and looked to the entrance. "Well, if it isn't my little brother Leo!" Cleomenes exclaimed, as he leaned back and considered Leonidas with narrowed, alert eyes.

"Sir," Leonidas responded.

"Come in," Cleomenes invited, gesturing with his hand. "Let me get a better look at the little hero."

Leonidas had seldom hated his brother more than at that moment; but he had been raised in the agoge, and he knew how to hold both his tongue and his feelings in check. He could hear the voices of his instructors and his eirenes echoing in his head: "Speaking in anger is as dangerous as fighting in anger." "Anger will expose your vulnerabilities." "Anger makes you careless." "Always keep a tight rein on your emotions." "Ride emotions like a powerful stallion, controlling them for your own aims."

Cleomenes did not like what he saw, either. Leonidas was anything but "little." He was at least as tall as Cleomenes himself, possibly a fraction taller. He had light brown hair that was thick, coarse, and slightly wavy, but cut short, because Leonidas was only twenty-one and on active service. (He would not have the privilege of growing out his hair in the Spartan fashion until he went off active service at thirty-one.) He was tanned, broad-shouldered, and unpleasantly reminiscent of Cleomenes' most hated rival: the darling of the city throughout his youth, Leonidas' older brother Dorieus.

"So, what brings you here, little brother?" Cleomenes asked.

"I've come to ask permission to serve with the perioikoi reconnaissance—since I can't lift a hoplon on account of this fracture." He lifted his splinted arm off his chest and then rested it on his rib cage again.

"Serve with the *perioikoi*? An Agiad prince? But then, you never were very proud, were you?"

Leonidas held his breath, repeating to himself the lessons of his youth: "The better man endures insults rather than distributing them." "Insults are a sign of weakness."

Cleomenes could sense he was not having the effect he wanted. Leonidas was not rising to the bait and getting agitated, as either of his brothers would have done. "You're not like your brother Brotus, are you?"

"No, sir."

Suddenly Cleomenes threw back his head and laughed, admitting, "I don't like him, either! I wonder: does that make us allies?" Leonidas looked at him uncertainly but said nothing. Cleomenes waited, but Leonidas remained silent, so Cleomenes asked, "So you want to come with us?"

"Yes, sir."

"Good. Then come along. You can assist the priests. They are always complaining that they have too much to do."

"Yes, sir."

"Find Asteropus and tell him I have assigned you to be his assistant."

"Yes, sir," Leonidas replied dutifully, while inwardly asking Kastor (whom he viewed as his special protector) what he had done to deserve this. The maiden that Leonidas was in love with, Eirana, had told him just last year that she preferred Asteropus, and ever since then he viewed the young seer with antipathy—despite hardly knowing him.

———

"Another cock!" Asteropus ordered anxiously, his face red and running with sweat, while blood soiled his long chiton.

"We've killed two already," Leonidas pointed out.

"Just bring another cock!" Asteropus snapped back, adding, "A black one, and be sure he's clean!"

That could only mean the signs were bad, Leonidas concluded, making his way toward the back of the camp where the helots were camped with the supply wagons and livestock. Around him the light of a thousand campfires lit up the night, and a low murmur like the humming of deep-pitched bees filled the air. They had reached

Eleusis, inside Attica. The allies were no longer in doubt about the target of this campaign, and Leonidas gathered from remarks he'd overheard that they were not pleased.

Athens was the most populous of the Greek cities, and one of the most powerful. She could field twenty thousand hoplites, it was said, and she had twice that many light troops. Attacking Athens was not something to be done lightly, even if one had a good reason for doing so—which, as far as Leonidas could see, the Spartans and their allies did not.

Only a few years ago, his brother Cleomenes had helped drive out the Athenian tyrant Hippias—a move consistent with Sparta's long-standing policy of toppling tyrants. Furthermore, important Athenian exiles had requested Spartan intervention, and the oracle at Delphi had ordered Sparta to drive Hippias out. But things were different now. There was no tyrant in Athens, and no judgment from Delphi in their favor, either. Leonidas was not surprised that the allies were angry—or that the signs were bad.

He reached the supply camp with only Beggar at his heels, trotting along happily; it being so late, he had already sent his attendant Mantiklos to bed. Here, too, the helots had rolled themselves in their blankets and stretched out beside the fires. He had to go from bundle to bundle in search of the helot in charge of the sacrificial animals.

The position of keeper of the sacrificial beasts was a prestigious and hereditary one among helots. The men who held it were specialists. They not only had the right to commandeer any animal they thought particularly beautiful and suited for the honor of serving as a sacrifice to the Gods; they also bred animals especially for the purpose. They were proud of their animals—and, not surprisingly, a little protective of them as well.

"What?" the old helot growled at Leonidas. "Another one? What do they want to do? Slaughter them all in a single night? Don't they see that if the Gods say "no" they mean "no," and the slaughter of every cock in Lacedaemon will not change that?"

Leonidas personally agreed with the helot, and he envied him the right to say what he thought, to refer to them as "they" and feel he was no part of them. "They," however, was Leonidas' brother. Leonidas nodded ambiguously, and the old helot sighed. He knew that Leonidas had no more power to change things than he did. He flung off his blanket, and with an audible groan dragged himself to his feet. He stuffed his feet into the old, muddy shoes beside his pallet and, muttering to himself, went in search of a new victim.

Leonidas waited, absently patting Beggar's head, as she stood with her tongue hanging out one side of her mouth. He found himself looking out at the camp spread out across the valley, noting that it was easy to identify the part of the camp occupied by the Spartans. The Spartans laid out their campfires in lines and at regular intervals. The allies, in contrast, were scattered unevenly—like the stars. They were louder, too, Leonidas registered, and restless. You could see men moving around the fires in large groups, and horses cantered back and forth. He frowned. Even if the allies were less disciplined, there was no real excuse for the amount of activity he could detect.

"Here!" The helot thrust a burlap sack at him. It was tied closed with twine at the neck, but the body was leaping and wriggling. The cock was wildly trying to break free.

Leonidas thanked the old man and took the sack in his good hand. He started back toward his brother's tent, Beggar habitually sniffing the ground, her tail upright and wagging slowly in general contentment as they went. The Spartan camp seemed like an island of calm in a growing storm, Leonidas thought—and then a horse came galloping straight at him. He had to jump aside, almost losing his balance because his broken arm hindered him and the cock was struggling so violently. He glanced up just in time to see that the rider was King Demaratus.

Leonidas wondered why the Eurypontid king was riding out of the Spartan camp in the middle of the night, and he turned to follow him with his eyes. Demaratus hauled his horse to the right, toward the Corinthian camp. Leonidas watched in astonishment as he plunged in among the fires. He saw men make way for him as he rode deeper and deeper into the camp. Then abruptly he drew up before a particularly large tent lit from the inside, and the Corinthians swarmed around him. Demaratus jumped down and disappeared inside the tent.

Leonidas considered this a moment, then continued on his way. He turned the sack over to Asteropus. Asteropus snatched it from him and tore it open to remove the cock and inspect it critically. Leonidas had the feeling he was hoping to find something wrong with the animal, so he could send Leonidas back to the perimeter again. Yet he was also in a hurry and asked irritably, "What kept you? The king has been asking after the cock every five minutes."

Leonidas treated the question as rhetorical and withdrew. Outside he looked again toward the Corinthian camp. Things seemed to have calmed down somewhat, though there were still large numbers of men around the tent that Demaratus had entered.

Leonidas considered what he had seen and could not really make sense of it. Not from here. He looked down at Beggar. Seated beside him, she at once looked up and met his gaze. "Shall we go and see what all the fuss is?" Leonidas asked her. She jumped to her feet, her tail wagging, as if to say: Whatever you want to do, master!

Leonidas walked away from the Spartan camp and entered the Corinthian one. In the darkness, no one could see the color of his himation. He wrapped the himation close, as if he were cold, to cover his splinted arm, and joined the back of the crowd.

"—I tell you, they don't have the right!"

"The Treaty says we must follow the Spartans wherever they lead!"

"*If* they're threatened!"

"Where does it say that?"

"Who in Hades do you think decides if they're threatened? The f**ing Spartans, I tell you!"

Leonidas recoiled at the vulgar language. Expletives, he had been raised to think, were always superfluous. They added no value to any communication. Even adjectives and adverbs, while considered somewhat frivolous in Laconic speech, provided additional information, but expletives did not. Expletives were merely outbursts of uncontrolled emotion, and as such they reflected poorly on the speaker. Of course, most youths went through a phase when they punctuated their speech with as many of these scorned words as possible, just to show they didn't care what their instructors, their parents, and the city officials thought; but Leonidas had outgrown that stage. He associated bad language with teenage immaturity, and it surprised him to hear it on the tongues of bearded men. Meanwhile, the Corinthians were still blustering.

"We've no quarrel with Athens! Why should we fight them?"

"If we refuse to fight, what then? You don't think the f**ing Spartans will take it lying down, do you? The bloody f**ers will kill us all!"

Leonidas looked hard at the speaker, and the expression on his face frightened him. The man's eyes burned with hatred. Hatred, Leonidas registered with unease, directed at Sparta, at him. It had never occurred to Leonidas that Sparta was hated by her allies. He had been raised to think that Sparta's constitution, its orderly society, its superior educational system, and, of course, its superb army were admired throughout the world. It came as a shock to think they were seen as brutal men, capable of slaughtering their allies if the latter did not follow their lead.

"We outnumber them! As long as we stick together—"

"The pissing Tegeans are Spartan lap dogs! They'll never risk defiance!"

"Then who gives a shit! I say, *we're* free men, not slaves! What right have the mother-f**ing Spartans got to tell us who to fight?"

Leonidas had heard more than enough. He edged his way past the agitated crowd of debaters to try to get a glimpse into the tent. The two hoplites guarding it, however, were alert and very forbidding. He moved away from the entrance and slipped around to the back of the tent. It was dark and still and smelled like a latrine. He tried to walk carefully, but the tent attracted him as a light did moths. Enlarged and distorted by the light of the interior lamps, the silhouettes of several men undulated on the walls of canvas as they gestured and paced.

With shock, Leonidas recognized the voice that was speaking. It was not Demaratus, but the father of the youth who had been gored by the boar. What was his name? Archidemos? Archi-something.

Leonidas had been rather intimidated by the Corinthian pole-march the first time they met. He had ridden up on a fretful stallion and scattered orders like Zeus casting thunderbolts. He had taken little note of Leonidas initially, his concern (understandably) being his son. Only as he mounted to follow the cavalcade with the stret-cher had he paused, looked around, and then ridden over to thank Leonidas. It had not been very heartfelt, more good manners than anything else, and he had reached for his purse. Noticing at the last moment that it was missing, he offered to "send someone around with a suitable reward."

Leonidas had turned him down. "I did not act for the sake of reward, and I do not need it."

The Corinthian made no protest. Rather, distracted with worry for his son, he had ridden away without another word. Leonidas would have had to walk back with his broken arm if Alkander hadn't been there. Alkander had helped him mount the borrowed horse and then jumped up behind him.

Leonidas noted now, however, that Archilochos was a good orator. He had a clever way with words. What he said was not so different from what the men outside the tent were saying, but there was poetry as well as sentiment in his words. Leonidas had never heard a man talk like that before, and at first it entranced him.

In Archilochos' mouth, the campaign was an outrage and an insult. The free cities of the Peloponnese, which had once allied themselves with Sparta for the common good, were now being exploited for the sake of aggressive and reactionary policies. They were being asked to sacrifice their young men on the altar of Spartan ambition. To take part in this campaign was to surrender their sovereignty to Spartan hegemony and to trample underfoot the honor of their fathers, who—heroes all—had fought for freedom and democracy in the Peloponnese.

After a while, however, the flood of words started to make Leonidas dizzy. The words were seductive by the sheer beauty of their melody, alliteration, and rhyme. But the longer the man talked, the more exhausted Leonidas became. He could no longer remember the beginning of the speech. The words were tumbling over one another, obscuring their predecessors. Leonidas longed for a clear conclusion.

Instead, another speaker started talking. He was less gifted but equally long-winded. Leonidas sighed and decided he had seen and heard enough. The allies were restless. They did not want to proceed. Worse, they were hostile to Sparta, full of mounting hatred. And the signs were bad.

He moved as unobtrusively as possible toward the front of the tent again. The crowd here had thinned notably, and the men who remained were more morose than agitated. They were awaiting the outcome of what was going on in the tent. Leonidas slipped away in the darkness, heading for the Spartan lines.

Lost in thought, he did not register that someone had come up behind him until a voice remarked gruffly, "What are you doing here, Leonidas?"

Leonidas spun around sharply. Demaratus was looking down on him from the back of his tall horse.

"How did you recognize me?"

"That ugly bitch doesn't trail anyone else." Demaratus jerked his head in the direction of Beggar, who wagged her tail, oblivious to insults. "Now, answer my question. What were you doing here? Spying for your brother?"

"Should I be?"

"Tell me: how many men does Sparta have here?"

"Two thousand Spartiates and that many perioikoi."

"And what is the strength of our allies?"

"Eleven thousand, four hundred and—I believe—ten."

Demaratus laughed. "You made that up."

"Did I?"

"It doesn't matter. You know as well as I do that the allies outnumber us by more than two to one."

"Yes, sir."

"So what, young man, does it mean if they refuse to march any further?"

"That fighting Athens will be difficult."

"Difficult." Demaratus repeated. "Difficult ... You've never stood in the line, have you, Little Leo?"

"No, sir."

Demaratus nodded. "Difficult indeed. Let me tell you something, Leonidas, son of Anaxandridas: Without our allies, we are a little, insignificant city." He pressed his calves more firmly on his horse's flanks and galloped past Leonidas into the darkness of the Spartan camp.

Leonidas continued doggedly. Four thousand men against twenty thousand. And the signs were bad.

"Halt!" The command was called by a sentry, who abruptly blocked Leonidas' path.

"It's me," Leonidas answered. "Leonidas, son of Anaxandridas."

"Password!" the sentry snapped back, although he had gone to the agoge with Leonidas and must have recognized him.

"I haven't a clue," Leonidas admitted. He was not attached to any unit, did not do sentry duty, and had no need to know the password.

The next thing he knew, the sentry was pointing a sword at his throat and ordering him not to move, while shouting for reinforcements. A moment later, two other young men jogged up. "This man was trying to enter and doesn't know the password!"

"I'm Leonidas, son of—"

"Tell it to the lochagos," one of the newcomers advised, adding, "Come with us, Leo."

Leonidas sighed, annoyed but not worried. Since he was not with his unit, he was not subject to any restrictions on his movements. He had no reason to dread a confrontation, he thought— until the tent flap opened and he found himself face to face with Kyranios.

Kyranios had a reputation for being one of the best tactical commanders in the Spartan army. His lochos was often assigned the most difficult position in the order of battle and frequently given difficult independent tasks. Ambitious officers longed to be assigned to his lochos.

Leonidas was too young to dream of that. He could not aspire to officer status for years, and as with all ordinary rankers, his initial assignment was based on family and clan ties. He was in the Pitanate Lochos because he was an Agiad; Kyranios commanded the Mesoan Lochos.

The reason Leonidas found a confrontation with Kyranios intimidating was personal, not professional. Kyranios was the father of the girl with whom Leonidas was in love. Furthermore, the last time they had come face to face, Leonidas had been a mere eirene and had come courting—when he should have been with his charges. Kyranios had made him feel worthless for neglecting his duty.

The escort reported formally, "This man tried to cross the perimeter and could not give the password."

"I expect not," Kyranios answered evenly. "Dismissed."

The sentries withdrew.

"So, son of Anaxandridas, what were you doing lurking around outside the camp at this time of night?" the lochagos inquired, inspecting Leonidas closely with his eyes.

"I noticed considerable commotion in the allied camp, sir, particularly among the Corinthians, and went to see if I could find out what was happening."

Kyranios considered the young man in front of him critically. He had long held a low opinion of Leonidas because of the company he kept. Alkander had been an inept stutterer as a boy, and when his widowed mother became too poor to pay the agoge fees, he should have been expelled and excluded from future citizenship. Instead Leonidas, although only a boy, had paid for Alkander's school fees from his own considerable fortune and enabled Alkander to gain his citizenship. He hadn't turned out so badly in the end, Kyranios admitted; but Leonidas' other best friend, Prokles, had. Through negligence and self-indulgence, Prokles had been responsible for the death of one of his charges last year when he was an eirene—and that was unforgivable. Prokles had been rightly sentenced to exile for twenty years. Finally, the fact that Leonidas had left his charges unattended to come courting was something Kyranios considered reprehensible.

Nor had this recent incident with the boar done much to change his opinion. As far as he could see, it had been pure chance that brought Leonidas and Alkander to the scene and, if one was objective about it, their rescue efforts had been badly flawed; first, they failed to kill the boar in the initial assault, and second, Leonidas failed to avoid the front hooves when delivering the coup de grace.

Yet for all that, Kyranios liked what he saw now, and he liked the answer Leonidas had just given him. It spoke well for the young man that he had noticed what was going on in the other camps. Too many young men never seemed to see anything that happened outside of their own mess-tent! Even more impressive was that it had aroused his curiosity. As a leader of men, Kyranios had long since learned that curiosity was by far the most reliable indicator of intelligence. Education, even literacy, could be drummed into the dullest brain with persistence and sanctions, but curiosity could not. Finally, the fact that Leonidas had gone to investigate suggested initiative and courage. Courage was not in short supply in the Spartan army, but Kyranios felt initiative too often was.

"What did you find out?" Kyranios asked.

"The allies are very angry with us, sir. They think this campaign is unjustified and that we are misusing the provisions of the treaty for our own benefit."

Kyranios nodded. He knew all that, but it never hurt to have one's opinions confirmed. It showed that Leonidas had indeed kept his eyes and ears open.

"And Demaratus was there consulting with Archilochos," Leonidas added a little gratuitously, since he had not been asked. He simply couldn't help thinking of Eirana and how he would need her father's approval if he were ever to bring her home as his bride.

"What did you just say?" Kyranios asked sharply.

"King Demaratus took part in a meeting at Archilochos' tent in which the allies poured out their grievances."

"Did he say anything?"

"I did not hear him." Leonidas hesitated, but then added, "He overtook me on his return, however, and indicated he considered it foolish to proceed against Athens without the allies."

"Without them it is inadvisable; with them it would be madness."

"Sir?"

"Did you learn nothing at the agoge?" Kyranios snapped irritably. "The last thing a commander needs when he commits to battle is untrustworthy troops. They break away just when you need them most, disrupt the order of battle, weaken your line, or expose your flanks. Perhaps worst of all, they have the potential to demoralize or confuse even your best men. They almost certainly lead to chaos and defeat. I would rather fight at a three-to-one disadvantage with reliable troops than achieve superiority in numbers with untrustworthy men. If the allies do not want to fight, we should let them go. We will be stronger without them."

Although what Kyranios said made sense, Leonidas still found the thought of fighting Athens alone daunting. His expression betrayed this.

Kyranios, of course, could have dismissed him, but instead he found himself explaining, "Think about it, son of Anaxandridas.

War is almost always a failure of diplomacy. It is always better to get what you want by negotiation rather than aggression. But it is particularly foolish to use bloodshed to try to obtain something that cannot be sustained. Look at your own father! He recognized that we had more to gain by making Tegea an ally rather than a subject. The hotheads wanted to conquer Tegea. They wanted to make the Tegeans slaves and divide up the land among themselves. And then what? The Tegeans would have been no less resentful of our rule than the Messenians. We would have faced a series of uprisings, which the Messenians would have joined. We would have been bogged down in nearly continuous internal warfare—impoverished, weakened, bled. Chilon saw that and he, with Athena's help I'm sure, convinced your father that it was wiser to make a friend of Tegea than a perpetual enemy.

"The situation is very similar now. We gain nothing by forcing the allies to fight. If their hearts aren't in it, they are worthless militarily, and each casualty will become a grievance against us that will fester and swell into bitter hatred. Hatred is dangerous."

Leonidas pictured the faces of the men in the Corinthian camp and remembered his own fear; but in the agoge they had been taught that hatred, like any violent emotion, was more dangerous for him who had it than for him who provoked it. He had been taught that hatred was like "taking poison and expecting someone else to die of it." At last he ventured to ask, "But isn't it more dangerous for the allies than for us?"

Kyranios cocked his head and considered Leonidas. There was no question: the young man was growing on him. "In the first instance, yes. If, for example, the allies in their outrage over this unjust war were to attack us tonight or in the morning, what do you think would happen? They would fling themselves upon us, screaming hysterically like barbarians—and be cut down like wheat as we, relying on discipline and drill, form up and fight as a unit. And then what? The survivors would return home, abrogate the treaties of alliance, and start negotiating with one another. The next thing we know, we would be ringed by enemies who share the common goal of humiliating us. Argos would gladly join them, and the Messenians could be counted on to stab us in the back. We might still win every battle, but not

without losses. And since each battle would be an unnecessary one—
one we could have avoided simply by not forcing the allies to fight
now—each casualty would be for nothing. In the long run, we would
be weaker, and all for nothing."

"How do we stop that from happening, sir?" Leonidas asked.

Kyranios smiled. "Good question; and thanks to you, we are a
step nearer than I thought an hour ago."

Leonidas looked puzzled.

Kyranios reached for his helmet and then his himation and
announced, "I'm going to see Demaratus." He paused. "Do I need to
arrest you, or can I trust you not to warn your brother?"

"If you arrest me, you can be certain that I do not betray your
trust—and I won't have to answer to my brother for being disloyal."

Kyranios laughed. "I'm beginning to like you, Leonidas. You are
welcome to stop by my kleros when we get home. I can't for the life
of me understand what Eirana sees in that sour-faced seer, and maybe
this incident with the boar will lend you a little more glamour in
her eyes. Meanwhile, you're under arrest. The wine is over there, and
there's some leftover bread, too. Help yourself."

Kyranios then ducked out of his tent.

———

It was rapidly turning into the rowdiest Assembly Leonidas had
ever witnessed. According to the Spartan constitution, laws had to be
introduced by the Council of Elders, or Gerousia, but no law could
be enacted without the ratification of the Assembly. This gave the
Assembly the final say over legislation. The fact that the Assembly
could not introduce amendments or riders to the proposed laws did
not mean there was no discussion. On the contrary, the very fact that
the proposed legislation had to be accepted or rejected in its entirety
made the discussions on controversial laws fierce.

The majority of Sparta's citizens, those who had not participated
in the campaign against Athens because they were already full citizens
and in the reserves, were appalled to discover that behind their backs,
the entire structure of their alliance system had suddenly changed.
Before this bungled campaign against Athens, the allies had been
required to "follow wherever Sparta led." Now, it seemed, the allies

were to be given the right to vote on whether to campaign—or not. Representatives from all alliance members would decide by majority vote whether a campaign would take place, and Sparta—like all other cities—would have just one vote. A majority vote against Sparta could result in the allies thwarting Spartan ambitions and undermining her policies.

Men were shouting "Shame!" and even the usually popular Kyranios was shouted down with shouts of "Coward!" and "Traitor!" when he tried to speak.

Leonidas was shocked and unsettled by the uproar. First of all, Kyranios had convinced him that the proposed changes, which effectively turned the loose alliance of cities into a more formal "League," made sense. Second, he thought it was unbecoming to shout insults at men who had so often proved their worth and loyalty. Most importantly, this kind of shouting and insulting did not further discourse. As boys in the agoge, they had been taught silence, respect, and economy of speech—and here the whole citizen body was acting riotously.

Well, not really, he reflected, looking around the stoa again. The outrage was loud and vehement where it was voiced, but it was not dominant. Leonidas could see many older men putting their heads together and muttering. Many middle-aged men were also frowning and shaking their heads—although it was hard to know if they disapproved of the proposed League charter, or just the ruckus caused by the opponents of it. Most of the noise was coming from the younger full citizens, those just out of the army, and a sprinkling of vocal older men.

The chairman of the ephors was calling for order so he could give the floor to the city treasurer. Nikostratos was a man now in his midfifties, with thinning hair and an increasingly frail body. His shoulders had become rounded and his skin pale from hours spent over accounts rather than on the drill fields. Leonidas knew him well because he was the chairman of Leonidas' syssitia, or dining club. He knew that Nikostratos had a sharp mind, a delightful sense of humor, and a profound understanding of what was good for Sparta, but he feared Nikostratos' virtues were not as widely recognized as they ought to be. He waited tensely as the treasurer stepped forward to stand at the front of the stoa and face the Assembly.

"Peers," Nikostratos opened. "What is more valuable? A free man or a slave?"

The question could have been rhetorical, since no one in this forum was going to claim a slave was worth more than a free man; but the shouts of "Free men!" came loudest from the same party that had opposed the League charter.

"Then the value of our alliance system has just increased dramatically," the treasurer concluded, adding before anyone could object, "What angers you is not that we now have free men as partners but that this campaign, for which you voted, had to be called off—"

"We came home like a dog with its tail between its legs!" Lysimachos shouted. Lysimachos had been Leonidas' eirene when he was ten—and a singularly selfish and self-serving one at that. He was now thirty-one and had just gone off active service. He had not been with them on this campaign.

"That is because you did not secure the consent of the allies before marching," Nikostratos started to point out.

Someone else shouted, "No! Because our kings were seen to be bickering! We were exposed as internally divided!"

Leonidas had to lean forward to see who had said this, and recognized a certain Orthryades. Orthryades had been a company commander in the army, but he had failed to be appointed lochagos when a position became vacant earlier in the year. He had immediately retired in evident protest. He was proud, ambitious, and popular with a faction of the citizen body that felt Sparta was "going to the dogs" and needed to "remember her roots." Nikostratos claimed Demaratus had prevented Orthryades' promotion because he distrusted the "aggressive conservatism" of Orthryades. Now, Leonidas surmised, Orthryades was getting his revenge. In a voice that sounded like a clarion call he shouted, "This debacle is one man's fault! Demaratus'!"

Orthryades was echoed at once by Lysimachos, who called out: "Demaratus showed the allies we were weak and divided!"

Leotychidas, Demaratus' bitter rival, worst enemy—and heir— joined the attack, raising his voice to ask mockingly, "How much gold did Athens have to pay you, Demaratus, to buy your—"

Demaratus was on his feet, shouting furiously. His reaction was so violent that it made Leonidas wonder for a moment if the accusation were true. But what use did Demaratus have for gold? He already had more money than he could use in a society that proscribed displays of wealth. Leonidas believed that the Eurypontid king's opposition to the war was personal, not venal; Demaratus hated Cleomenes even more than he hated Leotychidas. And just as they had learned in school, the hatred was eating away at Demaratus more than at his object. Even now, as though the whole debate had nothing to do with him, Cleomenes was sitting coolly on his throne, unperturbed by the heated debate around him. He looked as if he were above it all, as if it were no concern of his whatsoever.

Orthryades had evidently struck a chord, however—not in attakking Demaratus personally, but with respect to the humiliation of revealing internal divisions to strangers. Within moments the debate had shifted focus, with many arguing it was fatal to have "two captains on one ship." This debate was more general, with many more citizens participating. While old men whined about this being Spartan tradition, the divine origins of the dual kingship, and so on, the men in their prime, joined by many from the younger age cohorts, were insisting that there should be only one supreme commander on any campaign. This, however, was not the law that had been introduced. Eventually the chairman of the ephors managed to quiet the Assembly enough to vote on the League Charter.

To Leonidas' astonishment, after all the protests it passed by a large majority. Henceforth, Sparta could not take her allies to war without the consent of the majority, and a law to prohibit more than one king campaigning outside of Lacedaemon, and then only under the supervision of two ephors, was put on the agenda for the next Assembly.

Leonidas thought this was a good outcome, but as the crowd dispersed he noticed his twin brother Brotus barging his way through the crowd to Orthryades and Leotychidas. It crossed his mind that they were an evil pair, and it would be a bad thing for his brother to become friendly with them.

CHAPTER 3

DOMESTIC AFFAIRS

WINTER WAS THE SEASON OF THE year in which men devoted themselves to their families and their estates. For the reserve units, drill was reduced to just an hour a day; and even the young men, those on active service and required to live in barracks, drilled only half-time. More welcome still, the army was kept at only two-thirds strength. One pentekostus, or company, of each lochos was granted a month's leave each month. This gave every man the time he needed to visit distant estates, take care of family matters, or attend to other private affairs.

Leonidas was not slated for leave until the second month of the winter, but he was quick to use his greater free time to visit Kyranios' kleros and resume his courtship of Eirana.

The first time after the army's return that he ventured to call on her, his arm was still in a sling. Eirana's mother greeted him enthusiastically, drawing attention to his arm and requesting that he tell them what had happened; but Eirana clearly wasn't interested, so Leonidas kept his answer short. He tried to turn the conversation to Eirana herself, asking what she had done over the summer, but she just shrugged and said, "The usual." Her mother frowned and tried to make up for her daughter's rudeness with a flood of gossip. Leonidas appreciated what she was trying to do, but it could not salve the wound that Eirana's obvious indifference toward him had reopened. Discouraged, he turned to go, and Eirana's mother ordered her to "see Leonidas to the gate."

Alone with her as they walked down the drive past the paddocks (Kyranios, like many of the Spartan elite, was a horse breeder), Leonidas collected his courage and remarked, "I never see you in the city. Why don't you come more often?"

Eirana shrugged. "It is too far to walk."

The answer made no sense to Leonidas. "But you can ride or drive." He gestured to her father's powerful horses grazing on either side of the drive.

Eirana had wrapped herself deep in a wool himation and clutched it around her with her arms crossed over her chest. She gazed at the lanky horses grazing on the brown, brittle grass in their shaggy winter coats, and shook her head. "My father breeds horses for their height. Look at them! There isn't one that isn't taller at the withers than the top of my head. And they are all so temperamental! I cannot drive them, and I'm not a child anymore who just clings to the back of some aging warhorse and lets him carry me where he wills. I want a gentle mare that heeds what I want of her. My father does not know what that is." She sounded bitter.

Leonidas stopped and looked at her as she gazed across the pasture, clutching her himation around her. Her expression struck him as one of infinite sadness. "I expected you to be married by now," he told her bluntly.

She started and looked over sharply. "And I would have liked to be!"

"What has stopped you, then?"

She shrugged and looked away, her lower lip trembling as if she were trying not to cry. Leonidas waited for her to get control of herself. After a moment she swallowed and took a deep breath, but her voice was strained when she answered. "That is the worst thing about being a woman: you have to wait on men for everything."

Leonidas was left not knowing if she was waiting for her father's permission to marry—or waiting for Asteropus to ask for her.

———

Of course, some women waited longer than others. It was not

long after this trip to Kyranios' kleros that Brotus started bragging about having taken a bride. Since he was barely twenty-two, like Leonidas, he could not actually live with his wife yet; but he had, as custom required, snuck out of his barracks after curfew one night, "broken into" his bride's father's house, and claimed her, before returning to his barracks and morning roll call.

Brotus was the first of the age cohort to take a wife, and he clearly thought this gave him some distinction. He even predicted that he had gotten his wife pregnant on this first night. "You know what they say. The more pleasure a woman has in sex, the more likely she is to conceive! And you wouldn't *believe* how eager she was!" he bragged in the gymnasium, loud enough for those who were not particularly interested to hear. "She could hardly wait for me to get out of my clothes. I can't wait for curfew!"

Leonidas pretended he hadn't heard his brother's bragging, and so did many others. Brotus' bride Lathria had a reputation. She had been a wrestler as a maiden, and she had challenged more than one youth to a match. Leonidas had once been trapped into one, and it had left him in no doubt that she wanted more intimacy than the sport accorded. He did not believe that Brotus was the first to satisfy her sexual cravings. But if Brotus didn't care, what did it matter to him? Moreover, he supposed there was a certain justice in the marriage: Leonidas believed, though he had no proof, that Brotus had been instrumental in the "accidental" death of Lathria's brother Timon.

Alkander was another young man who had no intention of keeping his bride waiting. Alkander had been in love with Hilaira for years, indeed since before they knew what being in love was about. As she was the younger sister of their friend Prokles, Leonidas and Alkander had cheered her at the maiden races, applauded her performance in dances and choruses, admired her attire at festivals, and comforted her when her brother was sentenced to exile. At some point, however, it had become clear that while Hilaira loved Leonidas as a brother, she loved Alkander as a man.

Because her father seemed to blame Leonidas and Alkander for his son's disgrace, Hilaira and Alkander had been meeting secretly for more than a year—which generally meant in the city. Whenever

Hilaira could find an excuse to get away from her father's kleros, she did so, sending a helot to Alkander's barracks with word of where to meet her. Leonidas found it hard to believe her parents didn't know what was going on; but then again, they lived a withdrawn life since their elder son's disgrace. Nor was it always true that the older age cohorts knew what their juniors were up to. Although Sparta was a close-knit society, the lives of young and old were sufficiently segregated for something that was common knowledge among young men to sometimes surprise the older men.

Not long after Brotus announced his marriage, Alkander informed Leonidas that he, too, intended to marry soon.

They were both in the steamy massage room, lying side by side on the marble benches. "What does Philippos say?" Leonidas asked about Hilaira's father.

"I haven't dared ask him," Alkander admitted, while a bath slave rubbed oil into his back. After a pause, he added, "Hilaira says she'll go with me even without his permission."

Leonidas didn't answer. He didn't doubt it. He was envious of it. If only Eirana loved him like that! But there were risks in it, too. Lathria's father had been more than pleased to have an Agiad prince, second in line to the throne after Cleomenes' young son Agis, take his daughter to wife. Furthermore, Brotus' wealth was equaled only by Leonidas' own and that of a handful of other families. Alkander's situation was different. He had only his state kleros and his ties to Demaratus—which were tenuous. Alkander's sister Percalus, beautiful as she was, had yet to give Demaratus an heir. If she failed, the Eurypontid crown would fall to Demaratus' cousin Leotychidas— who had been Percalus' betrothed and had never forgiven Alkander for letting her marry Demaratus in his absence. In short, Philippos had good reasons not to favor Alkander's suit for his daughter.

"You aren't against us, too, are you?" Alkander pressed Leonidas.

"Of course not! It's just that if Philippos makes a fuss—calling it rape or abduction—and hauls you up before the magistrates... You could get into real trouble."

"They'd have to at least listen to what Hilaira says. We're not in Corinth or Athens, where women are chattels with no say over their fate!" Alkander countered defensively.

"Of course they'd listen to her; but you know as well as I that the judgment of the magistrates—much less the kings—is not always just."

They dropped the subject until after they had left the baths. Back outside in the brittle sun of a cold, short day, Alkander pulled his himation around him from the inside like a cocoon and told Leonidas in a low voice, "I want to take her to one of your estates. My kleros is the first place they'll look for her."

"And mine is the second!" Leonidas countered, alarmed by the thought. "They know how close we are!"

"But you have so many estates. They won't know where to start."

"They know it will have to be close by. You can't miss morning roll call."

"I think we have a twenty-mile radius."

"You can't walk forty miles between evening and morning roll call!"

"I can ride it. Hilaira will have two of her father's racehorses waiting for us."

"I don't think this is a good idea."

"Prokles always said you were too obedient to our laws," Alkander observed, looking off into the distance.

Excessive obedience was a far worse insult than the reverse, but Leonidas hotly pointed out, "Look where Prokles' disregard for our laws got him!"

"I'm going to marry her, Leo." Alkander turned his gaze back on his friend. "Whether you help us or not. If you don't help us, it will make no difference—either to my determination to marry Hilaira or to our friendship. I know how much I owe you. I know I wouldn't be wearing this himation if it weren't for you. If you had not paid my school fees, I would have ended up apprenticed to some trades-man at best, and more likely sold into slavery. You saw those boys in Corinth?"

Leonidas frowned. He had indeed seen the boys hawked in the Corinthian agora like female prostitutes. Although they had been warned, it had still disturbed him.

"If we take the racehorses, people will look for us as far from Sparta as possible." Alkander brought Leonidas' thoughts back to the present. "That is why I thought the best place to hide would be at your ruined kleros."

Leonidas had inherited so much private property that the Spartan treasury felt he could afford to receive as his official state portion an estate that had been devastated by fire five Olympiads earlier. It was located near the city but had been vacant for two decades, since only someone with other sources of income could afford to fix it up.

"It's not habitable!" Leonidas protested.

"Three of the rooms are," Alkander reminded him. They had visited it together several times as Leonidas tried to recruit helot tenants and decide where to start fixing it up. "We can put braziers in the room under the stairs, and I can fix up the shutters beforehand. You wanted to do that anyway."

Leonidas knew he had no choice. No matter what Alkander said, Hilaira would never forgive him if he did not help her now, and if she were against him she would turn Alkander against him. Leonidas couldn't bear the thought of losing Alkander's friendship. His parents were dead. His brothers were his enemies. And he had lost his other good friend, Prokles, to exile. He couldn't afford to lose Alkander.

"Will you wait until I go on leave? At the next new moon?"

"Of course. I want to get as much fixed up as I can in advance— like set up a nice soft bed with lots of warm blankets." Alkander grinned at him.

———

When the new moon came, Leonidas departed on the long-postponed tour of his estates. He had not had enough leave to visit those of his properties located deep inside Messenia since he came into his inheritance a year earlier. He had a steward, Phormio, who made regular tours of his estates; and naturally each property had a manager, usually a perioikoi who shared in the profits; but Leonidas was curious to see his properties himself. With the survey map the Agiad steward had turned over to him at his inheritance, he set out with his dog Beggar, a mule loaded with provisions, and his attendant Mantiklos.

Mantiklos was himself Messenian. He had walked over a hundred miles to offer Leonidas his services, and many had advised Leonidas against hiring a Messenian. In the year they had spent together, they had slowly learned to trust one another; but the relationship was still an uneasy one, marred by the overpowering suspicion that all Spartiates harbored against their resentful subjects. More than once this past year, Leonidas had regretted his decision to hire the taciturn Mantiklos.

Now, as they tacked up their horses and dressed warmly in double layers of himations for the trip across snow-capped Taygetos, Leonidas asked the other youth, "Are you glad to be going home?"

Mantiklos glanced across his horse's back at his master and considered his reply carefully before answering. "That will depend on what I find."

Mantiklos was a dark-haired youth with dark brows and skin. He no longer wore his hair shoulder length as when he'd first come to Sparta, but it was still rather wild and shaggy, while his face was almost always dark with stubble.

They mounted and set off with Beggar trotting happily along behind them, her white-tipped tail wagging upright in the air. The road to Messenia zigzagged up out of the Eurotas valley, rising steeply. The horses strained, stretching out their necks, and their warm breath vaporized in the cold air like billowing smoke. They passed various temples, springs, and the marble quarries before midday. By now they were high enough for snow to have collected in the shadows, and it became perceptibly deeper as they continued the climb. Eventually it covered the earth beneath the trees so completely that dead leaves and fallen branches were obscured. The road was visible only because it was a cleared white path that snaked between the barren, gray trees.

This pass to Messenia was closed completely by blizzards at least once or twice most winters. In bad winters it could be closed for several weeks or even months on end. Leonidas didn't like the low clouds that seemed pregnant with fresh snow, and they pressed on with only very short breaks to snack from their cold provisions and relieve themselves. That way, they managed to put the pass behind them before dusk and benefited from the longer daylight west of the peaks. But when it became completely dark, they had no choice but to find a relatively sheltered fold in the mountains and settle in for the night. They tethered and fed the horses, and then dug themselves into the leaves to set up a tent. They cooked a meal over a fire they built at the entrance to the tent, then crawled inside and lay down with Beggar between them.

After a moment Leonidas asked, "Is this safe?"

"The fire will keep away the wild beasts," Mantiklos assured him.

"I was thinking of your countrymen," Leonidas answered, remembering with unwanted vividness all the childhood stories of Messenians slitting the throats of unsuspecting Spartans. It even occurred to him that Mantiklos, up to now kept in check by the fact that they had been with the Spartan army where Leonidas was surrounded by his comrades, might have been awaiting this opportunity.

"You are well armed and well trained. It is unlikely that the kind of men who live in the wilderness could kill you. And there is Beggar, too."

The bitch lifted her head at the sound of her name, looked over at Mantiklos, then yawned and flopped her head back down, obviously intent on sleep after the long, hard journey.

"Do you regret your decision?" Leonidas asked abruptly, the cold keeping him from sleep.

"No. But sometimes I wish I were not so alone."

"Alone?" Leonidas turned on his side and propped himself on one elbow to look at his attendant. They were never alone. They lived in barracks, drilled in units, went to the baths and gymnasia in groups, and sang in chorus. The rarest thing in the life of a young Spartiate and his attendant was solitude.

"The others, the attendants, they're all Laconian. They look on me with as much suspicion as you do. Not to mention your comrades! Sometimes I get very tired of all that suspicion and hostility."

"It's hard to forget two hundred years of warfare."

"Especially when you declare war on us every year!" Mantiklos snapped back.

"That does not seem to bother the Laconian helots," Leonidas pointed out. "And we only declare war on you because you are so hostile. We live in peace with the perioikoi, and Tegea, and all the cities of the League, which were our enemies once," Leonidas pointed out.

"But not with Argos!" Mantiklos reminded him. "You only make peace with people who submit to you. Like hounds, the others have to lie down and offer you their jugular. Then you accept them as long as they run in your pack. But if men are as proud as you, then you cannot abide them, and you fight until one or the other of you is destroyed."

"Then all Messenia needs do to have peace is to submit—truly submit—to us."

"But that doesn't make sense! You admire courage above all else. You should respect us more for not being submissive! You should admire our spirit."

"But you would never be satisfied with our admiration. You want control of your country back. You want independence for Messenia."

"Of course we do!"

"But we can't afford to give it to you. We can't support the Spartan army—not in today's world where other armies are so well equipped—without the riches of Messenia."

"Then you will always live in fear of us."

They were silent for a few moments, each following his own thoughts. After a while Leonidas asked in a low, earnest voice, "Why did you want to serve me?"

"I wanted to learn what the Spartan army was really like, from the inside. I wanted to understand what made it so good, so I would know how to fight it."

Leonidas held his breath for a moment, registering that this was more dangerous than the murder he had feared. He should have thought of this earlier. "And now you will stay here and start training rebels?"

Mantiklos laughed. "If only it were that easy!"

"What do you mean?"

The other shrugged, then sat up to readjust the sheepskins he had spread over himself to help keep warm before asking, "Do you think there are many Messenians like me?"

"I have no idea."

"You will see. Most of my countrymen are craven. They want their freedom only if *others* are willing to fight and die for it. They want independence only if it does not *cost* them anything. The bulk of my countrymen are whiners—always complaining and moaning about their fate, but unwilling to take any risks to change it." With these words, Mantiklos lay down again and turned his back to Leonidas.

The next morning, stiff and unrested from a cold and uncomfortable night, they made their way down from Taygetos to the Gulf of Messenia. They spent the night in Kardamyle, a pretty town on the east shore of the bay with a good anchorage and a well-appointed inn. The horses and mule were put up in a proper stable, while they had a hot meal and slept with the other guests around a large hearth that burned through the night.

The following day they kept to the coastal road following the shore of the Gulf, and at last Mantiklos seemed to lose his inhibitions and began to talk. He started hesitantly, but when he realized that Leonidas was interested, he talked more and more expansively. He told Leonidas about the battles that had taken place in the surrounding countryside during the First and Second Messenian Wars.

Of course, Leonidas had already heard about these battles. They were an essential component of agoge curriculum. But he pretended otherwise, responding rather with wonder and pressing Mantiklos for details, because Mantiklos' version of what had happened was very different from what was taught in the agoge.

Leonidas did not discard what he had learned in the agoge. He thought that the agoge version could not be so far from the truth, or he would be Mantiklos' attendant and Mantiklos the wealthy hoplite—not the other way around. But he realized that the way one was told about the deeds of one's ancestors had a huge impact on one's perception of oneself.

Mantiklos stressed again and again that his forefathers had been heroic freedom fighters, while Leonidas' forefathers represented brutal and corrupt power. Mantiklos' ancestors had been crushed by greater numbers, greater wealth, superior weapons—never by the cleverness or courage of their adversaries. Yet when Leonidas looked around him, he saw that Messenia was richer and more prosperous than Laconia. Messenia should have had numbers and wealth on her side. As for weapons, it does not take long to imitate the weapons and tactics of one's adversaries. They taught *that* at the agoge, too: if the enemy has something that you find hard to defeat, then learn what it is and how to counter it—fast.

"What is your agoge like?" Leonidas asked, interrupting his attendant's description of the Battle of the Boar's Grave.

"What?" Mantiklos asked, disconcerted by the interruption.

"What is your agoge like—your upbringing, your schooling?"

"I cannot say what it is like for everyone, because each father has charge of his sons' education. As you can see, my father taught me well, but not everyone is so lucky."

No, clearly not, Leonidas reflected—and that gave Sparta a significant advantage over other city-states. The agoge assured that all Spartan boys, regardless of the wisdom, wealth, and virtues of their fathers, enjoyed the same education—provided their fathers could pay the agoge fee. And the agoge enabled the able sons of mediocre fathers to win recognition and advance in life. Furthermore, all the boys were required to attain a high standard of education, both physical and mental, and all gained fundamental knowledge about their city and the world around them.

Of course, the agoge was only as good as the instructors that ran it, but no institution in Sparta, not even the army, was more carefully monitored and regulated. The Paidonomos was elected to his office and therefore subject to dismissal if he was found wanting, and his assistants were selected as carefully as officers in the army.

"What of your leaders?" Leonidas asked next. "Were they ever elected?"

"Of course not. Messenia was a kingdom when you crushed her."

"And you are descended from Messenia's last king?" Leonidas remembered Mantiklos claiming this the first time they met.

Mantiklos frowned. "Aristomenes was never officially king, but he came of the line of the Messenian kings."

"Aristomenes: your freedom fighter, my mass murderer," Leonidas summarized with a faint smile.

"Is a military commander called a murderer merely because he is successful with his tactics? Because he surprises his enemy when he sleeps?"

"When his enemies are schoolchildren, certainly."

"That was only one incident! Aristomenes did many great deeds besides that! And why do you never give him credit for getting past your guards and being able to strike in the heart of your city?"

"Maybe because at the time we had no guards in the city. We did not learn the need for them until Aristomenes slaughtered the children of the agoge."

"Do you honestly think that Sparta's army never kills children?"

"I don't doubt it has happened. I doubt if it was policy."

"You are naive—sir."

Leonidas laughed.

On the evening of the third day, they reached the estate Leonidas most wanted to see, his horse farm located on the far western peninsula of the Peloponnese. The manager of the estate had inherited the position from his father and his father's father before him. He had been warned by Phormio that his master was coming, and although he could not know the exact day to expect him, he had taken precautions to be ready for him.

Leonidas and Mantiklos were welcomed with wine and bread the moment they dismounted, and their horses were spirited away by efficient grooms before they could turn around. Leonidas was shown to the master quarters, where fresh linens and fresh flowers awaited him. A young boy was sent with him to take his dirty clothes, offer him a fresh, clean chiton and towels, and show him the way to the bath. Mantiklos was shown the way to the helots' hall, where he could wash himself and receive clean clothes from his equals.

Leonidas welcomed the bath more than the wine. He felt filthy after three days on the road, sleeping in the open or in public inns. The heat in the steamy chamber (for the bath was located in a small, windowless room), at last thawed the chill that had sat in his bones ever since that cold night on Taygetos. He stepped into the marble-lined bath and sank down in the steaming water with a sigh. He closed his eyes and floated in contentment, relaxing and enjoying the solitude.

After an undefined time, Leonidas noticed the water was cooling, so he roused himself. He submerged his head and rubbed his hair clean with his fingers. Then he stood and stepped out of the bath.

The little boy who had been sitting on the floor clutching his knees at once jumped to his feet with a look of alarm on his face. He looked up at the naked, dripping-wet Spartiate looming over him with obvious fear in his eyes. Leonidas grinned at him and asked for a towel. The boy scrambled to get it, handed it to him, and then backed away.

Leonidas rubbed himself and his hair dry, and then nodded toward the marble ledge running around the room and asked the boy, "Can you oil me down?" Oil and scrapers were provided on a wooden shelf, obviously laid out in readiness for a bather.

The boy nodded vigorously, although his expression was wary and he swallowed several times. Leonidas stretched out on his belly.

The boy took one of the vials of oil, poured it into his other hand, and then rubbed his hands together before rubbing Leonidas' back. His hands were small and he worked rapidly and timidly.

"You can press harder," Leonidas told him, missing the expert massage of the public bath slaves in Sparta's better baths.

The boy tried to do as he was told, but he apparently did not have the strength or experience. Leonidas accepted this and resigned himself to getting the oil without the massage, closing his eyes. The boy reached for more oil, but the vial slipped through his already oily hands and shattered on the floor, scattering shards. Leonidas started at the unexpected sound, rearing up slightly in instinctive alarm. The boy leaped backward and then ducked down into a crouch, lifting his arms as if to ward off a blow. "I'm sorry, I'm sorry!" he gasped out, wincing in anticipation of a blow.

Leonidas just stared at him.

The silence and the absence of physical violence made the boy peer frightfully over the edge of his arm to see what was happening. When he met Leonidas' gaze, he first ducked his head back down, but then seemed to register that Leonidas' look was not threatening or angry. He looked up again questioningly.

"Who beats you, boy? And what is your name? Where do you come from?"

The boy's eyes widened in wonder. He started to stammer out, "Crius, master. My name is Crius."

"Come here, Crius—but be careful not to step on the shards."

Crius slowly got to his feet and tiptoed nearer to Leonidas, who swung his feet down from the ledge and sat facing him. The boy stopped about a yard away, as if hoping he were still out of range of Leonidas' fists.

"Where are you from, Crius?"

"From here, master," the boy answered, puzzled.

"Are you a helot? Messenian?" Leonidas asked.

The boy nodded.

"Your parents live on this estate?"

The boy nodded again.

"Who beats you?"

Crius looked nervously over his shoulder and around, as if he thought the walls might have ears. Then he dropped his voice and whispered, "The master, master. I mean Master Melampus, master."

Melampus was the manager.

"Are you the only one he beats?"

The boy shook his head vigorously.

"Does he beat your parents?"

The boy nodded.

"What does your father do?"

"What can he do? The master has a right to beat us, doesn't he?"

"I meant, what is your father's job."

"He's a groom, master."

"And your mother?"

"She works in the helot kitchen. The master says she's not pretty enough to serve him."

"I see. Does he beat the other helots?"

The boy nodded.

"All of them?"

The boy thought about this for a moment and then decided, "I don't think he has ever hit Grandma Tima—she is very old, almost a hundred. She is blind and toothless and I don't think he has ever hit her. He just told us to stop feeding her, but my mother sneaks her things."

Leonidas rubbed his face with his hands. This was a nightmare. He took a deep breath. "Crius, I want you to clean up the shards and the spilled oil very carefully and put them there on the shelf, and then I want you to continue oiling me down."

Crius nodded and did as he was told, while Leonidas lay back on his belly. The boy had just gotten to his calves when there was a knock on the door and Melampus stuck his head into the bath. "Is everything all right, sir? Can I get you anything? Wine? A girl? We have several fine fillies here!"

Leonidas opened his eyes and looked back toward the smiling manager. He shook his head. "Not at the moment. I knocked that vial off the shelf earlier; could you remove the pieces?"

"Of course, sir." Melampus rushed in to gather up the shards on the shelf, casting a suspicious look at Crius, who cringed, betraying his guilt. Melampus cuffed him across the back of his head. "You careless whelp! I can't trust you to do even the simplest task!"

"Leave the boy alone. I told you, I broke it."

Melampus knew Leonidas was lying. "The boy is worthless! He is frightened of the horses and no use in the stables. I thought he might be of use here in the house, but he drops things all the time! I can't have him serve at table or half the dinner lands on the floor! And now he can't even see to a guest in his bath. It would be better if we could sell helots like this! He's worthless to us here, but he might bring a good price as a whore; his backside isn't bad."

The boy blushed violently.

"It is illegal to sell helots as chattel slaves," Leonidas answered evenly. "Let him finish; I am anxious to dress and have something to eat."

"Of course, sir." Melampus withdrew.

Crius seemed to hesitate, and Leonidas had to insist that he continue. Very timidly the boy resumed oiling his calves.

"Do you have something wrong with your hands, Crius?"

The boy stopped and stared at Leonidas. Leonidas sat up again. "Show me your hands."

Crius held them out to him.

Leonidas could see nothing wrong with them. He held out his own hands palm upward, but with his fingers curled. "Hook your fingers in mine and pull." The boy glanced up at him curiously, but then did as he was told. The boy had hardly any strength in his hands at all. "Do they hurt?"

"It hurts to grasp things, master. To close them tight." The boy tried to make fists while staring at his own hands, but stopped himself when it became too painful.

"Has Melampus ever abused you?"

"Master?"

"What he said about your backside. Was he speaking from experience?"

The boy's blush seemed to belie the shake of his head—until he added in a whisper, "Not him, one of his guests. A horse trader from up north."

"Help me get dressed, boy."

"Yes, master." The boy scurried to collect a fresh-pressed chiton and Leonidas' belt. As he helped him into them, he ventured, "I don't want to be sold, master. Please don't let the master sell me. My mother says my hands weren't always like this. Maybe they will get better."

Leonidas went down on his heels to be eye to eye with Crius. "Melampus has no right to sell you, Crius. It is against the law. Where can I find you again?"

"Find me? But I'm supposed to sleep outside your door in case you have need of something, master."

"Very good."

Back in the chamber assigned to Leonidas, Mantiklos was waiting, washed and changed and obviously impatient. "May I go pay my respects to my parents, sir?"

"I'll think about it," Leonidas answered, and Mantiklos' expression instantly turned sullen. "Stop it," Leonidas ordered in exasperation. "Of course I'm going to give you leave to visit your parents, but not until you've told me more about Melampus."

Mantiklos' expression turned wary. "What do you mean?"

"You grew up around here. You must be able to tell me something about his reputation. Is he respected?"

"As a horse breeder? Certainly. People come from all over Hellas to breed their mares with his studs."

"And otherwise?"

Mantiklos' expression closed. "What else matters to a Spartiate?"

That was too much for Leonidas. "Go on, then!" he dismissed Mantiklos. "Go visit your parents, but don't bother coming back!"

That sent a visible shock through the young Messenian. "But—why not, sir?"

"If you don't know me after a year together, then you're too boneheaded to be of any use to me. Surely you've learned all you wanted to about the Spartan army. Why not start a rebellion right away?"

"Maybe I will!" Mantiklos shot back and then stamped out the door.

Leonidas was left feeling confused and angry. "Damn him!" he muttered under his breath.

———

In the andron, Melampus had a feast waiting for Leonidas. The elegantly appointed chamber was aglow with light from what seemed like a hundred small lamps. Added to these was a large lamp in the shape of a pentekonter, which hung from the ceiling and emitted lights from the oar-holes. There were also tall standing lamps in all four corners, with lifelike bronze snakes coiling up to hold a broad, shallow bowl full of glowing embers. The couches were made of wooden frames with rattan surfaces, covered with cushions. Leonidas had never dined in such luxury before, but he pretended it was ordinary.

There were just the two of them for dinner. They were served by two boys wearing wreaths of myrtle. First they poured water from jugs over the diners' hands and handed them pressed linen towels. Then they rolled in the tables laden with savory-smelling dishes, swathed in clouds of steam when the lids were taken off. The scents made Leonidas' mouth water and his stomach growled at him, reminding him he was hungry.

Melampus was graciously identifying his dishes: snow-white wheat rolls, lamb casserole, baby birds in a flaky pastry, and grilled tuna steaks. Leonidas felt almost dizzy just looking at it—and he had the uneasy feeling from his host's smirk that Melampus knew it.

Still maintaining a façade of sophistication, Leonidas helped himself to a small portion of each dish, but firmly refused the offered wine, insisting on water only. His stomach was going to have enough trouble digesting the fragrant sauces and rich fare without wine on top of it. Besides, he needed his wits about him.

After the meal was served, Melampus launched into a well-prepared report on the estate, stressing how prosperous and famous it was, while carefully injecting hints on what needed to be improved. "The worst thing, sir, is being required to use the labor tied to the estate rather than being able to purchase qualified slaves."

"That's the law."

"Not all Spartiates are so—shall we say—scrupulous?"

"No?"

"Your brother Cleombrotus, I hear, has discreetly authorized the manager of his estate near Pylos to sell off worthless helots in exchange for some first-class Scythian and Thracian slaves."

"It is a common mistake for people to assume that because Brotus and I shared the same womb at the same time, we are otherwise similar."

Melampus took the hint and let the topic drop—at least for the moment. They talked again of horses: the number and age and reputation of the stallions, the fact that even Demaratus had sent mares here, and that one of the horses that had drawn Demaratus' chariot to victory at the Pythian Games had a dam from here. Melampus felt Leonidas could breed racehorses if he invested a little more...

"The Games do not interest me. Let Demaratus have his victories. I would rather concentrate on horses for our army."

"Draft horses?" Melampus gasped, appalled.

"Scouts. Reconnaissance is critical, and mounted scouts are the best."

Melampus was disappointed, but he swallowed down any protests for the moment, saying only, "You must see the horses yourself, sir."

"I intend to."

Noting that Leonidas now called for wine, however, Melampus guessed that he was tired of business and ready to relax. "Would you welcome some entertainment, sir?"

"Entertainment?"

"I regret that without knowing the date of your arrival, I had no time to hire musicians for the evening, but perhaps a couple of the fillies from the estate might amuse you?"

"All right," Leonidas agreed, inwardly uncertain. They had been warned about "entertainment" in Corinth, but he had never had an opportunity to experience it.

At Melampus' signal, three girls entered nervously. Their bodies were almost naked, but their faces were laden with heavy makeup—white paint base with rouge on their cheeks and lips and thick, dark lines outlining the eyes. Shimmering shadows darkened their lids, and they reeked of heavy perfume. If their bodies had not been so unformed, still juvenile, Leonidas would have thought they were older women. They performed an awkward dance in which they gradually removed their scanty clothes.

Leonidas could feel his host watching him anxiously, so he kept his eyes on the girls and sipped his wine slowly. They did not particularly arouse him. In fact, he found himself thinking of how much lovelier Eirana and Hilaira were when they ran or rode in short chitons. When the girls finished, he nodded simply and thanked them.

"Would you like one of them to join you in your chamber tonight?" Melampus asked.

"Are they chattels?"

"No, helots," Melampus responded, surprised. "If you would authorize me to buy chattel slaves, I could improve the quality—"

Leonidas waved him silent and addressed the embarrassed-looking dancers. "Go to your own beds."

They scuttled out.

"That bad?" Melampus asked, with raised eyebrows.

"I didn't say they were bad, but I have never taken a girl against her will and I don't intend to start now."

Melampus' narrowed his eyes slightly. "Such a paragon of virtue!" The sarcasm was hard to mistake. "Have you no vices?"

Leonidas laughed, thinking of his brothers and their opinion of him; but to Melampus he simply replied, "Undoubtedly. I am tired and will retire." He swung his feet down, and Melampus sat up to see him out. Leonidas waved him back down. "I can find my own way."

When he reached his chamber, he found Crius curled up in a ball on the naked floor outside the door. He had neither a pallet to sleep on nor a blanket to keep off the chill. Leonidas bent and lifted the boy off the floor and carried him into the chamber. He put him onto the bed and pulled a blanket over him. Then, taking a couple of the extra blankets, he stretched himself out on the mat before the fire on the floor.

———

As always, Leonidas woke at first light. For a moment he was disoriented and could not remember where he was—inside a fine house but lying on the floor. Then he remembered and got to his feet. The boy was snuggled deep in the covers, sleeping soundly. Leonidas peered out the window at a gray day, with low clouds scuttling across the sky on a brisk wind. He removed a clean chiton from the mule pack, wrapped his leather corselet around his torso for warmth more than protection, tied it down his left side, and then drew the broad shoulder flaps down and tied them one at a time to the front. He shoved his feet into his high sandals and pulled the laces tight before wrapping himself in his best woolen himation. This he had not worn on the journey, so it was relatively clean. Thus dressed, he went to the bed and gently shook Crius awake.

The boy reared up, alarmed, and stared around in bewilderment. "Where am I?"

"I put you to bed last night. Come, dawn is breaking. I want you to take me to your parents."

Crius scrambled down from the bed and led him eagerly. The house was still and filled with shadows, but Crius moved silently, and Leonidas followed as stealthily as he could. Only as they approached the helot tract did the first sounds of life reach them—the clatter of pottery being set out and the smell of bread baking. Crius popped his head into the kitchen and looked around, but then shook his head and led Leonidas across the muddy yard, where the chickens pecked and cackled, to the row of low thatched cottages. Smoke drifted from the chimneys, and someone came to the door of one cottage to empty a bowl of something. A youth, relieving himself in the bushes at the end of the row, looked over in astonishment at the approach of Leonidas and Crius.

Crius led them straight to the second cottage from the right, bursting through the door and calling out, "Mom, Dad, the master is here!"

Leonidas had to duck to enter the dim room, which was smoky and dingy. He surprised a family sitting at benches around a wooden table. There was a man, two youths, and two little girls, both younger than seven by the look of them. A woman was standing with a heavy pot in one hand and a wooden spoon in the other, apparently preparing to dole out porridge into the waiting wooden bowls set before the others. They all stared at the apparition in the doorway. Then the man struggled to his feet, and his sons hastened to follow his example.

"Sit down. May I join you? It smells good."

They gaped. The woman dropped the spoon in the pot, reaching for another wooden bowl from a shelf behind her. She put it and a spoon on the table, hissing at the two girls to make room for the master.

Leonidas addressed himself to the head of the household. "Your son Crius has been looking after me, but he is shy. He did not tell me your name."

"Pelopidas, master. And these are my sons, Polychares," the larger of the boys nodded his head, "and Pantes." The younger teenager nodded. Then, turning a bit, he nodded toward the woman: "My wife, Laodice."

While Pelopidas looked wary and the youths just plain dumbfounded, the woman met Leonidas' gaze with alarmed eyes. Leonidas nodded to her, remembering what Crius had said about her not being pretty enough to serve in the main house. She was certainly no beauty, but nor was she an ugly old hag. She was neatly dressed and covered her hair with a simple linen snood, and there was intelligence in her expression.

"Crius tells me you are a groom," Leonidas addressed himself to Pelopidas.

"Yes, master."

"You look after the stallions?"

"No, the mares and foals mostly."

"You were born here?"

"Yes, master."

"How many helot families are tied to the estate?"

"Seven."

Leonidas pictured the line of cottages. There were only six. One family either lived in the main house or had a separate house. To be sure he had not misread the situation, he asked, "Are you the senior family on this estate?" (One helot family usually took precedence over the others by virtue of their former status in Messenia, or because they were descendent from the firstborn son of the original family settled on a particular property.)

Pelopidas shook his head.

"Have you been a groom all your life? Have you any other experience?"

"What do you mean, master?"

"Can you drive a plow or reap grain?"

"Of course. We all help as needed. The boys mostly handle the sowing and harvesting, but I can drive a team of oxen." Pelopidas knew this was something to be proud of; not all men could manage it, but Pelopidas was broad-beamed.

"And your sons? Are they both grooms?"

Pelopidas shook his head. "Pantes is a trained carpenter. He is building the new horse boxes in the south barn and has fixed all these shelves and that cabinet there." The father pointed with pride, and the son looked down humbly.

Laodice seemed to suddenly remember herself during this exchange and started serving out the porridge, starting with Leonidas.

"Polychares will follow me in the stables," continued Pelopidas, volunteering information for the first time. "He's good with horses."

"Crius tells me that you work in the kitchens," Leonidas addressed Laodice directly; but she looked down, embarrassed, and her husband answered for her.

"She is the best cook on the entire estate!" Pelopidas declared emphatically. "Go ahead and taste this porridge, master. And she can bake pastry as fine and flaky as the fancy things they sell at Methone."

Leonidas dipped into the porridge and nodded, satisfied. It was as good as any he had tasted, given the simple ingredients. Indeed, she had added something that improved the red-cabbage base significantly. He made up his mind. "How would you feel about running an estate on your own?"

Pelopidas stared at him, and Laodice dropped the spoon into the pan.

"But we couldn't displace—"

"I don't mean here. I have a vacant kleros in Laconia. There was a house fire five Olympiads ago and the helot family was killed. No one has had the money to rebuild, and no one has been settled on it. I am looking for a family to settle there and take it over."

"You mean as the principal family?"

"As the only family. It's a state kleros. It's about a fifth the size of this estate, and it is not a stud farm. You would have to help rebuild everything. There is a lot of work to be done—especially for a carpenter." He addressed this to a wide-eyed Pantes. "But you would be entitled to 50 per cent of the harvest. And your sons would inherit it." He looked at Polychares as he said this.

The sons turned sharply to look at their father and then their mother, but Pelopidas was frowning. "Leave here altogether and go to live permanently in Laconia?" He asked this as if he couldn't believe it.

"Yes," Leonidas answered, watching the faces of the others. Crius looked as if he were holding his breath while he awaited his father's decision, and the middle boy looked even more eager, while Polychares said outright, "That would be wonderful. A place of our own!" He looked to his mother for support. She looked at Leonidas as if searching for something.

Leonidas pushed back the bench and got to his feet. "I will leave you to discuss it among yourselves. You can give me your decision tomorrow. Thank you for the porridge." As he ducked out of the door again, Crius remembered that he was supposed to be waiting on the master. He called, "Wait for me!" as he tried to get out of the seat he'd taken between his brothers.

Leonidas turned and put his head back inside the cottage. "Finish your breakfast. I'm going to the stables."

For almost five seconds no one moved, and then they were all talking at once. "Dad, this is fantastic! This is what you and Mom have talked about—"

Laodice cut off her eldest son, looking hard at Crius. "Did he touch you? Like that other man? Did he?"

"No! He's not like that! I broke a vial and he told the master it was his fault, and last night he let me sleep on his bed while he slept on the floor—"

"Why would he do that? I don't understand. He's not just Spartiate, he's an Agiad prince!" Pelopidas retorted, frowning, because he thought his son was lying.

"Mantiklos says it's different in Laconia," Polychares chimed in. He was only a year younger than Mantiklos, and they had been friends before Mantiklos went away. "He says none of the helots *there* grovel before their masters. He says they joke together and the Spartiates treat them like real men. He says in the army they are allowed weapons and eat the same food, and the helots are treated by the surgeons, too. On the estates they live like masters—like Melampus does here! We could have all that!"

"Not so fast," his father warned. "We've never been to Laconia. Are you going to believe everything that windbag Mantiklos tells you just to puff himself up? Helots are helots. And this estate Leonidas talked about, the house burned down and everyone was killed. I don't like the sound of that. The shades may still haunt it and resent us coming. Besides, how can we rebuild a whole house—"

"I can do it, Dad," Pantes spoke up eagerly. "If you and Polychares help, I'm sure we can—"

"Don't interrupt! There's more to building a house than carpentry! At least we know what we've got here—"

Laodice interrupted her husband, her eyes flashing with fury. "Indeed—and it can hardly get worse than this!" She turned again to Crius. "Swear by all the Gods, Crius, you are telling me the truth! He did not touch you?"

"I swear, Mom! And he sent the girls away, too! Melampus was upset with them and slapped them around for not looking "willing" enough. He said they had disgraced him. And he asked about my hands. He guessed right away that I wasn't just clumsy. He asked if they hurt."

Laodice looked at her youngest son for a long moment. She remembered the state he'd been in just six months ago when the other guest had abused him. He had nearly drowned himself in a frenzy to get clean again, and when she had coaxed out of him what had happened, he had admitted he was sure he was going to die because it had been so unnatural. He had vomited with revulsion over and over. She did not think he could now have turned into a docile whore.

Thus, even though she could not understand why an Agiad prince would single them out for such a favor, she turned to her husband and said firmly, "We must take this chance, Pelopidas. The Gods are not generous to the likes of us very often, and they will be very angry if we turn away their gift. I don't care how hard it is, and I don't care if we freeze this first winter, and I will deal with the shades of the dead helots when they come; but I will not let that man do to our little girls what he did to—others."

It was only three days before the end of his leave when Leonidas finally returned to Sparta. He had enjoyed the trip more than he had expected, but it was good to be coming home, too. He looked forward to telling Alkander all the things he'd seen and learned. He wanted to consult with Nikostratos and Phormio; and most of all, he wanted to give Eirana the mare he'd found for her.

She was just thirteen hands tall at the withers, black with a white star and one white sock. She was six years old and as sweet-tempered as a lamb. Leonidas had bought her very cheaply because her small size was considered a defect; but all he could think of was Eirana's complaint about her father's horses being too tall. Leonidas had not ridden her himself because of her small size, but she was very docile to lead and did not shy even when the other horses did. She submitted to having her hooves picked without the slightest fidgeting, and she rapidly learned (as Beggar had) that Leonidas was generous with edibles if she nuzzled him. He was certain that Eirana would love her.

It was a crisp but sunny winter's day when he and Mantiklos made it to Sparta. Mantiklos had shown up before he left the horse farm and had taken up his duties as if no words had passed between them. Leonidas, too, pretended they had not fought, but he knew now that he would never really trust Mantiklos—just as Sparta could not trust Messenia. Mantiklos was leading the mule, while Leonidas had Eirana's little mare on the lead.

The market was open and crowded for a winter's day. The sunny weather had attracted people, if only to stroll around and exchange gossip. Leonidas decided to detour around the agora area to reach his barracks. Then he planned to go to the baths and get his hair cut to make himself presentable for Eirana. Tomorrow, on the second to the last day of his leave, he would take the mare over to Kyranios' estate and present her to Eirana. He would trim her mane, too, he thought, glancing back.

"Leo! Leo!" The woman's voice took him by surprise and he looked around, confused, until he spotted Hilaira waving to him from a side street. She had a basket of eggs over her arm, and a cart that was offloading tiles into the second story of one of the houses blocked her way, but most noticeable was her short hair: that could only mean she was a married woman. He drew up and waited as she navigated around the obstacle, taking care with her precious cargo of eggs. As she reached him, he jumped down and was rewarded by a hug and a kiss on his cheek. "Thank you so much, Leo! It was the most romantic thing a girl could imagine! No nosy mothers-in-law or prying helots. Just the two of us! Alkander had everything so beautifully fixed up, and though there were snow flurries that night, you wouldn't believe how wonderfully cozy the corner room is! We left everything there for you—well, the bed and the blankets and the lamps, though there's not much oil left," she admitted, laughing.

Her happiness was infectious. Leonidas laughed with her. "What did your father say?"

"Oh, I think he was expecting it—maybe even waiting for it. My mother and grandmother have been nagging him for months, telling him he was being purposelessly obstinate. Everyone knows that you and Alkander were good influences on Prokles. My father just couldn't swallow his pride. But once we just did it, he welcomed Alkander back and it's like it was before—only better." She giggled. "You have to come at the next holiday. My father told me to tell you that! He wants you to visit us."

"Where are you living?"

"I'm back home for now, but we're looking for a flat in the city so we can see each other more often. Alkander's kleros is too far out of town to be practical when he's on active duty."

Leonidas nodded understandingly. "Look at this mare." He drew attention to the little black mare on the lead.

Hilaira's father raised horses, too, and Hilaira had a good eye for them. She nodded approvingly at once. "Oh, she's very pretty, but isn't she too small? How old is she?"

"She's six. I bought her for Eirana because she said her father's horses are too tall for her. She should be perfect, don't you think? And she's very sweet tempered." He looked across at Hilaira, smiling, and saw that her smile had melted away. "What's the matter?"

"You haven't heard."

"What?"

"Eirana married Asteropus."

"Married?"

Hilaira nodded.

He just stood there, feeling the joy drain out of him and the warmth fade from the day.

"I'm sorry, Leo."

"What does she see in him? What does he have that I don't?"

Hilaira swallowed. If she hadn't loved Alkander, she would have loved Leonidas. She did not understand how Eirana could reject him in favor of the long-faced, dreary priest. "I don't know," she admitted. Leonidas looked so hurt that she wanted to reach out to him, but already he had turned away from her and announced that he had to report back to barracks.

He sprang onto his own horse and was gone. She was left with her basket of eggs, staring after him as he rode away. What a fool Eirana was!

———

Leonidas was glad that he had to report to his syssitia for dinner. He knew if he'd been on his own all evening, he would have spent it trying to figure out why Eirana had rejected him. Instead, at his syssitia he was distracted by the curiosity of the others about his travels and by their news.

They were nineteen altogether, from the chairman, Nikostratos, to the two youngest members, Alkander and himself. Tradition required young men to apply for membership to a syssitia on attaining their citizenship at age twenty-one, and each syssitia had to vote unanimously to accept new candidates. Leonidas and Alkander had decided as boys that they would join the same syssitia and had, after serving as mess-boys in one after another as custom demanded, selected this one—mostly because the chairman, Nikostratos, was wise and well educated, and had been kind to the ridiculed Alkander.

Nikostratos was now fifty-eight and had been elected city treasurer for many years running. He had thinning gray hair and his eyesight was going, too, particularly in the dark, so he used a walking stick, but his wits were still as sharp as ever. Leonidas found himself relying on Nikostratos' advice more and more.

But the first person to greet him at the syssitia was Alkander. His friend, no less than Hilaira, greeted him with exuberant thanks for his reluctant help, and reinforced all his wife had already said—their wedding had gone well and Hilaira's father had forgiven them any alleged misdeeds.

One by one the others arrived, hung their himations on the hooks by the door, and slipped out of their sandals to recline on the benches, glad of the braziers burning in the center of the room. They welcomed Leonidas back warmly, and quickly brought him up to date on Cleomenes' renewed agitation to campaign against Athens and on rumors of Argive infringements along their common border.

"It's because of this disaster with our allies!" one of the members of the mess insisted. "The Argives don't believe our allies will support us if we are attacked. They think they can strike with impunity."

"They are eager to test us. We will have to respond sharply, or they will only become bolder."

"They are using hit-and-run tactics. They go ashore, plunder an isolated farm, burn down the buildings, and then return to their ships and disappear again. By the time the fire is seen and troops arrive, they are already gone. We can't be everywhere at once."

"The perioikoi say we need a stronger naval presence to intercept the Argive ships before they can land their raiding parties."

"The perioikoi want a stronger Lacedaemonian fleet to protect their trading interests!" someone shot back.

"And what is so wrong with that? We profit from their trading as well."

"Do we? I wonder if we wouldn't be better off living from our own resources. Foreign trade only brings foreign entanglements. We have enough trouble with Messenia."

"Leonidas just returned from Messenia," Nikostratos said, entering the conversation. "Let's hear what he has to say. Leo?"

Leonidas was not unprepared for the question. He had spent much of the last month consciously trying to form his opinion in order to articulate it here. "We are hated there; and some of that hate is traditional, passed from father to son in the stories children are told, just as we learn of Messenian atrocities in the agoge. But some of the problem is the men we leave there to manage our estates. Some of these men are merely mediocre, and so resented by men who think themselves better. Others are outright cruel and arbitrary, reaping deserved hatred that grows and festers."

Nikostratos was pleased with the answer. "Quite right! I have argued this many times. As absentee landlords, we often rely on petty tyrants who do us more disservice than service."

"Yes, but if you do not ride the Messenians hard, they will rob you blind. They do not think they owe us rent at all," one of the others protested; and soon a lively discussion of the Messenian problem developed—which led, naturally, nowhere.

———

When dinner was over, Nikostratos caught Leonidas by the arm and asked him to walk home with him. "I cannot see as I should; you don't mind guiding me the few steps to my townhouse?"

"Of course not."

Outside, the others dispersed rapidly into the darkness; while from all the other syssitia lining the road to Amyclae, men likewise emerged in laughing groups that then melted into the darkness. At the outskirts of the city itself, silence enveloped them except for a dog's distant barking—which made Beggar tense and raise her ears, then drop her head and continue walking beside Leonidas as if to say she had chosen him. "I thought I should tell you that Eirana, daughter of Kyranios, married this last month while you were away."

"Yes, I heard."

"Ah, that's why you looked so dejected," Nikostratos surmised and stopped. They faced each other. "She was a worthy choice, Leonidas, but you must put this behind you. You are still very young. I don't know why you young men are all in such a hurry to wed these days.

I was twenty-six before I took a wife, and we still had plenty of time to found a family."

Leonidas nodded dutifully. Nikostratos had two children, a son and a daughter, both of whom were married and had children of their own. Nikostratos himself was widowed and lived alone in a couple of rooms over a shop so he could attend to his civic duties, because his kleros was halfway to Gytheon. Leonidas thought he was a lonely man who buried himself in his work in part to avoid the emptiness of his private life—but he dared not say that. Instead, he remembered, "You wouldn't have use for a pretty little mare? I bought her for Eirana, because she said her father's horses were too tall. Now I can't bear the sight of her."

Nikostratos answered after a slight pause, "I have no use for her, but I will ask around." He changed the subject. "You made a wise choice to settle Pelopidas and his family on your kleros. They are very grateful and anxious to make a success of it. However, you need to be sure they have the building materials they need. They think you expect them to buy it themselves."

Leonidas sighed. In his present mood, his kleros and the helot family were just a burden, another problem, but he said dutifully, "I will visit them tomorrow."

"Do not be discouraged by the rejection of one young woman, no matter how worthy she was," Nikostratos reiterated. "Sometimes I think it is good for us to be denied what we think we want. We all too often get fixated on a single goal and become blind to all else."

Leonidas nodded politely, not really in the mood for this fatherly talk. Then again, his father had died when he was very young, and he had often wished for an older man to give him advice when he was confused. He also reminded himself that Nikostratos had never given him bad advice.

"I used to be very ambitious," Nikostratos continued. "I could see that the state finances were in chaotic disarray and that the city was always bankrupt despite being rich. All I wanted was to become treasurer so I could put things in order. Now I have done that, and I realize that I have only made things worse. Now your brother has the means to pursue his reckless adventures. In your father's time, I could always tell the kings, "Sorry, we can't afford that." But your brother knows the treasury is full—thanks to me." He laughed sadly. "Ironic, isn't it?"

"Do you never long for a democracy like Athens, with no kings at all?"

"Heavens, no! Why, they even elect their polemarchs! Can you imagine that? Turning the fate of the city over to the man who has the best dinner parties or pays the potters and papyrus-makers more than his rivals? Our kings may be a little eccentric at times, but they still have the blood of Herakles in their veins. I have not yet seen a Spartan king who lacked courage or did not have the instincts of a warrior."

"My brother included?"

"Your brother included. He has the right instincts—he is bold, cunning, quick to see his enemy's weaknesses, and merciless in exploiting them. He simply allows himself to get distracted too easily and is not as steady of purpose as he should be. He could use a little more of your stubbornness and tenacity." Nikostratos paused, smiled, and added: "And you could use a little more of your brother's capriciousness. Then maybe you would quickly find another maiden to court."

Leonidas only sighed.

"This is far enough. I can see my own way home from here. You don't want to be late." He nodded toward the broad, straight street leading to Leonidas' barracks, and they parted.

CHAPTER 4

THE IMPORTANCE OF BEING PRETTY

GORGO WAS SEVEN WHEN SHE WAS confronted by the fact that she was not considered pretty. The priestesses from the shrine to Helen at Therapne had all the girls between the ages of seven and fourteen muster on the Dancing Floor in order to select which ones would take part in the Heleneia this year. The selected maidens would be garlanded in flowers and walk in the procession, followed by flower-studded straw chariots carrying the prettiest maiden from each of the five villages of the city, to the shrine.

There were usually twenty girls chosen as "flower girls," and Gorgo was eagerly looking forward to taking part now that she was at last old enough. It never occurred to Gorgo that she might not be chosen; but when the priestesses walked along the rows of eager and expectant girls, pointing a finger at the girls they found worthy, they walked past her without a glance. The look on their faces was indifferently dismissive—as if she were no more worthy of consideration than a mule among horses. Gorgo was stunned.

She ran to the fountain house, clambered up on the stone trough, and gazed at her reflection in the water. But her image was shattered by the next helot girl who plunged an amphora into the water to fill it. She ran out again, starting for home, but at the agora she paused to look at her reflection on the burnished bronze face of a massive hoplon hung up for sale. Her face was distorted in the hammered, convex surface, and she ran on, frightened.

She reached the Agiad royal palace by the back entrance and scampered into the stableyard, deftly dodging the men offloading hay from a wagon in the alley and ducking under the belly of one of her father's chariot horses, who was being groomed at a spot that blocked her path to the kitchen stairway.

"You're old enough to know better than that!" the startled groom scolded, frightened to think what would happen if the king's precious child were kicked by the powerful beast. Fortunately the stallion was dozing contentedly in the sun, only barely interested in flicking at flies with his tail.

Meanwhile, Gorgo was already halfway up the stairs and running (now a little breathlessly) down the corridor of the helots' quarters toward the inner courtyard and the private dwellings of the royal family. "Mama! Mama!" Gorgo called as she skidded around the corner into her mother's chamber.

"Hush!" her mother admonished angrily. "You'll wake your baby brother!"

Her mother, as usual, was hanging over the cradle of her youngest child. Gorgo had lost two younger siblings already: one when he was a toddler and the other when he was just a few weeks old. The latter had been so sickly that everyone shook their heads and whispered that the elders wouldn't accept him anyway. Now there was another baby brother in the cradle, and Gorgo found it hard to take an interest in him. To her he did not look any different from the others, red and wrinkled and squalling all the time. She did not really think he would live very long, either, so why should she pay him much attention? Obedient to her mother, however, she lowered her voice and whispered loudly, "Mama! They didn't pick me."

"For what? What are you babbling about?"

"To be a flower girl!" Gorgo insisted, utterly uncomprehending how her mother could forget something as important as this. "For the Heleneia!"

"Oh, that! I thought I told you not to bother? Besides, this year Demaratus will be making the sacrifice. It wouldn't be seemly for you to be among the maidens in the procession."

Gorgo frowned. She understood about the eternal rivalry between the two royal families of Sparta, and that it was important never to suggest that the rival line had some sort of precedence over her own house; but her mother was missing the whole point. "But mother, they didn't even *want* me!"

"Of course not; something like that is only for pretty girls. Why, even that hussy Percalus did it." Percalus was the Eurypontid queen, and Gorgo's mother hated her with a bitterness that far exceeded the everyday rivalry between the Agiad and the Eurypontid rulers. As soon as the name Percalus arose in connection with the flower girls, Gorgo knew she would get no sympathy from her mother; so she gave up and ran down the hall to her grandmother's chamber.

She was relieved to find her grandmother at her loom, as Chilonis was an active woman and often away from the palace during the day. "Grandmama!" Gorgo called out as she rushed to fling herself at her grandmother, certain of a receptive hug.

Chilonis was caught a little off guard by the unexpected arrival of her granddaughter, but she managed to open her arms just in time. The impact of the seven-year-old was enough to almost knock her off the stool, however, and she found herself admonishing the child, "Not so rough! You're too old for that!"

But Gorgo felt her grandmother's warm arms close around her skinny body, and she knew the older woman was not really angry with her. She ignored the scolding, looked up into her grandmother's square face, and pleaded hopefully, "Grandmama, I'm not ugly, am I?"

"No, of course not," Chilonis assured her firmly. "Have some of the boys from the agoge been teasing you or something?" Chilonis, confident that this was just a childhood misunderstanding, even dropped her arms and turned back to her loom.

"It wasn't the boys," Gorgo told her urgently. "It was the priestesses of the shrine of Helen. They didn't even look at me—for the flower girls for the Heleneia!" Gorgo's distress, as well as her words, drew her grandmother's attention back to her. She was looking up at her grandmother with wide-set eyes, and Chilonis registered that the child understood fully the difference between the taunting of children and the judgment of grown women. She sighed and took Gorgo back into her arms.

Gorgo understood that, too. It meant it was true: she was ugly. She clung to her grandmother in fright. She knew it was terrible for a girl to be ugly. Hadn't her mother become queen because she was the prettiest maiden in Sparta at the time? And the same was said of Queen Percalus—that she was the prettiest maiden of the next "crop," so pretty that King Demaratus had taken her with*out* a dowry.

Chilonis could read Gorgo's thoughts, and she freed one hand to ruffle the top of Gorgo's head of unruly bright-red hair. "It's all my fault, Little One. You take after me."

Gorgo frowned and looked up in indignation. "But *you're* not ugly!"

Chilonis smiled faintly. "Thank you, but that's not what your grandfather thought. Your grandfather would not have been half so reluctant to take me to wife if he had found me more attractive. And had I been a beauty like your mother or Percalus, then he would no doubt have visited my bed more often—no matter how difficult his first wife, Taygete, made life for him at home. No, my child, there is no point denying it: I was never considered a beauty, and you seem to have taken after me rather than your own lovely mother."

Gorgo, still frowning, thought about that. She had never thought of her grandmother as in any way deficient. She certainly wasn't *ugly* the way some old women were. She was not pock-marked, she had all her teeth, and she had no warts or birthmarks or other deformities. She had a pleasant face and hair the color of bay horses, now streaked with gray. Gorgo did not think it was so bad taking after her grandmother, if it meant she was like her in other ways as well. "Am I as clever as you are, too, Grandmama?"

Chilonis laughed at that and ruffled her hair again. "You are twice as clever as I ever was, child."

Gorgo broke free of her grandmother's arms, but only in order to be able to face her more firmly. "Don't make fun of me!" she demanded, frowning more fiercely than ever. "Papa says *you* can write poetry and do geometry and read the language of the Egyptians!"

Chilonis laughed again. "I tried to learn hieroglyphics from an Egyptian merchant one winter, but without much success, I fear. And I can teach you geometry if you like, but it was *my* mother who was *really* clever at mathematics. She was a student of the great scholar Pythagoras."

"Daddy says all his brains come from your side of the family," Gorgo insisted, still trying to come to terms with not being pretty, talking herself into being proud that she took after her not-pretty grandmother.

Chilonis understood, and so she did not contradict this statement. Instead, she suggested that Gorgo and she go out for an excursion. Gorgo eagerly agreed. There was nothing she liked more than going places with her grandmother, unless it was going places with her father. Chilonis wound a himation expertly around her neck and shoulders and fastened it with a large silver clasp decorated with the face of a gorgon. Then she took Gorgo by the hand, went back down to the stables, and ordered her two-horse chariot made ready for them.

Gorgo eagerly helped the grooms. She expertly ran her hand down the back of one mare's legs and picked out her hooves, one after another. She combed out the tail and vigorously brushed away stable stains from knees and hocks. Then she climbed aboard the chariot as the grooms backed the team into the traces. At last they were ready, and Chilonis deftly turned the team to face the exit and clicked at them to walk forward.

It was a hot, sunny day and the air over the city was laden with fine dust: stirred up by the supply wagons trundling through the narrow lanes, kicked up by the herds of boys at play, and blown in desultory clouds from the drill fields across the river. Chilonis turned the chariot away from the river and headed north, past the ball field surrounded by its moat and plane trees. She took the northwest road leading gently up into the narrows of the Eurotas valley.

As Chilonis drove she explained to her granddaughter, who had fallen silent and appeared to be brooding again, "The fate of pretty women is not always pretty. Take the most famous of all Spartan princesses, Helen. When she was still a girl, she was abducted by Theseus and had to be rescued by her brothers. Then she was coveted by so many men that her father held a contest among her suitors to auction her off to the one who found his favor. Because of her irresistible beauty she was abducted yet again, this time by a foolish foreign prince, and held captive for ten years in Asia. Even if she was, as some say, seduced rather than abducted, she must still have suffered to see the horrible war she caused. In contrast, her less attractive cousin, Penelope, was courted by and married to the good Odysseus, the man of her own choice. You see," Chilonis continued, as she drew up the chariot before a small and ancient monument showing a woman wrapped in a himation, "it is said that on this very spot Penelope pulled her shawl up over her head to indicate to her pursuing father that she went willingly with Odysseus."

Gorgo stared with new interest at the ancient statue in the shade of the simple Doric temple. "Is that how our custom of stealing brides started?" she wanted to know.

Chilonis smiled, pleased by the notion. "Yes, maybe. I don't think anyone knows, but it could go back to Penelope. After all, Helen was given to the man of her father's choice and then turned adulterous—whether by force or free will. Penelope married the man of her *own* choice and was true to him—a much more Spartan pattern." This said, she clicked her tongue to the team, and they continued on their way out of the city into the surrounding well-cultivated countryside.

"I am going to confess something to you, Gorgo, that I have never told another soul, not even your father." She paused and Gorgo gazed at her expectantly. "I want you to know that I was not at all unhappy that your grandfather visited me so seldom. I was much happier having my own household and doing much as I liked, than I would have been with all the obligations of a queen. So, you see, there are some advantages to being not-so-pretty—at least here in Sparta, where women have so much freedom."

Gorgo seemed to consider this very carefully, her brows drawn together in concentration. Then she nodded solemnly. "You don't *act* unhappy. And I cannot change it, can I?" She looked up as if hoping for one last promise of things getting better.

Chilonis shook her head and laid a hand on her granddaughter's fragile shoulder. "No, you cannot change the color of your hair or your eyes, nor can you make your mouth small and full and red. You will never be a great beauty; but if you have the sense to know that a woman is more than a façade and that her value is not in the beauty of her exterior but in the soundness of her mind, body, and character, then you will discover that men who share these qualities—like the good Odysseus—will recognize those qualities in you."

CHAPTER 5

FIRST BLOOD

PELOPIDAS' FAMILY HAD MADE REMARKABLY GOOD progress since arriving in Laconia. At first they had lived in a lean-to shack and fetched water from the Eurotas, but soon they had cleared the well, and room by room they started making the helot quarters habitable. As they systematically cleared away the rubbish from the fire, they carefully salvaged anything that might be reused. Beams that were charred only at one end were cut down and the good portions saved. Tiles were sorted carefully, and where clean breaks and large pieces made it possible to piece them together again, they were saved. Using only these salvaged materials, the Messenians made the helot kitchen habitable, and they soon had the hearth and ovens working again. Meanwhile, Pelopidas cleared the scrub brush from several acres of land and readied them for plowing.

As the spring equinox approached, Leonidas spotted Pelopidas in this cleared field between the house and the river, driving the oxen hitched to a plow. Beside him, pushing a hand cart, was Polychares. It was hard work trying to break up earth that had been unturned for decades, and the oxen strained and staggered as they ran up against roots, tree stubs, and rocks. Polychares, like his father wearing only a loincloth, struggled to remove the stones turned up by the plow and load them into the hand cart. As Leonidas watched, Pelopidas shouted and stopped the team, took an ax from the handcart, and

started to hack at a tree stump. Leonidas shook his head unconsciously. There seemed so much more to do than he had anticipated.

At the house Leonidas tethered his horse on a sapling. The sound
of hammering and sawing came from the tract of outbuildings that
Pantes used as a workshop, while the two little girls squabbled in their
high-pitched voices as they trampled on clothes in a large wooden
vat in the courtyard, holding their hems up out of the water. Smoke
wafted from the repaired chimney, and the smell of something delicious enveloped Leonidas. Beggar lifted her nose and ears, her nostrils
quivering in anticipation. Leonidas couldn't resist the scent, either.
Rather than ducking into the workshop to see what Pantes was
working on now, he went to the kitchen instead.

Laodice was bent before the open oven, removing a metal sheet
on which baked goods were carefully placed. They were swollen and
glistening with fat and smelled of cinnamon, apple, and honey. She
had wrapped rags around her hands to be able to handle the hot tray,
and sweat dripped from her red face, her hair completely covered by
her snood. She backed away from the oven with the tray and turned
to set it on the brick counter beside the oven.

Leonidas was behind her, and she had not registered his presence.
He couldn't resist reaching around her and snatching one of the
pastries from the tray, popping it into his mouth.

Laodice jabbed an elbow backward in a sharp but well-practiced
motion as she scolded, "Keep your filthy paws off them! They aren't
for you!" The tray down, she turned around to finish telling off her
younger son, and was confronted by the sight of her master jumping
from one foot to the other as he tried to chew and let cool air into
his mouth at the same time. The shock of having jabbed and shouted
rudely at her master was completely obliterated by the sight of him
hopping around like a small boy, and she laughed without thinking.
Then, terrified of what she'd done, she covered her mouth and held
her breath, fear replacing amusement.

"That's the first time I've seen you smile," Leonidas observed as
he swallowed down the apple tart.

"I'm sorry, master—"

"I'm not. Those are *delicious*! You could make a fortune selling
them in the market!"

"That's what I hoped, master. I wanted to take as many as I could bake to market tomorrow. When you snatched one, I thought you were one of my boys, but you are welcome, of course. Just let them cool a little."

Leonidas looked at the pastries, and his mouth, despite his burned tongue, was watering again, but he knew he should not steal Laodice's source of income. He knew they needed many things to make this ruin a home. He looked away from the apple tarts and focused instead on Laodice. "Is there anything I can help you with?"

Laodice seemed to start, then she looked away. She wiped the sweat from her face with the rags on her hands and then pulled the rags off, her eyes down. "You have given us so much already, I don't think we can ask for anything more."

"This kleros is worthless to me without you," he reminded her simply; and his eyes surveyed the barren kitchen, looking for something they might need. They had brought their household goods—utensils, cutlery, pottery, and linens—with them in the ox-cart in which he had sent them to Laconia. Leonidas had also ensured that building materials were delivered, along with straw and hay for the oxen and staples to sustain them until the first harvest.

"Master, there is only one thing…" Her voice drifted off.

"Yes?"

"Crius. His hands. If there were something we could do to heal his hands, then he would be more use to you."

"Of course. I'll take him to see a surgeon. Where is he?" Leonidas looked around, surprised that he had not seen him earlier.

"He is mucking out the stables."

Leonidas went out to the stables. The manure was being carefully heaped upon the bed of the ox-cart so that it could be hauled out onto the field. Pitching the heavy, soiled straw up onto the wagon was hard work for the little boy, particularly since his grip on the heavy pitchfork was awkward and uncertain. He was working naked, sweating and breathing hard.

"Crius!"

The boy turned around and grinned at once. He dropped the pitchfork and ran forward to throw his arms around Beggar. The bitch licked his face and wagged her tail in equal enthusiasm.

"Get yourself cleaned up," Leonidas ordered. "I'm taking you into the city."

Crius didn't wait to be asked twice. He rushed out of the stableyard and down to the river's edge, Beggar running beside him. The river was still cold. Crius stopped when he was just knee deep, bent down, and plunged his hands into the water to splash it over his shoulders. Then he rubbed his hands and arms to clean them while Beggar frolicked about in the shallows. When Crius came running back, Beggar bounded after him, shaking herself dry as she came into the yard again.

Crius started chattering excitedly, "Can I ride on your horse with you? What are we going to see? Is there a market? Can we go to the temples?"

"We're going to see a doctor."

Crius went silent.

"Come on." Leonidas tossed the boy the chiton he had left carelessly on a bench, and started for his horse. When he reached it, Laodice came out with a little satchel of things. Leonidas looked at her questioningly. "For you and the doctor." Leonidas looked inside; it was filled with her apple tarts. He looked at her again, questioningly. "I can make more," she insisted. Leonidas knew that she didn't have unlimited supplies of the ingredients, especially not the expensive cinnamon; but he understood her need to thank him the only way she knew how.

Leonidas took Crius to the lochos physician and returned to barracks to stable his horse before going to the baths. He was met by Mantiklos before he had even dismounted. "I was about to come fetch you, sir! We're under marching orders! Tomorrow at first light."

"Why? Where? What's happened?" Leonidas jumped down, catching the mood of excitement at once.

"Kythera. The Argives have landed troops on Kythera and are burning everything in their path."

The island of Kythera and the eastern shore of the Malean peninsula had all once been part of the Argolid. Piece by piece over the centuries, Spartan blood and persistence had wrested them from the hands of Argos. The Argives wanted them back—every single rock, tree, and well.

Up to now, however, the Argives had confined themselves to hit-and-run raids, plundering isolated farmsteads and then setting them on fire, or capturing Lacedaemonian ships that had the misfortune to cross paths with Argive warships. Because Cleomenes was agitating for yet another campaign against Athens, however, the Council had decided to deploy only a single lochos to the Argive border. The idea was to discourage Argive incursions while keeping the bulk of the army in Sparta, ready to march north. As spring came and the campaign season approached, ambassadors had been sent forth to the allies in an effort to forge a majority in favor of war with Athens. The border with Argos had remained surprisingly quiet. Now they knew why.

"How many men are we sending?" Leonidas wanted to know.

Mantiklos shook his head helplessly. No one had told him. Leonidas searched around the courtyard for someone who might know and caught sight of his company commander, Diodoros, who was giving orders to the quartermaster. He waited politely until his commander was finished. As the latter turned to leave, Leonidas addressed him. "How many troops are we sending, sir?"

"Just two pentekostus for now. We're to report back on the strength of the enemy and send for help if we need it."

By dusk the next evening Leonidas' hundred-man company was embarking on three small ships, one enomotia per ship. The ships, known as penteconters, were owned and manned by perioikoi and had just a single bank of oars and twenty-five rowing benches, unlike the three-banked triremes that had become masters of the seas in recent decades. They were painted bright colors with huge eyes flanking the battering ram, which lay in the wet sands as if looking out to sea. They were beached side by side on a sandy cove in the Laconian Gulf east of Gytheon.

Leonidas had not boarded a ship since his ill-fated adventure as a boy, and he was reminded briefly of that embarrassing episode; but this was very different. They boarded by unit in neat files that ascended from the beach to the deck of each ship by ladders reaching down from the high, curving sterns to the hard sand of the beach.

The ladders were long, and they sagged and bounced under the weight of the men. Leonidas was glad that his armor and arms were being boarded as cargo.

The attendants, Mantiklos included, had to wade out into knee-deep water, holding their own and their masters' equipment in bundles over their heads. Sailors hooked the bundles onto the end of a rope that was fed through a block and tackle at the end of the yardarm. At a signal, men on deck hoisted each parcel up above the rail, while other sailors swung the yard fore and aft so the bundle could be lowered onto the deck. This procedure had to be repeated hundreds of times. Night had come by the time they were fully loaded.

Conditions aboard the penteconter were very crowded. Each enomotia numbered roughly thirty-two hoplites; with their attendants and support helots, that made for close to one hundred men. All had their equipment, and both men and parcels had to be kept out of the way of the oarsmen. They were literally crammed into every corner, and they sat or stood between the banks of oars and crowded together on the quarterdeck and the foredeck. Leonidas worked his way to the bows and swung a leg over the side to sit astride it. This freed him from the press of people around him and gave him a better view.

The careful planning that had gone into even this simple operation became evident as the tide came in and started to float the now-heavy penteconter off the sand. As part of the crew shoved and pushed the ship down the beach, a wave came in and the whole vessel rolled drunkenly. At a shout the sailors scrambled to get back aboard the vessel and the oars started to bite into the water, oozing the ship into the bay.

One of the other penteconters had gotten away already and was leading, while the third was still loading. There was a brisk breeze and the swells were running quite high. Whitecaps curled here and there in the darkness, and the snout of the penteconter churned the dark seas white as it cut and battered its way forward.

Before long the first men started to feel sick and tried to squeeze their way to the railing. Some made it, others didn't. There was considerable cursing as the vomit splattered on other men and the deck, making it unsafe and slippery as well as vile-smelling. Others followed Leonidas' example and scrambled onto the railing itself—although this was hardly a safe perch as the ship rolled and pitched its way forward.

Leonidas concentrated on the horizon. He was amazed by how clearly it could be seen despite the darkness. It was a cloudless night, and the stars were so bright that they turned the heavens a distinctly lighter shade of blue than the heaving seas, much less the ominous shore. The bow-wave was a brilliant white—just like the white caps and the snows of Taygetos that one could see looming out of the darkness behind them. On the shore, the occasional smudge of orange marked a farmhouse or a village where torches, lamps, and hearth fires burned.

Gradually Leonidas became aware that something dark blotted out the stars to starboard, and then he realized that it was edged with white. It could only be the island of Kythera itself. It loomed up sharply with steep, uninhabited slopes. The captain swung the bows to starboard to steer a course directly between the island and the Malean peninsula. This meant they were running broadside to the waves, and the rolling of the penteconter became alarming to the landlubbers crowded on her decks. Here and there men lost their footing and slipped and fell, now and then taking others with them, accompanied by a short spasm of violent cursing. For the most part, however, they were packed so closely together that they had no room to fall down.

At last the bows swung to starboard yet again, and the little ship surged on a series of waves that overtook them and passed them by, leaving them wallowing in the trough before the next wave lifted them up and pushed them forward for another few yards. The oars occasionally bit into air, but they made good progress, and soon a long, white beach was visible before them. An island started to shield them from both wind and waves, and the captain ordered every other oarsman to rest as he slowed the ship down to a crawl. To their left, one of the other penteconters was also cautiously nosing its way forward.

A sudden swirl of white in the darkness off to starboard alerted Leonidas to danger. Rocks and reefs stretched far out into the bay. A sailor scrambled up the mast and sat astride the yard, shouting instructions down to the helmsman. They maneuvered cautiously into the bay, approaching the shore at a decorous pace until they were about two hundred paces away. Here the penteconter pivoted around neatly, and then the oarsman backwatered the ship toward the shore. One of the deck officers shouted, "Get inboard! On deck! Now!"

Leonidas and his companions barely managed to get their feet on the deck before the stern of the ship struck the shore with a loud crunching and creaking. Everyone was thrown forward. Leonidas would have lost his footing if they hadn't been pressed so closely together. The ship crunched to a stop. The waves broke around her bow and swept up the beach to the hissing sound of frothing water and tumbling, clacking stones turning over on themselves.

The Spartan officers took over from the seamen. Even before the oars were fully shipped, the hoplites were ordered over the side. Leonidas was one of the first to scramble up over the railing and drop onto the stony beach below. He fell into water that was still bitterly cold and came up to his groin, sucking at him and trying to pull him back down the beach as it retreated. He had to struggle to keep his footing on the rolling, shifting stones, and for a panicked moment he thought he would fall.

Around him others were dropping into the water with loud splashes and the same kind of flailing about. From the deck overhead someone was shouting at them to move out of the way. "Get ashore, you idiots! Move up onto the beach!"

Leonidas started slogging through the foam, fighting against the undertow. How did men ever do this wearing armor and carrying their arms? How could you slog up a beach defended by an enemy? Indeed, how could they be sure the Argives weren't here? Leonidas looked around in the darkness, expecting a phalanx of Argives to emerge any moment. Fortunately, it didn't.

Instead, more and more Spartans splashed into the water and waded up onto the shore. As the three ships, all of which were now beached, became lighter, their crews followed the soldiers overboard to haul them fully out of the water. When the ships were completely beached, the helots began offloading the equipment.

Gradually, order started to vanquish chaos. The hoplites formed up by unit. Roll call was taken. Arms and armor were brought. They were ordered to kit up and did so wearily, their attendants helping with hands clumsy from lack of sleep. It was approaching dawn and they had been up nearly twenty-four hours straight. They were all tired. Leonidas thought of the times in the agoge when they had been made to stay on their feet all day and all night, marching, standing watch, marching again. It had seemed sadistic at the time. Now he was thankful for it.

The eastern horizon paled and the stars were fading away. At a shout, the first enomotia started forward, to the distinctive clank of bronze on bronze as the aspis carried on their backs jostled against one another. But then they started singing, and the clanking of hoplons was drowned out by the chorus of men.

Leonidas was in the second enomotia, and their turn came next. They were marching in four-by-eight formation, the commander in the front rank on the right. Leonidas, as one of the youngest men in the unit, was in the middle, sandwiched between men more experienced than he.

They marched northwest along the shoreline toward what appeared to be a small city or fortified town. The town was apparently still sound asleep, and Leonidas mentally derided the fools for their poor watch. With Argive troops operating on the island, they should have had men manning the walls, ready to challenge any approaching force, regardless of the hour of the day. How could they be so certain that these three hoplite formations were their own?

The singing of the first company faltered and died away. Then the front ranks of Leonidas' own enomotia fell silent. Leonidas glanced to his left and then to his right. He knew the men beside him intimately after eighteen months in the same thirty-two-man unit. They were Sperchias, from his own age cohort, and Aristandos, who was just a year older. Aristandos was a bit of a braggart and a showoff who thought he was destined for command and fame. Sperchias was more modest, but with a wonderful wit and a sunny temperament. The looks they gave Leonidas, however, were identical, and they reflected his own thoughts: something was wrong.

They passed between the square crenelated towers that flanked the gates, and the smell of charcoal was strong. All that was left of the heavy gates were the hinges. They entered a ghost town. Everything

in it was black with soot if it had not burned to ash. Nothing lived.
Not even a stray cat or dog. They drew up in what had once been
a broad square. The very temples were blackened from the smoke
of the fires, and the roofs had caved into the sanctuaries. Diodoros,
their company commander, ordered them to stand at ease, and with
the three enomotarchs went from building to building around the
square. When they were finished, they were ordered to march out
again.

They set up camp outside the walls with great care. None of them
were in doubt anymore that they were at war.

———

The hoplites were given ample time to rest and eat, because their
commanders wanted intelligence before moving in any direction.
Most especially they wanted to establish contact with the Heraklid
Company, which had set out several hours ahead of them but had
landed on the western shore of the island. While one of the penteconters was sent back to the mainland for provisions, the other two
were sent on reconnaissance along the coast, with the primary task
of locating the Argive ships. Meanwhile, helot scouts were sent out
into the countryside to try to find locals who could give them information.

By noon intelligence started to flood into the Spartan camp in
the form of shepherds, fishermen, and farmers who seemed to crawl
out of the earth itself. They came filthy, hungry, exhausted, and full
of tales of horror. There were a few women or children among them,
but these were clearly terrified beyond tears and lamentations. Even
the children were eerily silent—too terrified to cry anymore.

The Argives had landed more than a week ago. They had landed
on this beach, but not with penteconters or triremes. They had come
disguised as merchants and had set up an open market not far from
where the Spartans now camped. The unsuspecting townspeople had
come out to shop. They had left the gates to their city wide open
behind them. The Argives had slipped men, still dressed as merchants,
into the city. Then abruptly they threw off their friendly demeanor,
drew their swords, and started killing people fast and furiously. Only
rarely had anyone been able to defend himself. Some people, those

telling the story, escaped into the surrounding hills. From here they had seen how the Argives plundered the town haphazardly, putting to the torch anything that did not gratify their immediate wants and needs. Anyone who fell into Argive hands, regardless of sex or age, was killed. The girls were usually raped first, but they were killed afterward. The Argives were taking no prisoners.

Horrifying as the tales were, however, they were not very helpful. The Spartans needed to know where the Argives were *now*, but all these survivors could tell them was that they had sailed away. One or two told of trying to get to relatives in other towns, but said they had turned back when they saw smoke in the sky, indicating the Argives had gotten there first. They felt safe here, because there was nothing left that would entice the Argives to come back.

———

Brotus was with the Heraklid Company, which landed on the west shore of the island. Here they went ashore in the narrow mouth of a steep gorge and toiled their way up from the shore single file along a narrow, stony path. They found no evidence of Argive incursions except some slaughtered cattle, until they reached a fountain house cut into the side of the slope near a natural waterfall. The Argives had evidently taken the place by surprise, presumably in the early morning before news had gotten out about their presence. There was no evidence of any kind of resistance, indeed no male victims at all. All the corpses were female, women come to fetch water.

The women had evidently been rounded up, collected in one place, and then forced to strip. Their clothes were all together in a single heap. They had then been collectively ravaged—old and young, pretty or plain—before being killed. By the state of decay, the Spartans calculated that the massacre had taken place at least two days earlier. Now flies feasted, particularly in the eyes, mouths, and bloody crevices between the legs of the victims.

Brotus found the sight of all these naked women, sprawled around with their legs apart, fascinating. He was particularly drawn to one woman. She was not the youngest of the victims; in fact, she was matronly with enormous breasts. She lay draped backward over a wall, and her breasts hung down in the wrong direction. He circled back to get a second look at her because the sight quickened his loins. He decided to ask Lathria to hang like that off the edge of the bed next time he visited her.

The helots were tasked with burying the women and the Heraklid Company continued inland, past a burned village that perched on the top of the cliff with a view to the west. They encountered straying farm animals, including some cows, lowing with pain from not having been milked. As the attendants rounded these up and milked them, Brotus watched the way they pulled at the udders and the milk spurted. He wondered if women's milk spurted like that if you squeezed the breasts of a nursing mother. He pictured grabbing the big breasts of the dead woman and squirting warm milk into his mouth.

"Here, have some!" A helot handed him a black mug with fresh milk in it. Brotus gulped it down and turned away before anyone noticed he had an erection.

Brotus lay down to sleep like the others, his himation wrapped around his helmet to make it softer, and the helmet under his head. The day was warm. Bees hummed in the nearby olive orchards. Goat-bells tinkled in the distance. Brotus saw the breasts of the dead woman swaying before his eyes. He brushed the flies away and reached for one. He put his mouth to the nipple, closed his lips around it, sucked in—

"Up, up!"

The section leader was kicking them awake. "Up, up! The Argives are just five miles away. Fighting kit!"

Brotus started shaking. The excitement was overwhelming. Although every man knew exactly what he had to do—although they had practiced it dozens, scores, hundreds of times—this was different. Brotus could sense it. This was it. The real thing. He was about to engage in real combat.

At the edge of the camp, the company commander swung himself onto one of the scout horses and galloped away, apparently intent on seeing the enemy for himself before making his final dispositions. The enomotarchs were left with the task of forming up their troops.

Brotus' attendant could see his master was trembling so violently he couldn't re-pin his chiton at the shoulders. He reached forward to help, but Brotus knocked his hands away, furious that his temporary weakness had been noticed. "Get my aspis, you asshole!" The man withdrew sullenly. There were times he pictured hitting Brotus back or just abandoning him, but he had a wife and two children. He couldn't risk it. The best he could hope for was that the Argives would take care of Brotus for him. He glanced to the east. The front ranks of the company were forming up, shields on their arms and their helmets down, but spears still at the slope.

Brotus squirmed his way into his bronze breastplate and snapped the metal hinges shut, closing them with a metal pin. He yanked his helmet down over his face and grabbed his shield.

The company commander was back. He signaled the three enomotarchs over to him and gave orders, gesturing. A moment later the other two enomotia marched out, but Brotus' was left standing in the sun. Their enomotarch came over. He inspected them critically. Brotus felt the officer pause much too long in front of him, and he started sweating profusely, wondering if something was out of order; but then the commander moved on without comment. When he was finished, he ordered, "At ease. The other two enomotia are going to surround the Argive patrol and drive it this way. We'll see if any live long enough to face us."

"Shit!" someone said, putting their collective emotions into words. It was easier to do something than just to wait. Standing here on the road and waiting for the enemy was nerve-racking. But they did it.

The sun was getting higher and warmer. The bees had gone silent. So had the goat-bells. Brotus strained his ears for the sound of conflict. When he stopped expecting it, it finally came—on the wind from far away. Shouting; the clang of weapons. His blood quickened in his veins. Why wasn't he there?

As abruptly as it had started, it was over. Everything went silent again. A turtledove was calling from somewhere. A rider trotted up. The Argive patrol had been eliminated except for two prisoners. "We should have all the information we need out of them within an hour or two," he predicted.

The men were stood down, but Brotus could no longer sleep. He drifted to the command tent.

The other two enomotia returned. There had been no casualties. They were in good order and except for a cut forearm here, a bleeding lip there, the odd pulled tendon in knee or ankle, there were no casualties. The men were relaxed and joking. "Like killing fish in a barrel!" they bragged. "They squirmed a bit, but they didn't have much bite."

One of the prisoners screamed like a stuck pig, but he didn't tell them anything. The other proved more intelligent. The Argive force was almost one thousand strong, minus the troops guarding the ships. It had taken and burned the port of Skandia and was besieging the walled city on the hill behind it. Those who had managed to escape from Skandia had sought refuge here, and the city was hopelessly overcrowded. From what the Argives could see, there were hardly any fighting men in the city, just a bunch of farmers and merchants with makeshift panoply—and women, of course. The Argives had surrounded the city and cut off the water supply. They figured the city would surrender soon, and meanwhile they were feeding themselves on their spoils from the surrounding countryside.

The Spartans killed the informant and his more courageous companion and left the bodies to the scavengers. The troops were ordered to have a meal and rest.

"What?" Brotus asked, incredulous. "The Argives are just a few miles away! What is this? An army or a holiday excursion?"

"Are you a Spartan or a loud-mouthed Argive?" came the sharp retort.

Brotus frowned and looked over his shoulder to see who had insulted him. The man was tall, wiry, and good-looking. He was barely two years older than Brotus, but he was already a section leader and had a reputation as an exceptional fighter. Brotus bit his tongue, but noted the man resentfully. His name was Dienekes.

———

Leonidas felt as if he had only just drifted off to sleep when one of the sentries woke them. "Strike camp! Form up by unit! Marching kit!"

Aristandos cursed as he rolled to his feet.

Marching kit meant that they wore their breastplates and their swords, but spears, hoplons, greaves, and helmets were carried on their backs. While the hoplites got their kit rolled and stowed in their backpacks, the helots were taking down the tents and preparing to transport these and all the other accouterments of camping, from provisions to the pots and fire for cooking them. They had brought no pack animals on this expedition and would have to hump everything themselves.

They marched out by enomotia; and very shortly after setting off, they turned sharply to the right and started winding up the barren mountainside on a narrow track. One of the senior rankers, a man close to going off active duty, called over to Diodoros, "Where are we going, then?"

"We are to find the Argive ships and kill any Argive that makes it back to them. The Heraklid Company has been charged with making the assault on the Argive camp."

A ripple of discontent was audible in the ranks. The Heraklid Company, always the Heraklid Company, was to have the glory of the fight, and they were just to sit around and mop up any cowardly Argives that fled to their ships.

The steepness of the climb soon silenced them, however, and all that was heard was their heavy breathing and the occasional clatter of a dislocated stone rolling down the mountainside from the track. They marched inland first, and then along a plateau. The low scrub brush of the barren slopes near their landing beach gave way to richer vegetation. There were olive groves and other orchards, some already in bloom, their white blossoms like a distant mist on the face of the hills in the darkness. However, the farmsteads were darkened and abandoned. No sheep or goats grazed in the fields, and no hounds sounded the alarm as they trudged past.

After roughly four and a half hours' marching, they came to a fortified town. Here people were awake. Torches along the ramparts were waved to and fro and they could hear horns blowing, apparently as signals. As they approached the gate, a voice shouted down at them from the tower, "Who goes there?"

"Diodoros, Kastor Company, Pitanate Lochos," their commander replied simply.

"You're Spartan?"

"Do you have to see the color of our cloaks?"

The men on the tower huddled in consultation. Not surprisingly, they suspected a ruse. After a moment they shouted down, "Send us a herald, and we will speak with him."

Diodoros nodded, turned, and called for Sperchias.

Sperchias' family had property on Kythera, and Sperchias had visited more than once on holidays. He slipped out of his rank and file and reported to Diodoros. Diodoros gave him the herald's staff and sent him toward the gate.

"Remove the rest of your men a hundred paces!" ordered the man on the tower; and by the gleam of the torchlight on the ramparts overhead, Leonidas could see a man aiming an arrow at Sperchias, the tip following his every move.

A small door cut into the massive gate cracked open, and Sperchias was yanked inside before it slammed shut again.

"Well done," Diodoros remarked, nodding with approval.

They waited. Gradually, as the sky lightened behind them, Leonidas became aware of more and more noise coming from behind the walls, as if the whole city were coming to life. It almost sounded like cheering. Diodoros called them to order. "Helmets!"

The gates creaked open, and the sound of cheering became less muffled. On the ramparts, too, people started cheering. Sperchias came out of the gate grinning. Behind him the streets of the little town were filling with people, all of them shouting and cheering, "Spar-ta! Spar-ta!"

Diodoros turned and walked along the front rank, redressing it with a gesture here and there, then inspected each of the remaining twelve ranks. "This may not be Sparta and you aren't in parade dress, but try not to look like a bunch of Argives!" he admonished them before turning on heel and ordering, "Right march." A moment later they took up a song to help keep themselves in step.

The inhabitants of the town were going crazy. The boys were jumping up and down; some had even climbed onto the rooftops. Women and maidens were waving shawls from the balconies. Youths and men reached out from the packed crowds on the sides of the streets to clap them on the shoulder and call out thanks.

Sperchias, back in his place in the ranks, muttered to Leonidas,

"I don't think they're going to be very pleased when they find out we aren't staying."

——◆——

They weren't. The town elders were outraged that their presumed "defense" was moving on. They showered protests, bitter recriminations, insults, and outright threats on their erstwhile saviors. One of the older men was weeping tears of rage as he insisted Diodoros had no right to leave them undefended.

"My orders are to secure the Argive ships and ensure that none of the enemy escape alive. You should not wish to hinder us in that task."

"They may have killed us all by the time they get to their ships! We have only survived so long because they are laying siege to Acro-Skandia. We cannot defend ourselves against them! Look what we have here!" He indicated the handful of armed men collected around him. They were armed with a ragtag collection of old weapons, and their armor was even worse—mostly scruffy leather corselets. Not one had hoplite panoply. On their faces, fear cast a strong imprint, overshadowing their individual features.

"You stood your ground against us today. Behave no differently to the Argives, and you will have nothing to fear."

"Why not fight them here? Why take a chance that they will do to us what they have done to so many other towns?"

Diodoros was getting annoyed. "I have my orders, and I do not have to explain them or myself to you. We are here to rid you of the Argives, and we will do so in our own way. Be thankful for the results and stop bickering about the means!" He still faced unanimously sullen and resentful expressions from the native men. "Damn it! Trust us!"

"Trusting you has resulted in half the towns on the island being turned into charnel houses!" the old man reminded him.

——◆——

Brotus' company was roused at sunset and marched out at dusk. The sun had set, but the sky glowed a luminous blue in which the first stars glittered. A stiff, cold breeze came off the water. They were ordered to march in fighting kit, and despite the grumbling, most men were not unhappy with the order. It meant their commanders expected to fight tonight.

Brotus had control of his nerves. He fell into his position in the file with a grin at the men beside him. They grinned back, although Brotus thought Alexander, the man on his left, looked nervous. Forgetting his own bout of nerves earlier, Brotus sneered inwardly at the young man, calling him "old woman" in his mind, although he was a year younger than Brotus.

After about two hours the battalion was split up again. The Argives were besieging Acro-Skandia, they had been told, and had completely surrounded it. The Spartans wanted to attack in at least three places at once.

After another couple of hours' march, the commander ordered his men to stack up their breastplates and spears and darken their arms and legs with mud. Leaving the armor and spears defended by their attendants, the hoplites then went forward armed only with their shields and swords. They were under orders to remain as silent as possible: no singing, no talking, no running.

The Argive camp was readily visible by the campfires, even though these were burning low this time of night. Most of the men slept out in the open under the stars, but here and there were tents, evidently for the noblemen and officers. Some of these were still lit from the inside, indicating their inhabitants were awake.

The Spartans stopped a second time. Selected men were sent forward to take out the sentries. Only after these returned, wiping the blood off their short swords, was the order given, with a silent gesture, for the rest to advance. No one had to explain the objective to the Spartan troops. They were to kill as many Argives as quickly as possible without raising the alarm. They could accomplish this best by moving by stealth between the campfires and carefully slitting the throats of the sleeping men. This was not work that could be done in rank and file. It was not about walls of bronze. This work required the stalking and cunning of the hunter.

As they approached the perimeter of the Argive camp, the men spread out. Those that immediately encountered a victim bent to slay him; others penetrated deeper into the camp, seeping like water between the fires. Each man searched for a victim, and then another and another.

Brotus had his eye on one of the tents. He was an Agiad prince, and he wanted to kill men worthy of him—officers and noblemen. He briefly fantasized about killing the Argive commander. Not while he slept, but in a man-to-man duel—after Brotus had killed his attendants and the Argive nobleman had had time to arm himself, of course. Snatches of the *Iliad* describing the encounter of Achilles and Hektor came to mind: *"Come nearer, so that sooner you may reach your appointed destruction." "…Weaker as I am, I might still strip the life from you with a cast of the spear…"*

Brotus approached the tent purposefully, only vaguely conscious that sounds were starting to bubble up from around the camp. Here a gag, there a short groan or a startled word, abruptly cut off. He pushed back the tent flap with his drawn sword. Subconsciously he registered several chests, and armor hung on some kind of a hook rigged from the tent frame, but his eyes were focused on the bed. A man and a woman lay stretched out on it. Both were naked. Not the noble fight he had imagined, but Brotus did not hesitate. In two strides he was beside the bed. The man lay on his side with his right arm and right leg thrown across the woman, pinning her down to the bed as he slept.

The woman was awake. She looked straight at Brotus as he plunged his sword down into the neck of her companion. The woman reared up. She was young and big-breasted, and between her breasts someone had recently cut, with deliberation and careful cruelty, the letter "alpha." The wound was still red and inflamed, but a thick crust had formed on it.

An Argive whore, Brotus thought to himself; he caught her by the throat and pressed her back onto the bed with his left hand as he straddled her with his knees. Blood flooded her face, but she struggled, tearing the edges of the scab away from the wound between her breasts. Fascinated, Brotus put a knee on her stomach and watched the way the alpha stood out ever more clearly as her dark blood oozed from the edges of the scab onto her white skin. She was making choking sounds, however, so he closed his hand more firmly until her tongue started to protrude, her eyes rolled back into her head, and her limbs went limp.

Instantly Brotus released his grip on her throat, dropped his sword, and slipped his left arm out of the grips of his aspis. He reached down and hooked a hand under each of her knees. He pulled them up and shoved them apart. The pressure in his loins was so intense that it was blinding him, obliterating all other thoughts and sensations. He did not realize another man had entered the tent until the kick hit him hard in the rib cage and sent him crashing off the bed. The second blow connected with his chin and flung his head back so violently he heard his neck crack. A foot thumped down on his belly just below the end of his rib cage, pinning him to the ground beside the bed.

The woman was gone in a swirl of linen, and he was staring up at a crested helmet and a sword—a short Spartan sword. The man in the helmet hissed furiously, "We haven't finished fighting!" Dienekes! Brotus recognized his voice.

Dienekes reached down and yanked Brotus to his feet, spun him around in the direction of the still-open tent flap, and put his boot in Brotus' backside with so much force that Brotus staggered clear out of the tent. He stumbled over something, went down on his knees, and only then started to come to his senses.

The bitch! The whore! She had bewitched him! Distracted him from his duty! He'd dropped his sword and left his shield inside the tent!

Frantically, Brotus looked around and found the sword of one of their slaughtered enemies, but he could not be seen without his aspis! It would be utter disgrace. He circled back around the tent, cut his way inside, and recovered his shield. Then he started running toward the sound of fighting, because by now some of the Argives had indeed woken up, raised the alarm, and offered increasingly organized resistance.

Brotus flung himself into the melee in the dark with frantic fury. He had to wipe out the shame of letting that Argive bitch seduce him. He should have killed her. Why hadn't he just killed her? She had bewitched him! The vile, sex-crazed succubus! But he had kept his helmet down. Dienekes could not have recognized him, he consoled himself. No one would ever know about the incident. He would redeem himself with blood. So he slashed and hacked and gutted anything that came in his way.

———————

By midafternoon Kastor Company had begun their descent to the coast. Informants had reported that the Argive ships were sheltered inside a steep gorge that emptied into the sea near the village they were now approaching. The gorge, their informant had told them, was so deep that the masts of the Argive ships did not rise above the edge. The base of the gorge was allegedly shallow and sandy, allowing the Argive ships to rest softly. The mouth of the gorge, however, was so narrow it could not be seen unless one was looking straight into it.

No sooner had they reached the coast than they were again confronted by destruction. It came in the form of a small farmstead that for some reason—perhaps a sudden burst of rain or a too-hastily lit fire—had not been gutted by the flames. This meant that the bodies of the victims were rotting out in the open. The stench was vile, and Leonidas was not the only one to taste his breakfast in his throat. Sperchias couldn't keep it down at all and was sick. A child was draped over a stone wall like a discarded chiton, his or her limbs swollen like sausages from decay. An infant had been strung up by his feet from a ceiling beam and slit open. His guts hung out of his open belly across his face and a heap of innards lay on the floor beneath him, buzzing with flies. His mother lay spread-eagled on the floor. Her face was turned toward the infant, petrified in expressive agony. A hammer handle had been jammed up her vagina. The image would haunt those who saw it for the rest of their lives.

They dug graves and wrapped their himations around their mouths and noses as they got the corpses onto planks and set them in the earth. There were four children all together. The two men, apparently brothers, had at least died fighting, but they had been hacked to pieces in the process.

"If Greeks can do this, what is it like to fight barbarians?" Sperchias asked Leonidas when they at last turned their backs on the Farm of Horrors (as Leonidas would always remember it).

"Did you know them?"

Sperchias shook his head. "Our property is much further south." He gestured vaguely with his arm. "Now I am afraid to go there."

They reached a wide, sandy beach and, careful to mount sentries, they stacked their arms ready for rapid use. Then the men were allowed to swim while the helots prepared the evening meal.

Leonidas and Sperchias swam out together into the swells. "What is the point of torturing people for sport?" Sperchias asked rhetorically. "I can understand doing it to get information, but what more could they take from those people? They took away everything they had lived for and loved, and then they took their lives. Why did they have to torture them first? They weren't even Spartan! If they did it to us, maybe you could call it revenge. But these were *perioikoi*! What could that young mother ever have done to the Argives to justify what they did to her?"

"Nothing. Nothing could justify what they did to her. Nothing," Leonidas repeated, and they swam back to shore as the sky grew purple with the sunset.

———

They were woken in the middle of the night again, and it started to dawn on Leonidas that this was a deliberate policy. Sparta forbade the use of artificial outdoor lighting in the city, and the Spartan agoge and army trained for night maneuvers, but most other Greeks were uncomfortable moving—much less fighting—in darkness. Attakking at night gave the Spartans an advantage. Furthermore, the use of darkness enabled them to disguise their movements and their weakness in numbers.

They were given orders to keep silent to the extent possible, but to don full panoply. Their attendants were likewise ordered to arm themselves with whatever missile weapons they had; some had bows, Mantiklos his sling. They were then informed in whispers by their section leaders that the Argive ships had been located. The ships were protected by a "substantial body of troops." The sides of the gorge were too steep to enable any approach except at the mouth—where, obviously, the Argives had set up sentries. Those attendants who were good with bow, javelin, or sling were sent up onto the heights above the gorge to shoot down into it as soon as it became light enough to distinguish friend from foe. The hoplites were going to have to make a direct assault up the mouth of the gorge to seize control of the ships.

The certainty that he was about to face combat for the first time in his life put Leonidas' nerves on edge. He had felt cheated when the boar broke his arm and he had been ordered back to Sparta the previous year; and since landing on Kythera a fight had seemed probable, but not—until now—certain. The moment of truth was at hand.

This had been his destiny since birth—since the day the elders agreed to let him live because he was presumed healthy enough to grow up to perform this function. Certainly he had been training himself for this moment since the age of four or five, when he had first started to absorb the stories and the ethos of the civilization that nurtured him. More concretely, the last eight years had been spent in intensive and highly specialized training for this event. But he had not been tested. Now, before dawn, he would find out if he was worthy of all the efforts invested in his upbringing.

As they left camp, Leonidas was pursued by nagging doubts. Maybe he was as worthless as his mother and elder brothers had always asserted. If he failed in any way today, it would certainly prove them right—and he was certain he would not be able to live with himself.

Marching in a file just two wide and fifty men long, they followed a narrow trail that skirted the edge of the steep cliffs until they came to the mouth of the gorge. Here the cliffs turned sharply inland, and the mouth of the gorge lay low and white before them; but although the cliffs were gone, the winter storms had heaped up loose stones and sand into a tall bank that was cut only in the very middle, where a stream emptied its water into the sea.

They continued forward to cut off the entire mouth of the gorge; but just when the first four or five pairs of men had crossed the stream, a shout and then a blazing arrow lit up the sky. One of the Argive sentries had sighted them.

Instantly the men who had crossed the stream turned back and rejoined the main body of troops. Although they could not see the enemy, they could hear shouts, horns, and the clatter of arms. To Leonidas' inexperienced ears, it sounded like hundreds of men. Already they were being ordered to advance four deep and twenty-five across rather than take another two to three minutes to form up twelve by eight. What this meant was that Leonidas and the other novices found themselves in the rear of the four ranks rather than in the middle.

Leonidas didn't have much time to think about it. Advancing up the steep bank was treacherous. The stones rolled and slid under their feet, sometimes giving way and dragging them down. The line was not as firm and solid as it should be. Furthermore, the steepness of the incline made it impossible for the men behind to lean their shields into the backs of the men ahead and help them. The ranks became increasingly separated.

And then, to his horror, Leonidas registered that the Argives were pouring down the bank on their left, just beyond the stream. There appeared to be hundreds of them, all shouting and howling with rage like a pack of wolves. Sperchias, with Leonidas immediately to his right, was on the far left-hand side of the Spartan formation, and so was closest to the Argives. Leonidas could see the Argives start to form up, and he realized that in a matter of moments they would be in a position to fall upon the Spartans from the rear. Worse, if the Spartans continued their advance, they would find themselves trapped inside the gorge by the Argives.

The order to counter-march did not come a moment too soon. At a single command, the Spartan line reversed direction, and the order for double-time was unnecessary. They were all stumbling, falling, and sliding down the slope, the stones shifting under them, clattering and rolling. Here and there, little individual rock-slides half buried the men in front; and as some men were brought to their knees, the men behind them couldn't stop sliding and falling, so that the whole formation lost its cohesion.

Sperchias gave a shout of surprise as much as pain, and Leonidas saw him go down, the shaft of a javelin sticking up into the air. The man behind him made one attempt to grab Sperchias, but his feet were sliding with the stones, and the men behind him were pressing down on him. Leonidas only had a split second, but he managed to get hold of Sperchias under his arm and dragged him upward and forward in a single motion. He had not stopped. He was riding the rolling stones more than anything, acutely aware that his back was exposed to the enemy. The javelin throwers ...

At last he felt the earth firm up under his feet as he reached the bottom of the bank of stones. Gasping, his pulse pounding in his temples, sweat dripping into his eyes, he started running. He was still half-dragging Sperchias, although the other man had somehow managed to get his feet under him and was hobbling forward as fast as he could. Together they plunged into the breaking surf on the beach.

The head of the javelin was still lodged in Sperchias' thigh, but the shaft had broken off in the landslide. Sperchias cried out once as the salt sea water washed into his wound, but already the order to reverse again had rung out; this time the orders were for files of eight. Leonidas and Sperchias found themselves in the middle again, their leaders and the best men ahead of them, the rest of the older men behind them. Overhead a purple tinge lighted the sky and turned the whitecaps pinkish out in the bay.

Leonidas was relieved to hear the sound of shields clacking into position in an unbroken line, because already the Argives were nearing them. They were coming not as a phalanx in slow march, but running triumphantly in a disorganized horde.

The Spartans had hardly taken up their stance before Leonidas was staggered, even in his position three men back, by the onslaught of the Argives. All along the Spartan line, men grunted in surprise and effort as they leaned into their shields to break the momentum of the Argives. Sperchias let out an involuntary cry as the sudden pressure on his wounded thigh sent a searing pain up his body. Leonidas could see nothing but the back of his shield as he held it in the back of the man ahead of him for what seemed like eternity. His shoulder and calf muscles were tensed to the point of cramping. He was acutely aware that beside him, Sperchias was gasping with pain as he tried to stand despite his leg wound.

And then, incomprehensibly to Leonidas, they were ordered forward. With a Herculean effort they took a step, leaning forward, pushing against the man ahead and propelled forward by the man behind. The first step was the hardest. The second was just a fraction easier. The third was notably easier. And the fourth and fifth. They were stepping over Argive bodies now, and Leonidas brought his spear into play for the first time, jabbing downward with the butt to stop the writhing and wriggling of the Argives they were walking

over. He didn't think about it particularly; it was a motion they had
drilled a thousand times.

They were advancing up the bank again, but slowly; in a compact
unit it seemed easier somehow. One step at a time, they went up the
treacherous slope until, abruptly, they were over the crest and the order
came to pause. Leonidas needed to catch his breath, and Sperchias
was crumpling slowly on his left. Diodoros ordered the wounded to
fall out, and wherever a man was missing, the men behind moved
forward so that the phalanx was again compact and dense. Then they
started down the bank into the Argive camp.

Leonidas had no sense of the total picture, but they were advancing down a much shallower slope than they had gone up, and the
walls of the gorge were closing in. The sky overhead was lightening,
and the darkness of the shadows seemed more intense.

The Argives were no longer fighting. They were in flight.
Leonidas could hear shouts and the cracking of underbrush coming
from farther up the slopes to left and right.

The bows of a ship loomed up in front to the left, and soon they
were marching past the big merchantman, beached here as if tossed
up by a storm and left listing to port. They squeezed between two
other ships, penteconters, and kept moving forward until they were
at the very edge of a fast-flowing stream and the walls of the gorge
were almost closing over their heads. There was no sign of Argives
anywhere.

Diodoros ordered a halt and allowed them to rest their shields
on the ground, prop their spears in the sand by their butt ends, and
drop down onto one knee behind their hoplons. It was a huge relief
to arms and shoulders to share the weight of the shield with the earth.
Drinking water was passed out to the hoplites by those attendants not
above them on the heights of the gorge.

But before they had fully caught their breath, shouting from
overhead broke out. They looked up. Their attendants were calling
and pointing. The Spartans looked back and saw that the two penteconters they had passed earlier were lurching forward. Some of the
Argives had evidently managed to circle back to the ships and were
now trying to launch them.

Yet again they reversed their direction and started down the gorge on the double. But with daylight breaking over the valley more and more, they were seen almost at once. The Argives scrambled aboard their ships, pulling the ladders inboard with them. A moment later the Spartans had surrounded the two ships, and the Argives were firing missiles and insults at them.

Diodoros ordered his troops to withdraw out of javelin range and called the enomotarchs over to consult. To Leonidas, the thought of trying to assault the ships was intimidating. It was no easy thing to board a ship. To do so against opposition and without so much as a ladder seemed impossible. But Leonidas knew they would be asked to do it.

"Do you think shouting and banging one's shield really makes one braver?" Aristandos asked, frowning.

"It must," Leonidas concluded. The silence that their own training and ethos required of them certainly only allowed fears to fester and nerves to tense almost beyond endurance. Leonidas kept eyeing the steep sides of the Argive ships and trying to imagine climbing up them in full armor. If they attacked amidships where the freeboard was lowest, they would also be at that part of the ship where the Argives could muster the most men to oppose their assault. If they tried to attack bow or stern, where there was room only for a handful of defenders to block their way, they would have to scramble up almost twelve feet. Leonidas did not know how it could be done.

The sun broke over the horizon behind them, and sunlight was reflected brilliantly off the Argive shields. Almost immediately afterward, the first missiles started to rain down from the edges of the gorge. The Lacedaemonian light troops were at the extreme edge of their range and their weapons were not very effective, but at least they had the effect of making the Argives duck and throw their shields up, some of their swagger shattered.

Diodoros appeared. He walked along in front of their line, his helmet shoved back so they could see his face, and stopped in the middle. "We have two options," he announced conversationally, his back contemptuously turned toward the enemy to show he feared them not at all. "We can assault the ships and try to capture them and whatever loot they have aboard, or we can burn them. Burning will cost us little and is a horrible way to die."

"It's what they've done to the poor people here," one of the older men pointed out.

"Indeed. But Lacedaemon could use those ships."

"Then let's take them," Aristandos shouted out in a burst of youthful bluster, and Leonidas looked at him, frowning. He didn't value this kind of thoughtless bravery.

"Your bark is worse than your bite, puppy," one of the front rankers snarled back, but no one actually voiced a contrary opinion.

"This enomotia is in favor of assault?" Diodoros asked, his eyes sweeping along their line, seeking each man's eyes. Several men in the front rank shrugged. Again Aristandos replied in the affirmative. No one contradicted him. Leonidas wondered if he were the only one reluctant to attack. Maybe his fears were a reflection of his lack of leadership abilities? Maybe he was a coward. No one else seemed to be afraid of the assault. He held his tongue.

Satisfied, Diodoros went on to the next enomotia, and shortly afterward Leonidas' enomotia was charged with seizing one of the two penteconters. Planking had been dragged from somewhere, possibly from the "Farm of Horrors," and a couple of grapples with rope had been found as well. One was given to Leonidas' enomotarch.

The latter announced that he would lead up the plank, and asked who wished to have the grapple. Aristandos volunteered. No one fought him for the honor. Leonidas thought that was a bad sign. Aristandos was, after all, still relatively inexperienced. Surely there were veteran hoplites who could climb up the rope of the grapple in armor and fight single-handedly on gaining the deck? If none of them were prepared to take the risk, then the risk must be very high, he reflected.

They prepared for the assault. Spears would be useless. Swords were the only weapon for this kind of work. "It's up to you whether you want both hands to climb up the plank or want to go up with sword drawn," their enomotarch told them. Their shields, however, were slung over their backs to protect them from missiles and blows as they scaled up the plank.

They formed up in the order of the assault. The enomotarch went first, followed by the other men in the order of their ranks: the best first, the youngest in the middle, and the other older men behind, with the deputy commander, Euragoras, bringing up the rear. Leonidas' position—now that both Sperchias and Aristandos were out of the line—was eighth from the rear. It was not the place of honor, but he did not resent it.

The assault was signaled by pipe. There was no beating of shields and no battle cry. They did not even sing the paean to Kastor. They ran forward, secured the planking, and rushed to get enough men onto the board to make it too heavy for the Argives to push off at the top. The enomotarch was the first man off the plank, and he was instantly surrounded. It was up to the rest of them to keep pouring up the plank to ensure that he was not overwhelmed.

There was no time for more self-doubts. Leonidas sprang onto the plank when his turn came and went up it as fast as he could on all fours. The plank was stained scarlet near the top, but there was no Argive at the railing anymore. He stepped onto the wet deck over the corpse of his enomotarch, who had been rolled into the gunnels, bleeding from a score of wounds. The men who had preceded Leonidas, however, had already pushed the Argives halfway down the foredeck. Leonidas had time to draw his sword and pull his shield off his back and onto his arm before he met the enemy.

Between him and the line of fighting men were a half-dozen other corpses—or bleeding bodies. Most were Argive, but as Leonidas stepped over one in Spartan scarlet, blood bubbled out of the man's mouth and nose and he coughed. It was Aristandos, and he had a sword thrust clear through his guts, just below the end of his cuirass. His eyes were wide open and they met Leonidas'. They seemed full of reproach—or was it just amazement? Leonidas had no time to reflect upon it. He flung himself into the melee on the foredeck, driven in part by the fear that he had somehow shirked his duty. If he had volunteered, he would be lying on the deck coughing up his guts.

Gradually, the Spartans forced the Argives off the foredeck and onto the narrow gangway that ran down the center of the ship to the mast, and then beyond to the quarterdeck. There was room for barely three men with their shields, and with the column already eight deep, it hardly made sense to just throw himself behind the others. Leonidas glanced down the length of the ship. The banks of oars were empty, the sides of the ship abandoned as the Argives clustered on or near the central gangway, trying to repel the Spartans advancing along it.

Leonidas jumped down onto the nearest oar-bank and then, with long, running strides, leaped from one oar-bank to the next until he reached the stern. Slinging his shield onto his back, he scrambled up onto the quarterdeck, thereby positioning himself to the rear of the fighting Argives. As he paused to catch his breath and pull his shield back onto his left arm, he was joined by Euragoras.

The deputy enomotarch shouted into his ear, "Wait for the others! This isn't the *Iliad*!"

Within minutes, however, eight of them were collected on the quarterdeck, and Euragoras had them form up three across to advance against the Argives from the rear. Some of the enemy, when they realized they were being attacked from behind, jumped down into the oar-pits and then tried to scramble over the sides of the ship to escape. A small group fought with the dangerous frenzy of men who know they are going to die and wish only to take as many of the enemy with them as possible. The battle for the ship was soon over.

———————

By midmorning all the fighting was done. Company casualties were "just" five men dead and eleven seriously wounded. For the sake of five ships loaded with valuable plunder including gold and silver, cloth and weapons, the price was not exorbitant. Then again, one of the enomotarchs had been killed, and the second badly injured falling from an assault plank.

As they collected to bury the dead in a grave dug into the bluffs above the gorge facing north to Sparta, Leonidas was conscious of being badly shaken. He felt no euphoria whatsoever over their victory. The bravest had paid the highest price—from the enomotarchs to the foolish Aristandos. The Spartan rear rankers had come away almost unscathed, while the most cowardly of the Argives had escaped altogether and would terrorize the countryside until they were hunted down like mad dogs and killed one by one. There was a good chance his company would be here all summer clearing them out, Leonidas reflected with a sigh. He had trained all his life for this, and with consternation he realized he didn't particularly like his profession.

CHAPTER 6

THE RUNAWAY

GORGO'S THIRD LITTLE BROTHER DIED, TOO. It was late autumn. The winter solstice was approaching, and the weather had turned bleak. Her mother's laments merged with the howling of the winds coming down off Taygetos, and Gorgo's father escaped by going hunting in Messenia. Gorgo tried to play with her elder brother, Agis, but they quarreled (as they often did). So as soon as the rain stopped, Gorgo ran away.

She did not intend to stay away forever. She planned to come home as soon as she heard her father was back. Meanwhile, she took a sack of food to keep her for a day or two and headed for Amyclae. She wanted to go first to the great Temple of Apollo and bring the God her most precious possession, a pretty stone a stranger had given her. She thought she would talk to the God and convince him to stop killing her baby brothers so her mother wouldn't be so unhappy. When her mother was unhappy, her father stayed away, and then they were all unhappy.

When she reached the southern outskirts of the city, she was distracted by a flogging. One of the boys from the agoge was down in the sandpits about to be flogged for some transgression. Not being in a particular hurry, Gorgo joined the spectators. As usual, the crowd consisted mostly of the other boys in the miscreant's own herd and any other herd that happened to be passing by, along with a sprinkling of idle citizens and the odd stranger. You rarely saw perioikoi or helots at the floggings, because they generally had business to attend to when passing through Sparta, and the floggings were too common to interest them. The boys and citizens watched because they knew each other and were supposed to take an active interest in who had done what and how well they stood up to their punishment. The strangers, however, came to gawk, because the concept of flogging citizens' children in public was unique to Sparta and widely abhorred in the rest of the world.

The boy who was to be flogged was at that awkward age between "little boy" and youth. He was clearly older than Gorgo herself by several years, but it was hard to tell if he had passed his fox time already or was just on the brink of it. He was shaved, of course, and skinny and dirty and, this being the end of the year, his chiton and himation were in very ragged condition.

Gorgo had never seen Spartan boys his age look any other way, and she was not offended by his appearance. She calmly found a place on the surrounding wall to sit, folded up her cloak as a cushion, and settled down with her feet dangling. Taking an apple from her sack, she sat swinging her legs, waiting for the entertainment to begin.

It was a moment or two before she realized that the men behind her were strangers and they were talking about her. They spoke Greek with a funny accent, and one of them said in disgusted outrage, "Why, that's a girl!"

"Probably just some slave girl," an evidently older man answered.

"With a purple himation?" the younger man countered, scandalized.

Gorgo looked down at her cushion, feeling a little ashamed of herself. She had taken her best himation because it was the warmest and softest and she liked it best, but now that the stranger drew attention to it, she felt a little guilty, too. It was dyed with the most expensive dyes and had a gold border. She knew her mother would scold her if she tore it, lost it, or got it too dirty.

At once she felt a hand roughly shake her shoulder. "Girl! Where did you get that cloak? You stole it, didn't you?"

"Why should I steal it?" Gorgo asked back angrily, looking up at the strangers with her brows drawn together in indignation. They were dressed like perioikoi women, in bright-colored chitons with fancy embroidered borders and short himations of equally gaudy design. They smelt of musk oil. But the worst thing about them was that the younger man was fat. Gorgo had never seen a fat young man before, at least not that she could remember. The youth who had noticed her, however, was too young to grow a beard but apparently old enough to carry a sword, because he did—and he was all white flab. Gorgo gazed at him in horror—to match his own, as he realized that she was not only a girl, but a girl who stared him straight in the eye.

"How did a stray like you come by such a fine cloak, then?" the young man demanded.

"It was given to me!" Gorgo answered truthfully.

"A little whore, are you, then? With patrons who give you pretty things?" the youth sneered. "Let me see your wares!"

"We don't have whores in Sparta!" Gorgo told the stranger indignantly, full of innocent conviction.

"What? No whores? Father, what am I to do for entertainment tonight?"

"Stop demeaning yourself by chattering with slave girls. The flogging is about to begin," his father answered sternly.

Gorgo, too, turned her attention back to the sandpits where the boy, now stripped naked, was taking up his position, with his back to the audience and his hands firmly grasping the bar between the stands. Two of the mastigophoroi, assistants to the headmaster of the agoge, waited at the ready, with canes cut from river reeds in their hands.

A woman from the crowd—Gorgo guessed it was the miscreant's mother—asked what the boy had done wrong. She was told that he had used a citizen's horse without his permission and then—and this was the real crime—on returning it had not seen that it was properly walked out or watered. Gorgo was indignant. Why even she, at eight, knew better than to do that! In fact, the only reason she hadn't taken Shadow with her on this adventure was because she had been afraid she wouldn't be able to take care of her properly while she was away from home. She directed her attention to the boy in the pits with a sense of witnessing the administration of justice.

The boy braced himself, and except for an inevitable twitch and lifting of the neck and head, he withstood the first blows steadfastly.

"Look at her!" the stranger whispered behind her. "She looks like she's enjoying this!"

Gorgo stiffened, realizing she was being talked about again.

"Aren't you?" the father answered. "Admirable discipline these Spartans have. Admirable."

"But look at the girl! It's unnatural for a girl to watch something like this! No girl should witness a boy getting humiliated!"

"It's more unnatural for those matrons over there!" his father countered.

"To them he's just a boy," the youth replied unconcerned, still obsessed with Gorgo. "But this girl is younger than he is. How will she respect him after seeing this?"

Gorgo was grateful to hear an elderly woman intervene. "That depends on how he bears himself. If the boy bears up well, he gains in reputation, and if he does not he is shamed, as he should be. That is exactly why our girls *should* watch—so they can choose husbands worthy of them!"

"*Choose* their husbands? You let brainless girls *choose* their husbands?" The youth found this idea so ridiculous, he burst out laughing.

"*Our* girls *aren't* brainless," came the dry retort, but the youth and his father were both laughing too hard to hear it.

Gorgo couldn't take it anymore, however. She jumped down from the wall, grabbed her himation, and fled.

She followed the river path beside the Eurotas, still heading south, away from the city. The path weaved amid the reeds, imperfectly following the banks of the river. Here and there other paths crossed it, used by people going to the river to wash or swim or fish. Gorgo passed a number of helot women working knee deep in the muddy water and beating at their dirty clothes with river reeds. She also passed a number of boys from the agoge, lying on their bellies and fishing (or attempting to) with their hands or with small, self-made nets and spears.

The further she went, however, the less disturbed she was by people. Instead she encountered frogs and storks, mice that dashed for cover into the reeds, and hawks that wheeled overhead. She was quite happy until she heard an eerie mewing sound coming from the river. The sound was so full of pain—almost like the whimpering of her dying brothers—that it sent a chill down her spine, and she stood stock-still in the towering reeds, frightened. Was it the spirit of her brother, whom she had neglected and resented, come to haunt her? Or maybe some helot girl who had turned out her unwanted baby on the riverbank?

She stopped and listened again, torn between the desire to run away and the duty to go and see what it was. Running away would be cowardly. Gorgo did not want to be a coward. Cowards were disgusting! And what if it was a helot baby? Helots belonged to the city. No helot girl had the right to throw a healthy baby away. Gorgo pictured herself rescuing the child and taking it to the ephors and being praised for saving a life for the city. But what if it wasn't healthy? What if the baby was blind or deformed? Gorgo took a step backward, and then was so ashamed of herself for her cowardice that she plunged through the reeds, ignoring the mud and the mice. Her headlong plunge brought her to a burlap bag lying on the sandy bank—and moving.

Something inside it was still alive. But it was not a child. It was too small for that.

Gorgo reached out and pulled the bag toward her. There was something heavy in the far end, but in the middle something moved and mewed. With the knife she carried in her belt, she slit the bag open and revealed three dead puppies and one lone survivor. It stumbled out of the bag, lifting its wet head to sniff the fresh air and blinking in the light of day. Gorgo fell in love instantly. She swept the puppy into her arms, and it started trying to suck milk from her soft white flesh wherever it could. When she lowered her face to it, the puppy reached up and tried to suckle from her neck, her ear, her nose.

Shouldering her supply sack, Gorgo purposefully retraced her steps back to the main road. Here, as expected, she soon came upon a tavern, and she entered with the intention of asking for milk for the puppy. In the doorway, however, she stopped dead. The room was filled with men, and some instinct said that these were not the kind of men who filled her father's andron or the many syssitia along the road. They smelled and they stared. Gorgo backed out—and she didn't for an instant think she was being cowardly. Her appearance and retreat was met with a volley of laughter and rude comments from the men in the tavern, but she was forgotten as quickly as she had appeared.

She continued down the road to a smithy. The smith was working beside his forge and one could hear the clang of the hammer on glowing metal, while several horses, held by a helot boy, waited patiently in the yard. Gorgo went past the forge and to the back of the cottage. Here a woman was tossing slops to a pig in a pen while fowl pecked around the kitchen yard. "Hello!" Gorgo began.

The woman looked up and straightened, watching Gorgo warily.

"May I have some milk for my puppy?" Gorgo asked.

"Your puppy? Come show us!" The woman gestured Gorgo over.

Gorgo obeyed, holding out her puppy.

"What did you do? Rescue it from the river?"

"Yes, the other three drowned, but you see how strong he is? He survived and he deserves to live."

"He's got a white hind leg; that's bad luck. Throw him back," the woman advised.

"NO! I rescued him and I'm going to keep him!"

"Well, that's up to your mother, I daresay, but I'm not wasting any of my precious milk on a worthless pup!" the woman replied, and turned her back on Gorgo to indicate the subject was closed.

Gorgo stood for a moment, considering a protest, but then gave up and headed for the next tradesman's cottage.

Eventually she did get milk for her puppy. The kind woman who gave it to her also taught her to soak the corner of a rag in it and then offer this to the puppy to suck on. Unfortunately, after the puppy had had enough to drink he urinated on Gorgo, so she had to go wash herself in the river—which was very cold this time of year. It was also getting dark and the wind had picked up.

Although she dried herself off and wrapped herself in her himation, Gorgo's teeth started chattering, and the puppy was whimpering again, too. She held it close, suddenly aware that she was miles and miles from home and it was getting dark and she was cold and hungry and all alone. She looked around and saw nothing familiar. She started to fear she had missed the turnoff to the Temple to Apollo in her search for milk.

Gorgo was afraid. As the light of day faded rapidly, she remembered all the stories they told about wolves and rebellious helots. She remembered that the Messenians, who had slit the throats of the girls and boys in the agoge, had come at night through the Taygetos mountains that loomed up ominously on her right. She had to seek shelter. She made for the light of a torch burning beside a building of undecipherable purpose. When she reached it, she discovered it was an inn.

Her appearance in the door went unnoticed at first. She approached the counter, where a heavy woman was serving out wine and savory-smelling meals. At once the woman demanded unkindly, "What have we here? If you've come begging, you've come to the wrong place. Go on! Get out!"

"I'm not a beggar!" Gorgo protested. "I just need a place for the night."

"Alone? Who's paying, then?" The woman looked around as if expecting to see the girl's father or brother appear, perhaps having gone to stable the horses after sending the girl in ahead.

"I walked down from Sparta alone. My father's hunting," Gorgo tried to explain. "But he'll pay you when he gets back."

"Sure he will!" the woman replied sarcastically. "Now get out before I throw you out!"

The exchange had drawn attention to Gorgo, and again strangers started talking about her. "These Spartans really do just let their daughters run around wild, don't they? Why, they must be like bitches in heat when they reach maturity, lying with anyone and everyone they meet on the street."

"I wish we'd run into some of *those*. All I've seen is filthy little runts like that!" another dismissed Gorgo with contempt.

A third man, middle-aged with a graying beard, stood up and came over to Gorgo. Squatting down before her, he asked: "Are you lost, child?" His voice was gentle and his face kindly.

"No; I just don't know where I am!" Gorgo answered, harvesting a laugh from everyone who had heard her reply.

Even the kindly man laughed, although he stopped first and suggested calmly, "If you tell me your father's name and where he dwells, I will see that you get home safe."

A male voice answered from behind her before Gorgo could get a word out: "Thank you, stranger, but that won't be necessary."

Gorgo spun around and with immeasurable relief recognized her favorite uncle. She ran to him, clutching her puppy. "Uncle Leonidas!"

Leonidas bent and lifted her into his arms, puppy and all, and then nodded again to the stranger, who had also come to his feet. "Thank you again for your offer to help, stranger."

As Leonidas turned and carried Gorgo out of the inn, the people behind them were still muttering about the way Spartans let their children run wild and what an unhealthy system of education it was.

"How did you find me, Uncle Leonidas?" Gorgo asked, leaning her tired head against his warm, strong chest with a sense of relief that betrayed how frightened she had been.

"We are returning from an exercise, and I just happened to see you go into the inn," Leonidas explained.

Out in the street Leonidas' entire eight-man section was milling around, waiting on him. They looked surprised to see him carrying a child, and even more surprised when he said simply, "My niece." Adding, "Chi, take the puppy so I can carry her on my shoulders."

One of the other young men came forward and scooped the puppy out of Gorgo's arms, making a face as he did so, which brought laughter from the others. But Leonidas ignored them, firmly turning Gorgo around in his arms and lifting her up over his head to sit on his shoulders.

Gorgo didn't mind. Her father often carried her like that, too. Leonidas had hold of her ankles, one in each hand, and she held on to his head, a little dismayed that his hair was so much shorter than her father's that she couldn't get her fingers into it properly. But she felt completely safe, and the countryside went by much faster at the easy marching pace of the young men. After a few moments one of the men started singing a melodious marching song and the others joined in, including Leonidas in his warm, deep voice. Thus they sang her all the way home.

Although by the time they reached the Agiad palace Gorgo was *very* tired and hungry, she was still sorry to arrive. Inside was all the gloom that she had fled this morning, and she knew she might have trouble talking her mother into letting her keep her puppy—not to mention the scolding she would get for being away so long without telling anyone, and for her dirty clothes. But Leonidas swung her down, and the young man handed her back her distressed puppy, and the meleirenes at the gate pushed open the heavy gates without hesitation to let her back inside. Her adventure was over.

CHAPTER 7

OBLIGATIONS

THE SOLSTICE WAS BEHIND THEM NOW and the days were getting longer, but it was still cold. Morning drill left the young men chilled through, because the sweat they worked up cooled the moment they stopped exercise. As a result, the young men flooded the baths as soon as drill was over. They sought the steam baths to warm up, and then let the bath slaves massage them down with oil to drive the muscle aches away.

Before Alkander married, Leonidas and he had come together to the baths, but now Alkander preferred to go straight to the town-house Hilaira kept in the heart of the city. There she prepared a hot bath and a hot meal for him, especially on days like this. Leonidas rarely saw Alkander before dinner at their syssitia anymore, and he increasingly spent his free time with Sperchias.

Today Euryleon, one of the youths who had been in the unit Leonidas commanded as an eirene, joined them too. Euryleon had received his citizenship at the solstice and was just finding his footing in the army; it was natural that he attach himself to the familiar Leonidas.

"… so we're going to put the roof on during the Achilia," Leonidas explained, lying on his belly while the bath slave oiled him down. The Achilia was one of Sparta's lesser holidays. Dedicated to the hero Achilles, it lasted only five days; but since it was not accompanied by elaborate choral, dance, or athletic contests and occurred in the winter when campaigning was rare, it was a good time to get work done on one's estate. With the agoge closed and the army furloughed except for a small emergency guard, many families used the holiday to travel to Messenia or other outlying estates.

"Are you going to get married soon?" Euryleon asked, making the connection between Leonidas getting his kleros fixed up and starting a family.

Leonidas frowned because it was a sore subject, and Sperchias answered for him. "Getting the roof on is only the prerequisite for fixing up the interior," he told Euryleon with a warning look.

Euryleon took the hint and asked, "Do you want us to come help you?"

"You don't need to. Pelopidas has talked most of the helots from neighboring estates into helping." Leonidas considered this fact, adding, "Pelopidas was very good about lending out the oxen, or sending Pantes over to do carpentry work, when his neighbors needed help. He's made himself liked and respected, despite the initial hostility to strangers."

"Not to mention the impact of Laodice's cooking!" Sperchias added with a grin, sitting up on the bench and swinging his legs. "Will she be cooking for the workers?"

"Of course. She's in town today buying raisins, almonds, and other stuff so she can cook some things in advance."

"In that case, I'll definitely come," Sperchias announced, and Euryleon nodded, adding with a glance at Leonidas, "Unless I'm on duty, of course."

"No, you're not on until the Chalkioika." As section leader, Leonidas knew the duty schedule; his friends did not.

The sound of excited voices at the entrance penetrated to the inner chamber of the baths. Leonidas thought he heard his name mentioned. He lifted his head and cocked an ear. Beggar, who was resting with her head on her front paws under the bench, immediately followed her master's lead.

There was clearly some commotion that brought laughter from some of the younger men and then a rebuke from Alcidas, one of the agoge officials. Leonidas signaled to the slave that he was finished and sat up.

"Leonidas, son of Anaxandridas?" Alcidas called sternly.

Leonidas stood and walked into the next room. A meleirene, one of the nineteen-year-olds that served the city as sentries, messengers, and the like before assuming the responsibilities of eirenes at age twenty, stood in the doorway, but it was the deputy headmaster who addressed Leonidas in a reproachful voice. Alcidas had been one of the agoge officials whom Leonidas had disliked when in school: a humorless, petty-minded stickler for regulations. "Young man, you are wanted at the magistrate's office," he intoned ominously. "One of your helots has been arrested."

Leonidas caught his breath. Ever since their joint trip to Messenia, he harbored suspicions that Mantiklos might turn rebellious. Instantly he pictured Mantiklos refusing to obey orders or even back-talking someone. If provoked, Leonidas realized in growing alarm, Mantiklos might even strike out with his fists.

Meanwhile, Alcidas lectured in a self-righteous voice, "You should have better control of your helots, son of Anaxandridas! You give them too much freedom and they get ideas! They think they are more than the miserable worms they are!"

That was certainly true of Mantiklos, Leonidas noted, wondering not for the first time if he should dismiss him. But first he had to find out what he had done.

"Helots reflect on their masters," Alcidas continued; "wherever you find uppity helots, you also find a lax master. Inferiors need to be ruled with an iron fist, and if you don't, you don't deserve to rule at all."

Leonidas had heard this rubbish before. Alcidas was just like Brotus. They both thought you could solve every problem with brute force. But Leonidas held his tongue. In silence he turned to the shelves lining the wall, found his bundle of belongings, and dressed. Sperchias and Euryleon did the same.

As the three young men stepped out of the warm, humid baths into the chilly afternoon, however, Leonidas was astonished to be confronted by Mantiklos himself. "Sir! Come quick! Laodice has been arrested!" The Messenian's face was darkened by a scowl of barely suppressed anger.

"Laodice?" Leonidas found himself asking stupidly. He couldn't imagine it. Women didn't get arrested—except for soliciting. Laodice was the last woman he could imagine soliciting.

"Come quick!" Mantiklos insisted, already turning and pushing his way through the early afternoon crowds.

Leonidas looked at his friends. He did not know what the hard-working, honest Laodice could have done to get herself arrested, but he was certain he was going to need the advice of someone wiser than himself; so he ordered, "Euryleon, go find Nikostratos and ask him to come to the magistrate's office."

Euryleon nodded and started in the other direction, while Sperchias fell in beside Leonidas. "You don't suppose it's illegal to cook as well as Laodice does, do you? Maybe it's against the law to make black broth that you don't actually want to puke out again?"

Leonidas cast Sperchias a smile of thanks for trying to cheer him up, but inside he was worrying that *he* had broken the law in some way by settling the Messenian family here in Laconia. But if that was the case, why hadn't anyone said anything before this? Why arrest Laodice rather than Pelopidas?

They reached the lovely colonnaded square on which the court buildings were located, only to find a larger-than-usual crowd. Fortunately, the attention of the crowd was directed to the corner where the public pillory was set up in front of the temple to Zeus of the Council. In fact, the crowd was so thick that Leonidas could not get even a glimpse of the criminal who was attracting so much attention. He noted that surprisingly, there were more adults than boys in the crowd, although it was usually the other way around; but he was too worried about Laodice to give it much thought.

Leonidas hastened past the temple of Athena of Counsel, casting his eyes and prayers in the direction of the third temple on this square, one of several in the city dedicated to the Divine Twins. Leonidas sent a prayer to Kastor, adding mentally, "You probably wish I'd picked another God to be my protector."

Mantiklos, who had forged ahead, was awaiting him impatiently, at the foot of the stairs up to the colonnaded structure that housed a series of chambers in which the magistrates heard cases. He pointed up the steps. "Talthybiades is the magistrate you have to see," Mantiklos told his master, and Leonidas did not ask how he knew. He just

ordered Mantiklos to keep hold of Beggar—dogs were not welcome
inside official buildings—and started up the steps, adding, "You
better stay here too, Chi."

As he entered the corridor, several men recognized him and
pointed him in the right direction. "On the right. The second door."
They seemed more amused than hostile or disapproving about
whatever had happened.

Leonidas entered the identified office. Talthybiades was a man
in his forties with a tall forehead and a sharp nose. He was wearing
a long blue himation, the mark of his office, and Laodice was sitting
on the bench at the side of the office with her wrists tied and tears
running down her face.

"Oh, there you are at last! We've been looking for you for hours!
This woman says she works for you."

It was hardly a secret that Laodice worked for him. At least once
a week she sold her sweets in a stand in the agora. Leonidas looked at
Laodice, but she would not meet his eyes. She sank her head lower,
her shoulders folding in as she bent over and the tears dropped onto
her lap. Her hands were trembling, too. "She does," he confirmed.
"What are the charges?"

"She tried to give the whore water!"

"What whore?" Leonidas asked, bewildered. Prostitution was prohibited in Sparta, and the punishment for soliciting in public places
was draconian enough to keep it out of sight—which, of course,
meant it flourished in the surrounding perioikoi towns and villages.

"The bitch we have out in the stocks!" Talthybiades snapped
back. "She was found soliciting on the steps of the Olympian Aphrodite in broad daylight by your twin brother! Fortunately, he brought
her straight to us before she had caused a greater disruption! What
would have happened if she had still been there when curfew ended
and the older age cohorts of the agoge had been on the loose?"

Leonidas treated the question as rhetorical. He did not believe
Talthybiades seriously thought the youths of the agoge were unfamiliar with commercial sex. Furthermore, Leonidas had never known
his twin brother to be particularly prudish, and technically he had
no right to be around during curfew, either. But Leonidas was not
here on account of the whore or his twin, but because of Laodice.

He wanted to be sure he understood the situation. "You arrested my woman for giving water to someone in the stocks?"

"To a whore!" Talthybiades insisted.

"Does that make a difference?" Leonidas asked.

"Legally, no, but it does make me wonder what sort of household you run!"

Leonidas ignored the jibe. "What's the fine?"

"Two hens or a bushel of olives."

"I'm good for the hens. Let her go."

Talthybiades did not lower himself to personally cutting the prisoner free; he rang a bell and a meleirene answered. The meleirene was ordered to cut Laodice free. Leonidas gestured for her to follow him, and returned through the grinning crowd with Laodice in his wake.

As he emerged from the building, Beggar bounded up the stairs to rejoin him, and Mantiklos and Sperchias got to their feet. "What on earth…?" the latter wanted to know, but Leonidas shook his head. Laodice was stumbling, and he sensed she was barely able to keep herself going. Furthermore, the crowd of spectators around the stocks was larger than ever. He recognized Dienekes, debonair as ever, pushing his way through the crowd with a heavy frown of disapproval on his face. Despite his youth, Dienekes was an influential man, a popular section leader. Leonidas didn't want to explain himself—or Laodice—to him, and he hustled Laodice out of the square.

"Mantiklos, go home and fetch Pelopidas. Have him bring the cart to Alkander's townhouse," he ordered. Then he took Laodice by the elbow and guided her firmly in the direction of Alkander's house, with Sperchias trailing them.

He could feel Laodice trembling, and she kept murmuring under her breath, "I'm sorry, master. I'm sorry. Please don't throw us off the kleros. Please, master. Pelopidas is a good man. A good man. It's all my fault, master. Please."

She kept repeating the litany no matter what Leonidas said, so he fell silent and concentrated on guiding her, because she was stumbling, blinded by her tears.

When they reached Alkander's house, the housekeeper took one look at Laodice and exclaimed as she let them in: "What's happened?

Has there been an accident? Here, I'll take her!" The woman reached
out and took Laodice into her arms at once. "Have you hurt yourself,
dearie?" she asked, adding, as she led her away without giving Laodice
a chance to answer, "You're chilled through, you poor thing. Come
in by the fire."

The sound of voices in the courtyard drew Alkander onto the
balcony of the upstairs room, and at the sight of Leonidas he called
something over his shoulder and then started down the wooden stairs.
Hilaira emerged at once and followed her husband downstairs, but
then continued to the kitchen, leaving her husband to see to Leonidas
and Sperchias.

Hilaira knew Laodice well. Because Leonidas had no wife, Hilaira
made a point of checking up on things at his kleros "from a woman's
point of view." She soon realized that Laodice had things very well
in hand. Indeed, she had developed a strong respect and affection for
the helot woman, and sometimes wished the helots on Alkander's
kleros were half as hard-working and pleasant as Laodice and her
family.

Laodice sat by the hearth with her back to the door. She had
dropped her face into her hands and was sobbing uncontrollably, while
Hilaira's housekeeper patted her ineffectually on the shoulder. Hilaira
put an arm around the helot's shoulder, asking warmly, "What's the
matter? Has something happened to Crius?" Hilaira knew how much
Laodice worried about her youngest son, whose hands made him
useless and whose uselessness made him impudent.

"It's all my fault," Laodice stammered in reply. "I'm so—please,
Mistress Hilaira!" Laodice twisted sharply around to look Hilaira
straight in the eye. Hilaira recoiled at the almost wild look on her face
and the sheet of tears that glimmered on her cheeks. Laodice reached
out and gripped Hilaira's hands, and Hilaira was alarmed by how
fiercely she clutched; the strength in her wiry hand hurt Hilaira unin-
tentionally. "Please! You can talk to the master. Tell him I'm sorry! I'll
pay back the two hens."

"Laodice, calm down," Hilaira urged, dropping on her heels
beside the helot woman. "What hens? Did some hens get killed by
accident—"

"No, no. The hens he had to pay for my release. It was so—so—

stupid of me. I should have known better. But when I saw that girl, and she is so young—just like I was—and you know she didn't want to. If Pelopidas wasn't such a good man. Such a good man!" Laodice broke down into uncontrollable sobbing, clutching her fists to her eyes and howling in misery like a small child.

Baffled, Hilaira stared at her equally perplexed housekeeper; and then she pulled Laodice closer into her arms, while her housekeeper set about mixing herbs into hot wine to calm Laodice's nerves.

By the time the hot spiced wine was ready, Laodice had gotten some control of herself. She was no longer bawling, just hiccupping, as the tears continued to pour down her red and swollen face.

"Won't you tell me what happened?" Hilaira pleaded with her. "From the beginning?"

"Melampus," she choked out. "Melampus—raped—all the girls."

"Who is Melampus?"

"The manager—in Messenia," Laodice got out, and Hilaira was starting to understand. Leonidas had told them about his horse farm and the manager, who treated the helots badly and let guests abuse Crius.

"He raped you?" Hilaira asked intently, holding Laodice's hand in hers.

Laodice nodded, but would not meet Hilaira's eyes. "When I was—was—fourteen."

Hilaira closed her hand around Laodice's more firmly and waited.

"He—he—made me—there were four of them."

Hilaira's eyes met her housekeeper's. The older woman came and laid a hand on Laodice's shoulder too, patting her with her big fleshy hand and muttering, "There, there."

Laodice was shaking her head. "I try not—to—remember. But the girl—out there. It could have been me. You see, afterward— my father—said he couldn't waste an obol on a dowry for—for—a whore. They pinned me down, you know," she continued as she wiped at her running nose with the back of her arm; "they pinned me down. I tried to get away, but there were four of them. My father called me a whore. He told me to "go earn my living" … If Pelopidas … Pelopidas is such a good man." Laodice dissolved into tears again, and Hilaira pushed herself upright. She was staring at her housekeeper. The old woman was shaking her head, but tears shimmered in her eyes.

"I'm going to talk to Leonidas," Hilaira announced.

———————

They had erected the framework and were already working on the latticework to hold the tiles when Crius—otherwise just getting underfoot—shouted up to Leonidas. "There's a lady here to see you, master!"

"Aha," Euryleon retorted, casting Leonidas a glance while wiping the sweat off his face with the back of his arm. "So there *is* a future mistress we are doing all this work for. I suspected as much!"

Leonidas pushed himself upright to get a look into the yard. The short flash of hope that it was Eirana driving the chariot fled; his stepmother Chilonis was at the reins. "Can't you just imagine my brother's face if I asked to marry his mother?" Leonidas replied to Euryleon, and left him gaping as he started down the ladder to the ground.

Crius was waiting for him at the bottom of the ladder, a linen towel over his shoulder and a bowl of cool water in his hands. Leonidas bent over the bowl, plunged his hands into the water, and threw it on his face. He grabbed the towel and dried his face and hands, and used the linen to wipe sweat off his arms and neck as well. He was thinking that Crius was becoming a problem. The surgeon had said there was nothing they could do about his hands. It was a condition that would probably only get worse with age and was particularly bad in cold, damp weather. A helot boy with weak hands was not much use in the world. Crius could not grip any tool firmly enough to use it effectively. He also had no future as an army attendant, since he would need strong hands to be able to arm his hoplite, drive supply wagons, or use a bow. Not only was his future very murky, but his present development was all bad. Rather than have him dropping and breaking things all the time, his father and brothers tended to just send him away. As a result, he was becoming wild and impudent. He grinned at Leonidas and asked boldly, "Will you give me a ride in the chariot? I've never done that!"

"No!" Leonidas told him, amazed at the boy's cheekiness. None of the boys in the agoge would have dared talk to him in such a tone! He didn't even address Leonidas as "sir," much less "master."

Crius obviously didn't believe Leonidas, because he kept grinning and tagged along as Leonidas went over to greet Chilonis.

"I'm sorry," she opened the conversation. "I obviously came at a bad time."

"Not for me. I needed a break. Come sit in the sun, and Crius will bring us some refreshments." Leonidas addressed the latter remark to Crius, scowling sternly. Crius laughed and ran off, tossing the water away so he could run better and forgetting the linen towel so that it blew off his shoulder and fluttered to the ground. With a sigh, Leonidas excused himself to collect the towel, and then returned to join Chilonis on the bench in the sun on the back terrace.

Chilonis was admiring the view. "This kleros will be beautiful when you get it fixed up," she greeted him.

Leonidas took a moment to look at his view and nodded, still gazing out across the Eurotas to the backdrop of the blue-hued Taygetos. "If only I had someone to share it with."

"Good heavens! You're only twenty-three. You have plenty of time to find the right maiden."

"I did find her, but she preferred someone else." He smiled in self-contempt, still not meeting Chilonis' eyes.

"That is most definitely *her* problem," Chilonis retorted firmly.

He turned to look at her at last. "I'm sure you did not come to discuss my marriage prospects."

"No, I came to thank you. Twofold, actually. I have owed you thanks for nearly two years." Leonidas looked puzzled. "That sweet little mare you brought back from Messenia the winter before last," she reminded him. "I bought her for my granddaughter, and Gorgo adores her. She learned to ride easily on such a gentle mare, and now she rides around the countryside as if she were a little centaur. With another horse I would worry about her far more. And it is on Gorgo's account that I am here today. Thank you for bringing her home the day she ran away last month." The excuse was—and sounded—lame. The incident had taken place weeks ago.

Leonidas shrugged and shook his head. "Anyone would have

done it, but it was lucky I happened along and spotted her. What on earth was she doing way down beyond Amyclae on her own?"

"She'd run away from home—from her mother's grieving."

"I'm sorry about this last child."

Chilonis nodded. She believed him. Unlike his two brothers, Leonidas clearly did not covet Cleomenes' throne.

"She could have come to harm." Leonidas brought attention back to Gorgo's ill-advised escapade. "There are a number of taverns and inns along the route that are frequented only by strangers. There are many strangers who do not understand our ways and would never have believed Gorgo was a Spartiate, much less a king's daughter."

Chilonis sighed. "I know. And I'd like to think she has learned a lesson. She was frightened—or she would not have been so grateful for your rescue. She's talked of nothing but you since."

Leonidas laughed. "Well, at least there is one Spartan maiden I have captivated—even if she's only eight. Did her mother let her keep her puppy?"

Chilonis sighed. "Not really. We've hidden it in the stables for now. Gorgo spends all her time there—between her mare and her puppy." A burst of shouting from overhead drew their attention; Chilonis realized there was much work still to be done, and the day was half gone. She got to her feet. "I shouldn't keep you from your work any longer. I just felt I ought to thank you, since neither my son nor my daughter-in-law will have the courtesy."

Leonidas stood, perplexed as to her purpose for coming since the reason she had given seemed unconvincing, and asked politely, "Are you sure you won't stay for a snack? Laodice is the best cook in Lacedaemon."

"I know!" Chilonis smiled. "I buy from her whenever I see her stand in the agora, but your work crew needs the refreshments more." She hesitated, and finally overcame her own reluctance to say what she had come for. Even if it wasn't her business, she liked Leonidas, and she wanted to warn him. "People are talking, Leonidas."

"About what?"

"That whore you bought. It does no man's reputation any good to be *seen* with whores—much less maintaining one in his household."

"Kleta is no more a whore than Cassandra or Andromache! She

was a prize of war—the Argives even carved an alpha in the flesh between her breasts to give her a permanent brand of ownership! And I'm *not* sleeping with her!" The truth was, he didn't even want to. The thought of sleeping with the girl was abhorrent to him, because it would have put him on the same level as the men who had abused her—the Argives he hated.

Chilonis looked at Leonidas sharply, impressed by the outrage in his voice and the vehemence of his reaction. Then she told him, "That's not what your brother is saying."

"What does Cleomenes care?"

"Not my son; Brotus."

"Brotus?" Leonidas repeated, looking at her hard. "Did it never bother *anyone* that Brotus was the *only* one who saw Kleta soliciting?" Leonidas paused to let this sink in, and then continued, "Kleta claims she was at an inn far outside the city limits. She says Brotus brought her to the city, promising her a place in his home—only to turn her over to the magistrates instead. She says she wasn't soliciting inside the city."

Chilonis was shocked. "But why would Brotus lie like that?"

"I don't know. I've never been able to understand how his mind works."

Chilonis considered this a moment and then shook her head. "Even if you're right, Leo, it doesn't change anything. It's your reputation—not Brotus'—that is on the line. Brotus is seen as the "upstanding, conscientious citizen" who turned a whore over to the authorities, and you are cast in the role of the oversexed bachelor who keeps a whore in his own home. I believe that you mean well; but there are times when it is wiser to sacrifice our personal preferences in order not to court public disgrace. You could be ruined by this act of kindness."

"And what happens to Kleta if I throw her out? She was raped by a horde of Argives when she was hardly out of childhood, then rejected by her own family, and driven to prostitution just to eat. She was betrayed by a customer, sentenced to humiliation in public, and ridiculed by every passer-by. If I throw her out, she'll have nowhere else to go but back to the streets—and from what Laodice tells me, she's more likely to kill herself. I don't want that on my conscience."

Chilonis sighed and opened her hands to indicate she didn't have an answer, but added, "I hope you aren't making a mistake. Thank you again for helping Gorgo." She climbed aboard her chariot, took up the reins, and carefully turned it around in the drive. Then she waved and set off at a trot. Leonidas stood and watched her drive away, then returned to working on the roof.

———

Chilonis, however, was disturbed by what Leonidas had told her; and taking advantage of the sunny day, she decided not to return to the palace just yet. Instead she turned south at the road and headed farther from Sparta, enjoying the brittle winter sunshine and the solitude. She was in no hurry to return to the royal palace, because the atmosphere there was oppressive. The problems were much deeper than the death of the youngest infant.

For some time it had been evident that Cleomenes had a mistress, a perioikoi woman in Messenia, and he was spending more and more time with her—using any and every excuse to go to the far side of Taygetos. Chilonis sighed. Although she had never warmed to her daughter-in-law, Gyrtias, she did not approve of her son's infidelity. Furthermore, his infidelity was itself only one of many symptoms of his increasing self-indulgence and inconstancy. Chilonis had doted on Cleomenes as a child, but he had always been willful and baffling to her. They had clashed often when he was a teenager, and since becoming king before he was old enough to be a citizen, her influence on him had waned sharply. Cleomenes was polite to her, but he did not heed her—and much less did he heed the hapless beauty he had selected (against her advice) to be his wife.

As for poor Gyrtias, she knew about her husband's infidelities— or at least suspected them—and husband and wife fought bitterly. The loss of this third son only made things worse. Gyrtias' grief was genuine, but it also made her difficult to live with. She was obviously never going to win back Cleomenes' affections if all she ever did in his presence was scream or weep.

The situation had the added negative effect of disturbing the two older children—as this incident with Gorgo proved. Gorgo, as Leonidas so rightly pointed out, had been in real danger. A lone child was easy prey for any number of predators, the worst of which were the barbarian and Greek slave traders that frequented the taverns Leonidas had talked about. Gorgo could have disappeared, and they would not even have known where to look for her. She could have been kidnapped, put aboard a ship bound for any port in the world, and lost to them forever before anyone noticed she was gone.

And then there was Agis. Chilonis sighed again. Her son's firstborn and heir was turning into a terror. He was more self-willed than his father had ever been. He was hot-tempered and violent and seemed utterly immune to discipline. Not that he was subject to overmuch of that, Chilonis thought with another sigh. Both his parents spoiled him, and even when she or one of the ephors or councilmen made some effort to bring the boy to order, his response was irrational screaming and boundless fury. It frightened her to think what sort of king he would make.

She shook her head. It made no sense for Sparta to evolve and nurture such an excellent system of public education—and then deny it to their future kings. Chilonis was certain that Agis would have benefited from the agoge. It was exactly what he needed—the pressure of a herd to make him respect his fellows, and the discipline of the eirenes and instructors to make him respect the law and accept that he could not always get his own way. It most certainly would do him no harm to go to the pits once or twice to learn to endure pain and humiliation with dignity! In retrospect, Chilonis acknowledged that Cleomenes, too, would have made a better king had he gone through the agoge as his half-brothers had done. His half-brothers had all gained in stature and popularity by successfully completing that long, hard testing ground.

She thought again of Leonidas, by far the best of her husband's sons. From the first day they had ever exchanged words in the courtyard of the royal palace, Leonidas had surprised her with his level-headed intelligence, his sound understanding of human nature, and his rock-solid instinct for right and wrong, all combined with a natural warmth. All of this explained why he had rescued this perioikoi girl accused of soliciting, she conceded. And now that she thought about it, she had heard Dienekes remark mysteriously and disparagingly that "Brotus had his reasons" for wanting the girl discredited.

Dienekes had added that Leonidas was "sharper than his reputation." But she couldn't make sense of his words, nor shake the sense that it was a dangerous mistake. In a small city like Sparta, a man's reputation was quickly ruined. Then again, a man had to be true to himself. It had to be some sort of divine joke that the only Agiad prince uninterested in power was the one most suited to kingship. Or was the fact that he was disinterested what made him so well suited?

Chilonis was so lost in her thoughts that she had already driven past the man sitting by the side of the road before she noticed him. The red of a citizen's himation, however, eventually penetrated to her brain, and she pulled up to look back over her shoulder.

Her subconscious had not been mistaken. A gray-headed Spartiate was sitting on a boulder by the side of the road. Just sitting there, gripping his walking stick. It was rare to see anyone idle in Sparta—particularly out in the middle of nowhere on a chilly winter day. Chilonis carefully backed the chariot up until she was directly opposite the man, who looked up at her.

It was the city treasurer, Nikostratos; and with a small intake of breath Chilonis noted that his high forehead was badly bruised, his cheek scratched, and his beard dirty.

"Sir! What happened to you?" Chilonis asked in alarm.

Nikostratos frowned and pressed his lips together in disgust. Then he took a breath and admitted, "I tripped and fell coming out of the Menelaion." He was referring to the temple to Menelaus and Helen that was perched on the hill behind him. "I was just trying to collect myself a bit before continuing."

"Are you hurt?" Chilonis asked, sensing that he did not need to "collect himself" if all he had was a scratch and a bruise or two.

Again Nikostratos sighed. Then he opened his himation, which he had been clutching around his torso, and thrust out a naked leg that revealed an already swollen and discolored ankle. He had removed his sandal because the swelling made it uncomfortable, and red indentations marked where the sandal straps had been.

"Wait while I turn the chariot around," Chilonis ordered; and then, with considerable skill, she backed into the turnoff to the Menelaion and maneuvered the chariot next to Nikostratos. As she halted beside him again, he hauled himself off the boulder using his walking stick, then reached up and grabbed hold of the side of the chariot. With Chilonis' help he clambered up beside her, shaking his head and muttering about being a "worthless old man" the whole time.

"Don't be ridiculous. It could have happened to anyone," Chilonis admonished.

"It happens to me far too frequently," he countered. "I broke it more than twenty years ago when I was still with the army, and it has never been the same since."

"Maybe you should ride more and walk less," Chilonis suggested gently.

Nikostratos shook his head, hesitated, and then admitted, "Can't afford the damn beasts."

Chilonis stared at him. "The man who saved Sparta from bankruptcy can't afford a horse?"

"You don't avert bankruptcy by spendthrift habits," Nikostratos pointed out rather sharply, not meeting her eye.

"True," Chilonis agreed and decided to let the subject drop, since the treasurer was clearly embarrassed. They continued in silence until Nikostratos, feeling guilty about his rudeness, remarked, "I hope I am not diverting you from some important task."

"None at all. I was just enjoying the day after stopping to look in on my stepson."

"Leonidas?"

"Yes. I came to thank him for bringing Gorgo home. You know she ran away a couple weeks ago, and Leonidas found her south of Amyclae in one of those inns?"

Nikostratos gazed at Chilonis in alarm. "That's dangerous! Is she all right?"

"She's fine. She even rescued a puppy that someone had thrown into the river to drown—and she adores Leonidas, talks of him all the time."

Nikostratos smiled at the image and nodded. "She's got spirit."

"Indeed... You know Leonidas is roofing the main house of his kleros—he was up on the roof with several friends, helping the helots."

Nikostratos nodded with satisfaction. He was always pleased to hear good things about Leonidas, because he had long believed in the boy—even when most of the city still thought of him as the "runt of the litter" and adored Dorieus and Brotus instead. To Chilonis he remarked simply, "He's a good young man."

"He said something about a girl turning him down. Who would be so foolish? I would have thought he was the most eligible bachelor in all of Sparta at the moment."

"Eirana, Kyranios' daughter, turned him down to marry Asteropus instead—but that was two years ago."

Chilonis didn't like the sound of that. "You don't think there's any truth to the rumors that he bought that whore to satisfy his lust, do you?"

"Good heavens, woman! Where did you hear such nonsense? Leonidas was pressured by Hilaira, the daughter of Philippos, into buying the woman. I was there. Hilaira and that helot cook of his set on him like the Furies themselves, insisting the woman was not really a whore. Besides, Leonidas and Sperchias were shaken by what the Argives had done on Kythera. When they heard she'd been abused by the Argives, who carved an alpha between her breasts with a knife, they were determined to rescue her."

"Brotus is spreading all sorts of unsavory rumors about Leonidas," Chilonis told the treasurer.

Nikostratos looked at her with an inscrutable look, and then announced, "That, my good woman, is because Brotus is mired in unsavory rumor himself. But I will see what I can do."

They fell silent again for a few moments, and then Chilonis had another idea. "Since I have you captive, sir, I wonder if you could answer a question."

"You are welcome to ask. Whether I have an answer to *any* question is another matter altogether," Nikostratos returned.

Chilonis laughed. "There is hardly *anyone* in Sparta whose opinion is more respected than yours."

"Well, that may be because I never answer questions, but let people answer them for themselves," he told her with a flicker of amusement.

Chilonis laughed again, and this time Nikostratos cracked a small smile of his own, giving her a sidelong glance.

"Sir, as the widow of a Spartan king, is there any property I can call my own? A widow's portion? A kleros as the other widows have?"

Nikostratos looked over at her, horrified. "Don't tell me your son wishes to expel you from his home!"

"No, no, no. This is entirely my own idea—but, you know, it is never good for a mother-in-law to live with a young couple. I should have moved out years ago."

"Madam, you are the most sensible person in the Agiad palace. I cannot—as a responsible Spartan citizen—support your desire to abandon your station," Nikostratos stated firmly, shaking his head.

Chilonis laughed. "I'm flattered, but let's be honest with one another. I will be just as sensible wherever I happen to live, and since my influence on my son is currently nil, it might be worthwhile seeing if it would increase for being less common."

Nikostratos stared at her—until a rut in the road jolted the chariot and caused him to wince in pain and grab hold of the rim of the cart. After the road had become smoother, he announced, "Madam, this is a very bad day. First I make a fool of myself falling head over heels into the dirt. Then I learn that Brotus is slandering his own twin for an act of kindness. And now I hear that the sensible and wise queen mother of our exceedingly erratic and temperamental Agiad king feels she has no influence on him."

"I'm sorry to contribute to your woe, sir, but could we return to the issue of what property I am entitled to as a widow?"

"Unfortunately, there is no state portion for a queen or former queen. If your husband did not provide for you in his will..." He seemed to be thinking. "Hmm...I might be able to find a precedent... But..." He was frowning and started rubbing his beard. In the process he found it was dirty and, blushing with embarrassment, started to comb it clean with his hands. "Why didn't you tell me my beard was filthy!" he snapped rhetorically at Chilonis.

Once in the city, Chilonis wanted to take Nikostratos to a surgeon, but he steadfastly refused. "Believe me, I know my ankle. It's just the damn tendons and ligaments, which are stretched out of all useful shape. Have been for years, which is why they give way at the slightest provocation. A little unevenness in the pavement, the ankle buckles and I land on my face. It is acutely humiliating, but I assure you it will heal without any expensive doctoring."

Chilonis didn't like the sound of that, either. Was he saying he couldn't afford a doctor any more than a horse?

Nor would he let her drive her to his home. "Stop right here," he ordered.

"But you can't walk on that ankle."

"I most certainly can! I would have walked the whole way home if you hadn't happened along. I live just up the end of that street, and there is no reason why you should have to maneuver this chariot down a narrow alley. I thank you most sincerely for your kindness, good lady, but I don't want to become even more indebted. Debt is against my principles," he added, with a little smile that sought to soften the harshness of his refusal. Then he eased himself carefully but determinedly off the back of the chariot onto his good foot and hobbled away, leaning heavily on his walking stick.

Nikostratos had a hard time hobbling to his syssitia that evening. By the time he arrived, he was sweating, and his left armpit was bruised from leaning so hard on his crutch. The other men were solicitous, but they respected his refusal to make a fuss about things. It was only as they stood to leave that Nikostratos called on Leonidas to help him.

Leonidas was no longer the youngest member of the syssitia. They had accepted Euryleon at the solstice, on his graduation. It would have been more correct for Nikostratos to ask for Euryleon's help, but the latter was shortsighted and had trouble seeing in the dark. Thus although Euryleon dutifully offered his help, at a nod from Leonidas he withdrew.

"You don't mind seeing me home tonight, do you?" Nikostratos asked as he laid an arm over Leonidas' broad but soft, warm shoulders. They were so much more comfortable than the top of his walking stick!

"No, of course I don't mind. Euryleon will tell Euragoras why I'm late." Euryleon was in Leonidas' section and could report to the enomotarch.

"I wanted to talk to you about something," Nikostratos confided.

It was pitch dark, and although it had been one of those bright, sunny winter days that promised the return of spring, with the sunset winter seemed to have returned with a vengeance. Leonidas paused to wrap his himation more tightly around him.

"When your father died," Nikostratos started, "did he make no provision for his second wife, for Chilonis? I mean, your mother was most generously endowed, as I remember."

"My mother went to her own estates. She wanted nothing to do with anything that had belonged to my father. She felt he had betrayed her."

"I see." Nikostratos was lost in apparently unhappy thoughts.

"What is the matter?"

"The queen mother, Chilonis. She wishes to move out of the palace and retire. But she owns nothing, it seems. No one has provided her with anything she can call her own."

"Why does she want to move out?"

"Ah, leave it to you to go straight to the heart of it. Why, indeed? I am not sure. The answer she gave me was ..." He looked for the right word. "Facile. She did not tell me the whole story. But she is not a frivolous woman. If she feels she should move out, then she will have her reasons."

Leonidas nodded in agreement.

"Another thing," Nikostratos went on as they continued their slow, tortured way along the road back to Sparta: "It is not good for you to keep that perioikoi girl, the one picked up for soliciting, on your kleros. People are talking about you."

"People, or my brother Brotus?"

Nikostratos frowned and insisted, "People—including your brother Brotus." He stopped and faced Leonidas. "You're a bachelor, Leonidas; you can't keep a whore on your kleros without people talking about it."

"You mean it would be better if I were married?"

"Yes—because then your wife would be in charge of your kleros; and since no self-respecting woman would let her husband keep a rival under her roof, people would recognize that, whatever else the girl did, she did not warm your bed."

"I don't see how the temperature of my bed is anyone's business."

"The morality of every Spartan citizen is the business of us all," Nikostratos reminded him.

"The girl was thrown out of her own home for being a victim of Argive brutality, and you want me to throw her out again just because some tongues are wagging behind my back? Listen: if you hear anyone say a word against me, tell them to say it to my face!" Leonidas was getting worked up.

"Stop being stubborn, Leo; this doesn't have to be blown out of proportion. This girl isn't your kin. She's perioikoi. You are not in any way responsible for what happened to her."

"Aren't I?" Leonidas stopped, making Nikostratos stare at him. "Aren't we all? What happened on Kythera was *our* fault. We left it undefended, then took over a week to respond. All the while, the Argives were rampaging across the island—plundering, burning, raping, and murdering. There were scores of girls who suffered what Kleta did, only most of them are now dead. Because we failed them."

"We can't be everywhere at once."

"We collect taxes and tolls from the perioikoi, don't we? We demand their absolute loyalty and require them to send their sons with us as auxiliary troops whenever we operate outside our borders, don't we? We even expect them to help put down helot unrest if necessary."

Nikostratos was frowning. "What are you driving at, Leo?"

"That we made a pact with them, a simple two-part pact: First, they receive the exclusive right to engage in trade and manufacturing in exchange for paying high taxes and tolls. Second, they support us militarily without question in exchange for protection. When we let the Argives sack most of Kythera this past spring, we failed to keep our end of the bargain."

Nikostratos considered the younger man and nodded. "There is truth to that."

"Then you must also admit that if it happens too often, we will deservedly lose the loyalty of the perioikoi, and our own strength will diminish accordingly."

"You are probably right," Nikostratos conceded, impressed that Leonidas could be this foresighted; but then he added firmly, "But that has nothing to do with the fate of this girl. She's already been rejected by her own family. What happens to her will have no impact on perioikoi loyalty one way or another."

"Maybe not, but I feel personally responsible for what happened to her, and for that reason I owe her all the compensation I am capable of giving."

"What you're doing, Leo, is just digging in your heels and refusing to see reason on this out of sheer orneriness!" Nikostratos retorted; then he patted Leonidas' shoulder to calm his protégé before he could reply. "You don't have to just dump her out onto the streets. You own scores of properties—including, if I remember correctly, a majority share in a flax mill near Kardamyle."

"What does that have to do with anything?"

"I've never met the girl, but most perioikoi women are excellent weavers. This girl must have spirit and brains, or she would not have survived—or escaped the Argives. Give her some capital and let her set herself up in business as a weaver, attached to your flax mill. That gives her an honest way to earn her living—and puts her on the other side of Taygetos, too far away for even the most hostile detractor to impute sexual motives on your part."

Leonidas thought about it for a moment, and then admitted, "No wonder you have been elected treasurer again and again. That is a very good idea, and I will speak with my steward Phormio about it tomorrow."

"Good man," Nikostratos nodded, satisfied and relieved, mentally thanking Athena for the inspiration. Then he raised the other topic that was bothering him. "Have you heard about your twin's wife, by the way?"

"You mean the rumors that Lathria was overly friendly with a certain helot from the lumberyards while Brotus was away on the Argive border this fall?"

"Ah, so you do keep an eye on your brothers." Nikostratos sounded pleased.

"No," Leonidas corrected. "I am forced to hear about them constantly from others."

Nikostratos acknowledged the rebuke with a small laugh, but persisted. "What do you make of it?"

Leonidas sighed. "Lathria is hot-blooded. Brotus was, as you said, away until late this fall. It does not task my imagination to think she sought amusement elsewhere while my brother was away."

"With a *helot*?" Nikostratos sounded shocked, and he stopped to stare at Leonidas.

It was too dark to see the younger man's face, but Leonidas shrugged and answered evenly, "What Spartiate would risk the rage of the second in line to the Agiad throne? I think a *helot* might have found it far more difficult to resist Lathria's inducements."

"But what Spartiate woman would lower herself to such a liaison?" Nikostratos still seemed incapable of imagining it.

"The helot involved was allegedly a very fine-looking young man, exceptionally well-made and strong as an ox."

"Was?" Nikostratos raised his eyebrows.

"He was found dead the other day, and no one is asking any questions—not even the lumberyard owner."

"And you think it possible that your sister-in-law willingly took this helot to her bed?"

Leonidas shrugged. "I don't have any trouble believing it at all, actually." Leonidas thought back on his own encounters with the sexually charged Lathria.

"You will not be alone in thinking this," Nikostratos concluded.

"No," Leonidas considered and then added, "I'd say every Spartiate under the age of thirty and over the age of eighteen knows about Lathria's proclivities."

"Except your brother, it seems."

"I suspect my brother knows—now."

Nikostratos had been guiding them as they walked, and he stopped in front of a narrow two-story building in the alley behind one of the army barracks. Leonidas assumed they were taking a shortcut to someplace more respectable, but Nikostratos removed his arm and started fumbling in the dark with the door. Leonidas exclaimed in some confusion, "You live here?"

"Yes."

"But where?"

"Above this shop. If you could help me up the stairs..."

"Nikostratos! I would carry you, if you need me to, but where is your attendant? Your daughter? Your daughter-in-law? Do you mean you live in this —this is not even a *perioikoi* dwelling!"

"No, it belongs to a freedman, a former Arcadian slave who escaped here and somehow bought his freedom—or not. I don't know exactly. I am his tenant, not his interrogator. As for my daughter and daughter-in-law, I do not like to impose on their hospitality."

"Hospitality? But you must have a kleros of your own!"

"It is halfway to Gytheon and supports my young grandson. How could I attend to my duties or come to the syssitia if I lived there? Horses eat too damn much, and where would I keep one here in the city? This is fine. What more does an old man need than a couple of rooms?"

Leonidas could think of many things—the warmth of a hearth fire, for a start, and someone to cook and clean for him. Meanwhile, Nikostratos had opened the door and hobbled down a dark corridor to a cramped, unpleasant courtyard. The whole place had the musty smell of mildew and rubbish and improperly cleaned latrines, although it was too dark to see much.

Nikostratos looked up a narrow wooden stairway with no railing, in obvious despair.

Leonidas went around to the open side and slipped his arm under Nikostratos' shoulder to help heave him up the stairs. He got the old man into his bed and then stood looking around. There was almost nothing here. "Where is your attendant?" Leonidas asked again.

"I let him go."

"What do you mean?"

"He was an old man and he wanted to go home."

"Home? Where?"

"To Messenia."

"Your man was Messenian?"

"Yes."

"You didn't tell me that when I asked you about Mantiklos."

"It was irrelevant. But this past summer, my man asked me to let him go home. After the Karneia. I didn't have the heart to stop him. He was going home to die. Kidney problems."

"Does my brother Cleomenes know how you live?"

"Why should he?"

"Do the ephors and Council know?"

"Why does it matter?"

"Because you are one of the most important officials of this city!" Leonidas responded forcefully. "It is not right that you should live like this!"

"What do you propose? An official apartment with household help and catering for all city officials? That would just turn every post into something coveted for the wrong reasons. Lycurgus knew what he was doing when he said our city officials should serve for honor— not pecuniary rewards—and all citizens should be equal in wealth," Nikostratos retorted.

"But we aren't equal in wealth!" Leonidas protested. "The constitution has been corrupted and circumvented, and we are living a lie! We wear the same clothes and call ourselves equals, but we're not!" Leonidas was angry, as he always was when confronted by a reality that did not match his ideal image of his city.

"I'm sorry to have distressed you, Leo," Nikostratos declared sincerely. "That was not why I brought you here. I have been neglectful of myself. Thank you for reminding me. I will endeavor to improve."

"Should I send you a helot youth to look after you?"

"I'd rather have more of those sweets you brought the other night to the syssitia."

They both laughed, and Leonidas left it at that.

—————

The next morning Nikostratos had considerable difficulty getting himself washed and dressed on account of his bad ankle. There was not always something to hold onto when he needed it, and if he used a crutch, it meant he lost the use of one hand, too. The ankle was swollen terribly now, and his toes were black. He gave some thought to going to a doctor after all, but then decided on the baths instead. The bath slaves had salves, the kind of things they rubbed into the aching muscles of the young men after drill.

The visit to the baths did him good, and one of the slaves even bound up his foot after applying a heavy poultice. Feeling much better, Nikostratos went to his office behind the Ephorate, and started searching through the records for some precedent that would help

Chilonis. By late afternoon, hungry and frustrated, he had to concede to himself that he had not found anything. He had hoped he would. He had looked forward to taking the good news to Chilonis. Maybe he should drop by and tell her what he had found? At least she would know he'd tried. It wouldn't be right for her to think he had not made an effort. She might feel hurt or slighted if she thought that.

Having convinced himself that he had a good reason to seek out the queen mother, he combed his beard with his hands and patted at his braids to be sure they were still tidy. Then he wrapped his himation around himself carefully and set off, limping painfully.

It took him a long time, with many pauses, to reach the Agiad palace. Outside the palace Nikostratos took the steps one at a time, reaching the shade of the portico with relief. Here he paused to adjust his himation and pat his braids again before requesting admittance. The meleirenes on duty opened the doors to the city treasurer without question, and once inside, Nikostratos simply stopped the next household servant he saw and asked him to fetch Chilonis. He then eased himself down to sit on the bench running around the entry hall. As he waited, he started to feel ridiculous. Why was he bothering the queen mother with the news that he had found nothing?

A moment later she was coming toward him, smiling so sincerely that he forgot his own embarrassment. "I'm afraid I don't have particularly good news," he started at once, lest she thought his appearance meant something it did not.

Chilonis did not smile any less. "The news that you are here is good enough for me. Come, join me for some refreshments and we can chat. How is your ankle doing?" She looked down at it.

"It feels much better," Nikostratos lied.

"Did you see a doctor?"

"Not necessary. A bath slave was more than good enough."

Chilonis looked skeptical, but held her tongue. She led him to a chamber with a central grate in which a fire glowed more than burned. There were benches around the walls, and small tables on wheels. Chilonis bid Nikostratos make himself comfortable, then took one of the tables and disappeared. Nikostratos was left to contemplate the room with its ancient murals. They must be hundreds of years old, he calculated, dating to an age before Lycurgus and the Great

Reforms. It was a sobering reminder of how ancient the Spartan royal lines were. Cleomenes was the fourteenth king in his line; and if one assumed an average reign of twenty-five years, that took the Spartan kings back 350 years. It was not wise to break with something that had worked so well for so long, was it?

In Athens nowadays, he reminded himself, the Council of Five Hundred was selected by lot rather than elected. This meant the Council, which both prepared bills for debate and implemented laws passed by the Assembly, was chosen at random. Furthermore, no man was allowed to serve more than twice in the Council, so even those randomly chosen were not given a chance to learn their duties and exercise them professionally. Finally, the chairmanship changed daily to prevent anyone from abusing power.

Two aspects of these reforms unsettled Nikostratos. On the one hand, the concept of appointing people to positions of power by lot suggested a fundamental belief that all men were equally capable, or that the Gods would always ensure that the lot fell to the most suitable. Nikostratos did not believe in either circumstance. The Gods were always fickle, and it was patently obvious that not all men were equally capable of deliberation, reason, and governance. Thus the idea of a lottery for government seemed ridiculous to Nikostratos. No one would choose a cook or a physician by lottery, either. Yet neither a cook nor a physician could do as much collective damage as a bad government. Nikostratos considered this latest Athenian innovation an insult to the concept and profession of government itself.

The other aspect of the reform, however, unsettled him even more. If, as he suspected, the selection by lot degraded the importance of the Council of Five Hundred as a whole, then there would be a corresponding increase in the importance of the Assembly. The older he became, the more Nikostratos distrusted the Assembly. The larger the crowd, the more easily it could be manipulated—as if some herd instinct took over, enabling a demagogue to harness the majority to any cause, no matter how foolish or dangerous. Too often in his life, sensible ideas had been ignored and foolish plans acclaimed just because a clever speaker or some other kind of irrational influence swayed opinion in the Assembly.

On the other hand, Nikostratos found himself intrigued by a third aspect of the Athenian reforms, namely an extension of the franchise. As a man who had many dealings with the perioikoi, Nikostratos found himself wondering whether Sparta would benefit from giving them a voice in government. By restricting the franchise in Sparta to the Spartiates, who were by law hoplites, they cut themselves off from their economic power base and so from the wisdom, common sense, and vast experience of men of trade, industry, and finance.

Nikostratos was shaken from his reverie by the reappearance of Chilonis, pushing a little table laden with grapes and olives, fresh-baked bread, goat's cheese, yogurt, and honey. The sight of it made Nikostratos realize how hungry he was. His face lit up, and Chilonis smiled.

"I see the old wives are right: the way to a man's heart is through his stomach."

"Why would any woman want to find her way to my heart?" Nikostratos countered, first helping himself to the bread and then folding cheese and olives into it before popping it into his mouth.

"Curiosity?" Chilonis countered.

"Dangerous. It kills cats."

Chilonis only laughed. She sat down beside him and helped herself to the grapes. "So what news did you bring me?"

"Unfortunately, the only precedent I could find was the queen of Archelaos, who appears to have had her own household for much of her son's reign; but the properties she possessed then transferred to her younger son, and they may in fact have been *his* portion. Your husband did provide for his younger sons, after all."

Chilonis' face said it all.

"Obviously, I didn't mean that you should ask Cleombrotus or Leon—"

"I wouldn't ask either of them for as much as a bale of hay!" Chilonis interrupted sharply. "We threw them out of their home like rubbish when their father died. I've felt guilty about it ever since."

"They were both in the agoge," Nikostratos reminded her reasonably.

"That's immaterial. This was their home—and it *still* isn't mine." She got up and started pacing. Her hand reached out to the faded but once bright-colored murals with their rather heavy-handed depictions of battle scenes—the siege of Troy, Achilles and Hektor, Kastor and Polydeukes...

Nikostratos considered the proud woman and wished that he had someplace to offer her.

She seemed to intercept his thought, turning to look at him with a sad smile. "I will ask my son. He should not begrudge me one farm when he has so many. He may even be glad to get rid of me."

"Do not speak ill of one of my kings," Nikostratos countered.

The sound of shouting from far away made them both start and look toward the outer courtyard. They looked at one another, puzzled. "An Argive attack?" Nikostratos wondered out loud.

They could now distinctly hear someone asking for Chilonis personally, in agitated tones. A moment later a helot burst into the hall. Chilonis looked at him expectantly, recognizing her grandson's servant. Before he could speak, she guessed. "Agis. What has he done now?"

"Madam." The man was breathing heavily and he was sweating. He looked frightened. "There has been an accident."

"Has he been hurt?" Chilonis asked anxiously, and her hands curled in distress.

The man held his breath. "I—yes—he has been hurt. We must send for the king."

"My son is in Messenia," Chilonis countered. "Where is Agis? What happened to him? How is he injured?"

"He—he insisted he wanted to see the wrestlers better, madam." The man was licking his lips, and the sheen of his sweat was sickly. Nikostratos could smell him, and he smelled of fear. "I tried to talk him out of it."

"Out of what?" Chilonis pressed him, her expression increasingly alarmed but her voice firm.

"Climbing onto the roof of the palaestra, Madam." The man's voice fell away as he said it.

"He's fallen from a roof?"

There was no chance for the man to answer. From behind them, more voices announced the arrival of a large body of men. Nikostratos was on his feet. He hobbled toward the doorway behind Chilonis. He could see a large crowd—mostly citizens, a couple of whom were still naked and covered in sand—apparently they had been exercising in the palaestra when the accident occurred. They were carrying something between them on a stretcher.

Someone, apparently one of the women of the household, had fetched Queen Gyrtias. She rushed out of the peristyle into the courtyard and bent over the limp body on the stretcher. Nikostratos' view was partially blocked by the crowd of servants that were gathering around the cluster of men already escorting the stretcher. But Gyrtias' piercing shriek made his hair stand on end.

Chilonis plunged into the crowd.

The queen was hysterical. She was screaming inarticulately in a high-pitched wail, and then she started literally tearing at her hair and scratching her face. Chilonis was giving orders. Nikostratos stood and watched in horrified admiration while she ordered the queen's women to take her away and the men with the stretcher in another direction, and then started questioning the witnesses. They told what had happened with wide, expansive gestures, looking up over their heads and indicating a fall.

Suddenly a small voice piped up, making Nikostratos jump in surprise. Nikostratos looked down and found little Gorgo standing beside him. She was wearing only a short chiton that revealed dirty knees and feet. Her bright red hair was coming out of its braid, and her freckles were very evident on a pale face that looked up at him with wide hazel-green eyes. "What's happened?"

Nikostratos took a deep breath, instinctively stroking the back of her long, bony neck. "I fear something terrible has happened to your brother, Agis."

"Agis?" She looked at the commotion in the courtyard, standing on tiptoe and craning her neck to see more, but the stretcher had already disappeared. She looked back up at Nikostratos. "You mean he's done something *really* terrible?"

"In a way, yes," Nikostratos agreed. "I think he has hurt himself very badly."

Gorgo was frowning up at him.

He took a deep breath. "I think he is dead."

———

The word reached Leonidas at the baths. Someone coming straight from the gymnasium where the accident had happened broke in, telling everyone within hearing. Although Leonidas was in the next room, someone who knew he was there rushed to tell him, "Your nephew Agis was killed in an accident!"

Leonidas, who had been sitting comfortably in the warm water to counter the muscle aches from drill, sat up sharply and turned to look at the messenger. But already other men were spilling into the chamber, chattering. Some were still talking about the accident itself—that the boy should never have been allowed to climb up onto the roof, that the boy was too willful, that the roof was slippery with mist. Others were asking where Cleomenes was and speculating what he would do.

Leonidas splashed out of the water and searched for a towel, which Mantiklos hastened to hand him. He rubbed himself dry as fast as he could. Alkander burst in: "Leo, have you heard?"

"Of course! Where's Brotus?"

"Brotus?" Alkander looked at Leonidas as if he were mad. The twins rarely had anything to do with one another.

"Brotus just became heir to the Agiad throne, and it would be just like him to start gloating! I'd better find him and sit on him for a while! Mantiklos!" he shouted at the helot, who was returning the towels he'd just used to a bin. "Take word to my section!" Turning to Alkander he asked, "Coming?"

"Coming where?"

"To find Brotus, of course."

"You can't stop him from gloating, Leo. He's—"

"I can try to keep him from being obvious about it until the funeral is over. Where are my things?" He was looking around irritably, unable to identify his own clothes on the partitioned wooden shelves on which the bathers left their bundles. At last, finding his stuff, he pulled his chiton on over his head and tightened his belt before reaching for his sandals.

Outside it was already dusk, and Leonidas calculated that it was no more than an hour to dinner. Leonidas decided he would check the gymnasium where Brotus often practiced boxing, and if he wasn't there, try to intercept him outside his syssitia. He started through the city with Alkander and Beggar at his heels.

There were half a dozen gymnasia around the city and although all were opened to all citizens, each also had its own clientele, largely determined by the trainers available at each. Leonidas usually avoided Brotus' favorite gymnasium, the one at which a former Olympic boxer trained young men most attached to that sport, but he made straight for it now.

Naturally everyone here had already heard the news, too, and they were standing about in a cluster, spilling out of the entrance into the street. As Leonidas had expected, Brotus was grinning in the center of the crowd.

"Come to pay homage to the crown prince, have you, little brother?" he called out at the sight of Leonidas.

"No, I've come to close your trap!"

The crowd parted instantly before Leonidas. If the Agiad twins were about to fight with one another, no one wanted to be in the way—but they waited avidly on the sidelines.

Brotus' face drew together into a scowl at his brother's retort, and he thrust out his lower jaw belligerently. "You can't stop me from doing a damn thing!" Brotus told his twin.

"Watch me," Leonidas countered; and in the same instant that Brotus lashed out with a fist, Leonidas sidestepped, twisted, wrapped his arms around the boxer, and flung him down to the ground. Brotus was partially winded by the maneuver, but he still struggled furiously. Leonidas took a blow to his face that broke his lips on his teeth and set his nose to bleeding, but he had his knee on Brotus' groin and pressed down hard, while using his hands to pin Brotus' throat to the earth until he started to choke. Brotus' eyes bulged in his head and he flailed with his arms and legs in ever greater panic. Leonidas just held him down, the blood from his own nose dripping on Brotus' face and neck, until Brotus' arms flopped down in exhaustion. Then he let go and stepped back and up in a single motion.

His brother stared up at him, gasping, his hands unconsciously holding his throat. There was absolute silence around them.

"You may be crown prince until Cleomenes has another son, but there is no need to remind anyone of how little they want to see you become king," Leonidas told him bluntly—eliciting protests from

Brotus' friends. He then turned on his heel and stalked away, leaving them to pick up his brother.

Alkander caught up with Leonidas several strides up the street; and after they were out of hearing, he ventured to ask, "Why did you do that? Brotus hates you enough already."

"Better that he hates me than Cleomenes."

Alkander thought about that. "You can't seriously think he would try to challenge Cleomenes?"

Leonidas stopped in his tracks and turned to face Alkander. It was almost dark and the pipes were whining, signaling dinner. "Don't you know what they found at his kleros this morning?"

Alkander shook his head.

"Lathria at the foot of the outside stairs—stone dead."

"Dead?"

"Just like Agis."

"But Brotus wasn't anywhere near the palaestra this afternoon!"

"No, and of course he says he was in his barracks last night—but the helots tell me otherwise."

"Leo! Are you sure?"

"About Lathria, yes. He came to his kleros in the night long after curfew, and he quarreled violently with Lathria. Brotus called her a whore. She called him various unsavory names in return, and he started hitting her. She ran out of the bedroom and started down the stairs. He caught up with her and hurled her off the stairs onto the flagstone courtyard a good ten feet below. The helots came running and he ordered them away. He told them if any of them told what had happened, he'd see to it they disappeared."

Alkander was staring at Leonidas in horror.

"He killed her brother, too, remember?"

Alkander opened his mouth to speak, but found no words. He shook his head. Finally he asked, "What are you going to do?"

"What can I do? I was not there. I did not even find the corpse. The helots are terrified. They will never tell a magistrate what they said to me in private. They only confessed to me because they have known me all my life, and they were in shock over what had happened. But they are terrified, Alkander. My brother has bullied them too long. And you can be sure his friends and superiors will verify his alibi. Officially he was in barracks last night, miles from his kleros."

"But are people going to believe it was an accident or suicide?"

"People will believe what they want to believe. And someone has to bring charges. After the rumors about her sleeping with a helot, she had hardly any sympathy in this city. Her own parents disowned her, while people like Talthybiades, Lysimachos, and Alcidas were calling on Brotus to divorce her, afraid that a helot brat might be raised as a Spartiate. No one is going to look into what happened last night on my brother's kleros."

"So your brother gets away with a second murder?"

"Alkander! What do you want me to do?" Leonidas asked back angrily. He hated this, too, but he didn't see any alternative.

Alkander waited a moment for Leonidas' anger to cool, then said in a very low, almost inaudible voice, "You should tell someone else about your suspicions—the ephors perhaps or, better, members of the Council of Elders. They have to know what you think, even if they too can do nothing."

"Why?"

"Because Brotus is now the heir to the Agiad throne."

"What he has done does not alter that."

"Maybe not, but it might convince the ephors and Council that something else has to be done to ensure he does not become king."

"What do you mean?"

Alkander shrugged and looked away, unwilling to meet Leonidas' eyes. What he meant was that someone might "discover" that Leonidas was the elder twin. What he said was, "Maybe Cleomenes could be persuaded to take another wife, one who will give him healthy sons. There is the precedent of your father, after all."

"And create that kind of intrafamily rivalry again?" Leonidas countered. Then he conceded. "I'll talk to Nikostratos about it."

Alkander had to be satisfied with that.

CHAPTER 8

THE HEIR TO THE THRONE

WHEN CLEOMENES RETURNED, HE WAS OVERCOME with grief. He threw himself on the floor beside the couch where the little corpse was laid out, and banged his head on the tiles. His screams resonated through the palace and the servants fled in alarm. In a fit of guilt, the king drew his hunting knife and started to systematically cut incisions over his heart, as if he wanted to tear it out. His wife managed to stop him only by pulling him into her arms and wrapping her himation around him. He sobbed into her breast and then her lap until she took him back to her chamber, where he spent the night with her.

The next morning a messenger was dispatched dismissing the mistress in Messenia, and the king made a point of appearing everywhere in public with his queen. He started showering her with gifts as in the early years of their marriage. Cleomenes also granted his mother a large, prosperous estate opposite Amyclae, and she was given permission to remarry. Many saw this as an indication that Chilonis had been to blame for "poisoning" her son against his wife and that she had been sent away in disgrace. Her marriage to Nikostratos aroused a brief flurry of gossip, but it was generally accepted as a perfectly sensible thing for both of them.

The only person who suffered from the arrangement was Gorgo. She felt guilty for not really missing her brother Agis, and she felt neglected by her parents and betrayed by her grandmother. She wanted to run away again, but she was afraid. She sought out her mare, Shadow, and her puppy, Jason, and spent hours talking to both.

One morning while she was standing on an overturned crate so she could trim Shadow's mane, her father came up behind her. "So this is where you disappear to!" he exclaimed.

She spun around, delighted at the sound of his voice, and her smile broadened when she saw that for once he was alone. Her mother was not with him. She had him all to herself. She flung her arms around his neck, and he lifted her off her crate and spun her around. "Does my princess want to come for a ride with me?"

"Oh, yes, Daddy! Of course! Where are we going? Can I ride Shadow?"

"Yes, if you wish; but I rather hoped you would sit in front of me on my horse, like you used to do when you were little."

Gorgo was torn only for a moment. She could ride Shadow this afternoon or tomorrow, but it had been ages since her father had taken her with him, and she did not know when she would have another chance. So she nodded eagerly, and he carried her over to his favorite white stallion. The grooms were just brushing the last pieces of straw from his tail and picking out his hooves.

Cleomenes swung his daughter up onto the horse's back and then, from a mounting block, jumped up behind her. He took the reins, and as soon as they were in the street outside he took up a canter. The eager horse sprang forward willingly and they tore down the streets, scattering everything in their way, from chickens and helots to boys of the agoge.

Gorgo would have been frightened if her father hadn't been holding her so tightly in his left arm. They were galloping north, past the theater and ball field and on toward the temple to Penelope. When they left the main road and started up a rocky, zigzagging path, Cleomenes let his horse fall into a walk. He also let Gorgo talk.

Gorgo babbled without pause about all the things she had wanted to tell him for weeks and months and years. She told him about her puppy and made him promise she could keep it, and she told him about her adventures when she ran away. Cleomenes seemed to find it all very amusing. Maybe it hadn't been so dangerous after all? She asked why her grandmother had moved out, and if she could go visit her—to which her father said she could visit as often as she liked, without answering the question of why she had left.

They left the forest behind and rode across a meadow in which the first of the wildflowers, heralds of the nearing spring, were blooming. Amid a semicircle of cypress trees stood the Temple of the Horse Grave. This ancient Doric temple marked the spot where Helen's suitors had been made to swear that they would support whichever one of them became her husband. Here Cleomenes jumped down and pulled Gorgo into his arms, before turning his horse loose to graze.

They went together to the simple, weathered stone altar, and Cleomenes made an offering of wine that he had carried in a satchel over his back. Then he removed some prunes and considered them before deciding they could be "better used" to feed himself and Gorgo.

Gorgo entered the temple to admire the beautiful bronze statue of a horse with raised head, pricked ears, and one foot outstretched as if anxious to come toward her. It reminded her of her beloved Shadow.

"Gorgo! I'm hungry!" her father called.

Gorgo patted the bronze horse on his shiny nose (which proved she was not the first to have patted him) and went back out into the pleasantly warm sunshine. They sat down on the steps, looking across the broad field before the temple. Although the field was blooming and the surrounding trees were budding, leaves blown off the surrounding trees by the winter storms still lay at their feet like a carpet.

Gorgo wiped sweat from her brow with the back of her arm as she had seen the boys do.

"Thirsty?" her father asked. She nodded vigorously. Her father produced a skin of wine and with a smile, offered it to his daughter.

She eagerly took a sip and then made a face and spat it out. "Yuck! That tastes terrible!"

Cleomenes threw back his head and laughed in delight. "It's neat wine, precious. Just the way I like it." He took a large gulp, smacking his lips demonstratively as he finished.

His daughter was frowning at him, and so he pulled her into his arms and tousled her hair with his hand.

"Stop that!" she protested. "You'll mess up my braids."

"What braids?" her father teased. "You mean this mess is supposed to be braids?" He held up one braid by the frayed tip. Large loops had long since escaped around her cheeks, and the braid itself was halfway unraveled.

"Yes!" Gorgo insisted, pulling it out of his hand and then deftly pulling the strands apart to start rebraiding her hair.

Cleomenes stopped her by holding her tightly in his arms and kissing the top of her head. "My little princess!" he declared proudly. "Do you know what you are now?"

"What?" she asked suspiciously.

"Why you, my precocious princess, are the heir to the Agiad throne."

"But I'm a girl," she protested. "I can't command the army."

Cleomenes threw back his head and laughed in delight. Then he gave her a short hug and turned her around in his arms to kiss her nose before saying, "No, but whoever you *marry* will command our army; and you, of course, will command him!" He pinched her nose playfully.

Then, already bored, Cleomenes stood up. "Come, let's ride on!" He whistled to his stallion, who at once lifted his head and then came trotting over to get the apple Cleomenes always kept ready for him.

Cleomenes again swung his daughter up onto the broad back of his stallion and climbed up behind her. As he turned away and asked his stallion for a trot, he thought smugly to himself that Tyndareus had been very lucky, but also very wise. After all, sons were unpredictable—they could die young, be weak or whiny or overly self-willed. What father could ever be sure that a *son* would be all he wanted him to be? But a *son-in-law*—the grown man that a father could choose for his daughter—could be exactly right. It made no difference that Gorgo was not a beauty, as Helen had been. For the prize of commanding Sparta's incomparable army, men would willingly overlook her deficiencies.

CHAPTER 9

THE GAMES

THE WINTER HAD BEEN MILD, AND the earth sprouted and turned green earlier than normal. The unseasonably warm weather brought everyone out into the fresh air, casting aside with relief their winter clothes and mood. This being an Olympic year, every ambitious athlete took advantage of the weather to start training as soon as possible.

Leonidas was under considerable pressure to compete in wrestling. He had always been good; and there were those who said that if he would just train a little harder, he stood a real chance of a victory. But when Leonidas was feeling lazy, he would argue that Sparta had enough other contenders for the laurels without his efforts. Demaratus was entering a four-horse chariot, and his chances were widely thought to be excellent. His team could beat anything that came up against it in Sparta, for a start; and Leonidas would also point to his old herd leader Ephorus, who was now a world-class discus thrower, and Brotus, who had won at boxing when still a youth. Brotus was determined to take the crown home again, this time as an adult. He spent every free minute at his gymnasium, battering bags or people. In short, Leonidas told those pushing him to compete, Sparta had more than one good chance of a victory and did not need his efforts.

But Alkander harassed him when they were alone together, insisting: "It would not be good for you if Brotus claims another Olympic victory while you have nothing. If you get one, too, it will largely neutralize any benefit he would otherwise derive from an Olympic prize."

"Why do you insist on seeing us as rivals?" Leonidas retorted irritably.

"Because you are—whether you want to be or not," Alkander replied, and it was true. It had always been true.

So although Leonidas was undecided about competing, he did start training harder. What this meant was that he spent nearly all his time either at drill or in the palaestra. He almost never made it to his kleros anymore, much less his other properties.

One evening as he came out of the palaestra, he was astonished to see Crius running down the street. Worse, a whole herd of boys from the agoge were pursuing him, shouting threats and insults and even throwing things at him. The boys of the agoge were raised to look down on helots, and they were certainly not above beating or otherwise intimidating and harassing helot boys their own age or younger. Fearing the worst, Leonidas immediately stepped between Crius and the boys and ordered at the boys to halt.

There was nothing the boys of the agoge hated more (as Leonidas well knew) than the interference of Spartiate citizens in their games and free time. Their life was hard enough, between training and sports and lessons, without having to answer to every passing citizen. But the law was the law, and they knew that Leonidas had the right to stop them, question them, and—if he thought they were rude or disrespectful—report them to the Paidonomos, who would see that they were punished.

Reluctantly, resentment written all over their dirty faces, the boys drew to a halt in a ragged cluster and stood waiting for him to address them.

"What's going on? Why are you chasing my helot?"

"Sir?" one of the boys ventured with a quick upward glance. The boys were standing, as required, with their eyes cast down and their hands at their sides.

"Are you the herd leader?" Leonidas asked.

"Yes, sir."

"You were chasing one of my helots. I want to know why."

"He was mocking us, sir! Taunting and calling us names! He does it all the time!"

Leonidas turned to look behind him. Crius had halted and was standing a good hundred yards farther up the road, grinning.

"Crius! Come here!"

Crius obeyed readily. He was clearly not afraid. It was hard to believe that this lanky boy on the brink of youth was the same creature who had cowered in the baths at Leonidas' estate in Messenia just three years ago. He was very cocky now.

"These boys say you were mocking them," Leonidas told the helot boy firmly. "Is that true?"

"All I said was that they were lame-asses."

Leonidas nearly choked. Helots had no business saying things like that to their betters. The boys of the agoge allowed themselves little smiles of self-righteousness.

"What made you say something like that?" Leonidas demanded furiously.

Crius shrugged. "I was watching them race down at the course, and they *are* all lame-asses!"

Leonidas couldn't take it any longer. He cuffed Crius hard. "You address me as "sir" or "master!" Just because you're worthless—or should I say *especially* because you are otherwise worthless—is no excuse for disrespect."

The boys of the agoge were grinning now.

Crius shook off Leonidas' blow like a duck shaking off water. "They're still lame-asses—*master.*" He made it sound like a sneer, and Leonidas felt he had no choice but to hit him again, harder this time.

Crius ducked his head, so that the blow only partly connected, and took flight at once. Leonidas was caught off guard, and as he started after the boy he realized that Crius was sprinting away from him with apparent ease. He called out to a meleirene farther up the street to stop Crius. The meleirene, twice Crius' weight and wearing leather armor, brought Crius down easily, but by now they were attracting attention. People on the street stopped to see what was going on, and the shopkeepers came out of their shops and craned their necks.

"Bring him here!" Leonidas ordered. The meleirene obligingly wrenched Crius' arms behind his back and held onto both his wrists while he pushed him forward to stand in front of Leonidas. The boys of the agoge who had been chasing Crius watched with open triumph and anticipation written on their faces. It was not common for them to get such exalted help as this from a Peer and officer.

Crius was finally beginning to look sullen rather than impudent, which meant he had at least acknowledged that he had to submit for now.

With the meleirene holding Crius in front of him, Leonidas asked, "What are you doing here in the city?"

Crius frowned, shrugged, and shuffled his feet. The meleirene brought his knee up hard into Crius' butt, and the boy straightened up with widened eyes that gazed at Leonidas in outrage. Leonidas saw a flash of understanding in those eyes: the late realization that although Leonidas might have indulged him in the past, he *could* command him. "I was just here, sir. I—" he shrugged—"don't have anything else to do."

The boys of the agoge started laughing and calling him a liar. Helot boys started working as soon as they could walk. A boy as old as Crius, who was clearly ten or eleven, would usually be burdened with chores. Helots did not enjoy leisure. But Leonidas knew that Crius was telling the truth. "You were loitering around in the city. Is that what you usually do?"

"I like watching the games and the races. Sir," Crius told Leonidas, looking up with wide eyes that were openly pleading now, reminding Leonidas of his handicap, playing on his sympathy as he had so often before.

"And you called these worthy sons of Spartiate citizens insulting names?" Leonidas asked, trying to break the pattern of pity and indulgence.

The boys of the agoge looked smug.

Crius glanced at them, impudently tossing his long hair out of his eyes as he looked straight at Leonidas. "Yeah. Because they are slow as mules! I could beat any of them—I could probably lap them!" Crius bragged, his little chest swelling out as he spoke.

The meleirene kicked at the back of his knees, and Crius dropped onto the street. His astonishment was greater than his pain, and the boys of the agoge laughed in delight. Even the onlookers hissed, and several shouted at Leonidas that it was time the boy was taught a lesson.

Leonidas recognized the voice of his former eirene Lysimachos, who (as always) advocated punishment: "Take his impudent hide off him, Leonidas!"

Leonidas did not respond. He remained apparently unmoved. He just looked down at Crius, who was now looking up at him with tears in his eyes and a quivering lip—but not from pain, from rage. "It's true!" Crius insisted furiously.

"Prove it!" Leonidas answered. With a flick of his hand he gestured for the meleirene to pull Crius to his feet; and turning to the boys of the agoge, he nodded. "Go on, back to the racecourse. He's going to race you right now."

The boys were surprised, but Leonidas was a Peer and officer. None of the boys dared contradict him, no matter how unprecedented such a contest might be. And many of the passers-by—those that had nothing better to do—followed along curiously, although Lysimachos shook his head disapprovingly and went in the opposite direction.

At the racecourse there were many agoge units engaged in training and informal races, but Leonidas cleared them off the course with a single shout. He had the boys of the agoge unit that had been chasing Crius select their three best runners. He ordered them and Crius to strip and to line up at the start between the statues of the Divine Twins, Kastor and Polydeukes. The Twins stood naked and at the ready, with opposite feet forward, smiling at one another under stone helmets. Leonidas ordered the selected boys to race the length of the stadium.

Crius pulled ahead of the others from the start, and never gave up his lead. The spectators looked at one another and started chattering. The Spartan admiration for athletic ability was warring with their inbred contempt for helots. Leonidas looked around at the boys from the other herds who had also gathered around to watch. "Who wants to race with him?"

The clamor of the volunteers was great. A second race took place. Again Crius took an early lead and kept it.

Now several other citizens came over to Leonidas and demanded to know what he was doing.

"Crius claimed he could beat his betters. I am making him prove it."

That raised eyebrows, but no one stopped him. Now volunteers from older age cohorts were demanding the right to put Crius in his place. Leonidas hesitated, but Crius was defiant. "I can beat them, too!" he insisted.

And he did—if by a smaller margin.

Word had spread, as it so often did in a close-knit society like Sparta, and one of the Olympic trainers showed up and asked what was going on. Leonidas explained, adding that Crius was tired now, but that he had beaten everyone so far.

"What are you thinking, Leonidas? We can't enter a *helot* in the Games!"

"I wasn't thinking of the Games. I was thinking of the army. Good, fast runners are worth their weight in gold."

"Hmm. Let me see him run."

Leonidas ordered someone to fetch Crius water, and one of the boys dutifully trotted over to the fountain house located under the shade of some large plane trees beside the course. He brought back one of the tin cups, brimming with water. He did not hand it to Crius, however, as this would have been too demeaning. He gave it to Leonidas, who gave it to Crius. Crius was breathing hard and sweating from his last race, but he was also looking pleased with himself.

The trainer selected one of the boys, who looked to Leonidas to be three or four years older than Crius. He told the boy to strip, while Crius was given time to catch his breath. Then he told the boys to race a diaulos—that is, from one end of the stadium and back again, requiring a turn at the far end.

Crius reached the far end first, but lost his advantage at the turn. He trailed the other youth most of the way back, but then with a supreme effort managed to overtake him at the very last minute. Cheers broke out in amazement—the spectators' admiration for the sportsman at last overcoming their reluctance to acknowledge a helot.

Crius was too spent to even acknowledge the cheer. He bent over double, holding his knees, and his whole body swayed in time with his gasping lungs. He had his mouth wide open, gulping in air, and the sweat dripped from him onto the sand like rain.

Leonidas looked only at the trainer, who was standing with his hands on his hips and pursing his lips. At last he turned to Leonidas. "Would that he *had* been born Spartiate," he said simply. "I've waited all my life for a boy like that. He has wings on his heels!"

So the Gods had given him a gift after all, Leonidas thought. "Don't tell him that. He's cheeky enough as it is."

"But we can't ignore such talent!" the trainer replied, professionalism vanquishing prejudice. "For a start, he would help train up the others. He would make them all try harder! And if you want him for the army, he needs to be able to run distance, not just sprint. We have yet to see if he is up to that."

"He's yours if you want him, then. He's no use to me."

"Seriously?"

"He has some sickness in his hands and can't grasp things. He's always dropping and breaking things."

"Ah! The Gods are mean with their largess, aren't they? They never give us anything without taking away something else."

———

Just two days before the Olympic athletes were due to leave for Elis and the final stage of training near the sacred site, Leonidas injured his shoulder in training. It was nothing serious, just a dislocated left shoulder, but it precluded his participation in the Games. Many in Sparta were sour about it. Brotus sneered that his brother was afraid of facing real competition, as he set off with his trainer and no less than three helot attendants. Alkander, too, thought Leonidas had done it intentionally.

"What were you doing training Euryleon at dusk in the rain anyway?" Alkander wanted to know.

Leonidas sighed and massaged his injured shoulder with his other hand. "He's the weak link in our file. He needs to get stronger or he endangers us all."

"Drill masters and eirenes have been trying to strengthen him since he was seven—and they have all failed. What makes you think you can do any better?"

Leonidas tried to shrug, but it hurt, and he frowned in irritation as he answered, "Because I *have* to succeed. It's my ass he's covering!"

"Why don't we just admit that not everyone born of Spartiate parents is meant to be a hoplite? Why can't we let our young men be what they *want* to be? What they are best at, as in other cities? Why shouldn't Spartiates be poets and architects and sculptors—not just beasts of war?"

"What are you talking about?" Leonidas protested. "Are you a beast? Am I? We've spent the better part of our lives learning to use our brains and use them with discipline and precision—at least as much as our arms. Spartiates are poets and architects and sculptors. Have you forgotten—"

Alkander cut him off. "Yes, but we still have to fit the mold—we have to be perfect, interchangeable hoplites in the line—before we can be anything else!"

"What's got into you?" Leonidas wanted to know.

"I have a son," Alkander reminded him simply. The infant had been born to Hilaira just two weeks earlier, and Alkander felt an overwhelming sense of protectiveness toward the tiny life entrusted to him. He had never expected to feel this way. In fact, he had at first resented the fact that Hilaira was pregnant and would soon be too busy being a mother to be a wife. But when Hilaira had placed the squalling infant in his arms and he had seen the tiny fingernails and the miniature toes, he had been unmanned by a sense of wonder. He realized that just as the infant had fingers and toes, he also had a heart and a mind: that he was a whole *person*. That realization filled Alkander with an intense desire to make sure that this little person had a better life than he'd had. At the same time, it terrified him that the child might at some point fail to meet the high demands placed upon Spartiate youth. Alkander had endured several sleepless nights until the elders passed the boy fit to live.

Now he said to his friend, "I hate to think of my son suffering in the agoge as I did."

Leonidas sighed. He knew that Alkander had suffered because he was not terribly athletic and had stuttered as a boy. While Leonidas had for the most part enjoyed his upbringing, for Alkander the years in the agoge had been unmitigated hell. But it also depressed Leonidas to think that Alkander had a son already—when he himself did not even have a wife. So they said no more.

———

The spectators began to assemble in the fields around the sacred precinct almost a fortnight before the start of the Olympic Games. Men started to trickle in from all over the world, some spectators coming from as far away as Tarentum, Egypt, and Phoenicia. The locals catered avidly to their needs, selling food, wine, herbs, clothes, shoes, and utensils, as well as the usual souvenirs and tin or clay figurines for votive offerings or as good-luck charms.

As more and more spectators arrived, tents or shacks were set up in rows along improvised streets, and men of the same city congregated together; for example, there were Boiotian, Euboean, Samian, Delian, Naxian, Arcadian, and Argive quarters. The largest quarters were the Corinthian and the Athenian.

There was great rivalry between these two trading cities, a rivalry that had intensified in recent years; both were maritime cities with large and growing fleets of both merchantmen and triremes. Both were dependent on imported grain and exported finished products. They competed head-on in many crafts such as pottery and bronzework, and in trades such as slavery. The Olympic Games always brought such competitiveness to a peak. This year the usual rivalry was sharpened by the fact that the reforms in Athens had brought many brash young men of poorer backgrounds into positions of power—while Corinth remained an unabashed and proud oligarchy, in which "the best rather than the rest" reigned, according to the Corinthians. Topping it all, both cities thought they had the best runner: the man most likely to win the short sprint, which was the origin of the Games, the most prestigious contest, and the one whose winner gave the next four-year Olympiad its name.

At the bookmaker tables in the shanty town outside the sacred precinct, the betting was lively. Different bookmakers specialized in different sports, and they shouted out the odds to the milling crowds that collected to place bets or simply to sightsee. The Spartan king Cleomenes caused a minor sensation when he rode through on his white stallion and insisted on betting ten to one *against* his co-monarch, Demaratus. There was also much pushing and shoving at the table taking money on the boxers, as the Spartan Cleombrotus and his Rhodian rival, Periander, had faced off twice before and shared the victories equally, although a large minority of island Greeks insisted that the dark-horse Naxian contender, Lakrates, was going to put the two favorites to shame.

The chair litter, therefore, had some difficulty making progress. It was carried by two black slaves, and a young man who walked with a limp and a foppish cane escorted it. Inside, to the surprise of those who bothered to glance up, was a young man. It was rare for young men to let themselves be carried around. If they were too lazy to walk but rich enough to have slaves, they usually rode horses. But a glance at this young man suggested he was ill. His face was aged prematurely and etched with a crooked grimace that came from the pain that never quite left him.

The young man walking beside the litter, entertaining him with his chatter, was plump and cheery. He kept up a commentary for his companion as if he were afraid of silence. At the booking table for the runners, the youth in the litter waved for his slaves to halt. "Find out the odds on Aristeas, Chambias," the young man in the litter asked his friend.

Chambias nodded eagerly and lurched toward the table to comply. He soon reported back, "Seven to four; the Athenians have two runners they think can beat him."

Lychos took his purse from his belt and removed ten drachma, which he then handed to Chambias. "Put these on Aristeas."

Chambias nodded and plunged back into the crowd, going straight to the head of the line, since the other men appeared to be poor craftsmen of no importance. The Athenians, however, protested loudly, and two of them laid hands on the Corinthian youth, thrusting him roughly toward the end of the queue.

Chambias was outraged. These men stank of sweat and garlic, and they had no right to touch him at all—let alone push him around. "Who the hell do you think you are?" he demanded, outraged.

"We're Athenian citizens!" one man barked back proudly.

"Citizens!" Chambias scoffed. "You wouldn't know how to wear panoply—much less use a spear—even if you could afford it!"

"But we can send a trireme's ram into the heart of any ship we choose!" came the loud answer, supported now by cheers from the other rowers.

The information only made Chambias more distressed to have been touched by these rude men—mere thetes, the lowest class of Athenian citizen. The fact that they manned Athens' fleet of triremes did not in any way endear them to Chambias. Athens' fleet was paltry and inept compared to the proud fleet of Corinth. Furthermore, in Corinth the men who hired on for the fleet, while freemen, were considered the lowest filth of the city—men without land, property, or families. They certainly didn't vote in Assembly, and they wouldn't have dreamed of laying a hand on a priest! Chambias could only conclude that in Athens these men had been given so much power that it had gone to their heads. He tried a different argument: "Have you no respect for a cripple?"

"Oh, you don't look too crippled to stand in line!" an Athenian retorted bluntly, adding to his compatriots with a sneer, "These spoiled aristo boys whine about everything."

"That's because they spend so much of their time bent over, they can't stand up anymore!" another replied with a snicker.

Indignant and full of contempt for Athens—a city that gave men such as these the power to sit in judgment on their betters and make policy—Chambias went to the back of the line.

Lychos, the young man in the litter, hadn't noticed what was happening to his companion, because his attention had been drawn by shouting and laughter over to his left. There, in front of the brothel stalls, one of the pimps was with one hand holding back a young Spartan, who was evidently trying to escape, while with the other hand he was holding on to the bare breast of one of his whores. The crowd was roaring with laughter at the discomfort of the young Spartan, who was blushing bright red and tripping over his own feet in an effort to escape. Lychos joined in the laughter as the Spartan fell and the pimp used the opportunity to push the whore down on top of him. The guffaws of the crowd swelled as the Spartan struggled to free himself from the embraces of the whore, who was playing to the crowd by clutching the youth in a lewd embrace.

"Haven't had a woman yet, eh? What better time to start than now? Make this an Olympics to remember. I'll give you a discount, seeing as you have so little experience!"

Attention had been so riveted on the struggle between the whore and the young man on the ground that no one noticed another Spartan who had pushed his way through the crowd. In a swift movement he reached down, hooked his elbow around the woman's throat, and with no apparent effort dragged her off his countryman. The young man on the ground picked himself up and brushed himself off, still blushing in shame. His companion released the whore, pushing her in the direction of the pimp, and took the embarrassed young man by the arm. Together they pushed through the surprised crowd, the one still red-faced and the other grim.

Lychos was suddenly reminded of the day he had nearly died. There had been two Spartans that day, too. He couldn't remember it well—everything was a confused blur—but something about these two young men reminded him of his rescuers.

Chambias was back from the betting tables, complaining about the Athenians and indignantly relating how they had treated him, but Lychos wasn't listening. "Do you remember the Spartans who killed the boar?" he asked his friend.

"What?" Chambias couldn't follow his thoughts.

"The boar. Two Spartans killed it. I was wondering if they might be here, but I can't remember their names—only that one was King Cleomenes' younger brother. Do you remember their names?"

Chambias shrugged. "No, I've forgotten."

———————

Leonidas and Euryleon didn't speak until they were halfway back to the Spartan camp. Then at last Euryleon ventured, "I got lost, Leo. Really, I did. I didn't mean to go there. I just—got lost."

Leonidas believed him. Euryleon wasn't intentionally a trouble-maker; he just consistently got himself in trouble because he couldn't see properly. Left on his own he got lost, or stumbled in the dark, or knocked things down ...

When Leonidas didn't answer, Euryleon ventured another remark. "Did you see them, Leo?"

"Who?"

"Those—those slaves." He looked sidelong at his section leader and then asked, "Was it just my eyesight, or were they really just children?"

Leonidas nodded grimly. "There were several children."

"But that's sick!" Euryleon protested angrily.

Although Leonidas agreed with him, he felt it was his duty to be more diplomatic and remind his subordinate that other cities lived by different laws. "Lycurgus' laws are not followed outside of Sparta."

Euryleon thought about this in silence until they reached their camp. "We are very different from the others, aren't we?"

"I don't know." Leonidas smiled sidelong at Euryleon and admitted ruefully, "I don't know much beyond Sparta."

———

Asteropus was unhappy. As usual, Cleomenes wanted good signs, and there were none.

"Then make another sacrifice!" Cleomenes ordered, adding ominously, "Or maybe I need another priest."

The threat of dismissal made Asteropus break into a cold sweat. He was happy in Delphi, far away from the rigor of Spartan life. It wasn't just the discipline of the barracks, drill fields, and gymnasia that he was glad to escape. Worse than the army and its physical constraints was the fact that in Sparta, even thought was disciplined! Asteropus loved idle talk and debate about frivolous topics. He liked to get lost in words or to let his thoughts wander in any direction they fancied. He delighted in tossing unfinished ideas about and even discussing total nonsense—all of which was considered bad taste in Sparta. There, discourse was supposed to be "productive," and one was expected to remain silent rather than make a facile or inadequately considered remark.

Asteropus loved the theatrical offerings of Delphi, too. Plays provided so much greater freedom of expression and feeling than the traditional dances and choral singing of the Spartans. Of course, the Spartans commanded the traditional arts well. Hardly anyone could match the precision and harmony of a Spartan chorus or the beauty of a troupe of Spartan dancers, whether it was the maidens recreating the beauty of wind in a field of flowers with their bright dresses and shawls or the awesome sight of Spartan swordsmen dancing by torchlight. But Asteropus had come to like dissonance, irregular rhythm, and the unpredictable beat of music that was less controlled, less predictable, more radical. In Sparta everything was *communal*; in Delphi he was free to be himself.

"You would be ill served if I made up an omen in order to mislead you, sire," Asteropus reasoned.

"I didn't say make something up; I said try again—harder."

Asteropus took a deep breath. "I will have to find a pure animal, sire."

"Don't we have enough already?"

"I will have to go and find one, sire."

"Forget it, then. Leave me alone."

Gratefully, Asteropus withdrew from the king's tent. But the sight that greeted him beyond the tent was hardly designed to cheer him up. The Spartans, of course, didn't camp with the other Greeks. They had set up their own camp almost half a mile away, and it was laid out exactly as the Spartan army would camp on campaign—except that the weapons were absent. The whole atmosphere remained, however, *disciplined*, and therefore abhorrent to Asteropus. All these healthy young men laughing around their campfires, sharing jokes and bad food! The sight disgusted him, and it reminded him of how different he was from his countrymen. If only he'd been born in Athens or Corinth or Thebes!

He turned his back on the Spartan camp and made his way toward the bright lights of the chaotic, vibrant main camp. Asteropus breathed more deeply and more freely the farther he got from his countrymen. You could literally smell the rich diversity of the other camps! There were so many different sorts of things cooking—garlic and onions, cinnamon and cloves, pork fat and goat's cheese. And lanterns lit up these tents from the inside, turning them into bright-colored beacons. Torches moved between the tents, too, in contrast to the near darkness of the Spartan camp, while the clamor of voices was intoxicating: all the different dialects of Hellas blended and competed like different instruments, punctuated by the occasional sound of a foreigner. Asteropus loved it.

He plunged into the narrow, crooked alley between the outer rows of tents, watching his step to avoid all the refuse dumped out into the walkway, and he did not mind even this. The refuse was a tribute to freedom! In the Spartan camp everything was regimented, right down to where one was allowed to urinate and shit, he thought resentfully.

Asteropus deftly skirted the part of the shanty town where the gambling and whoring houses were set up. Although he was not interested in visiting such establishments, he approved of their presence because they represented the freedom to enjoy life, to indulge oneself, even to ruin oneself. He thought that no man was truly free unless he had the freedom to destroy his health and fortune with excessive drink, excessive sex, and senseless gambling. Only by proving that a man could *of his own free will* despise these excesses, did a man demonstrate true character. Since Spartans did not have the opportunity to overindulge, their abstinence proved nothing. Rather, they were like children, slaves, or women—inferior creatures who had to be guided, regulated, and controlled by their parents, owners, husbands, or—in the Spartan case—by their officers, ephors, Council, and kings.

The thought reminded Asteropus of his own wife and daughter. He missed them and wished he could bring them to Delphi to live with him. Other priests brought their wives, but Eirana had not liked Delphi the one time she visited. She complained that she had nothing to do there; and of course the libraries, theatres, and symposia were all closed to her, being open to men only. She had complained that he spent every night with his friends, drinking and talking, and came home drunk at dawn—unwilling to understand that to have done anything else would have demeaned him in the eyes of the other Greeks. She had complained that he did not fulfill his "marital duties" often enough, and accused him (most unjustly) of having sex with flute girls and whores just because she had heard these creatures were brought as entertainment to the symposia he frequented. In short, they had fought frequently, until she threatened to leave him if he did not take her home. To avoid such a scandal, he dropped everything to escort her back to his kleros in Sparta.

Asteropus sighed at the memory. He had expected marriage to be different. He had imagined Eirana waiting for him every evening (or morning, as the case might be), anxious to hear all that he had to tell, a source of comfort and encouragement. Take tonight: Cleomenes was clearly displeased with him. He would have liked to talk to Eirana about it and hear her tell him all was well, that he understood the Gods, and that he had no need to fear. But without someone telling him that, it was so easy to doubt himself…

"Asteropus!" The sound of his own name startled him out of his thoughts, and he looked around in astonishment.

The man smiling and waving to him was familiar, but at first Asteropus could not place his face. He waited hesitantly as the man lifted up his elegant long chiton to make his way carefully over and around the refuse in the alley. "Don't you recognize me? I'm Cobon, son of Archiphron."

Asteropus was immediately embarrassed. Cobon was incredibly rich and very influential in Delphi. Asteropus bowed his head and answered readily, "Sir, I am honored that you know my name! What can I do for you?"

"Why, come join me in my tent. I was just on my way there, but I am not ready for sleep. Let us drink together for a bit."

Asteropus was flattered that Cobon even knew who he was, much less that he would extend an invitation of this kind. He had certainly never invited Asteropus into his home in Delphi.

As if reading his thoughts, Cobon remarked, "We have seen far too little of one another in Delphi. Entirely my fault, of course. I meant to invite you over, but you know how things are—one thing after another got in the way. What a fortunate circumstance that I should run into you here. Come, this way." Cobon's slave trailed him, holding up a torch, and this made the going much easier. They proceeded to a large tent conspicuously guarded by two burly Nubians. Only very wealthy men could afford this luxury. Then again, only very wealthy men needed to take such precautions.

Inside the tent, Cobon kicked his other slaves awake and ordered them to light the lamps and pour water and wine. In a very short time, Asteropus found himself comfortably settled on a low couch softened by thick pillows. On a low table in front of him, a broad kylix had been placed along with a bowl of figs, dates, and raisins mixed with nuts.

"You must tell me how you found your king," Cobon remarked jovially. "Is he still intent on interfering in Athenian affairs?"

Asteropus grimaced and took a deep drink of the rich black wine; then, shaking his head, he declared, "You have no idea what a difficult man Cleomenes is. He is vain beyond reason! It isn't a matter of interfering in Athenian affairs. He does not take a genuine interest in Athens or anywhere else—he cares only about whether an affair makes him look good." It all started to pour out of him—the things he had imagined saying to Eirana.

Cobon nodded sympathetically, encouraging Asteropus with well-placed words of agreement or exclamations of distress at appropriate moments. He also kept the wine flowing and the snacks plentiful.

Late into the evening, Cobon asked the young priest, "And what is this I hear of your wife? Is it true she has left you?"

"No, no! She simply does not like living in Delphi. She has returned to her father's home."

Cobon shook his head in disapproval. "A wife should not put her own likes and dislikes ahead of her husband's welfare. I can assure you, no Phocian girl would have been so selfish—or rather, so foolish. A wife who leaves a young, virile husband alone is inviting him to take a concubine. There are many poor men in and around Delphi who would be delighted to sell you their sweet virgin daughters to keep your bed and house if your own wife is so neglectful of her duties."

Asteropus stiffened and was about to reply that that was not the custom in Sparta, but he stopped himself. Another stupid Spartan custom! Another restriction on a man's freedom! The other Greeks were so sensible! Of course a young man needed a woman in his house and bed. "Good girls, you mean? Not whores or slaves?"

"No, no! I wouldn't think of letting some common whore into my house either! After all, I have daughters, and you never know what diseases they bring with them. No, I mean well-brought-up, modest girls whose fathers are simply too poor to come up with a dowry. Just the other day a poor farmer came to me in bitter distress because unexpected bad times mean he can no longer pay the dowry he promised his neighbor. Now the neighbor will not take his daughter as planned. The girl is already fourteen, and he sees no hope that his fortunes will improve in the short term. Or there was another fellow who came to ask the oracle what to do because he has twin girls, both twelve, and he cannot provide *both* of them with dowries, but he says they are so alike he cannot select between the two who should be rewarded and who punished. I'm sure either father would bless you the rest of their days if you would promise to take their daughter into your house and treat her properly, like a concubine and not some slave girl."

"Even knowing that any children would be illegitimate?"

"Well, it is up to you whether you expose or provide for the children. Their fathers would have no objections whatever you do, I assure you, as long as the girls are honorably taken off their hands."

Asteropus was tempted, but the idea was still so strange that he could not wholeheartedly embrace it. So he nodded and said he would think about it. They talked of other things, notably the fact that the deposed Athenian tyrant Hippias had found refuge with the Persian satrap in Sardis. Cobon reported that Hippias had been given a huge palace filled with slaves and a dozen women for his personal use and was living almost as well as the satrap himself. "It is said by those who have seen him that he is more tyrannical than ever—and bitterly determined to regain control of Athens. He brags that he is learning from the Persians how to rule."

By the time Asteropus made his way back toward the Spartan camp on rather unsteady legs, he was feeling very pleased with himself. He had clearly impressed Cobon with his intelligence and his insight. Asteropus imagined being included in Cobon's famous symposia. He imagined being counted among the great man's inner circle of friends. How it would improve his status in Delphi! Who needed Cleomenes, Asteropus asked, if a man like Cobon valued his friendship and advice? Soon he could picture himself living an independent life in a lovely villa overlooking the Gulf of Corinth. He would have his own library and his own chef. What a thought—to never again have to eat black broth! And there could be a sweet Phocian girl—all smiles and humble adoration—to listen to him and admire him and share his bed. Why, with Cobon as his patron, he would be able to afford to let their offspring live, and they would be surrounded by happy children.

"What's the matter with you?" a sentry demanded. "Been drinking neat wine?"

The challenge, with the sneer in it, intensified Asteropus' hatred of his own city. "And what if I have?" Asteropus threw back. "Sparta is the only city in the world that does not trust its grown citizens to drink wine! Indeed, the whole world laughs at Sparta for its *fear* of wine."

"Until they face our spears!" came the retort.

"We can't fight the whole world," Asteropus scoffed back. "Sparta is nothing but a quaint provincial town! We only make ourselves ridiculous by pretending we do everything better than everyone else and are more virtuous, too!"

"If you have so little liking for our laws, why do you wear Spartan scarlet?"

"Why, indeed?" Asteropus asked himself, and turned his back on the sentry to find his way to his own tent.

———

The boxing was scheduled for immediately after the dolichos, the long-distance race in which the runners had to run twenty-four lengths of the stadium. It was always hard to guess how long the dolichos would last, and since it was a rather boring event, many spectators skipped it to secure better seats for the boxing. The bulk of Spartan spectators chose this option, because they had no strong entrant in the dolichos but were hoping Cleombrotus would give them a victory in boxing. Leonidas, however, declared his intention to go to the dolichos.

"But if we go there, we'll never get a good seat for the boxing!" Sperchias protested.

"Why should I fight with half of Greece for a place from which to watch my brother beat someone up? I can see that in Sparta without any trouble any day of the week."

Sperchias opened his mouth three times to find an answer, and finally settled on, "But the dolichos is so boring."

"Not really. You go ahead to the boxing, if you like."

Sperchias and Euryleon wordlessly followed Leonidas. They joined a small contingent of other Spartans, friends of the one Spartan competitor, Oliantus. No one really thought the young man, who was in the age cohort ahead of Leonidas, had much of a chance against the Corinthian Aristeas or the Athenians, who were rumored to have not one but two outstanding runners, Pheidippides and Eukles.

Leonidas and his friends made themselves comfortable partway up the slope beside the stadium. These were not the best seats, but their interest was only moderate. Below them was a very large crowd of rowdy Athenians, who at the moment were divided into two factions that were shouting insults at one another. It was hard to hear exactly what was being said, but it sounded as if some of the men had invented little rhyming ditties that made rude remarks about their rival. These brought roars of approving laughter from their own faction and counterinsults from the other faction.

There was also a large Corinthian contingent, but this was more orderly, and the front-row seats near the finish line had been cordoned off. Only just before the start of the race did the men for whom these seats were reserved arrive in a small group, escorted by slaves. One man was even carried in on a litter, which the slaves set down so he could sit. The slaves then stood and held an awning over the spectators so they were shaded from the hot sun. Refreshments had evidently been brought along as well.

Sperchias shook his head in disgust.

There were almost twenty contenders for the race, and they set off rather like a herd of cattle, thundering down the length of the stadium. There were the inevitable collisions at the turn, shouts of "foul play," and protests, largely ignored, as the leaders pulled away in the second lap. After four laps, the field was spreading and thinning out. The favorites were justifying their odds and the Spartan was holding on to fifth place, which was fine at this stage. By the end of ten laps, a couple of men dropped out of the race altogether, and the majority were running only for the sake of honor with no hope of victory. The contest was down to a six-man race: the two Athenians, the Corinthian, the Spartan, an Ithacan, and a Samian.

A slave reached the Spartan spectators and leaned over the man sitting nearest the edge. The man turned and pointed toward the back, and the slave made his way up the slope. "Leonidas, son of Anaxandridas?"

Because of his poor eyesight, Euryleon couldn't follow the race, so he was watching the spectators. He heard the question and nudged Leonidas.

"Leonidas, son of Anaxandridas?" the slave asked again.

"Here!" Leonidas answered.

"My master, Archilochos of Corinth, invites you to join him over there." The slave pointed to the Corinthian section on the other side of the stadium, with the awning held by slaves.

"Why?" Leonidas wanted to know. Although he recognized the name, he also remembered Archilochos had engineered the revolt of the allies against Sparta's dominance in the League. While he understood Kyranios' logic about not fighting with half-hearted allies, he still did not feel particularly friendly toward a man who had called Sparta insulting names. "I'm perfectly comfortable here."

"His son Lychos would like to meet you, sir," the slave explained.

Leonidas thought about that for a moment, and then stood up.

"You're going?" Euryleon asked, amazed.

"Why not?" Leonidas countered.

Euryleon sighed and got to his feet.

"You don't have to come."

"Over there I might be able to see something," Euryleon retorted.

Leonidas couldn't argue with that, and he was not unhappy to have Euryleon with him. Leonidas would have preferred Alkander; after all, Alkander had helped kill the boar. But Alkander had stayed home in Sparta to enjoy the holidays with his wife and newborn son. "Chi?"

Sperchias shrugged and pushed himself off his feet. Together the three friends followed the slave, harvesting curses and complaints for treading on other people's toes and things and blocking their view.

They reached the Corinthians as the race went into the twentieth lap. It was now getting exciting. The two islanders had fallen almost a lap behind. The Spartan Oliantus and one of the Athenians, Eukles, were half a lap back. Fighting for the lead were the Athenian Pheidippides and the Corinthian Aristeas. The Corinthian crowd was correspondingly on edge.

Leonidas paused to get a good look at where he was going. He quickly found Archilochos, who had not changed much in four years. He was still a handsome, vigorous man in his prime. He was darkly tanned, and although he wore rich clothes, they were not gaudy or excessively ornate like those of some of his countrymen. Nor was it hard to identify Chambias. He looked much the same, only softer and plumper. Lychos, however, was a shock. He sat twisted in the litter in which they had carried him. One shoulder hung lower than the other. He was very pale, and his face was lined prematurely from pain. Leonidas shuddered inwardly, wondering if he had done the young man a service—saving him for a life like this.

The cheers around them grew in intensity. The runners were on their twenty-second lap. Just two more turns. The Spartan seemed to be gaining on the leaders, and from across the stadium the few Spartan spectators were standing and cheering him on by name: "Oliantus! Oliantus!" Leonidas was glad for him. He was a quiet, rather ugly man who hardly ever drew attention to himself. A conscientious soldier, Leonidas knew, who had been passed over for promotion every year. He felt it would only be fair if Oliantus won a surprise victory here—and it served the rest of his countrymen right for preferring to secure seats for Brotus' fight rather than support this underdog.

The slave who had sought out Leonidas was, however, urging him to hurry up, and the spectators around them were cursing them for being in the way.

Leonidas and his friends arrived as the runners went into the twenty-third lap, and even Archilochos was perfunctory in his greeting. "Here, here." He and Chambias made room for them. In this cordoned-off space people were not really crowded. "We'll just watch the end of the race," Archilochos told them. "Aristeas is leading!"

Leonidas and his companions were happy to comply. The Corinthian had indeed taken the lead and Pheidippides was losing ground, while Oliantus was still gaining. Leonidas hoped for an upset. As they completed the last turn and started back toward the finish on the last lap, however, the two leaders put in a final effort and started pulling away from him again. Leonidas felt sorry for him. He'd put in an excellent effort, far better than anyone had expected of him. Victory had appeared to be within his grasp, but it slipped away on the heels of Eukles and Aristeas.

As the two runners swept past Leonidas, they were like a single beast, with all four limbs flailing the air and their beautiful bodies glistening with sweat and oil. They were over the finish line, and Archilochos turned to look at his son, asking, "Who won? I couldn't see. Who won?"

Archilochos was not alone in his uncertainty over the outcome. The Athenians were wildly declaring Eukles the winner, but the Corinthians insisted it was Aristeas. The judges had their heads together, consulting; then the herald was called over and Aristeas of Corinth was declared the winner. At once the Corinthian spectators went wild with enthusiasm, while the Athenians protested: "Not true! Not true!" "Cheaters!" "Liars!" "The judges have been bought with Corinthian gold!"

Athenian spectators poured out onto the floor of the stadium. While some swept their champion onto their shoulders and started to parade him around like a victor, refusing to admit he had lost, still others started rushing toward the judges' stand shouting, "Cheaters! Takers of bribes!" They tore away the barricades set up to protect the judges from the crowd.

The judges fled, clambering over their seats and trying to get away from the angry Athenian mob. A couple lost their himations, and one was pulled down by the hem of his chiton, while another was caught by the ankle. Soon their screams for help were as loud as the Athenian protests and insults—only shriller.

Archilochos was terrified that something would happen to his crippled son. He signaled to the litter carriers, but it was impossible for them to make progress down the steps against the flood of frightened spectators pouring upward. He shielded his son with his own broad and well-muscled body, while roughly shoving Chambias up the slope. Pipes were shrilling, trying to restore order, but a brawl had broken out between the Athenians and some of the poorer Corinthians.

Archilochos was shouting in Leonidas' ear, "Get my son to safety!"

Leonidas looked over and assessed the situation. The stream of people determined to get away from the brawling were too concerned about their own safety to give way to the litter. Even as he watched, someone thrust Chambias aside so roughly that he fell. His cane rolled down the slope out of his grasp. One of the slaves holding the litter put down the handles to fetch it for him. Behind them, the sound of the brawl was getting worse. The shouting of insults had been replaced by grunts, the unmistakable sound of fists hitting flesh, and the groans of the injured.

"Hold on!" Leonidas grabbed Euryleon and trusted Sperchias to follow him. They locked arms and formed a human shield against the other spectators who were fleeing in panic. Thus protected, the slaves and Chambias collected themselves and started up the slope again. In a few moments they were over the brim of the bowl and the crowd was dispersing around them. They could look back down on the stadium and see how the Athenian mob had swarmed over the judges' stand, knocking over their chairs. There was no sign of the judges themselves. Some of the game officials had arrived, however, and with whips were starting to restore order.

Archilochos gestured for the Spartans to come with him. Sperchias protested weakly, "We could still make the boxing"; but Leonidas shook his head, and Euryleon wasn't going anywhere without him. They soon found themselves in Archilochos' large, well-appointed tent.

Lychos was protesting that he was fine. "Don't make such a fuss, father! Nothing happened to me. Look to Chambias."

Indeed, Chambias had scraped his elbow and wrist when he was pushed down. Slaves were sent for water and bandages, while Lychos dragged himself across the tent to the three Spartans. Leonidas could see his eyes scan all three of them, and with a slight smile he focused on Leonidas. "Are you Leonidas?"

"Yes."

"Then I owe you my life. I am glad I now have the opportunity to thank you personally. And your friend?" He dismissed Euryleon, who was half hiding behind Leonidas, and looked at Sperchias closely, expecting Alkander. But although he had no memories of the youth, he had been told by Chambias how beautiful and fair Alkander had been. Sperchias didn't fit the description, and he was vigorously shaking his head.

Lychos looked surprised, but he said no more. Instead, he signaled to the slaves to bring refreshments.

Somewhat warily, the Spartans sat down on the folding chairs provided, and soon Archilochos and Chambias joined the circle, too. A krater was brought, and water mixed with wine. Chambias looked shaken and he kept repeating, "I warned you about the Athenians! They are worse than barbarians. Did you see them? They attacked the judges and Aristeas, too! Dogs! Wild dogs!"

"I hope this spectacle will convince your countrymen that these so-called 'reforms' in Athens are very dangerous," Archilochos remarked to Leonidas.

Leonidas raised his eyebrows. "Are you saying my brother was right after all, and we *should* have driven Kleisthenes out of Athens three years ago?"

Archilochos frowned; in retrospect, Corinth's elite did see Kleisthenes' reforms as a dangerous precedent. If ordinary Athenian citizens could make laws and pass judgment on their betters, how long before the Corinthian hoi polloi started demanding the same rights?

On the other hand, Archilochos could not regret the coup carried out against Spartan leadership in the League. Corinth would never give up the control they had wrested from Sparta there. "No. I would not go that far. Your brother sought to restore Hippias—and Corinth has felt the oppression of tyrants. Sparta has no business trying to impose tyrants on others, since it goes to so much trouble to ensure not even your two kings have as much power as one tyrant. But Sparta should keep a close watch on what is happening in Athens. These reforms have unchained demons of the worst kind: ambition and greed among the undisciplined and uneducated masses, the very class of men governed by base urges and shortsighted conceptions of their own good."

Leonidas looked rather blankly at the Corinthian merchant, which annoyed the latter. Archilochos frowned more darkly. "Mark my words: if things continue the way they are going in Athens, Sparta will not have the luxury of ignoring it. The Athenians grow arrogant, and it is only a matter of time before they try to take what is *not* theirs. Kleisthenes has opened a Pandora's box of new and dangerous forces. Surely you agree?"

"I've never been to Athens, sir."

The answer surprised Archilochos—not because he had expected a young Spartan to have been to Athens, but because most young men had opinions about everything, whether they knew anything about a subject or not. "Would you like to go?"

"Very much, sir," Leonidas admitted, the old urge to travel bubbling up in his breast more powerfully than ever. He still felt cheated, in a way, that the campaign of three years ago had disintegrated before he could get much beyond the Isthmus. He thought, too, of the way strangers who came to Sparta spoke of other cities that were bigger and richer. They spoke of temples and monuments more magnificent than any in Lacedaemon. They laughed at the Spartan acropolis and disparaged Spartan homes as "quaint" and "old-fashioned," or even "primitive." Leonidas wanted to defend his city, but how could he if he had nothing to compare it to?

"I'll take you, if you like. I'll be taking a cargo up to Piraeus as soon as we return from the Games. You could travel back with us to Corinth and take ship with me to Piraeus. I expect to have a return cargo within a fortnight and be back in Corinth by the new moon."

Lychos at once seconded his father enthusiastically. "Yes! That's an excellent idea! I'll be on the second ship, won't I, Father?"

His father nodded—albeit uneasily, as if he wanted to say no.

"We could see the sights together," Lychos continued to Leonidas; "that is, if you don't mind being seen with a cripple." He added the latter with a twisted smile.

"How can I object, when I am to blame?"

"Blame?" Lychos frowned and cocked his head. "You did what you could. I do not blame you for not coming earlier."

"But if I had come later, you would not be suffering now."

"What a Spartan thing to think and say—that it would have been better to die than to live as a cripple. That's what you meant, isn't it?"

Leonidas nodded once.

"Come to Corinth. I will show you, you are wrong. My life is probably better than yours—if all the things I hear about Sparta are true."

"I'll try to get permission," Leonidas promised sincerely, adding with a glance at his companions, "but my friends would like to see the boxing, if you will excuse us now."

As soon as they were out of the tent, Sperchias shook his head. "You're mad, Leo. They'll take away your section if you ask for furlough. Besides, you'll be taking a huge risk. What if you develop a taste for neat wine and whores and fancy food with spices and sauces?"

"I could always desert," Leonidas suggested with a wicked smile.

"Leo! Don't even *say* that!" Euryleon protested in obvious distress.

Leonidas at once threw his arm over Euryleon's narrow shoulders and laughed. "Don't worry. I'll be back, if only to tell you fools what it's like."

———

The boxing had not gone as people expected. The Rhodian had been knocked out in the first qualifying rounds, and the Naxian had danced over one opponent after another without taking a single blow, while Brotus had to beat his way to the finals by sheer, dogged force. By the time Brotus faced the Naxian his nose was bleeding, one eye was swollen shut, and half his teeth were loose.

Brotus hated the sight of the young Naxian. He was grinning and relaxed! Through his remaining eye Brotus noted that the Naxian was beautiful—just the kind of sunny boy all the girls fell for, Brotus thought resentfully. He became determined to break the pretty boy's nose and ensure that he would never smile quite like this again.

Brotus' trainer was giving him tips as he rebound his hands, but Brotus wasn't listening to anything but the rush of blood in his veins. "Pretty little pimp," he kept thinking. "I'll teach him to respect Sparta."

As they bowed politely to one another like model athletes, the Naxian whispered, "I'm going to show you stupid Spartan swine what boxing really is."

Brotus swung at once. The Naxian was caught off guard. He'd become overconfident because of his easy victory over the famed Rhodian boxer. Brotus connected, and the Naxian staggered backward, dazed more by surprise than by the force of Brotus' fists. Before he could recover, Brotus landed a second and a third blow.

The Spartan spectators were cheering. "Bro-tus! Bro-tus!"

The Naxian spectators (and many others) were shouting advice at the Naxian, telling him to get his guard up, to step left or right or duck or whatever—anything but let the Spartan win.

Sweat stung Brotus' eye as he moved in, and then suddenly he was down and the sky was falling. He got his feet under him in a second and jumped upright again, but then a second crack hit the back of his head and he not only went down on his knees, he lost his vision for a few seconds. But he wasn't out yet. In a maneuver practiced so often at the agoge he didn't even have to think, he dropped on one shoulder, rolled onto his back, and then flung himself forward onto his feet again. His vision had returned.

The Naxian hadn't expected the move and his guard was down, just long enough for Brotus to smash his fist squarely into the pretty face, shattering his nose. The Naxian staggered backward, a hand going to his face as if to assure himself of what had happened.

Brotus jeered. "You won't ever be pretty again, pretty boy!"

The Naxian took advantage of his gloating. A fist hit Brotus' good eye.

Brotus reeled, his balance knocked askew along with his vision. The next blow hit his lower jaw with a crack audible even among the spectators. Brotus felt blood pour into his mouth, and for a moment he could hear shouts of "No! NO!" as he lost his balance and fell. He could hear someone panting. Something wet was dripping onto his face. "Pig. Stupid Spartan pig!" The judges were counting...

"I'll kill him," Brotus thought in the darkness and silence that surrounded him. "I'll kill him." But the crown of olives had slipped away.

CHAPTER 10

HOMECOMING

GORGO'S MOTHER HAD FORBIDDEN HER TO go far from the palace. The Olympic victors, King Demaratus in the chariot racing and Ephorus in the discus, were expected to arrive sometime in the course of the day. The city had planned an elaborate welcoming ceremony, and the Agiad queen was determined not to be outdone by the Eurypontid queen. As soon as the men returning from Olympia reached the shrine to the divine Lacedaemon, a runner who was waiting there would sprint to the city, and heralds would blow a signal. Then the whole city would begin to assemble; and the Agiad queen expected her daughter to accompany her since, inadequate as she was, she was all the children Gyrtias had left.

But the waiting was terrible; and so, confined to the precinct around the Agiad palace, Gorgo wandered around aimlessly. She was drawn first to the grave and monument to Alkman, because the girls' chorus that was to sing in honor of the victors had come to give sacrifices to the great poet so he would favor them with a good performance. Gorgo hoped that when she was old enough, another three or four years from now, she would pass the audition for this chorus, because it was the most prestigious in the city—and you didn't have to *be* pretty, just have a pretty voice. Gorgo took satisfaction from noting all the girls in the chorus who weren't particularly pretty. She decided that more than half of the girls were plain.

Next she found herself, almost against her will, at the Temple to

Helen. Gorgo was at war with Helen. She hated her. She embodied everything that Gorgo hated: beauty, vanity, stupidity, infidelity. As far as Gorgo was concerned, Helen had never *done* anything worth admiring, and she didn't see why there should be monuments to her all over the place! "I'm certainly not bringing *you* any sacrifices!" Gorgo thought defiantly to the statue of Sparta's famous queen. To her irritation, however, she noticed there were lots of votive offerings collecting before the altar—everything from wilting flowers to little figurines and shards with prayers scratched on them. Feeling very daring and impudent, Gorgo reached out and snatched up one of the offerings to read what was written on it. "Helen, make me beautiful so Polybius will love me! Euridike." Angrily, Gorgo threw the shard back into the bin with the other offerings and fled back outside.

Although it was still early in the morning, it was obviously going to be a hot day. Not a breath of wind moved the heavy air, and all the leaves on the plane trees were coated with dust. In another couple of hours it would be far too hot for anyone to want to do anything strenuous in the sun. Gorgo glanced down at her dog, Jason. He was panting already, his tongue hanging out of the side of his mouth. "Shall we go to the racecourse?" she asked him.

Gorgo knew perfectly well that that was much farther than her mother wanted her to go, but at least there would be something going on there. Jason, as always, looked up at her with adoring eyes. She reached down and stroked his head, and he lifted his snout to lick her face.

Gorgo laughed, jumped down from the steps of the temple, and started running down the street, with Jason racing delightedly at her heels. He seemed to think she was playing with him, and now and again he leaped up to bat at her chiton. They dashed past the sanctuary of Athena of Vengeance Deserved and the ancient statue of Ares in Chains. According to legend, Ares would never desert the Spartans as long as they kept him captive, symbolized by this statue of the God in chains. Gorgo thought that it was a silly idea. How could you keep a God captive? They came and went where and when they wanted and could not be grasped, much less held fast. Besides, putting chains on anyone only made them desperate to escape and hate the person who chained them. What better way to ensure that victory always evaded them forever than to put Ares in chains?

Gorgo passed the tombs of her ancestors, the Agiadi, and the oldest house in the city, older even than the two royal palaces. People said it had once belonged to Menelaos. It was made of massive stone with sloping walls and very small windows. It seemed a grim, cheerless place, and Gorgo was glad she did not have to live there. The current owners were one of the oldest and richest families in Sparta, but they rarely lived here, either, preferring their estates. Just opposite, however, was a statute to Herakles that was particularly beautiful. It was where the boys of the agoge liked to bring offerings for success in their many trials and competitions.

Gorgo reached the gymnasia that surrounded the racecourse; and here, in contrast to the parts of the city she left behind, there was a lot of activity. Men, towels draped over their necks or shoulders, were coming and going. Their skin glowed with oil, and they smelled of sweat and olive oil mixed with thyme and bay leaf. Gorgo loved the smell, but she did not pay much attention to the men themselves.

Beyond the gymnasia on the racecourse, the youths of the agoge were playing sports. At the start of the racecourse stood two tall and graceful statues to the Dioskouroi, Kastor and Polydeukes. The twins stood, one on either side, arms outstretched like runners preparing to start a race. What Gorgo particularly liked about these two statues was that rather than staring straight ahead like most Kouroi, they looked toward each other and smiled—like friends sharing a remembered joke.

A herd of naked boys were jostling one another at the start, preparing to run a race. Most of the spectators were at the other end of the course, where the finish would be. Gorgo walked around to join a group of girls her own age.

Before her brother died, Gorgo had gone to school with these girls, although she had never been allowed to sleep in the agoge with them. Now her mother did not even let her go to school. The girls, therefore, acknowledged her only with nods or not at all. One of them, Alkyone, sneered audibly, "Oh, if it isn't the precious little princess." Only Phaenna risked a timid smile at her. Gorgo placed herself next to the friendly Phaenna and tried to ignore Alkyone.

With a shout, the boys at the start of the course set off in a ragged herd. The girls leaned forward to see what was happening. Nausica's brother was among the runners, and she started jumping up and down, cheering him on. "Neokles! Neokles! Come on! Faster!" Some of the other girls had other favorites. Gorgo didn't know any of the boys. "Who is the boy out in front?" She put the question to Phaenna, but unfortunately Nausica overheard her and burst out laughing. "That's a helot, silly!" And then, louder for the other girls, she added, "Our princess fancies a helot! Gorgo is in love with the helot Crius!" They all laughed at her. "Gorgo is in love with a helot!"

Gorgo felt the perfect fool. First of all, she didn't fancy *any* of the boys, much less love one. And how was she to know that the fastest boy in the whole pack was a helot? They were all naked with shaved heads. Phaenna reached out and squeezed her hand in sympathy, whispering, "Crius is faster than *anyone*." Sure enough, he won this race and the next, but the other spectators paid no attention to him; they were only interested in who came second.

By now the sun was high and oppressively hot. The other girls were collected by the widow who looked after them and herded back toward the city to bathe and change. They left Gorgo standing without so much as a goodbye—except for Phaenna, who half turned and waved at her over her shoulder. Gorgo waved back and then looked around, wondering what to do next.

How much longer could it be before the signal came? She looked down at Jason as if he might be able to answer her, and he responded by pawing her. She wrapped her arms around his neck and laid her cheek on his head until he squirmed free.

She noticed a helot woman clinging to the shadows of the closest gymnasium. She had her veils up over her head, as was more typical of foreigners than Laconians. She also had a heavy satchel across her back and held a pitcher in her hand, which she had apparently just filled with water from the nearby fountain house. The fountain house itself was overflowing with boys, clamoring for a drink and dunking each other under the spouts, or otherwise noisily splashing water around to the accompaniment of high-pitched squeals of delight.

The helot boy did not dare go there. He would have been thrown out or even beaten if he tried. He went instead to the helot woman, and with a smile she handed him the pitcher. He lifted it to drink directly from the spout and then, his thirst quenched, he poured the rest over his head with a laugh. The woman, whom Gorgo presumed to be his mother, reached out and patted his shaved head as if she weren't used to the sight of it. He responded with a toss of his head, shaking off extra water like a dog. His mother took her satchel off her back and offered him something that he eagerly accepted. Then someone shouted something, and he darted away with only a hasty wave to his mother, still eating what she had given him.

The helot woman put the pitcher back inside her satchel and swung it up onto her back. As she did so, her eyes met Gorgo's. She smiled at her. "I expect you'd like a sweet, too?"

Gorgo's face lit up, and the helot woman brought the satchel down again and opened it up to remove a nut-and-honey square. Gorgo popped it into her mouth, and at once her eyes widened. "That's delicious!" she exclaimed, with her mouth still full. The woman laughed at her. Gorgo remembered her manners and covered her mouth with her hand.

"They better be," the helot woman said as she again shouldered her burden. "I want to set up a stand near the Dancing Floor and sell them this afternoon."

"Do you live around here?" Gorgo asked, falling in beside her.

"No, on the other side of the Eurotas."

"And that boy—the one who is so fast he wins every race—is he your son?" Gorgo looked back and gestured vaguely.

"Yes, my youngest boy. He has a sickness in his hands and has never been any use to anyone, so I am very grateful to the Gods that he can run. Our master says that when he grows up he can be a runner for the army. I never thought things would go so well for him. That is why I am going to stop here and give one of my cakes to Herakles to thank him for giving my little boy a gift after all." They had reached the statue of Herakles. Gorgo regretted losing such a wonderful sweet to a God who couldn't possibly enjoy it, having neither tongue nor stomach anymore. Then they continued on together.

"And who are you?" Laodice asked.

Gorgo was surprised. Everyone else seemed to know who she was without asking. "I'm called Gorgo," she admitted.

"What an odd name!" Laodice exclaimed.

"My father said it was because I screamed so loudly from the moment I was born."

Laodice laughed. "And who is your father?"

Gorgo shrugged in embarrassment, sensing that if she told the truth this woman would shy away from her. "He's a Spartiate, but he won't let me go to school—Oh, listen! That's the signal! I have to go home and change!" She started to run away, feeling guilty for being so far from the palace. She had gone three strides before she stopped, turned back, and called to Laodice, "Thank you for the honey square! I'll look for you later and buy some more!" Then she ran as fast as she could back to the Agiad palace.

She was late, of course. Everyone warned her that her mother was looking for her. So she burst into her mother's chamber with an excuse on her lips: "Mom, I'm sorry—"

She couldn't finish before her mother interrupted with an exclamation of horror: "Where have you been? You look like something the cat dragged in! Your filthy dog has been jumping all over you, hasn't he? I warn you: if you don't stop letting him ruin everything you own, I'm going to sacrifice him to Hera!"

As if he could understand her words, Jason instantly turned tail and darted out of the room. Gorgo called after him, in a voice sharp with fear for his life, "Go lie down!"

Gyrtias was sitting before her dresser while one of her women dressed her hair. It was being braided and then looped up and pinned with bronze pins in the shape of lilies. Her jewel box was open before her. She ordered one of her women to "see to Gorgo," and her daughter was hustled into the next room.

A large terra-cotta tub filled with rose-scented water stood in the middle of the room. Water stains splattered around it were evidence of her mother's recent bath. Gorgo was ordered to strip out of her dirty chiton and get into the bath. Her mother's servant even made her put her head right under the water and scrubbed at her head and hair. When she finished bathing and was drying herself off on a linen towel, her mother emerged. She was wearing a lovely white peplos with a border of palm leaves in gold thread. A fine Egyptian-cotton himation in the deepest of blue and purple tones hung off her shoulders, clasped with two huge brooches shaped like Gorgon faces. At her neck was a large gold collar with rolled amethysts. She also wore a tiara and long dangling earrings with amethysts. On both hands she wore several rings. Not at all what Lycurgus, the Spartan lawgiver, had prescribed for women, Gorgo thought. She remembered learning that Lycurgus had said Spartan women were not supposed to wear gold or silver at all, much less rouge their cheeks and lips, as her mother had clearly done. The more self-righteous women refused to wear any kind of jewelry—although the majority were happy to wear bronze, rolled stones, alabaster, ivory, glass beads, and the like.

"Come here, child!" Gyrtias ordered her daughter, shaking her head in despair. "What are we going to do with you? You look like a drowned rat!" She sat herself down on the foot of the bed with Gorgo between her knees and started vigorously combing Gorgo's wet hair, while giving orders to her women to bring this and that.

Within a short time Gorgo was outfitted in a lovely bright-green chiton with bright yellow trim. She had been given pretty sandals with green beads sewn atop the leather. Meanwhile, her mother combed her hair until her whole head hurt, and then braided it while still wet into six tight "cornrows" that clung to her scalp until they reached the back of her head. Here the ends were woven together and looped up and pinned with a single large tortoiseshell hairpin. Her mother then turned her around and started pinching at her cheeks, while calling for her coal pencils.

Gorgo protested. "I don't want to wear makeup!"

"Nobody asked you if you wanted to!" her mother replied bluntly. "You'll do as you're told. I want your father to be proud of you when he comes home."

"But he likes me the way I am!" Gorgo insisted.

"Don't be silly! All men love beauty and, Aphrodite is my witness, you don't give me a lot to work with. We must cover these ugly freckles," she remarked over her shoulder to one of her women, who at once went to get a white paste to smear all over Gorgo's face.

When her mother was finished with her, Gorgo felt like a painted statue. It was horrible. She didn't recognize herself in the mirror her mother held up to her, and everything itched! But her mother knew how to make her behave. "If you wipe anything off, I'll have that wretched dog of yours hung up in the garden by his ears and make you watch while the crows eat him!" Sometimes Gorgo had the feeling her mother *wanted* her to disobey, so she would have an excuse for killing Jason.

But there was no time to fuss. The parade of returning athletes and spectators had reached the outskirts of the city, and everyone in the palace was streaming out to take up positions along the route. Gyrtias hustled Gorgo down and into the state chariot so they could take their places on the steps of the Council House.

The streets were full of people. Banners hung from the balconies. The maidens were garlanded with flowers and the boys of the agoge looked scrubbed and clean—their eirenes having chased them down to the Eurotas not only to wash themselves, but their chitons as well. The young men were in full panoply of bronze, their helmets glistening to perfection and the black crests freshly brushed and stiffened with wax. The older men wore either their armor or, like Nikostratos, a comfortable but good-quality chiton. Gorgo smiled and waved at him and her grandmother, and they waved back but kept their distance. Gyrtias did not particularly like her mother-in-law.

Eventually the sound of singing grew steadily closer, and the crowd in the main square settled down. The chorus of youths leading the procession came into the square first, followed by Demaratus, driving his victorious team with the wreath of olives on his brow. The horses were garlanded with wreaths of oleander (which seemed to be irritating them, since they kept shaking their heads and fretting). Standing beside him in the car of the chariot was Ephorus, likewise crowned with olives. Demaratus halted the chariot before his own wife, who like Gyrtias was seated on a throne before the Council House. She rose, a lovely figure with bright blond hair in a fluttering pale-blue peplos. Holding a large kylix in both outstretched hands, she descended the steps to her husband. He drank from the kylix and then lifted it up and poured the rest of the wine out in a gesture of offering to the city.

Ephorus was greeted by the senior member of the Council, who followed with a short speech praising the victors and urging the youth of the city to strive harder for perfection so they could honor their city at future Games.

Gorgo wasn't listening. First she waved to her father in the second chariot, and then she looked at the other athletes, those who had participated but not won anything. Among these was her uncle Brotus, wearing a huge bandage around his head, apparently because of a broken jaw. One eye was completely swollen shut and the other badly discolored and half closed. He looked very mean at the moment, Gorgo thought, her latent dislike reinforced. She looked in vain, however, for her favorite uncle, Leonidas. Then she remembered that he hadn't participated, and therefore would be somewhere in the crowd of spectators farther back in the parade.

Even after the official part of the homecoming was over, however, and people were mixing together freely, Gorgo still couldn't find Leonidas. Everywhere people were welcoming home those who had been away, and hearing blow-by-blow descriptions of the events. Many were buying the delicacies offered for sale by enterprising helots and perioikoi. Gorgo had managed to slip away from her parents and even wash her face off in a fountain house. She sought out her grandmother and Nikostratos and led them to Laodice's stand so they could buy some of her nut-and-honey squares.

Laodice recognized her at once, and her face broke into a smile. "Why, it's little Gorgo! Are these your parents?" she asked, surprised, since Chilonis had long been a loyal customer and Laodice knew she was the mother of one of the kings.

Chilonis laughed. "Grandparents," she answered. She then obligingly bought some of Laodice's wares, chattering with her amiably about how things were going at the kleros. Gorgo thought it perfectly natural that her grandmother knew everyone. She was just like that.

"We've roofed all the balconies now," Laodice announced proudly. "I wish the master would come and see. The house gets prettier every day. We see far too little of him. It has been more than two months since his last visit."

"Oh," Nikostratos entered the conversation for the first time. "You won't be seeing him for a bit more. He was granted leave to travel to Athens with that Corinthian youth whose life he saved."

Laodice looked blankly at him. The incident in which Leonidas killed the boar had happened before Laodice and her husband came to Laconia. But Chilonis remembered the incident well, and she asked with interest, "So the boy survived?"

"Apparently he and his father were at Olympia and invited Leonidas to travel back with them to Corinth and on to Athens, where they are traveling on business. Leonidas was granted a month's leave—and Euryleon was ordered to travel with him."

At the mention of Leonidas, Gorgo's ears pricked up sharply.

Her grandmother was saying, "I'm so glad for him! He's wanted to travel ever since Prokles was exiled. I wonder why they sent Euryleon with him?"

Nikostratos laughed. "To keep an eye on him, of course—and make sure he has a constant reminder of his duties here in Sparta. Euryleon is just the kind of young man to get himself into trouble in Athens, and Leo will feel obliged to look after him. Nothing could be a better guarantee that he won't stray too far himself."

Chilonis looked at her husband skeptically.

"Believe me, my dear, responsibility is a far greater bond than slavery."

Gorgo was sorry she wouldn't be seeing Leonidas today, but then she had a happy thought. "We'll make him come and tell us about Athens, won't we? As soon as he gets home," Gorgo addressed herself to Nikostratos as the chairman of Leonidas' syssitia. "You can order him to come when I can be there," she advised the older man self-confidently.

"All right," Nikostratos agreed readily enough—smiling at her and wishing with all his heart that she had been born a boy.

CHAPTER 11

ATHENS

THE ACROPOLIS IN ATHENS SAT MAJESTICALLY at the top of a sheer white cliff that separated the Gods from the filth, noise, and chaos of the teeming, overcrowded city clinging to its feet. Acrocorinth also towered above the modern city, but it was much farther away and looked only like a distant fortress. The Athenian acropolis, in contrast, rose out of the heart of the city, and the roofs of the temples were a jumble of decorated tiles that peered over the fortress walls, hinting at the treasures within.

Sparta had nothing to compare with it. Leonidas didn't see any point in pretending otherwise, and openly admired the magnificent temples—and the view. To be sure, there were some spectacular views into the Eurotas valley from the mountains surrounding Sparta, but nowhere could you look down right into the agora and see the people in the stalls haggling with their customers or watch people loitering around the theater.

Leonidas leaned out as far as he could over the thick wall to get a better look. Athens was huge. Not only did it spread around the foot of the acropolis but, like water, the houses seemed to be seeping out from the center into all the surrounding valleys. Even beyond the city walls, buildings not only lined the roads, but formed whole neighborhoods in sporadic clusters, apparently around wells, temples, or gymnasia. Inside the city walls, except for the public areas around the agora and theater, the houses were crowded so close together that it was hard to see streets as such, just cracks in the "pavement" of roof tiles. The courtyards were small, and there were swaths of the city with no trees at all. The gymnasia beyond the walls of the city were all the easier to find, because it was only here that large stands of cypress and plane trees stood out boldly, oases of green in the carpet of ragged terra cotta and stone. And somewhere in the distant haze to the south was the sea.

"It's incredible!" Euryleon exclaimed beside him. Euryleon was not looking out across the city, but back at the acropolis itself. The temples here were so richly decorated that even Euryleon could see they were brightly painted, although he could not see the detail with his poor eyesight.

Leonidas turned back to consider the temples, admiring the lifelike quality of the sculpture. Most of Sparta's temples were old, dating back twenty-five Olympiads or more, and they were consequently adorned by rather stiff figures in almost passive poses. Here, warriors fought and maidens danced, horses galloped, and men struggled with Amazons on the friezes and pediments. Every image exuded vitality, as if it had been alive only a moment before and suddenly turned to stone by an evil spirit.

Lychos was sitting on the steps to the Parthenon waiting for them. He was dwarfed by the columns framing him, which rose easily to seven times the height of a grown man. Men entering or leaving the temple bustled past him as if they did not see him; certainly they took no note of the slight figure. Many may even have mistaken him for a beggar, Leonidas suspected, because he was so unassuming and obviously crippled.

Leonidas, however, had come to respect the young Corinthian. Lychos was frequently in pain. Sometimes a sudden motion or a too-eager gesture would tear a grimace from him, or he would catch his breath or break out into a sweat. Whenever Lychos saw that Leonidas had noticed, he would smile and insist, "It's worth it. I'll show you."

And in many ways he had. In Corinth, he had shown Leonidas his library. He admitted he had not been much interested in the sciences before "the accident," but during the sedentary years of his slow recovery he had come to love reading. Leonidas had glanced through some of the documents, but they seemed very long-winded and hard to follow. Leonidas had more understanding for Lychos' enthusiasm for his herb garden. Lychos explained that he had become interested in medicinal herbs, and he had overseen the planting of his own garden of healing plants. Leonidas could relate to that.

But Lychos' greatest joy was sailing. He had a small fishing smack that, with the help of a two-man crew, he could maneuver with amazing agility and daring. When first launched, the little craft had been tossed about by the wind and the waves, never steady for an instant, terrifying Leonidas, while Lychos laughed as the wind ruined his otherwise well-tended hair and clothes. With the sail set, however, the boat steadied and began to pound through the waves with bone-jarring force. When the bows smashed down, water was flung up and inward, soaking them all; and all the while the leeward gunnel sliced the sea, gurgling and frothing. Eventually, Leonidas started to enjoy it—somewhat—but the sea was far too unpredictable and capricious for him to be comfortable. Lychos, in contrast, seemed to be made whole again by the sea—and to have an uncanny feel for it. He gave his orders with certainty, and he seemed to smell a change in wind or weather long before either hit. Nor could Leonidas understand where he got the strength, for just a few minutes at the tiller had taught Leonidas that steering a boat required both skill and muscle.

Commanding one of his father's ships to Athens had been a major step forward for Lychos. He admitted to Leonidas the night before they sailed that it was the first time his father had given him the privilege, although he'd been nagging him for almost a year. "I've traveled with him everywhere this past year, and our helmsmen are all trustworthy men. They are loyal and would never let harm come to me intentionally. Yet my father resists letting me out of his sight. He let me have a ship this time only so as not to shame me in front of you—and because it's such a short run."

They made Athens in a single day, on a good following wind, with a cargo of timber from Arcadia. They put in at Kantharos, the commercial port of Athens; so Leonidas did not get a good look at the naval shipyards in Zea, to the east of Piraeus, as he would have liked. Archilochos, however, kindly insisted that he would deal with business and their luggage, and sent Lychos on into Athens with the two Spartans and their attendants. Flanking Lychos' litter, Leonidas and Euryleon with their helot servants had walked into Athens and, after stopping for some light refreshment from a street vendor, headed to the acropolis.

With a nod to Euryleon, Leonidas descended from the wall and sat down beside Lychos. "Magnificent," he commented simply.

Lychos nodded. "It is, isn't it? There's no place quite like it in the whole world. Not even in Persia or Egypt. Although the pyramids in Egypt have their own grandeur, they are dry and lifeless compared to this. They were built to dead gods, while our Gods are still living." He raised his head to look toward the ceiling, and then turned around to look back into the temple at the gigantic figure of Athena, with her glistening helmet and bright gown. "We'd better get back into town, or my father will start to worry," Lychos decided.

"May I make an offering to Athena first?" Leonidas asked, and Lychos nodded.

Leonidas entered the temple, leaving the bright sun and the refreshing breeze behind. He took his time gazing up at the tall statue of the Goddess, who wore a bronze helmet with a real horsehair crest shoved back on her head. She was very impressive, undoubtedly more so than their own main statue to her in the Temple of the Bronze-house Athena on the acropolis of Sparta. That likeness of the Goddess looked dowdy compared to this. Leonidas dropped his knapsack off his shoulder onto his feet and reached inside for some bread he had saved from lunch. He placed this on the altar, with a silent prayer to the Goddess to open her city to him in friendship and allow him to learn as much as he could without disgracing himself or his own city. Then he returned outside to his friends and asked, "Do you know where to meet your father?"

"Of course. We always stay with a guest-friend of his: a certain Demothenes. We need only ask. Everyone in Athens knows the way."

———

By the time they arrived, Leonidas was thoroughly confused about direction. He was used to navigating by the sun and the mountains. Sparta had a simple north-south orientation, with the acropolis in the north and Amyclae in the south; it was impossible to get lost. But in Athens the streets were so narrow that you didn't always have

a clear view to the acropolis, and the surrounding mountains and sea
were far too distant for navigation. Leonidas didn't like the feeling of
not knowing where he was or what direction to go to get home. It
wasn't that he felt any desire to go home just yet, but it was unsettling
not to know what direction to walk should he want to.

When they finally reached the house of their host, Leonidas and
Euryleon were tired, sweaty, and ready for some peace and quiet, but
they found neither. Instead, they entered an oppressively opulent
house where the door frames were carved and painted, the floors
were mosaics in elaborate patterns, and the walls were adorned with
frescoes—but which, to young men who had spent so much of their
life outdoors, seemed cramped, dark, crowded, and noisy. Because
the windows were small and looked out onto the narrow streets—
which actually meant at the walls of the next house—artificial lighting
was needed, even in the glaring light of noon. The courtyard was so
cramped that all but a tiny square lay in shade. It was also overcrowded, with a well, washing tubs, grinding stones, barrels, handcarts,
and general clutter. The smell of the stables, which opened directly
onto the courtyard, was powerful enough to pierce into the rooms
facing the courtyard. Only deeper in the house did incense and dried
herbs improve the smell.

Leonidas and Euryleon were shown up to the old nursery in the
rafters of the house and told they could make themselves comfortable here. Lychos would sleep with his father in the guest chamber.
There were two beds in the nursery as well as a crib. Children's toys—
rocking horses, tin hoplites, dolls—were neatly lined up and gathering dust in the anteroom. Clearly there had been no young children
in the household for a long time.

Young Spartans travel light and they had little to unpack, so
Euryleon and Leonidas soon found themselves back in the courtyard. By now it was starting to get dark, and they were directed to
the andron for dinner with their host and "a small circle of friends."
Their attendants were pointed the way to the kitchens.

The andron was the most elaborately decorated room in the
house, with fine couches and soft cushions, large bronze lamps, and
a marble-tiled floor. Their host, a man in his early sixties, greeted
them warmly: "Any friends of Archilochos are welcome guests." The

young men were shown couches farther down the room and were soon joined there by the son of the house, Kallixenos.

Kallixenos was in his early thirties, tall and slender, with rather gaunt features and long, curly dark-blond hair. He wore a long linen chiton with a wide border of woven hawks and hounds, over which he had slung a two-toned gauze himation with a floral border that glittered in the lamplight. "So you're from Sparta!" he greeted the two guests. "How fascinating! I've never actually *met* a Spartan before. You must tell me what it is really like there. You know, we hear so many *horror* stories about life in Sparta—but I'm sure they can't all be true. You look quite normal." He laughed at his own joke. Leonidas and Euryleon looked at one another.

"Please, please, make yourselves comfortable," Kallixenos urged them, indicating two couches. Leonidas bent and untied his sandals so he could swing his feet up onto the couch. Euryleon followed his example.

Already a slave was hovering, offering hot white rolls and an olive relish garnished with mint and coriander. Lychos and his father arrived, and while Archilochos remained at the head of the chamber with their host, Lychos joined the young men. He clearly knew Kallixenos, but their greeting was decidedly cool, even vaguely embarrassed. Shortly afterward other guests started to arrive and they were introduced one after another.

Most of the guests were roughly their host's age, men of obvious wealth and power. Among these worthy gentlemen the conversation soon turned to politics. Leonidas tried to follow what they were saying, but not knowing much about the situation in Athens, it was difficult. All that he was able to glean was that there was to be an Assembly the next day, and that someone was at risk of being "ostracized." Leonidas had no idea what that meant and had to ask Kallixenos about it.

"Oh. Don't you have ostracism in Sparta? No, I suppose not. It's quite new to Athens, too. Kleisthenes introduced it. One of his better ideas, really. It's terribly amusing. The best reason for going to Assembly at all nowadays."

"But what is it?"

"Oh, a public vote to exile someone."

"For what crime?" Leonidas asked, shocked, thinking of Prokles.

"No crime," Kallixenos shrugged. "That's the fun of it. Anyone can be named, and since there doesn't have to be a crime, no one even has a chance to defend himself. If you can buy enough votes, you can get rid of your worst enemy without them putting a foot wrong."

"Buy votes?" Leonidas asked incredulously. He could not imagine selling this precious privilege for any sum of money. "But who would sell his citizen's rights?"

Kallixenos shrugged. "Most of the poor citizens don't give a damn if one rich man or another has to leave the city, so if you offer them a drachma or two, they'll take the shard you give them with the name you've already scratched into it. Half of them can't read anyway, and so don't know what you've written. At least one man was enterprising enough to prepare shards with his enemy's name on them and stack them in different piles. He then gave the shards out to the illiterates regardless of what name they *said* they wanted. He nearly got lynched by the mob when they found out." Kallixenos laughed at the memory.

"And who is going to be ostracized tomorrow?" Leonidas asked.

"Well, we won't know until the votes are counted, but my father's all in a dither," Kallixenos nodded dismissively in the direction of his father, "because Kleisthenes' supporters have targeted one of his old cronies. You'll have to come along to Assembly with us tomorrow and see which of them manages to manipulate the mob best. Generally Kleisthenes can talk them around, but my father's friends have deeper pockets. If people are hungry enough, they'll take the drachma and to hell with Kleisthenes' pretty words."

At the other end of the hall the conversation had turned to the price of grain. Athens was dependent on imported grain, mostly from cities along the Black Sea. There were rumors of a drought in the north that made everyone nervous about this year's grain crop, and apparently some people were starting to hoard grain, driving up prices. It occurred to Leonidas that if one had to have money to buy grain, then money would play a more important role in society. In Sparta, on the other hand, everyone had their own kleros, so that Spartiates and helots alike generally could be sure of enough to eat, and it was easy to do without money much of the time.

Meanwhile, the appetizer of honey-glazed shrimp had been

served. Leonidas had never had anything so delicious, and Euryleon announced appreciatively, "This beats black broth any day." Due to a lull in the conversation, even the older men heard the remark, and everyone laughed.

"I'm pleased that you are enjoying the meal," their host called down to them. Leonidas and Euryleon nodded politely.

The next course was brought, and the conversation of the older men turned to astrology and the extent to which the course of the stars reflected or predicted events. If an eclipse or a comet was an omen, did that mean that all that happened afterward was unavoidable? Or could men by their actions avert impending disaster? Could a comet, for example, wake up a city to a threat, inspiring them to avert the disaster predicted by the comet?

Although Leonidas was interested in the discussion, the main course of eels in mulberry sauce and stuffed lamb's kidneys arrived. Besides, Kallixenos had no intention of letting him listen to the older men, but rather started harassing the Spartans with questions. "Have you ever eaten eel before?"

"No," Leonidas admitted. He was having some difficulty getting this dish down. The diet of other Greeks was dominated by fish; and while he liked shellfish well enough, eels, oysters, and sardines appeared to be an acquired taste.

"And the kidneys?" Kallixenos pressed him.

"Oh, we eat lots of kidneys," Euryleon declared, "but we don't stuff them with pine nuts and coriander. We normally stew them with hearts and lung."

"How ghastly!" Kallixenos exclaimed with a look of disgust.

"Not really," Euryleon assured him. "You throw in carrots and leeks and season with bay leaves or—"

"Good heavens! You make it sound like you cook it yourself!" Kallixenos exclaimed in horror. "Don't you have kitchen slaves?"

"Not in the agoge. We did a lot of our own cooking in the agoge."

"How revolting! Why on earth should you be made to do the work of slaves?"

Euryleon looked uncomfortable and tried to explain, "Well, we don't have slaves in the agoge, so it makes sense to learn to cook." Because of his poor eyesight, Euryleon was a poor hunter, and so he had often been stuck with the chore of cooking for the boys of his herd. Over time he had developed a certain talent at it, which in turn had won him the affection of his herd mates.

Leonidas had learned to appreciate Euryleon's culinary talents during his year as Euryleon's eirene. Sensing that Euryleon was hurt to have one of his few talents devalued as "slave work," Leonidas remarked, "Feeding an army is as important as arming it."

Lychos smirked, hiding his amusement behind his kylix, but Kallixenos frowned. "What does that have to do with whether a gentleman should demean himself with cooking?"

"In Sparta, we respect any skill that contributes to the readiness of our troops."

"I see. Including cooking."

"Exactly. Army and syssitia cooks are hereditary professions, passed from father to son along with many recipes and secrets on how to improvise in the field and adapt dishes for different types of game."

"So you respect your armorers and mule-team drivers and the camp followers, too?" It was not a serious question, and Leonidas thought it was beneath his dignity to answer.

Euryleon, however, felt deeply insulted by the mention of camp followers and burst out, "We don't have whores with our army! They sap a man's strength, the opposite of a good meal."

Kallixenos laughed. "How would you know? I'll wager a tetradrachma you've never visited a whore!"

With the incident at Olympia fresh on his mind, Euryleon flushed, and Leonidas spoke more harshly than appropriate in order to draw the attention away from his friend. "And *you* have never been to war!"

Kallixenos snapped his head around to sneer at Leonidas, "Don't pretend you and this boy have!"

Lychos burst out laughing, and enlightened their host with obvious relish. "Wrong, Kallixenos. They beat the hell out the Argives last year."

"Sparta's army may have, but not these gentle youth—"

Lychos was nodding smugly, enjoying the fact that Kallixenos was in the wrong. "Our dear friends here have blood all over their gentle hands, so show a little more respect."

Kallixenos raised his eyebrows and then bowed his head. "Well, well, a toast to our warriors, then;" and although not everyone was finished eating, he signaled to a slave for wine. As soon as his kylix was full, he tossed the contents over his shoulder in the vague direction of a house altar as a flippant libation, and the slave at once refilled the kylix, which he then raised with the words, "To our Spartan guests!"

A slave was filling the kylixes of the others, and Leonidas tried to cover his cup—with a glance at the older men, who had not started drinking wine yet—but as soon as he removed his hand, the slave filled it anyway.

"It's black wine from Crete," Kallixenos told him. "Try it; you'll like it."

"Is it neat?" Leonidas sniffed at it.

"Oh! You mean it's true you never drink wine neat in Sparta?" Kallixenos sounded astonished.

"Yes."

"Why?"

"Because neat wine makes a man dull of tongue and slow of motion."

Kallixenos threw back his head and laughed. "We will see about that! Tomorrow evening I'll take you to a little symposium with some of *my* friends. I'll show you just how nimble neat wine makes *us*!"

"We'd be delighted to attend," Leonidas agreed at once. He was very curious about this kind of event.

"Good, but for now have one little bowl," Kallixenos cajoled. "Surely you aren't afraid that a single sip or two of strong wine will unman you? Here in Athens, you will find, we respect a man who can hold his liquor far more than a man who abstains. After all, any slave can be sober simply by being too poor to afford good wine; but a man who, having tasted the finest Dionysus has to offer, can still perform like a true man is admirable indeed!"

The meal appeared to be over. Demothenes was also signaling the slaves to pour wine. Leonidas sniffed tentatively at the wine in his kylix.

"If you don't drink that, I will think Sparta is populated entirely by women!"

Euryleon at once lifted his kylix, tossed the contents down his throat, and smiled at Leonidas provocatively as he held out the kylix for more, to the approving cheers of the others.

Leonidas capitulated. It was easier to sip it slowly than to remain the focus of attention. So he tasted the wine, nodded his approval to the host, and the conversation moved on.

Kallixenos asked, "Is it true you steal food to keep from starving in your agoge?"

Leonidas opened his mouth to deny it, but Euryleon beat him to it. "Oh, yes, *that's* true. We all got quite good at stealing, didn't we, Leo?"

Leonidas gaped at his countryman and didn't know what to say. He didn't want to flatly contradict Euryleon, but he didn't want to confirm such a preposterous assertion either. "Up to a point," he tried to explain. "During the Phouxir it is quite common, but I wouldn't say we *all* do it." He glared reproachfully at Euryleon.

"Well, I did!" Euryleon told him defiantly, emboldened by the wine, and sensing a way to redeem himself in the eyes of the Athenians. "I did it quite a lot, or the food would have been even worse!"

"And is it true you let yourselves get flogged senseless?" Kallixenos asked next.

"Of course not!" Leonidas hastened to answer before Euryleon could say something foolish.

"The flogging was only if you got caught, you know," Euryleon pointed out, obviously relishing this opportunity to educate the arrogant Athenian. "One of my mates had stolen this fox, and just when he was about to make off with it, the owner of the estate showed up. So to avoid getting caught and flogged, my friend stopped and chatted with the old man. He had the fox wrapped in his cloak that he was carrying over his arm, as we sometimes do, and he crushed the fox against his stomach to keep it from squirming or yelping. Fortunately it was dark and the old man couldn't see too well." The longer he talked, the bigger the eyes of the Athenians grew; while Leonidas started drumming his fingers on the edge of his couch, because he was pretty certain Euryleon was making the whole story up. Euryleon was good at this kind of thing and had often entertained his herd over their campfires with similar "stories."

"Anyway," Euryleon continued, "he got away with it. He just

stood there and chatted to the old man like he had all the time in the world. But when the old man finally went inside his house, my mate crashed to the ground with a groan. We rushed over to him and discovered that the fox had chewed right through the cloak and his skin and was gnawing at his insides the whole time he had been chatting!"

The foreigners made exclamations of horror and revulsion, although Kallixenos' face suggested fascination, too, as he asked breathlessly, "And then? What happened then? Did he get flogged for stealing the fox, too?"

"Of course not! That's the whole point of the story! He hadn't been caught, so he wasn't flogged, even though he had obviously stolen the fox!" Euryleon retorted, frowning at the Athenian's lack of comprehension. Then he shrugged and added, "Of course, he died from his wounds..."

Leonidas choked on his wine, stunned by Euryleon's audacity in making up a tale like this. He wanted to tell the others that it was a ridiculous fabrication, but the conversation at the other end of the hall had suddenly become heated.

"They are all slaves!" the youngest of the guests near their host insisted passionately. "To bow before the 'great king' and grovel at his feet is slavery!"

"Nonsense! Only the tyrants themselves, who have to deal with the Darius personally, have to grovel. Most citizens live no differently than they did before. Perhaps better, since the Persian fleet protects their merchantmen and they can buy grain from the vast reaches of the Persian empire."

"At exorbitant prices! Don't think they get a discount because they are subjects of the same king," another man scoffed.

"It shames all Greeks for our brothers to be subjects of a barbarian race," the younger man insisted. Leonidas noticed that he was more weathered than the others, and suspected he was a sea captain.

"The tyrants have bartered away the freedom of their citizens," another man argued in a more moderate tone. "The citizens are largely innocent victims of the selfish policies of the tyrants."

"That is simplifying the situation. Not all the cities that have paid homage to Darius are tyrannies. But they are too weak on their own to defy him. For the most part, they are small cities with a few hundred citizens. They cannot hope to stand against the might of Persia. Why, all of Hellas, even if united, would not be able to field an army half the size of Darius' own."

"And Hades will freeze over before Hellas unites!" an old man with a long white beard and a bald head threw in with a snort of contempt.

"Are you saying we are condemned to being subjugated one by one?"

"Of course not. Why should Darius covet our poor, rocky peninsula? He has enough rich lands elsewhere. If we leave him alone, he'll leave us alone."

"You know he has given refuge to Hippias?" the younger man asked angrily. "The Persian satrap Artaphernes at Sardis has received him like a lost son and showered him with gifts and women. Hippias promises to deliver Athens to the great king, if only Persia will give him enough gold to enable him to regain power either by bribes or with mercenaries. If he succeeds in winning Darius' support, we will not have the choice of 'leaving them alone.' We will be fighting for our freedom, not just from Persia but from tyranny!"

"Calm down, Melanthius. It has not come to that yet," their host advised.

"Mark my words! It will come to that sooner than you think!" Melanthius turned and called down the hall to the Spartans. "And what would Sparta do if the Persians backed Hippias? Would you still welcome him back, although he is not just a tyrant but a Persian slave and would bring Persia into Hellas?"

Leonidas was uncomfortably aware that the strong wine was already having alarming affects on him. He found it hard to focus his eyes, and his tongue felt heavy. He wasn't sure he would get his words out right and feared he would make a fool of himself.

"Leo!" Euryleon hissed at him. "Say something!"

Leonidas shrugged. "The Assembly will decide."

"I thought you were an Agiad prince. Can you not speak like the son of kings?" Melanthius taunted.

"No; I am a Spartan Peer."

Melanthius lost interest in the obviously stupid young Spartan and turned back to his fellow Athenians. "If Sparta is no longer able or willing to lead Hellas, then we must seize the leadership! We must show the Persian despot that we are not afraid of him. We must not leave our brothers enslaved!"

The old man shrugged. "I haven't noticed anyone rising to rescue our brothers in Messenia."

There was an awkward silence, and all eyes turned again to look at the Spartans. Leonidas cursed himself for accepting the neat wine. He knew he ought to have a ready retort for this, but his mind and tongue failed him. He licked his lips and swallowed, his mind blank.

Archilochos came to his assistance. "Let's not be hypocritical, gentlemen. Which of us does not own Greek slaves taken in one war or another, or captured by pirates? The only thing that distinguishes the Spartan subjugation of Messenia from our own enslavement of fellow Greeks is the scale. No other city has dared to—much less succeeded at—conquering one of its neighbors. But we all keep Greeks enslaved on a smaller scale.

"The issue," Archilochos continued, "is whether we can allow substantial portions of Hellas to be conquered by a *barbarian* power without endangering our existence in the long run. Democracy is a fragile plant, and while it can survive—indeed, thrives upon—rivalry and competition and small-scale wars among ourselves, I doubt it can endure if it falls under the shadow of an oppressive foreign power like Persia. The Persians are nothing like us, and they have different gods. Yet the Persian Empire has grown so strong that it can crush us anytime it chooses to. If the Persians are indeed persuaded to support Hippias, then we will have no choice but to fight them. The alternative would be the slow obliteration of our Gods, our way of life, and our very civilization. We will have to fight Persia or allow our entire culture, our heritage, and our hopes for our sons and grandsons to be obliterated."

———

Leonidas was relieved when the symposium ended and he could slink away to his bed. He felt unsteady on his feet, and he desperately needed to relieve himself. When he at last made his way back up to the nursery he remarked to Euryleon, "Kallixenos is an ass, but you shouldn't have accepted that first cup of neat wine!"

"You didn't have to follow my example," Euryleon replied, flopping down on the bed.

"Of course I did. That was solidarity. You broke the line."

"Don't be ridiculous." Euryleon turned his back on Leonidas.

"And what was that nonsense about the fox?" Leonidas demanded. "I've never heard so much bullshit in my whole life! Who the hell would want to steal a *fox* in the first place? I can't believe they swallowed it!"

Euryleon giggled and turned back to face Leonidas, propping his head on his hand. "I couldn't, either—but when they didn't question me, I just couldn't resist going on."

"Did you have to go to such extremes? We may be able to set Lychos straight, but Kallixenos will be telling that silly story to all his friends—not as an example of how tough we are, but rather how *stupid!*"

"Well, you know it did sort of happen. A couple of years before you joined us, Xenos trapped this fox cub and tried to tame him, but one day when he was holding him he bit deep into his stomach! He had to go to the surgeon, and he nearly died."

Leonidas just shook his head in disgust and turned his back on Euryleon.

Euryleon yawned and lay on his back. Then abruptly he lifted his head and remarked, "And you have to admit the wine tasted delicious. Just like the food. I'm never going to be able to enjoy black broth again."

Leonidas sat up in bed. "Euryleon!"

"What?"

"Swear you won't drink neat wine ever again."

Euryleon didn't answer, as if he were already asleep.

"Euryleon! Swear!"

Euryleon sat up to glare at Leonidas. Then he nodded. "I promise never to drink neat wine again." He lay down, turned his back on Leonidas and added, "After we leave Athens."

Leonidas was out of bed and on top of him. Euryleon didn't have much of a chance—being weaker, smaller, and taken by surprise—

but he struggled enough for them to both fall off the bed. The sound of them crashing onto the floor brought their attendants from the adjacent room and shouts of alarm from below. "What's happening? Are you all right? What's going on up there?"

"Now you've made fools of us!" Euryleon hissed to Leonidas, while trying to stop laughing.

"I'm disciplining a ranker for insubordination!" Leonidas called back to his host. Then he gave Euryleon another cuff and got up off him. They returned to their beds and fell quickly asleep, contented.

———

Leonidas and Euryleon slept later than ever before in their lives. There was no changing of the watch ringing out the hours, and the sun was hidden from them by the high walls of the city. Consequently they had no sense of time, and they only staggered out of bed when the call of nature roused them. To Leonidas' astonishment, the sun stood so high in the sky that it was shining directly into the small courtyard, and the slaves had evidently been up for hours. Savory smells wafted out of the kitchens, washing was hanging out to dry, manure recorded the coming and going of delivery carts, and an old slave woman was spinning in the shaft of light that spilled in over the high walls. It struck Leonidas that she was the first woman he had seen here, and he felt a little embarrassed that he had not yet had an opportunity to pay his respects to the hostess. Maybe today.

Mantiklos had found out where the household bath was, and he took his master there to wash and change. He had been up earlier and had already accompanied some of the household slaves on a shopping expedition. "You've got to go to the agora," he advised his master eagerly. "You've never seen anything like it. It doesn't matter what it is: shoes, belts, cloaks, shields, cooking pots, buckets and barrels, even glass! They've got dozens of craftsmen selling it—not just one or two, but *dozens*! And everyone carries coins around with them on their belts and buys what they fancy. And the pottery! It's beautiful, like you wouldn't want to eat from, like paintings." Leonidas knew what he meant; he'd noticed it the night before at dinner.

"The food isn't half bad, either," Leonidas remarked, remembering dinner.

"What *you* get, you mean," Mantiklos answered tartly.

"What do you mean? Didn't you get the leftovers?"

Mantiklos snorted. "I expect *someone* got the leftovers, but not the household slaves. We were given slops worse than anything I've ever had before in my life—campaigning included."

Leonidas gazed at him. In the army, the Spartans always shared their meals with their helots. The Spartiates got served first, and the helots ate afterward. That meant the food might be cold and the best bits taken already, but it was not intrinsically less nutritious or tasty. Helots on the estates ate as well as they liked—Laodice certainly made sure her family ate better than many Spartiates!

"The women get different food, too," Mantiklos added. "They don't get any wine at all, no meat, no fish, no spices! Just the same slops we got, only with white bread and more butter and cheese."

"That was just the slaves."

"No, it wasn't!" Mantiklos insisted. "It was the meal they made specially for the old and young mistresses."

"What do you mean, the old *and* young mistresses?"

"The old man and his son are both married and their wives live here. The young mistress is pregnant with her first child and due in a month or two."

Leonidas supposed that might explain why he hadn't seen her. Some pregnant women preferred to live secluded in the last months; but he was surprised she was living with her mother-in-law. Spartan wives generally stayed in their father's home until they set up their own household on their husband's kleros.

"Let me give you a shave and trim your hair, sir. You look shaggy."

Leonidas gladly submitted to Mantiklos' barbering. The Messenian had become quite good at it. Besides, it was a good opportunity to gather more intelligence. "What else have you seen here?"

"The slaves live rotten lives," Mantiklos told him bluntly.

"Don't tell me worse than Messenians?" Leonidas opened one eye to observe his squire.

Mantiklos grimaced. "I hate to admit it, but they do. Can you believe it? Slaves are not allowed to testify at a trial of a citizen *unless* they have been tortured! So anytime a citizen gets accused of one thing or another—as they are all the time around here—the *slaves* of the household are tortured either by the prosecution to make them testify against their masters, or by their own masters to make them vindicate him! Everyone in the household is terrified that in these unsettled times, their master will get into some lawsuit, and they will be put on the rack and stretched until they come apart at the joints or hung over a fire until the skin falls off their feet. The former housekeeper was put to the rack a couple of Olympiads ago, and he can hardly walk anymore. It's the most barbaric custom I've ever heard of! At least you Spartans only kill us outright for what *we* have done or not done, not for what you accuse *each other* of doing!"

Leonidas laughed at this conclusion, but Mantiklos only glowered at him more furiously and continued, "None of them are allowed to marry. They are locked up at night to keep them apart from the women—like animals."

"I don't expect that's terribly effective," Leonidas remarked, thinking how easy it was for lovers to meet at other times and locations.

"But if a slave girl gets pregnant, the child belongs to the *master*, not the father. Usually, if the master doesn't want it, he leaves it in the agora for anyone who does, or puts it to death right away. And the young Athenian men are no better about keeping away from the slave girls than the Spartans in Messenia. The young master here has had all the women at one time or another, except his old nurse."

"I thought you said his wife lived here."

"She does, but that doesn't stop him from taking his pleasure with the slaves."

"She must be a singularly stupid woman. Imagine what Hilaira would do to Alkander if he looked sideways at one of the helots on her kleros!" Leonidas laughed at the thought, because it was unimaginable that Alkander *would* look at another woman—but if he did, Hilaira would make his life hell!

Mantiklos, however, only shrugged. "What should the poor girl do? She's only just turned fifteen, and according to the slaves she hardly dares say a word to anyone, though she's been here almost two years. I caught a glimpse of her and she is very frail and sickly-looking—pale white skin and an enormous belly. In fact, she seemed to be all eyes and belly. I don't expect she'll survive childbirth. She's too little and weak for it."

Leonidas stared at Mantiklos. He had been raised on Lycurgus' laws, which required that girl children be fed like their brothers and that they exercise in order for them to grow into healthy mothers. The laws furthermore said that no girl should be married before she was "old enough to enjoy sex" because, the lawgiver had reasoned, she would otherwise give birth to sickly children. Leonidas had been raised on that philosophy without thinking about it particularly.

Mantiklos, however, had moved on to the next subject. "The worst thing about the slaves here is that they are all cut off from their families. They have been bought and sold—sometimes more than once. They don't know who their fathers or brothers are. They don't know the stories of their ancestors or the names of their household Gods. They are all just individuals struggling to survive in a strange place. They don't even all speak the same language. There's a slave here who came from someplace in the far north and knows only a few broken phrases of Greek, and another who is from Africa and talks to himself all the time in his own barbarian tongue. It drives the others crazy, because he is vicious and they are afraid of him. They say he once carved up a man—first killed him and then carved up his body into little pieces and cooked them in a big pot."

"Here in this house?" Leonidas asked in horror, sitting bolt upright.

"No, before he came here; but they swear it is true."

Leonidas looked skeptical, and Mantiklos let it go. Although he was now finished with Leonidas' haircut and shave, they were content to continue gossiping, sitting side by side in the only patch of sun available in the courtyard. "Because they all come from diffe-rent places, they are always bickering among themselves. The Greeks think they are much better than the rest, of course, but some of the barbarians are just as proud. That is why, although they all hate the Athenians, they will never be a threat to Athens as we Messenians are to Sparta."

"What do you mean?"

"Well, if you go out into the streets you'll see. There are many times as many slaves and metoikoi as Athenians, but they are so different from one another that they would never unite against the Athenians. We Messenians, on the other hand—"

Leonidas knew about Messenia. He wanted to understand more about Athens. "What are metoikoi?"

Mantiklos scratched his head and thought about it. "They're free men from somewhere else in the world. Athens seems to attract human rubbish. I was told they have to find a patron and get themselves registered with a community if they want to live here permanently, and they have to pay a special tax. Anyone who lives here without being registered or who fails to pay the taxes is arrested and sold into slavery. The paidagogos here is an old Thespian who moved here to set up a school for boys but somehow fell on hard times and couldn't pay his taxes, so he was sold into slavery."

"The Paidonomos?" Leonidas asked, horrified—thinking of the headmaster of the agoge, one of the most revered and powerful of all Spartiates.

"No, the paidagogos. I was told all the wealthy men here in Athens have them: slaves that look after their school-aged boys. You know, escort them places, carry their things for them, recite the *Iliad* to them, and the like."

"Did you meet the man?"

"Yes. He's almost blind and just sits about."

"May I meet him?"

"I don't see why not. Shall I fetch him for you?"

"I'll come with you."

Mantiklos shrugged, although he knew perfectly well it would cause a minor sensation. In the short time he had been here, it had become obvious that Athenian gentlemen never entered the slaves' quarters. Leonidas had to duck to get through the kitchen doorway; and the sight of him, freshly bathed and in a fresh chiton, made one of the kitchen maids shriek. A ripple of agitation swept the room, and then a better-dressed middle-aged man rushed over, asking what the "honored guest" was looking for. When Leonidas said he was seeking the paidagogos, everyone turned and stared at a man sitting in the back of the kitchen, holding a walking stick between his knees. They called to him. He lifted his head and looked about, bewildered. "What? What?"

"What do you want with him, sir?" the officious housemaster asked.

"I would like to talk with him."

"Please, sir, make yourself comfortable in the courtyard. I will send him to you."

Leonidas was content to comply. The kitchen was smoky and humid. He was glad to retreat into the courtyard, cramped and cluttered as it was. Here he settled onto the rim of the well with Mantiklos beside him.

Euryleon, coming out of the baths, spotted him there and came over. "What do we do now?"

"I want to meet an Athenian schoolmaster."

Euryleon looked at him as if he were mad. "Didn't you get enough schooling in the agoge?"

Leonidas just laughed; but then he stood out of respect for the older man, who was tapping his way forward across the cobbles, clearly blind.

"Here, father." Leonidas went forward and took his elbow.

The slave started and looked up with cloudy eyes that tried to focus on Leonidas. "Where are you from, young man? Why do you call me father?" For a moment he seemed to hope that Leonidas had come from his home, from Thespiae. Perhaps he hoped he was the son of some distant and forgotten liaison, or a nephew or other relative, someone who had come to set him free.

"Lacedaemon," Leonidas answered him.

At once the blind man deflated and looked down. "Then why— why did you call me 'father'?"

"We are taught to honor all older men," Leonidas explained, embarrassed that his habitual speech had unnecessarily aroused false hopes. To distract the old man, he added, "I was told you once had a school of your own and are a learned man."

The blind man sighed deeply. "Once had. Once had." He shook his head as he let Leonidas lead him to the bench on which the woman had been spinning earlier. The sun had already shifted, and the bench was now in the shade. Then the man nodded, "Yes, young man, I once had a school. I came to Athens, you see, because I had been told that in Athens they honor learning over all things, and I thought I would have many rich pupils eager to learn."

"And isn't that what you found?"

He sighed again. "I wanted to teach algebra and geometry, but the young men of Athens have no time for such things. They want only to learn how to make clever speeches so they can deceive their fellow citizens, or how to wrestle and run to win the admiration of lovers, who will spoil them with gifts. No one here is interested in abstract learning."

"You should have come to Sparta," Leonidas told him, only half in jest.

"Do you learn anything there at all—besides how to kill, I mean?"

Leonidas was taken aback by the slur, and he looked over at Euryleon a little helplessly. Then he said simply to the old man, "Test me any way you like."

The old teacher squinted up at him. "What are the angles of an equilateral triangle?"

"Sixty degrees."

The teacher started. "How do you know that?"

"I told you I went to the Spartan agoge. Geometry is considered one of the most important sciences."

"And do you know your Homer as well?"

"*Now the Trojans came on with clamor and shouting, like wildfowl, at daybreak, bringing the baleful battle to them. But the Achaean men went silently, breathing valor, stubbornly minded each in his heart to stand by the others.*" Leonidas quoted the first passage that came to mind, for he had memorized many.

The old teacher looked astonished, but then frowned and admonished, "You have edited that to suit your Spartan love of brevity. But you have the essence right. And can you sing as well?"

"Don't ask!" Euryleon protested. "Once he starts, he doesn't stop!"

"And you learned it all at the Spartan agoge?" the Thespian asked, obviously still skeptical.

"Yes, and much more, as Lychos here can attest." Leonidas smiled at Lychos, who was limping toward them with his tortured gait. "This is a former schoolmaster and tutor, I presume, to Kallixenos."

Lychos sat on the other side of the Thespian slave. "What am I to attest?" he asked, amused.

"This young man knows his geometry and his Homer and he can sing, and he claims he knows much more as well."

"Indeed, he knows how to kill wild boar and how to bind up wounds, and how to make a fire with only a flint."

"And how to steal," Kallixenos added, joining the crowd. "It's time to go to Assembly. We want to be near the front where we can see what's happening. They need six thousand citizens for a quorum. You can't see anything at the back of such a crowd. Have you ordered your litter?" he asked Lychos.

The latter shook his head. "I'm not coming. I don't like crowds."

Kallixenos shrugged and swept toward the gate in an apparent hurry. Leonidas stood and thanked the Thespian scholar for speaking with him. "Is there anything you would like from the city? I am going to the agora."

"You don't mean to steal it?" the blind slave asked, bewildered by Kallixenos' remark.

"No, that was a poor joke. I am Prince Leonidas of Sparta, and can afford to buy you anything you wish."

It was a foolish thing to say, and punishment came instantly. The old teacher went down awkwardly onto his knees right there in the cobbled courtyard and begged, "Buy me my freedom and take me back with you to Sparta. I wish to see the school that produced you and offer my services to the schoolmaster."

Euryleon made a face behind the old teacher's back; and Leonidas, embarrassed, hastened to help the man back to his feet, saying vaguely that he would see what he could do.

As soon as they were out of hearing, Euryleon protested, "You and your bragging! We can't take that old man back with us. He can't walk that far, and the Paidonomos will laugh himself sick at the sight of him."

"If you hadn't told Kallixenos that we learn how to steal in the agoge, he wouldn't have provoked me!" Leonidas defended himself; then they hurried to catch up with Kallixenos.

They soon found themselves in a flood of people, all moving in the direction of the agora. The atmosphere was more festive than tense, but the press of people was uncomfortable. Leonidas and Euryleon had never been in such a crowd before, even at Olympia. Furthermore, hawkers of food, drink, and various other items of greater or lesser utility took advantage of the crowd to try to push their wares. They held things right under the nose of any prospective customer, and Kallixenos warned his guests to watch their purses: "The crowd is full of pickpockets!"

It was a rowdy crowd, too, reminiscent of the Athenians at Olympia, and everyone seemed to be talking at once. Spartan Assemblies were usually orderly affairs. Only when a subject was hotly debated could the crowd start to get loud and sometimes aggressive, but rarely disorderly. Here, even before anything started, everyone was arguing with everyone else, or so it seemed.

The other thing that struck Leonidas was the diversity of the citizens. In Sparta the young men always attended Assembly in armor, and most of the reservists came in Spartan scarlet. They were all soldiers, and they looked like it. Only very old men sometimes came in long chitons. In Athens the crowd came in everything: from the expensive, brightly-decorated robes of Kallixenos and his father to the half-chitons of the smiths and tanners, who arrived with naked torsos still smelling of their shops.

"Are those men citizens?" Leonidas asked with a nod to a cluster of burly men with dirty hands, naked feet, and long, tangled beards hanging to their chests. They looked more barbarian than Greek to Leonidas, used as he was to the cropped hair of young men and the braids and trimmed beards of reservists.

"Disgusting, isn't it?" Kallixenos retorted. "You see, men of substance with country estates often can't make it into the city for an Assembly. The shopkeepers and craftsmen and off-duty sailors, in contrast, have no trouble attending, so they dominate the crowd. It is their votes that one has to secure if one wants to control public policy."

Leonidas considered the crowd again. The craftsmen were in a clear majority of the assembled citizens. Large as the crowd seemed when crammed into the narrow streets, it wasn't really larger than a full Spartan Assembly. On the other hand, that meant only about one-fifth of Athens' citizens were actually attending. A Spartan Assembly usually drew eighty to ninety per cent of her citizens, with only the ill, infirm, or those away on their distant estates or on garrison duty absent.

The ostracism debate itself was also an unruly affair, with men shouting insults and demanding the expulsion of one man or another. Theoretically, one person from each of Athens' ten tribes could be nominated, Kallixenos explained, but at this time there were only two names "in contention" for the dishonor of expulsion. Rather as in a sporting event, the tension between the two factions grew steadily, infecting even those, like Leonidas, who did not have a stake in the outcome.

Kallixenos, despite his pretense the previous evening of finding everything so amusing, was obviously displeased with the outcome. His father's friend had been ostracized and would now have to leave Athens for ten years. "The mood is getting worse every day," he complained. "You can look after yourselves for a bit, can't you? I want to talk to a friend."

Leonidas and Euryleon were not unhappy to lose Kallixenos' company, and they contentedly wandered around the commercial center of the city. They admired the diversity and quality of the wares offered for sale. They also visited the potters' quarter to see the famed Athenian ceramic painters at work. When they wearied of that, they made their way back to their host's home and found Kallixenos awaiting them impatiently. He was going to his gymnasium and had been told by his father to take them along.

Although glad of the opportunity to exercise, Leonidas was aware of Kallixenos' resentment. He also felt badly for Lychos, who was again left behind. They rode to the gymnasium, which was located outside the city, the visitors each provided with a mount from their host's stables. Kallixenos set a fast pace at first and then slowed and fell in beside Leonidas. "How can you stand being around Lychos all the time? He depresses me."

"I am to blame for his condition."

"I thought you saved his life?"

"Such as it is. If I had come later, he would not have survived to suffer."

"I hate being surrounded by cripples and ugly things. I love beauty; which, incidentally, you will be privileged to experience in unusual measure tonight. The host of tonight's symposium has secured the attendance of Therapne. You can't know what an honor that is! She is probably the most expensive and coveted hetaera in all Athens at the moment. She belongs to Melanthius—you know, the man who is so anxious to go to war with Persia? He only lends her out to people he wants to influence, so you must be grateful to our host's father for being on the list of people Melanthius wants to befriend."

Leonidas nodded.

Kallixenos laughed. "You don't look like you're impressed, but you will change your mind once you've seen her!" He put his heels to his horse and sprinted away.

"Maybe we shouldn't go to this symposium tonight, if there are going to be whores at it," Euryleon suggested.

Leonidas thought about it. "I think we should go, but stay sober."

Euryleon made a face at him; then they picked up the pace to catch up with Kallixenos.

Gymnasia were much the same all over Greece, and the two Spartans easily oriented themselves. They stripped, oiled, and went out on the track for some running. Afterward they splashed themselves down under the fountains, and then sat in the shade of the stoa for a bit, listening to a man lecture on medicine. The speaker approached the subject from a much more theoretical standpoint than the Spartans were used to. He talked about the need to ensure the proper balance among the elements of fire, water, earth, and air, and argued that imbalance led to poor health. Leonidas found this far more difficult to comprehend than what he had learned as boy about what individual plants did for the human body. Meanwhile, Kallixenos was talking and laughing with friends.

They noticed a surprising number of older men standing about, fully dressed, in the shade of a second stoa opening onto a second complex of sports fields. These men evidently had no intention of engaging in any kind of sport; and, curious, Leonidas and Euryleon went over to see what they were looking at. They found that the second complex was reserved for boys. These came with their slave escorts and trainers. It was soon obvious from the comments around them that the interest of the spectators was largely erotic.

"They act like the older agoge cohorts watching the girls," Euryleon remarked.

"They don't *have* any girls' races or wrestling, so they have little choice," Leonidas observed.

"But they have so many whores," Euryleon protested.

"You can't talk to women," Kallixenos explained, coming up behind them unexpectedly and hanging a hand on the shoulder of each. "Except for the rare ones like Therapne, they don't have a brain in their heads, so boys are more fun. You play with them, get a little sexual relief, and then you can chat with them, teach them silly ditties or show them tricks, and ..." He shrugged, his eyes hungrily fixed on a laughing boy with fair hair.

"What about your wife?" Leonidas asked.

Kallixenos looked at him startled. "What about her?"

"Can't you talk to her?"

"I don't know. I've never tried. Why should I? She's about to provide me with an heir—at least I hope it won't be a girl. What more is a wife for? Surely you don't talk to your wife?"

"I would, if I had one."

Kallixenos just laughed at him. "You may know about war, Leonidas of Sparta, but you know nothing about women."

"It would seem I know more than you, since I *have* spoken to many."

Kallixenos raised his eyebrows in obvious disbelief. "Seriously?"

"Seriously. My stepmother was a student of Pythagoras and is literate in the language of the Egyptians as well as in Greek."

Kallixenos stared at him skeptically, then shrugged. "The women in Sparta must be different. Here they are all illiterate and dumb as sheep. Believe me, my wife hardly knows how to add two and two together, and I don't think I've ever heard her say a whole sentence at a time. Therapne is an exception. Come, we should go to the baths to be ready for tonight."

———

It was well after dark before the party of young men set out for the symposium. Lychos was perfumed, carefully coifed and dressed, while Kallixenos had never looked better. His hair had apparently been curled and he gleamed with scented oil. He wore wide, elaborately embossed bracelets on both his wrists, and the gold embroidery on his chiton glittered in the light of the torches. Four slaves of their host accompanied them to clear the way for Lychos' litter and provide lighting, but the Spartan attendants had been dismissed to seek their own pleasure.

On arrival the young men were ushered into the andron and provided with wreaths of myrtle. Some of the guests were already there, and they welcomed Kallixenos loudly, demanding introductions to his "Spartan friends." Two men were sharing their couches, one with a youth of fourteen or fifteen, the other with a much younger boy. Leonidas instantly felt sorry for the little boy, who looked frightened and tense despite the reassuring petting of his companion. The latter stroked the boy's shoulders and thighs and whispered repeatedly in his ear.

The food again was exquisite: fresh plaice in coriander crust, chicken stuffed with olives and grapes, savory cheese cakes, and honeyed mushrooms. It was served on the finest of Attic pottery, but this time the scenes depicted meticulously and artistically in the bowls and on drinking cups were explicitly pornographic. There were also girls playing the aulos in the background. Unlike the night before, when the conversation had been more serious, tonight it was fast and witty—except for the little boy, who sat silently with his eyes down.

When they had had their fill of the food, the tables were rolled away, and slaves quickly swept up anything that had fallen on the floor. Water and linens were brought for the guests to wash their hands. Garlands of fresh flowers were passed around to one and all, and the host offered a libation to the Gods. Finally a krater of wine was rolled in, and slaves went from couch to couch, pouring for the guests.

Leonidas covered his kylix with his hand and insisted firmly, "No, we are drinking water."

"Only water?"

"Only water."

"Why?" the others wanted to know, astonished.

Kallixenos answered for him: "It is to be a contest of who is most nimble at the end of the evening: stone-sober Spartans or drunken Athenians!"

"Aha!" His friends cheered and clapped and called for more wine so they could "start competing."

Meanwhile, someone brought out a lyre and played on it a bit. When finished, he passed it to the young man on his left, who in turn played and passed it on. They were all very good at it. Leonidas declined when his turn came, and the hosts graciously refrained from either pressing him or making derogatory comments. Euryleon, too, declined the lyre, but he struck up the duet of Kastor and Polydeukes when his turn came, and Leonidas with a laugh had to join in. The duet was well received, as both young men sang well, and Euryleon's tenor blended well with Leonidas' bass. When they had all finished performing, someone asked about Therapne; but their host shrugged and assured his friends, "Melanthius promised she would come."

They started a game of tossing wine at one another from their kylixes, a highly skilled undertaking that usually succeeded only in splashing wine on the floor and splattering the target with stray drops. Their host, however, produced great gusts of laughter when he landed a cup full in the face of the little boy. While the target was left gasping and wiping at the wine that dripped off his face, soaking the front of his expensive and now ruined chiton, the others roared with delighted laughter. Then several men at once started urging the little boy to remove his wet, spoiled clothes "so we can admire you fully."

The little boy clutched his stained and dripping chiton in obvious distress, tears brimming in his eyes; but his lover, more responsive to the urgings of his friends than to the misery of his "beloved," whispered in the boy's ear as he shoved the chiton off his shoulders.

Leonidas couldn't bear watching and looked away. Kallixenos caught his eye and remarked, "See what I mean about being nimble when we drink?"

"I'd be more impressed if your friend landed a spear with the same accuracy," Leonidas retorted, trying to keep his anger in check. Anger is as dangerous as drink, he reminded himself.

"Do you think we can't?" Kallixenos countered, his eyes glinting with hostility to match Leonidas' own. "Don't underestimate us," he warned.

An eruption of exclamations distracted them. In the doorway was a female figure completely swathed in a sober, dark gown and shrouded in heavy black shawls. She paused dramatically for a moment, then let these outer garments drop to reveal a sky-blue silk himation with red trim. On her arms were gold bracelets, while her throat was completely encased in the metal, and a gold tiara glittered against her black hair. Even her sandals appeared to be of gold—at least they glittered with gold decorations. As she stepped deeper into the room, she shed her himation, revealing a golden gauze gown so transparent that it revealed more than covered the body underneath. It was the kind of body to inflame any man's loins: heavy on top, slender in the waist, and gently rounded at the belly and hips over long, graceful legs. She stood in the middle of the room, smiling from one man to the next, and they cheered and clapped and toasted her. "Incomparable Therapne!" "Aphrodite's rival!" "Helen's reincarnation!"

When her painted eyes fell on Leonidas, she stopped and cocked her head. Leonidas felt his pulse race. She walked straight toward him, and his mouth went dry. But then she reached out to stroke his head like a hound, and Leonidas instinctively pulled back sharply. The room hooted in derision. Therapne silenced them with an imperative gesture of her hand as she addressed Leonidas. "You are no puppy, Spartan. What is your name?"

"Leonidas."

"And well it suits you! A lion among the pampered lap dogs." She tossed the insult casually over her shoulder, and the others groaned or protested, but she ignored them. "May I join you?" She prepared to recline upon his couch.

Leonidas shook his head. "I don't think that would be in your master's interests."

"Sorry?" She raised her well-traced eyebrows.

"As I am a stranger, your owner will have no particular benefit from my friendship." Leonidas was testing her. He was hoping she had chosen him for himself, but he was very wary of being used. He was also aware that sexual desire could be as enslaving and as humiliating as drunkenness.

"On the contrary: to a man intent on war, no ally could be of greater value than Sparta."

It was not the answer he had hoped for but now that he knew she was only acting on the orders of her master, he found it easier to resist. "I am only a Spartan Peer."

"Funny. I was told you were a Spartan prince, the brother of Cleomenes, whom my master would be *most* interested in befriending."

"Then I am the last man you wish to please, for my brother heeds me not at all."

"Why ever should he ignore such a splendid brother?" she teased, smiling at him intimately.

Leonidas laughed but retorted, "It is a long story. Do your master's bidding with someone else."

Several others at once started clamoring for her to come to them, and Therapne shrugged and turned to smile at them; but Kallixenos said for all to hear, "You are a fool or a coward, Leonidas. You could have enjoyed her first and *then* told her she was barking up the wrong tree. What *true* man turns away pleasure like that when it comes crawling to him!"

"What is the pleasure in being another man's pawn?"

"Don't be so puritanical! What pleasure is more basic or universal than sexual satisfaction?" Kallixenos challenged him.

"Satisfaction of the loins is animal, while the joys of love cannot be purchased."

Kallixenos looked at him, uncomprehending; but Therapne spun around and, clapping her hands slowly, declared: "And the lion has claws! Well said, Leonidas!" She went toward him again, her hips swaying provocatively and her eyes fixed on him. "But tell me, if you scorn the pleasure I offer you, where *do* you take your pleasure? Have you a mistress to whom you have sworn fidelity? Or is there some boy who has turned your head?" Her lips curled in a sneer and her eyes fell contemptuously on the little boy, who sat naked on his lover's couch, blushing bright red with natural shame.

"Mine is the pleasure of the sun breaking over Taygetos after a long, chilly night on watch; the pleasure of diving into the cool waters of the Eurotas after a morning in the dust and sweat of the drill fields; the taste of my helot's apple tarts; or the sight of my dog, bursting with pride, when she brings me a stolen duck."

Kallixenos broke out laughing. "You are going to give your countrymen a reputation for garrulousness with answers like that."

Leonidas looked down, embarrassed and ashamed of himself. He had indeed said too much.

Therapne reached out and stroked his thigh, smiling at him. "Are you sure?"

"You can see for yourself you have aroused me, but I still prefer Beggar with her stolen duck," Leonidas retorted stubbornly, lifting his chin and staring her in the eye. His loins were full to bursting, and he was acutely aware of wasting his youth as a bachelor, but his obstinate streak had taken over. He was full of sexual energy and resented the fact that he had no place to expend it in his current lifestyle, but he hated even more the feeling of being manipulated. These Athenians wanted to see him turned into a mere animal, panting and gasping in his desperation to satisfy the hunger of his loins.

The Athenians protested that he had no right to insult such a magnificent example of womanhood, while the hetaera stared down at Leonidas with narrowed eyes, now full of hatred because she felt insulted. "I came here to make a friend, but you have made an enemy. Are you so certain that was in your city's interests?"

"I am certain that my city cannot be bought any more than I can. If Sparta fights the Persians, it will be in her own interests and not those of Athens or your master."

"We shall see!" she told him, and went at once to the host's open arms. She lay on his couch and rolled him onto his back to kiss him in front of all of them. This seemed to be a signal for the flute girls to sidle up to the other couches with their painted smiles and practiced gestures, while the little boy was now all but smothered by his lover.

Leonidas could take no more. He swung his feet down and slipped on his sandals.

Euryleon looked over at him in protest. "Do we have to go *already*?"

"Stay if you like. I am leaving."

To his surprise, Lychos also slipped from his couch and, with a gasp of pain, bent to tie his sandals. Leonidas waited for him, then took his arm to help him out into the courtyard.

They stood side by side in the cool night air. A breeze had sprung up from somewhere and rustled the few leaves of a scrawny tree, struggling for life in the cobbled yard. "Thank you," Lychos whispered.

Leonidas looked over at him, unsure what he meant.

"I hate it, too. And Kallixenos knows it. But I—I have never had the courage to say 'no.'" He fell silent and then admitted, "My father makes me go. He wants me to 'enjoy myself with men of my own age and class.' There is so much I can't do anymore, so he feels it is all the more important that I do what I can—like drink and whore. But you are right! There is more pleasure in a sunset over the Aegean or running before a brisk breeze on a rolling swell or in a starry night! Why, even the sounds of the springs and lines creaking as a ship rises and falls at her berth in port on a cool, dark night like this is more magnificent than a dozen Therapnes! Oh, that we could go down to the *Heron* and just lie on her deck under the stars!"

Leonidas thought about it a moment. He certainly had no desire to return to the cramped, stuffy room under the eaves where he had sweated through the previous night. The thought of a night in the open on the warm deck of a ship was much more appealing. "Why don't we?"

"We'd have to rouse my litter slaves, and they can be so subtly resentful and will tell my father."

"I can carry you. Climb on my back." Leonidas went down on his heels and offered his back to Lychos.

Lychos hesitated only a moment; then he wrapped his arms around Leonidas' neck and his feet around his waist. Leonidas stood. "You have to tell me the way."

"I could find my way to the sea if my eyes were blind and ears deaf. Here! To the right!"

———

They caused a small commotion when they reached the ship, and at first the helmsman was angry. He insisted on sending a crewman to tell Archilochos where his son was; but eventually the crew calmed down and went back to sleep, while Leonidas and Lychos settled on the deck between the steering oars. Leonidas accepted wine in his water, and they talked while the stars turned slowly overhead.

"You see what a favor you did me that day by Acrocorinth?" Lychos pressed Leonidas.

The latter shook his head.

"I was on my way to becoming just like Kallixenos. Indeed, I admired him and tried to imitate him. I looked up to him so much that I allowed him to be my lover, when I was younger—a sporadic affair that lasted almost until I was sixteen. I was still under his spell when the boar got me." Leonidas stirred uneasily, and Lychos looked over at him. "Did you never have a lover? A man you let use your body any way he pleased because you thought he was the most wonderful thing in the world?"

Leonidas sensed it was almost rude to tell the truth, but he was poor at lying. "No. Sparta is different."

"So everyone says," Lychos agreed, staring at the stars. "One day maybe I will be able to visit there."

"You are welcome any time. You can stay at my kleros, and although our cooking is not so sophisticated as here, my housekeeper is an excellent cook."

"I love simple food. When sailing, we usually catch fish during the day and grill it at night over an open fire. It is better that way than in any sauce or fancy crust." They both reflected on this for a moment, and then Lychos continued, "You aren't married yet, are you?"

That was a sore subject, particularly since Brotus had married for a second time before heading for Olympia. Leonidas shrugged and answered, "No more than you."

"My father has arranged it," Lychos admitted, not looking at Leonidas. "Most Corinthians don't marry until they are in their thirties, but he is afraid I won't live that long and is desperate for an heir. The wedding was to take place after the Games, but we postponed it when you accepted our invitation."

Leonidas at once felt guilty. "I'm sorry to have disrupted your plans. Why didn't you say something? We could—"

"I don't mind the postponement," Lychos assured him. "I wouldn't mind waiting for years. I'd rather not marry at all."

Leonidas didn't understand. "Why?"

Lychos shrugged, clutched his knees, and looked at the stars.

"Don't you like your bride?" Leonidas ventured.

Lychos shrugged again. "I've only met her once. At the betrothal. She seems nice … It must have been terrible for her when she learned her father was giving her to a cripple."

Leonidas thought about that a moment, impressed that Lychos could see things from the girl's perspective, but he still couldn't understand Lychos' reluctance to marry. "But?"

"It seems like a lot of responsibility," Lychos admitted. "I'll be responsible not just for her well-being but for her reputation and her happiness."

"I don't think Kallixenos sees marriage that way," Leonidas remarked dryly, his disapproval obvious.

"No," Lychos agreed. "But I don't want to be like him. Why aren't you married?" Lychos asked.

"I'm still on active service and have to live in barracks," Leonidas answered, hoping Lychos had not heard that many Spartiates married anyway.

"That sounds horrible," Lychos admitted candidly.

Leonidas thought about it. "You'll laugh, but in a way it makes me enjoy the rest of life more."

Lychos laughed, but remarked, "Now, perhaps, you understand about my pain! It is horrible, but it reminds me that I am alive. And without it, if I were dead, I would not be sitting on this warm deck with a cooling breeze and my first real friend beside me."

"I'm honored. But what of Chambias?"

"Chambias?" Lychos looked up at the stars. "Chambias has always been my friend because our fathers want it; but, you see, tonight he would have been like the Athenians—"

"And Euryleon!" Leonidas snorted.

"Yes, and Euryleon. He would have justified staying and drinking until he couldn't walk in a straight line and had to vomit in the street while slaves guided him home. That's what they're all doing now, you know? They will drink until they can't see straight or stand upright, and then they will stagger home, feeling miserable but telling themselves they are 'real men.' What does being pissing drunk have to do with manhood? I don't understand it."

Leonidas didn't understand it either, so they were comfortably silent together until Lychos remarked, "When Kallixenos was my lover, he often hurt me. He knew he was doing it, yet he did it intentionally—just to see how far he could go, to test just how great my love for him was."

"Then Kallixenos is more than an ass, he is a bastard."

"He will be a very powerful bastard," Lychos reflected. "He is the kind of man who would be a tyrant if he could be."

"You know that the sexual misuse of a child, male or female, is against our laws, don't you?" Leonidas asked.

"And do all Spartans live by your laws?"

"Of course not. There are as many cruel and selfish men in Sparta as anywhere; but at least they have to do it in secret and fear the scorn of their neighbors and officers if they are discovered. If a child's parents find out, for example, they can demand terrible punishment."

Lychos thought about that and nodded. "You know, it sometimes seems as if you Spartans live your whole lives in fear of your neighbors and officers. You have so little chance to be yourselves, for better or for worse. You must all wear the same clothes. You even have to wear your hair and beards the same way! And you must behave in set ways and follow the same profession."

Leonidas thought about this carefully, because there had been times when he had resented all these things; but he asked back, "Is it really all that different in Corinth and Athens? Don't potters' sons become potters and tickers' sons tinkers? And it seems to me the dictates of fashion are as stringent as our traditions.

"On the whole, yes, but there is no compulsion about it. I think what horrifies outsiders about Sparta is that it is all enforced by law and custom and is so, well, brutal."

"But it was Kallixenos who hurt you," Leonidas pointed out. "And Spartans aren't really all the same. In fact, the reasoning behind us all having a kleros of the same size and all dressing in the same manner is that then the real differences—those of character rather than mere wealth or station—are more evident. On the surface, Kallixenos is a well-educated, well-mannered young man. I imagine that his good clothes and good looks deceive many about his true nature."

"Yes," Lychos admitted; "but so do your clothes and looks deceive, Leonidas. When we see you, muscular and tanned and standing straight as a spear, we see only a stupid Spartan hoplite, but you are far more subtle and complex than you appear to be."

"I suppose we all are," Leonidas concluded. They left it at that and drifted off to sleep.

———

They were back in Athens by midmorning. As on the day before, the household had been awake for hours, but the masters were nowhere to be seen. The kitchens were already steaming and busy with the preparation of the evening meal, and Leonidas was reminded of the old schoolmaster he had met the day before. He asked Lychos what he thought of the whole situation. "I can't take him with us. Euryleon and I will walk back to Sparta. Could he travel with one of your father's freighters?"

"I'm sure it could be arranged, if that is what you want. Now I'd better go find my father and reassure him I am all right." Lychos went deeper into the house; and Leonidas mounted the stairs up to the attic room, where he found Euryleon sprawled across his bed, snoring. He was half dressed, and Leonidas, in disgust, shook him hard. "Wake up, you drunken fool!"

Euryleon started out of a deep sleep, sat up sharply in alarm at the rude awakening, and then groaned and grabbed his head. "By all the Gods! What have they done to me?" His breath stank of both wine and vomit.

"Nobody did anything to you!" Leonidas answered in disgust. "You did it to yourself!"

"Don't remind me!" he moaned and then cried in alarm, "Help! I'm going to be sick!" He clapped his hands over his mouth and his belly heaved, but he swallowed it down. Sweat glistened on his forehead.

"Mantiklos! Alkios!" Leonidas called for the two helots.

They came stumbling in, disheveled and rubbing sleep from their eyes.

Euryleon was moaning again. "I think I'm going to die."

"Stop it!" Leonidas ordered. Then, turning to the two helots, "Go fetch water and a bowl he can be sick in!"

Euryleon was swaying in agony. "My head feels like it's going to fall off!"

"Well, it isn't much use to you, so it wouldn't be much of a loss," Leonidas reasoned.

"Don't shout at me so!" Euryleon pleaded, although Leonidas had not raised his voice. "You don't know what this is like!"

"What, in the name of Kastor, happened last night after I was gone?" Leonidas wanted to know.

"I don't remember!" Euryleon whimpered, shaking his head. "I don't remember a thing!"

———

It took them half an hour to get Euryleon on his feet and down to the baths and another half-hour, after he'd vomited a couple of times, to clean him up. Alkios brought him dry bread from the kitchen to settle his stomach, and he slowly started to feel better. Leonidas insisted on their going to the gymnasium. Euryleon was in no state to argue. Docilely he followed along behind his former eirene and current section leader. They went in silence, surrounded by the cacophony of the great city.

Leonidas let his eyes sweep along the shops, spilling their wares into the streets almost like refuse. Real refuse lay underfoot, making the pavement slippery and treacherous. Slaves and craftsmen haggled and bickered loudly all around them. People pushed and jostled their way forward, shoving aside the old and the infirm without so much as an apology. More than once Euryleon and Leonidas had to jump out of the way of someone riding recklessly through the narrow streets. Apparently the very affluence that enabled a man to keep a horse entitled him to ride down anyone in his way. There were beggars, too, cripples and old crones pleading for their "orphaned" children. Leonidas supposed that not everything they said was true, but surely no one went begging for the fun of it? There was, in short, desperate poverty living beside the glorious wealth of the men like their host and in the shadow of the gaudy acropolis.

Leonidas felt as if he had gorged himself no less than Euryleon had; he had gorged himself on new impressions, sights and smells and sounds. He looked up toward the acropolis, and it had lost its splendor for him.

"I think it's time we went home," he told Euryleon.

His friend stopped. "You don't want to go to the gymnasium?"

"I mean, home to Sparta. We'll go to the gymnasium now, but tomorrow we should start for home."

Euryleon nodded and they continued.

Beyond the city walls the air was better and there was less congestion, although the many carts and wagons turned up the dust badly. The two Spartans left the road to walk beside it. They stopped for water at one of the many fountain houses, and reached the gymnasium to find it almost empty. It was still before noon, too early for most Athenians.

It was only on the way back from the gymnasium that Euryleon remarked out of nowhere, "She said women can't enjoy sex. She said there was nothing for them to enjoy."

"What are you talking about?"

"The girl last night."

"I thought you said you couldn't remember."

"I can't—or not much of it. But there was this girl. I guess she was one of the flute girls."

"And she said she didn't enjoy sex? If you believe that, you'll believe anything!" Leonidas scoffed.

"But that's just it, Leo. She didn't. You could see. Her face was just painted on and her eyes ... they were ..." Euryleon was frowning, looking for the right words. He decided: "They were like the eyes of the fish they feed us all the time here. There was no life left in them at all. She let anyone do anything they wanted to her, even the most disgusting and humiliating things; and she endured it all from anyone and everyone without the slightest sign of repugnance or even shame, but without a flicker of pleasure, either. It was horrible."

Leonidas looked at his friend, but Euryleon wouldn't meet his eye. He was looking down at the dusty road, and he looked tired and sad and much older than the day before. Leonidas nodded. "We'll go home tomorrow."

CHAPTER 12

THE STONE WALL

LAODICE WAS IN THE KITCHEN MAKING cheese. Since Polychares had brought home a wife this past winter, she spent more of her time cooking. Polychares' bride, Melissa, had taken over the bulk of the other household chores, the cleaning and washing and mending. Laodice was pleased with Melissa, and with her eldest son for his good sense in choosing her. She was not the prettiest of the helot maidens who had made eyes at her eldest son, but she was one of the brightest. More important, she was hard-working and ambitious. She had not married Polychares because he would inherit so much, but because she wanted to make even more of what he had. From the first day, she had offered to take over the heavy work so Laodice could concentrate on the cooking that brought them extra income. With the help of Laodice's two daughters, who at ten and eleven respectively were starting to be a real help in the household, Melissa kept the whole house and their clothes in the best order and sparkling clean.

Laodice glanced out the kitchen window toward the Eurotas, where she could hear the distant voices of her daughters. They sounded as if they were protesting something. Melissa was hard on them sometimes, chasing them around and scolding them to do their share of the work, but Laodice supposed she had been too lenient on them—just as she had been with Crius.

She still could not get over how well things had turned out for Crius. For a helot boy with crippled hands to end up living in the gymnasium and training with sons of Spartiates was a miracle of sorts. She knew Crius was happy—even if he missed her food and his former freedom. He complained, of course, that they were hard on him in the gymnasium and that the food was terrible. He complained that the boys hated him because he could beat them all, and that he had no friends. The trainer only used him as you would a whip or drum or any other device to make his real charges perform better. But Laodice did not listen to his complaints. Things could have been so much worse.

Nor was she frightened for her girls anymore. Again she looked out the window and tried to get a glimpse of them. After the incident with the poor girl who had been captured by the Argives, Laodice knew once and for all that Leonidas would never touch them. More than that, he would protect them from other male predators. The mere fact of being Leonidas' helots ensured that no other Spartiate, much less a helot, would dare take liberties with them. No one wanted to make an enemy of an Agiad prince, and people knew instinctively which Spartiates looked after their helots and which didn't.

Dangers still lurked, of course. The perioikoi lived enough outside the close-knit community not to necessarily know the unwritten laws. More seriously, many strangers passed along the road to Epidauros Limera. But at least here in the heartland of Lacedaemon, only a couple of miles from the drill fields of the Spartan army, they did not have to fear raids or pirates.

Laodice paused for a moment in her work to think again of Kleta, who had been ravished, tortured, and enslaved by the Argives. When she first saw her in the stocks, Laodice had been reminded of her own rape twenty years earlier. She had identified with Kleta. After Leonidas had paid for Kleta's release and brought her home, however, she came to realize how much worse Kleta's experience had been. This insight had helped Laodice put her own trauma into perspective. Laodice's humiliation had lasted only a single day. Melampus had sent for her one night after he had been drinking with "customers." They had each raped her in turn. She had gone home to her parents, and her father had rejected her. But already the next day, Pelopidas had declared his willingness to marry her, and the hurt and shame could be buried and ignored until grass grew over it. Kleta, in contrast, had been used by the Argives for two weeks—tortured, humiliated—and when her family turned her out, there had been no honorable man to marry her and let her return to a normal life.

It was good that Leonidas had found a place for her to work far away from here, Laodice concluded. Despite her pity for Kleta, it would not have been right to have her living in the same house with her daughters. At some point they might have become too curious about her past—or Kleta's bitterness might have infected them.

Laodice turned her attention back to the cheese, but her thoughts soon drifted to Pantes. She was also going to be strict with him, she told herself, pounding her cheese firmly. Pantes was doing very well with his carpentry, which also brought in extra income. In fact, he was doing so well that he had notions of renting a shop in the city and starting a carpentry workshop. He promised to still give his father half of what he earned until he reached age twenty-one, but he did not want to live at home. He said he would get more commissions and sell more if he had a shop in the city, and it was hard to deny this. But Laodice suspected that the real reason he wanted his own establishment was so he, too, could take a wife and start a family.

No girl would want to be the third woman in a household, subject to both Laodice and Melissa, but there were lots of girls eager to marry a young craftsman with his own shop and apartment. Yet how were his father and brother to get along here on the kleros without Pantes' strong back and hands? Pelopidas wasn't getting any younger, and they had more and more work to do as they reclaimed more of the land that had been left to go to seed in the years of vacancy. More land meant more income and security. It was more certain income than what Pantes could earn with his carpentry. Besides, Pantes was full of grandiose plans and dreams. His father and elder brother often had to curb his extravagance and bring him back to earth. Laodice feared that on his own, he would buy too much wood and spend too much time building pretty cabinets in the hope of finding a customer, rather than taking mundane commissions for the repair of wheels or the construction of workbenches. She feared, too, that a wife would not want to see 75 per cent of her husband's earnings go to someone else—50 per cent to Leonidas as the master, and then half of what was left to Pantes' parents. It was a recipe for trouble and strife.

The cheese finished, she set it in the pantry to cool and checked the milk supplies. They now had two cows and no less than six goats for milking. They were definitely prospering—better than she had ever dreamed when they left Messenia five years ago. No sooner had she thought this than she heard muffled shouting, and her heart missed a beat. She could tell instantly that something terrible had happened. She should have known better than to take the Gods' goodwill for granted. Nothing can go so well for very long!

She left the pantry and stepped into the kitchen yard, raising her head to decipher the direction from which the shouting came. She could make out the whinny of a horse, the barking of a dog, a man shouting, and what sounded like a girl screaming hysterically. Her daughters!

She ran through the kitchen and out the back door, but she had not gotten more than a few feet before she saw Pelopidas coming toward her with the limp body of a child in his arms and a dog yapping at his heels. Beyond him two horses were running around, one of them with a broken leg that swung loose inside the intact skin of his long lower leg while he threw himself around on three legs in panic and pain. The other horse was galloping around in alarm, whinnying in apparent sympathy with his wounded comrade. Polychares was running down from the upper barley field to catch the horses, leaving the oxen standing before the plow, while Melissa was trying to help another boy, who was sitting in the mud near the stone wall to the next estate. One of her own daughters was shrieking hysterically—apparently at the sight of the wounded horse.

"Chryse! Hush this instant!" Laodice called to her silly daughter, and started toward her husband. As he came closer, she realized that the body in his arms was not one of the boys of the agoge, as she'd assumed, but one of the Spartan girls. They wore the same short chitons and went barefoot like the boys, but no one shaved their hair, so this poor creature had a long red braid.

Recognition dawned. "It's little Gorgo!" she exclaimed, coming up beside her husband and falling in beside him. "What happened?"

"She was riding that big mare over there and tried to jump the stone wall. The mare hesitated, but she pressed it on. The mare refused at the last minute, throwing her over the wall and snapping her own leg in the process. The other mare refused, too, and ran away, dumping the other girl on the ground; but she isn't seriously hurt, just bruised."

They were back inside the courtyard, Gorgo's dog at their heels, and Laodice pointed for her husband to take Gorgo right up and into the master's bedroom. Although the master was rarely here, he did maintain a well-appointed room, and it was the only appropriate place for a Spartiate. Laodice stripped the pretty woven covering she had made herself off the bed, and her husband lay the little girl down on the clean linen sheets. As he did so, Gorgo groaned and stirred, to the relief of her rescuers.

"How badly is she hurt?" Laodice asked, as she stroked Gorgo's face and started her own inspection. She had clearly hit her head and was bleeding from the abrasion on her temple. She also appeared to have broken her collarbone, and her left hand was swelling up already.

"We must send for a surgeon," Pelopidas concluded. "I'll go at once."

Laodice nodded. "Tell Melissa to bring the other girl here, too, and fetch water and clean linens!"

Her husband nodded, and Laodice gently straightened Gorgo's chiton and stroked her forehead as she groaned again. Her dog pushed his way forward and tried to lick his mistress's face and hand. Laodice let him, knowing it was just concern and might actually help revive the patient. Inwardly, she was thinking that this is what came of girls being given too much license! The girl should never have been riding a horse, much less jumping stone walls! But that did not make Laodice less sympathetic to the little girl on the bed.

Gorgo's eyes fluttered open and she looked, frightened, into the dim room. "Where am I?" she asked, and then before anyone could answer, "What happened to Goldie? Is she all right?" She wanted to sit up.

Laodice held her down. "Lie still. I think you have broken several bones. We have sent for a surgeon."

Jason whined and raised his paw onto the bed, so that Gorgo turned and smiled at him. "Jason!" But when she went to pet him, she gasped and looked at her hand, only now becoming aware that several fingers were broken.

At that moment Melissa entered with the other girl. Gorgo saw her and called out at once, "Phaenna!"

Phaenna was dirty and disheveled from her fall, and she had a scraped and bleeding knee and elbow, but she was not really hurt. She ran forward to Gorgo. "Are you all right? I was afraid you were dead or had broken your neck!"

"What happened to Goldie and Shadow?" Gorgo countered.

Phaenna burst into tears. "Goldie broke her leg! It snapped clean in two. They'll have to kill her!" she sobbed.

Gorgo sat bolt upright, grimacing at the pain, but with her eyes wide with horror. "No! Oh, no! Poor Goldie!" And then another thought struck her. "My father will kill me!" she wailed, and tears started down her face—whether from pain, grief, or fear was unclear.

"I told you we shouldn't take a horse without his permission!" Phaenna retorted, and burst into a new flood of tears.

"And old Kallias will get in trouble, too!" Gorgo realized next. As her sense of guilt grew, her tears flowed stronger.

From this exchange, Laodice concluded that Gorgo had been riding without her father's permission and that probably a helot groom would be punished for giving in to the young mistress. Laodice disapproved of such behavior; but children were children all over the world, and she only hoped that this incident had taught Gorgo a lesson. At least she sounded distressed that someone else would get in trouble for her foolishness.

"Lie down, Gorgo," she urged firmly. "It is too late to change what you have done. Lie still while I see to your friend." Laodice took a linen towel from Melissa and dipped it into the cool jug of water. She set about cleaning off Phaenna's scrapes and sent Melissa for some pitch to spread over them. Then she wiped Gorgo's head wound clean and dried her tears, too; for Gorgo was lying flat on her back, crying silently.

Polychares put his head into the room. "Is she going to live?"

"Yes, yes. Just a few broken bones. Your father has gone for the surgeon."

"I've got both horses tethered out back, but one will have to be put down. The sooner the better. Who does she belong to?" The question was directed at his mother, but she could only turn to the two little girls. It was Phaenna who answered in a timid, frightened voice, "King Cleomenes."

Laodice caught her breath and looked over at Gorgo in alarm.

"He's at Delphi, and Mom doesn't understand anything about horses," Gorgo told the helots. "You'd better send for my grandmother, Chilonis."

———

The queen mother arrived in her chariot before the surgeon, because she lived closer. Polychares took her around at once to see the wounded horse. She gave permission for it to be put down, and promised she would inform the king that everything had been done properly. She then urged Polychares to get his oxen out of the orchard, where they had wandered after being left standing so long, and return to his work.

Only then did she go in search of her granddaughter. Laodice backed away a little nervously when the queen mother stood over the bed. "Well, you've ruined a perfectly good horse with your foolishness, child. A beautiful, fine creature with so much life in her is right now having her throat cut because you had less sense than she had. If you were a boy, I'd see you got sent to the pits for a good flogging!"

"I know," Gorgo sniffled miserably, rubbing away her tears with the back of her still-good hand as she squirmed on the bed in guilt.

"Your mother is likely to respond very badly, you know. She might take Shadow away—or kill poor Jason here!" Chilonis glanced at the dog sitting patiently beside his mistress. Jason lifted his ears and cocked his head at the mention of his name.

"Please, Grandma! Don't let her do that! Please! You can flog me if you like! Really, I'll go down to the pits just like the boys. I deserve it, I know—but don't let Mom take Shadow or Jason away! Please!"

"I'm afraid that is for your mother to decide."

"Then keep them safe at your kleros. Hide them from her! If she kills either of them, I'll kill myself!" Jason looked back and forth between his mistress and her grandmother, aware he was being talked about but not understanding what was being said. To be on the safe side, he thumped the floor with his tail.

Chilonis looked at the dog and knew she couldn't bear to have her daughter-in-law kill him, or the sweet little mare Shadow, either. "I will keep Jason for a few days, but you should know that Shadow pulled a tendon, by the look of things. I think she will recover, but she'll probably never be the same again."

"Oh, no!" Gorgo called out, and then with a gasp turned her head away and started crying miserably.

Chilonis couldn't bear the sight; she caved in. She reached out and patted Gorgo's shoulder, and then stroked her head. "Hush, child. I'm sure your uncle will let her stay here in the care of Pelopidas. You know he worked at your uncle's horse farm in Messenia, don't you? He's an excellent groom."

The surgeon arrived at last, and Chilonis took Phaenna out and drove her home to her own parents. By now Phaenna was very nervous about what would happen to her, and she explained to Chilonis that it was Gorgo's fault. Gorgo wanted to ride Goldie and jump the wall. Chilonis let her talk, and then assured her that she would not be held responsible at the palace. "What your own parents do with you is their affair." She then went to the Agiad palace to break the news to Gyrtias.

As was to be expected, her daughter-in-law reacted badly: first hysterical with worry, then angry about Gorgo's foolishness. She at once threatened to take her daughter's horse away from her, but Chilonis told her not to be silly. "A girl needs to be able to ride. It is better Gorgo keeps the mild-tempered Shadow than be tempted to take one of her father's horses again." Gyrtias next swore to punish the head groom, but Chilonis dissuaded her from this, too. "You will only incur my son's displeasure if you do that. He trusts the old man. Besides, the loss of such a fine mare will be punishment enough for him. Indeed, I doubt he will feel kindly toward Gorgo ever again. You know how he dotes on his four-legged charges."

This settled, she swung by Leonidas' kleros on the way home to see what the surgeon had to say. Gorgo was bandaged and patiently awaiting her punishment. Having told Gyrtias that Gorgo probably shouldn't be moved, Chilonis felt no guilt about loading her on her chariot and taking her home to her own kleros for the night.

It was dark now and they had to drive slowly, Jason trotting alongside them. The horses nickered as they smelled their own barn, and the household helots spilled out into the yard as Chilonis pulled up. "We were worrying, mistress!" they confessed.

It was quite chilly, and Gorgo was shivering in her grandmother's himation, the shock catching up with her now. Chilonis ushered her into the main hearth room and settled her on a bench beside the fire, while someone went to fetch her wine and a snack. Chilonis had her own meal brought to her here and sat beside Gorgo, with Jason at their feet. Gorgo impulsively laid her head on her grandmother's shoulder, unable to embrace her because of her broken collarbone, held rigidly in place by the bandages. "I'm so sorry, Grandma. I'll never forgive myself for killing Goldie. But, you know, the worst is, I'm afraid now—of jumping, I mean. I'll never be able to jump a stone wall after this."

Chilonis laid her arm gently over her granddaughter's shoulders and told her gently, "It is not a good thing to be afraid, Gorgo; but sometimes it is better to know your own limits than to take unnecessary risks just for the sake of proving one's courage."

The sound of Nikostratos returning from his syssitia brought Chilonis to her feet. She rose, flinging the end of her himation over her shoulder, as she went toward the hallway to greet him. Gorgo could hear their low voices as her grandmother told her husband all that had happened to her this day.

"But the girl's all right?" Nikostratos asked anxiously.

"Yes, yes. I think she's learned an important lesson."

They came into the hearth room arm in arm, and Gorgo got to her feet dutifully. Nikostratos came over to look down sternly at her, but then he smiled, and called for wine for all of them. "There must be something about that stone wall," he remarked with a laugh. "Leonidas damn near killed himself trying to jump it a few years back, too. Speaking of which, the Guard list was posted today and Leonidas wasn't on it."

"Were you expecting him to be?" Chilonis asked, surprised.

Nikostratos weighed his head from side to side. "Leonidas is an exceptional young man. He's not just brighter than most of his generation, he combines intelligence with justice and common sense."

"And since when were those criteria for the Guard?" Chilonis wanted to know. "I thought it was all about who was strongest, fastest, and best at drill?"

"Rare as it is, my dear, you are wrong. Theoretically at least, guardsmen are supposed to be able to think and act independently. They should be officer material. Which is why it disturbs me that Brotus was on the list."

"Brotus?" Chilonis exclaimed, incredulous. "But what has he ever done to deserve such an honor?"

"Nothing, unless you count winning the laurels in the boxing at Delphi during the last Pythian Games," Nikostratos pointed out. "The problem is that the selection is up to the three hippagretai; and a certain Orthryades, the same man who resigned from the army when he was passed over for lochagos, was appointed by the ephors to replace Akrotatos. Orthryades is very thick with Leotychidas, and they both seem to think that Brotus is a useful ally."

"I'm not following you," Chilonis admitted.

"Leotychidas and Brotus are heirs apparent to the two reigning kings, respectively. Brotus has never fully accepted that Cleomenes should be king, you know, and Leotychidas will seek to exploit his discontent to use against Demaratus."

"But Demaratus and Cleomenes hate each other."

"True, but don't underestimate Leotychidas' deviousness. What he lacks in raw intelligence, he makes up for in instinctive cleverness."

"What can he possibly gain by backing a dim-witted brute like Brotus?" Chilonis wanted to know.

Nikostratos lifted his shoulders in helpless acknowledgment of his own uncertainty. "I don't think there is any specific plan as yet, just a general sense that men opposed to the status quo need to band together and support one another. By the selection of Brotus for the Guard, his standing—and so his potential value to Leotychidas—has been increased. At least that's the best sense I can make of it.

"Changing the subject, we learned today in Council that Athens sent an embassy to the Persian Artaphernes, demanding that he send Hippias back to Athens in chains."

"Not very likely, I wouldn't think," Chilonis retorted rather flippantly.

"No chance at all," her husband replied, "but it is the kind of request that will provoke the Persian ire. They don't like 'insignificant little towns' making demands of them. And almost more importantly:

if the Athenian Assembly has been moved to make this demand, how do you think it will respond to a negative answer? I suspect they will get all worked up about it. A mob is generally more arrogant than even the vainest king."

"Does bad blood between Athens and Persia really affect us in any way?" Chilonis wanted to know.

"Maybe not," Nikostratos admitted with a shrug, but his expression belied his words.

"Any other news?" Chilonis pressed him. She loved this hour of the night, when Nikostratos told her all the gossip of the city.

"Oh, this will interest you: That Thespian slave Leonidas bought Leonidas bought in Athens really *is* a clever mathematician. Epidydes was skeptical at first, but he says that in three hours of interrogation this Thespian put all the agoge instructors to shame. Imagine letting such a learned man slide into slavery for the sake of a tax!" Nikostratos shook his head in bafflement and disapproval.

"Don't sound so smug. You know there are many good men here in Sparta who may lose their citizenship only for want of enough money to pay their syssitia fees."

"They may lose their citizenship, but they are not sold as slaves! This man was sold like some barbarian on the open market! He was lucky to be bought by a rich man as a paidagogos, but even then he had little chance to actually teach. He says the young man of the house showed him no respect, laughing at and playing tricks on him! You will want to talk to him yourself. Epidydes has agreed to give him a room at the agoge and let him teach the boys who are interested and sharp enough—not as part of the regular curriculum, but for those who show particular talent with numbers."

"Do you think we have many of those?" Chilonis asked skeptically.

"A score or so, no doubt. I certainly intend to see if he can teach *me* anything useful."

"Then I will tag along," Chilonis agreed, pleased at the thought of doing something together with her husband. They had found each other so late in life that it was important to share as much as possible, and what could be more satisfying than learning something new together?

"There is also a rumor going around that Asteropus—the Agiad permanent representative to Delphi—has taken a concubine. They are saying that he paid some poor farmer a handsome sum for his fourteen-year-old daughter, and she has now moved into his house to keep his hearth and warm his bed just as if she were his wife."

"Can he do that?"

"He couldn't get away with it in Sparta, but who is to censure him in Delphi? Other Greeks do this kind of thing all the time—sometimes keeping a concubine under the same roof as their legal wife."

Chilonis looked at him in skeptical disapproval.

"*Your* son is hardly the type to be too harsh on a man for keeping a mistress," Nikostratos pointed out.

Chilonis glanced a little nervously at Gorgo. With relief she saw that her granddaughter had drifted off to sleep, with her good arm over her panting dog. Chilonis smiled. "We'd best put her to bed, poor child."

Nikostratos went over and lifted Gorgo into his arms. He carried her to the bed at the back of the hearth room. Chilonis brought an extra blanket and tucked it around her, while Nikostratos brought a bowl of water and some old bread for Jason. The dog settled down for the night, while the older couple returned to the fire and sat holding hands as they talked late into the night of a dozen other things.

CHAPTER 13

MARRIAGE

USUALLY, THE PERIOIKOI STEWARD OF HIS estates sought out Leonidas at his barracks. Leonidas' days were filled with his duties as a citizen, and he devoted what free time he had to the activities he enjoyed: relaxing at the baths with his friends, practicing for the next festival with his chorus, bird hunting with Beggar, or riding out with his friends. Managing his estates was not on Leonidas' agenda. He had not learned about it while growing up a virtual orphan, nor was it necessary to learn after he came of age, since he had an excellent steward in the person of Phormio.

Phormio had been recommended to Leonidas by the steward of the royal Agiad estates. Even then, six years ago, Phormio had been an experienced administrator, no longer in his youth, but his previous position as one of the hired officials responsible for procurement for the Spartan army had not given him sufficient scope to unfold his talents. Leonidas, in contrast, had given him a free hand to manage his dispersed and diverse properties as he saw best. Leonidas' only requirement had been that his mess fees be paid punctually, and he could afford whatever was needed to fix up his kleros.

Phormio had soon proved his worth. Leonidas never lacked for money personally, and on his occasional visits to his scattered estates, he had noticed that all his properties were looking more prosperous, better maintained, and somehow happier. That was all Leonidas cared about; he was not very interested in the details of the accounts. But on this sunny late-spring day, Leonidas needed to talk to Phormio.

Phormio, like most wealthy perioikoi, preferred not to live in Sparta. Spartiates had their own, unique lifestyle, which the perioikoi did not share. Perioikoi served only two years in the army, providing Sparta with reliable contingents of auxiliary troops; but at the age of twenty-one, just when the Spartiates were starting on a forty-year career in the military, perioikoi took up whatever profession they wished to pursue. Nor did perioikoi have to belong to syssitia or refrain from the pleasures of neat wine, loose women, and conspicuous consumption. Perioikoi towns reflected these differences, with a large number of taverns and brightly painted houses and inhabitants.

Thus Leonidas had to ride to Bryseiai, west of Amyclae, to find Phormio. Bryseiai crouched at the foot of Taygetos, surrounded by flowering orchards at this time of year. Phormio's house was one of the largest in the little town, a sprawling, two-story structure with imported red tile roofs, complete with decorative corners that reared upward just as on the temples in Athens. Covered balconies ringed the upper story, and covered outdoor stairways led up to these directly from the street. The façade itself was freshly plastered and painted a bright white down to three feet above the pavement, then red-brown so that dirt splattered by passing vehicles would be less visible, while the window frames, doors, and shutters were painted a bright red.

Leonidas' arrival caused a minor stir; a slave boy took his horse while another rushed up the stairs to inform the master. Leonidas himself was ushered down a short but narrow hallway into an atrium paved with splendid mosaics in every color of the rainbow. The sun poured in, glinting on the water bubbling up from a central fountain set in a square pool. Around the pool were blooming potted plants, while the walls of the walkway around the atrium were painted with vivid scenes from the *Odyssey*. Because this house was newly built and decorated, to Leonidas it seemed more splendid than the royal palace in which he had grown up. It was certainly more pompously decorated than his own kleros.

Phormio emerged on a balcony overlooking the atrium and called down jovially to Leonidas. (Leonidas had never known the man to be anything but good-humored.) "What a surprise! Come up to my office!" Phormio gestured toward a stairway at the corner of the atrium.

Leonidas bounded up the stairs to be met at the top by his steward. Phormio was very fat by Spartan standards. His face was round under longish, curly hair, his shoulders were soft, his stomach extended, and he waddled more than walked; but his smile was heartwarming. "If you'd warned me," he admonished, smiling, "I could have fixed things up for you; but since you choose to take me by surprise, you will see me as I really am." From his tone, he was not the least flustered or ashamed. "Come this way." He led Leonidas into a spacious room faced with a long balcony looking toward the mountains, now in shade. There were cubbyholes for documents on one of the interior walls, and two scribes behind a long desk got to their feet at the sight of Leonidas, obviously more flustered than their master.

Phormio dismissed the scribes with a wave of his hand and indicated a leather sofa to Leonidas. "Wine? Water? Fruit?" he asked his guest.

"Water and something light would be nice," Leonidas confessed.

Phormio went back onto the balcony and called down, "Water and a light snack!"

Then he returned and seated himself expectantly opposite his employer. "I assume you had some urgent reason for honoring me with this visit," the steward concluded, still smiling. "How can I be of service?"

"When I was little, I had a nurse. A wet nurse, actually, because my mother was nearly fifty when I was born, and everyone assumed that caring for twins would be too much for her."

Phormio just nodded. He knew all this.

"The girl was dismissed as soon as I went to the agoge, and I've never seen her since. Yesterday, however, one of the laundresses from the palace stopped me on the street to tell me she is in desperate straits. There must be some way I can help her. She was always good to me."

"What did this laundress tell you exactly?"

"She said Dido had married and had two sons, but her husband died young and the boys didn't turn out well. One, she said, had gone to sea and had never come back. The other is even worse because he doesn't work, just lives off his mother, taking from her every obol she scratches together from the honey she sells. The laundress said she was ill, but didn't know the details."

"It sounds as if providing a pension would only enrich this ne'er-do-well son," Phormio observed dryly.

"Couldn't we bring her to my kleros or settle her on another estate? She was very good to me," Leonidas repeated, feeling guilty for not looking after Dido earlier. It was six years since he had obtained citizenship, and he had not once inquired after her.

"We will need permission of not only her estate owner but her family as well—which in this case would be that same ne'er-do-well son."

"That's crazy," Leonidas protested.

Phormio raised his eyebrows and his lips twitched, amused. "What do you mean, crazy?"

"Dido must be old enough to be a grandmother by now. Why shouldn't she have control of her own fate?"

"Because she's a woman."

"What difference does that make?"

Phormio tilted his head to one side and considered his employer with amusement. "You do realize, I hope, that you Spartans are the only people in the whole world who think women are intelligent enough to make rational decisions?"

"But it's perfectly obvious they do," Leonidas countered, annoyed. "Besides, we're talking about a mature woman and a worthless youth. How can it be reasonable to let the bad fruit ruin the tree?"

Phormio laughed outright now, and promised, "I'll see what I can do. What is her name?"

"Dido."

"Dido. That's all? Do you know who her father was?"

Leonidas shook his head, feeling foolish.

"The village she was from?"

Leonidas shook his head again, adding, "But the laundress who told me about her will know where to find her."

Phormio nodded. "Of course. Don't worry. I will find her."

Leonidas thanked him and at once got to his feet, anxious to continue downriver for an afternoon of bird hunting.

Phormio stopped him. "Wait! Before you go! Damn it! Where did I put…" Phormio pulled himself up and started looking about the room, picking up wax tablets, moving cushions, and opening chests until at last, in a corner, he found what he was looking for. With a satisfied "Aha!" he returned to Leonidas and, beaming, handed over a bundle wrapped in burlap and tied together with twine. "Here! Take a look at this!" he urged.

Leonidas took his eating knife and cut the twine easily. Unfolding the burlap, he found a dark-blue linen cloth with a border of white "Λ"s: the lambda of Lacedaemon—or Leonidas. It was reasonably nice, but not something he would have chosen for himself. Leonidas cast Phormio a puzzled look.

Phormio laughed. "No ideas? Don't you remember the whore—"

"Kleta!" Leonidas made the connection at last.

"Exactly. I stopped by to see how she was getting on. She is really getting quite good at the weaving—as you can see. She's not so good with the books, of course, being illiterate, but the manager of your flax factory is taking care of things for her."

"And cheating her, no doubt," Leonidas shot back.

Phormio raised his eyebrows. Their eyes met. "She's not capable of looking after herself."

"She might be, if he wasn't taking such a large cut, don't you think?"

Phormio considered Leonidas intently, slowly reseating himself opposite his young employer without for a second breaking eye contact. He had liked Leonidas from the start, and he had been delighted to be given such a free hand managing things. His own ethics prevented him from cheating Leonidas, especially since he had no need to. The estate was vast and varied, offering ample opportunities to increase his own percentage-based income without ever taking more than his contractual share. But not until today had he seen any indication that Leonidas was even aware of the potential for being cheated. "Do you distrust all of us so much?"

"No. Should I?"

Phormio laughed and then, still smiling, he cocked his head, his eyes both alert and amused, and said, "The only way to stop from being cheated, good sir, is to take a more active interest in your estate."

Leonidas took a deep breath, and held it. Outside it was a beautiful spring day. Beggar would be making a nuisance of herself by trying to get at the household hens. His colt would be fidgeting and pretending to spook at every sudden sound. It was four hours to dinner. He wanted to spend the afternoon chasing down the wild geese that invaded the Eurotas this time of year, laying their eggs in the high reeds. He let his breath out slowly. "All right. Tell me."

Phormio smiled. "Let's start with Pantes."

"Pantes? Pelopidas' younger son?"

"Exactly. He's a very good carpenter."

"I know."

"Well. Let him do it full time. Hire someone less talented to do the heavy agricultural labor. Loan Pantes what he needs to set up his own shop in Sparta and travel to the major markets throughout the Peloponnese."

"That sounds expensive," Leonidas protested.

Phormio ignored him. "If you let him do what he *wants* to do, you'll find he works much harder, produces much better products, and repays your investment a hundredfold."

Leonidas nodded slowly. Phormio continued. "Then there's your bronze foundry. It needs a new, larger, better-lit and better-ventilated building."

"But I thought you said it was unprofitable?"

"It is. That's why I went to visit it this spring. The reason it is unprofitable is that the conditions under which people currently work are too cramped. There are frequent accidents and morale is terrible. A new building would enable the work to be done without so many accidents; but most important, morale and productivity—and so, ultimately, profitability—would increase."

Leonidas was a soldier. He understood the importance of morale. But he still hesitated, because this sounded extravagant.

Phormio pressed his case. "As it is, the factory helots are always running away, joining outlaw bands, becoming thieves and trouble-makers. If, on the other hand, they had good working conditions and were paid higher wages, they would settle down, get married, raise families, and stop being troublesome."

"You're saying the best way to prevent helots from becoming restless and rebellious is to pay them off?"

"No," Phormio countered. He was now very, very serious. He knew he had Leonidas' attention, and had just discovered that Leonidas was sharper than he had given him credit for. "What I am saying is, the best way to prevent them from becoming rebellious is to give them respect and dignity."

"Which is expressed by higher wages," Leonidas insisted.

"Which is expressed by treating them like the skilled workers they are, rather than disposable, contemptible beasts."

"But what will that cost?" Leonidas insisted.

Phormio considered him. After a moment he admitted, "You won't even notice." He let this sink in, and then continued. "According to legend, you know, that is the very foundry in which the bronzeworks for the Temple of the Bronzehouse Athena were produced. It is a proud tradition. Worthy of an Agiad prince."

"Your point?"

"You don't have to confine yourself to smelting bronze for military equipment; you could hire craftsmen capable of manufacturing works of art, such as we used to export around the world."

"Hire from where?"

"That will depend in part on what you pay."

"And what else?"

"Apollo," Phormio replied with a quick smile. "Talent sometimes lies undiscovered in the gutter. With the good will of Apollo, we will find such a person right here in Lacedaemon. But nothing attracts talent so much as talent. You need to build up a reputation, and to do that you have to want to do it—and to commit resources."

"Will there be anything left for me?"

Phormio considered Leonidas very seriously, and then concluded, "That depends, young man, on what you want." He paused. "Do you want to be rich like your twin, who lets whole harvests rot in his warehouses while his helots kill their newborn children for fear they cannot bring them through the winter, or do you want to count your wealth not by what you hoard but by the fame of Lacedaemon itself?"

"It's a pity you can't speak at Assembly," Leonidas countered, with a smile that was not as flippant as he wanted it to seem. "Maybe you could influence my other brother."

"King Cleomenes, you mean? He is a shrewd administrator. Like you, he is more concerned with results than means, and he encourages trade. He is willing to provide loans to enable investment, and his appreciation for quality production has resulted in a number of new initiatives. Think of the pottery painters he invited from Corinth: they have set up their own factory in Tsasi." Phormio paused. Leonidas nodded but said no more. So Phormio was forced to ask point-blank, "May I do it?"

"Yes. Anything else?"

"I think that's enough for today—if you want to have time for bird hunting."

Leonidas was a little ashamed to think he was so transparent, but also relieved that the afternoon was indeed still young. He thanked Phormio, who escorted him to the top of the stairs. Leonidas started down, and from overhead, Phormio called after him. "It's time you married, master. Only a man with children really plans for the future."

———

Leonidas was on his way to his syssitia with Alkander when Kyranios, his white-crested helmet in the crook of his arm, flagged him down. Leonidas pulled up and waited respectfully but warily for the senior officer.

"I'd like a word with you alone, if I may." Kyranios glanced at Alkander, who at once took the hint and departed with the words, "I'll see you at dinner."

Then, when Alkander was out of hearing, the senior officer addressed Leonidas earnestly. "I am here on a personal matter." Leonidas tensed. "Once, six or more years ago, you indicated an interest in my daughter Eirana." Kyranios paused and looked at Leonidas inquiringly.

Leonidas was compelled to concede, "Yes."

"You have not married since."

"No. But she did."

"To a man unworthy of her!" her father told him sharply. "I

opposed the match and so did her mother, but Eirana insisted. Now he has humiliated her! He has taken a concubine into his house in Delphi and lives openly with her."

Leonidas had heard the rumors. He said nothing.

"She spent the winter in Delphi. Trying to set things right. But Asteropus refuses to send the other girl away. He says *she* has done him no wrong and does not deserve disgrace!" The father's voice vibrated with indignation. "Eirana had no choice but to return to us. And now this other woman—the daughter of some man too poor to provide a dowry!—has given Asteropus a son. I'm told he dotes on the boy—neglecting his legitimate child! He has broken my daughter's heart! There is no chance of reconciliation. So I have asked the magistrates to recognize a divorce." He paused and looked sidelong at Leonidas, as if expecting a response.

"I am sorry for her," Leonidas commented stiffly.

"Yes." The lochagos waited, but when no more came, he continued, "You are still a bachelor. Would you consider taking my daughter to wife? You know her bloodlines are among the best in Sparta, bar the royal families. I am prepared to provide a large dowry."

"I do not need property, sir, and I would never take a bride for her dowry. There is no question that your daughter is in every way suitable to be my bride, but what does *she* want?" Leonidas paused and looked hard at Kyranios. The older man's face was clouded, unreadable. So Leonidas continued, "She preferred another man six years ago. I will not take her now unless that is her wish—not yours."

"Fair enough. Talk to her yourself."

———

Leonidas could not put either his thoughts or his feelings in order. He tossed and turned so much during the night that some of his comrades cursed him, and Sperchias sat up and told him bluntly to go outside and leave them in peace. So Leonidas rose and with only Beggar for company, walked the deserted streets of Sparta for over an hour.

Twice the meleirenes on patrol called out to him and then, recognizing him, rapidly faded away. They were supposed to watch for helots or strangers who had no business prowling the streets after curfew—and for boys of the agoge and men on active service, who were supposed to be in barracks. But the reality of power relationships meant that no meleirene was going to risk reporting a man of Leonidas' stature. It wasn't being a prince or even a section leader that protected him. If he had developed a reputation for bad living, arrogance, or bullying, they might even have enjoyed reporting him and seeing him humiliated. But Leonidas had a good reputation, and that meant he was safe from harassment.

Leonidas wandered listlessly to the Spartan acropolis and to the Temple of Athena. According to legend the temple had been started by Tyndareus, and his sons had continued to build it but had died before it could be completed. So the Spartans had finished it. Unlike the Temple to Athena in Athens, all the artwork was done in bronze, rather than stone. But this was an advantage, because Spartan stoneworkers of the previous century had been unable to produce work comparable to what the Athenians did now; while Lacedaemon's bronzeworkers, in contrast, were a match for the Athenian stonecutters. More than a hundred years ago, Spartan artisans had produced works in bronze equal in liveliness and character to what the Athenians did in stone today.

Leonidas found himself studying the bronze friezes closely, the words of Phormio in his head. He was intrigued by the thought that Lacedaemonian craftsmen might be capable of producing works like this again: the miracles of Herakles, and a particularly moving depiction of Hephaistos freeing his mother from her fetters. Why shouldn't Lacedaemon be renowned for her men of bronze in more than one way—as the products of her factories as well as her agoge?

Leonidas went around to the back of the temple, where the lives of Kastor and Polydeukes were depicted. He sank down on the steps and gazed up at the night sky, littered with bright stars. Beggar, as always, was content just to be with him, even if she did not understand this strange night outing. She sat herself down between his knees and he scratched her absently behind the ears, as he tried to decide what he wanted.

He was hungry for marriage and children, but he disliked being anyone's second choice. He was not even sure if he was in love with Eirana anymore. Yet all the pretty maidens that Alkander and Hilaira pointed out to him were more off-putting than attractive. They ran around in loud, self-confident hordes, always so full of themselves, and they all seemed alike. Of course, he knew objectively that this wasn't true, but to stop and watch them and try to find one he liked would arouse too much attention. He couldn't ask a young woman the time of day without the whole city speculating on his intentions!

After a while, however, he was stiff and tired and none the wiser, so he went back to the barracks and slept until the watch woke them. After morning drill, he bathed and changed into a clean chiton made by Laodice from the cloth Kleta had sent him. Wearing only a belt and baldric, but no armor, he walked to Kyranios' kleros.

He had the feeling everyone was expecting him, because no one was there but Eirana herself. She met him at the door and asked him in—"... or would you rather walk together?"

Leonidas preferred the outdoors.

It being a warm, early summer day, Eirana took no outer garment. She simply pulled a scarf up over her head and closed the door behind her. She set out toward the pastures, and Leonidas fell in beside her. She had aged in the last six years. Her eyes were sunk deeper in her face and she had put on weight. She was no longer the fresh young maiden he had fallen head over heels in love with when he was still an eirene.

"I wasn't sure you would come," Eirana admitted when Leonidas remained silent.

"I wasn't sure you wanted me to."

She stopped and looked up at him, tears quivering in her eyes. "You are right. I treated you poorly, and I have no right to ask for your kindness now. I would not have done it! It was my father—"

"Then I will not torment you any longer." Leonidas turned to leave.

"No! Please! That's not what I meant!" The anguish in her voice was real, and he stopped and looked back at her. The tears were escaping from her eyes and running down her face. "I meant I had no right to *ask* you to come! Not that I didn't *want* you to come! Please, Leonidas! Please don't reject me—even if it is what I deserve!" She dropped her face in her hands and started sobbing miserably.

Leonidas didn't have the heart to resist her. He went back, wrapped his arms around her, and held her until she had calmed herself. It felt remarkably good to have her in his arms. She was warm and soft, and his whole body responded. How much he wanted a wife! He wanted to spend his nights in her embrace, not listening to the snores of his comrades. He lowered his head to nuzzle at the back of Eirana's bent head, probing her responses. She lifted her face to his, flung her arms around his neck, and kissed him passionately. It was more than he had expected.

The excess of emotion on her part and the sense of wasted youth on his led them both to seek immediate gratification of their desires. The day was warm, the grass soft and thick. The grazing horses were benevolent spectators. If Eirana's parents or helots were watching from the windows of the house, they were clearly approving.

Only after they were lying in the grass, dozing and listening to the crickets and the breeze in the pine trees, did Eirana speak again. Her voice was tight, still filled with tears despite Leonidas' embrace. "You will take my daughter, too, won't you? She's so hurt because her father doesn't love her anymore..." She broke off, starting to cry again.

Leonidas stroked her head. "Of course. Why shouldn't I?"

———

The news that the master had taken a wife and that she would soon be coming to take up residence at his kleros sent Laodice into a panic. For the last three years, ever since their own quarters were finished, she had been making the main house ready for a mistress— but that was very different from the prospect of actually meeting her. In reality, Laodice and her family had become used to being "masters" of their own house. The master's occasional holidays on the farm had been like having an honored guest. A woman living here permanently would be something else again.

Laodice was suddenly certain that a *woman* would find fault with everything. She looked around the house and noticed all the little things that hadn't been done yet. Oh, they had the rebuilt and plastered walls. The roof was strong and leaked nowhere. The floors were well surfaced with practical local terra cotta—but nowhere a mosaic scene or even a pretty patterned walkway. And the walls were simply whitewashed—no frescoes or even pretty stenciled borders. Most distressing to Laodice was the realization that all the furniture had been built by her son Pantes. He was very proud of his work, all the more so now that the master had loaned him the money to set up his own shop. Maybe he really was good, Laodice thought, looking at his creations with their very sparse but "strategic" decorations in a new light. But what did she know? The new mistress might find it all very primitive and beneath her dignity.

The master had told them, full of pride, that his bride came from a "very good" family, that her father was one of Sparta's lochagoi, and that she had been married to a priest of Apollo at Delphi. That sounded very exalted to Laodice. She was desperately afraid that the mistress would find many things to complain about at the kleros.

At least her arrival would be in the dark. The master had explained the peculiar Spartiate marriage custom of "capturing" the bride by night and leaving her at his residence, only to return to his barracks before morning roll call. It seemed a very funny custom to Laodice, and she had heard the helots from the surrounding farms laughing about it. It saved the Spartiates huge amounts of money in wedding feasts and presents, the helots joked; but how many times had the bride woken up and discovered she'd been carried off by the wrong man? The Spartans all looked alike in their cropped hair and training armor, they teased. And the girls cut their hair and dressed as boys, too—so they could get by the watch more easily.

Pelopidas, Polychares, Mantiklos, and the new field hand Leonidas had brought from one of his other estates to replace Pantes doubled up laughing when Polychares told the story about some ardent bridegroom who had failed to get the girl's father's permission. The father, an officer it seemed, found out about the planned elopement and made sure the meleirenes knew when and where to look for the young man and his daughter. The amorous couple were caught, arrested, and put in the stocks—to the amusement of the entire agoge, who came to taunt them there. Laodice didn't find the story funny. All she could picture was poor Kleta.

With a sigh, Laodice left the men to their gossip, and set her mind to what she should cook for the mistress the first day. The master said she had a four-year-old daughter. Children liked sweets. She would be sure there were plenty of sweets ready, but there wasn't much time.

The master was clearly in a hurry now that he had found the woman he wanted ...

———•———

Hilaira found out about Leonidas' marriage from the woman that sold baskets in the agora, who had heard it from the cooper on Lycurgus Street, who had it from the dye merchant around the corner. By the time Alkander was home for his midday meal, she was ready to grill him. "And did everything work out for Leonidas last night?"

"Give me time to catch my breath and wash up, would you, woman?" Alkander answered in mock reproach.

Like most married men, Alkander went straight from morning drill to his wife's home—whether that was a nearby kleros or, as in Hilaira's case, a rented apartment in the city itself. While bachelors went to the public baths or down to the river to swim and took their midday meal at a tavern or street stall, married men let their wives bathe and feed them, since even men on active duty had the afternoons to themselves until dinner at the syssitia and reporting to barracks for the night. Most Spartan children were conceived on these leisurely afternoons, and not—as foreigners thought—in hasty night trysts, when the men were technically AWOL from their units.

As he stripped, Hilaira took Alkander's filthy, sweat-soaked chiton from him and dropped it in the wicker hamper. Alkander stepped into the terra-cotta tub in the middle of the sunny courtyard, sinking down into the cool water with an audible sigh of contentment. Hilaira came around behind him and started massaging his neck. Then, as he relaxed with a sigh, she dunked his head under the water. Alkander came up sputtering.

"Tell me!" she insisted before he could get a word out. "Did Leo finally carry Eirana home, or didn't he?"

"Of course he did," Alkander answered, still scowling at his wife for the dunking.

Hilaira kissed his frown away, and with a smile returned to her massage, but now she wanted to know. "And?"

"What do you mean, 'and?'"

"Well, what was he like this morning?"

"Happy; what do you expect?"

"And that's all?"

"Do you think we give one another a blow-by-blow description of our wedding night?"

"I always suspected it…" she teased, inwardly confident that it was not true. She had heard too many men scorn Brotus for "talking too much" and others for being "lewd" to think they indulged in too much indecent talk about their wives.

"Leonidas says everything went well, and that is all we need to know," Alkander told her primly. "Eirana is now on his kleros, and her father has delivered two splendid mares and a chariot as her dowry. Her daughter and the girl's nanny will move in with them in the next couple of days."

"I think I shall go visit her," Hilaira declared.

"Good idea. I'm sure Eirana would like that—but don't let Thersander eat too many of Laodice's sweets. If you spoil him too much, he's going to have a terrible time adjusting to the agoge."

"Don't remind me!" Hilaira protested. She dreaded the day when she would have to give little Thersander up to the harsh nurture of the Spartan agoge. Already she was planning to retain this townhouse even after Alkander went off active service, so that she could be near her children—providing a ready and nearby haven from the vagaries of life in the herds and the injustice or incompetence of adolescent eirenes.

"Where is the rascal?" Alkander wanted to know, standing up and reaching for a towel that was hung out to dry on a laundry line stretched from one side of the courtyard to the other.

"He wore himself out this morning with a temper tantrum when I wouldn't let him near the bullpen in the agora. He went to sleep right after lunch." Hilaira always fed her son before her husband came home for his midday meal; but usually the boy waited eagerly for his father, and Alkander played with him for a few minutes before he was put down for a nap while the adults had their meal together.

Alkander tiptoed into the nursery to check on his son and found him, as his mother said, sound asleep and breathing deeply, with a serene expression on his face. Alkander smiled. He was a beautiful child—all bright blond curls and soft, pale brown skin. Alkander's protectiveness knew no bounds. He knew that he would give his life without thought or regret for the boy's sake—and he would defend the boy from the cruelty and injustice of any eirene or instructor or herd leader, too! But he also knew that the very best defense he could give the boy was proper preparation for the years ahead. He knew he had to prepare him both mentally and physically to be strong enough to endure the hardships of the agoge: the cold, hunger, sore muscles, blisters and cuts and bruises, and above all the ridicule and teasing. If he could just help the boy *not* to be the butt of all jokes, as he had been, he would have given him a valuable start in life, Alkander thought. The problem was, Alkander wasn't sure how to go about that. Closing the door behind him very softly, he turned to smile at his wife.

Hilaira slipped into his naked arms and lifted her face to his. He kissed her and then bent and lifted her into his arms. He carried her up to the loft room that served as their bedroom. He set her on the bed and lay down beside her. She stood, but only to remove her peplos and lie down again, naked. He turned toward her and started to caress her.

They took their time because there was no rush, and then they lay talking on the bed. They discussed Hilaira's mother's waning health, and her father's misfortune in losing his best young stud stallion in a freak accident. "And you heard Leonidas tracked down his old nanny Dido?" Alkander asked. "Apparently she was living in dreadful straits, terrorized by her own son into giving him everything she earned. Leonidas has arranged for a pension to be paid via her cousin, Brotus' nurse Polyxo, so her son can't get his hands on it. He wanted to bring her here, but—"

"Daddy! Daddy!" Thersander broke in on them. He rushed to the bed and crawled onto his father. "We saw the Minotaur today!"

Alkander laughed and swept his son into his arms. Sitting up, he tossed the boy into the air. The three-year-old squealed with delight, while Hilaira swung herself out of the bed and hastened to dress again. As she combed out her hair, her son babbled nonstop to her husband, who was now dressing himself. He was a good father, she thought, with gratefulness and a glance down at her belly. It was two months since her last period. She was very likely with child again.

Somehow the days and weeks slipped away from her. There was no longer any doubt that she was again with child, and preparing for the new addition to the family preoccupied her in a pleasant way, weaving and sewing and fixing up the cradle. So it was a couple of months before Hilaira finally organized her visit to Eirana, on a day when Alkander's enomotia had been detailed to provide a ceremonial escort for some visiting dignitary, so that Alkander would not be able to visit her at all. The summer heat had broken and the first rains of autumn had fallen, refreshing the parched countryside and giving the fields an almost spring-like green.

Hilaira loved the autumn more than any other season, for it heralded the time of year when Alkander would be with her more often than any other. Beautiful as spring was, for Hilaira (and many other wives in Sparta), it was the precursor of the summer months, when the men were often away on long maneuvers—if not actually campaigning. Twice now, Alkander's pentekostus had been engaged in hostilities against the Argives, and those were summers Hilaira preferred not to remember. The dread of bad news had soured even the loveliest day, for she could never quite forget that Alkander was at risk.

But today she rose early and ordered the housekeeper to make a picnic lunch for them. Then she and the housekeeper set out together right after breakfast, with Thersander on the hefty housekeeper's back. The housekeeper was a middle-aged helot woman from Hilaira's father's estate who had come to run Hilaira's town establishment after Thersander was born. She was widowed, but had brought five children into the world and buried three of them. The housekeeper's son was Hilaira's father's second attendant, and her daughter was a kitchen maid on a large estate. She was a big help to Hilaira, doing all the heavy work from housecleaning to washing, chopping wood, fetching water, and baking the bread. Broad of face and beam, she was not a particularly bright woman, but she had a ready laugh and a good heart, as she had shown that day Leonidas brought Laodice to them after Laodice had helped Kleta. As they made their way out of the city, she entertained her mistress with local gossip.

Beyond the bridge they had to stop and let Thersander watch the army units at drill. The men were in training armor, but they were drawn up into opposing forces. Again and again they clashed with one another while officers prowled around watching for breaks in the line, files that didn't close up properly, or any other detail that failed to meet their standards.

Thersander was fascinated by it all, and Hilaira was reminded of the many hours she had spent on the opposite slope watching the boys of the agoge struggling with learning the intricacies of the phalanx in the clouds of choking dust. The girls had usually brought skins full of cool water and even apples or nuts and raisins to snack upon. When they were old enough to have sweethearts, they shared these treasures with their favorites during the short breaks. Alkander had always been surrounded by maidens offering him refreshments, and Hilaira had often shared her snacks with her brother and Leo instead. But she'd first suspected that Alkander really liked her best when he took another girl's water but winked at her even as he drank.

Eventually Thersander lost interest and they continued down the east bank of the Eurotas, past the giggling pubescent girls splashing naked in the shallows. Not long afterward they reached Leonidas' kleros and turned into his cypress-lined drive, leaving the main road behind. One of the helot girls, out with the goats, saw the visitors first and ran back to announce them. By the time they made it to the courtyard Laodice was coming out of the kitchen, drying her hands on her apron. Laodice welcomed Hilaira earnestly. "What a pleasure to see you, mistress. Why didn't you send word that you were coming? I would have made something special."

Hilaira laughed. "Everything you make is special," she assured the helot, trying to ease her apparent distress. Hilaira remembered when Leonidas' kleros had been a ruin, and she appreciated how much the helot family had done to turn it into a very pleasant home. She remembered even more vividly the way Laodice had looked the day she was arrested for giving water to that poor girl who had been in the stocks. The rescue of Kleta had made the two women conspirators despite the difference in their status. Hilaira did not like to see Laodice looking so worried.

Laodice, meanwhile, was asking her to come into the courtyard and promising to get her refreshments and the mistress. "Melissa!" she called to her daughter-in-law, "Come take the boy!" Thersander, who had fallen asleep on the housekeeper's back after the excitement of the drill fields, at once woke and started wriggling and whining. The housekeeper untied the shawl that held him onto her back and set him down on the ground. "We'll make ourselves comfortable in the kitchen," she assured Laodice, so that Laodice could see to Hilaira.

The courtyard was by far the nicest part of the main house, because it offered a spectacular view across the Eurotas to Taygetos. There were benches lining the house, enabling people to sit out here and enjoy the view while working, and a table, too. At this time of the day the benches were still in shadow, and the air smelled of the rosemary growing in large pots between the benches. Hilaira was surprised not to find Eirana out here enjoying the lovely morning. She was sure that this was where she would have sat to spin. Indeed, she would have dragged a loom out here so she could weave, Hilaira thought. Laodice urged her to sit down while she went to fetch the mistress.

Eventually Eirana emerged from the upstairs bedroom and came down the outside stairs to greet Hilaira. "How kind of you to come! Forgive me! I—I had a bad night. I have a headache. I'm sorry. Sit down. I'll have water and refreshments brought." Eirana seemed flustered and her hair was in disarray, as if she had indeed just gotten up. Her movements were slow, too, as if she were just waking up. Leonidas must have been here during the night, Hilaira surmised with amusement. But she couldn't blame him. After waiting so long to marry, he was undoubtedly an ardent lover, and since he had been promoted to enomotarch during the summer, he took less of a risk than Alkander by going AWOL at night.

Eventually the two women settled themselves on benches at the large table. Fresh grapes and bread were spread out on a linen cloth before them along with a flask of cool well water. Hilaira asked Eirana how she was settling in and if there was anything she lacked.

"No, no," Eirana assured her. "Laodice and Melissa are exemplary helots. Indeed, they spoil me. They are so kind and efficient. And the girls, as well. If only..." She broke off and looked around as if missing something. "Excuse me." She stood and disappeared into the house. Hilaira heard her talking, scolding it sounded, and she heard a child whine, without understanding exactly what was said. After a few minutes Eirana emerged, pulling a petulant girl by the hand. The girl was pouting and hanging back. "You will say hello to Lady Hilaira!" Eirana insisted.

The girl stamped her foot and said, "No!"

Hilaira smiled at the little girl. "I'm not really that terrible! Come let me look at you!"

"NO!"

Eirana cuffed her sharply, then pushed her forward.

The child took advantage of her mother's letting go of her to dart away, right back into the house. With an exclamation of exasperation, Eirana went after her, leaving Hilaira feeling embarrassed. She hoped she would never have such a difficult child—and her hand went automatically to her belly, wondering what the next little being would be like. She thought it was a girl, which was fine, except that Thersander was terrifyingly vulnerable. She lived in constant fear of him being taken from her by a fever or accident, a scorpion or snake or—as he grew—the hardships of his upbringing.

Eirana returned without the child, looking very tired. "I'm sorry. I apologize. You have to understand, she was so hurt by her father..."

Hilaira looked blankly at Eirana, who sank down on the opposite bench, clutching her shawl around her shoulders, although it was by no means cold. "Asteropus..." Eirana gazed blindly toward the Taygetos and swallowed.

To her horror, Hilaira saw the young bride blink back tears at the mere mention of her first husband. Hilaira didn't like this. She loved Leonidas like a brother, and any slight to him was a slight to her. "And what of Leonidas?" she asked, more sharply than she intended.

Eirana looked back at her as if bewildered by the question. "He is so good! He has done everything he can for us. He has been patient with Cleitagora, too—but she—she—doesn't trust men. Not even my father. I don't know..." Her voice and gaze drifted away again. Hilaira could not understand the other woman. She seemed depressed, as if all she cared about was her daughter—when she had a husband anyone could be jealous of and an estate that no one but the kings themselves could match.

"I'm sure Cleitagora will grow out of whatever ails her," Hilaira declared firmly.

"You think so?" Eirana asked anxiously.

"Of course! If she sees how happy you are with Leonidas."

"Yes, yes. I suppose you're right," Eirana admitted, sounding unconvinced. "I believe I may already be with child," she added, with a quick glance at Hilaira.

"Congratulations! That is wonderful news! Have you told Leonidas?"

"No, no. I am not truly certain."

"But still, you must be very excited," Hilaira insisted. "You may be carrying an Agiad prince!"

"Yes. Maybe. Not that it matters. Cleombrotus' boy Pausanias is very healthy, and I only had a daughter last time. I might disappoint him."

"You know Leonidas isn't the kind of man to scorn a daughter. And you can be sure he'll be with you if he can, when the time comes; he even came out to my father's kleros to sit with Alkander when Thersander was on his way." Hilaira laughed at the memory. Her parents had told her afterward that the two friends had drunk a whole amphora of wine in their hours of waiting through the night and—as they got drunker and drunker—had engaged in various childish contests that only they seemed to understand and appreciate.

"How is Thersander?" Eirana finally thought to ask. "And you, too, are expecting again, aren't you?"

Hilaira was happy to talk about her son and her condition, so the two women found common ground at last; the morning drifted away until Hilaira decided it was time for her to start back to the city. She collected Thersander and her housekeeper from the kitchen and headed back for Sparta.

———

They found a nice knoll for a picnic, and as they settled down with their cheese and bread, the housekeeper shook her head and remarked, "It's not good, mistress."

"What do you mean?"

"What Laodice told me."

"What?" Hilaira asked, alarmed.

"That young woman, Leonidas' wife—she means no harm, but she has bad spirits."

"Don't be ridiculous," Hilaira scoffed, but the hair at the back of her neck stood up. The old helot woman had put into words something she, too, had sensed.

"You know," the helot continued, unperturbed by her mistress' words, "Laodice and her family have lived on that kleros six years now with nothing but good fortune. They have had good harvests, and their livestock has been healthy and productive—no locusts or cattle sickness the past six years, no floods or drought. They are good, hard-working people, and the spirits clearly have nothing against them. But since that woman has moved in, the dead have returned."

Despite the sun overhead, Hilaira was chilled through. "What are you talking about?"

"That woman, she sees fire in her sleep. Fire and people dying! She wakes up screaming every night when Leonidas isn't there—and he can't come all that often. Not at night. He usually comes afternoons, and his wife hides her nightmares from him. But it has to be the souls of the dead, the ones who were killed there in the fire that destroyed the house six Olympiads ago."

Hilaira stared at her housekeeper in horror. Why would the spirits resent Eirana and not Pelopidas and his family? She and Alkander had spent their wedding night in the ruins, too—and it had been a night full of romance and passion, fragrance and starlit skies, without a hint of horror from beyond the grave. It made no sense.

But there could be no question that Eirana was not happy as a bride ought to be. Something was not right, and Hilaira couldn't shake the feeling that Eirana would not make Leonidas happy as he deserved.

CHAPTER 14

A MAP OF THE WORLD

It was not often that King Cleomenes sent for Nikostratos, so he responded quickly—but warily. He hoped the interview had nothing to do with a recent argument between Chilonis and her daughter-in-law, Queen Gyrtias, because the last thing he wanted was to get involved in women's affairs. On the other hand, Nikostratos reflected as he made his way to the Agiad palace, it would be worse if Cleomenes wanted an accounting of the state treasury in private. Such a request would suggest that Cleomenes was planning something again. Cleomenes was bored and fractious and clearly looking for a new adventure—if not domestically, then abroad.

Nikostratos mounted the half-dozen steps onto the broad porch of the palace, and the meleirenes on duty came to attention out of respect for his office and age. Inside the two-story entry chamber, Nikostratos was directed by the household steward to one of the back courtyards, where he found Cleomenes stripped down and engaged in a wrestling match with his personal trainer. Personal trainers were common in the rest of Greece but were generally superfluous in Sparta, where the agoge provided instruction to youth. As the heir apparent, however, Cleomenes had never attended the agoge, and he had been accorded personal trainers by his father throughout his youth. The man wrestling with him now was only a half-decade older than he, a foreigner from Halicarnassus and a good instructor. Nikostratos stood in the shade of the surrounding peristyle and watched until the match was finished.

Cleomenes won, and got up grinning, dusting the sand from his knees. "I'll be right with you," he called to Nikostratos and went over to the fountain, which spouted water from bronze lions' heads into a large marble basin on the far wall. He plunged his hands into the basin and splashed water onto his face and over his shoulders; and then, on second thought, in an easy, fluid motion, he swung his legs up and over the rim to drop into the water. He submerged completely and came up, wiping the water away from his face with his hands. While still seated in the fountain, he squeezed the water methodically from his long braids, starting at the top of his head. When he reached the back of his head, he grasped the braids together and wrung them out like a washerwoman does clothes. Finished with this, he swung himself out of the fountain. A helot was waiting with a towel, and as he dried himself he gestured for Nikostratos to come over to him. He was still smiling, apparently in a good mood—which only made Nikostratos more nervous. Cleomenes was altogether too moody for his liking.

"Have you heard?" Cleomenes asked (stupidly in Nikostratos' opinion, as there were always many rumors floating about the city, making it impossible to know which one the king was referring to). As if reading his thoughts, Cleomenes added: "A ship escorted by two triremes dropped anchor at Limera yesterday, with none other aboard than that tyrant-turned-liberator Aristagoras, son of Molpagoras of Miletos himself."

"And what does he want?" Nikostratos asked in alarm. The last thing Sparta needed was for this volatile and cagey Ionian politician to come seeking asylum; but since the man had recently had a falling-out with his Persian "allies," this was the first thing that came to Nikostratos' mind.

Cleomenes laughed. "That was what I wanted to ask you! All I know is that he told the port captain he was on his way to see me— *me*, note—not the ephors or the Council or Demaratus. What do you think of that?"

Nikostratos spread his himation so he could sit comfortably on one of the marble benches around the courtyard, propping both hands on his walking stick between his knees, while Cleomenes started oiling himself down. "There was a time, you know," Nikostratos started—in a narrative tone designed to give himself time to think—"when Miletos was torn by civil war, much as Lacedaemon was in our Time of Troubles. Lacking a wise man in their midst such as Lycurgus, they chose arbitration from outside. These arbiters traveled around and looked for estates that were well tended and prospering despite the civil strife, on the premise that men who had kept their farms in good order would be good at government. But they found very few such estates, and so they found very few men whom they thought fit to govern. The best of these was a certain Histiaeus. So a council was set up with Histiaeus at its head. Unfortunately, Histiaeus is being held in a golden cage in Susa by the Persian King Darius, and Aristagoras, who is his nephew, rules in his stead."

"What is the point you are trying to make?" Cleomenes urged his stepfather impatiently.

"Well, first, that the Miletans have accepted a very restricted olig-archy, indeed a quasi-tyranny, in which Aristagoras rules more by default than by right. Second, that this same Aristagoras first made friends with the Persians and urged them to help him meddle in Naxian affairs; but when that expedition came to naught, he fell out with the Persians and is now said to be fomenting rebellion among the subject cities of Ionia."

"So I've heard. But why would Aristagoras want to see *me*—and not Demaratus or the Council and ephors?"

"Well, without ever having met the man, I suspect it is because you were so interested in interfering in Athenian affairs in the past, while Demaratus and the ephors stopped you. Aristagoras no doubt sees you as the one powerful Spartan who might be receptive to the idea of a foreign adventure—which is not necessarily a compliment," Nikostratos hastened to point out.

Cleomenes frowned at him, but did not contradict him. "Our young men are spoiling for a fight."

"That is why Lycurgus very wisely created a Council composed exclusively of men over the age of sixty—and the kings—to check the hotheaded tendencies of our young men in Assembly," Nikostratos shot back.

Cleomenes laughed, but then added more seriously, "The Council cannot stop me from asking for volunteers."

Nikostratos cocked his head. "Our constitution is a sacred text, Cleomenes. It was sanctioned by Apollo himself, and it cannot be altered at the whim of any king. But since it is not written down, but rather memorized and passed on from generation to generation, there is no one alive today who remembers all its clauses. We tend to know only those parts of it that we use daily. However, there are some *very* old men in the Council who might unexpectedly *remember* something from our constitution that *does* prohibit kings from taking citizens too far away from Lacedaemon without the consent of the ephors—whether or not they are volunteers."

Aristagoras impatiently paced the deck of the large freighter while the anchor was wound in. Although his ship still lay in the shadow of the massive rock island that hovered just offshore, the sun had broken over the horizon, and its long rays stretched over the sea beyond the bow to spill onto the village on the shore. This early light was still reddish, and it turned the whitewashed buildings a gentle pink. It was a pretty sight, this coastal village snuggled along the edge of the sea with limestone hills rising sharply behind it. On the narrow plane between the steep rocky slopes and the sea, the land had been cultivated, producing a rich green plane of orchards and barley in the ear. The whitewashed houses had red tile roofs and blue shutters, and the fishing boats, drawn up on the shore for the night, were brightly painted, with eyes on their bows and red, blue, or yellow gunnels.

But for all its charm, Aristagoras had eyes only for one thing: a spot of coppery light on the shore that burned so steadily it was like the light of a beacon in the darkness, although it was visible now in full daylight. He gestured to the seaman manning the stern spring. "What is that light?"

The man squinted as he followed Aristagoras' pointed finger, but he shook his head and shrugged. "Never seen it here before, my lord," he answered.

The anchor was manhandled inboard, and the small foresail set to maneuver the vessel alongside the only quay. Amidships, several slaves were wrestling with an awkward wooden box almost three feet by four feet and a foot deep. They were bringing it out of the hold so it could be taken ashore, along with the many other chests containing Aristagoras' clothes, toiletries, gifts, and traveling gear. An elderly man pulled himself up with difficulty from the main deck to the afterdeck and came to stand beside Aristagoras.

Aristagoras frowned at him. "Tell me again what I am doing here. This village wouldn't merit a mark on the map of Ionia! The Persians would not even notice it was here! We have been kept waiting two days already, and for what? Corinth has a larger fleet and Athens more wealth!"

The old man nodded. "It is not that long ago that Lacedaemon ruled the Aegean. Besides, Ionia does not lack fleets or money. It lacks hoplites."

"Didn't you tell me there were only eight thousand Spartans? Corinth has almost three times that number of citizens, and Athens more than five."

"But many of Athens' and Corinth's citizens are men too poor to pay for hoplon and helmet. All eight thousand Spartans are, or were, hoplites."

"How is that?"

"Because of the land reform carried out forty Olympiads ago, which gave each Spartan citizen sufficient land to support a hoplite and his family. If a man cannot maintain himself and his equipment, he loses his citizenship. Only age releases him from his duty."

Aristagoras cast the old man a skeptical frown; but they were now moving steadily closer to the shore, and his attention was still riveted on the curious spot of light. It was starting to disintegrate into a line of lights, and he saw it was a phalanx of troops drawn up eight across and four deep. The hoplons and helmets were catching the morning sunlight, suggesting a high-degree burnishing; yet more impressive, the only things that moved in the whole formation were the black horsehair crests, which quivered in the breeze off the sea. The soldiers themselves were as immobile as if they had been turned to stone. Aristagoras had never before seen such a disciplined troop of men. He glanced back at his companion and the latter smiled with satisfaction, noting: "You have been honored, my lord. Those are Spartiate hoplites—full citizens, not perioikoi auxiliaries."

At the quay they were met by the port captain, a burly man with a gray-streaked beard. He gestured immediately to the troops drawn up beside the quay on the beach, saying in a low, gruff voice, "Your escort has arrived, sir." Then, pointing in the opposite direction, he indicated several wagons and a chariot that had also been made ready for the guest. Aristagoras nodded, gave instructions to one of his men to see to loading their luggage, and started toward the escort. He was followed by his uncle and two bodyguards.

Up to now, the helmets of the escort had been shoved back, their spears sloped—resting on the men's shoulders—and the shields leaned against the men's knees. At an order, the men pulled their helmets down over their faces, took their shields on their arms, and brought their spears upright. A man separated himself from the rest and came forward to meet Aristagoras. He alone still had his helmet shoved back to reveal his face and kept his spear slanted backward. Although from his behavior Aristagoras assumed he was the commanding officer of the escort, nothing about either his panoply or his clothing suggested any particular status—unless you considered the fact that his helmet crest had a tuft of white horsehair at the front, before turning black like the rest. Aristagoras next noticed that every aspis was identical. Rather than having an individual or family device on the face of their shields, these men all carried an aspis with a lambda on it. And all men wore their armor over red chitons.

"Welcome to Lacedaemon, sir," the officer greeted him. "King Cleomenes sent us to escort you to Sparta. Do you care to inspect the troops?"

Aristagoras considered this man, the first Spartiate he had ever met face to face. He was young and handsome in a rugged, healthy way, with brown hair and hazel eyes. He was tall, but so was Aristagoras, so they stood eye to eye. Aristagoras nodded in answer. He was eager for a closer look at the wares he had come to buy.

He started down the first rank with the officer at his heels. At this range he could see that the men had individual breastplates and helmets, some of which were older, others more decorated. Likewise, although all chitons were dyed red, they were in fact individually made, so they were of different lengths, cloth, and cut; and many had white, black, blue, or yellow patterns or borders. Without being able to see faces, it was impossible to know the ages of the men; but Aristagoras was impressed that the ranks were well organized so that men of roughly the same height stood shoulder to shoulder, thereby ensuring the best possible shield protection. And they still stood perfectly still.

"A nice touch, the lambda—but how do you tell your men apart?" Aristagoras asked the officer pacing him.

In answer, the officer started introducing his men by name.

"Ah, but you know the order they are in *now*," Aristagoras remarked. "In battle it would be different."

"Why?"

"Because you won't know the order they are in once the melee starts."

"Why wouldn't I?"

"Have you never been to war?" Aristagoras asked, irritated. "The confusion is quite indescribable."

"No doubt you are more experienced than I, sir, but I have not yet seen a Spartan line scramble."

"*Have* you ever been in a battle?"

"Three times now, sir."

Aristagoras snorted and turned away from the escort to start back toward the waiting chariot. "How long will it take us to get to Sparta?"

"That will depend on you, sir. If you wish to ride ahead, ten of us can be mounted to ride with you, and we can make Sparta tonight. If you wish to stay with your baggage, it will take roughly eighteen hours."

Aristagoras opted for the latter. He did not want to arrive without the gifts he had brought for Cleomenes.

So they set off in a long convoy: the escort leading, followed by Aristagoras, his bodyguards, and his uncle/chancellor in the chariot, and then the baggage train with Aristagoras' things and his slaves. For the march, the escort had removed their breastplates, helmets, and greaves and stacked these on a wagon along with their aspis. They then formed up two abreast and sixteen deep. Bareheaded and using their spears as walking sticks, they started up the winding road. A man with a flute in a satchel across his back brought up the rear.

The first part of the journey was inhospitable. The narrow road switchbacked its way up the side of steep hills covered with scrub-brush. The heat of the sun made it particularly unpleasant, and men and beasts were soon sweating profusely. The horses provided Arista-goras were good quality, however, and Aristagoras caught occasional fragments of conversation, joking, and laughter carried back on the wind from the escort. With their helmets off, he could see they were all young men, and they maintained an impressive pace despite the terrain. At regular intervals the entire convoy halted for water.

Eventually they crested the mountain range that ran down the Malean peninsula and started to descend very gradually, using a path that ran almost parallel to the spine of the Parnon range as it slowly lowered itself into the Eurotas valley. The landscape had changed dra-matically, and Aristagoras was amazed. Somehow, all the reports of Spartan austerity—schoolboys forced to go barefoot and owning only a single himation, the image of boys stealing to keep from starving, and even the adult citizens huddling together in common messes that served only horrible black broth—had encouraged Aristagoras to expect a poor country. Unconsciously he had pictured a place parched to desert in the summer and nakedly cold in winter. He had expected everything to be brown, dusty, and wind-blown, and the dwellings to be hovels. This was not what stretched out before him.

The broad bowl of the Eurotas valley was richly cultivated and dotted with prosperous farms. Everything was green, right up to the tree line of the massive range of Taygetos on the far side of the valley. The Eurotas sparkled when it caught the sunlight as it wandered and weaved its way slowly toward the sea—as if reluctant to leave this pleasant valley behind. On the floodplain itself wheat and barley grew thick, while the slopes on both sides of the valley were terraced and planted with olive and fruit orchards: apple, pear, lemon, and plum. The abundance of water was evident not only in the vegetation, but in the many springs and fountains. They were able to stop regularly to water the horses and oxen and to fill their own skins from natural springs bubbling with clean, cool water. Spartan slaves also regularly replaced the water in a large wooden barrel containing wine amphorae to ensure the wine was kept properly chilled.

Nor was there anything inhospitable or unpleasant about the

large, rambling rural dwellings that they passed at frequent intervals. Except for Doric colonnades fronting their porches, they were largely unadorned. No sculptures, terra-cotta figures, or mosaics garnished them, but they were solidly built of local limestone and utilized the local cream-colored tiles for roofing. They seemed to glow warm and bright against the green vegetation around them. Furthermore, although whitewashed rather than elaborately painted, their proportions were consistently elegant—as if designed by mathematicians or master architects rather than just built. Many had wide terraces and long balconies. Finally, these homes made up for their lack of decoration by incorporating natural beauty into their layout: flowering trees, potted palms, flowering tamarisk, myrtle and oleander bushes, cypress trees, and fountains.

The day cooled rapidly after the sun sank behind the peaks of Taygetos, and when it was completely dark, the officer of the escort called a halt and came back to suggest that they camp for the night. Aristagoras readily agreed. He was hungry and stiff from the day in the chariot. One of the many natural mountain springs splashed invitingly into a crude stone basin to their right, and a grove of chestnut trees enclosed them in a pseudo-courtyard.

As soon as the orders went out, Aristagoras' household slaves set to work erecting his tent, spreading out carpets and setting up his bed, chairs, and tables. While he made himself comfortable in these abundant and well-appointed furnishings, his cook and two assistants started a fire and began preparing his meal. Aristagoras took no interest in this as it was routine for him, but he watched the way his escort likewise set up camp, their arms stacked in the middle and the small tents, apparently for four men each, erected in a neat circle. Four fires were soon burning, and water and wine was passed out.

The officer of the escort appeared for the first time without helmet or spear. "Is everything to your satisfaction, sir?"

"Yes, fine. Why don't you join me for dinner?" Aristagoras suggested.

The young man's eyes shifted sharply. For a moment he seemed about to decline, but then he nodded. "Just let me tell my deputy where to find me." He was gone before Aristagoras could answer, and so Aristagoras went inside his tent. His bodyguards would eat outside with the slaves, but his chancellor was waiting for him. "I've asked the escort commander to join us," Aristagoras told the older man as he washed and dried his hands with the water and towel brought by a slave, then reclined on a couch.

The older man nodded and stretched out on his own couch before asking, "What is your first impression?"

Aristagoras sipped the wine poured for him into a kylix and admitted, "Not what I expected. I am most curious what this Spartiate will have to say—if we can get him to talk, that is. Aren't they supposed to be terribly taciturn?"

The arrival of their guest cut off the conversation. He was given water and a towel to wash his hands, and then offered water and wine. When he was settled and the first course of olives and pickled octopus was brought, Aristagoras opened, "Do tell us a little bit about yourself. I do not even know your name." It was a question.

"I am called Leonidas, commander of the Achillean Enomotia of the Kastor Pentekostus, Pitanate Lochos."

"I see. And that is how you define yourself? Who was your father? Have you no brothers? Are you married? Have you sons?"

"My parents are both dead. I have two brothers still living, one dead. I am married and have two children, twins a year old."

"Sons?"

"A son and a daughter."

Aristagoras considered the young man opposite him and concluded that for some reason, he did not want to talk about himself. He tried another tack: "If I have been informed correctly, Lacedaemon has the finest army in the world. Half a century ago you were masters of the Aegean; and even Croesus, King of Lydia, was not too proud to seek Spartan aid in his wars with Persia. Indeed, the whole world looked to you for soldiers to help them win, whatever their cause. But now your army never shows itself anywhere, and it seems to be quite useless. I mean, maybe you could explain to me what it is for these days? No one has dared attack you here in generations."

"The Argives are constantly trying to regain the shore just behind us, and Kythera, too, while the Messenians would rise up in revolt if they thought we were not strong enough to defeat them again."

"Ah, yes, the Messenians. A bit of a problem, aren't they? How do you—as the great liberators of Greece, the opponents of tyrants, and all that—justify the oppression of an entire city-state of fellow Greeks?"

"I don't," Leonidas retorted.

"Meaning?"

Leonidas shrugged. "Meaning the situation is as it is. I did not create it, and I cannot change it. Sparta defeated Messenia many generations back. The liberation of Messenia would destroy our economy as it is now structured. In short, it is not in my interest or that of any of my peers to change it."

"But if you freed Messenia, you would not have to fear the enemy at your back, would you? You would be free to use your army for other purposes—maybe even for causes that could bring you greater fame, glory, and wealth. Have you never thought of that?"

"Have you been to Messenia, sir?"

"No," Aristagoras admitted.

"Then you cannot know what wealth is needed to outstrip it."

Aristagoras only laughed; and then in answer to Leonidas' stony gaze, he patted his arm condescendingly and noted, "And you have seen nothing of the wealth of Asia."

"True. Tell me about the Persians. Why did you fall out with them?"

Aristagoras frowned, and his answer was sharp for the first time: "Because they are an insufferably arrogant people. They think they are superior to every race on earth! They think all other peoples are not merely different, but uncivilized. They *use* other peoples for their own ends, but they do not respect them."

Leonidas held his tongue. He thought this description would fit the Athenians—or the Spartans themselves, for that matter. Didn't every city think it was the best in the world? That its laws and its gods were the finest?

"You will have heard of my Naxian expedition," Aristagoras continued in a still agitated voice. "That pompous Persian ass, Megabates, went snooping around the fleet and found one Myndian vessel on which there was no watch set. And why should there be? We were on the offensive. No one knew where we were bound. We had not even set course for Naxos! But that arrogant asshole ordered the captain of the vessel to be put in *chains* with his head sticking out an oar-port! He turned a venerable gentleman into an object of ridicule for the whole fleet! A Greek trireme captain! A man who had raised the entire sum to lay down the keel and who paid every man-jack aboard, oarsman and marine alike—treated like a mere slave, humiliated before his own crew! It was an outrage against all men of means! If such things are allowed, who will want to raise money for a trireme ever again? I freed him with my own hands, and Megabates—although he was under *my* orders—reproached me for it! Then when we came to Naxos, he pouted in his tent like Achilles and waited until all my resources had been exhausted in the futile siege, and *then* he went home, having ruined the enterprise!

"Yet rather than blaming Megabates as he deserved, Artaphernes demanded that *I* pay the expenses of the Persian force that had sat around eating and drinking, but so singularly failing to support me! To have paid such a debt would have ruined Miletos! So what other choice did I have but to turn against such unreliable friends?"

Leonidas listened in patience to this flood of self-justification and was impressed by Aristagoras' ability to excuse his despicable behavior, but he doubted that even Cleomenes would be impressed by the story.

"You understand the situation?" Aristagoras asked when Leonidas said nothing.

"No, sir. If any commander failed to set a watch, we'd put him in the stocks, too."

"A senior commander? A polemarch?" Aristagoras asked incredulously.

"Especially a polemarch—except it would not come to that, because each section leader sets his watches, so no polemarch has to. Not even I need worry about the watch. I know I can rely on my four section leaders and my deputy. But, of course, I *did* check before I came to see to your wishes. You can come with me now if you like and ask each of my four section leaders what the watch is for tonight."

"Tonight? Who are you afraid of?"

"Indiscipline."

Aristagoras stared at him, uncomprehending, and then shook his head. "You do what is senseless just to keep yourselves from being free to follow your own pleasures, as is perfectly normal for any free man."

"No, we do what is necessary for the freedom of all of us by ensuring that we cannot be taken by surprise."

"A man who is forever constrained to do what he does not want is no better than a slave," replied Aristagoras, dismissing Leonidas' answer with an irritated wave of his hand.

"A man who follows only his baser instincts is worse than a slave: he is an animal."

"If he follows only his baser instincts, perhaps," Aristagoras conceded, adding, "but a free man can choose between his baser instincts and his nobler sentiments—and it is that freedom to choose that makes him free."

"Perhaps," Leonidas conceded, but then he smiled and got to his feet. "And, therefore, I hope you will respect the fact that I now choose to check on my men." He walked out of the tent, but did not go directly to the campfires. Instead, he stood breathing in the smell of the pines and looking up at the stars, remembering what Lychos had taught him about navigating by the constellations.

Aristagoras had succeeded in making him feel enslaved. He longed to be with Lychos—who might be anywhere the sea could take him, Crete or Byzantion, Cyprus or Naukratis. Then, with a wince of guilt, Leonidas realized that he had not wished to be home with his wife and babies. For six years he had imagined married bliss; and after only two years of enjoying it, he was already tired of it. He told himself he loved his twins. He had even named his daughter "Kleopatra," beloved of her father; but the truth was that their screaming and fussing and Eirana's obsession with them tired him out.

Eirana was a good mother. She seemed to live for nothing beyond the welfare of her three children. She could not sleep at night for listening for their slightest whimper, nor could she sit down for a glass of wine without jumping up a half-dozen times to do something for one or the other of her babies. She threw questions at him, but her attention was drawn away before he could draw breath to answer. In consequence, she knew nothing of what was going on in his life or in his head. Worst, she claimed his kleros wasn't good for the children. There were "vapors" from the Eurotas, and "chills" from Parnon, and there were too many snakes in the cellar, and the stairs were too steep, and…He couldn't remember it all. She had moved to one of his larger estates on the far side of Taygetos. He could only get there on the longer holidays, which he sometimes thought had been her real intent in moving…

No, his marriage was not a success, he admitted to himself with a deep sigh, as he started toward the campfires.

He was stopped by his second in command, Oliantus, who emerged out of the darkness before Leonidas reached the firelight. Oliantus seemed doomed to always being second best. Leonidas had watched him nearly win the crown in long-distance running at Olympia, only to be defeated in the last lap by the Athenian Eukles, who was now a famous runner, and the Corinthian who had carried away the crown. On taking command of the enomotia, Leonidas had found Oliantus a silent, introverted man, apparently still brooding over that defeat. Leonidas, however, had rapidly discovered that while Oliantus was not the best hoplite—the two best hoplites of each squad made up the front rank—he was conscientious and reliable. For this reason, Leonidas had appointed him his deputy and made him responsible for everything that went on behind the lines. He was the man who made sure that the cooking fires never went out, that their supplies were not damaged by rain or lost to mice, that their pack animals were fed, shod, and sound, et cetera, et cetera.

In the last two years Leonidas had come to value him immensely, understanding that the ugly, shy man was devoted to his duties and all the men in a way that was selfless and, too often, thankless. The natural tendency of men was to complain about everything from their bedding to their food, without ever giving a thought to how difficult it was to organize these necessities. "Is everything all right, Leo?" he asked out of the darkness.

"With our guest? I think so. He brought enough luxuries and slaves to be comfortable wherever he goes."

"Have you found out what he wants?"

"I haven't tried—but he hates the Persians for petty reasons and is curious about us. I think he will ask us to help him fight the Persians."

"And what will your brother say?"

Leonidas shrugged. "I expect that depends on what Aristagoras promises him. It's not that Cleomenes is venal, but he *is* vain. He might like the title of 'liberator.'"

———

They reached Sparta by midafternoon the next day. At that time, the drill fields on the east bank of the Eurotas were occupied by boys of the agoge rather than by troops. Leonidas tried to hurry past, feeling that the boys, scruffy and sloppy as they were, made a bad impression. It took a decade to train troops up to the standard expected in the Spartan army, and none of the boys on the drill field were near to it yet.

Leonidas could make out some sixteen-year-olds being given instruction in the intricate art of deploying from line of march into phalanx. This meant shifting from a formation two across by sixteen deep to an eight-by-four square. They were making an absolute hash of it, and all he could think of was his own remark about never fighting "scrambled." These boys didn't seem to have caught on to where they ought to be, even in the initial formation! Nearby, some fourteen-year-olds were struggling with the "simple" task of— on command—reversing the grip on their spears from underhand to overhand. Whenever the command came, the clatter of dropped spears followed—and then came the shouts of exasperation and the bobbing of the line as the youths retrieved their dropped spears. The youngest boys on the drill fields at this time were being shown the basics of keeping in formation with shields (wicker in this case) and spears at the ready. They were so inept that they looked more like a bunch of farmers harvesting hay, or wheat waving in the wind, so unsteady and uncoordinated were their spear-tips.

Aristagoras paused to watch.

"They're just the boys in training, sir," Leonidas apologized.

Aristagoras gazed at him with raised eyebrows. "I can see that. I thought you ran around wild as boys."

"Only some of the time."

"And the rest of the time you are out here." He nodded toward the drill field.

"No, actually we spend a lot of time in chorus, dancing, and other lessons as well," Leonidas answered wearily. Why did foreigners

always focus only on those aspects of their education that were most
outlandish?

They continued into the city, and the baggage was sent directly
to the palace, but Aristagoras insisted on a walking tour of the "most
important sites" with only his bodyguards and Leonidas in attendance. Although he tried not to show it to the arrogant young escort
commander, Aristagoras was impressed. No, Sparta wasn't Athens,
Memphis, or Sardis. It was a relatively small city. But Aristagoras
felt he had been misled by those who claimed Sparta was "not a real
city." Technically, this was true. It had no walls (which was one of
the characteristics used to define a city), but it did not lack any of
the other characteristics—not the public buildings nor agora, not
the gymnasia nor baths, not the theater nor public fountains, not
the monuments nor temples. Most impressive was the stoa with the
"thousand" columns where the Assembly met—the Athenians, after
all, still met in the open. He also found the stately buildings of the
Council House, the Ephorate, and the administrative buildings of
the agoge impressive for their combination of symmetry, proportion, and Doric simplicity. While the sculptures on the pediments
were stiff and heavy by modern standards, they were far from primitive. Furthermore, these buildings were ancient, which lent them
a certain dignity divorced from artistic taste. Sparta certainly didn't
lack for palaestra and gymnasia, public baths and athletic fields.
Aristagoras found the racecourse, with two charming statues of the
Dioskouroi, particularly attractive; and the unique ball field, with
two bridges over the moat—one adorned with a statue of Herakles
and the other with a statue of Lycurgus—very interesting. All in all,
there were far more monuments in the city than Aristagoras had
expected.

What impressed Aristagoras most, however, was the behavior
of the citizens. The boys, as he had expected, were shaved, barefoot
and scruffy—but he had never met such well-mannered youth in
his whole life! Even the poorest urchins in Miletos were rude and
impudent, while the sons of the rich were spoiled and self-centered.
Here, all Leonidas had to do was call to any of these boys, and they
came and stood at attention before him with their eyes down and
their hands by their sides. They answered every question he put to

them with "sir," and they were quick to offer help, too. When they had stopped so Aristagoras could dismount from his chariot, boys had come out of nowhere to hold the horses.

The young men, whom they encountered predominantly on the athletic fields and at the baths, were impressive, too. Again, they behaved with marked deference and respect when Leonidas introduced them. Every one of them welcomed the visitor, wished him a pleasant stay in Lacedaemon, and assured him that he need only ask "any of us" if he needed something. They were all, furthermore, in outstanding physical condition. Aristagoras told himself that there had to be fat, lazy, weak, and ugly Spartiates, but they were not in evidence.

What *was* in evidence everywhere were the women. Hadn't Homer described Sparta as the "land of beautiful women"? Evidently, he had not been referring to Helen alone. Aristagoras was utterly amazed—and a little disconcerted—to discover that women dominated the Spartan agora. In other Greek cities, the agora was not just a place of commerce, but above all the place for men to congregate, exchange news, and discuss everything from politics and court cases to the latest theory of alchemy. In Sparta, in contrast, there were no citizens in evidence at all—only craftsmen, merchants, farmers selling their goods—and women.

At first Aristagoras was not entirely certain just who these women were. On the one hand they wore old-fashioned peplos, which meant they showed quite a lot of leg when moving rapidly; but there was nothing lewd about them. They generally wore a himation up over their head (though not shrouding their faces), and they appeared more intent on striking a good bargain with the salesmen than on attracting attention to themselves. In other words, they were not whores. Because they were shopping and wore neither gold nor silver, they might have been household slaves, he thought; but most wore very expensive fabrics beautifully dyed in rich colors, set off with bold borders, and clasped with heavy bronze, silver, and ivory pins. Furthermore, they walked upright and seemed very self-confident. "Who are these women?" Aristagoras asked at last.

"Mostly citizens' wives."

"Your *wives* have to do the daily shopping?" Aristagoras gasped in shock. He would never have let his wife go down to the agora and haggle with craftsmen and other charlatans. She couldn't add two and two together, anyway. "Your own wife comes here?" Aristagoras pressed him.

"Of course." When she is in Sparta, Leonidas added mentally with a sigh.

"Have you no slaves?"

"The helots do the heavy work, but it is usual for a Spartiate wife to make most household purchases."

"So your women have driven the men out," Aristagoras concluded; because obviously, men would not willingly congregate where they would be surrounded by a bunch of gossiping women.

"It is considered bad manners for a young man to loiter around the agora," Leonidas replied.

"Why? What can be bad about meeting with one's fellows and discussing developments in the world?"

"We can do that in our syssitia—not here in the open where helots, perioikoi, and strangers may see and hear. Besides, there is a prohibition against Spartiates having coins and 'engaging in trade,' which some of our more conservative citizens interpret to mean even daily shopping. Our wives are not subject to the same prohibitions, because they have control of the household finances and must be able to both buy and sell goods as needed."

"But—that is madness! You let women control your finances?"

"For the most part, yes, our domestic finances. The city has an elected treasurer, of course—a highly respected man of great knowledge in mathematics and accounting."

"Yes, but how can you let women run your private affairs? Their brains are underdeveloped, and they are not—no matter how much they try—capable of understanding higher principles. Why, if I let my wife run my household, we would have nothing but sweets and pretty baubles, and we would all starve."

Leonidas shrugged, "We've been letting our wives run our households for the last forty Olympiads, and our prosperity is unimpaired."

The evidence appeared to support Leonidas. Lacedaemon was certainly prosperous, but Aristagoras could not believe women had

anything to do with it. He concluded that the Spartans only pretended this was the case, for reasons only they could know.

While the mature women were baffling and incomprehensible
to Aristagoras, the girls were delectable—and they appeared to run
around everywhere. He could hardly credit his eyes when he first
spotted them watching the boys at drill outside the city, dismissing
them as younger boys watching their elders. But at the baths and
then the racecourse, there could no longer be any doubt. Nubile and
even younger prostitutes were put on display in a most unusual way.
Namely, they were allowed to strip completely naked and then take
part in sports alongside the young men. Apparently, by the time they
got to be sexually mature they were sequestered away for their paying
clients, but the young ones were evidently put on display like this to
encourage youths and men to bid for first rights or the like. It was an
intriguing custom, and Aristagoras was about to ask more about it,
when one of the girls walked right up to them.

She had just finished bathing, come ashore, dried herself down
in full view of everyone, and then pulled on a simple chiton. She was
still rubbing dry her bright red hair when she came over to them.
"Excuse me," she said shortly to the stranger, and turned at once to
his companion. "Uncle Leo, may I ride Cyclone in the Gymnopaedia?" Then, before he could get a word in edgewise, she hastened
to assure him, "I know it's my own fault that Shadow isn't up to it
anymore, but she couldn't have won even before the accident. She's
sweet, but she's not really fast. Not like Cyclone. If you let me ride
her, I'll bring you the laurels! Cyclone is the best mare in all of Lacedaemon! You won't be riding her yourself, will you? I asked Eirana
last time I saw her, and she said she didn't ride anymore. Please let
me ride her!"

"I'm not going to make a decision now," Leonidas told his niece
sharply, because he was embarrassed by the way she had plunged in,
ignoring the stranger. Pointedly he added, "This is your father's guest,
Aristagoras of Miletos."

Too late, Gorgo realized that the man with her uncle was someone
important. She had been so determined to make her case to Leonidas
that she had dismissed the man with him as "some stranger." Now she
turned her attention to Aristagoras, frowning slightly, and noticed his

gold rings and bracelets, his woven chiton—and the scandalized look on his face. Embarrassed, she realized her hair was a mess and her chiton falling off one shoulder. Self-consciously she pulled the chiton back in place and reached up to comb her fingers through her hair. "I'm sorry to have interrupted, sir," she stammered, then turned and darted away.

"Who—who—was that—girl?" Aristagoras stammered in utter confusion. It was one thing for a girl-whore to address a favored customer as "uncle," but to be told he was her father's guest was outrageous. He was here to see a king!

"That was my niece Gorgo. My brother's only child, since his son and heir died in an accident five years ago. He spoils her, I'm afraid." Leonidas paused, laughed, and added, "We all do."

"Your brother's child? A Spartiate's daughter? By a slave girl, then?"

"No, by his wife." Leonidas turned and looked Aristagoras straight in the eye. "You didn't think these girls were slaves, did you?" Aristagoras' expression was answer enough, and Leonidas continued firmly, "They are all the daughters of citizens. They are dressed simply and barefoot only because they are in the public upbringing." Leonidas was angry because he could tell how shocked Aristagoras was, but he was angry with himself, too. He should have known how the foreigner would react. He should have made a point of telling him about the girls. And Gorgo didn't make things better by being so bold. But it was too late now. "I think it is time I took you to my brother."

"Your brother?"

"King Cleomenes."

Aristagoras stared at him. He tried to remember if he had said anything to this young man that betrayed his intentions, and then thought angrily that it was no wonder the young man had said so little about himself! He had been sent by Cleomenes as a spy, and Aristagoras had fallen for the ruse—hook, line, and sinker. He felt very foolish.

They returned in silence to the Agiad royal palace with its long, low columned porch and the ancient Kouroi flanking the main door. The meleirenes came to attention for Leonidas, and then one of them said: "Sir! You are to take the stranger to the Tyndareus chamber. His things and slaves are there already."

They passed out of the sunlight and into the cool shade of the interior. Aristagoras could sense how old the palace was. The ceilings were lower than was now fashionable, with timber beams made of rough-hewn trees. Underfoot were mosaics so ancient that they were little more than crushed stone, rather than neat squares. At least there were frescoes on the walls here, albeit very old ones in the antique style and rather faded.

There was no doubt that Leonidas knew his way about, however. He led around several courtyards to a nice, small, well-planted one; and here Aristagoras was greeted by his own staff as if they had feared for his life, despite the bodyguards that still shadowed him. As Leonidas took his leave, Aristagoras could not resist tossing after him, "Going to report to your brother?"

Leonidas paused, turned back, and answered: "No, my company commander." Then he walked out.

———

Aristagoras could not complain about Cleomenes' hospitality, although he was now wary of Spartans generally and did not trust his host's apparent cordiality. The dinner served was excellent—maybe not as refined, and with less fish than Aristagoras preferred, but the meat was excellent and garnished with chestnuts and leeks. It was served on what he was assured was native pottery, which was lighter in color than the products of Athenian workshops, but boasted lifelike scenes. His host shared his excellent wine unmixed, and they had a very pleasant conversation in which Cleomenes asked many questions, giving Aristagoras an opportunity to show off his wide knowledge of the world.

The next morning there was a proper inspection of the army. This was a formal occasion, with the men in their battle panoply drawn up by lochos for their kings—Demaratus made an appearance, too. Aristagoras took the parade in front of the Council House and then followed by chariot to the drill fields, where maneuvers were held for his benefit.

It was impossible not to be impressed. These large units demonstrated the same precision of movement and discipline that the little escort had displayed. From the slope of the hill on which he stood, Aristagoras could hear none of the verbal commands—only the salpinx and flutes—but the speed with which units wheeled, shortened or expanded the distances, and the fluidity of their deployment from one formation to the next, suggested mastery of the art of marching far beyond anything Aristagoras had seen up to now. At length he turned to Cleomenes and remarked, "Very pretty; but can they fight?"

Cleomenes, as intended, was offended and drew a deep indignant breath. "Choose any man you like!"

"I don't mean man to man, I mean as an army. Does your army ever really fight?"

Cleomenes was boiling with rage. "Of course we do. Have you heard nothing about my campaigns in Attica and the Argolid?"

"Not really. I heard you got besieged on the acropolis once and had to turn back the next time for lack of allies—and indeed, domestic opposition." Aristagoras looked pointedly at Demaratus, who was talking to one of the lochagoi. "But I have not heard of the whole Spartan army going anywhere and doing anyone any harm in the last five Olympiads."

Cleomenes was furious, but he had no answer.

————

It was not until the afternoon that they got down to business.

For the official audience, Aristagoras was received in the ancient throne room, which was relatively low and dingy. The pillars here were thick and painted darkly. There was a hearth at the front of the room, open to the sky (and empty at this time of year), and the throne itself looked as old as the *Iliad*. It was flanked by two potted trees, a palm and an olive, that undoubtedly had some symbolic significance lost on Aristagoras and which no one bothered to explain. Cleomenes didn't sit on the throne. Instead he had couches and tables brought in, and they settled down comfortably.

Aristagoras opened his appeal: "I hope, Cleomenes, that you are not too surprised by my visit. After all, Sparta is the leading city in all Greece, and you are the Spartan king with the greatest intelligence and vision." Cleomenes bowed graciously at the compliment, although he had far from forgotten the insults of this morning.

"Now, the fact is this," Aristagoras continued: "the Ionians have become slaves to the Persians. This is not only their shame, but yours." Cleomenes raised his eyebrows. "It is *your* shame, King Cleomenes, because—as I said earlier—the Spartans are the leaders of Greece; and if any Greek is enslaved, then it diminishes your own glory."

"Ah," Cleomenes remarked ambiguously.

"But if you do that which is pleasing to the Gods and come to the aid of your oppressed brothers, you will find rich rewards. I do not speak only of the rewards of glory and fame—although these would be yours in abundance—but also the rewards of riches quite beyond counting."

"We have highly trained accountants here," Cleomenes corrected the impertinent stranger.

"So I heard—your women." Aristagoras laughed to show he recognized this was a joke. Cleomenes only frowned.

"Please, may I show you something I had made and transported all this way merely to show you where your own interests lie?"

Cleomenes was scowling now. "What?"

"If I may send to my quarters?"

"Of course."

Aristagoras asked one of the attending helots to go to his quarters and ask his own slaves to bring "the map."

Shortly afterward, four of Aristagoras' slaves appeared, carrying the awkward box offloaded at Limera. Cleomenes was curious, and he got up to stand over the slaves as they pried open the wooden box, revealing a large bronze sheet on which a map of the world had been etched. "Here," Aristagoras explained, pointing, "are the Gates of Herakles. Here is Italy and Sicily, and here is Hellas, with this dot representing Sparta."

Cleomenes pointed, "And that is the Isthmus, Corinth, and there is Athens."

"Exactly! Now look here. These are the oppressed cities of Ionia. Here is the Persian provincial capital of Sardis, and here—all the way over here—is the principal seat of the Great King, Susa. But his Empire does not end here. It goes on and on and on to the very ends of the earth in the East. The riches of all this vast Empire would be yours, if only you defeat the Persians in Ionia."

Cleomenes gave the tyrant-emissary a skeptical look.

"I have seen your army and I have heard that it is the best in the world—that is why I wonder so much at its staying here idle when your brothers cry out to you to save them from the Persian yoke. You will have no trouble *beating* the Persians. They fight in turbans and trousers, and their weapons are bows and short spears hardly better than their arrows. They are softened by a life of luxury and rich foods, nothing like your tough young men! If you defeat these effeminate men with their perfumed hair and painted faces in Ionia, you will not only have freed your brothers, but this whole, vast Empire will be yours for the taking." He gestured with his hand.

"Odd that these perfumed men with painted faces have conquered such a vast empire, then, isn't it?" Cleomenes noted.

"That was decades ago, under Cyrus. The new generation is soft." Aristagoras dismissed Cleomenes' objection and pointed to the map again. "Look, here is Lydia, a fine, rich country where the noblemen have houses filled with gold; and then Armenia, rich in cattle; here are Assyria and Cilicia and Media; and here Arabia, rich in spice, Phoenicia, the master of the Mediterranean, and Egypt, with all the riches of the Nile; here is conquered Babylon and humbled Media. Here, beyond the banks of the Choaspes, is Susa." He pointed to a star on the map. "This is where the Great King lives and keeps his treasure—the tribute paid by all these subject states and peoples. But beyond is still half the Empire—there is Parthia, Bactria, and India." He paused again and looked at Cleomenes' face. Cleomenes' eyes were narrowed, and he appeared to be calculating.

"Look!" Aristagoras drew his attention back to the lower left-hand quarter of the map, where the Greek peninsula was etched onto the bronze. "Isn't it time you stopped squabbling over this insignificant rocky scrap of land and turned your attention—and your superb army—to places of great fertility and wealth? Why do you shed the blood of your beautiful young men in interminable skirmishes with the Argives and Arcadians? Why not set before them a task worthy of their skills and courage? There is no gold or silver to be taken from Messenia or Arcadia—poor, rocky places that they are.

But here!" He pointed again to Persia and Susa. "Here are treasures beyond imagination, and all waiting for whoever is bold enough to seize them."

Cleomenes' eyes were swinging from Greece to Susa and back again. At last he asked, "Just how far is it from Sparta to Susa?"

"Your troops, I am told, march very fast. I was told that they can be in Messenia in a day or Athens in three. So if they were to set off from Miletos marching at that pace, they could reach Susa in three months." Aristagoras was being generous. Even Persian royal messengers using relays of horses took a month. He did not really think a Spartan army could cover the distance in three months; but he thought this sounded plausible enough to impress upon Cleomenes how vast the Persian empire was.

Cleomenes, however, took a step back from the map, which he had been examining closely, and announced sharply, "Stranger! Your proposal to take the Lacedaemon Army three months' journey from the sea is highly improper! You must leave Sparta before sunset!"

Aristagoras had not been prepared for such an abrupt dismissal. Things had been going so well up to this point. How could this one fact overturn all the rest of his arguments? But Cleomenes had already turned and stormed out of the throne room.

Aristagoras, seeing all his hopes retreating with Cleomenes, grabbed a small branch of the potted olive tree and tore it off. He hastened after Cleomenes, carrying this symbol of reconciliation and calling for him to stop. Cleomenes paid no heed. He stormed into a courtyard—where the girl Aristagoras had seen at the baths the previous day jumped up to greet him, announcing breathlessly, "Father! Uncle Leo says I can ride his mare Cyclone in the Gymnopaedia! I'm—"

Cleomenes laughed and threw an arm over the girl's shoulder, pulling her to him in a gesture of paternal indulgence and pride. "So I can lay wagers on you, can I?" he teased, ruffling her disorderly red hair as he asked.

"Sire, please hear me out," Aristagoras begged stiffly, embarrassed to be witness to such an unseemly domestic scene.

Cleomenes turned around to look at Aristagoras, dropping his arm from his daughter's bony shoulders and instantly becoming serious. The girl, however, stood beside him, also staring at Arista-goras—evidently too stupid to understand she had been dismissed.

"Send the child away," Aristagoras snapped irritably, gesturing with his head to the girl.

The girl looked at her father.

"Say what you wish and pay no attention to my Gorgo. She knows how to be silent," Cleomenes retorted with a stern look at his daughter, warning her to behave. Gorgo bit her lip and held her breath.

Aristagoras was furious. He felt ridiculous, standing like a suppli-cant with an olive branch in one hand in front of this half-wild girl, dressed in a short chiton that exposed her legs from the knee down. Part of him wanted to turn around and leave them both standing, but then the image of that immaculate escort flashed through his mind. He reminded himself of the brilliant maneuvering of the larger units this morning, and his desire to control such splendid troops overcame his sense of dignity. "You need not march all the way to Susa to see your own reward, sire."

Cleomenes raised his eyebrows.

"Your rewards would start at once. I could, from my own treasury, advance you ten talents. I have it with me at this very moment."

Cleomenes shook his head sharply.

"Twenty talents, then—but that is all I have on me at the moment."

Cleomenes shook his head again.

"Twenty talents, as I said, is all I have with me; but there would, of course, be another twenty waiting for you when you reached Miletos."

Cleomenes could be heard taking a deep breath, and the girl looked from him to Aristagoras and back in alarm.

"That's forty talents for you alone, sire, just for coming to Miletos with an army to liberate your Greek brothers from the Persian yoke. The other riches would then be yours for the taking—merely by sending your splendid bronze youths against the Persians in their silk pants."

This time Cleomenes did not shake his head. He frowned as if tempted.

"Make it fifty talents, then," Aristagoras conceded. "Twenty now, and thirty when you reach Miletos with an army at your back to bring freedom to Ionia."

"Father! You had better go away, or the stranger will corrupt you!" Gorgo burst out, unable to keep quiet any longer.

Cleomenes turned and looked at her as if he had forgotten she was there. Then, swinging back to face Aristagoras, he ordered, "Leave Sparta at once, stranger! I will not receive or listen to you ever again!" Then he stormed off through the next door, slamming it behind him.

Aristagoras was left in the anteroom with the despicable girl-child. These Spartans—so martial and masculine to the eye—were indeed ruled by their women! Even a girl-child, who in any proper home would have been ashamed to be seen, let alone heard, in the presence of a strange man, could tell a grown man—a king!—what to do!

Aristagoras was filled with rage and hatred for both the men, who were so weak and foolish, and even more these unnatural women. He was angry that he had come here, and furious that he had humiliated himself by asking for Spartan help. He burned with shame, and wanted nothing more than to be gone as quickly as possible. He turned on his heel and rushed back to his own quarters, angrily tossing away the olive branch as he stormed out.

Gorgo was left alone in the courtyard with a chilly feeling of having done something wrong. The stranger's look of hatred had been like a spear thrust to her gut. She sensed that he hated her not because she was ugly and had said something wrong, but just for being alive. And her father was angry with her, too. He had taken her advice, but he would not thank her for it. It occurred to her that she had come in the middle of something, and maybe she hadn't understood all that was going on. Her father had explicitly warned her to be silent. She had behaved like a child—blurting out the first thing that came into her head. Although it was summer and hot, she shivered—and decided she had better go tell her grandmother and Nikostratos what she had done. Maybe they could find a way to put it right.

CHAPTER 15

TRIAL BY FIRE

IT WAS THE DRIEST, HOTTEST SUMMER in memory. The crops were slowly parching in the fields, baked daily by the blistering sun and brittle from thirst. The helots tried to irrigate, but many of the smaller creeks and brooks had dried up altogether and some of the springs had run dry, while the level of the wells sank alarmingly. Men looked more and more anxiously toward the western sky, hoping for a cloud that would presage rain, but the sky was clear.

Laodice was terrified. She could not sleep at night for listening and praying for rain. She began each day with an inventory of what was left in their pantry. Why had she wasted so much flour on pastries and bread to sell in the market just so they could buy useless luxuries? She should have hoarded it instead. If they had no harvest this year, they would not make it through the winter. They would have to slaughter all their livestock just to have enough to eat. But what would they do without the oxen when it was time to plow and plant again?

Pelopidas, Polychares, and the youth Kleon worked themselves mercilessly in the oppressive sun to dig a ditch to the Eurotas, and then built a crude pump powered by an ox. With this they managed to get a trickle of water up to the lower field. They took turns driving the ox to power the pump, while the others raked or funneled the water to first one row of barley and then the next, and so on, until this one field came back to life. But Laodice watched her husband, her son, and Kleon shrink as they sweated away flesh. At the end of the day they fell into their beds, exhausted beyond thought or conversation.

At least Pantes' shop was prospering and, as Laodice had expected, he had taken a wife. Yet while Pantes no longer worried her, her concern for her daughters had grown. They were now at that dangerous pubescent stage when they were moody and boy-crazy. More than once she had caught them sneaking down to the Eurotas to watch the boys of the agoge swimming.

Laodice had lived in Laconia long enough to know that the sexually active youths of the agoge considered helot girls "fair game." Not that many of the youths of the agoge would actually rape the girls (though it happened now and again); most knew that using force against the helots working for another Spartiate could get them into serious trouble. The fact that Laodice's girls were Leonidas' helots made the situation even clearer. It was well known that Leonidas would not tolerate any abuse of his helots, and any youth who went too far would lose his hide.

The problem was that Laodice's girls seemed to have picked up the Laconian attitude toward these youths—namely, that it was an honor to be deflowered by a true Spartiate. The neighbor girls candidly argued that there could be nothing better than a Spartiate lover who paid you in game he had hunted or trapped, or even made the girls pretty trinkets with rolled stones and carved figurines.

Their mothers had nothing to say against the practice. It seemed they had all done it in their youth, and could point proudly to this or that item that had been a gift of this or that Spartiate—now respectable citizens with wives and children and honors. So the mothers encouraged their daughters' promiscuousness, saying that it added to the family diet and income, while the girls themselves loved being courted and bedded by the "golden" youth of the agoge.

The smarter girls even built up a dowry from the gifts of their Spartiate lovers to make them more attractive to their own class. To Laodice's incomprehension, the offspring of such unions carried no particular stigma. They were simply raised like other helot children, either by the girl's family or by the girl herself after she married.

To be sure, helot youths sometimes resented the deflowering of their future brides by their masters if they already fancied a girl, but there wasn't much they could do to stop it. Mantiklos had gotten into a terrible fight because he caught the girl he was courting with a meleirene. He'd attacked her in his rage, provoking her brothers to come to her defense. Mantiklos had ended up with a broken nose, several cracked ribs, and more simmering hatred toward the Spartiates than ever. But Laodice knew that the more mercenary helot youths actively encouraged their sweethearts to get as much material gain from their lovers as possible.

Laodice, however, sided with Mantiklos on this issue. She found the Laconian customs disturbing. She thought it was wrong and unhealthy for a girl to sleep with anyone other than her husband, and she wanted her girls to go to their marriage beds as virgins—as she would have liked to have done herself. So she fretted about her daughters and about finding them husbands before they got seduced by one of the Spartiate youths, while she anxiously watched the radiant blue sky for some hint of rain.

———

As the summer progressed, even the Eurotas shrank to a ghost of its normal self. With baskets of washing on their heads, the helot women had to cross the mud flats left behind on the riverbed as the water retreated. The mud clung to their legs and drew them deeper into the morass with each precarious step. When finished, they had to trudge back with the wet laundry on their heads, and sometimes women lost their balance in the treacherous quagmire, spilled their laundry, and had to start all over again.

For the youths of the agoge, the low water meant they had to wade through the stinking mud just to go for a swim at all—and then wade through the mud again afterward, getting dirty and sweaty again. The boys therefore chopped down trees and built a precarious walkway across the mud to the deeper parts of the river; but this only led to fierce fights between gangs of boys defending the bridge and those trying to take it. Generally they all ended up in the mud flats on either side of the bridge, coated in mud like piglets.

Disgusted, the teenage girls withdrew and found their own swimming hole farther downstream. The currents of the river, flowing over the roots of some ancient plane trees on a little island, had carved out a deep pool. The girls could reach the island with dry feet, because the channel on the eastern shore had dried up and the girls could leap across the narrow gully. The maidens stripped down, hanging their chitons on the trees, and with squeals and giggles of delight slipped into the cool water. They sank under the surface and let the water sweep their long hair downstream, then popped up again to catch their breath and wring the water from their hair. Their high-pitched chattering and giggling seemed to carry for miles.

The girls were soon discovered by some off-duty meleirenes, who didn't bother with the detour around the eastern shore and plunged right into the river, chasing the girls back to their island and their clothes. It was a silly game, as far as Gorgo could see. Disgusted with the brainless behavior of her friends, she grabbed her things and fled. One of the meleirenes tried to cut her off at the gully, but she gave him a kick in the direction of his groin that he just managed to deflect and told him bluntly, "I'm not interested!" Her tone of voice was too decisive for him to mistake it as flirting. He let her go.

Gorgo ran barefoot across the floodplain, which was now starting to bake and crack, and scrambled up the far bank, pulling herself up on dusty saplings. Only when she reached the road did she untie her sandals from around her neck and put them on her feet. She started tramping at a good marching pace in the direction of her grandmother's kleros. When she arrived half an hour later, the staff greeted her with exclamations of dismay. She usually rode over, and today she looked much the worse for wear. "Good heavens, girl! You look like something the cat dragged in!" her grandmother's old house-keeper exclaimed with humor.

Gorgo was reminded of the way her mother had always said that to her. She snapped unkindly at the old helot woman, "Maybe I *am* something the cat dragged in! Leave me alone!"

Overhearing this remark as she arrived, Chilonis exclaimed sharply, "Gorgo! You've no right to use that tone of voice to poor Irene! Apologize at once!"

Gorgo was in no mood to apologize to anyone. "Why should I?" she retorted. "She says I looked like something the cat dragged in, and all I said—"

"I heard what you said! It's not what you said but the way you said it! What on earth has got into you? Apologize to Irene and then come with me."

Gorgo had been late to mature. At thirteen, many had mistaken her for a child of ten or eleven. She had not started her monthly flux until this past spring, as she turned fifteen, and her breasts were only just starting to develop. Chilonis had therefore already diagnosed teenage moodiness and insolence, and she doubted if there were much she could do but wait for Gorgo to grow out of this unpleasant phase.

Gorgo turned to the helot and said in an angry, uncontrite voice, "I'm sorry if I was rude to you, but I don't think it's particularly nice to call someone 'something the cat dragged in.' I'm sure you wouldn't like it if I said it to you!"

The woman opened her mouth, flabbergasted, and then looked at her mistress, who sighed and said simply, "I'll deal with her, Irene. You go back to your work."

Chilonis then led the way out of the kitchen to her own study and sat down to face the now sullen Gorgo. "If you're going to go around dressed like a boy of the agoge, with your hair hanging unkempt about your shoulders and your feet filthy, you deserve to be told what you look like."

"Well, what do you want me to do? Sit around combing out my hair and oiling my skin for all the boys to see, like Nausica and Alkyone and Phaenna?"

Chilonis noted that now Phaenna, Gorgo's one and only friend, had apparently joined the clique of girls who were taking a pronounced interest in the opposite sex. That was normal. But she understood Gorgo, too.

Gorgo plopped herself down on the bench by the door, her long, lovely legs thrust out in front of her, but with her shoulders hunched and her head hanging as she picked absently at her frayed belt, and complained, "The *only* thing they can talk about is boys, boys, boys—who's won what race, who's had to go down to the pits, who's been caught with some helot girl. It drives me crazy!"

"Um," Chilonis commented. It could indeed be tedious—but it was also biological and inevitable. "Aren't you interested in any of them?"

"The meleirenes?" Gorgo asked, horrified. "A bunch of pimply little runts, whose only interest in us is sex! And they don't care which of us they get their hands on, either!" Gorgo shot back.

Chilonis laughed—because it was so true.

"I don't see what's so funny!" Gorgo demanded, her green eyes flashing and her lips thrust out in a stubborn pout. "*You're* the one who always said a woman isn't just a bedmate or a breeding factory— not to use the language *they* do!"

Chilonis sighed. It wasn't easy being fifteen. So she suggested simply, "You're right. Why don't you come with me to my geometry lesson?"

"Geometry lesson?"

"Yes, Nikostratos and I are learning geometry from that Thespian schoolmaster your uncle bought in Athens several years ago."

"I heard he didn't want to teach girls."

"He didn't at first; but then someone pointed out that one of his favorite students, whom he had mistaken for a boy of the agoge, was in fact a girl. And, of course, he couldn't say no to me. I think he has adjusted somewhat. Why don't you come? You were good at math."

"I need to change and comb my hair first," Gorgo suddenly decided.

"Well, wash your feet off in the trough and then go up to my room, comb out your hair, and take any of my peplos."

"OK." Gorgo sat up and was gone at once. With a sigh, Chilonis sat thinking things over before following. She caught up with Gorgo in her own bedchamber, where the teenager was looking through her chest of clothes.

Chilonis reached into the chest to pull out a bright green peplos with a border of yellow bees embroidered on it. "This would suit you. It will bring out your green eyes and the highlights in your hair."

"You want me to look pretty for a blind slave?" Gorgo challenged.

"Ibanolis is no longer a slave; your uncle bought his freedom. And you are to make yourself pretty to please *me*—and yourself. Let me help you."

Chilonis had Gorgo strip out of her dirty chiton with its worn belt and pulled the peplos out of the trunk, folded down a broad piece, and then wrapped it around her granddaughter. She used two strong bronze pins to clasp it at Gorgo's shoulders. She took a long silk sash and tied it at her waist, and then bloused the peplos over the sash and considered her work. Satisfied, she directed her attention to Gorgo's hair. It was darkening with age and had lost its bright red tones to become richer in color, particularly when wet. Chilonis made Gorgo sit down at her own dresser and, standing behind her, gently combed out her hair. "You have beautiful hair, Gorgo. Don't let anyone tell you otherwise. It is much more interesting than the bright blond that so many of your friends have."

"You're just saying that," Gorgo retorted, although she was secretly pleased and her grandmother knew it.

Rather than braiding her hair, Chilonis left it free, but clipped out of her face with some hairpins with the same bee motif. Together grandmother and granddaughter went back down to the courtyard, where the helots had already hitched two horses to the chariot in preparation for the trip into town.

As they drove past Leonidas' kleros, Gorgo remarked, "I think it's mean the way Eirana refuses to live here, after all the trouble Uncle Leo went to fix it up for her."

Chilonis cast her granddaughter a sideways glance. She quite agreed, but she wasn't sure it was good for Gorgo to take a dislike to her aunt.

"He really loves the place, you know, and now it's half boarded up and neglected again."

"Pelopidas and Laodice keep it in the best of order!" Chilonis defended the helot family.

"I didn't mean the farm. I know they keep that up, and their own quarters; but look, you can see the main house is shuttered up." Gorgo pointed and Chilonis knew it was true. She had seen it herself day after day.

"And she's not really a good mother, either," Gorgo continued in her self-righteous teenager tone; "she is too protective. Leo's son will get creamed in the agoge!"

"Gorgo, don't you think you're talking a little out of turn? I mean, what do you know about child-rearing?"

"Well, I know I wouldn't hover around *my* children all the time so that they couldn't take a single step on their own! And I wouldn't rush over and coddle them every time they fell and scraped their knee or just failed to get what they wanted!"

Chilonis felt she ought to reprimand Gorgo for passing judgment on her elders, but the girl was right. Eirana coddled and pampered her children. Hilaira had mentioned it, too, saying she knew how hard it was not to spoil and cosset one's children, but she thought Eirana carried it to extremes.

"What's that?" Gorgo asked, distracting Chilonis from her thoughts. She looked over to where Gorgo was pointing.

At first she thought it was a welcome cloud, but then she realized that it was too dark, and it billowed upright from somewhere beyond the mountain. It was smoke. Somewhere up in the mountains a fire had started, and in this dry weather it was sure to spread.

———

By nightfall they could see the glow in the sky from throughout the Eurotas valley, and the first firefighters, perioikoi from the villages nearest the fires, were on their way. However, a strong wind was blowing out of the northeast, driving the fires south and west.

By the next day the smudge of smoke hung over the sky to the southwest; and more and more residents in the southern Eurotas valley, helots and perioikoi alike, were dropping their farm tools and heading into the mountains to try to fight the fire. On the second night the southwestern sky was ablaze, and together light and smoke blotted out the stars in that quadrant of the heavens.

A runner reached Sparta the following morning. He was black with soot and streaked with limestone dust. He dropped to his knees, vomiting, before he could get the message out. "Out of control," he gasped as they passed him water to sip. "Completely—out—of—control." And then, when he had got control of his heaving chest again, "Threatening—Arna."

A company of the Conouran Lochos was dispatched at once, but by late afternoon they had sent for reinforcements. Reportedly, the whole western flank of the Taygetos was ablaze to the south. Arna had been consumed by flame, and the fire, fanned still by strong winds, was devouring the parched forest as it came closer and closer down the slopes toward the cultivated areas. Two more companies were dispatched, including the Kastor Company of the Pitanate Lochos.

They marched south to cross the Taygetos via the lower, gentler passes opposite Gytheon rather than take the brutal, direct route through the gorges. It was an eerie march, however; although they left after darkness, the unnatural glow in the sky above the mountains enabled them to see their way remarkably well. Not until they had put the spine of the Mani peninsula behind them, however, did they grasp the magnitude of the threat they were facing. Never having seen the like of it before, they had not been able to imagine what the previous messengers had been talking about. All the villages farther up the slope had been devoured by fire, and the flames were spreading still, feeding on the tinder-dry forest. The fire was coming relentlessly south, pushed by the northeast wind.

As they turned north to deploy, they saw how sparks carried by the wind rushed ahead of the main fire and, time and again, ignited the crown of needles in tree after tree with a whoosh of flame. This meant the fire was leapfrogging forward. While the main fire progressed at a steady pace, these forerunners lit scattered fires farther down the slope.

"By all the Gods! What can man do to stop it?" Oliantus exclaimed in horror. "Nothing will stop that until it reaches the sea!"

But there were scores of farms and several villages between the fire and the sea. "Has someone given the order to evacuate?" Leonidas asked Diodoros, but the company commander shook his head; he didn't know. A man galloped by on a horse, heading back for Sparta and more reinforcements.

They went forward, wearing their leather armor and armed with axes, shovels, and picks, to try to clear a firebreak ahead of the next village, Thalamai. They found themselves engulfed in smoke, the sun rising behind a curtain of soot. Daylight remained murky, and the sun was a dirty blood-orange. Soon they were coughing and retching from smoke inhalation. The thirst was terrible.

The company of the Conouran Lochos was finished. They staggered down the hillside, half sliding, half rolling, unable to stay upright, and they were black as Ethiopians with red eyes.

A rumor started that the ephors had finally grasped the gravity of the situation and that the whole army was on the march. Leonidas didn't believe it. They couldn't leave their backs exposed to the Argives.

By afternoon Leonidas could hardly stand, and his men were dropping to their knees from exhaustion. The heat and roar of the fire was so great it was like working inside a furnace, and they were so dehydrated they could neither spit nor piss. They were coughing dry, shallow coughs, their lungs filled with filth. Overhead the smoke billowed black and ominous, blocking out the sun, and then the first sparks started hitting them. A shout went up, and they knew what it meant even before the salpinx sounded retreat.

Like the company of the Conouran Lochos before them, the companies of the Pitanate and Limnate Lochoi fell more than walked back out of the smoke to be replaced by the complete Amyclaeon Lochos—all four pentekostus—fresh in from Sparta. Leonidas and his men staggered to the fountain at Thalamai to drink before they fell into the sea—without bothering to first strip off their leather armor—to cool off.

When Leonidas had pulled himself together, he found Oliantus, and together they made a quick assessment of their men. Many were suffering from minor injuries—twisted ankles, broken fingers, and burns. All were coughing up black phlegm. "We ought to work with wet cloths over our mouths," Oliantus suggested, and Leonidas nodded, grateful as always for his deputy's diligence in trying to take care of them all. Not for the first time, Leonidas conceded to himself that he couldn't manage without the ugly man. He looked around, wondering where they were going to get wet cloths, and noted that some of the villagers were loading wagons and preparing to evacuate. He went over to one of the men, who was hoisting his little children up to a woman already aboard the wagon. "Has the order been given to evacuate?"

"Do you think I'm waiting for some bloody order? I'm no boneheaded Spartan! I'm a free perioikoi, and I'm not standing around to see my family incinerated. I'm heading north on the coastal road while it's still clear!"

The road north led through Leuktra to Kardamyle, and between the two lay Leonidas' estate where Eirana had chosen to raise their children. Leonidas had time only to thank the Gods that the wind was blowing hard from the north, and not threatening his wife and children, before he was called to a conference.

There were now three full lochoi deployed to fight the fires here in Messenia, but fires had also started in Laconia itself; and the company of the Conouran Lochos was being ordered back to Sparta to help deal with the fires there, while the Mesoan Lochos moved to the Argive border to ensure the Argives didn't take advantage of the situation—and to address any fires that might break out on the Parnon range. The entire Peloponnese was a tinderbox.

The conscientious Oliantus made sure the men got a meal, and they got some sleep, too; but by dusk they were woken and sent back into the fight. Making use of a natural gorge over a now completely dry riverbed, the firefighters had cleared a strip of land almost two thousand yards wide. By midnight the sparks from the fire on the other side of the gorge were falling on the cleared areas, starting small fires among the underbrush, trunks, and roots left behind, but unable to take hold. It looked as if this firebreak was going to hold, and the firefighters sank onto the ground to watch—prepared to take action if necessary, but for the first time daring to hope it would not be. Their state of exhaustion was so great, however, that it was several minutes before someone realized the reason the sparks were no longer threatening them: the wind had shifted.

"The wind's backed around to the south," someone exclaimed in alarm.

Leonidas raised his head, unable—unwilling—to believe it. But staring at the fire, his eyes confirmed the report. The flames were blowing away from them. They struggled to their feet even before an order was given, their smoke-filled brains and exhausted bodies slowly grasping the significance of the shift. There was no danger that this firebreak would fail, but to the north there was nothing whatever to stop the fire.

Orders were passed down the line to return down to the coastal road. They obeyed, still dazed and exhausted. The Amyclaeon Lochos had already moved out, heading north. They were ordered to follow at once. It was, however, impossible to see how dangerous the situation was, because smoke obscured the entire slope of the mountains.

Just before daybreak they came upon a completely incinerated wagon, with the charred corpses of the horses still in the traces and the black lumps of former humans in the box of the wagon. The fire had swept over them with such intensity and speed that they had not even had time to disembark and run to the sea, only a hundred paces away. Everything was burned right down to the beach. The paving stones they were marching on were hot.

Leonidas felt ill. Eirana and his children were on a farm in the line of the fire, and there was nothing he could do for them but pray. He prayed that the Amyclaeon Lochos had managed to get ahead of the line of fire and that someone had sent messengers warning the inhabitants to evacuate.

When they finally caught up with the support train of the Amyclaeon Lochos and the ragtag collection of volunteer firemen from the surrounding countryside, they were informed that Arkines had been lost—everyone in the village had burned to death in their own homes or while trying to escape the conflagration. The firefighters were again trying to create a firebreak, this time about eight miles north of Arkines; but the speed of the fire was as fast as a man could walk, and the erratic wind sent it now northward, now westward in unpredictable gusts.

Climbing up from the coast onto the slope, Leonidas and his men were gasping for breath long before they even reached the fighting line. On arrival, they found that at least half the men they were relieving had already collapsed, unable to stand any longer. No one spoke. The Amyclaeons dragged themselves off, and the Pitanates took over with a sense of desperation tinged with helplessness. They were exhausted and thirsty before they even started. If the wind didn't veer again or let up, it was obvious that they would not be able to contain the fire here.

Still, they tried. They widened and lengthened the firebreak for over three hours, and Leonidas was on the brink of thinking they would succeed, when a sudden gust of wind sent a flurry of burning twigs and branches over their heads. Trees exploded into flame more than a hundred yards behind them. The auxiliaries panicked instantly, flinging down their heavy tools and running straight down the slope in sheer terror. The orders for the Spartiates to withdraw came almost at the same time, the salpinx wailing withdrawal and senior officers shouting and pointing furiously. They had to move fast to avoid being trapped. Already the flames were on three sides of them. The heat started to blister their skin. Leonidas didn't know where they suddenly found the strength to jog out of the trap.

Leonidas' first duty was to his enomotia. Twenty-odd years of discipline kept him from losing his head. He had to get his men to safety, and every one of them needed water and rest. But mentally he envisaged the flames, which were now encircling the stretch of mountain on which his estate stood. No matter which way the wind blew, it was endangered.

But surely Eirana had already left. For all he knew, she had left days ago. She might have returned to Laconia as soon as the fires broke out, he told himself. But another part of his brain whispered, "Why should she have done that while the wind blew from the north?" He wanted to think she would come "home" for safety as soon as any danger loomed; but the truth was, she didn't seem to view him—much less his kleros—as home or safety.

They collapsed on the shore of the sea, and Oliantus went in search of fresh water and food, while Leonidas went in search of someone who could tell him the evacuation status of the villages and farms on the endangered mountainside. The Amyclaeon lochagos didn't have the foggiest idea of the status of the civilians, but the perioikoi head councilman of Kardamyle said that refugees had been passing through the village all night. He wasn't sure where they had come from, but many had surely gotten through, heading along the coastal road, which was still open.

Leonidas returned to his men. Eirana was an intelligent woman, and she was very protective of her children. She would not take unnecessary risks. She was also a good driver and had several carts and strong draft horses on the farm. The helots on this farm were sullen but not rebellious, and it was in their own interest to get off the farm if it were endangered. Leonidas told himself he had every reason to assume that Eirana and the children had made it to safety. He dropped down beside his platoon, and Oliantus handed him a jug full of warm water. "Drink it slowly!" he ordered his superior. "One sip at a time."

Around him his men lay as if dead—sprawled on their backs,

their sides, their stomachs, their arms and legs flung any which way. They were filthy, stinking, and done in. But the sun was blotted out by the smoke, and even the air around them was thick with heat and falling ash. Oliantus handed Leonidas a chunk of bread. He took a bite, started chewing, and then fell back and lost consciousness.

Someone shook him awake. Nothing had changed. He might have been asleep for only a few moments—except that he was very stiff. The Mesoan Lochos had just arrived. The Argolid was also aflame, and the ephors had decided they no longer needed to defend the border. Kyranios had already taken overall command of the fire-fighting efforts. He ordered the two already exhausted lochagoi to get to work cutting a firebreak around Kardamyle itself, with its precious warehouses and port facilities, while he took his comparatively fresh lochos farther up the slope to protect the springs above Kardamyle.

Leonidas just managed to speak to Kyranios before the lochagos set off with his men. "The last I knew, Eirana was on my farm up there," he told his father-in-law. To his own ears, his strained voice betrayed his fears.

Kyranios nodded and replied calmly, "She's not a child or a fool. She will have had the sense to get out while she could." Then, seeing the look in Leonidas' eyes, he laid a hand on his arm and reminded him, "We're doing all we can."

They got to work on the firebreak. There wasn't one of them without some injury, and their muscles were so stiff they couldn't respond more than woodenly. At least they had relatively easy access to water here, and Oliantus had their attendants working in relays to bring them water every half-hour. He had organized bread, cheese, and sausage, too. Although the air was bad, the heat was more endurable, now that they weren't working in the direct proximity of the flames.

By midafternoon the flames had reached the upper firebreak, but the break appeared to be holding. The two lochoi near Kardamyle were given a hot meal and then sent to reinforce the Mesoan Lochos at the upper firebreak.

The fire was raging across the face of the mountain, nipping already at the last trees on the far edge of the tree line. Beyond that, it would burn itself out on the limestone. But Leonidas' estate was obliterated. He couldn't even locate the buildings in the charred, still smoking devastation left behind. If Eirana hadn't made it to safety...

They stayed by the firebreak through the night, watching the flames slowly starve for lack of anything left to consume. The wind had died down, too, helping to stabilize the situation. At least here. The night sky was still marked by lurid light coming from other fires to the north and east. Weary beyond caring, Leonidas wondered who was fighting those fires. Then his watch was over and he fell asleep.

He awoke, disoriented. The sun was bright for the first time in days, and bizarrely, Alkander was bending over him. "Leo," he woke him gently. "Leo."

Leonidas sat up. His whole enomotia was on their feet, already awake but doing nothing, just standing around looking strange. Apparently Oliantus had woken them, but not him. Oliantus' ugly face was deformed even further by an expression of deep worry, while Mantiklos hovered beside him anxiously as if he'd been sick. And where did Alkander come from? He was with the Conouran Lochos. Were they back? Apparently.

"Leo, I've been sent to tell you we found them."

"Found who?" Leonidas still wasn't fully awake. Then he remembered. "Eirana and the twins? Are they in Kardamyle?" He dragged himself to his feet, his aching muscles protesting painfully.

"They didn't make it out, Leo."

They stared at one another. Leonidas wanted to deny it, say it couldn't be true—but obviously they wouldn't have sent Alkander otherwise.

"Where are they? Where were they found?"

"Search parties went in at first light. Kyranios sent men to your estate straight away. All that is left of the house and outbuildings are the cellars."

"What do I care about the house? Are you sure she was there? Are you sure she didn't get away in time?"

"She wasn't in the house, Leo. We found her and the twins about two hundred yards from the house—and her daughter by Asteropus another hundred yards away. It looked as if the elder girl had run away, and Eirana went after her, but we can't be sure what happened. Only that they are dead."

"I want to see them," Leonidas told him.

"No. Not really. It would be better if you didn't," Alkander told him honestly; but he did not expect to be heeded.

Leonidas roared at him that he had a right to see his wife and children, no matter what state they were in; and Alkander dutifully led him away with a last look at Oliantus, who nodded understanding.

———

Chilonis stopped by Leonidas' kleros to tell Laodice the news. "I just wanted you to know," she explained to the helot woman, who stood drying her hands helplessly on her apron. "He might not say anything himself; and without knowing what happened, you might have said something that hurt or angered him inadvertently."

Laodice nodded, her hands wringing her apron in distress.

"Is something else the matter?" Chilonis asked.

Laodice shook her head. Between them Pelopidas, Polychares, and Kleon had managed to save the main field of barley with their pump; and the apples and pears were coming, smaller than normal, but they would yield. They would have an olive harvest, too, though the wine was uncertain. Laodice wasn't worried about herself at the moment, only Leonidas. "Will the master come back, do you think, ma'am?"

"I think so," Chilonis answered, but she wasn't sure. He had spent his wedding night here; his two children had been conceived and born here. He might not want to come back. "I hope so," she added with a sad smile to Laodice. "You've done so much to make it lovely."

Laodice shook her head. "The garden's ruined, ma'am. We couldn't waste water on useless plants this year."

"Of course not," Chilonis agreed, following the helot's gaze to the brown, brittle wrecks of rosebushes and oleander that bordered the terrace. "But you might be surprised. Plants are more resilient than we think—and people, too."

———

Laodice didn't hear him come. She awoke in the middle of the night, as she so often had this horrible summer, and sat up listening for what had disturbed her. Pelopidas was lying on his stomach with one hand on the floor, snoring softly. He had every reason to sleep hard, and she slipped out of bed carefully so as not to disturb him. Pulling on the chiton she had worn the day before, she tiptoed out of the room, past Kleon fast asleep by the hearth, and glanced at the bed under the loft where Melissa lay curled in Polychares' arms, the cradle in easy reach. Their infant slept as soundly as his parents.

Laodice went up the first several rungs of the ladder to get a look in the loft and check that both the girls were there—not off trysting with some hot-blooded and foolish meleirene. But to her relief, two pairs of feet stuck out at her on the bed the girls shared.

Still, she could not shake the sense that something was amiss. She was standing in the middle of the cold kitchen, trying to decide what to do, when something snapped outside the kitchen window, and she caught her breath in alarm. Something was indeed moving just outside the kitchen; but the longer she stood still and listened, the more certain she became that a horse was tied up outside. She slipped outdoors and found Leonidas' stallion loosely tied to the railing of the barn, doing his best to graze on the sunburned grass. He raised his head at the sight of her and nickered, expecting feed. Laodice dutifully returned to the pantry and selected one of the shriveled-up, worm-eaten apples that she kept in a special barrel. She brought this back to the stallion and then moved cautiously toward the terrace to find his master.

She saw Beggar first. The bitch was sitting in front of the bench, looking into the shadows with mute concern. Leonidas was entirely lost in the shadows cast by a rising moon. Laodice hesitated. He clearly wanted to be alone with his memories and ghosts. She had no right to intrude. But an instinct stronger than reason compelled her forward.

He had leaned his head back against the whitewashed plaster of the house, and tears were trickling down the side of his face. She sat down beside him, taking his left hand in both of her own without a word. He didn't start or open his eyes, but he closed his hand around hers while the tears streamed in a heavier flood. Laodice found she was crying as well, but it didn't matter. Beggar looked from one to the other, tapping the terrace tiles with her tail in confusion.

Eventually he swallowed and lifted his head, opening his eyes. Laodice at once withdrew her hands and stood to leave.

"It's all right," he told her. "Sit with me a moment more."

She sat down again, a little nervous now.

"It was a bad marriage," he told her simply. "She never loved me, and I'm not sure I loved her—not in the end. I did once, when I was young; but the rejection hurt, and I wasn't sure I wanted her when her father asked me. But at first she seemed so...loving. Later I realized she only wanted more children."

Laodice took his hand again and held it firmly.

"What kills me is Kleopatra and Kleodakos. I shouldn't have let her take them so far from me. I should have made her live in the city like most young brides, so I could see them daily. I should have watched them growing up, and been a father to them—like Alkander is to his boys. As it is, I know the children of every man in my enomotia better than my own. Isn't that sick?"

"No," Laodice told him firmly, shaking her head. "It was Apollo's way of protecting you. Your children were marked to die, master. The mistress had dreams about it. She knew the fire would consume her. She had dreams here every night. We all thought it was the old fire that haunted her, the fire that burned down this kleros; but, you see, none of *us* ever had nightmares. Now it is clear the dreams were a warning of what was to come."

"But if she'd stayed here, she would have been all right."

Laodice shook her head. "No, master. We can't run away from our destiny. If she had stayed here, we all would have died with her. The fires would have struck here and not in Messenia."

Leonidas gazed at the aging helot woman. He was not convinced about destiny—but he could see Laodice believed absolutely in what she said. He could see that she was grateful his wife had taken her curse somewhere else. The helots on the estate where she had chosen to live had all died with her. (And if they hadn't, Leonidas would have personally seen to it that they were executed for abandoning Eirana and his children.)

"Please come home, master," Laodice found the courage to beg him softly. "Next year when you go off active service, don't go and live somewhere else. Come back here. We'll fix up everything for you. I'll replant the garden."

Leonidas nodded and said "Thank you," ambiguously.

Laodice knew she had done as much as she could. She dared not press him further, so she slipped away. Returning to her bedroom, she pulled her chiton off over her head and lay down. Pelopidas turned over in his sleep and pulled her into his arms. His breathing resumed its normal rhythm. Laodice lay contentedly in his embrace; but her senses were too alert to let her sleep until she heard Leonidas collect his horse outside their bedroom, then ride at a canter up the drive to return to Sparta in the moonlight.

CHAPTER 16

FULL CITIZENS

AT THE WINTER SOLSTICE, THE MEN who had completed ten years of active service symbolically turned over their standard-issue lambda-bearing shields to the graduating class of eirenes and joined the reserves. For the first time in twenty-four years, the young men would not be required to sleep in barracks, and for the first time in their lives they would be eligible for public office. Alkander was looking forward to living on his kleros full time rather than simply visiting on holidays, and in the last fortnight before the solstice he spent all his free time fixing it up.

The smell of Hilaira's cheese balls wafted up from the kitchen to the loft, where Alkander was building beds for his two sons from reeds he had cut on the banks of the Eurotas. As he worked, he explained to his wide-eyed boys what he was doing. "The reeds are flexible but strong, so you can weave them together like this and then they'll hold together. See? Now we'll fill up the frame with straw and sweet-smelling sprigs of lavender, but when you're out camping you can use leaves, pine needles, or grass. And even if you can't find anything to fill it with, you can lay your himation over it, and at least the frame will keep you up off wet or hard ground."

"Hungry!" two-year-old Simonidas announced, completely bored by his father's long lecture on bed construction; already he was scrambling down the ladder from the loft with the agility of a monkey. His elder brother Thersander watched him go; but when he was sure his brother had run off in the direction of the kitchen and he was alone with his father, he asked in a low voice, "What is it like, Dad? The agoge, I mean." In just two weeks' time, when the holiday at the solstice was over, Thersander would enter the agoge for the first time, because he would turn seven in the course of the coming year.

Alkander had been concentrating on the bed, and the question took him by surprise. At some level he had been expecting this question since the day his son was born, but he hadn't been expecting it today, right now. It caught him like a kick in the gut, and he held back a gasp. Then he looked over into his son's earnest face and wanted to scream. Instead, he said, "It takes some getting used to at first, Sandy, but you'll find that it is mostly fun."

Thersander did not look convinced, and he gazed at his father with large, dark eyes that seemed to know he was lying. Alkander tried harder. "The agoge is where I met Uncle Leo. We did everything together when we were little—riding and swimming and cave exploring." All on holidays from the grim agoge, Alkander noted to himself mentally. "And you'll learn about tracking and trapping, and to play ball." He exerted himself more.

Thersander nodded solemnly, evidently still not convinced. He looked at the reed bed his father had made and rubbed the frame absently. "Did you have to go to the pits very often?"

"Just once in my whole life," Alkander assured him. At least *that* was an honest answer.

"Why?" Thersander wanted to know.

"Uncle Leo and I were supposed to fend for ourselves for ten days, if I remember correctly; only we'd been lazy and hadn't set enough traps, and so we got hungry and thought we'd steal some cheese from a helot family. But their geese caught us red-handed, and we had to go to the pits. Which was only right."

"And Uncle Leo?"

"He went to the pits with me."

"Just that once?"

"No, he got in trouble a second time, but that is a long story. I'm sure he'll tell you about it if you ask. But for now I agree with Simonidas. Let's go get something to eat." He smiled at Thersander, and the boy took the hint, scampering down the ladder as if he'd forgotten the topic.

Alkander, however, could hardly eat for inner agitation. As soon as they had put the boys to bed for their nap, he addressed Hilaira. "You married a coward and a liar," he opened in a rush of self-contempt. "I told our son today that the agoge is 'fun.' Fun!"

"What choice did you have? It wouldn't do him any good to be afraid of it," Hilaira reasoned.

"Are you sure? I don't know anymore." Alkander dropped his head in his hands and ruffled his still-cropped hair. After the solstice he would be allowed to start growing it out and would soon wear the braids of a full citizen.

Hilaira reached out and laid a hand on her husband's knee. "Not all boys hate it like you did. Prokles and Leo got on just fine for the most part. Sandy is strong and self-confident. There's no reason why he should suffer like you did."

"No other civilized city in the world does to their young children what we do!" Alkander replied, jumping to his feet and starting to pace around the hearth room. "It's nearly freezing out there," he continued, pointing to the shuttered windows, which only partially kept out the chill, "but we will make the boys go barefoot! They'll be expected to wear nothing but a coarse chiton and himation, and they will freeze! Some boys become so sick that they have sore throats and running noses from the first week practically to the summer solstice! Why?"

Before Hilaira could even draw a breath to answer, Alkander answered himself. "The idea of a public school is right, of course. When you hear Leo's stories about the way rich Corinthian and Athenian youths have private tutors and trainers while the poor cannot read or write, I know that the concept of a public school is a good and just idea. We ensure that every boy in the next generation learns our laws, our history, and our musical traditions, and we ensure they have the skills they will need as citizens, to reason and think logically, to argue cogently and express themselves succinctly. Their training makes them good hoplites, capable of withstanding hardship and privation when necessary and able to endure pain for the sake of the line. But why do we have to go to such extremes?"

"Maybe you don't," Hilaira suggested, looking her husband in the eye as he turned to stare at her. "My grandfather claimed that the agoge wasn't always as harsh as it is now. He said when he was young the food was better, for example; but then a Paidonomos came along who wanted to encourage trapping and hunting by making the food so monotonous that the boys wanted to hunt and trap. He said the Phouxir was shorter, too, and earlier in the year so that the weather was generally milder."

Hilaira had Alkander's undivided attention; her grandfather, Lysandridas, had been the closest thing Alkander had ever had to a grandfather (not having known his own), and he respected him greatly. "According to Granddad," Hilaira continued earnestly, "shortly after Chilon died, the Eurypontid King Ariston maneuvered his candidate for Paidonomos into the agoge. At the time, Leo's father was still too inexperienced to know how to oppose him. The new headmaster was a fanatic who coined the phrase, 'What doesn't kill them will make them stronger.'"

Alkander snorted, adding, "What rubbish! As if the boys can't become sick and maimed and carry lasting damage from bad diet and excessive hardship."

"He ran the agoge for almost two decades, making it harsher the older and more inflexible he became. I remember Granddad saying to my mother that we were lucky Epidydes took over shortly before your age cohort was enrolled. He expected Epidydes to change things."

Alkander gazed at his wife. As a schoolboy, Epidydes had seemed more distant and more powerful than the Gods. The Paidonomos held the fate of all the boys in his hands. He had the final say on whether a boy was punished and how, and on whether or not a boy was to be expelled and so excluded from citizenship. Even as an adult Alkander had long avoided Epidydes, acutely aware of his own inadequacies as a schoolboy and secretly suspicious that Epidydes had only allowed him to remain in school as a favor to the Agiads.

"Your grandfather considered Epidydes a good man?" he asked Hilaira again, watching her face closely.

"Yes," Hilaira insisted, removing her snood and combing her hair back with her hands, twisting it together at the back of her head, and replacing her snood. Then she faced Alkander down. "He supported

Epidydes actively in his candidacy for Paidonomos, and he was so relieved when he was elected that he got a little drunk. I remember it very well because he didn't get drunk often, you know, and I was just a little girl. I didn't understand much except that he was very happy for Prokles' sake."

"Hilaira," Alkander started very cautiously, afraid of her reaction, "what would you say if I told you I wanted to work in the agoge?"

"Why should I oppose it?" she asked back. "You can't just sit around here and get in my way!" She cast the retort at him with a smile and a laugh, making him laugh with her, but they both knew she was serious, too. She'd been running his affairs for nearly a decade. She did not need—or want—any interference from him now.

"Of course, the Gods only know, Epidydes might throw me out the door before I even finish asking. I mean, I'm a mothake—"

"Don't use that term!" Hilaira cut him off. "It's not your fault your father had a marginal kleros or that your mother wasn't good at running it. Just because she couldn't pay your school fees and Leo had to pay them for you doesn't make you any less a citizen today!"

"Do you have any idea how many young men are in my same situation now? This last drought has wiped out scores of families," Alkander pointed out. As someone who had nearly been thrown out of the agoge because his mother couldn't pay his fees, Alkander paid attention when he heard that one man or another had pulled his son out of school. He knew it was still happening, particularly in years like this, when terrible weather caused the crops on marginal land to fail.

"I know how lucky we are that your sister married the Eurypontid king and that he felt compelled to give us this excellent kleros. I know some kleros are so infertile that nothing a woman does can make them yield enough for her husband and sons. We are very, very lucky."

Alkander impulsively took a jar of milk and poured some out before the house altar with a prayer of thanks. After his mediocre performance in the agoge and his dependency on Leo, he could so easily have been given one of the marginal kleros that could hardly support a man, much less his sons. Instead, they were living on a sound kleros that turned a small surplus even in a year like this, just because his sister had fired the lust of King Demaratus.

But Hilaira had everything under control here. She could be trusted to keep her sons financially secure. Where the boys needed him was in the agoge. "Hilaira, I'm serious. I want to apply for a position as instructor, with the long-term goal of becoming at least a deputy headmaster or, eventually, even Paidonomos."

Hilaira nodded. "I can't think of anyone in Lacedaemon who would be better suited," she assured him.

"You might be biased," Alkander noted, pulling her into his arms with relief and gratitude.

———

Brotus stretched himself out on the cushioned bench beside the hearth and closed his eyes for a short nap. He didn't intend to sleep long, but drill had been exhausting in the muddy morass the drill fields had become; and after a hefty meal of his wife's crusty pork chops and bread drenched in herbal butter, the cozy warmth of the room made him sleepy. He left his flaky pastry, made with crushed nuts and honey, on the table beside him for when he woke up.

Pausanias peered around the door, his eyes on the pastry. His mother made wonderful sweets, but she never let him have any. Sweets, she said, were for adults. They ruined children's teeth, she said; besides, he wouldn't get any in the agoge and might as well get used to it, since he started in less than a fortnight. But Pausanias loved sweets.

He looked over his shoulder to be sure he wasn't being watched. He could hear his mother's stern voice reproaching the housekeeper for some fault. Helots were dumb and always made mistakes. His mother spent her whole day chasing after them and making sure they did their work properly.

He looked back at his father. His father appeared to be sound asleep. One hand had fallen off his belly and hung completely relaxed, the fingers stretched limply toward the floor. The other hand rose and fell with his barrel-shaped chest, encased now in nothing but his sweat-stained chiton. Pausanias took a step into the room and then paused. Except for his rising and falling chest, his father didn't move. Another step, and another. Brotus was starting to snore very softly in the back of his throat. Pausanias was within range of the honey pastry.

Holding his breath, the six-year-old reached out slowly. His hand closed around the pastry and he yanked his arm back. The pastry was his!

But a drop of honey had fallen on his father's forehead as he snatched the pastry off the table. Brotus came out of his dream with a confused grunt. He felt his forehead with his hand, then stared in confusion at the sticky, clear substance on his fingers. He looked so funny that Pausanias chortled in delight.

"Huh?" Brotus sat up and turned toward his son in a single motion, a frown clouding his face. He saw Pausanias stuffing the pastry into his mouth as fast as he could, hardly chewing in his haste to get it all inside before someone could take it away from him.

Brotus growled, "You impudent little rascal!" and sprang to his feet.

Pausanias bolted. Brotus' feared fist hit thin air, and that made him roar in rage. "You little bugger! I'll teach you a lesson!"

Pausanias nimbly slithered out a window and darted across the farmyard toward the barn. Brotus lumbered after him, still shouting insults. He burst into the barn and looked around, bewildered in the comparative darkness. The bull stirred uneasily in his stall. The milk cows blinked at him and moved their jaws in circles as they chewed. Brotus growled, "Show your ugly face, you little bugger, or you'll be sorry!"

High-pitched laughter tumbled down from overhead, and Brotus looked up to see his son comfortably crouched in the rafters, grinning at him.

"Don't think I'll forget about this!" Brotus shook his clenched fist at his son. "You'll get yours when you come down!"

Then he turned and stormed out of the barn, smiling smugly. The cub was all right, Brotus thought proudly. He liked the boy's impudence, because that showed courage, and he was proud of how agile and quick he was. Brotus made for the kitchen rather than the hall. "Sinope!" he called for his wife as he crossed the threshold.

"I'm right here; no need to shout!" came the tart retort.

Sinope was no beauty. She was tall for a woman, thin, bony, and flat. Her face was angular, with a mouth that was wide and a little crooked under an oversized, beak-like nose. But Brotus was pleased with her. She'd presented him with Pausanias less than a year after their marriage; and there were two more children in the nursery now as well, a girl and another boy. This production of offspring was a wife's most important function. Brotus felt his full nursery demonstrated his own virility and underlined his superiority over his twin brother, who was childless again.

But Sinope was more than a good breeder. She also cooked hearty, tasty meals, and she ran the kleros like a drillmaster. The helots got away with nothing here—she even collected the leftovers from every meal and fed them to the pigs rather than letting the helots feast on meat and white bread made for their masters.

"I want another pastry," Brotus announced, plopping himself down on the bench behind the kitchen table.

"Another?" Sinope asked back. "I don't know about that." Her gray eyes went pointedly to his waistline. "You don't want to get any fatter than you are already."

"I'm not fat, and I'll eat as much as I damn well please in my own house!" Brotus growled back, but he didn't really mind his wife's concern. It showed she cared about him.

Sinope raised her eyebrows, but she went over to the cupboard and took down the wooden tray with the pastries on it. She placed one on a plain pottery plate with black glaze, manufactured right in Amyclae. She was not one of those spendthrift wives like her sister-in-law, who insisted on buying Corinthian or even Athenian pottery, all painted with fancy figures of people doing any number of silly things. She brought the plate over and thumped it down in front of her husband. Standing before him with her hands on her hips, she asked, "And what were you shouting at Pausanias about?"

Brotus scowled up at her, but then gave up and burst out laughing. "You're right. He got my pastry, the little thief; but I'll give him a lesson he won't forget as soon as I get my hands on him."

"I see; which means he got away from you as well," Sinope concluded rightly.

Brotus laughed again, and their eyes met. They were both very proud of their firstborn.

Sinope sat down opposite Brotus. "While I have your attention,

I've been meaning to ask you: what do you plan to do when you go off active service?"

"Afraid I'll get in your hair, are you?" Brotus asked back, then laughed at his own joke. "Not a chance. The Orestes gymnasium wants me to take over the position of chief trainer. They think with me on the staff, all the aspiring boxers will come to the Orestes gymnasium. And I'm not half bad with discus and javelin, either."

Sinope nodded, satisfied. She had worried that Brotus might decide to just "retire." Her sister's husband was like that, and she had nothing but contempt for him. A man ought to be involved in public affairs in one way or another.

"And then I'm going to see that I get elected to one thing or another," Brotus added, breaking into her thoughts, after finishing off the pastry and wiping the crumbs away with the back of his fist.

"Such as?"

Brotus shrugged. "Whatever. It doesn't matter so much what, so long as I'm seen to be leading. I'm the rightful Agiad king and as soon as my brother dies, I'm going to take hold of my inheritance. It's good for people to get used to looking up at me. Being in the Guard was good, but I was one of three hundred there. I need to stand out more."

Sinope nodded approval; but before she could speak, movement at the door caught the couple's attention. Pausanias was back, grinning at them.

"Come in here and get what you deserve!" Brotus barked.

Pausanias' eyes shifted as if considering escape, but then walked straight up to his father and stood still in front of him. "Good boy!" Brotus praised, and then cuffed his son hard with the back of his hand.

Brotus' fists were those of a professional boxer and his blow, although only a casual flick from the wrist, was enough to make blood gush from his son's nose. Sinope made an annoyed sound and reached for a wet dishcloth to stanch the bleeding, but Pausanias made no noise; he just stared at his father.

Brotus smiled. "Good boy! Sinope, get our son a pastry."

"Brotus! That's not right. You know he'll get none in the agoge."

"Not unless he can steal 'em, huh?" He winked at his son.

Pausanias smiled, despite the blood streaming down his face.

His mother handed her son the wet cloth and ordered him to hold it to his nose until the bleeding stopped, while she fetched him the pastry her husband had ordered.

"There are some things you need to know about the agoge, boy," Brotus started in a fatherly tone while his son stood holding the bloody cloth to his nose. "First, you know each class elects their herd leader, don't you?"

Pausanias nodded.

"I was elected herd leader as a seven-year-old—and every year after that! I expect the same of you, or you're going to feel what my fists can do when I have a mind to! Understand?"

Pausanias nodded.

"Good. I was a Victor of Artemis Orthia, too, and the same goes for that."

Pausanias nodded.

"As regards the Phouxir, you shouldn't have any trouble with *that* the way you're going. Little thief!" Brotus laughed and reached out affectionately to ruffle his son's hair. Soon it would be shaved off, he thought; but Brotus had no fears for his son. He was going to be all right in the agoge. He already had all the makings of a leader.

———

They had been out all morning in a drizzling rain that threatened to turn to sleet at any moment. It was bitterly cold, and low-hanging clouds blocked the view of both Taygetos and Parnon, turning the Eurotas valley into a flat plain in the middle of nowhere. The drill fields had been a morass of mud, so the two officers stopped at the entrance to the chamber that served as the office for their enomotia to remove their mud-encrusted boots with fingers red and stiff with cold.

Inside the gloomy room, records and duty rosters were kept, along with some spare equipment and, fortunately, linens. Oliantus grabbed a clean, dry towel and handed it to Leonidas.

Leonidas took the towel, bent down, and started rubbing the mud off Beggar, who had started to shiver violently. He worked diligently, rubbing hard to stimulate the circulation in her paws—apparently absorbed in this task, but in fact trying to think of a way to break the news to Oliantus that he intended to quit the army when he attained full citizenship.

Leonidas knew that his deputy had only remained because of him. Oliantus could have retired last year, but Leonidas had begged him to stay on. Leonidas had told him that the enomotia would not be a happy unit without him; and Oliantus, who had never before been told he was important to anyone, had been persuaded to stay.

But now Leonidas intended to retire, and he knew Oliantus would feel betrayed. When he finished with the dog, he collected his courage and faced his deputy, who was rebraiding his hair after drying it with a towel, and took a deep breath. Before he got a word out, however, they were interrupted by the meleirene on duty.

"There's someone asking for you outside, sir," the meleirene reported.

Leonidas did not welcome the interruption. His decision to quit the army affected Oliantus more than anyone else, and he owed him an explanation. Furthermore, he was annoyed by the fact that the meleirene had expressed himself imprecisely. Any meleirene ought to know that an officer expected precise information in the fewest possible words. At a minimum, the meleirene should have informed Leonidas whether this was a citizen (a man who had completed his active service), a young man (one still in the army), a youth (a fourteen- to twenty-year-old), a boy (a seven- to thirteen-year-old), a perioikoi, or a helot. "Someone" was too vague a term. "Who is it, and what does he want?" Leonidas asked irritably.

"He didn't say what he wanted, sir," came the strangely hesitant answer; and then the information, "It is Meander, son of Diactoridas, sir."

The name meant nothing to Leonidas, but it sounded Spartiate, and Oliantus had already turned away. The conversation would have to be continued later. Leonidas signaled for the meleirene to let the man in, while he turned to toss the dirty towel in a corner.

"Give me your wet things," Oliantus suggested, adding reproachfully, "Where's your attendant?"

"Mantiklos?" Leonidas asked, as he handed Oliantus his wet himation and started to untie his leather harness to get down to his wet chiton. "He got some poor girl pregnant and is trying to talk his way out of marrying her."

Oliantus said nothing, but his expression said it all: he did not approve of Mantiklos or of Leonidas retaining him. But there was no time for further discussion, because a strange figure stood in the doorway.

Leonidas turned to face the visitor, and still did not know what to make of him. He was tall, slender, tanned, and young. Leonidas guessed he was in his late teens or early twenties, but his hair was not shaved like a youth of the agoge, nor was he in training armor like a young man. His clothes were far too simple for a perioikoi youth, but the way he stood—straight as a spear with his chin up—was not a helot stance. Not that he was impudent. He had his eyes down and his hands at his sides—just like a youth of the agoge, which he obviously wasn't.

"You asked to see me," Leonidas remarked, his leather cuirass now hanging loose.

"Yes, sir." The youth swallowed visibly. "I heard, sir." He licked his lips. "I was told, sir, that you once paid the agoge fees of a boy too poor to pay his own way."

"Yes," Leonidas admitted, his eyes studying the youth more intently than ever. He was in good physical shape, but barefoot, and his himation was very shabby. Furthermore, his fingernails were torn and ingrained with dirt, as if he'd been working in the fields.

"Sir, our crops failed after the drought this summer. My father saw he wouldn't be able to meet his syssitia payments, so he hanged himself." The young man said it emotionlessly, his eyes still down; but Oliantus caught his breath, and Leonidas glanced at his deputy. Meander was continuing, "I'll work without wages for the next nine years if you'll just pay the agoge fees."

"How can you work for me and attend the agoge, and why nine years?" Leonidas demanded.

"Because that's when my brother will graduate and get his own kleros, sir." Meander risked looking up for a split second, and Leonidas saw the desperation in his eyes.

"Your brother?"

"My younger brother Aristodemos, sir. He'll turn twelve at the solstice."

"How old are you, Meander?"

"Nineteen, sir."

"But you're not in the agoge."

"No, sir."

"Why not?"

"My father pulled me out three years ago, because he couldn't afford to have two sons in the agoge at the same time."

"He pulled his *elder* son out of the agoge, but let his younger son remain?"

"Yes, sir."

"Look at me," Leonidas ordered.

The young man lifted his eyes and looked straight at Leonidas; his throat was working.

"Why did your father do that?"

"He thought my brother was better than I, sir."

Leonidas had grown up being told that Dorieus and Brotus were better than he—that he was superfluous and second-rate. But he wasn't. He'd proved that, and he didn't think for a moment that the young man standing in front of him was second-rate, either. If nothing else, he'd had the courage to come here—and offer to work like a slave for nine years to keep his brother in school. Leonidas wondered if his brother would have done the same for him. "What does your mother think of all this?" he asked.

"She never contradicted my father, sir, and she hasn't lived with us for years. She lives in Messenia with her sister."

"What year did you say you left the agoge?"

"After my sixteenth year, sir."

Leonidas cursed very shortly but crudely, causing Oliantus to look at him in consternation. Leonidas was shaking his head. "There's no way you can make that up. I can't put you back in with the seventeen-year-olds. You should be an eirene next year."

Meander dropped his eyes and murmured, "I know, sir. I didn't expect that. All I ask is that you let me earn my brother's fees—"

"You don't have to earn your brother's fees!" Leonidas told him angrily. "I'll pay them; but what are we going to do with you?"

Meander, not knowing Leonidas, heard only the anger in his voice and assumed it was directed at him. He started stammering,

"I'm sorry, sir. I would have liked to stay in the agoge, but my father couldn't pay. I've worked as hard as I can." With each sentence the proud stance was crumbling. Before Leonidas' eyes he was shrinking, collapsing, turning from Spartiate into helot. "I tried to make the kleros pay. I don't know—"

Leonidas couldn't stand it any longer. "Stop it!" he ordered.

Meander went instantly still and just stood as if turned to stone. He had even stopped breathing. He didn't know what to do anymore. He'd tried being proud and being humble. Nothing seemed to work. He wanted to drop dead.

Oliantus dropped a dry, warm himation over Leonidas' shoulders and muttered into his ear, "Put him out of his misery and hire him as your attendant. He'd do a better job than that Messenian."

Leonidas looked at Oliantus and then back at Meander. "So, Meander son of Diactoridas, you passed the Phouxir?"

"Yes, sir."

"And Artemis Orthia."

"Yes, sir."

"You can handle javelin, bow, and sword, and you started to exercise with spear, but can hardly have mastered it."

"No, sir," Meander admitted.

"You've also learned trapping, hunting, and camping, but you never actually carried an aspis or wore bronze."

"Correct, sir."

"How would you feel about serving as my attendant?"

"Sir?"

"You don't have to. I don't have any other ideas at the moment, but there are probably lots of alternatives. However, serving as my attendant would have certain advantages for you. I might, for example, be able to teach you what you didn't learn in the agoge. Maybe there's some way..." Leonidas stopped himself and focused again on the youth. "What do you think? Would you be willing to do that?"

"Sir, I don't know how to thank you!"

"You're interested?"

"Of course, sir! It would mean—everything to me!"

"Then that's settled. Report—is tomorrow too soon?"

"No, sir!"

"Report tomorrow evening, at curfew. Bring whatever kit you have—and don't worry," Leonidas cut him off before he could even say it; "what you don't have I will provide. You can assure your brother his fees will be paid."

"You won't regret this, sir!" Meander assured him, looking more dazed than happy.

"No, I won't regret it," Leonidas told him firmly. "Now get out of here and let me get changed." Meander disappeared instantly, and Leonidas turned to stare mutely at Oliantus. What appalled him was that although he'd known about this problem ever since Alkander had almost been thrown out of the agoge for the same reason, he had acted as if everything were all right just because Alkander was saved. He had put his head in the sand and ignored all the others. "I'm going to talk to Nikostratos," Leonidas announced; and grabbing his himation, he stormed out with Beggar, who struggled to her feet to follow him.

Leonidas found the treasurer in his office, and Nikostratos listened patiently as he railed against the injustice of excluding good youths from the agoge just because of their fathers' poverty.

Nikostratos nodded agreement. "Somewhere between 160 and 240 kleros were marginal even before this last drought. With the drought, it will have crept up to 320 or more. Several hundred citizens could be facing loss of citizenship. A significantly larger portion don't enroll all their sons in the agoge. There are probably as many as one thousand youths who are entitled to attend the agoge, but can't afford to," Nikostratos summarized, adding, "but there's nothing we can do about it, Leo."

"Why can't the city pay their fees?"

"We could, but only at the expense of other things we need."

"What in the name of Apollo is more important than the education of the next generation?"

"I could think of one or two things—like clean drinking water, the roads into Messenia, and protecting our borders from the Argives. But even if we pay for their education, what then?"

"What do you mean?"

"They graduate, and there are no kleros for them."

"Why aren't there?"

"Because there isn't any arable land left that has not already been assigned or purchased. The only lands available for new citizens are those kleros that have become vacant because of a lack of heirs, but these rarely number more than a half-hundred in any one year. We couldn't find a thousand new kleros anywhere in Laconia."

"What about Messenia?"

"Most of Messenia is in private hands."

"But—what about state factories? Why couldn't a citizen draw his income from something other than agriculture? Why couldn't he be given shares in something like the state quarries? Much of my income is no longer agricultural."

"That's a very interesting idea," Nikostratos admitted, adding with a sigh, "but it's probably not constitutional—at a minimum, it would take a great deal of persuasion to get the Council to propose and the Assembly to accept such a radical change. Secondly, Leo, the Spartan state is bankrupt again. Revenues have declined dramatically in the last decade. We really don't know how to meet all the expenses we have already, even without taking on any new obligations." Nikostratos ran his thin, splotched hand over his balding head, and he looked more than his sixty-six years. "It would make more sense for wealthy individuals, such as yourself, to sponsor boys. If the one hundred or so wealthy families with a large surplus income sponsored ten boys apiece, the problem would be solved."

"But that's uncertain—it leaves things to chance, to the generosity of individuals, whereas the problem is systemic. Are we equals or not? How can we call ourselves Peers and let our younger brothers sink into poverty indistinguishable from that of helots? This youth Meander has been working in the fields! He was doing helot work, but on a farm too poor to yield anything! There are many helots richer than he—and people like my brother Brotus would rather watch someone starve than give up a single bushel of grain!"

Nikostratos raised his eyebrows, to indicate that Leonidas was exaggerating and that he did not approve.

"I'll go talk to Phormio," Leonidas declared, frustrated, and got to his feet again.

Leonidas took his fleetest young colt from the stables and set out for Bryseiai. As happened more and more often these days, Beggar could not keep up; and when Leonidas got too far ahead, she sat down on her haunches and howled in heart-rending protest. She was getting old, Leonidas registered—not for the first time—and went back for her. He dismounted, draped her over his shoulders, and remounted.

At Phormio's house there was unusual bustle, as imported pottery was offloaded into a warehouse and the wagons loaded again with products from Leonidas' bronzeworks. Leonidas, however, was a frequent visitor these days, and he knew his way around. He handed his hound and horse over to a slave boy in the stableyard, and took one of the outdoor stairways leading directly up to Phormio's office.

On this winter's day the office was closed against the outside, with shutters blocking out both the chill and the view; but inside, no less than three braziers kept the room warm, and oil lamps provided enough light to work. Phormio got to his feet, smiling at the sight of Leonidas. He ushered his master to the largest of the braziers, commenting, "You look chilled through. Let me order hot wine."

"I haven't had lunch," Leonidas admitted; "if you have anything left over—"

"Of course; and give me that wet cloak." Phormio took it from Leonidas and handed it to one of the scribes, with instructions to hang it out to dry in the kitchen and return with hot, spiced wine and a big bowl of barley and beef stew. Then he reached across the scribe's desk and picked up a large bronze krater, which he handed to Leonidas. "Before you tell me what you've come for, take a look at this."

"It's beautiful!" Leonidas exclaimed instantly, admiring the workmanship with eye and fingers as he turned it around in his hands. The krater had a foot with an elegant, leafy pattern, handles made by lions standing on their hind feet and pressing their front paws against the lip of the krater, and a beautiful bronze relief on the body involving one naked male and three female figures in beautifully draped peplos. "You don't mean to tell me it was produced in my works?"

"That's exactly what I'm going to tell you."

"What is the motif?"

"Eros and the Muses."

Leonidas looked skeptically at Phormio. "I don't think that is going to sell very well here."

"Maybe not; but it was the first design by a young artisan, Arion, who applied for the position of master. He's from Thespiae, and there they are devoted to Eros and the Muses. Besides, the idea was to produce bronzeworks good enough for export again, as in the age of Chilon."

"A Thespian, you said? What brought him all the way down here?"

"They just got badly beaten in a clash with Thebes. Apparently they had to cede a lot of territory to the victors, and this young man lost his home. He's looking for a new start."

Leonidas knew little of the conflict between Thebes and Thespiae, except that it was as old as Sparta's struggle with Argos. Dismissing it as not his affair, he said, "Make sure he calls on Ibanolis. The old man would be pleased to see someone from home again after all these years. Maybe the young man can even give him word of his family."

"Can I hire him, then?"

"If he can do designs other than Eros and the Muses. Ask him to design a shield for me. When I go off active service, I surrender my standard-issue shield to a graduating eirene, and will need a personal aspis as a reservist. If he can design a suitable bronze facing for it, he has the job."

"Good. I'll tell him. Now, what is it this time?"

"Did you realize that up to a thousand youths entitled to Spartan citizenship are in fact excluded because their fathers are too poor to meet their agoge obligations?"

"No," Phormio told him. "But it doesn't surprise me. Some of the kleros are very poorly managed. The soil has been completely exhausted on many. Others have been scandalously shorn of vegetation, overgrazed, et cetera, et cetera. You don't teach agriculture in your agoge, do you?"

"Our wives are supposed to manage our estates," Leonidas countered.

"Ah, yes." Phormio thought about this a moment. Although he wouldn't want to turn his business over to his wife, he was not blind.

"And many of them do it very well. Your mother was a genius when it came to keeping her properties profitable."

"What if I were to sponsor ten youths in the agoge?"

"If that's what you want," Phormio agreed at once—and too readily.

Leonidas cocked his head and considered his steward. "How many youths could I afford to sponsor?"

"What do you mean, afford?"

"Well, what if I carved up all my private estates into kleros that could each be assigned to a youth on graduation from the agoge?"

"I'd have to go back and look at the dimensions of each of your properties. It might be twenty, maybe twenty-five. Certainly not more than thirty."

"What if I sponsored youths with my other income as well?"

"What do you want to do without?"

"What if I just lived from my own kleros like an ordinary citizen?"

Phormio was no longer smiling. He looked Leonidas in the eye and spoke deliberately: "Are you *sure* that is what you want to do?"

"Tell me one reason why I shouldn't?" Leonidas asked back.

Phormio cocked his head to one side and considered his employer, weighing his words carefully before he spoke. Leonidas waited. Phormio was no Spartan, and he did not share their values; and for that very reason, Leonidas expected an answer he could easily refute. He could do without fine horses and kennels or fancy imported pottery.

"Because," Phormio said at last and very deliberately, "you could do far more good for Lacedaemon by using your wealth in other ways."

"What do you mean? What is more important than our youth?"

Phormio shook his head. "In the abstract, nothing; but in practice, all you would effectively do is impoverish yourself for the sake of a score of others—and what about the remaining hundreds? How are you going to select who is deserving and who is not?"

Leonidas said nothing, because this was the crux of the matter. If he could help only a score or more, he still failed to solve the fundamental problem.

"The only way to solve the problem as a whole," Phormio continued, "would be for the Spartan state to assume all obligations for its citizens, just as it does for the military equipment of active units."

"Nikostratos says we can't afford it."

"That is because the Spartan state tends to be excessively parochial. Look at Corinth and Athens. Their elites may be landowners, but they do not derive their wealth from agriculture. Their wealth comes from manufacturing and trade."

"Our constitution prohibits us from pursuing trades other than arms."

"I'm not suggesting you change your constitution or your lifestyle. You can all continue to live in barracks as far as I'm concerned. But we perioikoi do very well with manufacturing, and we could contribute a great deal more to the Lacedaemonian treasury—enabling it to fully finance your educational system if you wanted—if we received more support for *our* trading activities and interests."

"What do you mean? I thought you could trade as you pleased. We don't stop you, do we?"

"No, you don't. We all prospered for nearly thirty Olympiads. But times have changed. Lacedaemon is no longer allied with Samos and so master of the Aegean, as you were in the age of Chilon. More importantly, since the fall of Croesus and the rise of Darius, the situation has deteriorated dramatically. The Persians are an aggressive and hegemonic power. They want to *control* everything. They are not content to let others live and prosper outside their sphere of influence. They impose stiff tariffs on anything imported, and export duties on goods they sell. They charge port taxes just for laying alongside— and those are only the official fees! The *real* cost of doing business with the Persian Empire is the bribes. Every time you turn around, there is a petty or less petty official who wants his 'cut.' A merchant doing business from Memphis to Sardis has to 'settle' with the port captain, the customs officials, the officers of the watch, the tax collectors, and right on up the chain to the satrap himself. The costs of doing business across the eastern Mediterranean have exploded, and now there is this war."

"The Ionian revolt, you mean?"

"Yes. Ever since Aristagoras talked the Athenians into sending twenty triremes to help them sack Sardis, the entire Aegean has become unsafe. Our ships can go nowhere without risking attack from either the rebels or the Persians. Both sides treat neutral vessels as fair game. As our trade gets choked off, our revenues decline—and so do our contributions to the Spartan treasury."

What Phormio said made sense to Leonidas, but it also seemed far beyond his control—unlike paying the agoge fees for boys whose fathers were too poor. Leonidas protested, "There's nothing I can do about the Persians, Phormio, but—"

"Forgive me for contradicting you, sir, but there is," Phormio declared. He came to stand directly before Leonidas, and then stepped aside as a slave returned with a tray laden with hot wine and a bowl of steaming soup. The slave set the tray before Leonidas and withdrew.

Leonidas reached for the steaming mug of wine and held it between his cold, red hands. He inhaled the spice-laden scent of the steam and waited for Phormio to enlighten him.

"Sparta needs a fleet, not just an army," the perioikoi told him. "In your father and grandfather's day, you used to support significant shipbuilding on Kythera; you had sufficient ships to establish Taras, to transport an army to Samos, and to take your brother Dorieus on an expedition to Africa and later to Sicily. You were even able to land a lochos with perioikoi support in Attica during your first attempt to depose Hippias. But ever since then, your brother Cleomenes has seriously neglected maritime interests. That was a mistake. Sparta needs a fleet stronger than ever before to protect her merchantmen and to project Lacedaemonian power. If you had a significant fleet, you could deploy your troops wherever you liked, and bring them home again. Your influence in the world would increase—and so would your wealth."

"You're talking to the wrong Agiad," Leonidas protested. "Talk to my brother the king."

"First of all, I can't, and you know I can't. Secondly, your brother, for whatever reason, has contributed to the problem and is not likely to be part of the solution. Thirdly, you have a sawmill, Leonidas. For the price of just ten hoplites, you could double its capacity and enable us to lay down keels on at least five triremes."

"And who would man them?"

"Don't worry about that. There are more than enough perioikoi

youths eager to fight back against the Persian predators. But surely
you see: twenty, forty, even a hundred more hoplites in your already
invincible army will make no fundamental difference to Sparta's
power; twenty triremes, on the other hand, could be decisive."

Leonidas knew Phormio was right, but it didn't address the issue
of inequality and injustice for the children of the poor. Still, he had to
accept the fact that he could not solve those problems alone. Phormio
was right. As far as he could see, only if the state paid for the education of all children could everyone have the same opportunity, and if
the state was to pay it had to be able to afford it, and that meant more
revenues from the perioikoi.

He set the wine down and reached for the bowl, brimming with
barley and beef stew, in which carrots and leeks floated enticingly. He
stirred it once with the spoon provided and nodded. He resolved to
work on changing the way the agoge fees were collected, but to do
so he had first to get elected to public office. If he were Paidonomos,
for example, he could waive the fees of the poorer boys. If he were
an ephor—but that was getting ahead of himself. He took a spoonful
of stew and savored it before meeting Phormio's eyes and agreeing:
"Expand the sawmill and start building your fleet."

———

Officially the festival honored Helios, and the series of sacrifices
and choral performances was meant to coax Hellios back to Hellas.
At some point in the distant past, however, the Spartans started
advancing the age cohorts at this time of year. While the boys and
youths of the agoge moved up one grade, the eirenes received their
shields, and the oldest age cohort of young men gave theirs up and
retired to the reserves. With ball games between the best teams of
each age cohort and dances performed by the girls of the agoge, this
festival appealed particularly to youth; but it climaxed in a torchlight
ceremony in which each graduating eirene, called by name, went
forward to receive a cloak and shield as a symbol of their citizenship.

Usually Gorgo loved this particular festival, but this year she felt
depressed and lonely. Her parents had an official role to play, of course,
presiding at the ceremony from the steps in front of the Council
House along with the Eurypontid king and queen, the ephors, and

the Gerousia. These dignitaries stood behind the line of retiring men and faced the eirenes, taking their salutes when they accepted the shield. But there was no place for a king's unmarried daughter among the city's notables.

That had been true in other years, of course; but then she and Phaenna had together cheered their favorites in the ball games, and mingled in the crowd to buy themselves votive offerings, sweets, and ribbons for their hair. But Phaenna now had a sweetheart, one of the graduating eirenes, and of course they were trysting after his graduation. That made Gorgo a fifth wheel, and she felt like it.

In fact, as the sun slipped behind Taygetos after its shortest journey across the sky for this year, and the city was gripped with subdued anticipatory excitement for the final event of the season, Gorgo felt as if no one would notice if she went and hanged herself, or wandered off into the mountains and was set upon by wolves. She felt completely useless.

She picked up the silver mirror her mother had given her and looked at her reflected image on the polished surface of the metal. No, young men were never going to come from all over the world to compete for her hand. Her mother said they'd be lucky to find anyone to take her, while her father insisted she didn't have anything to worry about because "They'll come for the sake of commanding the Spartan army no matter what you look like." Somehow, Gorgo reflected, that didn't make her feel any better.

Listlessly, Gorgo combed out her auburn hair and pinned it up first one way and then another. She checked the results in the mirror, but nothing could please her. Maybe some of her mother's rouge? She looked for it—another gift long ignored—and rubbed a little on her cheekbones and lips, turning her head this way and that in the mirror. What was the point?

She stood and went over to her bed, where her maid had left out a lovely saffron-colored woolen peplos with a broad border representing green palms. The material had been very expensive, imported from Syracuse. She slipped the peplos over her chiton and her maid entered, apologizing for being late, to help her pin it at her shoulders. She used big bronze pins with suns on them. Her maid then helped her drape a rich green himation, with yellow suns woven across it, carefully over her shoulders. Gorgo enjoyed the softness of the wool and the way it flowed gracefully when she moved. Lastly, she slipped a jade bracelet with gold filigree lions' heads on her right wrist and hung golden lions' heads from her ears. The jewelry had been a gift from her father, and she treasured it. It seemed like such a long time since he had last given her anything. He was withdrawn and dissatisfied these days. She often saw him consulting with Asteropus or closeted with Leotychidas, the heir to the Eurypontid throne. She sensed that he was plotting something; but since that horrible incident with Aristagoras, her father didn't draw her into his confidence anymore. Gorgo sighed.

Gorgo left the palace by a side entrance and found herself out in the street. It was dusk now. The sky behind Taygetos still had a faint hint of purple streaked with fingers of black cloud, but to the east the stars were blotted out by light reflected from the big bonfires on which the sacrificial cattle were being roasted. The streets were crowded with people dressed in their best and warmest clothes. They streamed toward the Dancing Floor, where the final graduation ceremony would take place. Gorgo set off in the same direction, hoping to run into her grandmother. Nikostratos would be on the stairs with the other councilmen, so her grandmother would be on her own, too—if she came. Unfortunately, Chilonis had been suffering from a bad head cold this past week, and she had told Gorgo she wasn't sure she'd make it.

Here and there, youths and boys were singing. It was the disorganized, spontaneous singing of small groups of friends rather than that of formal choral performances. Sometimes the boys clapped in time with their songs; sometimes a soloist carried the song, supported only at the chorus by the others. The boys and youth were always in good spirits on this holiday. It meant the successful completion of a whole year, a step closer to citizenship—and ten days of holiday before meeting a new eirene and starting on the next stage of their long ordeal.

Gorgo envied the clusters of youths laughing and singing together. Why hadn't she been born a boy? If she had, it wouldn't matter whether she were pretty. She was sure she would have been good at *something*. If not a pan-Hellenic victor like her Uncle Brotus, at least an all-round good athlete like Uncle Leo. As far as she knew,

Uncle Leo had never been first in anything, but everybody liked him just the same.

Gorgo found herself looking for her uncles. They were both going off active service, and would symbolically hand a shield with the lambda on it over to one of the graduating eirenes. Searching the line of young men taking their places at the foot of the steps, she found her Uncle Brotus first. He was getting stocky these days, and he scowled a lot. As always. Gorgo tried to remember a time when he had ever taken any notice of her, but she couldn't.

Uncle Leo was different. He was chatting and laughing with several other young men whose names Gorgo couldn't remember at the moment. Gorgo thought his laughter looked forced, however, and she wasn't the only one to have noticed that Leo wasn't really happy anymore. Gorgo had heard her grandmother remark on it, and Nikostratos, too. They attributed it to the loss of his wife and babies this past summer, but Gorgo thought it had started before that. Eirana hadn't been good for Uncle Leo. She had never made him happy. He deserved better.

"Oh, my, aren't we all dressed up!" A voice sneered at her, and Gorgo looked over at her Aunt Sinope, Brotus' wife. "Didn't anyone ever tell you that a *good* Spartan woman doesn't tart herself up with jewelry and fancy imported fabrics? Oh, but I suppose you think you're a *princess* and so above our laws."

Gorgo was unprepared for the attack. It took her by surprise, and she didn't have a ready answer. She said the first thing that came into her head: "What makes you think you can interpret our laws better than my father? *We* have the blood of Chilon in our veins!" Gorgo then ducked into the crowd, conscious that she had been rude to an elder and done herself no favor. But it made her so mad! Why did Brotus' stupid wife think she had a monopoly on the interpretation of Sparta's constitution?

Still fuming inwardly, Gorgo sought to lose herself in the masses, as from the back side of the agoge administrative building came a rousing cheer. The sound was muted by distance, and yet the emotion was deafening: another class of eirenes had just had their last lecture from the Paidonomos and were forming up to march here and collect their shields.

It was so unfair! Girls didn't have anything like this. A girl's transition from girlhood to womanhood occurred not in public view, with proud parents and adoring sweethearts cheering, but in the dark of night and all alone, when a man stole her from her father's house. That wasn't the same at all! In fact, it was frightening and humiliating.

Gorgo particularly disliked the thought of someone abducting her because she had heard her mother talking about how it was *time* for Gorgo to marry. "The sooner she's settled," her mother had argued to her father, "the sooner you'll have a powerful ally against Brotus' ambitions. And the sooner Gorgo produces a male heir, the sooner you can put an end to Brotus' claims to the throne altogether."

Gorgo shuddered at the thought of giving birth. She could remember her mother's screams, and she'd heard horrible stories about women dying in agony and in pools of blood. It was so unfair! Young men didn't have to face anything like that when they became citizens and husbands!

A hush had fallen over the crowd as the eirenes marched into the square and started to take their assigned places. They looked splendid, as always. Gorgo looked for Phaenna's boyfriend, but couldn't find him. She wondered if Phaenna was really going to let him take her this year like she said, or if she would make him wait a little. She seemed in a terrible hurry.

The names were being read out. Gorgo watched her uncles turn a shield over to an eirene one after the other, still wishing she were out there in the square rather than wandering around on the fringes of the crowd feeling superfluous. She was so on the edge, in fact, that she did not even notice when the last name was read out.

Suddenly everyone was cheering, and then the whole crowd burst out into the Ode to Kastor. Gorgo noted that an old man nearby was weeping openly, though she couldn't know why. Memories of his own youth? Joy for a son or grandson? Or mourning for a youth who hadn't made it? There were always one or two of those: boys who were killed in accidents, youths who committed serious breaches of the rules and were forced to repeat a year, and—increasingly—young men whose families could not pay their agoge fees and so were forced to drop out.

The crowd was breaking up, dispersing. Younger boys were running to join their families, swept into the arms of mothers and sisters. Youths were going off in groups or swaggering proudly in front of younger siblings and admiring sisters. Young couples were disappearing around the corners into the darkness. Gorgo felt like going back to the palace and curling up in the straw beside her mare and hound, as she had done when she was a little girl.

"Gorgo! What are you doing? Come here!" The voice cut through her misery, and she looked up to see her Uncle Leo waving to her. He was with his friends, of course, and he was smiling, even though his tone was admonishing. As she joined his little group, he put his arm around her and drew her into his circle, asking in a low voice, "Is something wrong? You look so unhappy."

"I'm just jealous," Gorgo admitted. "I wish girls got to go through the agoge and graduate like that in public."

One of Leo's friends laughed outright, and another shook his head and remarked, "Believe me, it's not as fun as it looks!"

But Uncle Leo seemed to understand. He said, "You're right. At least in other Greek cities girls are the center of attention at their weddings, but we don't ever celebrate you, do we?"

"Better less celebration and more freedom," one of the women in the little crowd noted rather sharply.

"Of course," the other woman agreed, then smiled at Gorgo and added, "but what would be wrong with both? I'm Hilaira, by the way," she introduced herself to Gorgo, and then the others introduced themselves as well. Gorgo noted the names of Leonidas' friends Alkander and Sperchias and Euryleon. The latter suggested they go to the banks of the Eurotas, where the cattle had been roasting for hours, and join the feast. Since the other men were with their wives and Leo had none, Gorgo naturally fell in beside him. He chatted with her, asking about Jason and Shadow as if she were still a little girl, but that was better than being left out.

She asked him, "What are you going to do now that you're in the reserves?"

"I'm going to work in the agoge," Leo announced.

"Leo! You can't do that to us!" Euryleon protested, stopping dead in his tracks and gaping at his enomotarch.

"I can and have. I informed Diodoros this morning."

"Leo! You're mad!" Sperchias exclaimed.

"Why? You want a career in civil administration or diplomacy, not the army! Why is it wrong for me to want something similar?"

"Because you're a good officer, Leo—and an Agiad."

"What does that have to do with anything? Kyranios himself said that war is the failure of diplomacy. You do a good job as a diplomat, Chi, and we won't need a strong army."

"I'm not a diplomat yet; and the minute we lose the capacity to fight better than everyone else, the Messenians and Argives will crush us."

"We'll have a strong army whether I'm in it or not. Now, let's enjoy the food," Leonidas ordered; and the others knew better than to try to argue with him when he was in one of his mulish moods, as he obviously was.

Gorgo wasn't sure what to think, except that she wanted her uncle to be happy. Maybe he was right and he would be happier outside the army; but only, she thought, if he could do good for Lacedaemon. Uncle Leo was more like her father than he—or her father—liked to admit. Behind his façade of humility, he was actually very ambitious. What was more, she realized with a kind of awed surprise—even more than her father, he cared about Sparta, not just himself.

CHAPTER 17

THE GRAIN FLEET

THE EMERGENCY MEETING OF THE COUNCIL ended in midafternoon, at the very hottest time of the day. Nikostratos was thirsty and tired, but he wasted no time. He left the Council House with the others, and while they dispersed, he struck out across the square to the main administrative building of the agoge. Here he inquired where he might find Leonidas, and was told to wait in the Paidonomos' office while a boy was sent to fetch him.

Nikostratos waited in the anteroom until the two eirenes who were with the Paidonomos departed; then he stepped into the doorway and paused, leaning on his walking stick. Epidydes was absorbed in reading something and did not realize he had a visitor, so Nikostratos had a moment to consider him in peace. Sometime in the last decade, the headmaster had gone completely gray. Just like me, Nikostratos thought. We are getting old.

At last he interrupted the other with the words, "So, what's this I hear about you wanting to retire?"

Epidydes looked up, smiled at the sight of the treasurer, and retorted, "I'm only a year younger than you are." He gestured for Nikostratos to come in, close the door, and sit down. Nikostratos settled down on a bench with his walking stick between his knees.

"I'm too old for this job," Epidydes continued bluntly, adding, "I think I would be more use in the Gerousia."

"You'll have my vote," Nikostratos assured the headmaster at once. "But who do you see filling your shoes? Are any of your three deputies up to the job?"

Epidydes evaded Nikostratos' eye. "They're not bad men, but unimaginative. They want to do everything exactly the way they remember it when they were little. They lack vision and courage—especially Alcidas."

"What about the younger instructors? Leonidas, for example?"

"Aha!" The Paidonomos leveled his eyes at the treasurer with a reproving look, softened by a slight smile. "So that's why you're here. Because of Leonidas."

"True. I was wondering how he is doing."

Epidydes leaned back in his chair and considered the councilman warily. "Why do you want to know?"

"Oh, curiosity. I'm fond of the young man."

"Why is it that I don't believe you?" the Paidonomos asked rhetorically, but then reported willingly enough: "When Leonidas came to me before the solstice saying he wanted to join the agoge staff, I was delighted. Alkander had been here before him, you know, and Alkander is a good man. But everyone knows how Alkander struggled in the agoge, that he stuttered and that he was a mothake. Any attempt he makes at serious reform here—which we all know is his intention—will be blocked by the conservatives. They will discredit everything he tries to do because of who he was.

"Leonidas, on the other hand, is not only an Agiad, he's proven himself repeatedly. He's an exemplary citizen. He makes Brotus look like a dwarf and Cleomenes like a lightweight. He has Cleomenes' strength of intellect and his father's strength of character. In my opinion, Leonidas is without question the best of his entire generation, and he is popular. Whatever Leonidas decides he wants to do—in any field he chooses—he can count on support and assistance. I don't just mean the support of his friends. I mean he can genuinely sway public opinion; because even those who don't know him personally, know he represents something positive in our society."

"But?" Nikostratos prompted the headmaster, because clearly this whole exceptionally long speech was leading up to a reservation.

"But, he has a lot to learn about teaching. He is too softhearted, and the boys take shameless advantage of him. He believes any crazy story they tell him, and he hates disciplining them."

Nikostratos was astonished. "He did well as an eirene and had a good reputation in the army."

"Indeed; but as an eirene he had eighteen-year-olds, and in the army he was dealing with young men more or less his own age. He's good enough with the older boys, but he's soft on the little ones. Alkander is a much better instructor. He's patient but firm and knows when to use the cane. The boys respect him—and they adore him."

Nikostratos grunted. He wasn't surprised about Alkander, but he hadn't expected to hear bad things about Leonidas. "Just what do you have him doing? Leonidas, I mean."

"I've tried him at various tasks, but he's not doing well and he knows it, which discourages him further. I think—"

Before Epidydes could finish there was a knock on the door, and Leonidas himself entered. "You sent for me, sir?"

"No; Nikostratos did." Epidydes nodded toward Nikostratos, who was sitting with his hands resting on the T of his stick, considering Leonidas. The headmaster was right. Leonidas looked haggard and listless. He looked older than his thirty-one years, and he did not look like a happy man.

Leonidas was also confused. He saw Nikostratos every evening at his syssitia. What could the older man have to say that couldn't wait?

"I'm here on official business of the Gerousia, young man," Nikostratos answered his look. "You'd better come with me." He pulled himself to his feet and led Leonidas out onto the agoge porch. They stopped beside the ancient Kouroi, who smiled enigmatically as they supported the portico. In the shade, with the busy square spread out before them in the dazzling sunlight, Nikostratos stopped and asked as if casually, "Just why *did* you quit the army and take a position with the agoge?"

Leonidas shrugged. "If I am to have no children of my own, then I wanted to at least spend time with the children of others."

"What a lot of rubbish! There's no reason why you shouldn't have children of your own!"

Leonidas only shrugged again. "Theoretically."

"Now listen to me, young man! I understand you are still grieving for your wife and babies, but that is no excuse for talking as if you were *my* age! You have more than half your life ahead of you. You should and *will* marry again. It is your duty to Lacedaemon and to your house."

Leonidas smiled faintly. "My house is well secured by my brother Brotus, don't you think? Aside from Pausanias, he has a second son now—as his smug wife reminds me whenever she sees me. So what official business brings you to me?" Leonidas was in no mood to talk about his marital status, or about his brother and his growing nursery.

"A Corinthian ambassador arrived early this morning."

Leonidas was surprised. Usually news spread like wildfire in a tight-knit community like Sparta; but then again, he'd been inside all morning trying to impart the fundamentals of the constitution to unwilling and inattentive charges. He sighed unconsciously. He knew he wasn't doing very well, and he didn't understand why.

"It was Archilochos." Nikostratos had Leonidas' attention again.

Leonidas looked over hopefully. He'd begged Lychos to visit him for years, and the kleros was beautiful at the moment, with all the orchards in bloom. "Did he come alone?"

"With a slave or two."

"Lychos wasn't with him?"

"No; he rode very hard and through the night."

"What's wrong?"

"There's rioting in Corinth. Because the fires of last year destroyed almost all domestic grain production and the war in the Aegean has chocked trade, the grain stores are almost depleted. Corinth sent a powerful convoy, escorted by a squadron of triremes, to Byzantion to buy grain, but it was attacked on the return voyage by a Phoenician fleet under Persian command. A large number of the freighters were sunk, along with their cargo, and the Corinthians lost five triremes."

"And what does Archilochos want of us?"

"Roughly three hundred marines to protect the convoy they are now assembling for a second attempt."

"Do the perioikoi have that many marines?"

"Corinth doesn't want perioikoi marines, Leo. Archilochos wants Spartiates."

"We don't have trained marines," Leonidas countered. Marines used the same weapons as hoplites—spear and sword—but they were usually adept at javelin and bow as well. More significantly, aboard ship there was no room to form a phalanx; and on unsteady wooden decks, there was no way for hoplites to dig in their heels and shove, foot by foot and pace by pace. In short, the great virtues of the Spartan line—the discipline, strength and drill—could not come into play when hoplites were fighting in the role of marines.

Nikostratos noted, however, that the listlessness was now gone from Leonidas' stance. His spine had stiffened and he was standing more upright, his head had come up, and his eyes were alert. "Kyranios didn't balk," Nikostratos informed him.

"Kyranios is willing to take his lochos?"

"Kyranios will be taking an all-volunteer task force two hundred strong, and one hundred perioikoi marines," Nikostratos answered. "He said he would have to hand-pick the men because—and I quote—'Marines have to be more agile, more independent, more resourceful, and more spontaneous than hoplites.'"

"Volunteers?" Leonidas asked. "Active service only?" His expression was anxious.

Nikostratos shook his head slowly, amazed to find this was easier than he had expected.

"Reserves, too? I could volunteer?"

Nikostratos shook his head again, but before Leonidas could protest, he added, "You don't have to. Kyranios has asked that you be appointed his second in command."

———

It took them only three days to organize the task force. There were more than enough volunteers, just as Kyranios had predicted; so they hand-picked twenty section leaders and let them choose their own sections of ten and a deputy from among the plentiful volunteers. In addition to Leonidas, who was to serve as the more-or-less independent commander of ten of the sections, Kyranios appointed an experienced senior quartermaster for the entire task force, and Leonidas talked Oliantus out of retirement to be his own quartermaster. They took along a surgeon, two heralds, and two salpinx players. Each man was accompanied by his own attendant, of course; and so the little force was over 450 strong when it marched north at dawn on the fourth day.

Despite the early hour, with the city still cast in shadow as the sun had not cleared the Parnon range, people filled the streets to see them off. The boys of the agoge were like a noisy flock of crows, shouting and shoving and scrambling onto rooftops or into the plane trees for a good view. Some of the maidens formed a chorus and sang some of Tyrtaios' songs. Matrons waved from the balconies.

The men of the task force were in full panoply for the official march-out, their helmets, hoplons, and breastplates polished, their crests stiff with wax, their chitons fresh, and their sandals oiled. Everyone looked magnificent. The salpinx sounded "advance" and the flutes took up a melody, which the troops recognized at once and started singing.

Nikostratos, Chilonis, and Gorgo were standing in Chilonis' chariot drawn up in the road to Limera, which joined the Tegean road a little beyond the drill fields. As Leonidas came into view leading the second contingent of troops, they waved to him energetically. Leonidas waved back.

Gorgo was growing up, he noted with surprise. She was as tall as her grandmother, and she was developing a feminine softness he had not noticed before. The eirenes and bachelors were sure to start noticing her soon—if they hadn't already. Somewhat ruefully, he reflected that his brother was soon going to have a problem. As Gorgo was his only surviving child, any man who married her could conceivably claim—if not the throne itself—regency for any sons he had by her. If she married the right man, he would put an end to Brotus' ambitions altogether, Leonidas thought gleefully. But Cleomenes was going to have to choose his son-in-law very carefully...

———

They stopped to change out of their panoply after they had left Sparta behind, loaded the heavy gear onto the following carts, and proceeded at a vigorous marching pace that brought them to Corinth by nightfall. They re-kitted before entering Corinth, to enter in full splendor. The Corinthians expected them, of course, and the gates opened before them. Indeed, a large crowd welcomed them with torches, applause, and occasional cheers. Two oxen were sacrificed to Poseidon on their arrival, and the roasted meat with donated wine ensured a festive atmosphere in the city. The Spartans, however, continued beyond Corinth to rendezvous with the perioikoi marines, who had proceeded by sea from Gytheon. At Kenchrea, where the fleet was assembled, they set up camp.

Kenchrea was notorious for its taverns and brothels. The very air smelled sour with spilled wine, piss, and fatty food. Drunken men with slovenly women staggered around in the dark, and music escaped from the various locales with each opening and closing of the doors. But the hand-picked quality of the task force proved its value at once. Every one of the section leaders had his own men firmly under his eye, and Kyranios' reputation for discipline had discouraged men inclined to break rules from volunteering.

While the section leaders oversaw setting up camp, Kyranios and Leonidas attended a meeting with the officers of the fleet; they took their quartermasters with them. The meeting was held in the tollhouse at Kenchrea, and by the time they arrived, the room was crowded. Gathered here already were the trireme, penteconter, and merchant captains, the helmsmen, the rowing masters, the Corinthian captains of marines, and the perioikoi commander. Although, because of Spartan sensibilities, Kyranios was nominally in command of the entire expeditionary force, Archilochos was the actual admiral commanding the expedition, and he would be aboard the Corinthian flagship, the *Vengeance*. Another leading citizen of Corinth, Erxander, commanded the second squadron of triremes from the *Liberty*. Leonidas was pleased to see that Lychos was commodore of the six merchantmen from his father's merchant fleet sailing with the convoy. He would be aboard the largest of these freighters, the *Orcelle*. As agreed in advance, the Spartan marines were detailed to the triremes only. The Corinthian and perioikoi marines were placed aboard the merchantmen. Kyranios was stationed aboard the *Vengeance*, and Leonidas the *Liberty*.

After the full briefing, Archilochos signaled for the Lacedaemonians to remain while the others dispersed. The Corinthian then sketched the convoy formation for the Lacedaemonians on a wax tablet, and Kyranios assigned each of their sections to one of the triremes. The two quartermasters were dispatched to inform the individual section leaders of their assignments and make sure the provisions and stores that the Spartans had brought with them were properly distributed and stowed. Throughout these activities Lychos waited patiently, sitting at one of the toll-collection tables. Finally Archilochos and Kyranios left together, and the perioikoi commander excused himself as well, leaving Leonidas and Lychos alone together.

"I was hoping you'd come, but I hardly dared expect it," Lychos opened.

"We're all volunteers," Leonidas countered. "I was the first. How are your wife and children?"

Lychos was taken aback. It was considered rude in Corinth to ask after another man's wife, and he had never before known Leonidas to be intentionally rude. He concluded that maybe there was nothing wrong in Sparta with talking about a wife. Still, he couldn't bring himself to speak about his wife in public. So he answered, "They are growing very rapidly. Each time I return from a voyage they seem completely changed."

"How old are they now?" Leonidas forced himself to ask.

"Agathon is seven and Kallias four, their sisters five and two."

Leonidas realized he was too jealous to pursue this topic further, so he changed the subject. "Can you tell me more about the current situation?"

"What do you know?"

"Very little. I was told your grain reserves were almost depleted and the ships you sent to Byzantion last month were attacked by Phoenicians. Why? I thought Corinth was neutral."

"Corinth is, but Byzantion has joined the Ionian rebels, so the Persians declared an embargo."

"So why not buy grain elsewhere—Sicily or Crete?"

"First, it would take longer. Second, it would be much more expensive. If we are to fill our warehouses, we can't afford to pay the prices they are asking in Sicily these days! However, because of the embargo, prices in Byzantion have plummeted. Grain from around the Black Sea is piling up there. We really have no choice, though I admit we underestimated the risk. We had not realized the Persians had brought a Phoenician fleet into the Aegean."

Leonidas was thankful Lacedaemon did not depend on imported grain. It was bad enough that some citizens had been reduced to penury by the drought and fire of the last year, but there was no absolute shortage of grain in Lacedaemon—it was just unequally distributed. Men like Brotus profited from the poverty of others, but there was no need to import grain, and no risk of widespread starvation and riots. "What was this last expedition like?"

"A nightmare. The Phoenicians surprised us out of a fog bank. We didn't have time to get our triremes into line-astern on the exposed side, and we lost several freighters to that first onslaught. Another freighter went down to one of our own triremes that tried to cut through the fleet to get into position. The wind was erratic, coming first from one direction then another, so we couldn't get away. Furthermore, the Persians had placed archers aboard the Phoenician ships. So even ships like my own, which were not rammed or boarded, were subjected to barrages of arrows. We cowered behind whatever cover we could find as waves of arrows landed on the deck with a horrible racket—like hail, only worse. At some point I looked down through the gunnels at the water beside the ship and saw that it had turned red. There were men struggling amid the corpses and flotsam of a crushed ship, screaming and clawing at the sides of my vessel, trying to climb aboard. But we didn't dare stop to take them on board. I still have nightmares about it."

Leonidas said nothing. There were many images from his short military career—like that Farm of Horrors on Kythera—that he, too, preferred to forget. And then there was the image of the charred remains of Eirana and the twins... "What's Byzantion like?"

Lychos smiled. "You'll like it. Half oriental, half barbarian. I'll show it to you. And you'll love the Hellespont. It's the most spectacular sail you can imagine." He paused, smiled at Leonidas, and declared with feeling, "It will be good to have you sailing with us!"

Leonidas nodded; but it was time to get back to his men. He embraced Lychos and stepped out into the night. He walked along the line of crispy black seaweed under the curving sterns of the triremes lined up on the beach. The vicious, beak-like rams pointed out to sea, ready for launch. He could hear the water hissing in, rolling the stones on the beach, and then sighing as it retreated. Offshore, lamps swayed slowly in the rigging of the merchantmen. Now and then a seagull cawed, angry at being disturbed.

Leonidas was challenged at the perimeter of the Spartan camp, not by an ordinary sentry but by one of the section leaders Kyranios had selected, Dienekes. Even before Leonidas could answer the challenge, however, he was recognized and informed, "A Corinthian marine came looking for you, sir."

"Marine? You don't mean Archilochos?"

"Don't you think I know the difference between a perfumed Corinthian salesman and a hard-assed marine?" Dienekes answered, insulted.

"I expect he's a messenger of some sort. Where is he?"

"I sent him to your tent. Mantiklos is keeping a good eye on him. I didn't like the look of him, and I wouldn't turn my back on him if I were you."

Leonidas nodded, and without thinking dropped his hand to his sword hilt. Then, annoyed at himself, he took his hand away, but nevertheless approached his tent cautiously.

It was one of the privileges of command not to share a tent with nine other men. He shared his tent only with his quartermaster Oliantus and their two attendants. (Leonidas had left Meander behind on account of his youth and inexperience, much to the young man's disappointment.) Oliantus, however, was still seeing to the provisioning of the ships they would be boarding at dawn. The Corinthians had advised it might not be possible to stop for a midday meal, as was normal practice for triremes, and thus provisions for three days were being put aboard the ships.

As he entered, Leonidas saw Mantiklos first. The Messenian attendant was standing with a jug of something in one hand—and the other hand rested with his thumb looped through his belt, in easy reach of his knife. The guest was seated on Leonidas' sea chest, a wooden box filled with his gear that was ready to go aboard the trireme in the morning.

It was a "hard-assed" marine, all right. His thick, curly, unkempt hair and beard seemed to have a film of salt on them, and his skin was burnt leathery from the sun reflected off the waves on countless journeys. He had a scarf tied at his neck, as sailors often did, though

Leonidas did not know why. He wore a chiton of undefined color and poor quality and a leather corselet of better quality, but stained and worn. Against it, his sword was like a jewel set in cast iron—amber glowed in the knob of an ivory handle, and the silver sheath was elaborately embossed and highly polished. But the man's sandals were in bad shape, and there were bad scars on the man's legs. There was also a recent wound under his left eye that had discolored much of his face and swollen the one eye almost closed. Despite all that, Leonidas recognized him at once. It was Prokles.

"I guess no one calls you 'Little Leo' anymore, do they?" his boyhood friend remarked, without getting to his feet.

Leonidas didn't like his friend's looks any more than Dienekes had—if for different reasons. He saw too clearly the indications of bad times only partially withstood, and he saw bitterness on the prematurely aged face. But he was alive. And he was here. "Mantiklos, hard as it may be for you to believe, the man before you is a Spartiate—"

"Not so fast, Leo! I was born Spartiate, but no one ever gave me cloak or shield!"

"You can claim them as soon as your term of exile is up. You've passed the halfway mark already."

"I'm not coming back, Leo; and if you breathe a word of this to anyone besides my mother and sister, I'll find a way to have your throat cut!" Now Prokles was on his feet, and his entire posture was threatening. It reminded Leonidas of the savage barking of a dog that has been kicked too often. "Don't think I couldn't! I know all the cutthroats in the Mediterranean!" Prokles added viciously, and then laughed—a mirthless laugh.

"Sit down, Prokles, and finish your wine." Leonidas turned to an alarmed Mantiklos and assured the Messenian, "Prokles is an old friend. Give him the best wine we have."

"Unwatered!" Prokles ordered. "I don't abide by Spartan laws anymore."

Leonidas nodded to Mantiklos, adding, "Half and half for me."

Prokles reseated himself on the chest, and Leonidas sat on the cot that Mantiklos had set up for him. "Tell me what has happened to you since we parted."

"I didn't come here to talk about myself! I just wanted to—to hear about my family. Do my parents still live?"

"Your mother grieves for you every day. She thinks you have died in some foreign place. Why didn't you write?"

"I thought of writing now and then—especially at the beginning. I even composed letters in my head sometimes. But it was always the same: what I had to report would have brought joy only to my enemies."

"Enemies?" Leonidas asked. "Do you really think you had enemies?"

"The whole city was my enemy!" Prokles flung back.

"Alkander and I were never your enemies—much less your family," Leonidas reminded him softly, but Prokles only shrugged. Leonidas continued reasonably, "At least if you had written, it would have countered the rumors."

"What rumors?"

"That you took barbarian pay," Leonidas told him.

"Since when does Prince Leonidas of Sparta listen to rumor?" Prokles sneered.

"Since he has had no other source of information," Leonidas answered steadily.

Prokles turned his back on Leonidas and crossed the tent, to stand looking out into the darkness. After a moment he replied without turning around, speaking into the night: "No, I never took barbarian pay. But maybe I should have. There are things worse than getting rich on Persian gold!"

"Are there?" Leonidas asked, intending to provoke.

The trick worked; Prokles spun around and addressed him in a voice hard with fossilized anger. "You don't have any idea what I've been through, do you? You can't even *imagine* what it was like! I was born and raised on the estate I was told I would inherit. I was taught, from the time I could walk, only those skills and duties required of a Spartan citizen. I was drilled and tested and beaten to fit the form that Sparta demands of her citizens. But never—not for one day, one hour—was I taught how to earn a living if I *didn't* have a kleros, helots, a syssitia, barracks. Not for one minute was I asked even to think about *how* one earns money."

Prokles started pacing about the tiny confines of the tent like a caged lion. Mantiklos cast Leonidas an alarmed look, but Leonidas shook his head. They remained still and silent while Prokles raged. "And then, from one day to the next, I was cast out. Suddenly I had no mess to eat at, no estate to support me, and no skills to earn a living. I was taken across the border and dumped in a strange country, left among utter strangers living by different laws and customs. I had to find some way to fill my stomach and keep clothes on my back without a trade."

Prokles stopped again at the entrance of the tent and stood with one hand resting on the open flap, looking out into the night. After what seemed like a long time, he appeared to have curbed his anger, and he looked back over his shoulder. "Do you know? When other cities exile their citizens, the exiles sail away in ships laden with their valuables, and they settle in a colony or a friendly city where they can carry on their business as before. An Athenian potter or tinker or shoemaker can set up his shop anywhere in the world. But what in the name of Zeus is a Spartiate outside his unit?"

"A highly skilled hoplite," Leonidas pointed out softly; "one who can command the highest prices from all the kings and tyrants and cities of the world who depend on mercenaries for their survival."

"Not when they're a twenty-year-old youth who's never seen one day of combat!" Prokles shot back, spinning around on his former friend. "I might have known the use of every weapon and every formation drill ever dreamed up by bored instructors, but I had no *experience*. Besides, there was no war in Tegea and no tyrant in need of protection. No one wanted the skills I had to offer—and I was tricked and cheated and exploited by every kind of charlatan you can imagine, and probably some you can't. Was I supposed to write my mother and sister how I floundered about helplessly? How I made every stupid mistake a naive country bumpkin can make in a strange city?" Even after more than ten years, the humiliations he had suffered clearly still stung Prokles to rage.

"The hardest part for your parents and Hilaira was the uncertainty," Leonidas ventured in a low voice. "Your mother was haunted by images of you in need, and she wanted to help—but she didn't know where you were. They contacted all the people they had recommended you to, but you had been in touch with none of them."

Prokles snorted. "Did they really think I would go crawling to their rich horse-breeding friends? Did they think I'd offer my services as jockey or driver?"

"Your grandfather did," Leonidas pointed out.

"He was a slave!"

"He was an Olympic victor."

"I wasn't going to play poodle to their rich foreign friends!"

Leonidas had no answer to that. Prokles had always had an irrational, rebellious streak that Leonidas could not understand. Leonidas knew that if he had been exiled and put across the border with two horses and a long list of his father's aristocratic, foreign friends, he would have gone to these wealthy, influential men immediately. But Prokles was different. "So what did you do?"

"I gambled away everything my family had given me; and when I had nothing left to lose, I took work with a slave trader."

Leonidas stiffened involuntarily.

"Yes. That bad," Prokles admitted, meeting his friend's shocked eyes with a hard, almost hateful look. "I was paid to herd men around as if they were beasts. To chain and beat them for the slightest rebelliousness. I was younger and more slender than many of my charges, and they always outnumbered me. I had to make up for my weakness with brutality. And the whole time, my innards were cramped and gnawed by the terror that I would soon become one of them. I knew that if I didn't earn enough money to pay my debts, I would be forced to sell myself so someone else would have the problem of feeding me!"

"By all the Gods," Leonidas whispered, "why didn't you write? I would have found a way—"

"Never! You always lectured me on how I ought to behave! You always warned me I would get in trouble. Don't pretend you didn't think I deserved what I got when it happened! I didn't respect the laws. I was irresponsible. It was time I faced the consequences of my actions—wasn't it? And there were voices—do you think I didn't hear them?—that whispered I deserved nothing less than death."

"That was a minority," Leonidas insisted.

"Maybe, but at times I agreed with them. Or rather, I agreed that I deserved death if I couldn't make something of my life. The ephors decided that I had the right to a second chance, but that meant a second chance for *me* to make something of my life. *I* had to prove I had changed—not come crawling to you for help."

Leonidas was silenced, and Prokles continued in a calmer tone, "Slave traders pay badly. After all, they can always turn one of their purchases into an overseer. I think I was hired in anticipation of my going into debt to my employer so he could sell me. Instead, I refused to eat his meals or board in his lodgings, and went without wine or meat for more than a year until I had hoarded enough coins to risk leaving Tegea. I came to Corinth and found work as a marine with a pottery merchant."

"And you've been with him ever since?"

Prokles laughed his bitter, superior laugh. "You don't know a damned thing about life as a mercenary, do you? No mercenary ever stays with one employer for very long. There are always rumors of better pay, better berths, riches and women and adventure somewhere else. I've sailed as far as the Gates of Herakles and back again to the cities of the Levant. A mercenary is as fickle as an easterly wind, blown here and there, disappearing before the men he's cheated or the brothers of the girls he's seduced can catch up with him."

"Did you marry? Have children?"

"Bastards, you mean?" Prokles shot back, and then asked instead, "What about you? Have a full nursery? I'll bet you've got a boy or two in the agoge already." He said it with a sneer.

"My wife and two children were killed in the fires last year," Leonidas answered emotionlessly.

For the first time Prokles was taken aback. He caught his breath and looked hard at Leonidas. For a moment he seemed to notice that Leonidas, too, had aged and that not only laughter had lined his face; but then he shook himself and asked, "And Hilaira? How is she?"

"She married Alkander."

"Good. Have they children?"

"Two sons; the oldest, Thersander, entered the agoge this year, and Simonidas is three. She will be pleased to hear I've seen you—"

"No details!"

Leonidas made a noncommittal gesture. "She will not understand why you don't want to come home."

"Tell her I've gotten used to neat wine," Prokles retorted, thrusting his long-since empty kothon in the direction of Mantiklos. Leonidas nodded to the Messenian to refill it.

While Prokles drank deeply, Leonidas asked, "Which ship will you be on?" Leonidas nodded toward the door of the tent to indicate the ships lined up outside.

"I charge a drachma a fortnight; are you paying?"

"Certainly."

Prokles laughed. "You're still a fool, Leo. That's twice the going rate for the dregs like me."

"I'm not hiring the dregs; I'm hiring an experienced marine to train and coach an absolute novice."

"Aha; at least you know there's a difference between fighting on land and at sea."

"I know—and so do the ephors and Gerousia and Kyranios. But Corinth asked for Spartiates, and that's what she got—at least for the bulk of our force. We're two hundred Spartiates and a hundred perioikoi."

"Corinth had to come begging to you because the mercenaries are all taking Persian gold. The Medes can outpay any Greek. Half the Persian fleet is manned by Greek rowers and marines!" Prokles spat.

"You don't like Persians, it would seem," Leonidas observed, noting that Prokles was greatly exaggerating the situation. The Persians had little need to buy either oarsmen or troops, since they could conscript both and commanded the finest navy in the world.

"Do you know what they do with half the boys they capture? They cut off their genitals and make them serve as eunuchs in the harems. And the other half they sell into prostitution."

"I believe a substantial portion of Athens' wealth is derived from the slave trade," Leonidas countered.

"Athens? Athenians are all slave traders! They would sell their own mothers if they thought it would bring them profit! They crave wealth like Spartans crave honor. If Sparta had any sense, it would crush Athens before it gets any stronger. There is nothing greedier than the Athenian mob."

"For now, I would be satisfied with seeing this convoy safely to

Byzantion and back," Leonidas told him. "I'll sail on the *Liberty*. Will you join me?"

"For double wages? Certainly." Prokles stood, flung back the rest of his wine, and stalked out without another word.

"You're sure you want that man near you, sir?" Mantiklos asked skeptically.

Leonidas thought about it, but then he nodded. "Yes."

Mantiklos didn't look convinced, but he let the subject lie.

———

They had perfect sailing all the way up the Aegean to the Hellespont, with steady southwesterly winds and following seas that enabled both merchantmen and triremes to proceed under sail. Since they were not rowing even the warships, there was no need to stop at midday for a break and meal, and they sailed straight through the day. Of course, many of the Spartiates took a while to get their sea legs; but Leonidas was one of those least affected by seasickness, and with dolphins escorting them and the sun sparkling on the water, he began to understand Lychos' love of the sea.

At night they found a friendly shore, and the triremes beached while the merchantmen rode their anchors. The trireme crews built fires and bivouacked for the night, while the merchant crews sent boats ashore for fresh water and men to cook over an open fire. The well-protected convoy discouraged pirates; these rarely operated in groups of more than two or three ships. Ionian ships saluted and stayed away. Of the Phoenicians they saw nothing at all.

In Byzantion they were welcomed enthusiastically, because the embargo was cutting hard into the city's revenues. Here they learned that the Persians were busy in the eastern Mediterranean, where Cyprus was said to have joined the Ionian revolt. This was extremely good news for the rebels, since Cyprus not only was large and rich, but had provided many of Persia's ships and crews in the past. If the Cypriot ships came over to the rebel side, it would be a severe blow to Persian naval capacity.

Anxious to take advantage of the situation, the Corinthians loaded their ships as rapidly as possible and put back to sea, despite warnings from the older mariners that bad weather was afoot. Certainly the weather had changed. The sea seemed leaden. The clear, sunny days were gone, and they had to row through the Hellespont in pouring rain. On deck there was nowhere to keep dry, and below deck the air was clammy and suffocating. When the wind picked up, however, things went from bad to worse.

The wind churned the seas to a vicious chop, while visibility closed down to almost nothing. The poor visibility made any landfall excessively hazardous, and with so much of the day ahead of them, the decision was made to try to outrun the storm rather than put ashore.

But then the wind backed around to the northwest, and some of the merchantmen found it hard to sail close enough to the wind to hold course. On the triremes, the rough weather was making rowing difficult. One minute the oars bit only air, and the next water was pouring into the oar-ports, soaking the crew and accumulating in the bilges. The order was given to ship the oars of the lowest, thalamian, rowers, and the ports were closed. But the wind and seas continued to rise, and soon the heavily laden freighters started to founder.

The flagship signaled for the convoy to fall off before the wind and run downwind on storm sails. By the anxious lookouts posted in the rigging, however, Leonidas surmised there were hazards to leeward. Then night closed in around them.

In this roaring, heaving nightmare any encounter with land would be fatal, so no one thought of beaching. Instead, they plunged on through the night. The timbers of the *Liberty* groaned, anything not tied down rolled about underfoot, and the rigging slapped against the mast. The waves chased them, lifting up the stern until it seemed the bows were about to plunge forever into the deep. More than once, the ram of the trireme was completely submerged and they shipped water on the foredeck. Once a wave broke over the stern and washed the full length of the deck in a snarling, frothing mass. Leonidas saw a sailor lifted clear off the deck and swept overboard before his eyes. Men shouted and the man flailed wildly with his arms and legs. Just when they thought he was lost, he managed to catch hold of a streaming sheet that had come unraveled from the pin rail. His mates hauled the sheet inboard with the sailor clinging to it.

Leonidas looked around at his gray-faced men and ordered them to make themselves fast to the side of the ship. Prokles went around showing each man how to tie a lifeline around his waist with a knot that could be released by a single tug. "If she starts to go down, you just pull the release, see?" he told them. But they all knew that if the ship went down, they were lost with her. Paddling about in the Eurotas had not prepared them to survive in seas like these.

Below deck, conditions were even worse. The oarsmen on the lowest level, the thalamians, could not row, since the oar-ports were closed, but there was nowhere for them to go; so they sat on their benches, their feet in sloshing water, while above them the thranite and zygian rowers struggled to control their oars. This was easier said than done, with heaving seas that brought water crashing in on them at regular intervals and shoved the ship this way and that. Not a man was dry anymore.

Sometime during the night—they were all too drenched, cold, and bone-weary to know when—the *Vengeance* sent a signal by torch. With much cursing and foul language, the crew of the *Liberty* put the helm over, apparently to clear some island or promontory that stood in their way. This was more uncomfortable than running before the wind. Half the time they wallowed in the troughs between the waves with the wave crests looming over their heads. Leonidas was convinced that if one of the breakers ever caught the trireme in its teeth, the ship would capsize. On this course it was also much harder to keep an eye on the rest of the fleet. Once or twice, as they crested a wave, they had a glimpse of the ships nearest at hand, all struggling as they were. Once they thought they heard shouting and crashing noises, but it was hard to be sure over the roar of wind and wave.

When dawn finally broke, they found themselves completely alone on the ocean. Cursing, the captain sent a man up the mast to try to get a better view. Leonidas did not envy the sailor who had to scale the mast as it whipped around. He would not have had the courage to do it. The sailor tied himself aloft and scanned the horizon. After a few moments, he sighted something to windward and pointed.

They tried briefly to beat harder to windward, but the water breaking over the bows was too much, and the captain fell off the wind again. By now the thalamian oarsmen were doing nothing but bailing, passing buckets of shipped sea water to the zygians, who tossed it overboard past the thranites. The latter were the only oarsmen still actually rowing. The captain concluded it was too dangerous going any closer to the wind, and they resumed their previous course— the last convoy course—and held it as best they could. Sailors and marines were dozing fitfully in the gunnels, still tied to the side of the ship, while half the oarsmen slept upright on their benches and the others bailed.

Sometime in the late forenoon the wind started to back around to the south. They trimmed the sail, and gradually the trireme regained her mastery of the sea. They had removed enough of the shipped water for the trireme to be lighter; and while oarsmen slept, collapsed on one another, they set sail.

By afternoon, although there were still notable seas running, the captain was confident enough to put about and head back in the direction they'd come to search for their charges. The oars were run out, and two lookouts were sent aloft to scan the distant horizon in all directions.

They found one and then a pair of triremes, and then one of the penteconters. Lighter laden, the warships had generally outrun the merchantmen. It was late afternoon before they found the first of the grain carriers and then another six, all lashed together. By nightfall they had reestablished contact with the *Vengeance*, two penteconters, and nine triremes herding another dozen merchantmen. This meant that altogether they had found twenty-nine merchantmen, three penteconters, and fourteen of the triremes. The *Vengeance* signaled for ten of the triremes, including the *Liberty*, to stay with the merchantmen and get them to the next friendly shore for a rest and a meal, while the *Vengeance* and the other triremes sprinted off under oar to find the remaining merchantmen.

The triremes and penteconters with the convoy resumed their station around the reduced fleet and proceeded until they found a good harbor on Skyros. Here they replenished their water supplies and gave everyone a chance to sleep and eat. The Corinthians and perioikoi went in a crowd to the nearest village to purchase fresh fish and bread. The Spartiate marines sent one man from each ship to buy provisions for all and kept watch over their triremes.

The next morning, the *Vengeance* returned with six triremes and eleven merchantmen. After the men from these ships had been given a chance to eat and rest, Kyranios and Archilochos called Erxander and Leonidas to a command conference.

"Two of the merchantmen went down in the storm, but we found six more lame ducks—all have been damaged but are still afloat. They cannot keep up with the rest of the fleet, and we will have to leave them behind," Kyranios explained bluntly. But they didn't need a conference to explain this decision. Leonidas looked at Archilochos. The *Orcelle* had not yet rejoined the fleet.

"Two of the damaged ships are mine," Archilochos answered his look. "Although the *Orcelle* is undamaged, Lychos is keeping station with them, ready to take the crews off."

"Lame ducks are bait for pirates, and the islands east of here are full of them—more than ever since the revolt started," Erxander pointed out, expressing what they were all thinking.

"Can't we spare two triremes to stay with the crippled ships?" Leonidas asked, looking at Kyranios and then Archilochos. "Or at least the penteconters?"

"We're still missing one trireme and two penteconters at the moment," Kyranios reminded him.

"But we can't just abandon six ships, seven including the *Orcelle*," Erxander supported Archilochos unspoken wishes. "We've got to get as much grain as possible back to Corinth."

"The most we can spare is two triremes," Kyranios insisted.

"Then shouldn't we reinforce the marines aboard the merchantmen?" Leonidas asked.

Kyranios raised his eyebrows at Leonidas, but the Corinthians were enthusiastic. "Yes, that would be very helpful. Indeed, it's the only way. With two triremes we can't count on deterring pirates, but they generally withdraw if the fighting gets too intense. The mere sight of Spartan scarlet might discourage them altogether—if there is enough of it," Archilochos enthused.

"Sir, give me two men from each of the other triremes. I'll distribute them among the merchantmen. We can outfit our attendants with scarlet himations, and make it look like we are double the number of Spartiates. Word will have spread that we're with this fleet, but no one knows how many we are or on which ships."

"All right," Kyranios agreed. "Which two triremes?" he asked Archilochos.

Leonidas could see how much the older man was torn between the desire to stay with his son and his duty to the larger fleet. Erxander came to his aid. "I'll take the *Liberty* and the *Harmony*."

Archilochos nodded.

———

Prokles was on deck with Leonidas as they took station beside the tiny convoy of seven merchantmen. From the deck of the *Orcelle*, Lychos recognized the *Liberty* and waved at them.

"How did you ever become so friendly with that cripple?" Prokles wanted to know.

"Lychos is a first-rate sailor. Don't underestimate him," Leonidas answered.

"Are you really here to defend these ships?"

"Why else would I be here?"

"Look, Leo: That ship over there is all but foundering; if you slow down to its pace, we're all sitting ducks. If you want to save the others, you'd better cast that ship adrift. Then you'd better face up to the fact that those two ships, there and there, are in almost as bad shape. If pirates attack, they'll go for them first—but only to try to distract the triremes. The ship they'll really be after is your friend's ship. She's a prize worth taking—large, new, and loaded to the gills. What's more, even without sail set, the mast gives her away as a fleet ship. If they can, they'll try to lure the triremes away from her and then attack."

That made sense to Leonidas, so he called Erxander over and had Prokles repeat what he had said.

"They'd have to have three ships to do that," the Corinthian pointed out. "Still, it is a good point. We should order the *Harmony* to stay with the *Orcelle* regardless of what happens, while we retain freedom of maneuver. As for the slowest ship, we're not going to abandon it until we have cause. But we should tell the crew to be prepared to transfer to the nearest ship at the first sign of trouble."

"We should get the marines off her at once. If we know we're not going to defend her, then they should be stationed aboard ships we intend to defend—the other two slow ships, for example," Leonidas suggested.

"Good. But in a fight only the *Orcelle* has a chance of escaping; the others will have to fight. The best way to do that is if they form a single float. That way they help keep one another afloat, and marines can work together reinforcing whichever ship is attacked."

Leonidas glanced at Prokles. He shrugged. "That means you could lose them all."

"All or none," Erxander agreed. "Which is why it would be best if you transferred all marines to the merchantmen. I will be fighting both triremes as ramming vessels. I have no interest in boarding a pirate ship to take control of it, and unless I am trapped by several vessels at once I won't let another vessel close enough to board the *Liberty*, either. I need to retain my mobility; and marines, frankly, will just get in my way and add weight. It is the merchantmen who, if we are outnumbered, will be fighting hand to hand. They can't outrun anything and aren't maneuverable."

Although what Erxander said made sense, Leonidas hesitated to move all of his sixty Spartiates aboard the merchantmen, because the Council of Elders had specifically decided against this. Kyranios, too, had ordered that all Spartiates remain aboard the triremes. Was he being naive to take the Corinthian vice admiral's advice?

"What the triremes could use is archers. Are any of your men good with the bow?"

Leonidas nodded. "Our attendants fight as our auxiliaries and are well trained in both bow and javelin. I'll leave the twenty best archers with you, ten per trireme. That will put one hundred Lacedaemonians aboard the merchantmen. With the Corinthian marines already on board, we'll have close to two hundred men to defend the float."

"Agreed. If attacked, we abandon the lame duck and form a float made up of the others—except for the *Orcelle*. She must abandon the convoy and run for it."

Leaving the eldest of the attendants in command of the ten helots remaining aboard the *Liberty*, Leonidas redeployed his men as soon as the conference of captains was over. Leonidas himself went aboard the *Golden Dawn*, one of the two ships that had been partially dismasted in the storm. He kept Prokles and the salpinx player with him, so that he could give orders across greater distances.

The *Golden Dawn* was, except for the broken mast, in good condition. There were five Corinthian marines already on board, and the Spartiates were housed with them aft, in a low but dry and well-ventilated 'tweendeck space on which they could roll out their bedding and stow their panoply. The wind had died down, and the sea was settling.

———

Leonidas was woken by a boy violently shaking his shoulder. "Spartan! Spartan! Come quick!"

Leonidas rolled out of the bunk and crawled out of the 'tweendeck space to follow the boy up the ladder to the afterdeck. It was the middle of the night and the moon had set. On deck the air was fresh, and the sound of the escort's oars dipping and rising off their port quarter was like a whisper. Both the master and the chief mate were on deck, their attention focused to windward and away from the shore, where Leonidas had been told to expect the pirates.

"What is it?" he asked.

"Shhh! Sound carries better across water! Look!" They pointed to the west, across their starboard bows. Leonidas concentrated, and after a bit he decided that there might be a string of objects out there.

"What is it?" he asked again softly.

"It's a squadron of triremes—but we can't be sure whose—and we don't know if they've sighted us yet, either."

Leonidas looked across the convoy of cripples. Both Corinthian triremes were keeping station to eastward, because they had expected the danger to come from that direction. Maybe it still would. Who was to say these weren't Ionian rebels or neutral ships heading north for some legitimate reason? But he didn't like it. There were too many of them. All warships, from what he could see. He went back to the 'tweendeck "cabin" and woke Prokles. "Come on deck."

Prokles didn't ask questions. He came on deck. The Corinthians again pointed out the fleet. Prokles glanced at the stump of the mast left by the storm and then back at the fleet moving north. After a moment he he grabbed the secured but useless halyards and scrambled as high as he dared go. Given the and loose tackle, that was risky enough. He hung precariously in the rigging, one foot hooked around the lines, and focused his attention on the distant ships. When he returned to deck he announced, "Phoenicians. You can tell by the formation."

"Signal the *Liberty* and call all hands," Leonidas ordered, and went below deck to wake the other marines.

They took their panoply on deck and, lacking attendants, helped one another into it. Meanwhile, a signal flashed to the *Liberty* from a lantern shielded on three sides. It took longer than Leonidas liked to get her attention, but eventually the *Liberty* spun about and raced around the tail of the crippled convoy to surge up on the westward side of the *Golden Dawn*. By now, however, four of the Phoenician triremes had swung about and were making straight toward them. There was no need for silence anymore. The salpinx howled "alarm," and the captain of the *Golden Dawn* shouted across the water as the *Liberty* came alongside: "Phoenicians to windward! Phoenician triremes!"

They could see Erxander run to the far side of the deck and heard him start to shout orders furiously. All across the little convoy, they were calling "all hands" and the marines on all the ships were stumbling onto their respective decks, responding to the Spartan salpinx. Meanwhile, the *Harmony* pivoted sharply in place and shot through the convoy in a masterful display of seamanship. She fell in on the *Liberty*'s flank as the flagship swung her bows toward the Persian ships and surged forward with impressive determination.

The Corinthians were boiling through the water, leaving clean wakes in the starlight. All three banks of oars were working in unison with the precision of a Spartan phalanx. Not one oar was out of alignment or missed the timing by so much as a heartbeat. The oars swept forward and then dipped down into the water with an audible hiss. The two Corinthian triremes had set a course to intercept the Phoenicians and cut them off from the merchantmen—and they were rapidly closing the distance.

Leonidas wanted to watch the encounter. He longed to see these ships go into action, but he had to drag his eyes away and concentrate on his own task. The other merchant ships were closing on the

Golden Dawn, while her own crew was handing sail and preparing to throw grapples to the others. Meanwhile, the foundering ship was abandoned altogether. Contrary to orders, the *Orcelle* bore down on them, too, only to swing into the wind, her sail slack, as she came within hailing distance. "What are your orders?" Lychos shouted across the water.

"Flee!" Leonidas answered.

Leonidas could see Lychos turn to look over their flank, and he followed the gaze. The Phoenicians were shifting course, trying to slip past the Corinthian triremes, but Erxander adjusted for each movement perfectly. If the Persians turned to starboard they were headed away from the quarry, and if the turned to port they exposed their more vulnerable broadsides to the vicious rams of the Corinthian triremes. The sound of distant shouting and a faint clatter reached them. "Persian arrows," Prokles murmured into Leonidas' ear.

Lychos was calling, "I'll send my marines over!"

"No! You may need them! Set sail and flee!"

Leonidas could see how reluctant Lychos was, but he didn't have any more time for him. To starboard the first of the other ships had had been made fast, and another was nestling her prow between the two sterns and making fast in this position, with the fourth ship beside her. Further away, with a resounding, deep-timbered thud followed by a wrenching and whining as if the wood itself were alive and screaming in pain, the *Liberty* smashed into one of the Phoenician triremes. Moments later the *Harmony* struck a second. Yet already the *Liberty* had extricated herself from the damaged Phoenician, pivoted, and turned her dangerous ram on a third Phoenician. The latter, however, took flight. *Liberty* gave chase. The fourth Phoenician was making straight for the float of merchantmen at a terrifying speed.

Leonidas called for his marines to line up along the exposed side of the ship nearest the Phoenicians, but Prokles grabbed him by the arm and hauled him back. "Draw your line of defense here!" He indicated the *Golden Dawn*. "Now that we're lashed together, the other ship's not going down regardless. She's low in the water anyway. Whatever damage the ram does, you can repair it just by dumping some of the cargo. Fight here, and you increase the range for the Persian archers and make the Persian marines come to you! They'll either have to stop their archers or be killed by them!"

Leonidas had no time to argue. He changed his own orders and deployed his marines, Spartan and Corinthian together, along the side of the *Golden Dawn*, with the sailors behind them.

The *Harmony* was completely entangled with the Phoenician ship she had attacked; both ships appeared to be drifting, slowly spinning around like lovers locked together, while hand-to-hand combat flowed and ebbed across both decks. The *Liberty* was still chasing the third Phoenician, preventing it from engaging; while the first of the Phoenician ships, down by the bows and listing to starboard, was advancing at a slow but steady pace toward the float of merchantmen.

The fourth Phoenician smashed into the outer ship of the float with the distinctive thump, squeal, and crunch that Leonidas had heard for the first time only a few minutes earlier. This time it was much louder, and the impact sent all the men on the deck of the *Golden Dawn* crashing to their knees or backsides.

Barrages of arrows fell onto the deck ahead of them, but only occasionally did one fall among them. Then the first of the Persian soldiers scaled up over the side of the far deck, expecting immediate resistance, and hesitated at the sight of the empty deck. For a moment the Persians seemed to think the ship had been abandoned. Possibly they did not realize, given the darkness, that there were five ships lashed together in a giant float. In triumph, one of the leaders raised his arms over his head and shouted. From behind Leonidas one of the Corinthian marines released a single, well-aimed arrow. It went straight into the man's heart, and he crumpled onto the deck.

His dramatic death alerted his comrades, and they saw the line of marines defending the next ship in the float. They howled and rushed forward. Their approach took Leonidas by surprise. He had never fought Persians before, and he had no idea from which of the many nations that made up the vast Persian Empire these particular men came. They were not any of the subject Greeks, nor were they Egyptians; but they might be Medes or Babylonians, Lydians or Phrygians, or peoples from the eastern edges of the Empire whose race and country he had never heard of.

What struck him was that they rushed forward as individuals

rather than forming into a unit. They were shouting rather than silent, but the Argives had been vocal, and the Corinthians all around him were whipping up their courage with shouted insults and taunts. The clothing of the attacking men was, however, incomprehensible. They had covered their legs in cloth—which made no sense to Leonidas, since cloth provided no protection, but could get in one's way, or soak with sea water, sweat, or blood to weigh one down. The tunics they wore over their trousers were long-sleeved, and on their heads was a strange, close-fitting cloth hood. Except for their shields—odd-shaped and apparently lightweight—they had no protection for their vital body organs. Since their clothing was light, they advanced rapidly; but without any protection, they fell beneath the Greek spears like fish in a barrel.

In just minutes, a heap of corpses was piled so high on the deck of the other ship that the men coming after had to climb over the bodies of their comrades to reach the unbroken line of hoplites. Meanwhile, the archers had left the deck of the Phoenician trireme and started advancing, firing volley after volley almost on the level. The arrows generally stuck in the massive aspis, but here and there came clear through. Leonidas felt the prick of an arrowhead and the sticky flow of his own blood from the back of his left forearm. To his left, one of his men went down with a horrible involuntary cry when an arrow found its way into his eye. It was madness to just stand here and take this. Leonidas ordered the advance.

This was not simple. They first had to clamber up over the side of the *Golden Dawn*, and then step across the gap between the ships onto the slippery, unsteady heap of corpses on the other ship. Only beyond the human mound was there any chance of solid deck and the prospect of something steady under their feet.

Before they had made it that far, however, a shout of alarm from the sailors warned him that the damaged Phoenician trireme had swept around the stern of the float and was preparing to board them from the other side. That threat had to be faced, but to turn and face the new onslaught meant exposing their backs to the archers. Leonidas saw no alternative but to split his force. He ordered the Corinthian marines and the sailors to face the new threat, while he took his Lacedaemonians up over the side of the *Golden Dawn*.

Despite the unusual circumstances, thanks to a lifetime of keeping contact with their rank-mates and endless drill in adjusting their own movements to those of the men left and right, the Spartiates crossed onto the other ship in a line without serious gaps. That proved to be enough. When the archers realized that the wall of bronze was moving toward them, they broke and ran. Only the fastest made it. Anyone who slipped and fell on the bloody deck or tripped over rigging and scattered weapons was stabbed mercilessly by the "lizard stickers" of the Spartan spears.

When the line of bronze shields and scarlet cloaks appeared along the side of the ship, the Phoenician captain shouted furiously and the trireme backwatered wildly, pulling itself free of its victim. As it withdrew, the Corinthian merchantman settled into the water and started to list noticeably. Leonidas turned and led his men up the incline, to get back to the fight that was taking place at the far side of the float.

By the time they were back aboard the *Golden Dawn*, the enemy was pouring over the railing on the far side. There were bodies strewn across the deck of the far ship—Greek bodies for the most part. Arrows were pouring down on them again. It flashed through Leonidas' mind that he might die right here, along with every Lacedaemonian under his command. He could clearly expect no help from the two Corinthian triremes, which were both fully engaged. The sailors were proving surprisingly poor soldiers—something he hadn't expected, since they were defending their own ships and lives and had nowhere to escape. But there was no point thinking about it.

He called a halt to dress their lines. They were two men short—the man with the eye wound and someone else. No time to identify the casualties. At least they were on a level deck now and they could advance across it at a steady pace, drawing on their discipline and training.

The second Phoenician hadn't rammed, forcing the soldiers to climb over the bows one or two at a time, but had come alongside. The enemy troops poured over the gunnel along the whole length of the ship. Fortunately, they were the same poorly armed and unarmored men, and were just as undisciplined as their countrymen.

Oddly, there seemed to be more of them, and the hindmost men were stabbing the men ahead of them in their backs! They were Greek marines!

At last Leonidas' brain registered that there was another ship beyond the Phoenician trireme—the *Orcelle*!

The fool! But at the same moment, Leonidas felt such a rush of gratitude for the crippled Corinthian that it was as if he'd just been reinforced by the Guard. He increased the pace. Step and thrust, step and thrust. The enemy was going down before them with very little chance of defending themselves. The trick was to ignore the arrows, Leonidas decided. Raising his spear arm for the thrust, the man beside Leonidas took an arrow in the armpit and crumpled to the deck with a croaked-off wail. The man behind closed the rank with Leonidas without missing a beat. Step and thrust. They had cleared the deck of the *Golden Dawn*.

Ahead was a confused melee of sailors and an exceptionally large number of marines from the *Orcelle*, mixed with enemy archers and enemy marines. The sun broke over the horizon, and for the first time Leonidas could see that the Persians wore clothes of yellow and purple in bizarre stripes and chains of diamonds. It was the gaudiest sight he had ever seen in his life—all liberally splashed with red. And just beyond, the sun glistened blissfully on a calm and enchanting seascape.

By the time Leonidas made it aboard the Phoenician trireme, he realized that the Greek sailors had gained full possession of her after slaughtering the Phoenician crew. They cheered him and his marines as they crossed the trireme, heading for the *Orcelle*. Lychos was hanging over the side of his ship, clutching the rail. He was dressed in full panoply, and Leonidas knew that it must have half killed him just to put it on.

Leonidas shoved his helmet back and grinned up at the Corinthian from the deck of the captive trireme. "You stupid fool!"

"It worked, didn't it?" Lychos grinned back at him. "I think the Phoenician captain died of pure astonishment when he realized a freighter was attacking him!"

"I sympathize!"

"It helped that my marines are first-class archers and sent him to Hades with an arrow in his throat."

Leonidas threw back his head and laughed, then thought to ask, "Just how many marines do you have on board?"

"A lot. My father still won't let me go anywhere without all the protection he can buy."

"He'll wring the marine captain's neck when he finds out what you did!"

"But it was so beautiful, Leonidas! It was the most beautiful moment of my whole life—coming to your rescue."

———

By midmorning, the self-satisfaction at having won this first engagement had worn off. Although they had lost no ships—not even the one they'd abandoned—the *Harmony* had damaged her ram and lost almost a dozen sailors in the violent encounter with the Phoenicians. Furthermore, four of the Lacedaemonian attendants fighting aboard the *Harmony* had been badly wounded, while Leonidas had three casualties among his Spartiates. None were dead, but the man who'd taken the arrow in his armpit was probably not going to make it, since several ribs were broken and his lung appeared to be pierced. He was bringing up frothy blood and having difficulty breathing. The man with the eye wound would survive, but for the moment the pain was excruciating and debilitating. There were a score of Corinthian casualties as well, mostly sailors. All this would have been tolerable if they had been out of danger; but it was obvious that at some point the Phoenicians would wonder what had become of the four triremes they had detached. If they sent just one ship back to investigate, the Greeks could handle it. If they sent more, the Greeks were finished.

Furthermore, the freighter that had been rammed by the Persian trireme was clearly sinking, only kept afloat by the others. They were going to have to either abandon her or put about and try to limp to a friendly shore for repairs. The problem was that, according to Erxander, the closest "friendly" shore was more than likely a base for pirates. Still, this was the decision Erxander and Leonidas made together. Setting what sail they could, the whole awkward formation swung about and started making for the nearest island.

The wind was favorable. Despite sailing under jury-rigged canvas on broken masts, they made progress and had just started to convince themselves that they might succeed, when three ships were spotted on the horizon behind them—rapidly gaining.

Leonidas went aft and stood sweating in the afternoon sun, staring at the horizon until his eyes blurred over. He had removed his armor hours ago, and wore a linen corselet instead. Still, with the sun reflecting off the sea and no shade anywhere, even the wind couldn't cool him down. The sweat was particularly uncomfortable under the bandage on his arm, making it soggy. He stared at the dots on the horizon, while sweat collected in his eyelids and then ran down into his eyes.

It wasn't just three ships, it was four, and then six and then ten. How could the Phoenician fleet commander spare so many ships? But then Leonidas remembered they had only seen the Phoenician fleet in the night. Maybe it had been larger than they first assumed.

The hopelessness of the situation was laming. The *Orcelle* lingered for several minutes, but then crammed on all the sail she had and sped away, disappearing rapidly. The *Liberty* and the *Harmony* meanwhile turned about and took up a position astern of the convoy; here they lay side by side, bow to the Persians in the wake of the clumsy float, apparently undecided on how to proceed against ten—or was it twelve?—Phoenician triremes. Their oars dipped listlessly, just keeping them in position as the float drifted, more than sailed, eastward.

Prokles came up beside Leonidas. "Time to quit."

Leonidas looked over at him, uncomprehending.

"You can't fight all that."

"What else can I do?"

"Don't pretend you're *that* stupid, Leo! I expect the Persian admiral will make quite a fuss over you—a prince and all. You should be able to negotiate a good deal—if you handle it correctly."

"What do you mean?"

"No false modesty, for a start. Persians are hierarchical. Play up your bloodlines to the hilt. Descendant of Herakles and all that. Stress that you're mercenaries for hire. The Corinthians are about to be slaughtered, but that's no reason you can't offer the services of your Lacedaemonians to the Persian admiral. Throw your shields aside as soon as the Phoenicians have come close enough for the Persian trier-

archs to see what you are doing. In short, signal willingness to negotiate. The Persians will have heard about Spartans and will be curious.
They certainly won't dismiss the offer out of hand."

"If I did that, I could never return home," Leonidas told Prokles,
dumbfounded.

"You can't return home if you're dead, either."

When Leonidas continued to stare at him, Prokles asked sarcastically, "Are you sure all your men are as in love with suicide as you
are?" He nodded in the direction of the other Lacedaemonians, who
were silently gazing at the approaching enemy fleet. "Not all of them
have just lost their wife and children."

The remark lacerated Leonidas. He spun around and left Prokles
standing. He crossed the deck to Oliantus, who was staring at the
approaching triremes like the rest of them. As Leonidas approached,
Oliantus came to attention, expecting orders. "Sir?"

Leonidas signaled for him to come farther aft, where they could
talk unheard by the others. "We're all going to die here—unless we
surrender and offer our services to the Persians."

"Have you gone mad?" Oliantus gaped at him.

"No. I'm going fight. I just want the men to know that it's their
own decision. I won't be around to see who surrenders. Tell them
that."

"Sir, I won't insult any one of them by passing that message on!
Who have you been listening to? That exile?" He tossed his head contemptuously in the direction of Prokles.

"Don't sneer, Oliantus. He's talking sense."

"He's talking treason!"

"This has nothing to do with treason. One way or another, Lacedaemon is losing one hundred men. It ought to be up to the individual to decide if he wants to live a mercenary life in Persian service
or die here."

"With all due respect, sir: it makes a huge difference to Sparta's
reputation what we do here. The more Persians we take with us, the
less eager they will be to tangle with us again. We have a duty to
everyone at home to give the Persians reason to fear encountering
us—even when we're vastly outnumbered."

Leonidas was startled by this long speech from Oliantus, who was

generally a man of few words. Leonidas also realized he'd let Prokles
goad him with the dig about his lost family. All Oliantus had done was
to voice his initial thought: Prokles was a bad influence on him. He
took a deep breath and smiled. "Thank you. Let's kit up." The others
were watching intently while their commanders spoke together. All
Leonidas had to do was make the motion of setting a helmet on, and
the Lacedaemonians started back for the 'tweendeck space where they
had left their panoply.

By the time they were back on deck, the two Corinthian triremes
had pulled away. They were still side by side, but they were veering
westward to put themselves in a ramming position as the Phoenicians
swept in for the kill on the freighters. Leonidas tried to organize the
sailors; but the fear in their eyes and the nervous glances they made,
as if looking for a place to run and hide, suggested to him that they
would be of little use. The Corinthian marines were made of sterner
stuff and earnestly listened to his orders.

The basic tactic was to retreat to the ship in the center of the float,
the *Golden Dawn*, and to make the Persians come to them there.
Concentrated on the deck of this freighter, they would have almost
the mass of a good phalanx and would be fighting with overlapping
shields—a clear advantage. This would enable the second rank to
hold their shields high over the heads of the front rank, protecting
both of the first two ranks from arrows.

They got themselves into position with the sailors in the middle,
tested the formation, and then dropped their shields to rest. They
stood at ease while the Phoenicians closed the remaining thousand
yards. The *Harmony* took out the leading Phoenician and the *Liberty*
the second, with the now familiar sound of wood being smashed and
torn apart. The next two Phoenician ships made only a slight detour
around the pair of locked ships, and in a pincer movement closed on
either side on the float. They thudded hard into the outer ships, only
seconds apart. The marines were ready for them, all kneeling on one
knee so they wouldn't lose their balance. Grapples soared through the
air and clunked on the empty decks of the outer ships. The first wave
of arrows clattered around the Greeks bunched together on the deck
of the *Golden Dawn*.

Abruptly, a wild flurry of alarmed shouting erupted from the

Phoenician ships. The oarsmen started to backwater and the grapples were cut by the same men who had thrown them. The Greeks looked at one another in confusion. Then a trireme swept into Leonidas' line of vision. This trireme took the closest Phoenician as it was still trying to back off, and it was so close that Leonidas could see the ram smash right through the side of the Persian ship. Muffled shouting penetrated his helmet, and turning his head sharply, he saw another trireme on the opposite side of the float take out a second Persian. Turning completely around, he saw still more triremes in line abreast, sweeping toward the Phoenician fleet like Vengeance incarnate.

"Chians!" The word penetrated to his helmet and his brain. "Chians!"

They had just been rescued by an entire squadron of twenty Chian triremes—the rebel ships the Phoenician squadron had been looking for when they stumbled upon the damaged ships of the Corinthian grain fleet.

CHAPTER 18

A POLITICAL EXPEDIENT

"WHY DO YOU KEEP THE OLD bitch around?" Oliantus wanted to know, as he waited impatiently for Leonidas' dog to catch up with them. They were returning from the drill fields to the HQ of the Mesoan Lochos, where their company office was located.

By the time Leonidas had reached Sparta after escorting the Corinthian grain fleet home, he discovered that on Kyranios' recommendation, the five lochagoi had collectively named him company commander of the Menelaion Pentekostus in the Mesoan (Kyranios') Lochos—if he would accept the position. Furthermore, his exploits with the Corinthian fleet had been greatly exaggerated.

Leonidas understood why the Corinthians had lined the harbor walls and cheered themselves hoarse when the last seven merchantmen and their two escorts, all of whom had been presumed lost, limped into the harbor flying bunting from their jury-rigged mastheads. After all, those seven ships carried precious grain still desperately needed by the city, and their surprise survival seemed like a miracle. But Leonidas had expected the Spartans to be more sober about the whole affair. After all, he and his men would all have been feeding the fishes if the Chian squadron (which had been chasing the Phoenicians for days) hadn't caught up with them at that particular moment. Leonidas did not think he had done anything the least bit heroic. Lychos had. Even Erxander had—attacking when he thought he was outnumbered five to one—but not the Lacedaemonians. They had only done their duty and had had no real impact on the outcome of the engagement.

To his amazement, however, the Gerousia, the ephors, and many ordinary citizens saw things differently and openly congratulated him. Leonidas had been pressed from all sides to accept the offered company. Men argued that he now had very valuable experience fighting as a marine (the undamaged portion of the Corinthian grain fleet made it all the way back to Kenchrea without a single incident and so no fighting), and he had witnessed a full-scale naval battle between the Chians and the Phoenicians. That made him too valuable to the Spartan army to allow him to enjoy the luxury of living as a private citizen. He owed it to his city to remain on active service, they said.

Leonidas allowed himself to be talked into taking command of the pentekostus, because that was what he really wanted. Leonidas wanted to serve his city; and after the experience with the grain fleet, he was convinced that Persia was a serious threat to Hellas and that command of the sea was going to be vital. Now he understood what Phormio had been trying to tell him. He even fantasized about the Lacedaemonian fleet becoming a place for poorer Spartiates to serve, just as in Athens and Corinth. If the sons of poorer Spartiates could not afford the agoge fees, and so were not trained as hoplites, why not allow them to serve with the fleet?

But Leonidas was careful not to speak about his hopes and plans in this regard. Sparta was a society that did not welcome anyone talking "out of turn." Leonidas recognized that if he wanted to play any significant role in Spartan society, he first had to demonstrate his competence in leadership and collect political support among his fellow citizens. After his disastrous foray into teaching at the agoge, he also realized that he had the best chances of gaining respect and power in a military career.

So on the surface, everything had settled into a comfortable routine. After morning drill he stripped off his panoply, bathed, lunched, did paperwork, and then generally rode to one or another of his properties to check on things, followed by dinner at the syssitia, before going home to his kleros for the night. At thirty-two, he was exempt from sleeping in barracks, and took full advantage of the privilege. The company had two helot runners who in an emergency could reach him in less than half an hour.

Beggar, stiff-legged and gray at the muzzle, had finally caught up with them, and Leonidas bent to stroke her head and scratch her behind the ears, ignoring Oliantus' impatience.

"How old is that bitch?" his deputy asked.

"I don't know. I thought she was only a year or two old when she adopted me, but I now suspect she was older. She was probably the runt of a litter, or else the years living wild stunted her growth."

"One way or another, she's stiff and obviously in pain. She certainly slows you down."

"I'm not in a hurry."

"You have one of the best kennels in Lacedaemon. People from all over the world come here to buy whelps from them—and you go around with a mutt! It doesn't make sense. Why don't you select one of your own fine Kastorians?"

"Because they were born in slavery and know nothing else, but Beggar was born free and gave up her freedom to serve me."

They reached the HQ building, and the meleirene guards presented arms as they passed. In the long corridor, the sound of their footsteps echoed until they turned in to the company office. The room was lit by a single window through which light poured, showing the dust swirling in the air. Here they kept the duty rosters and disciplinary records, the inventories of equipment and supplies, and the lists of beasts of burden, vehicles, and everything else that was needed for the operation of the pentekostus. They even had two full-time clerks, perioikoi employees, one for accounting and the other for correspondence and record-keeping. These men were hard at work when the two Spartiate officers arrived.

The clerks muttered greetings and kept working, while Leonidas and Oliantus propped their spears against the wall and hung their training shields up beside their battle aspis. Leonidas' aspis, designed by the Thespian craftsman who had taken over his bronzeworks, showed the head of a roaring lion from the front. The relief was exceptionally high, and Leonidas knew the lion's snarling snout would get badly damaged in any real engagement, but the image had been so beautiful and lifelike he hadn't had the heart to tell the artist it was unsuitable.

Leonidas pulled his baldric off over his head and propped up his sword by the door beside the spears. He ran his hand through his long hair. It was almost shoulder length, and he would soon start braiding it like the older men did.

Oliantus was looking over the documents the clerks had waiting for him. "There is one section that consistently consumes much more wine than the others."

"How much more?" Leonidas asked politely, as he bent to untie his sandals.

"Roughly 20 per cent. Either they are very careless or they drink it almost unmixed—or some of them do."

"Hmm. Do you want to talk to them about it?"

Oliantus looked over at his commander, who kicked his sandals out of the way and started to loosen the cords of his corselet. "You know perfectly well that my talking to them will have little to no effect," Oliantus said patiently. He was perfectly aware that the bulk of the men in the pentekostus—like his comrades when he was a ranker and his classmates in the agoge—did not pay him much attention. He was not beautiful, in a society that associated beauty with virtue. He was not even particularly brilliant at philosophy or rhetoric or gifted at music, the other skills Spartans admired. And his only attempt at glory had ended in the dust at Olympia a decade earlier. His talents were more pedestrian, and he was glad that Leonidas valued them, but he had no illusions about being respected or admired by the population generally.

The conversation got no further, because Crius burst into the chamber. "Master! You better come quick!" Crius was one of the company runners, and entitled to burst in on them like this, but Leonidas had never seen him look this agitated. He was glistening with sweat and gasping for breath as if he had just run a long distance.

"What's happened?" Leonidas reached immediately for his sword.

"Dad caught Chryse with an eirene and Mantiklos beat him up—"

Oliantus burst out laughing and Leonidas put his sword back as they realized this had nothing to do with the company, but was merely a domestic crisis on Leonidas' kleros. Crius frowned and insisted, "Mom's afraid we'll all get in trouble for what Mantiklos has done, and Chryse's going to raise the dead with her screaming."

"All right, I'll come straight away. Oliantus, if there's anything urgent, you know where to find me. Crius, when you catch your breath, bring Beggar home with you." Leonidas re-donned his sandals, then went out to the HQ stables, collected one of his stallions, and set off for his kleros at a good pace.

Laodice was waiting for him at the head of the drive. He jumped down and led his horse, so she had time to tell him what had happened as they walked together to the house. "It's Chryse, master. I always suspected it, but I never could quite catch her—she's been sleeping with an eirene. Pelopidas found them together when he and Mantiklos were behind the mirabelle orchard, checking the fencing."

Mantiklos had married the elder of Laodice's daughters this past summer, and he spent much of his time on the kleros when they were not on maneuvers. Meander had rapidly learned his duties, and Leonidas preferred the young Spartiate as a companion because of his more cheerful temperament.

"Pelopidas grabbed Chryse and brought her home," Laodice continued, "but Mantiklos went mad and started beating the eirene, master!" Laodice was clearly horrified by this. "We know he shouldn't have done it, but Pelopidas didn't realize what he'd done till Mantiklos dragged the youth home—hogtied, bloody, and vomiting. They'll kill us, sir. They'll never believe Pelopidas had nothing to do with it! I've never seen Mantiklos like this before, either! He's gone completely mad."

Leonidas nodded. He remembered that a couple of years earlier Mantiklos had courted a girl who preferred a meleirene, and he was bitterly resentful of the liberties young Spartiates took with helots. Furthermore, while Pelopidas and Laodice had come to think of themselves as Lacedaemonian, even Laconian, Mantiklos still clung to his identity as a Messenian and saw Pelopidas' family as Messenian, too. For Mantiklos, this was a matter of national as well as family pride.

As they approached the house they heard Chryse's high-pitched screaming. Although it was somewhat muffled, the pitch was hair-raising. "I've locked her in the workshed, master; otherwise I don't know what she would have done. Pelopidas will take a horsewhip to her, I promise you, sir. We'll make sure she knows she's done wrong, but we have to get the eirene out of here first—only Mantiklos won't let us! If the magistrates find out—"

"I'll take care of the magistrates," Leonidas assured her. "Don't worry about that."

They entered the kitchen courtyard, where the sound of Chryse's screaming was louder and Pelopidas and Polychares were both arguing with Mantiklos—who stood over a naked youth stretched out on the ground with his hands and feet tied together behind him, while Kleon gaped at them all.

"Mantiklos!"

"This bastard was misusing Chryse! It's against the law, master! I want to see him in the stocks! I want to see you enforce the law!"

"So that's what this is all about." Leonidas met the Messenian's eye. They stared at one another. They both knew that the law against misuse of helots was a fine Lycurgan tradition—one that few Spartiates nowadays had any particular interest in enforcing.

"You're always preaching the law," Mantiklos told him with narrowed eyes. "Telling me that Sparta wouldn't treat Messenians badly if we didn't give you cause. I want more than words this time! I want to see you stand up for the law—your own law."

"First I have to establish the facts. Stand back and set the eirene free."

Mantiklos did this readily, because he no longer had any fear that the youth would escape. The eirene might have fled from helots, but he could not run from a Spartan Peer, much less a company commander.

As soon as the bonds came loose, the youth struggled to right himself. He was bleeding from his nose and mouth, and one of his eyes was starting to swell up. He had bruises on his stomach, too, and streaks of vomit and other fluids over his thighs. Leonidas nodded toward the horse trough: "Clean yourself up, eirene." Then he called Kleon over to take his horse around to the stables and sent Laodice to get a chiton for the youth to put on. While the eirene washed himself off, Leonidas went to the door of the workshed and called out: "Chryse! This is Leonidas. The longer you scream, the longer your lover will stand in the pits. Do you understand me?"

The screaming stopped instantly.

The youth pulled the chiton on over his wet body and, at a gesture from Leonidas, went through the colonnade into the main house. Leonidas led him to the hearth room, which looked out onto the inner courtyard but was darker and more sober. "First tell me who you are," Leonidas ordered.

"Temenos, son of Kephistodotos."

Leonidas had heard the name Kephistodotos, but it meant nothing to him. As for Temenos himself, Leonidas had no memory of ever encountering him before. He was not a particularly handsome young man—but not notably ugly, either. He was thin, as most eirenes were, and his hair, just starting to grow out, was fair, his eyes gray. "What do you have to say for yourself?" Leonidas asked next, expecting the usual excuses about the girl being just a "helot slut" who had been eager for the trinkets or food he brought her.

"I love Chryse, sir."

"What?"

"I would marry her if the laws allowed; but since they don't, I will not marry anyone else."

Leonidas decided there was no point in arguing with such nonsense. So he went on to the next issue. "I don't want you to press charges against my attendant. He had no right to do what he did, but public humiliation will only make him more sullen and resentful."

"All right, sir—if you promise me you won't harm Chryse."

"You insolent puppy!" Leonidas snapped back. "I'll do what I damn well please with my helots!"

"Chryse always claimed that you were different, sir—that you didn't treat her and her family like property. I'm sorry to learn she misjudged you."

The audacity of the answer took Leonidas' breath away. He would never have dared talk to a Peer like this when he was an eirene! "I said I'll do what I damn well please—that doesn't necessarily mean I'll harm anyone. But what her parents do to her is a different matter. Her mother is very angry."

"Her mother doesn't understand. Sir."

"Her mother is the smartest one in the whole family," Leonidas snapped back.

"But she wants Chryse to marry some helot. Sir."

"Of course. As your parents want you to marry a Spartiate."

"My parents couldn't care less what I do. Sir." The bitterness of the answer shook Leonidas, and he looked more sharply at the youth.

"I don't believe you," Leonidas told him, watching for the reaction.

The youth shrugged. "Go ask them, sir. But you may have to repeat my name several times before they even remember who I am."

"Where are your boys, and how old are they?"

"Thirteen-year-olds, sir. It's the Phouxir."

"Ah, of course." Leonidas had forgotten. That explained, however, how an eirene had time for "courting" in the middle of the day.

"All right. Dismissed."

"Sir?"

"Yes?"

"I meant what I said."

"What?"

"That I love Chryse, sir."

"Love is a dangerous emotion. Haven't your instructors taught you to curb it?"

"I won't give her up, sir."

"She isn't yours to give up."

"She is the mother of my child, sir."

"She doesn't have a child."

"She is carrying mine, sir."

"Then you have much to fear."

"Sir!"

"What?"

"Don't demean yourself with the blood of an infant!"

"You would be wise to leave before you say something else to harm your case."

"Yes, sir." The youth exited very promptly, but Leonidas followed him out, and before he could stop to say something through the window of the workshed, Leonidas called out after him: "Go *now*, Temenos! And don't come back without my permission!"

The eirene fled, and Leonidas told Pelopidas to unlock the shed and let him in. Chryse was sitting on the floor, clutching her knees and sobbing. Leonidas shut the door behind him and leaned against it with his arms crossed.

Chryse looked up at him. "Please don't punish him, master! What has he done wrong? The others do it all the time. Everyone does it! Why am I the only one who's not supposed to do it? Why is everyone against us?" She had raised her voice to a wail again, and the tears gushed down her face.

She wasn't exactly pretty in her present state, with her hair in disarray, twigs and leaves still clinging to her chiton, and her eyes and nose red, swelling, and running. But she was pretty, Leonidas knew. She was pretty and she was bright, and she was usually full of laughter. It was hard to see her like this, and he suspected Pelopidas would soften, too—long before he whipped her. "Temenos can't marry you. He will marry a Spartiate maiden, in ten to eleven years at the latest."

"But he can be mine *until* then!" Chryse insisted. "We can be *happy* until then! What's so wrong with that? Why do you begrudge us even a little happiness?"

That sounded more like Mantiklos than Pelopidas, and Leonidas wondered if it was wise to let the rebellious helot spend so much time here. Indeed, why keep him on at all, now that he had Meander? He was a bad influence. To Chryse he said: "I don't begrudge you a little happiness. As long as you assure me that Temenos never used force against you, the matter is closed as far as I am concerned."

"Of course he didn't use force! The other bastards would have, but he drove them off! He's the kindest, gentlest young man in the world! Mom doesn't understand anything! She thinks that only marriage is important—even if your husband treats you like dirt! I'd rather be Temenos' whore than be married to some stinking helot! Most of them are stupid and brutal and cruel! Temenos isn't like them at all!"

"All right," Leonidas said, opened the door, and walked out.

Pelopidas and Laodice were waiting anxiously in the courtyard. "What do you want us to do with her, master?"

"Nothing. At least not on my account. You must do as you see fit as her parents. But she has committed no crime. And nor has Temenos, Mantiklos," he continued, raising his voice to reach the

Messenian sulking around the trough. "I can't enforce a law that hasn't been broken. In fact, the only one who has broken any law here this afternoon is you—by attacking the eirene without cause, as it seems. Do you really want me to insist on the full enforcement of the law?"

Mantiklos growled something and stalked out of the courtyard.

"I don't like him living here," Pelopidas said as soon as Mantiklos was out of hearing. "Can't you send him back to Messenia?"

Laodice caught her breath, and Leonidas glanced at her. "If I send Mantiklos back to a job as overseer or the like in Messenia—which is what he's been after for a long time—he'd take your elder daughter with him. Is that what you want?"

Pelopidas frowned, and Laodice answered, "Let us talk about it among ourselves."

Leonidas nodded. "I'm overdue for a bath." He went around to the back of the house, collected his stallion, and headed for the city.

———

He was only halfway to the bridge when he ran into Alkander riding toward him. "I was coming to visit you," Alkander announced.

"Ah, the Phouxir's just started." Leonidas explained to himself how Alkander had time to come calling in the middle of the day.

"Yes; I've been doing some spot checks on relatives and the like."

Leonidas added, "I'm in desperate need of a bath. Will you join me?"

Without protest, Alkander turned around and fell in beside Leonidas, asking conversationally, "Does Laodice have everything secured this year?"

Leonidas laughed. When the Messenian family had first arrived in Laconia, they had had no idea about the Spartan custom of making the thirteen-year-old boys live outside of society for forty days. She had been completely unprepared for night raids on her pantry by half-starving teenagers, and had lost almost the whole of her pantry stores before she contacted Leonidas in a desperate panic. Leonidas had explained the custom to her and provided wooden bolts for the pantry door and windows. "What she *wants* to protect, she does. But she leaves some things out for the boys."

Alkander laughed, and then concluded, "She's a good woman."

Then he cleared his throat awkwardly, and Leonidas braced himself for another lecture on his bachelor status. "Have you ever thought of marrying your niece?" Alkander asked, not daring to look at Leonidas as he spoke.

"My niece?" Leonidas gaped at his friend. Alkander and Hilaira had tried to draw his attention to one maiden after another over the years, but this was really getting ridiculous. "Of course I haven't thought about marrying my niece! She's barely out of girlhood, and I can just imagine what my brother Cleomenes would say!"

"She's seventeen, actually, and the problem *is* your brother." Alkander still wasn't looking at him; but he was so pointedly looking away that Leonidas drew up sharply, making Alkander stop, too, and look at him questioningly.

"What do you mean?"

Alkander took a deep breath. "Your niece told the ephors this morning that her father is thinking of marrying her to a foreigner. To one of the Ionian tyrants, to be precise, in order to have an excuse for intervention in the Ionian revolt."

"He's mad! Whoever marries Gorgo will claim the regency—if not the throne—as soon as Cleomenes dies! He can't marry her to a foreigner!"

"There doesn't appear to be any law against it," Alkander pointed out.

"Then the Gerousia can damn well make one up!" Leonidas snapped back. "We can't put the Agiad heir in the control of some tyrant. If nothing else, Brotus would use it as an excuse to stake his own claim to the throne! And then we would have civil war! Cleomenes can't be serious!"

Alkander was pleased that Leonidas was so worked up about the topic. Most of the time he pretended to be completely indifferent to dynastic affairs. Gently Alkander remarked, "Gorgo was very wise to draw the attention of the ephors to the impending crisis."

"She's not stupid. In fact, she probably the best brain in the family—after Chilonis, of course."

"Um," Alkander agreed. "The ephors, of course, suspected that she had only raised the issue because she wanted to marry someone her father didn't approve of."

"As long as he's Spartan, why shouldn't she?"

"Oh, he *is* that," Alkander agreed.

"So why don't they just let her marry whomever she pleases, and eliminate the risk of Cleomenes marrying her to someone unsuitable?" But even as he spoke, Leonidas remembered how Alkander had opened the conversation.

Alkander saw his friend's eyes widen a split second before he answered steadily, "She named you, Leonidas."

There was a second of silence. The two friends gazed at one another. Then Leonidas spat out, "The little bitch!" before he sent his stallion galloping down the road furiously.

Alkander let him go, holding his own fretting colt at a standstill until the dust had settled. Then he eased up on the reins and let the colt stretch out his neck. Leonidas' reaction was not going to please anyone, and Alkander wondered if he should have handled the situation differently. Unfortunately, the damage was done . . .

———

Chilonis was weaving. The doors facing the terrace were open to let in the fresh air and light, but she had not moved the loom outside as she sometimes did. There seemed too much risk of a shower later in the day. Through the open doors and windows came the twitter of birds and occasionally the clang of a cowbell. She heard the hooves pattering on the drive, but she did not leave her work. She let Gorgo come to her.

"Grandma!"

"Come in."

"Did Nikostratos tell you?"

"My dear, the whole city is talking of nothing else."

"Grandma!" Gorgo stepped up beside her, and Chilonis looked up at her granddaughter. She had evidently ridden over rather than taking a chariot, and her hair was coming free of the thick braid. Furthermore, her peplos was dirty with dust and horse sweat. She smelled of horse. And yet she was lovely: straight as a spear, with well-muscled arms, a long, proud throat, and a symmetrical face with wide-set, intelligent eyes. "I don't understand why everyone's so upset! All I said was the truth!"

"Um hum." Chilonis turned her attention back to her loom.

Gorgo sank onto the bench beside her. "What did I do wrong?"

Chilonis drew a deep breath. "My dear child, you are only seventeen and can't be expected to think everything through, but if you want to know what you did wrong, I will explain it to you. First, you have turned the whole city against your father. I concede that he was being very irresponsible, and even cruel, to speculate about marrying you to Aristagoras—or was it Histiaeus? But you and I also know that your father often talks nonsense after a couple of cups of uncut wine, and that he has often speculated about marrying you to one man or another without any intention of actually doing so." Gorgo took a breath to speak, and Chilonis held up her hand to silence her.

"I quite agree that it is cruel of him. Indeed, he does it to provoke you, because sometimes he is very angry with you and it is his way of getting even. You do provoke him, too, you know?"

Gorgo frowned; part of her wanted to protest, but she was honest enough to know that what her grandmother said was not all wrong. She did provoke her father sometimes, and sometimes she even did it intentionally, because it drove her crazy the way he played with one idea after another, but never really kept to any course of action for long. He was ambitious and she knew he loved Sparta, but sometimes he seemed so lacking in principle and so cynical! And she hated it when he claimed that anyone—even the Gods— could be purchased. And sometimes she just craved his attention and affection, which had become rarer and rarer, especially since her encounter with Aristagoras four years ago. So in answer to her grandmother's question, Gorgo looked down and rubbed absently at the bench for a moment. They she looked up and asked anxiously, "But what about Leonidas?"

"Ah, yes. That was the second point I was going to make. You have probably ruined any chance of marrying him by your direct assault, so you had better start thinking about alternatives. The ephors and Council will now be very keen to see you safely married to a Spartiate at the earliest possible date, because you have alerted them to a danger they had ignored up to now. In short, your maiden days are numbered. I would say you'll be cutting your hair before the winter solstice—"

"But why not Leonidas?"

Chilonis sighed, stopped weaving, and turned to look at her granddaughter. There was a pity in her eyes now. "My dear child, if you would try to put yourself in his skin, I think you might understand. But if you can't do that, then take it from an old woman: no young man likes to have a girl publicly lay claim to him. You have robbed him of the status of hunter—and that is vital to a man's pride. If he were to marry you now, he would appear to be giving in to the whims of a mere girl—bad enough if he were a young man of twenty-one or twenty-two, but unthinkable for a full citizen and company commander! You really haven't left him any choice but to indignantly and forcefully refuse you."

Gorgo sat very still, and it took a moment for Chilonis to realize that her lips were quivering as she tried to keep from crying. "Oh, child, I'm sorry to be the bearer of bad news; but someone had to tell you," Chilonis rationalized, and then opened her arms and pulled Gorgo into them as the teenager broke into heart-rending sobs.

"But I love him," Gorgo gasped. "I don't want to marry anyone else …"

———

The entire syssitia fell silent as Leonidas entered, and they looked at him expectantly. He frowned. "If you're gossiping about me, I'll leave again so you can carry on."

"You'll do nothing of the sort!" Nikostratos countered.

Leonidas turned on his heel to leave. Nikostratos nodded to two of the youngest members of the mess, and they sprang to their feet to block the door.

"You'll come in and sit down with us and behave like an adult!" Nikostratos told off the younger man.

"I'm not going to talk about this nonsense."

"Calm down and have your soup!"

Warily Leonidas eased himself down on the couch and held out his hands to the mess-boys. One boy held the bowl while the other poured water over his hands, and then handed him a towel. Leonidas watched the entire ritual intently as if he were seeing it for the first time. The boys, both eight-year-olds, were very diligent, but just as they finished, one of them risked glancing up at him. Leonidas recognized the look of boyish delight at the prospect of hearing something worth telling their friends. Frowning, he sent the boys scampering back toward the kitchen.

A moment later they were back, rolling in the soup in a deep cauldron. The boys filled individual bowls with the thick stew while a loaf of warm bread was passed around. Leonidas tore off a chunk of bread and dipped it into the steaming-hot soup. Only after he had put the bread into his mouth did Nikostratos open his attack. "You realize your elder brother has outmaneuvered you, don't you?" he asked casually, not even looking at Leonidas—but there was no question to whom he was talking.

Leonidas looked up furiously, his mouth too full to retort, while Nikostratos continued, "King Cleomenes was called in to explain himself to the ephors, and he swore solemnly that you were his first choice for his beloved daughter—but that you wouldn't take her. It was only because you'd already turned him down—"

Leonidas swallowed what was left in his mouth and insisted, "That's complete nonsense. He's lying!"

"Oh, I don't doubt he's lying, Leo. That's not the point. The point is, he has now publicly gone on record saying that you were his first choice as husband for his daughter, and only because *you* refused has he been forced to look for alternatives. He insisted that his daughter is too intelligent, independent, and precocious—all of which is patently true—to give to anyone but a prince or, short of that, a ruler. He suggested that a Persian satrap would be more suitable than an ordinary ranker."

"That's ridiculous!" Leonidas scoffed.

"Maybe, but he has neatly shifted the blame for seeking a foreign bridegroom from himself to you," Nikostratos pointed out. "And made you look doubly bad, since you are well over thirty, unmarried, and childless, and so in open violation of the law already."

"Meanwhile, your *other* brother is talking divorce, so he would be free to marry Gorgo," Euryleon joined in.

"Brotus?" Leonidas asked, incredulous. "Brotus wouldn't last a day with Gorgo—she'd dissect him!"

Euryleon laughed, but retorted, "But she'd do it so intelligently, he might not even notice—thick as he is." The remark harvested a general laugh from their mess-mates.

Nikostratos, however, insisted seriously, "Well, as next in line to the throne, there is a certain logic to Brotus marrying Gorgo." He wiped the bottom of his bowl clean with bread.

"There is no logic to it at all!" Leonidas retorted hotly. "Besides, Brotus has no grounds for divorce—and Sinope will kill him if he even mentions it!"

"Well, in that case, for an Agiad prince there is always the precedent of two wives."

"That would only perpetuate the entire nightmare of two rivals for the throne. Pausanias would naturally claim the throne as first-born, and any child by Gorgo would claim it by right of his double-royal blood. The ephors can't be that stupid!"

Nikostratos shrugged and signaled for more soup. "Leonidas, you may very well be right. I admit the situation is unprecedented. Ever since the sons of Herakles came to this valley, there has never been a situation exactly like this. But you can't just look on this as a personal affair. There will be consequences to your refusal to marry your niece, and not all of them will be to your liking."

———

The ephors took much the same tack. The afternoon of the very next day, Leonidas was summoned to report to them. After morning drill he bathed and dressed in his bronze armor, and dutifully reported to the ephors with his helmet in the crook of his left arm.

The Ephorate was a relatively small building, not as imposing as the Council House, but it too was located on the main square. The Temple to Fear backed up against it. Some people claimed the juxtaposition of structures was because the ephors were supposed to fear the Law, and others that the citizens were supposed to fear the ephors. Leonidas suspected it was just an accident of indifferent city planning. Sparta was not a planned city, but rather one that had evolved haphazardly over centuries.

One entered the Ephorate by going up only a handful of steps and passing through a simple colonnade composed of four Doric pillars. The interior of the Ephorate was lit by windows set high in each of the three remaining walls or, at night, by a large, hanging lamp. Steps or seats lined the walls on the three sides facing the entrance. Five stone thrones occupied the center, facing two thrones just inside the door. There was also a sandpit toward the front of the chamber with a tripod on which entrails could be examined for signs. Blood in the sand suggested that the ephors had already consulted the Gods before calling on Leonidas to report.

The ephors themselves were all citizens more than half a century old. They had been elected at the last spring equinox and were due to step down at the next. Leonidas had voted for three of the five of them. The other two had been elected without his vote, as he had preferred other candidates, but he had no particular dislike or ill opinion of any of them. They were all solid, decent citizens with honorable service and grandchildren to their credit.

They sat on the thrones in a semicircle at the back of the chamber, while a Spartiate clerk was seated to one side to take minutes if called upon. Although most clerks in Sparta were perioikoi, perioikoi were not allowed in the Ephorate, because the decisions of the ephors were considered too sensitive to be shared with even one outsider. The Spartiate clerk was a man who had lost both legs in a horrible accident and had been exempt from military service ever since. He was now bent with age, and his face wore a permanent frown of pain and dissatisfaction.

The Chairman of the ephors opened: "Leonidas, son of Anaxandridas, you know why we have summoned you."

"I can guess."

"Then let us come straight to the point. We fully support your brother King Cleomenes, and it is our firm conviction that for the good of Lacedaemon, you should marry your niece Gorgo."

The man paused as if expecting a response. Leonidas refused to be drawn.

Another man took up the case. "Such a marriage would reunite the two branches of your house, healing the wounds of your father's double marriage."

Leonidas remarked sharply, "That double marriage was forced upon my father by the ephors of the time, and the evil it produced suggests that the ephors would do well *not* to meddle in the marriages of the kings! Had you not meddled then, my brother Dorieus—who was an exemplary young man and the best of his age cohort—would now be king, and would probably have male heirs in abundance."

"There's no way to know that. Besides, he was a hothead and too full of his own importance."

"Oh? And Cleomenes is not?"

"This arguing about the past serves no purpose. The proposal is a very reasonable one. You are a widower. Your niece is of marriageable age. There is a tradition of Agiad princes marrying their nieces; your own father did. What can you possibly have against the practice?"

"I have nothing against the practice, although it tends to produce dim-witted offspring, as Cleomenes has reminded me throughout my life."

The ephors ignored the remark. "Then what have you against the maiden herself? Has she offended you in any way? Has she conducted herself in an unworthy manner? We have heard nothing derogatory about her; but if you know some reason to think she is not suitable to be your bride, then tell us now and we will not press you any further."

"If Gorgo were a youth, she would be the most splendid scion the Agiads had ever produced."

"Then what have you against her?"

Leonidas shrugged. "Nothing in particular; but I'm not heir to the Agiad throne, and so there is no reason why I should choose my bride for dynastic reasons."

"It is good that you raise the issue of your bride; because, you know, we have been very lenient with you. It is two years since you lost your wife and children so tragically. You are now thirty-two, going on thirty-three. If you do not marry soon, we will have no choice but to subject you to the humiliations prescribed by the laws for men who fail to meet this most important of civil obligations. You will be fined, and you will have to parade naked through the streets and allow the women to taunt you, and henceforth you will be prohibited from attending the Gymnopaedia."

"It is not my fault my wife and children are dead," Leonidas retorted bitterly.

"We know. That is why we have been lenient up to now. We have not pressed you these past two years. But the time for mourning is past. You, Leonidas son of Anaxandridas, should have sons in the agoge by now. We cannot allow you to neglect your civic duties any longer. You are too popular, Leonidas. You are too much an object of admiration among our young men, youth, and boys. If you set a bad example, then it will have worse consequences than if someone else were to do so."

"That is to say: if I were a *less* exemplary citizen, you would turn a blind eye to my bachelor status? I can start neglecting my duties and adopt bad habits at once."

"Don't mock us!" the chairman barked, and a second stated firmly, "We are agreed: you must marry before the spring equinox, or you will be subject to sanctions."

"Anything else?"

The five officials looked at one another, baffled by so much stubbornness.

"Not at the moment."

———

Hilaira's tactics were gentler. She took Leonidas by the arm and walked with him along the banks of the stream that ran beside her kleros, Beggar stiff-legged but content at their heels. "You know I've tried to draw your attention to one maiden or another over the years. Sometimes I feel as if I have worried about matchmaking for you every bit as much as I have worried about my poor brother Prokles, or even my own children!" She laughed as she spoke, but Leonidas knew there was some truth in what she said. "And you must know that I *don't* care about dynastic politics or even your civic duty to procreate. All I want is for you to be happy."

"I know you mean well," Leonidas conceded. It was precisely because Hilaira had been so consistently concerned about finding him a bride that he did not take offense now. "But what you and Alkander have is rare," he told her. "Most married couples don't have it. Look at Sperchias, or Cleomenes and his poor queen. My own parents fought like cats and dogs for as long as I can remember, and my father completely neglected Chilonis as soon as she had served her dynastic purpose."

"Which was very much his loss, and reminds me of Nikostratos and Chilonis. You would not deny that they are happy together?"

"Of course not." Leonidas paused, because Beggar had stopped to wistfully watch a duck flap its way into the air and safety. It was a long time since she had been fleet enough to catch a duck, and he could sense her intense regret. He bent to stroke her head. "It's all right, girl. Old age will lame my spear-arm, too, one day." She looked up at him with adoring eyes, and he scratched her behind the ears so that she closed her eyes in contentment.

"When I see you with that dog," Hilaira told him sadly, "I see how much love you have in you, and it breaks my heart that you have no one to lavish it on but an aging bitch."

"What wife could ever be as adoring as Beggar?" Leonidas quipped back with a short grin. "Certainly not Gorgo! Why, she'd always be telling me off for being a fool, and admonishing me to do one thing or another!"

"That's not fair, Leo. She's not a bitch."

"No, she's just twice as smart as I am, and has never learned to hold her tongue. Imagine telling Aristagoras off to his face!" Leonidas laughed at the mere thought of it.

"Actually, the way Nikostratos tells the story, she told her *father* off—in the presence of Aristagoras."

"Which is just my point. If the child would do that to her adored father, think what the woman would do to a husband she despises!"

"Why should she despise you, Leo?" Hilaira asked, uncomprehending.

Leonidas shrugged. "Because I'm not half as clever as her father—as he has told me often enough. And I'm certainly not as clever as she is herself."

"Leo! Where did you get such a low opinion of yourself? You are certainly wiser than Cleomenes; and while Gorgo is witty enough, you are more than her equal in depth of understanding."

Leonidas continued walking. "That is kind of you to say, but in reality no one has ever accused me of being particularly bright."

Hilaira was so taken aback by this remark that she found no response. As they walked side by side in silence, she thought back to their childhood, remembering that Leonidas' brothers had never tired of telling him he was a disgrace to the family, the runt, the fifth wheel on the wagon...She realized there was no point in arguing about this, and tried a different approach. "You don't really think that we women fall in love because of some rational assessment of which young man is cleverer than us, do you? Besides, Gorgo has already made it plain she *does* want you. Whatever her reasons—"

"No!" Leonidas cut Hilaira off, his tone sharp for the first time in this friendly conversation. "Her reasons are *very* much to the point. The fact is, she is *using* me to foil her father! I don't doubt that she had good reason to fear he intended to marry her to someone she didn't want, and she brilliantly succeeding in interdicting that plan. I respect her—even admire her—for taking preventive action to avert something that was, from her point of view, a disaster. But when asked *whom* she wanted to marry, she was motivated by one thing only: she wanted to ensure the ephors did not dismiss her as a lovesick girl. She would have weakened her entire argument if she had named any other man in the city. They would have felt manipulated by a mere girl, and they might have dismissed the threat to her—and the city. Gorgo knew *exactly* what she was doing when she named me, but it had nothing to do with really wanting *me*."

Hilaira wasn't so sure; but since she knew Gorgo only superficially, she sensed that her protests would carry little weight. Instead she took Leonidas' arm again and walked with him in silence for several steps before remarking gently, "The wounds Eirana left still haven't healed, have they? You need to marry a maiden who loves you more than anything in the world—the way I love Alkander."

Leonidas' silence was answer enough.

"But how do you expect to win a maiden's heart if you never even try?" Hilaira asked him after a bit.

"All right. You can start parading them through again. The ephors have given me only till the spring equinox to find a bride, so I have no choice but to pay attention this time."

———

The nights were getting longer and colder, and the rains had started. It was lousy weather to be out in, Leonidas thought, feeling sorry for the thirteen-year-olds undergoing the ritual of the "fox time."

Dark, threatening clouds were sinking down from Taygetos as he rode home from his syssitia, and they reminded him of the horrible storm that had killed several boys in his own class during the Phouxir.

The rain struck just after he'd crossed the bridge. He got to his feet and waited, and Leonidas made a snap decision to jump down and take cover under the solid structure rather than ride on in the downpour. Rain this heavy rarely lasted for long. As he came under the arch, however, his stallion abruptly reared up and spun away, breaking free of Leonidas' careless grasp. The horse bolted down the road at a full gallop. Cursing, Leonidas knew it was pointless chasing after him. The stallion knew the way home to his barn and feed and companions, and he obviously had no objection to getting wet. So Leonidas turned to go under the bridge on foot, and a sudden motion made him realize why the horse had bolted: there was a boy already cowering there. The boy gasped when he realized Leonidas was coming back, and tried to get to his feet. He slipped on the mud and fell backward.

"Relax, boy!" Leonidas advised. "You haven't done anything wrong."

The boy looked at him warily, little more than the whites of his eyes visible in the gloom under the bridge, as he got his feet under him again and waited, his filthy himation clutched around his bony shoulders.

"I'll just wait out the worst of the downpour and then I'll be on my way," Leonidas assured him. "Sit down. Who are you?"

Warily the boy sat down again, still clutching his filthy himation around him. "Eurytus, son of Lysimachos, father."

"Lysimachos? Son of Tyndareus?"

"Yes, father."

That made this boy the son of his fourth eirene, a youth who had been selfish and arbitrary and whom Leonidas had come to hate. He would not have liked such a man as his father. He calculated that the boy must have been born when his father was thirty and asked, "Have you older brothers?"

"No, father, only two older sisters."

"Did your father teach you all you need to know to survive the Phouxir?"

The boy seemed to think about this, and finally answered with another question: "What do I need to know to survive, father?"

"There are many strategies. How do *you* plan to survive?"

"I thought I had stashed away enough food in a hideout I had made myself, but some of the other boys found it and stole it all." He hung his head as he admitted this, his words becoming mumbled at the end.

"That's bad. How long ago was that?"

"That was two days ago, father."

"Have you had anything to eat since?"

"No, father."

"That's bad. You have a fortnight still to go."

The boy hunched his shoulders further and said nothing.

They sat in silence, listening to the rain drumming on the paving stones of the bridge over their heads. Then Leonidas asked, "Don't your sisters put food out for you?"

The boy shook his head vigorously. "You don't know my Dad! He'd beat their hides off them if they broke the rules! He thinks I'm soft as it is. I've got to survive this or he'll kill me with his own hands."

"And what does your mother think of all that?"

"Mom's sick. She's been sick as long as I can remember. She can't leave her chamber anymore. My sisters think she can't last much longer. It'll surely kill her if I disgrace the family."

"Do you know who I am?"

"Of course, father. You're Leonidas, the Agiad."

"Do you know where my kleros is?"

"Yes, father; just down the road on the right before you reach the Menelaion."

"There's a toolshed beside the stables in which my helot housekeeper has been known to leave stale bread and other things she doesn't need."

With a sharp intake of breath, the boy's head came up.

"The rain's let up. I'll be on my way."

"Thank you, father!"

"Shhh!" Leonidas pulled his himation up over his head and left the cover of the bridge to start walking home.

Halfway there, he was met by Pelopidas with Beggar. The arrival of his riderless horse had alarmed the whole household, and the loyal helot had come looking for him. "I was sure you'd been hurt, master!" he explained anxiously, "and in the dark I wasn't sure I'd find you, but I knew Beggar would."

Leonidas bent and picked up Beggar. He carried her over his shoulders, her forefeet in one hand and her hind feet in the other.

Laodice met them anxiously at the door of the kitchen, and Leonidas explained again what had happened. He put Beggar down by the helot's fire, and asked Laodice to bring a towel so he could dry her off. As Laodice handed him a kitchen linen, he asked her: "Do you still leave bread out in the toolshed at this time of year?"

"Master! How did you know about that?"

Leonidas just laughed. "Can you leave a little extra tonight? I met a boy who is very hungry."

"Of course. Should I put in a little something sweet as well?"

"Cheese or sausage would be better for him. He's got to survive two more weeks."

"Did you tell him about your stepmother?"

"No. Does she set aside things for the boys as well?"

"Not really; she just gets 'careless and forgetful'—as she words it—this time of year."

Leonidas laughed.

"I've got some fresh apple tarts, master; would you like me to bring them to you?"

"No, I'll join you here." Leonidas gave Beggar a last pat and stood. The dog lifted her head in alarm, but when he sat himself at the bench beside the helot's own table, she dropped her head on the floor, sighed deeply, and closed her eyes to enjoy the warmth.

Melissa fetched a black-glazed one-handled kothon and set it before Leonidas, then fetched wine and water, while Laodice went to get her apple tarts from the cooling tray in the pantry. There were just the five of them: Pelopidas, Laodice, Polychares, Melissa, and Kleon. Mantiklos had left three days earlier for one of Leonidas' estates in Messenia, taking his wife with him, and Meander was sleeping in the barracks, as he preferred, because it made him feel almost Spartiate again. Chryse, however, should have been here and was not in evidence. "Where's Chryse?" Leonidas asked as Laodice returned with the tarts.

Her parents exchanged a look, but Melissa answered tartly, "You can't keep track of a bitch in heat."

"Melissa!" Laodice cried out in pain and rebuke. "How dare you!"

Polychares put his hand on his wife's arm to stop her from answering, and turned on his mother. "Don't shout at Melissa, Mom. She's only speaking the truth. Chryse sneaks away every chance she gets to meet with that—that—"

"Mind your tongue, lad!" his father interrupted, with a nervous glance at Leonidas, and Laodice ordered Melissa to help her put things out in the toolshed for the boys.

Melissa dutifully got to her feet and took a tray, which Laodice loaded with bread and cheese. Together they left for the toolshed (and a little talk, Leonidas suspected), leaving the men to talk about the harvest and impending slaughter.

When Laodice and Melissa returned, the conversation continued about mundane things while they drank more of their home-pressed wine, until Laodice ventured very cautiously, "Master, why don't you marry again?"

"I will. I have to. The ephors have given me only till the spring equinox."

"Will you bring Gorgo here?" Laodice brightened up at once.

"Gorgo? No. I don't know who yet," Leonidas told her.

The helot woman looked baffled, even a little alarmed. "Why not Gorgo, master? She's a good girl. She's always been kind to us. Why, she's even used her chariot to transport heavy things for me now and again. There aren't many Spartiate maidens, much less princesses, that help out helots like that. She's always been good to us, ever since she broke her collarbone jumping her horse over your stone wall."

Leonidas understood Laodice's concern. She had worried about Eirana, too. She was afraid of a strange woman coming in and taking over, ordering her around, insisting on changes. So he did not take offense; he just shook his head. "I haven't made up my mind yet, Laodice; but if my future wife, whoever she may be, is unfair to you, we'll move elsewhere."

The sound of a crash, a high-pitched cry, and then thuds and clatter, coming from the outbuildings behind the kitchen, brought them all to their feet. The helots each grabbed something heavy to use as weapons, while Leonidas led the way, his hand on his hilt. They didn't get very far. Just beyond, in the kitchen garden, they ran into Temenos struggling to hold on to a viciously fighting boy. "I caught him trying to steal from the toolshed!" Temenos announced excitedly to Leonidas, even as the boy wrenched himself half free.

"Let him go!" Leonidas ordered, annoyed, certain it was the same boy he had explicitly told to come here.

"But, sir! He's—" Leonidas cuffed Temenos hard enough for the youth to lose the last of his grip on the desperate thirteen-year-old. The boy dashed off into the darkness, and Leonidas could only hope he'd have the sense to try to collect the food later.

Temenos, meanwhile, stared at him in confused outrage. As an eirene, it was his duty to arrest thirteen-year-olds who broke the rules of the Phouxir.

"I ordered you not to return here without my permission," Leonidas said, distracting the eirene from the boy.

"But, sir—"

"I'm sick of hearing those words out of your mouth!"

"It's my fault, master," Chryse spoke up, emerging out of the darkness and coming to stand beside Temenos, clutching his elbow. "I was afraid to come home in the dark. I'd gone to meet Temenos in Amyclae, but then the rain came down so hard that we lingered. When it stopped it was dark and I was afraid."

"You shouldn't be in Amyclae after dark," Leonidas agreed simply. It was a bad part of town, frequented by foreigners and populated by pickpockets, thieves, and pimps. The fact that Chryse was known to be carrying on with an eirene made her all the more vulnerable. He was worried for her. Frowning slightly, he ordered her to go inside with her father and brother. The latter started berating her before they were out of hearing. Then the door closed, and the two Spartiates were alone in the darkness and the light drizzle.

"Sir, why won't you let me see Chryse here? You can't stop us from meeting, and this is the safest place."

"The best and safest thing for her would be for you to give her up. You know the others may use her to get at you."

"I've told her, sir, but she says she'd rather risk it than not see me. You can ask her yourself."

"I don't doubt that is what she would say; but if you love her so much, you should do what is best for her regardless of what she says. The truth is, you don't have the strength of character to give her up. You may love her, but evidently you crave her more."

Temenos was silent, and Leonidas sighed. He felt tired and old in the face of so much youthful ardor. At Temenos' age he had risked his fair share of reprimands and punishment to see Eirana—and she had not even returned his affection. What would he *not* have done for a girl who loved him and slept with him as well? He had to admit to himself that he would probably have risked almost anything. "You might as well come inside by the fire," Leonidas capitulated.

"Does that mean I am welcome here, sir? That I can come again?"

"'Welcome' would be putting it a bit strong, but you have permission to come here. I surrender."

Temenos did not look triumphant. Rather, he came forward only hesitantly, and when Leonidas turned and went into the house, he followed cautiously.

Inside, the Spartiates interrupted a tense family drama. Although the voices fell silent at the approach of the two Spartiates, they came into the kitchen to find Chryse in tears, Melissa looking self-righteous, Pelopidas looking beaten, and Laodice and Polychares both angry, while poor Kleon tried to make himself invisible in a corner. Temenos went immediately to stand beside Chryse, and Leonidas announced, "I have given Temenos permission to visit the kleros as often as he likes. It is safer for them to meet here than elsewhere. Pelopidas, if you do not want your daughter to see Temenos, you must prevail upon her to break off the relationship. Temenos will respect her wishes." As Leonidas said this he looked hard at Temenos, and the young man nodded vigorously.

"You can't talk sense to her!" Polychares protested. "She's lovesick."

"There are worse things," Laodice declared firmly.

"I'll turn in now," Leonidas announced, so that the helots and Temenos could sort things out among themselves. He retreated to the cool, dark portion of the house built for the Spartiate master.

It was a gracious house, two stories high. On the ground floor was the bath complex, and the long hearth room with a women's hall at right angles to it. On the first floor there were no less than four bedrooms. Leonidas went up the outside stairs, but rather than entering the bedroom he used, he wandered through the other three. The smallest had been used by Eirana's daughter from her first marriage, and the second had been the nursery for his twins. In the third, Eirana herself had slept when he did not visit, and here she had given birth to the twins.

The rain had turned heavy again and it made a dull, low-pitched rumble on the tiles overhead, while the gurgling of the drains was loud and higher-pitched. Leonidas hoped the boy he'd met tonight had the sense to spend the night in the toolshed, but he feared Temenos had frightened him away. He felt a renewed flash of irritation with the eirene for spoiling things, and then he realized that he was jealous. He envied Temenos with all his heart. He wished that he were twenty again, on the brink of manhood, and desperately in love with a girl who loved him back.

He'd had more than enough sexual energy then, and he resented that it had been largely wasted. Certainly he had never felt satisfied with casual affairs—or even, except for a short period before she became pregnant with the twins, with Eirana herself. He resented the empty nursery now, and his own empty bed.

But it was his own fault. He had chosen Eirana, and even after her death gave him a new chance, he had done nothing with it. Why? Why was he so reluctant to look at the girls Hilaira wanted him to meet?

He went back to his own room, stripped, and lay down on the bed. It was chilly enough for him to need the linen sheet and the wool blanket. He turned on his side facing the blank wall and, listening to the rain, eventually fell asleep.

———

Laodice woke him. "Master!" She was speaking right into his ear, her hand on his shoulder. She had her himation up over her head and clutched around her shoulders. It was wet with rain and her hair was loose, as if she had come from her own bed. "It's Beggar. She's having convulsions. I think the rain today was too much for her. I think she's dying."

Leonidas flung the covers off and ran down stairs and across the courtyard to the helot kitchen through the rain. Beggar was lying by the fire, as they had left her after bringing her in out of the rain, but her legs had gone completely rigid and were twitching erratically. The hound was making sounds as well, yelps of pain it seemed, although her eyes were rolled back in her head and she did not appear to be conscious.

Leonidas went down on his knees beside her and tried to massage her rigid muscles. He spoke to her unconsciously, telling her she'd be fine, saying she shouldn't have been out in the rain, asking if he'd failed to dry her properly. But she was beyond him. In a few minutes it was over. She went still and silent, the struggle with death finished. Leonidas drew back, staring at the corpse of his dearest companion, and he felt the intense cold of the rainy night in the dark, silent farmhouse.

———

The following day Leonidas went to visit his stepmother. It was still raining, although not so hard as the night before, and she ushered him into the hearth room, anxious for him to get out of the cold and wet. "You spent the whole morning out in this, and that's enough," she told him firmly.

He had, of course. The Spartan army drilled regardless of the weather, just as it was expected to fight in any weather. Being wet and cold and muddy was not an unfamiliar condition to any Spartiate. But it was still pleasant to be taken into a warm room and offered steaming water flavored with a squeeze of lemon and mint and a snack of cashew nuts with raisins.

"So, what brings you here on such a dreadful day?" Chilonis asked as she settled down opposite her stepson.

"Everyone in the whole city has tried to push me into this marriage with Gorgo—except you. I started to wonder why."

"Aha," Chilonis remarked. She stood, and started fussing with the hearth fire.

"Aren't you going to tell me?" Leonidas pressed her.

"I'm thinking about it."

Leonidas waited impatiently while Chilonis poked and played with the logs, causing parts of them to disintegrate into embers. At last she turned and looked straight at Leonidas. "Have you forgotten who I am? Or rather, how I came to be your stepmother?"

"No, of course not."

"Hmm." Chilonis looked skeptical, and she sat down again. "Let me put it another way. You grew up knowing how much your mother hated me and my son—"

"Actually, she hated the ephors most. You were just the instrument, not the source of her misery."

"Very well put." Chilonis bowed slightly to Leonidas. "The ephors wanted an Agiad heir, and they selected me as the vessel in which it was to be produced. I had no more say in the matter than a cooking pot. Your father, to his credit, protested vigorously at first, but he eventually gave in to pressure and took me to wife—for political reasons. He was, to be fair, always a gentleman. He showed me respect and consideration. He was kind and he was gentle. He never once treated me like anything less than his queen. But he did not claim or pretend to love me or even fancy me in any way. Intimacies ended with the confirmation of pregnancy. If I had been delivered of a daughter—or had Cleomenes died young, before the birth of Dorieus—they might have resumed. But with the birth of Dorieus at the latest, my utility was ended. My marriage, such as it was, ended, too. Your father visited his firstborn son regularly. He was courteous to his son's mother. But he never again treated me as his wife.

"Don't misunderstand me!" Chilonis reached out to lay her hand gently on Leonidas' arm. "I am not complaining for myself. I did not love your father any more than he me, and so I did not particularly miss or lament his absence. I actually quite liked having my own household, and control of my affairs and my son, without either spousal interference or financial concerns. It was a life of most exceptional independence, such as few women enjoy. But as someone who has lived through a political marriage, I have a very acute understanding of them. I didn't come to you to press a marriage with Gorgo because I love Gorgo far too much to want to see her pushed into a political marriage—whether it is to a Persian prince or to you."

"As her father's only child, she *will* be forced into a political marriage," Leonidas pointed out. "Whether you want it or not. Gorgo is the first to recognize that."

"Quite right. But that is the political reality. In my biased grandmother's eyes, she is a wonderful, even a remarkable, young woman. She is a very unique and special person, and—"

"Surely you know that I agree with you on that," Leonidas interrupted, taken aback by Chilonis' earnestness.

Chilonis frowned and shook her head. "Not really. You see her as a precocious child, perhaps; but you don't love her with all her imperfections and weaknesses as I do. I love Gorgo as only a grandmother can love. I love her more than I ever loved my son, and more than I loved her brother. I want her to be happy with all my heart."

"And you think marriage to me would ruin her happiness," Leonidas concluded sourly. It was not the explanation he had expected.

"Under the circumstances, yes."

"What do you mean by 'under the circumstances'?"

"Well, as a political expedient into which you have been pressured and harassed just like your father was. That is the whole point."

"But you just explained to me how happy you were in your political marriage."

"You weren't listening to me, young man!" Chilonis retorted sharply. "I said that after the marriage ended in all but name, I enjoyed independence and was content, but I was never in love with your father. Gorgo's marriage to you would be an unthinkable nightmare because she *is* so intensely in love with you. It's not some passing fancy or momentary crush, or even an adolescent sexual attraction. Gorgo loves you with a depth that is very rare in maidens her age. Your indifference to her, possibly even your hostility born of the political pressure brought to bear on you, would lacerate her to the quick. She would be tortured in ways she cannot imagine and does not deserve. What she deserves is to be married for herself—and not for reasons of state."

CHAPTER 19

ARTEMIS OF THE GOATS

HER GRANDMOTHER HAD TOLD HER THAT her uncle wanted to speak to her, but warned her not to get her hopes up. "He only wants to explain to you why he won't marry you."

But how could Gorgo not get her hopes up? She had not spoken to her uncle Leonidas since she had confronted the ephors almost a month ago with her father's plans for her marriage, and time was running out on them both. The ephors had already started to make alternative suggestions to her, and it was rumored Leonidas had been given a deadline of the spring equinox to marry or face the consequences. Gorgo felt she had nothing to lose by pleading her case with him face to face.

Much more difficult was deciding what to wear for such an important confrontation. Leonidas had stipulated that she meet him at the Temple of Artemis of the Goats on the precipitous hill just west of the city. It was an ancient and increasingly neglected sanctuary at the top of a very rugged and strenuous path—which was undoubtedly why Leonidas had chosen the location. It would almost certainly be empty during the afternoon watch, the time designated for their meeting, because most of the patrons of this Artemis were goatherds and travelers, who were more likely to make their sacrifices at the start or end of the day.

Gorgo could not exactly dress in something "courtly" if she were going to climb up that long, winding path, very likely in a drizzle.

She had to wear practical shoes, and even so she was likely to arrive with skirts muddy to the knee—unless she rode. If she rode, however, she could not wear court dress, either. Whatever she did, her outer garment was going to get wet and muddy, and if she rode, the garment underneath was going to get crushed. Her hair posed yet another problem: if she wore it free, it would get tangled and messy, but she felt she looked adolescent when she braided it. She didn't want to look like a little girl—but rather, an attractive young woman. She certainly didn't want to look like "something the cat dragged in."

But gazing into her mirror, she was not encouraged. She didn't like what she saw, and there was so little she could do about it. She tried brushing her hair this way and that. She tried various pieces of jewelry. She tried rouge on her lips and cheeks. She even thought of going to her mother and asking for advice; but their relationship was so strained that in the end she put on her favorite green peplos and wrapped herself in a voluminous rust-colored himation that had been oiled to make it less porous, and collected her mare.

The weather was actually clearing a bit, with weak rays of sun now and again breaking through the overcast. No one took any particular notice of Gorgo as she rode out of the city; she did it far too frequently. She passed the tombs of the Agiads with a little inner nod. Her ancestors, she reasoned, ought to be on her side. They should favor the marriage of two Agiads.

Farther on, she came to the monument of Tainaros, and then the impressive and more popular sanctuary to the Horse-Breeding Poseidon. The increasing popularity of horse breeding had brought new wealth to this particular temple, and everything here looked newly renovated. Beyond the temple, however, the trail became very steep, and Gorgo was glad she'd chosen to ride. This track was running with water in places, and here and there the trail had been washed away. She would have arrived looking like a drowned rat, and frozen through, if she had walked.

At the sanctuary itself, perched on the very top of the hill, she was relieved to find that Leonidas had not yet arrived. No other horses were tethered in front of the temple, and a couple who had been sacrificing at the altar hurried away at the sight of Gorgo. Gorgo tied her horse loosely to a large plane tree at the far edge of the large open terrace before the temple. She paused to gaze back on the valley below, largely lost in the mist and smoke rising from the hearth fires of the city, although the acropolis of Sparta was still discernible.

Gorgo removed her himation, since the weather was improving, and carried it over her arm as she entered the temple. She placed her offering on the altar and made a short prayer for success. Then she stood hesitantly in the empty temple and didn't know what to do with herself.

She was very nervous now. She told herself that she should prepare herself for the worst, so that she wouldn't make a fool of herself by crying or by begging. Then again, what did she have to lose by either? If Leonidas could not be moved by logic and reasons of state and just plain expediency, maybe a few tears would do the trick. What did she have to lose?

She glanced at the Goddess, depicted by a wooden statue. Artemis stood with her bow over her shoulder, but flanked by two goats rather than the more common deer and hound. Artemis was a virgin Goddess—not exactly the ally one wanted most in her present situation—and the fact that Leonidas had chosen this temple for their rendezvous was an ominous portent. It would have been more propitious to meet in one of Aphrodite's temples, Gorgo supposed; but then again, Gorgo hated that beautiful Goddess almost as much as she hated the beautiful Helen.

"The sun's come out; shall we sit on the porch?" Leonidas asked.

Gorgo spun around. "Where did you come from?"

"I've been here all along. You didn't see me in the shadows."

"But there was no horse outside."

"I walked."

He started for the exit and Gorgo went with him. The clouds were indeed tearing apart and the sun was bright, making all the wet limestone glitter, and offering surprising warmth in the still air. Leonidas sat down on the top step of the temple at the base of one of the Doric columns, and Gorgo sat down beside him, hardly daring to breathe.

Leonidas looked over at her, but she was looking down self-consciously at her hands. "Just when did you come up with this idea that I should marry you?"

She shrugged a little awkwardly. "It just sort of evolved... You know, when girls reach a certain age, they start looking at boys and speculating about which ones might make good husbands. We're expected and encouraged to do that. And, well, I looked just like the others did, but the boys all seemed so..." she shrugged and then admitted, "scrawny and silly and oversexed. I realized I wanted someone like you, so I looked at the older men. But most of them were already married, and there was none I liked as much as you. It dawned on me that I didn't want someone *like* you, I wanted you."

Leonidas looked at her skeptically.

"You carried me home on your shoulders when I was lost, remember? You let me ride your colts so I could win races. You put your arm around me and made me feel wanted when everyone else ignored me. And best of all, you never seemed to notice that I wasn't pretty." She looked down as she said this, ashamed to meet his eyes, because tears were forming.

"Because you *are* pretty, Gorgo. You are one of the prettiest girls in Lacedaemon. Who told you otherwise?"

"My mirror, for a start!" Gorgo told him sharply, looking up to see if he was mocking or pitying her. He met her gaze and she found herself adding practically, "No one ever picks me to welcome home returning heroes or Olympic victors!"

"Weren't you waiting for me when I came back from Corinth?"

"I cheated and rode ahead of the official welcoming event. Surely you noticed?"

Leonidas laughed and put his arm over her shoulder, drawing her to him. "At the time, I thought nothing of it. You were always a bit wild and self-willed."

"Is that very bad?"

"No," Leonidas told her simply. "When did you decide to force the issue by going to the ephors?"

Gorgo looked up at him uncertainly. His arm felt wonderful around her, and he seemed anything but hostile, and yet he was hardly acting like a lover, either. Just like her favorite uncle. "Well, my father started teasing me about who he was going to marry me to. One day it would be one tyrant, and the next day another. It was just a game to him. He liked to see me get angry and indignant. He liked to frighten me."

"I had no idea." Leonidas sounded upset—and that suggested a depth of sympathy Gorgo had not expected from any man.

"Grandma says I provoked it. She says I shouldn't have humiliated him in front of Aristagoras the way I did. Our relationship hasn't been the same since. In the last few years we fought a lot, and I often accused him of being fickle and ineffective. He drives me crazy with his cynicism and plotting."

Leonidas snorted, because he agreed entirely.

Gorgo continued, "But I suppose I shouldn't tell him what I think of him as bluntly as I do. If I were him, I wouldn't want me as a daughter, either," she concluded honestly, making Leonidas laugh and hold her more firmly.

She looked up at him uncertainly.

"Go on. When did you decide to go to the ephors?"

"After a particularly ugly scene with my father, when he said he had already sent word to Aristagoras offering me to him. Oh, Leo! If you knew the way that man looked at me! With *hate* in his eyes! He hated me just for being a *girl* and for hearing him plead with my father and then for speaking out. The thought of being married to him was unbearable!

"Of course," Gorgo admitted in a calmer tone, "I should have known Aristagoras would never agree to the marriage, since he despised me; but at the time, I was so upset I couldn't sleep. I tossed and turned all night, trying to think what I could do. I knew I had to tell someone who could stop my father. But who had *that* power? My father doesn't listen to anyone anymore, not even Grandma or Nikostratos. Then I thought of the ephors, and I realized they were the only people in all Lacedaemon who had the power to prevent my father from doing anything. I thought if they could force *your* father to have two wives, surely they could stop mine from giving me away to a foreigner.

"But I foresaw that they might ask who I wanted instead. And I thought, why not tell them the truth? Why not name you, since you were free to marry?

"Uncle Leo! Don't be angry with me anymore. Please! I know now that it was stupid of me. Grandma explained to me how stupid it was—how I put you in an impossible situation by naming you. But

I didn't mean to pressure you. Please don't be angry." She looked up at him and tears spilled out of her eyes, the emotional strain of the whole situation too much for her.

Leonidas reached up his free hand and wiped her tears away. "How can I be angry at you for using your brains to serve your heart?" He paused to reflect on what he had just said, and then added, "As I said to Hilaira not so long ago, you are by far the cleverer of the two of us; and if you honestly think that being married to me would be a good thing, then who am I to disagree?"

She swallowed and waited for the "but."

Instead, Leonidas continued, "So I've decided we should get married."

Gorgo started. "Just like that? But what do you want? I mean, why have you refused for the last month?"

"Stubbornness. Ask anyone. It is my greatest weakness."

Gorgo frowned. Leonidas was infamous for being stubborn—or tenacious, if one wanted to word it more positively. "But what do *you* want?" Gorgo insisted.

"That's just it, Gorgo. I want to be married and start a family; and when I started thinking about all the young maidens down there," he nodded in the vague direction of the city, "the bold ones flirting and preening and the shy ones blushing and awkward, I just couldn't imagine being married to any of them. Hilaira has tried to interest me in one or another of them often enough, poor thing. But when I thought about being married to you, I realized it would be the simplest thing in the world."

Gorgo looked at him, unsure if that was a compliment or not.

"But you know that in addition to being stubborn to a fault, I am notorious for being law-abiding. I will not break the law, even for you."

"But what law? Your father married his niece—" Gorgo started to protest at once, and Leonidas held up his hand to silence her.

"Lycurgus' laws say it is illegal to marry a girl too young to enjoy sex." Leonidas looked her straight in the eye.

Although she blushed slightly, she met his gaze and said very steadily and deliberately, "You will not be breaking the law if you take me to wife."

Leonidas nodded and looked away. "Then there is nothing to stop us, since your father solemnly swore to the ephors that I was his first choice as bridegroom—"

"He didn't mean it!" Gorgo pointed out indignantly, "and it makes me so mad that he would swear to a lie. He has no respect even for the Gods!"

Leonidas laughed. "I know. But he's on record approving my suit for you, so there is no way he can stop us."

Gorgo did not look convinced. "No matter what my father said, if he gets wind that you are coming for me, he might try to lock me up somewhere. He certainly won't give the watch permission to let you in. I suppose you might be able to convince the meleirenes—"

"It wouldn't be fair to put them in a difficult position; but don't worry about how I'll get in. I was born in that palace, remember? I spent the first six years of my life there. I know every way in and out, including ones your father probably doesn't. The question is: how soon can you be ready for me?"

Gorgo was taken by surprise, but she quickly concluded: "Tonight. There's really nothing to do..."

"Are you still in the same room you had as a girl, or did you move into your brother's room?"

"No, that would have been closer to my mother. I moved into Grandma's room after she moved out. It was a way of making me feel closer to her."

"Good. I know the room. I'll fetch you there sometime during the middle watch." (That was between midnight and dawn.)

She nodded, holding her breath, because she still couldn't believe that he meant what he said.

"There's one advantage to marrying an old man like me," Leonidas quipped with a grin; "I'm not subject to curfew." But then he grew serious again and considered Gorgo carefully. "You are sure about this? That there is no one else you'd rather have?"

"Yes. And you?"

"I'm not as quick as you are, Gorgo. My thought process is ponderous, but I am neither blind nor dense. You are the finest maiden in Sparta; and if you will have me, I would be a fool not to take you."

Gorgo was at first too stunned by the sudden turn of events to be nervous, but as darkness fell she started to fall into a kind of panic. When Leonidas had asked when she could be ready, she had feared to delay by even a single night, because she feared he might change his mind. But, of course, there were all sorts of things she really *ought* to do in preparation for her wedding. She was supposed to make sacrifices to Artemis and Aphrodite, for a start. It was also traditional to give away the symbols of her childhood, usually dolls and the like, but Gorgo had never liked playing with dolls. She had played with her dog and her horse instead, neither of which she was going to give away to anyone. Still, she had a bronze lion and a terra-cotta dolphin she had planned to leave on the altars of Apollo and Athena respectively. Under the circumstances, however, she decided that the Gods would accept the gifts after the fact as graciously as before.

Then there was the business of cutting her hair and dressing in boy's clothing. Because custom demanded that a Spartiate "steal" his bride from her father's home, and because most bridegrooms were young men on active service who were required to sleep in barracks, it had become tradition for the brides to cut their hair short and dress in short chitons like boys of the agoge or helots, so that they would allegedly "blend in" and attract less attention on the streets while being taken to their husband's home. That didn't entirely make sense to Gorgo, because of the curfew. No one but the watch and full citizens had a right to be out after curfew—most especially not helots or boys of the agoge. So why being disguised as one would help, Gorgo could not fathom. But tradition was tradition, and she was going to have to cut her hair and find a boy's chiton, all without attracting the attention of any of the palace servants or her parents.

It was a good thing, Gorgo noted, that her mother had always been too mean to give up one of her maids to serve Gorgo, even after she reached maturity. Normally, a girl her age would have had someone to look after her clothes, dress her in the mornings, and help her go to bed. But her mother kept the household women busy and only occasionally sent one to help Gorgo, so she didn't have to worry about deceiving any of the helots.

Gorgo wasn't much worried about her mother, either. She and her mother had never liked each other much, and Gorgo's appeal to the ephors had only poisoned the relationship further. Her mother accused Gorgo of being disobedient and disloyal (which Gorgo halfway admitted was justified). What really hurt was that her mother mocked her for naming Leonidas. "How dumb can you get?" her mother had asked. "I swear I knew by the time I was twelve that the *last* way to get a man was to announce to the world you wanted him! At *your* age you ought to know that the only way to ensnare a male is by flight! But then again, for all your alleged brains, you never did have more common sense than a goose, did you?"

Part of Gorgo wanted to go to her mother in triumph and say, "You were wrong! Leonidas wants me after all!" But then she would get weak knees at the thought that maybe he wouldn't come. So Gorgo decided the best thing to do was avoid her mother altogether. Since they did not have a close relationship, she expected no one would particularly notice.

It was harder to avoid her father. Cleomenes often sent for his daughter after he returned from his syssitia. After she had gone to the ephors, he had made a horrible scene in which he had shouted and raged at her. He had even threatened to put her in a cage and send her to Aristagoras as a present "to do with as he pleased" if she wasn't willing to marry him properly. But they had both known he was bluffing. No one in Sparta, certainly not the household helots, would have been his accomplice in such an outrage.

Far worse had been the next time he sent for her—when, after shouting for a bit, he broke down into tears. He had not been very coherent. He had lamented the death of her brother and then equated her to Helen (which Gorgo thought ridiculous, given her plain looks) and talked about holding a contest among her suitors (which she didn't have!) and a lot of other nonsense. Gorgo had tried to reason with him, but it was pointless.

He had avoided her for about a week afterward, apparently ashamed of having broken down in front of her or aware that he had spoken a lot of nonsense. Certainly the next time he sent for her he made no reference to the previous incident, and spent the entire evening discussing the Ionian revolt, its prospects of success, the implications Spartan neutrality would have on its position in the Greek world, and speculations about the prospects of invading Argos

successfully. Gorgo had been careful not to deviate from the prescribed topics and to tread very, very carefully, agreeing with everything
her father said without appearing to be merely echoing him.

Gorgo could not risk cutting her hair or changing into a boy's
chiton until after her father had retired and there was no risk of
him sending for her. But her father often kept very late hours, and
she started to get nervous as the dinner watch ended and the pipes
announced curfew.

Just as she had feared, her father sent for her very late.

By the time the summons came, she had "borrowed" a chiton
that had been left out to dry in the kitchen courtyard, she'd packed
her two favorite peplos and a himation, good sandals, and some toiletries into a satchel she could wear over her shoulder, and she had
laid out scissors and mirror in preparation for cutting off her hair. But
there was nothing she could do but answer her father's summons; to
have sent her regrets would only have aroused his suspicion.

Gorgo joined him, as usual, in the small reception room off his
sleeping quarters. The room was quite low, with fat, heavily painted
pillars opening to the atrium at one end and couches on the other
three sides. It was warmed now by a brazier with burning embers,
which let off a thin trail of smoke. The paintings on the walls had
darkened almost to non-recognizability under generations of smoke,
and it made the room gloomy.

King Cleomenes was already well into his cups. He lay on one
side with a large, white-glazed Laconic kylix filled with wine in his
left hand. "Ah, there's the little intriguer," he called out jovially as he
caught sight of his daughter.

Gorgo ignored the barb and came over to kiss the cheek he offered
her. He wore a full beard, which he did not trim like most Spartans.
His eyes were bloodshot. With a gesture he indicated the couch
nearest him on the right and irritably signaled one of the household
helots to bring Gorgo a kylix and wine. Gorgo accepted the kylix, but
asked for water only.

"Not allowed at my table!" her father countered, and gestured for
the helot to pour her wine.

Gorgo capitulated. Tonight was not the night to fight with her
father.

Cleomenes was mollified by her submission and announced in a cheery tone, "I've been thinking. You were absolutely right to reject these Ionian tyrants! Nothing but a bunch of jumped-up upstarts!" He made a rude noise, then laughed at Gorgo's embarrassed expression.

"Don't you like it when I do that?" he asked her, repeating the noise.

"No, because it demeans you, father."

"Oh, my, aren't we high and mighty tonight. It's not enough that you lecture me on what bribes I am allowed to take; now you want to tell me what sounds I'm allowed to make! It really is time to marry you off! Then you can bully your poor husband rather than me!"

Gorgo was very tempted to retort, but she bit her tongue.

"I must say it surprised me that Leonidas had the backbone to stand up to you. No doubt he was afraid of your tongue. Poor little Leo! Actually, you'd think he'd be used to tongue-lashings by now, seeing the way his mother, his other brothers, and I have lectured him on his shortcomings all his life; but I guess the thought of hearing it from his niece was too much even for him."

"Yes, I guess so," Gorgo agreed meekly, sipping her wine—and vowing that if Leonidas truly took her away from here and made her his wife, she would never, never, never insult or nag or demean him.

"What I was thinking…" Cleomenes' tone changed abruptly again, this time to the conspiratorial. Now he leaned toward his daughter with an eager smile and lowered his voice, as if he were afraid of being overheard. "I was thinking you are too good for these petty tyrants with the bloodlines of jackals! What you deserve, as the direct descendent of Herakles, is the Great King himself!" Cleomenes ended on a triumphant note.

"The Great King?" Gorgo asked. "You mean Darius of Persia?"

"Who else could I mean?" Cleomenes replied, as if she were dense.

"But he has dozens, or is it scores, of wives already!" Gorgo protested, outraged that he would even jest about such at thing.

"So, one more won't make any difference!" Cleomenes retorted cheerfully. "I'm sure he's so used to women nagging and badgering him that he is completely immune to it all."

"And I'm sure the ephors will be even more delighted by the

idea of giving Sparta to Persia on a silver platter, than by the idea of handing it over to a rebellious tyrant!"

"Don't think the ephors can protect you much longer, my dear. You have no idea how venal they are. I've got two of them in my pay already. Give me another month and some more of Darius' bride-price—which was very high, I might add, given the way you look—and I'll have the third ephor ready to sign the marriage contract—Where are you going?"

"To bed."

"I didn't give you leave."

"I'm going without it. Call the guard, if you like."

"Gorgo! Come back here!"

"No."

"Gorgo!"

She stopped, suddenly afraid he might come after her if she continued—and then he would see all the things she had prepared for her flight. But she did not turn around.

Her father's voice was suddenly sad. "How did we ever come to this?"

For a moment she felt sorry for him. She looked over her shoulder and met his bloodshot eyes. But she didn't have an answer. She just shook her head. "Let me go to bed, father."

He waved at her in dismissal, his expression suggesting disinterest or mild disgust.

———

Gorgo had to force herself not to run. The palace was still. All sensible people were long since abed, and the torches and lamps had been extinguished everywhere beyond her father's private quarters. At her mother's suite of rooms she paused and listened, but heard no voices within. She continued down the long corridor, which looked out through a second-floor colonnade at an interior courtyard, and noticed that there was a moon tonight. That was not good. The moon would light the streets and reveal them to the watch—assuming Leonidas came as he had promised.

She turned and slipped into her bedroom. Everything was as she had left it. Or was it? She sensed that something was different, even before a shadow separated itself from her cabinet. But the moment of tension was rapidly over; it was her uncle. "My father sent for me," she whispered. "I only just got away. I'm not ready yet."

"I'll wait outside, but hurry." Leonidas went onto the loggia.

Gorgo pulled her peplos off over her head, pulled the chiton on, and realized too late that in her haste she had forgotten a belt. There was nothing to do about that. She pulled her satchel over her head, then went to the dressing table. She pulled her hair together at the back of her neck with both hands, held it fast with her left hand, and with her right, blindly applied the scissors. She was certain the result was not flattering, so she did not even pick up the mirror. She simply hoped that Laodice (or more likely Melissa, in this case) would be able to put things partway right in the morning.

She joined Leonidas on the loggia, touching his elbow without a word. He looked down at her and smiled. Then he took her hand and led her deeper into the palace, back toward the kitchens, across the kitchen courtyard, and into the stables. Here, however, the horses stirred, and a man called out, "Who's there? Who's there? What do you want?"

"It's just me," Gorgo answered the old groom.

"Who's that with you?" The moonlight was lighting them up from behind, and the groom could see Leonidas' silhouette.

"It's me. Leo," Leonidas spoke very softly.

"Master Leo? How did you get in here? What's going on?"

"Shhh! Do you want to wake the whole household or provoke the meleirenes into sounding the alarm?" Leonidas asked in a low voice, coming nearer.

"But what's going on?" the old man asked in a whisper, peering up at Leonidas to be sure he was who he said he was.

"I'm taking Gorgo home with me," Leonidas told him.

Understanding dawned at last. The old man looked sharply at Gorgo and finally noticed her hair and dress. A wide grin spread over his face. "Oh, that's good, master! That's wonderful! Do you want to take some of the horses?"

"No, I have horses waiting at the company stables. But if you'll let us out the door, we can spare ourselves climbing into the loft and back down by the rope I used to get in."

The old man grinned and cheerfully let them out into the street.

Here Leonidas led, keeping to the shadows as much as possible. Although as a full citizen he had the right to move around the city after curfew, he did not want news of his marriage to become public before he went to the ephors to announce it. So at each crossroads, he paused to check for the watch before proceeding. Once he had to signal Gorgo sharply back and into an alley, while he hid in a doorway. The watch marched past, talking among themselves as they were not supposed to do. The officer in Leonidas frowned and he shook his head, but the bridegroom resisted the temptation to call them out for it.

At the company stables, Meander was waiting with two of Leonidas' horses. Leonidas helped Gorgo to mount one, taking her satchel from her, and then mounted the other himself. The footfall of the horses seemed very loud on the cobbles as they crossed the second half of the sleeping city, but Gorgo felt as if her heart were beating just as loudly.

At last they crossed the Eurotas, and Leonidas turned to assure her, "We're safe now. No one can stop us anymore."

"I don't think I'll feel safe until we're at your kleros," Gorgo answered, trying to stop her teeth from chattering. She had forgotten a himation as well as a belt.

Leonidas took off his own himation and flung it over her shoulders.

"I'm sorry," Gorgo told him; "I didn't plan very well."

Leonidas laughed. "I didn't give you a chance to plan at all. Let's get out of the cold as soon as we can." She nodded, and they started cantering down the road.

At Leonidas' driveway, they reined the horses in and rode up the drive between the cypress trees at a walk. The crickets were shrieking in a high-pitched chorus, as if they were trying to stop the onset of winter by sheer protest. The house was bright white in the moonlight.

Dogs started yelping as they approached, and Leonidas frowned and announced in annoyance, "That's the pair of puppies Alkander and Hilaira insisted on giving me to replace poor Beggar."

"I can bring Jason here, can't I?"

"Of course. What did you do with him tonight?"

"He sleeps in the kitchens. He won't notice I'm gone until I don't come for him in the morning."

Leonidas told Gorgo to go ahead into the house and that he would see to the horses, but she shook her head and came with him. They put the horses in the boxes, in which hay and water waited for them. Leonidas looked in at the kennels and tried to quiet the puppies, and then they skirted around the helot quarters and crossed the back terrace, bathed in moonlight.

"I know you won't believe me, Leo, but this really does feel like home," Gorgo whispered, a little overwhelmed by how true this was.

Leonidas was pleased, but he was also getting cold without his himation. "I hope it will feel as much like home inside," he told her, indicating the outdoor steps that led directly to his bedroom.

Inside, as expected, Laodice had put fresh-pressed linens on the bed and hung lavender from the ceiling. Pitchers and kothons waited on a chest beside the bed, along with a bowl of nuts and raisins. A brazier, glowing on the far side of the bed, had taken the chill off the air.

Leonidas closed the door behind them and considered his niece. She was clutching his red himation around her shoulders, and her hacked-off hair hung raggedly around her face. But she had never looked so lovely to him. She turned to meet his gaze and her lips were moist, catching the moonlight that filtered through the slats of the shutters over the window. Her eyes glistened in the light, too. She was smiling at him, albeit a little uncertainly.

He stepped closer and drew her into his arms, and she lifted her face to his. He kissed her on the lips for the first time in their lives, and she seemed to simply melt into him.

CHAPTER 20

GROWING THREATS

RETURNING FROM SUMMER MANEUVERS ON THE Argive border,
Leonidas' company followed the coastal road south, hoping to make
the turnoff for Thyrea before dark. Leonidas was pressing the pace a
bit because he was anxious to get home to Gorgo. Shortly before the
turnoff, the road looped inward behind a headland that blocked their
view of the Gulf and led through a dense forest. It had been a cloudy
day, but abruptly the clouds sank down and opened their bellies to
dump rain laced with hail.

Leonidas immediately ordered his pentekostus to seek shelter
amid the trees. Within minutes, however, the wind was tearing
branches down around them. Then, with a horrible screeching and
wailing, some of the trees started to break and fall. No one was concerned about staying dry anymore. They were drenched to the bone.
The issue was staying alive.

Leonidas sent all three runners and Meander out to find a suitable
place to shelter 250 men, one hundred Spartiate troops, their attendants, and the company helots. Crius returned first with the news
that a gorge up ahead would offer some protection; so Leonidas
ordered the troops forward, followed by the helots with the draft and
pack animals, but abandoning the wagons.

By the time they reached it, the gorge was running fast with the
sudden torrent of water rushing off the mountains. Still, the rocky
sides offered some protection from the falling trees and branches.

The hoplites found places to sit or at least lean against the sides of the gorge, and used their hoplons to protect themselves and their attendants from rain and flying objects. The bulk of the company helots got themselves up onto a deep ledge with sufficient overhang to protect them. This was too high up the wall, however, for the horses and mules. While the mules turned their haunches into the wind and dropped their heads, some of the horses were too high-strung and tried to bolt. One of the grooms broke an ankle when a fleeing horse dragged him several yards over rough terrain before he obeyed the order to let it go. Another helot broke his arm falling on the slippery rocks while trying to steady another horse.

Leonidas stayed with the helots attending the horses at the foot of the gorge, holding his own nervous stallion and one of the mules. As he watched the great dark clouds rolling and churning overhead, he shuddered inwardly. Although he was not naturally superstitious, this storm seemed especially ominous. It appeared to portend something particularly evil.

By dusk, however, the worst of the storm had passed; and since everyone was too bedraggled and tired to continue the march, Leonidas decided to camp where they were. He went back with the helots to collect the wagons, but since it was still raining there was no point in unloading supplies.

The men huddled in the gorge through the night, getting little sleep, as the wind still howled down the gorge and made the surrounding forest roar. They couldn't even warm themselves, because there was no dry wood with which to keep fires going. Without cooked food, they fed themselves on salted meat and hard cheese. Leonidas thought longingly of Laodice's cooking and Gorgo's bed, and told himself he would be there the day after tomorrow.

Sometime during the night the wind eased up, and dawn broke behind a bank of clouds that ended overhead. Within another hour or two they would have the sun again. Men unbent themselves and staggered up on cramped muscles, cursing and groaning as circulation returned to limbs that had gone to sleep in awkward poses. Leonidas and his enomotarchs started reorganizing and checking for serious injuries. They had lost three horses and one mule. Two helots had broken bones and one hoplite had sprained an ankle, but that was it. Nothing more serious than a cold, sleepless night, really—and it was over.

Knocking water from the crests of their helmets and wringing out their himations before reattaching them at the shoulders, they formed up. At first mud clung to their legs, chitons, and arms, but as they marched the sun broke clear of the retreating sheet of cloud; soon it had dried the mud, which then flaked off. The road turned back toward the coast and started descending. They were now no more than an hour from the turnoff inland at Thyrea, and some of the men started singing. The songs learned long ago in the agoge made the marching easier.

As a company commander, Leonidas no longer marched with his men. He was mounted and riding back to check on the supply wagons when the leading ranks of the column rounded the bend behind the headland. Ahead of them was a splendid view of the Gulf of Argos, glittering in the morning sun. The sight brought the front ranks to a halt so suddenly that the ranks behind collided into them. Cursing replaced singing—but only in the rear. The front rank had fallen ominously silent and seemed turned to stone.

Leonidas heard the song cut off abruptly. He looked over his shoulder, instantly sensed something was wrong, and spun his stallion around to canter forward along the side of the road. As he came around the bend, he pulled up in horror and gaped, just as his rankers had done before him.

Spread out before them on the curving, sandy beach of the bay were the carcasses of three ships, and between and around them lay the bodies of hundreds of dead. The bodies were being blown onshore by the wind, but then floated off by the tide. They rose and fell on the swells like flotsam. Nowhere in the floating carpet of dead was there even a faint flicker of life.

When they reached the beach, they learned why. The corpses were tied together by ropes around their necks, while their wrists and ankles were also bound. They had never had a chance.

"Slave transport?" Oliantus asked, staring at the carpet of corpses undulating on the swells.

"But where are the crews? Why didn't they set them free?" one of the section leaders asked.

The enomotarch who had gone farther up the beach to inspect the wrecks returned. "They weren't ships, but barges," he informed the others. "No form of propulsion. They were evidently being towed, and when the bad weather set in they were just cut loose."

"But there must be nearly three hundred slaves here! That's a huge investment. What merchant would risk losing so much cargo at once?" Oliantus had been tasked with organization too long not to think in practical terms.

"If it's their lives or yours..."

Leonidas had stopped listening. He had seen something that he did not want to believe; and so he waded into the water, kicking the corpses nearest the shore out of his way. His approach sent the seagulls soaring and protesting. He was swallowing back bile, but he had to be sure he was not imagining things. Then he stood directly over them—a chain of boys not more than ten, their faces still unfinished and smooth, their fine hair swirling around them in the eddies of the tide. All the little boys had been recently and brutally castrated. The salt water had washed away the blood and bandages, exposing the gaping wounds all the more clearly.

"Not slaves, captives. Persian captives," Leonidas summarized to the men he heard wading in after him.

Just before they had set out on these maneuvers, word had reached Sparta that the Ionian rebels had suffered a devastating naval defeat. The reports from Corinth claimed that after six years of tweaking the tail of the Persian Empire with their insubordination and audacity, the rebels had risked an open confrontation. If the accounts were credited, the rebels had mustered more than 350 triremes to face a Phoenician fleet of about 500 fighting ships at Lade, off Miletos. According to the Corinthians, when the fleets actually met, some of the Samian captains either lost their nerve or had taken Persian pay. In any case, before even engaging, they broke and ran. This naturally led to widespread panic among the rebel contingents. The Lesbians and many others followed the Samian lead and took flight rather than engaging. The 100 Chian ships and isolated remnants of their allies fought with determination and courage, but these forces were hopelessly outnumbered. Despite initial successes, the Chians were eventually routed. After this defeat, resistance to Persian rule collapsed across the Aegean, and Persia was seeking retribution.

Until this moment, however, Leonidas had not truly understood what the reports of Persian "retribution" meant. Now he was staring at the evidence of what befell the population of the once rebellious and now subdued Greek cities.

Leonidas believed the Ionian rebellion had been foolish. Sparta had refused to send aid for good reasons. As Gorgo, whose role in the decision had not been insignificant, pointed out, the rebellion had been led by tyrants more interested in their own fortune than in the freedom of their cities. But these children, Leonidas found himself thinking, had paid the price.

"We must bury them," he announced, "there beneath the temple." He pointed to the edge of the beach below a small ancient temple to Poseidon, then turned to splash his way back to the beach.

Oliantus nodded and started giving orders. No one seemed to mind that Leonidas did not stop to help as he usually did, but continued instead to the temple and sank down on one knee before the altar. He knelt for a long time, his head bent, lost in his own emotions. He could not forget that just over two decades ago and not far from here, he had briefly fallen into Persian hands. He might have ended like these boys. It shook him to his bone marrow. He had been saved by Prokles' grandfather, who had talked the perioikoi commander of the Eastern Squadron into launching no less than two triremes to rescue two foolish schoolboys. But Sparta had not been prepared to send a single ship or a company of infantry to save the island cities of Ionia...

Leonidas returned to the beach. The helots were hauling the strings of corpses onshore the same way fishermen haul nets, working in teams. As each corpse came within reach, one helot cut the neck rope binding the corpses to each other and the others lifted the body onto the back of a waiting colleague. This man carried it toward the long pit that had been dug by the hoplites in the soft soil under the bank.

Leonidas came up behind the men lowering the first of the corpses into the common grave. "Cut their hands and feet free. They may have died as slaves, but they are being buried as free men."

The enomotarch addressed looked over his shoulder, surprised to have Leonidas suddenly behind him; but he nodded, and without further instruction one of his men took a knife and did as Leonidas ordered.

Leonidas continued down the length of the grave, repeating the order to each commander.

Toward the end of the line he came upon Temenos. Temenos had graduated from the agoge and was now a citizen and soldier. He was helping cut the bonds of the corpses and looked as ill as Leonidas felt. Leonidas put a hand on Temenos' shoulder, and the young man looked over sharply.

"Greeks are capable of equal cruelty." Leonidas was thinking of the "Farm of Horrors" on Kythera. But he continued, "It is the scale of the Persian atrocities that is so terrifying—their ability to inflict so much suffering at once."

"But it *is* terrifying, sir." Although it was Temenos who spoke, all the men had stopped to listen to the exchange between the young man and their commander. Whether older men on the brink of full citizenship or young men like Temenos, barely out of the agoge, they nodded in agreement. Leonidas saw his own horror and fear reflected in their eyes.

"We have never faced an enemy like this before," Leonidas conceded.

"Are they our enemy, sir?"

Leonidas took a deep breath; he looked from the corpses back to the wrecks on the beach and then squinted as he looked farther east, beyond the horizon, where the Persian Empire stretched. It was an empire so vast that it would take six months of marching to cross from one side to the other. It was unimaginable. Perhaps more importantly, it was filled with peoples all prepared to obey the orders of a single man, their Great King—not a collection of squabbling city-states each jealous of its own territory, customs, and privileges. The Ionian revolt had not been subdued by Persia's famous cavalry, but by the ships and crews of Phoenicia in obedience to Persian orders.

Leonidas turned back to his troops. No one was working anymore; they were all waiting to see what he would say. "They are not our enemy today. But if they seek to cross the Aegean and establish themselves anywhere on the Hellenic peninsula, then they will become our enemy. Sparta cannot afford to tolerate a power such as Persia near at hand."

"Not even north of the Isthmus?"

"Not even there."

He nodded for them to get back to work, and returned to the temple of Poseidon to make a sacrifice and pray that the sea would stay between Persia and Greece.

———

Two days later, they were home. The gentle but solid Parnon range lay between them and the Aegean with its harvest of savagery. It was easy to pretend that Sparta was safe behind her mountain barriers, safe from retribution because she had not taken sides in the conflict between Persia and her subject Greeks, and safe because she had the finest army in the world...

Leonidas wanted to believe that. He marched his pentekostus into the city in full panoply, with shields and helmets gleaming. They were received by the casual cheers of boys and youths and idle citizens. At the barracks, the wagons and pack animals were turned over to the army helots, and the men and their attendants were dismissed. After maneuvers, units always had a fortnight leave. Leonidas rode straight for his kleros, Meander beside him.

It was sometimes hard to believe he had been married to Gorgo only two years. From the day she set foot on his kleros, Gorgo had belonged completely. Leonidas would never forget returning home on the first day after their marriage. He had left before dawn to report to his commanding officer and then to inform the ephors. As Leonidas had anticipated, the ephors were delighted and quick to spread the news. By the time Cleomenes woke from his wine-heavy sleep and discovered his daughter gone, it was too late to protest. Faced with widespread positive reaction, Cleomenes had little choice but to pretend great satisfaction in public. Privately he summoned Leonidas and swore he would never forgive him—or Gorgo.

That first day after his wedding, Leonidas had returned to his kleros exhausted and tense. When he walked through the door, however, he heard laughter coming from the kitchen. He followed the sound to find his wife sitting with Laodice, Melissa, and Chryse around the kitchen table, helping to shell nuts and apparently gossiping, as if she had lived there all her life. At the sight of him in the doorway, her face had lit up, and it was as if a curse had been broken.

Within weeks Leonidas could not remember what it had been like without her—except as a vague, gray dream he preferred to forget. When he compared this marriage to the last, it was like night and day. He had always been trying to please Eirana, always failing, always unsure of himself, and always disappointed. Gorgo, on the other hand, was so happy that he didn't even have to make an effort to please her; yet his simplest gestures, things he hardly thought about, made her even more affectionate and grateful. The positive spiral seemed to have no end. Gorgo had transformed his life without even trying. He still had ambitions and plans. He still took his work with the army seriously; but he knew that at some level the only thing that mattered to him was Gorgo.

Gorgo and their unborn child. Gorgo had brought him the news this past winter, brimming with pride and excitement. He was delighted. He wanted children, several children. He especially wanted a son he could raise as he imagined a father *ought* to raise his sons. And he wanted an heir, a son by Gorgo, who would checkmate any designs Brotus had on the throne. Gorgo's son would represent direct descent from the ruling Agiad king; and Leonidas was confident the ephors, Council, and Assembly would recognize any boy he sired on Gorgo as the rightful heir to the Agiad throne, bypassing Brotus.

But as Gorgo's time drew near, he couldn't forget that women died in childbirth more often than men died in battle. No matter how much he tried to suppress his fears of losing her, they were growing. Gorgo, he calculated, would be big and slow by now. Eirana had been virtually immobilized during the last month of her confinement. Of course, she had been carrying twins, but Leonidas understood that a child sapped a woman's strength—and Gorgo was only nineteen.

Furthermore, by now she might have become frightened despite her initial enthusiasm. Chryse had been like that. At first she had been defiantly proud to be carrying Temenos' child, but as the time for the birth drew nearer, she became frightened. She had been so terrified at the end that Laodice, who rarely asked for favors, begged Leonidas to send for Temenos. Leonidas, as an officer, could send for the young man, and he did. Temenos had then paced on the terrace all through the night, while Chryse screamed as if she was being tortured. It had been a bad night. Leonidas knew it would be worse when Gorgo was the one in agony.

They reached the top of the drive, and Leonidas could no longer restrain his eagerness. He let his stallion pick up the pace, leaving Meander trailing on his slower horse. To the left was a field of ripening grain, and to the right a half-dozen horses grazed contentedly, flicking casually at flies with their long tails. The air shimmered in the heat, and crickets screeched in the trees, but otherwise all was still. Everyone, Leonidas assumed, was resting during the noonday heat.

As they came close enough to see the front of the house, however, Leonidas was surprised to see two chariots waiting. The horses had been unhitched, explaining the large number of horses in the paddock; but Meander at once recognized Chilonis' driver lounging in the shade of the front colonnade, while the other chariot belonged to Hilaira. It was not unusual for Chilonis or Hilaira to drive over to visit Gorgo, but both at the same time? Leonidas flung himself off his stallion, leaving him to Meander's care without a word, and ran into the house only to collide with Melissa.

"Master! Where did you come from? This is no time to be here!"

"We just marched in. What's going on?"

"The mistress's water has broken. It won't be long now."

"Where is she?"

"Leo?" The voice came from the courtyard, and it belonged to Nikostratos. "Come here!"

Leonidas followed the voice. Nikostratos was sitting in the shade provided by a reed awning over the corner of the courtyard. As usual, he held his cane between his knees. Nikostratos was now seventy and increasingly blind. He had resigned as treasurer because of this, but his brain was as sharp as ever, and he remained an active member of the Gerousia. "Are you back already?" he asked as Leonidas emerged from the house.

"Already? I've been gone a month and we're a day late. We came upon four wrecked barges laden with dead Ionian captives. The

Persians had tied them together so when a storm struck they all drowned—hundreds of boys, recently castrated. It was one of the most horrible sights I've ever seen. Where's Gorgo?"

"Where do you think? Sit down here and keep me company."

"I want to see her—at least tell her I'm home—"

"I'll tell her that, master." Laodice emerged from the wing of the house, linens on her arm. "Mistress Hilaira is here and Mistress Chilonis. Everything is just as it should be. Welcome home."

"Why can't I see her?" Leonidas protested.

"You'd just get in the way and distract her, Leo," Hilaira reasoned, emerging from the side wing behind Laodice. "I assure you, you can't do a bit of good here."

"But how long will it take?" Leonidas asked, focusing his attention on Laodice, because she had gone through this at least five times.

The helot, however, dutifully deferred to Hilaira because of her higher status. "There's no way of knowing," Hilaira told him calmly. "It could take as little as a few hours or as long as a couple of days. Generally, first children take longer, so you should plan on staying away the rest of the day at least. You can sleep at our kleros if it continues into the night," Hilaira suggested. "Since I'll be here until it's over, I'm sure Alkander will be pleased to have company—and that way, we'll know where to find you."

"It's barely midday!" Leonidas protested.

"Well, this is certainly going to take all afternoon, so just go amuse yourself somewhere," Hilaira insisted, with a decisive and somewhat impatient gesture. She could hear Gorgo asking Chryse questions in the room behind her, and was anxious to get back to her. Chryse was only seventeen, after all; and although she had given birth to a healthy son a year ago, Hilaira did not think she was the best person to keep Gorgo calm.

Leonidas capitulated. Gorgo clearly had lots of support from her grandmother, Hilaira, Laodice, Melissa, and Chryse. So he turned to look rather helplessly at Nikostratos.

"It really is best to leave the women to it. I'll send your boy Crius for you as soon as it's over," he promised Leonidas. "Why don't you go to the baths? After a month of maneuvers, you could use a good bath and massage," Nikostratos noted, with a somewhat disdainful look at Leonidas' dirty, rank chiton and the salty and greasy braids of his hair. "I'll give you a report on her progress at dinnertime, but then I'll come back here, and you can go home with Alkander as Hilaira suggested."

"And from now to dinner?" Leonidas demanded. "I can't spend all afternoon at the baths, and Alkander's at the agoge this time of day," Leonidas reminded him with ill-disguised exasperation.

"Then go talk to Phormio," Nikostratos admonished. "You've been away a month, and I'm sure he has all sorts of things he wants to discuss with you. I think I heard him say something about a cargo of Egyptian papyrus, or was it sail canvas?"

No doubt Phormio did have all sorts of things he wanted to discuss, Leonidas conceded mentally, but Leonidas was in no mood for talking business. He wouldn't be able to concentrate. He had been away a month, and Gorgo might die without having seen him again. In addition to his fears for her life, he also remembered how the birth of the twins had radically changed Eirana's behavior toward him. After they were born, she had little time for—or interest in—him anymore.

Nikostratos' voice brought him back to the discussion. "You should also give some thought to Argos."

"What about Argos?" Leonidas asked, frowning because he could not follow Nikostratos' train of thought.

Nikostratos shrugged. "Your brother received an oracle telling him he will take Argos ..."

"I presume this was delivered by his own permanent representative at Delphi, Asteropus," Leonidas noted sarcastically. Leonidas had disliked Asteropus ever since he had been a rival for Eirana's affections, and increasingly he harbored suspicions that Asteropus had been bribed by his brother to deliver manipulated oracles.

"Yes," Nikostratos admitted, fully aware of Leonidas' suspicions, "but think about it all the same. We've been sparring with Argos for centuries. It's time we forced a clear decision."

"Why? The Persians have just ruthlessly suppressed the Ionian revolt, and left a warning in blood and brutality from Byzantion to Crete. Greeks should band together to oppose Persian ambitions— not kill each other!"

"Hmm. Possibly. But only after we've boxed Argos into submission."

"Why?"

"Because we will not be free to engage Persia until we have eliminated the latent threat of Argos."

"Kyranios says war is the failure of diplomacy. Has anyone ever tried to make an ally of Argos?"

"Not that I can remember—which is only to say it was probably before my time, not that it wasn't tried. Now, are you finally going to go and clean yourself up, or aren't you? I'll see you at dinner."

Leonidas gave up. He left Nikostratos in his spot in the shade, walked around the back of the helot quarters to the stables, and entered the low barn. Most of the horses were in the front paddock, but Meander had finished untacking and watering their riding horses. He was preparing to turn them out in the paddock and had each on a lead. "Is the mistress all right, sir?" Meander asked when he saw Leonidas.

"As well as can be expected, I am told," he replied, adding indignantly, "I've been ordered out of my own house!"

Meander smiled. "I guess that's normal, sir."

"When you let those loose, bring Red and whichever horse you want out of the paddock. We're returning to town," Leonidas ordered as Meander started out of the barn.

"Yes, sir; and Pelopidas says he needs to talk to you when you have a moment."

"Do you know what it is about?"

"Your mare," Meander replied, nodding toward the only stall that wasn't empty, and then he was gone.

Leonidas went to the stall. The black mare occupying it was one of his favorites. She had always been particularly intelligent and willing, but had suffered from assorted kinds of lameness. He had been forced to give up using her. Now she stood in her stall with her head down, looking distinctly miserable.

Pelopidas emerged from somewhere and came to stand beside him. Pelopidas was a hard worker and a good farmer, but his real love was horses. "Master," he started, "do you remember last summer when one of Kyranios' stallions got loose and it took weeks to catch him?"

Leonidas turned to look at Pelopidas, understanding the implication at once. "He was caught downriver and we never thought anything of it, but you can see for yourself."

"But in summer…" Leonidas looked back at the mare, but there no denying what Pelopidas said.

"She's due any day—just like the mistress."

Leonidas nodded. "Then if I have a son, he will have his first mount."

———

By the time Leonidas and Meander got back to the city, the main post-drill rush at the baths was over. Most men had moved on to spend their afternoon as they pleased in gymnasia or seeing to their private affairs. The bath slaves were cleaning up after the midday crowds—collecting discarded towels, mopping up water, sweat, and oil from the tiled floor, and rubbing down the marble benches.

Meander first unbraided and combed out Leonidas' hair, then helped him strip down out of his dirty clothes. At a nod from Leonidas, he then stripped himself and followed Leonidas into the water. When the baths were crowded, attendants were not welcome, but since Leonidas was almost alone, he did not expect any objections.

He had miscalculated. One of the few other bathers was Lysimachos. Lysimachos had been Leonidas' eirene when he was ten, and was father of the boy Leonidas had found under the bridge the year he married Gorgo. Although he had, as far as Leonidas knew, never done anything of note—never been promoted in the army or elected to public office—Lysimachos viewed himself as a defender of Spartan values. No sooner had Meander slipped into the cool waters of the large pool than Lysimachos reared up from where he was apparently dozing in the hot bath and shouted, "What are you doing, helot! You have no right to get into that pool! Get out! Out!"

Meander froze, then looked at Leonidas. Leonidas gestured for him to stay where he was, and turned in the water to address Lysimachos. "Meander is not a helot. He is the son of a Spartiate. Furthermore, he is my attendant, and we have been on maneuvers for the last month. There is no harm in him swimming when the pool is empty."

"Just because you are the son of King Anaxandridas doesn't give you the right to break the law! You're no better than I am, Leonidas! Tell your helot to get out of the water, or I'll come pull him out myself!"

Meander at once started to climb back out, but Leonidas laid a hand on his arm and stopped him. Instead, he got out of the pool himself, his hair hanging wet and limp to his shoulders and dripping water as he faced Lysimachos. Even in this state, Leonidas was an impressive figure. His muscles were well toned and his skin tanned. "Bring the ephors, Lysimachos, or call the whole damn Council: there is no law against attendants, particularly freeborn attendants, using these baths."

"You and your kind are undermining Sparta's strength and reputation in the whole world!" Lysimachos snapped back, pulling himself out of his bath and turning his back deliberately on Leonidas as he reached for his clothes. He was red with agitation. When he finished dressing, Lysimachos cast Leonidas a hate-filled look and snapped, "Don't think I'll forget this! You may deceive some people, but I remember what a little worm you were as a boy! You have always been soft on helots and tremblers! You even supported Corinth when they humiliated us and turned the League on its head!"

This was patent nonsense, since Leonidas had only been twenty-one at the time; but it was clear to Leonidas that Lysimachos was not being rational. This had nothing to do with an honest disagreement; it was personal animosity. Leonidas therefore did not bother answering, but he was inwardly stunned that anyone—especially anyone who knew him so little—hated him so much. He was reminded of the looks on the faces of the Corinthians that night thirteen years ago, when he had slipped into the Corinthian camp and overheard them ranting against Sparta. He had not understood the hate then, nor Lysimachos' hate now. What had he ever done to Lysimachos?

He was still standing there thinking about the exchange when Sperchias remarked from behind him, "You look stunned, Leo."

"I am," Leonidas admitted, turning to smile at Sperchias in welcome. The two men greeted each other with a quick hug, and then Sperchias drew back and remarked, "I only caught the tail end of that exchange. What was it about?"

Leonidas indicated a confused-looking Meander. "There's practically no one here, so I gave Meander permission to bathe. We've been on maneuvers for a month, and no one has worked harder than Meander. He's not even a helot; though, by Kastor, I'd have defended his right to be here even if he had been! What harm can it possibly do?"

Sperchias nodded and gestured for Meander to relax. "I'll join you," he announced, and stripped down to join Leonidas and Meander in the pool.

For several moments they were silent. Leonidas dunked his head underwater and ran his fingers through his hair from the scalp, as the accumulated salt from weeks of sweating in his helmet dissolved in the water. After a moment, he righted himself and swept his hands from his face to the back of his skull, pressed out the water, then caught his hair together at the back of his neck and wrung it out. Only when he was finished did he turn to consider Sperchias.

Sperchias was looking heavier these days, and his pleasantly round face seemed to sag a little, while his rough, red hair was already receding. But most disturbing, the once so cheerful Sperchias had eyes and lips with a permanently downward tilt that gave them a sad or discouraged expression. As they paddled around in the cool water, Sperchias remarked, "They're getting stronger, you know."

"Who?" Leonidas demanded.

"Leotychidas' faction."

Leonidas did not answer immediately. He was not blind or indifferent to politics. He was still a citizen with a vote in Assembly, but of late he had focused on his military career—and Gorgo. He had not been paying as much attention to politics as Sperchias did.

Sperchias had run for a half-dozen different offices over the last four years—and lost each time. Leonidas had repeatedly found himself assuring Sperchias that there was nothing wrong with him. But Leonidas could understand if Sperchias had become discouraged. Sperchias, meanwhile, had not lost his interest in public affairs, only his optimism. He had become increasingly cynical. Leonidas opted for a question now: "What does Leotychidas want?"

"He wants Demaratus disgraced and exiled so he can become king."

"I can see why Leotychidas would want that, but why would anyone support him?"

Sperchias weighed his head from side to side, considering his words carefully. "For a variety of reasons, not necessarily all compatible. Mostly they are malcontents, who don't like the way things are and believe Sparta is poorly led."

Leonidas thought a moment, reflecting on the remarks Lysimachos had just made about the change in the League charter, and then asked, "Because Demaratus sided with the Corinthians during the abortive campaign against Athens?"

"Yes. That was the start of it."

"But not the end, you mean?"

Sperchias was standing in the pool, his feet firmly on the bottom. He stretched his arms out and brought them together slowly, then repeated the gesture without comment, making small waves that lapped against the sides of the pool. Finally he said, "They have an agenda."

"What?"

"To 'restore' Sparta."

"As hegemon in the League?" Leonidas asked.

"More than that. It's also about putting the helots 'back in their place.'"

"What is that supposed to mean?"

"Well, they see prosperous helots and impoverished Spartiates, and allege there is a relationship. In short, they blame the latter on the former."

"That's absurd. The helots on the marginal estates are worse off than anyone."

"But helots like yours, Leonidas, are seen to be accumulating wealth."

"If my helots are industrious and talented, like Pantes with his excellent carpentry or Laodice with her sweets, why shouldn't they profit? They make me richer as well."

"That has been noted—and resented."

"That's even more absurd."

Sperchias shrugged. "I don't disagree..."

"But?" Leo prompted.

"You don't seem to recognize the danger. It does no good to say that they are irrational and that what they say is not true. They still say these things, and they are spreading bad rumors about you."

"Like what?"

"That you bought your promotion, for example."

"Chi! Are you serious? That would imply that all five lochagoi are corrupt!" Promotion of midlevel officers in the Spartan army was effected by consensus among the officers of the immediately superior rank. Enomotarchs were selected among promising section leaders by the company commanders collectively, and company commanders were appointed by the five lochagoi from the eligible enomotarchs.

"But you only needed three votes, didn't you? Euragoras says you bought two of them."

"Euragoras?" For the second time in a quarter-hour, Leonidas was stunned. Euragoras had been his own enomotarch when he was first in the army. He had always thought of Euragoras as a friend—not a close friend, but a friend nevertheless.

"It's just jealousy, of course."

Leonidas was silent. He could understand the frustration and jealousy of a man passed over for promotion. He remembered his own disappointment at being passed over for the Guard year after year. "They can say what they like. What difference does it make?"

"That's exactly my point, Leo: you underestimate them. This isn't about your personal reputation. It's about discrediting you so that you cannot get in their way."

Leonidas noted that this was a backhanded compliment, which imputed more influence to him than he felt he had.

Sperchias continued, "They have already bought Brotus with promises that he will be next. The idea is to bring down Demaratus first, and then Cleomenes."

"And then?" Leonidas pressed. "Just what do they want then? It is hardly as if my brother and Demaratus have agreed on anything. How can they be against them both?"

"They don't disagree with your brother's policies; rather, they believe he has been inept at implementing them. They want Sparta to abandon Chilon's policy of accommodation with our neighbors and return to an aggressive policy."

"So they support this war against Argos?"

"One hundred per cent; and they hope Demaratus will oppose it so they can expose him as 'cowardly.'"

"You said the faction was getting stronger?"

"Definitely," Sperchias agreed. "Look how they got their candidate for Paidonomos elected!"

Epidydes had retired the previous year to take up the first vacancy on the Council of Elders in three years. He had been replaced by one of his three deputies, Alcidas.

"And they are behind your election defeats," Leonidas concluded.

Sperchias did not meet his eyes, but Leonidas could read his expression.

Leonidas started up the steps out of the bath, and was met with a towel by one of the bath slaves. As he dried himself, he stated, "It will not happen again—if I can help it."

Sperchias joined Leonidas outside the bath and looked at him hard. "Does that mean you are going to take an active interest in this, Leo?"

"You have my word."

———

At dinnertime, Leonidas found Nikostratos waiting for him in front of the syssitia. "Any news?" he asked anxiously.

"Gorgo is doing very well, I'm told. She certainly has not made much noise, as these things go. In fact, I've heard laughing coming from the chamber, so she's kept her wit so far."

That sounded good, and Leonidas felt some of his tension ease.

"Oh, and one of your mares gave birth to a colt this afternoon, but she absolutely refuses to let it milk. She's kicked it away from her so consistently that Pelopidas has separated them and is trying to keep it alive by hand."

"Good man," Leonidas answered automatically, his thoughts still on Gorgo. It had only been six hours since she started labor. While Nikostratos was surely telling the truth and all was well so far, things could still go very wrong. He sighed, and Nikostratos patted him on the arm in sympathy as they went into the dining club together.

———

Leonidas left the syssitia with Alkander. Alkander suggested they stay at his townhouse rather than ride the seven miles to his kleros. He led the way through the back alleys to the narrow house, rented more than a dozen years ago to enable Hilaira and Alkander to meet while he was on active service. They retained it now because his eldest son, Thersander, was already in the agoge, and the younger boy, Simonidas, soon would be. Alkander and Leonidas stepped through the dark entryway into the courtyard, and Alkander called out to the housekeeper to bring them wine and water in the andron.

At dinner there had been much talk about Cleomenes' oracle, and Leonidas had reported on the corpses of the Ionian rebels, which led to a lengthy discussion of the Persian versus the Argive threat. Leonidas had taken a lively part in the discussion; and it was really only now, when he was alone with Alkander, that it struck him that Alkander, like Sperchias, looked tired and dejected.

"Is something wrong?" Leonidas asked. "You look discouraged."

Alkander nodded, reaching for wine before answering, "It's Alcidas."

Leonidas was not entirely surprised. Alkander had never gotten along with the senior deputy headmaster. Alcidas had always been a conservative, while Alkander had joined the staff of the agoge in order to reform it. "Something in particular?"

Alkander shrugged, "He's a tyrant, Leo. An insidious, subtle tyrant. He doesn't shout or scream, of course. He's Spartan. He was raised in the agoge the same as you or I. He has such firm control of his emotions that dealing with him is like dealing with a statue. His facial expression rarely changes, and his voice is always level, always soft, almost monotone. But he is…" Alkander looked hard for the right word, and finally concluded, "he is evil."

Leonidas started at such a bald accusation, but he said nothing. Alkander was not one for idle exaggeration. He looked hard at Alkander and awaited the explanation.

"I will give you an example: he has so intimidated the eirenes that they are afraid to come to him with their problems. I don't have responsibility for the eirenes." Alkander was the assistant deputy headmaster for the little boys, the boys aged seven to thirteen. "But Ephorus has confided this to me." Ephorus, once their herd leader, had become the supervisor of eirenes at the agoge. "Fortunately, in some matters they still feel they can go to Ephorus himself, but Alcidas has managed to make them ashamed of seeking advice; and Ephorus says the weaker youths, the very ones who need the most assistance, shy away from him."

Leonidas was appalled. He could vividly remember being an eirene himself. He remembered how much guidance and assistance he had needed from the experienced staff of the agoge. Before he could comment, however, Alkander continued. "Alcidas' answer to any kind of problem is to blame the person reporting to him; which, of course, only means that problems are *not* reported to him, and that instructors, eirenes, and youths try to avoid getting in trouble by taking as few risks as possible. Nobody nowadays would do what you did, for example, and turn the text for a public performance into an off-color caricature of the original. They wouldn't dare. You may say that isn't such a loss—and I'll grant you that your text was juvenile—but what I see is a creeping inhibition of initiative that could be fatal for Sparta's long-term agility in public and foreign affairs."

Leonidas nodded.

"Worse is the fact that the boys are being taught silence not so that they think before they speak, but to stop them from speaking at all."

"What do you mean?"

"Well, when we were growing up, we were never allowed to gossip, babble, or talk nonsense in class. We were supposed to speak only when spoken to; but then we were expected to give concise, coherent, and relevant answers. The emphasis was on responding to questions that challenged our intellect and made us think carefully about our answers before we opened our mouths."

Leonidas nodded slowly in agreement.

"What that meant in practice," Alkander continued, "is that the wittier we were—the more original, the more articulate, even the more impudent—the greater the approval we harvested. Don't you remember?" he asked, leaning closer to Leonidas, because darkness had crept into the little andron but neither man had thought to light a lamp. "You were so good at it! I can vividly remember one night in some syssitia when you were asked why only full citizens were allowed to wear their hair long, and you said, 'So the boys of the agoge will know whom to call "father" rather than "sir."'" Leonidas laughed, because he had forgotten the exchange.

"That's the point, Leo," Alkander told him intensely now. "They all laughed. At that moment, no one gave a damn whether you knew the correct answer; they appreciated a quick reply. In fact, as soon as we went back into the kitchen, they started discussing whether the tradition had indeed become nothing but an empty symbol of status.

"But under Alcidas, the boys are afraid of giving a 'wrong' answer. Alcidas wants them to learn everything by rote rather than think things out for themselves. He wants them to be silent not so that they think through their answers before speaking, but rather to silence differences of opinion."

"Are you sure?" Leonidas resisted the implications of what Alkander was saying. He had always been proud of his education, and most proud of the fact that it taught boys to think for themselves.

Alkander insisted firmly, "Yes. I am. Which is why I was not very interested in what you said tonight about the Persians, Leo. The Persians are very far away. Alcidas and his supporters are right here in Sparta."

"Chi claims Alcidas owes his election to the faction around Leotychidas. Do you agree with that?"

To Leonidas' surprise, Alkander agreed, "Absolutely! Leotychidas is like a venomous snake. He makes very little noise, and he prefers to wait for his prey to come to him. He strikes silently and without warning, and he is cold-blooded and devoid of compassion. He has been working against Demaratus for years now, and we never even noticed…" Alkander hesitated, but then he dropped his voice and admitted, "My sister came to me at the full moon. She confessed to following the urgings of her maid and seeking out a woman who lives in a cave on Mani. The woman is generally considered mad, but according to Percalus, she is a priestess to Gaia."

Leonidas looked at Alkander in alarm. He had never had a high opinion of Alkander's sister Percalus. She had Alkander's beautiful, fragile blond looks, but none of his common sense. Worse, she had let her good looks go to her head. She first enjoyed playing suitors off against one another; then, having given her promise to Leotychidas, she dropped him without hesitation when Demaratus beckoned with a crown. She had been married for fourteen years and had never once conceived, and this failure had induced her to make extravagant gifts to Eileithyia, the Goddess of childbirth, and Hestia, the Goddess of the hearth, as well as frequent sacrifices to Hera and Aphrodite—all without result. But Gaia was one of the old gods, and the Olympians were fiercely jealous. Leonidas did not think it was wise to seek out a woman who claimed to communicate with them.

"I agree," Alkander responded to Leonidas' look. "But she did, and this is the worst of it, Leo: the woman told her Leotychidas had put a curse on her womb. The woman said Leotychidas had himself come to her and paid her to perform the curse."

"And for a larger sum she would reverse it, no doubt," Leonidas scoffed. Whether or not it was because of his animosity toward Asteropus, over the years Leonidas had developed a low opinion of priests and priestesses. They were so greedy.

"I wish she had said that," Alkander answered in a voice that was almost inaudible. "That, at least, would have been transparent, and Percalus could have paid up and gone away happy—though none the more fertile. But she didn't." Alkander paused. It was pitch dark in the andron, but still neither of them thought to light a lamp. The darkness made Alkander's voice disembodied and more ominous. "She said it was too late, that a chain of events had already been set in motion. She told Percalus that she would live to be scorned by the man she'd scorned, but that Demaratus' fate would be worse: he would betray what he loved most, and be forced to watch while the barbarians reaped the harvest that he had sown with his treason."

———

The sky was graying in anticipation of dawn by the time Leonidas cantered up his drive in response to the summons by Crius. As he jumped down in front of the house, he turned his horse free and left him to find his own way back to his stall. He went inside and took the stairs two at a time, until the stillness in the house admonished him to silence. He stopped at the top of the stairs and listened. Nothing stirred. Cautiously he pushed the door open and peered into the room. Hilaira was stretched out on a pallet on the floor. On the bed, nestled in fresh, clean linens, was Gorgo, sound asleep with a bundle in her arms.

Leonidas tiptoed into the room and looked down at the bundle—which had a bright red face, wet lips, eyes screwed shut, and a shock of wet hair plastered to its forehead. He put out a finger to touch it, but then changed his mind and bent to kiss his wife instead.

Gorgo woke instantly. Her eyes widened, and then she smiled. "Leo! Have you seen her? Isn't she beautiful? She doesn't take after me at all! She's all yours!" She looked down at the bundle in her arms, full of pride, and Leo kissed her again.

"She's beautiful," Leo told his wife. "But not as beautiful as you."

"Leo—"

He silenced her with a kiss and then asked in a whisper, "Is there room for me in there, or do I have to sleep somewhere else? I'm exhausted."

Gorgo smiled and at once squirmed closer to the wall, taking the baby with her, while Leonidas pulled his clothes off and left them on the floor. It was a hot, sticky night and he did not try to take Gorgo in his arms; it was enough that—unlike Eirana—she did not send him to sleep elsewhere. He took her hand and she squeezed it. Her smile seemed to light up the darkness.

"What do you think we should name her?" Gorgo asked in a whisper.

"Agiatis," Leo told her without hesitation.

"You were expecting a daughter!" Gorgo guessed, almost offended; and then asked at once, anxiously, "Are you unhappy?"

"No," Leonidas lied. He wanted and needed a son—now more than ever, after what he'd heard today about Leotychidas and, by association, Brotus. He needed a son that he and Gorgo could raise to be a reforming king like Polydorus, a king with the blood of Chilon in his veins, as well as the blood of Herakles... But there was no point admitting that to Gorgo. It was not her fault. So he kissed her again, and pretended to sleep until he did.

CHAPTER 21

THE HEREDITARY FOE

THE PAIN MADE KYRANIOS CATCH HIS breath and cling to the edge of the table. For a moment his sight dimmed, and a trembling took hold of his left side; but then the crisis passed again, and he slowly let out his breath. These "fits" were coming more frequently, and it was getting more difficult to hide them from those around him.

As his breathing returned to normal, he twisted slowly to look behind him and see if anyone had noticed anything this time. Fortunately, the quartermaster was engrossed in going through the inventory with the clerk and the perioikoi responsible for procurement. They were in the final stages of topping up supplies in preparation for the campaign against Argos. If all went according to schedule, they would call up fifteen classes of reserves the day following the end of the Asclepia and march out three days later, roughly ten days from now.

A full call-up of this nature would enable Sparta to field five thousand Spartiate troops of the line, plus three hundred Guardsmen. It was Sparta's maximum striking force; and it left the defense of Lacedaemon in the hands of the perioikoi auxiliaries, and Sparta itself in the hands of the forty-six- to sixty-year-olds, supported by the eirenes and meleirenes.

It was rare for Sparta to field such a large force. Kyranios had never personally experienced it before, and he was extremely reluctant to admit his physical condition under the circumstances. To field a force this size, each lochos expanded from a standing force of four hundred men to a unit one thousand strong by absorbing reservists into their ranks. This was achieved by activating a fifth company and by swelling the four active companies with reservists until their strength doubled from one to two hundred men each. This, in turn, was achieved by each enomotia adding a section, to bring their numbers up to forty men each. The responsibility shouldered by each officer in such a call-up was enormous.

Kyranios had been a lochagos for twenty-three years, making him the most experienced commander in the Spartan army. Two of the lochagos were very junior, while the man closest to Kyranios in experience, Hyllus, was in Kyranios' opinion a pig-headed fool. Hyllus thought every battle could be won by sheer strength. He was fond of saying, "Turn off your brain, put your head down, and shove!" Hyllus was the last man Kyranios wanted to see in the de facto position of principal advisor to the commanding king, Cleomenes. Next senior after Hyllus was Arkesilos of the Limnate Lochos. While Arkesilos was certainly no bonehead like Hyllus, Kyranios was not sure he had the backbone needed to stand up to Cleomenes if the king started to do something crazy.

That they might need to stand up to Cleomenes was all too obvious to Kyranios. Cleomenes had always been erratic and prone to extravagant experiments. Despite the success of his first campaign against Athens, his latter expeditions had resulted in nothing but humiliation—first getting trapped on the Athenian acropolis and then having the allies abandon them. But getting humiliated by Athens was one thing; being defeated by Argos was another altogether.

Cleomenes' interference in Athenian affairs had not threatened the integrity of Lacedaemon—attacking Argos did. If they struck at Argos and failed to deliver a crippling blow, the Argives would take a terrible revenge. Kyranios had only to think of the raids Argos had delivered throughout the past decade, from Kythera to Thyrea. The Argives would love nothing better than the opportunity to regain control of the Malean peninsula and Kythera. They would, indeed, love to invade Lacedaemon and take Sparta itself. If they did, they would turn every Spartiate and his wife and children into Argive slaves. Kyranios didn't doubt that for a moment.

Which meant: if war with Argos was unavoidable (and it was, because Cleomenes was obsessed with it and the Assembly had endorsed it), then it had to be a singularly successful war. To be successful, the Spartan army had to deliver a knockout blow to the Argives—something so decisive that they would finally acknowledge Lacedaemonian hegemony on the Peloponnese. Anything less would only result in an escalation of the simmering hostilities—with dangerous consequences for the safety of all Lacedaemon, not to mention Sparta's ability to confront other threats such as Persia.

Kyranios' head was killing him. It felt as if one of the Titans had clamped his hand around Kyranios' skull and was pressing inward. Kyranios could picture the plates of his skull fracturing like an egg pinched between his thumb and forefingers. He put his fingertips to his temples and tried to rub the pain away.

Kyranios did not believe in the authenticity of the oracle Cleomenes claimed to have received from Delphi. He was not alone in his doubts. King Demaratus had openly scoffed at it, asking Cleomenes what it had cost him. This, however, had only led to a violent verbal exchange between the two kings that demeaned and discredited them both. Leotychidas, however, sensing a new opportunity to discredit Demaratus, had done all he could to ensure a majority in favor of war when the proposal came to the vote in the Assembly.

Had they all gone mad? Kyranios asked, closing his eyes to the pain and fear that was starting to unman him. No, not all. It had been a close vote, repeated three times; but the young men, like young men always, were full of themselves, cocky, spoiling for a fight...

A knocking on the door made Kyranios lift his head, drop his hands, and square his shoulders firmly. "Come in!" he barked, while his quartermaster and clerk looked briefly over their shoulders toward the door.

Leonidas entered, his helmet in the crook of his elbow, his leather corselet gleaming with oil, and his chiton fresh and clean—as was proper when a junior officer reported to his superior. "You sent for me, sir?"

Kyranios nodded and signaled Leonidas to come forward, but did not stand. He was afraid that getting to his feet would make him dizzy and that Leonidas might notice he was off balance. "I have bad news for you," he announced, watching Leonidas' expression closely.

Leonidas, he calculated, was thirty-five—exactly the age he'd been when he'd taken over the lochos. Leonidas admittedly had less experience as a company commander—just three years—but he had handled his company, and before that his task force during the expedition with the Corinthian grain fleet, splendidly. And Leonidas was an Agiad. Kyranios felt he had to take a chance on him.

Kyranios drew a deep breath. "You aren't going to like this," he told Leonidas bluntly, "but I have decided to appoint you my deputy; my current deputy will take over your pentekostus."

Leonidas started visibly and then asked simply, "Why?"

"I need you. That will have to be reason enough for you. Now, as my deputy, come with me to the Agiad Palace." Kyranios pushed his chair back and dragged himself to his feet, closing his eyes briefly as the room spun around him. When he opened his eyes again, Leonidas was holding out to him the white-crested helmet denoting his rank as lochagos and watching him keenly, but he said nothing.

They walked in silence down the long corridor and out onto the porch of the lochos headquarters. Kyranios kept waiting for Leonidas to say something. He knew Leonidas enjoyed command—just as he had. He was sure he did not want the position of deputy, which was a position without direct command authority, a position more like an adviser. But Leonidas maintained his silence as they descended the steps and crossed the crowded market square. The perioikoi, in anticipation of the campaign against Argos, were offering equipment and supplies—those that the Spartan army and her citizens would need on campaign—in exceptional quantity in the adjacent agora. Armorers and saddlers, shoemakers and bronze workers had all set up their booths here and cheerfully called out their wares.

Leonidas and Kyranios skirted the agora, heading west, past the theater and the Theomelida, which housed the tombs of Leonidas' ancestors. Leonidas seemed to nod to the dead of his house, but that was all. Instead he turned his attention to the smaller temple to Asclepius that stood opposite the Theomelida. Here, as in the main temple opposite the Cattleprice, preparations for the Asclepia were in progress. A wagon laden with bundles of freshly cut centaurea was being offloaded, and a cage full of live snakes waited under the portico, apparently delivered but not yet collected. "Have you thought of seeking Asclepius' help?" Leonidas broke the silence at last, indicating he knew more about Kyranios' illness than the latter wanted.

Kyranios nodded. "I will spend the night in the temple." More than that he could not do. He dared not consult the military surgeons, for fear they would declare him unfit for active service, and his wife's home remedies had all proved worthless. But Asclepius' great love of mankind, which had once led him to try to make men immortal, had not been extinguished by Hades' hatred—only inhibited. At certain places, such as Epidauros and Kythera, his spirit still stretched out from the Underworld to touch humans; and on the eve of the Asclepia, people had been known to experience miraculous cures to long-standing illnesses right here in Sparta. It was Kyranios' last hope—along with Leonidas.

As they approached the front entrance of the palace, they greeted the other four lochagoi, Hyllus, Arkesilos, Niokles, and Diodoros, each with his respective deputy. As a group they mounted the palace steps, then entered past the meleirenes on duty into the reception hall, with the benches around the edge and scenes from the *Iliad* fading on the walls. They waited here in silence until a household steward led them deeper into the palace, where King Cleomenes awaited them.

Cleomenes had elected to receive the five lochagoi and their deputies in one of the sunny, modern halls in the newer part of the palace. Four doors opened along one side to a garden with a fountain; sunlight and the fresh smell of moist earth and flowers seeped into the high-ceilinged room along with the faint sound of the bubbling water.

Cleomenes' eyes rested instantly on Leonidas, and he asked as if in alarm, "What brings you here, brother?"

Kyranios answered for him, "I've appointed him my deputy."

Cleomenes raised his eyebrows, and Hyllus frowned, but that was all.

They got down to business. Cleomenes had a map of Laconia and the Argolid. Cleomenes announced that the perioikoi would be reinforcing the entire border region and strengthening the garrisons on Kythera and at Limera. In addition, they would hold the passes to Messenia and have messengers ready to warn of any sign of unrest in Messenia. The Tegeans had been informed of Lacedaemon's intentions in a secret embassy, and they had pledged neutrality.

Hyllus grumbled about that, saying something about not trusting any "strangers"; but since Cleomenes had clearly already sent the message, there was little point discussing it.

They turned to discuss the march route and expected rate of advance. Hyllus wanted to go in by the fastest route—like a single deadly thrust to the heart of the beast, he said. Arkesilos asked whether, since Tegea already knew their intentions, they couldn't first march north and then turn east, crossing Tegean territory to take Argos by surprise from the northwest. Diodoros suggested that they divide up the army, sending two lochos by the northern route while the remaining three headed directly for Argos. If the movements of the first two lochos were kept secret, he argued, the Argive army might be drawn west to meet the three lochos invading directly, and could then be outflanked by the two lochos traveling via Tegea.

"If we had enough ships, we could embark the army here at home, and no one—least of all Argos—would know where we were going until we got there," Leonidas remarked softly, more to himself than to the illustrious company.

"We don't have that many ships, and who wants to risk a sea voyage anyway?" Hyllus dismissed his remark, but Kyranios looked sharply at his deputy.

Arkesilos was still considering the idea of dividing the army. "What if—"

Cleomenes cut Arkesilos short with a gesture. "What did you say, little brother?" He was staring with narrowed eyes at Leonidas.

"If we had a fleet, we could embark our army from any port in Lacedaemon without alerting Argos to our intentions. We could land near Tiryns and have a far shorter march."

Kyranios felt as if the tension in his head were easing, even as Hyllus barked, "What's the advantage of a shorter march? Have our young men grown lazy and afraid of a good hike?"

"A shorter march gives the enemy less time to deploy against us," Kyranios dismissed his knuckleheaded colleague, while his eyes remained focused on the Agiad brothers. Leonidas wasn't just standing up to Cleomenes; he was outright confronting him, which was more than Kyranios had expected—and extremely encouraging.

"What good is that if we're all seasick?" Hyllus scoffed, while Cleomenes and Leonidas continued to stare at each other.

Then, abruptly, Cleomenes seemed to come back to the discussion, and decreed: "We'll take the whole force straight in. Coordination is too difficult across these distances, splitting up too risky. Was there anything else?"

They discussed other details for almost an hour, and then the ten officers were dismissed. They left the palace and dispersed in the direction of their respective headquarters. Kyranios and Leonidas again walked side by side in silence, until Kyranios asked, "You understand what needs to be done, don't you?"

"You want me to keep my brother in check."

"Yes, I do."

"I'm not sure it will work. He doesn't respect my opinion—as you saw this afternoon."

"What I saw was that you made him stop and think for a very long time. That's a good start. Not many men can do even that anymore."

Leonidas sighed and nodded.

Leonidas put his horse away in its box stall and then went to the neighboring stall, where the unwanted colt was kept. The colt was a dapple-gray so dark it was almost black, with enormous feet and a head that was too big for its age, making it ugly. For almost six months Leonidas and Pelopidas had been hand-feeding it; and their success could be measured in its growth, for the colt was so much bigger than normal that they called him "Elephant." He came at once to Leonidas and nuzzled him, expecting feed. Leonidas, who never came empty-handed, gave him an apple. Elephant wanted more and pushed him with his head, making Leonidas laugh at his surprising strength. Offended, the colt turned and bounded to the far side of the stall, then stood looking at him over his shoulder with his ears pricked forward hopefully. When Leonidas left the stall door, Elephant rushed back to the door, kicked it to attract Leonidas' attention, then hung his head over the stall door, stretching out his neck. Leonidas took another apple from the barrel and handed it to the impudent colt. Then he went around the helot quarters to enter the back of the main house, following the hearth light that spilled in golden squares out of the windows of the main house onto the terrace.

This was Leonidas' favorite time with Gorgo, after Agiatis was in bed and the helots had withdrawn to their own quarters. As they settled down beside the hearth, Leonidas announced, "Kyranios isn't well," remembering the way the commander had looked earlier in the day—with dark circles under his eyes and lips pulled so tight that the lines of his face sharpened, making him look old and sour.

"Do you think he won't make the campaign?"

"He doesn't think he will. He wants to position me as his successor."

Gorgo hesitated, tried to see what was wrong with that, and couldn't; so she asked earnestly, "Isn't that good?"

"It could be. It depends what happens. There is nothing quite so ruinous to a commander's reputation as a lost battle," Leonidas noted with a smile. Then he grew serious again and added, "He thinks I can influence your father." Leonidas watched his wife's reaction carefully.

Gorgo did not even seem surprised. She nodded and snuggled closer to him and then, annoyed by the leather ties on his corselet, she drew back and undid them deftly, opening the stiff leather armor at the side and slipping her arms inside. "Kyranios is very wise, Leo. My father doesn't take advice well, but that doesn't mean he doesn't hear it. And even if he doesn't always heed good advice, he doesn't always ignore it, either. Besides, he likes you—sometimes."

Leonidas looked down at his wife, remembering the threats Cleomenes had made after their elopement. She was leaning her cheek contentedly on his leather breastplate, and he could see only a tangle of auburn curls. "What makes you think that?"

"He told me," Gorgo answered simply. She shifted in his arms to look up and meet his eyes. "You have to try, Leo. He gets these crazy ideas sometimes, and if there is no one there to tell him off, he can become obsessed with them." She paused, and then she added, "I love you for spending so much time with me and Agiatis, but I understand that your first duty is to Sparta."

The Asclepia was the first festival in the spring—even before Artemis Orthia, which in turn preceded the major summer festivals of the Hyacinthia, Gymnopaedia, and Karneia. It did not attract large crowds of foreign spectators, largely because travel was still uncertain at this time of year and because it was planting season, when most Greeks liked to ensure all went well on their estates. But this did not mean it was an unimportant festival in the Spartan calendar. As with other festivals, men on active service got home leave and the agoge was closed, so both men and boys were home with their families. Anyone who was ill spent the eve of the festival in a night-long vigil in one of the temples to Asclepius. The following day extended families, neighbors, and friends celebrated together over large feasts. Newborn lambs or kids were roasted whole over outdoor pits; and then as the stars came out, the guests gathered around the bonfires, swapping jokes and stories over last year's wine.

On the second day of the Asclepia, however, there were performances in the theater. Girls draped in centaurea performed a variety of dances, accompanied by a woman's chorus. After this the youths took the stage to the music of flute, cithara, and drum.

Seventeen-year-old Aristodemos was flushed with excitement as he peered, through a crack in the canvas dividing the orchestra from the stage, at the growing crowds pressing into the theater. They were lucky. This year the weather was exceptionally mild, and there was not a cloud in the sky. That made people more willing to stay for the later performances than in wet, cool years.

"It's practically the whole city!" one of Aristodemos' fellow dancers exclaimed with enthusiasm.

"And both kings!"

"Are they spitting at each other yet?"

"Not yet—they just act as if the other stinks."

"Places!" Euryleon ordered. The previous year, at the retirement of the old chorus master, Euryleon had taken over as choreographer of the youths' dance company. His shortsightedness was no disadvantage in this role, as he seemed to see the whole picture more clearly, while his hearing had always been particularly acute to compensate for his weak sight. Furthermore, while Euryleon had never been taken very seriously by his peers because of his underperformance as an athlete and hoplite, the boys of the dance troupe were in awe of his willingness to try radical new formations and moves.

At the center of today's performance was Aristodemos, because he had a solo performance that required a series of dramatic leaps and kicks. He had practiced them so often that he sometimes thought he did them even in his sleep; yet he was nervous as they took their places in the chorus line, preparatory to taking the stage.

A silence slowly descended over the theater—until even the screeching of the crickets, from the olive trees surrounding the temple of the Bronzehouse Athena on the hill behind the theater, could be heard. Then the drum started its slow beat and the company took the stage.

The youths were dressed in leather training armor over black chitons, but they wore no cloaks and carried no weapons. They were barefoot, although they wore leather greaves and leather helmets over their shaved heads to give them a martial look. The dance started slowly, with the whole line of sixteen youths carrying out the same steps, then broke into two lines of eight that faced each other, filed through one another, and then broke again into half-sections of four. These formed a four-spoked wheel that turned upon the stage, then broke apart to form a circle, and broke again into a long line; all the while, the pace had been increasing.

At last Aristodemos' moment came. He detached himself from the line, moved to center stage directly in front of the kings, and started his solo performance, while his fellows and eventually the whole audience clapped in time to the music. Before long the clapping started to break up into applause. Aristodemos felt the applause in his veins like uncut wine. It rose to his head and he leaped higher and faster than ever before. And then it was all over, and he was gasping for breath and almost slipped on his own sweat as he stepped back into the line for the final group figures.

The audience was on its feet in approval.

"Isn't that your brother Meander?" one of Aristodemos' fellow dancers asked out of the side of his mouth as they took their bows.

Aristodemos glanced up and to his horror, saw his colleague was right. Meander had pushed his way to the edge of the stage and was clapping wildly and calling out to him.

Aristodemos hastily looked down and pretended he hadn't seen him. How could his brother embarrass him like this? Now, at the moment of his greatest triumph! What an idiot! Did he have to draw attention to himself, hardly better than a helot, and so remind everyone that Aristodemos was just a mothake?

The troupe of dancers was withdrawing from the stage, making way for the last performance of the day. They crowded into the tent behind the orchestra, chattering excitedly. "Well done," Euryleon praised them all, nodding contentedly. "Well done! Good job!"

"Aristodemos! Aristodemos!" The voice pierced through their own excited noise.

"I can't believe he's doing this to me!" Aristodemos protested generally, looking in distress from left to right for a place to hide.

"Aristodemos!" Meander called again, pushing his way through the crowd, grinning from ear to ear. "You were wonderful!" As he reached his brother, he threw his arms around him in an enthusiastic hug. "I was so proud of you!"

Aristodemos tried to shrug off the offending embrace of a non-Spartiate. "Yeah, thanks," he muttered. He was so busy avoiding his brother's eye, and freeing himself of the unwanted intimacy, that he did not realize that Leonidas and Gorgo had followed Meander into the tent.

Leonidas had come to congratulate Euryleon on a brilliant debut as choreographer, but he did not like Aristodemos' reception of his brother.

"Did you like it?" Euryleon eagerly asked his mentor, anxious for the praise he thought he deserved.

"The line was excellent," Leonidas answered Euryleon, smiling and clapping him on the shoulder; then, without honoring Aristodemos with a single glance, he added, "but the soloist was too showy—too taken with himself, I think."

"But, sir!" It was Meander who protested, while Euryleon simply looked astonished, and Aristodemos flushed with anger and shame.

Leonidas turned to Aristodemos at last and remarked, "I trust my life to your brother, *boy*." The use of "boy" for a youth already seventeen was intensely insulting, and Aristodemos flushed hotly while Leonidas continued, "Until I say the same for you, I would—in your shoes—treat your brother with more respect."

Both brothers stared at him, stunned; then Leonidas nodded again to Euryleon and departed the tent with Gorgo in his wake.

It was almost pitch dark. Behind them, by the light of torches, the traditional pantomime narrating the life of Asclepius was being performed by a mixed company. Ahead of them, the sky glowed a brilliant blue behind the sharp silhouette of Taygetos, and the stars were coming out over Parnon.

"Euryleon deserved better than that, Leo," Gorgo ventured. "His whole life he's struggled to make up for deficiencies that aren't his own fault by excelling in other fields. The performance tonight was revolutionary in its complexity and verve, and it finally brought him widespread acclaim. But he cares most about *your* praise."

"I'll be sure he hears it; but that *boy* was only out on that stage because his brother came to me and was willing to work like a slave to keep him in school! Meander is worth ten of him! And then, rather than being grateful and honoring his brother for the sacrifice he made, he treated him like dirt! What the hell are they teaching the boys in the agoge today? That fame is more important than solidarity? If so, the Spartan army will disintegrate and collapse when Aristodemos' generation takes the field!"

"Just because one seventeen-year-old lets his success on the stage go to his head is no reason to infer a complete failure of our educational system," Gorgo cautioned.

"Of course not; but you know what Alkander says about Alcidas and his new regime! This is just another symptom of it! " Leonidas would have said more, but out of the darkness a voice caught them by surprise.

"So. You've harnessed yourself to your brother's chariot after all."

Leonidas and Gorgo turned toward the speaker, startled. Demaratus separated himself from the shadows of the trees. He was dressed in showy armor, with elaborate brass reliefs on the breastplate and the cheek-pieces of the helmet. Leonidas wondered what had made him leave the theater before the last dance ended, but he answered Demaratus' remark steadily, "No more than any other officer and ranker in the Spartan army."

"Except you aren't just an ordinary ranker anymore. You are deputy commander, Kyranios' chosen successor, and an Agiad prince. Did you learn nothing from the fiasco in Attica?"

"My brother learned not to trust our allies—or even the perioikoi—which is why we're taking a pure Spartiate army against Argos."

"And risking the slaughter of two generations. Have you thought of that?"

"What do you want of me, Demaratus?"

"Be careful, Leonidas. They want to pull you down, too. Leotychidas and Brotus are working together. They are behind this whole campaign. Leotychidas ensured that Talthybiades was one of the two ephors appointed to accompany the army. He thinks Talthybiades will be able to manipulate your brother Cleomenes."

Leonidas had voted against Talthybiades, but he had belonged to the minority on this point. The man was very, very clever, and had a long record of service to the state. Leonidas could not even say for sure why he distrusted him so much. His mistrust was completely intuitive, and that made it impossible to voice.

"He may be surprised," Gorgo spoke up, drawing the attention of both men. "My father is not easily manipulated by anyone."

"No," Demaratus conceded. But then he added, "But don't underestimate Talthybiades and Leotychidas, either. They are subtle and poisonous—and Leotychidas hates you, Little Leo."

———

The Spartan army in all its splendor—fifty-three hundred citizens in full panoply, each supported by one to two helot attendants, a supply train piled high with spare spears, swords, aspis, and armor, wagons with grain and sacks of flour, dried meat, cheese, and more— stood stalled at the river Erasinus on the Argive border. The weather was perfect. It was exceptionally warm and dry for this time of year, which while bad for agriculture, was good for campaigning. There was no sign yet of the Argive army. The way into the Argolid lay open before them like a welcoming bride.

And King Cleomenes refused to order the advance across the river Erasinus.

"Actually," he announced in a conversational tone of voice—his eyes, as usual, looking at something in the distance rather than at the faces of the men drawn up around him—"I rather admire Erasinus for refusing to betray his countrymen." He referred to the river's god.

"This is preposterous!" Talthybiades protested.

"Do you want to take such a decisive step against the wishes of the Gods?" Cleomenes asked as if astonished. "The omens, I tell you, are not favorable."

"The omens?" Hyllus asked, incredulous. "But what about the Oracle? We are destined to take Argos once and for all. What do we care about a petty God like Erasinus if Apollo is on our side?"

"Don't be impious!" Cleomenes admonished prissily, making several men roll their eyes, given Cleomenes' reputation for impiety.

Kyranios grabbed Leonidas' arm. "What is he up to now?" he demanded in a hiss that no one else could hear.

Leonidas looked hard at his elder brother and answered his commander, "He's playing with us."

"Meaning?"

"He has no intention of abandoning this campaign any more than we do."

And at the front of the little crowd, Cleomenes announced, "All the same, the Argives will not get away with things so lightly. We'll look for another ford."

Kyranios let out his breath.

"There isn't another ford!" Hyllus protested, but Cleomenes ignored him, and gave orders to start marching south on the west bank of the Erasinus.

Hyllus was right. There was no other ford, and they marched all the way to the Gulf of Argos, reaching the coast as the last of the light was fading. Despite the deepening dusk, however, it was still possible to make out the row of triremes and penteconters drawn up on the shore. Their rams were pointing out to sea ready for launch, and ladders were already extended to receive troops. Some of the men laughed at the sight of the ships, remarking on the cleverness of the

Agiad kings. But Kyranios glanced at Leonidas and commented, "Do you still think you have no influence on him?"

Leonidas was struck by the brilliance of the plan. While Lacedaemon did not have enough ships to transport their full force anywhere, from here the ships could shuttle back and forth across the Gulf. The Pitanate Lochos embarked at once and established a bridgehead, while the ships returned for the remaining four lochos one at a time. By dawn the following day, the entire Spartan army was deep inside enemy territory and less than a two-hour march from Argos itself.

———

Dawn came upon them too soon, revealing that the night deployment had been less successful than expected. Somehow (and some men were already muttering about treachery) the Argives had found out where the Spartans had landed and encamped. The Argive army had come south out of the city to face them in full force, positioning themselves just outside the village of Sepeia.

Kyranios was summoned at once to consult with the king and the other lochagoi, while Leonidas, his eyes scratchy from too little sleep, went to wash in the nearby stream. They had come for battle, and it awaited them today. It was time to wash and prepare oneself for death.

The whole army seemed to be in the stream, splashing water onto their faces and then stroking it out of their beards. With a fifteen-class call-up, the reservists outnumbered the active-duty men, and they, like the officers, had long hair that they wore braided. Leonidas, like the others, took the time to undo his braids, and with Meander's help combed out his hair and rebraided it neatly from his forehead into six rows that hung down his back, longer than the tail of his crested helmet.

Back at the command tent, Leonidas pulled a clean red chiton over his head. Then he sat and pried open his leather-lined bronze greaves with his thumbs, one at a time, to fit them onto his shins. When he finished, Meander was waiting with his bronze breastplate, which he helped Leonidas wriggle into, and then pulled the sleeves of his chiton out through the armholes to reduce the discomfort under his arms. Next came the baldric, with the sword already in the sheath.

Leonidas partly withdrew the sword in an automatic test that it sat correctly. Finally he took his leather-padded Corinthian helmet, with the distinctive black-and-white crest of a company commander, and pulled it down first to check the fit; he then pushed it upward by the nosepiece, so that it sat with the back edge rested on the base of his neck and the nosepiece on his forehead.

Kyranios was still not back from the command tent, so Leonidas made a tour of the lochos. Temenos was on guard with the Kastor Company, and Leonidas paused beside him. "Is everything all right?"

"Yes, sir." Temenos thought a moment and then asked, "Isn't it, sir?" The look of doubt in his eyes reminded Leonidas of his own first engagement more than a decade ago. He, too, had been frightened he might disgrace himself.

"Fine," Leonidas assured the younger man, and started to turn away.

"Sir?"

"Yes?" He turned back.

Temenos looked nervous. "Sir, if something happens to me, Chryse's parents will make her marry—I mean, I want her to marry, but my son ... I mean, a helot stepfather won't be able to teach him about us. I want him to know—to grow up knowing—that his father—"

Leonidas' waved him silent. "Don't worry. As a young man, your position in the file is at least five deep behind the leaders from the active army, with the reservists at your back. By this time tomorrow, you will probably feel cheated, because you will have seen very little except the back of your shield and the back of the man in front of you, and you'll be complaining about nothing more than aching shoulders and cramped calves. But if *ever* something happens to you and I am still alive, I'll be sure your son knows about you."

"Thank you, sir. I'm sorry—"

Leonidas again waved him silent, and turned to return to the tent.

Although mist still lingered in the valley, the sun rose like an aspis of burnished copper above the murk. Just before he reached the command tent, the Spartan salpinx wailed out, calling for the men to form up by regiment. Leonidas felt a twinge of irritation with his brother for calling the men to fight without their breakfast, but he supposed his brother wanted to get this over with. Waiting could tear at one's nerves, and Cleomenes' nerves tended to be overwrought. He was not known for his patience. So Leonidas turned his attention to his lochos, watching for any sign of confusion as it fell in. Their position was to the right of the Pitanate Lochos, which held the center of the line, with the Guard and Cleomenes in their midst. To their own right was the Amyclaeon Lochos. Left of the Pitanate was the Limnate Lochos, and the Conouran was on the far-left flank.

As the Spartans started to form up in their regiments, frantic shouting erupted from the Argive camp. Soon men could be seen pouring out of their tents and starting to form up on the double. In some cases men took their places in line while still arming, their slaves carrying their hoplons and helmets for them.

Abruptly the pipes ordered the Spartans to stand down for breakfast after all. Apprehensively Leonidas watched the Argives, while behind him his men obeyed the order and returned to their camp. After a moment of apparent disbelief, however, the Argive lines also disintegrated, and the Argives set aside their armor as they settled down to have their breakfast as well.

An hour or so later, with the sun now yellow as it rose above the mist and the air turning decidedly warm, the Spartan pipes called again for the Spartan units to form up. Again Leonidas went to stand at the front, his eyes watching the Argives as much as his own troops. The Argive response was amazingly alacritous—as if they could read the Spartans' own signals.

Kyranios was beside him. He looked gray and his eyes were bloodshot, but there was nothing wrong with his mind. "They're reading our signals," he concluded, just as Leonidas had done.

As if to prove his point, the herald blew for the Spartan line to stretch out, thinning to just five men deep, and instantly—with much shouting and running around—the Argive line also started to lengthen. Kyranios cursed and called for his horse.

One of his helots brought a sturdy black gelding over to the lochagos, and Kyranios tried to fling himself onto its broad back. He failed with an audible groan. Leonidas instantly went to help him. Kyranios looked at him with an unfathomable expression and made another attempt to mount. This time Leonidas shoved him upward from behind, so that he managed to land on the patient gelding's back; he then pulled himself upright and turned the horse to canter toward Cleomenes in the center of the line.

Meanwhile, the Spartans were in position. The troops stood at ease, with their hoplons resting against their left knee and their spears stuck butt-end into the earth. They wore their helmets cocked back while the officers inspected. Then they settled down to wait. The mist had burned off entirely, and the day was getting very hot. The men sweated in the sun.

While the army helots stayed in the camp with the baggage, the individual attendants were expected to bring water to their hoplites at regular intervals, as well as to have reserve spears handy, and to provide first aid when the battle actually started. All along the line, men were taking an offered goatskin and drinking eagerly. Leonidas noticed that he, too, was thirsty and looked around for Meander. The young man came instantly. He was grinning. "Your first engagement, isn't it?" Leonidas realized.

"Yes, sir!"

"Well, no doubt it will take that grin off your face," Leonidas predicted. "Remember, once we engage, no one is going to pay attention to anything but what is ahead of him. If you move in to pull the wounded out, watch out for the butt ends of the spears from the rank ahead. More than one attendant has been mortally wounded by the butts of fighting front-rankers."

"Yes, sir." Meander looked only a fraction more sobered, and Leonidas could not entirely blame him. For the products of the agoge, this was the ultimate test; Meander had been in the agoge long enough to absorb the ethos, even if his father's poverty had denied him the right to stand in the line.

It felt as if they had been standing in position for almost an hour when yet another signal sounded. It was to sit down. Not more than a thousand paces from the enemy, it was a gesture of contempt, intended to signal that the Spartans were so unconcerned about the enemy and so confident of their ability to respond rapidly that they did not need to remain at the ready even when in sight of the enemy. The Argives, however, parroted the move and settled on the ground, too.

Kyranios returned. He was no longer sitting upright in the saddle, but slouched to one side. He drew alongside Leonidas. "In a few moments, the pipes are going to order the midday meal. The Amyclaeon and Conouran Lochoi are going to peel off each flank and start back to camp. The Limnate and Mesoan Lochoi are to about-face and start marching back. If—as expected—the Argives also start to break up and return to their camp, the Pitanate will attack at once. Meanwhile, we take only ten paces in the wrong direction, then reverse again and support the Pitanate. Pass the word to ignore the salpinx, await verbal orders, and keep silent."

With an inward bow of respect, Leonidas noted that his brother was very canny—although the maneuver was highly risky as well. It would, in effect, break up their line into five regiments that would then each attack independently at slightly different times. If the Argive line truly broke up, it would work, since each lochos could fight well as an independent phalanx. But it all hinged on the Argives breaking up their formation...

Leonidas passed Kyranios' orders to the five company commanders and saw them bring it to the enomotarchs just in time. Then the signal to stand brought the Spartans (and Argives) to their feet, followed by the signal for "meal."

As planned, the Amyclaeon and Conouran Lochoi fell out toward the flanks, and the Mesoan and Limnate Lochoi about-faced. Ten paces was an eternity in this situation. Leonidas felt as if his back were exposed to the javelins of ten thousand men. He could hear noise from the Argive line, but he did not know what it heralded until, at last, they had covered the distance, and Leonidas gave the verbal order to about-face again.

As soon as they faced the enemy again, they could see the Argives had indeed turned their backs and dropped their guard. The Pitanate Lochos, which was now twenty paces ahead of the Mesoan Lochos, advanced at a jog, the fastest the Spartans ever moved in attack. The Spartan shields overlapped and the lines were almost straight; but because they were not singing or shouting, the Argives didn't realize they were coming until it was too late.

The king's lochos, with the Guard at the forefront, fell upon the unheeding Argives in a block that was not as compact as a standard phalanx, but dense enough to run over anything in its path for thirty paces. The first three Spartan ranks, using an overhand grip, stabbed down at anything standing; and the remaining ranks kept their spears vertical but in an underhand grip, ready to finish off the crumpled bodies of the men the front rankers had wounded and dropped but failed to kill outright.

The Spartans killed silently, but the Argives were screaming, shouting, and cursing furiously. Furthermore, because they had returned to the camp they had used during the night, they were tripping over scattered equipment, screaming as they stumbled into the still-burning coals of their own fires, and tearing down tents as they fled. The deeper the Pitanate Lochos penetrated into the disintegrating Argive ranks, however, the less cohesion the Spartan regiment could retain. Tents, cooking pots, and campfires blocked its path, too, tearing a hole in the line and forcing it to spread out.

The Limnate Lochos on the left, on the other hand, had neatly turned to one side in an evident effort to stop the Argives from fleeing to the safety of a nearby wood. But beyond the camp, some Argives were reforming into a compact phalanx about 150 across. Leonidas glanced around for Kyranios, but didn't spot him. He hesitated only a second, then gave the order himself by simply tapping the shoulder of the nearest enomotarch and pointing to the Argives falling into formation. That was all. The order rippled through the ranks. The phalanx pivoted slightly to advance directly toward the Argive formation, each man adjusting only as much as was necessary to retain the solid, unbroken, and unbending line now aimed directly at the Argive phalanx.

As they came nearer, Leonidas could hear the enemy shouting orders. Behind the Argive front rank, spear tips waved and men jostled one another as they moved into position or changed their slots. Leonidas looked again for Kyranios, but could not spot him. By now they were committed to this fight, and Leonidas had no intention of breaking it off unless he received a direct order to do so.

The enemy was still apparently adjusting their lines—trying to strengthen the center, perhaps? Or perhaps some men were just losing their nerve. As on Kythera, some of the Argives started to shout insults. Leonidas could see their open mouths, red and black holes framed by bared teeth between the bronze of their cheek-pieces. Their eyes were lost in the dark holes cut away in their helmets. Their noses were protected by the bronze hanging down between the eye sockets. The open mouths were the only part of their faces that was still human. Shouting like this, however, made them look bestial. Meanwhile, the Argive rear ranks were beating their spears against their shields, creating what they evidently thought was a threatening clamor. It reminded Leonidas of the chattering of giant teeth—and suggested that the rear ranks were not pressing in as closely as they should.

"Ready spears," Leonidas ordered. The first three ranks reversed the grip on their spears and raised them to shoulder height.

The Argives could take no more. With a wild roar they started rushing the Spartan line, screaming inarticulately with rage and to give themselves courage.

Although running robbed the Argives of their cohesion, a body of heavily armored men could still run over almost anything in their path. To stop from being bowled over, Leonidas ordered his own men to pick up their pace and lean into the attack. After that order, it was up to the front ranks. He dropped back to advance with the fifth rank, and it was from here that he heard the crash of shield on shield in an uneven, ragged crunching noise that staggered many men on both sides.

The Spartans recovered first. They put their weight behind their shields, thrusting their left shoulders forward as they drew their spears back, and then started jabbing downward at the enemy's second line. The length of the spears meant that men in the front rank aimed for the enemy's second or third rank, while the men in the second and third ranks aimed for the men in the enemy's first and second ranks. Three deep, the spearheads sought eyes and throats, while the Argives pushed back, grunting and thrusting their spears, likewise seeking Spartan flesh.

The clash had ended all forward momentum, and the supporting ranks pressed up close behind the front ranks, the entire formation compressing. Here and there a man went down, and the man behind had to step into the gap, over the dead or wounded body of the man ahead. Elsewhere spears broke. When this happened in the Spartan ranks, the disarmed man defended himself with the splintered remnants until the man behind could hand forward his own spear. This man, in turn, received a spear from the man behind him, all the way to the back, where the man in the last rank could shout to the helots for a spare.

The Argives did not seem to have a similar system. When their spears broke, they tossed them away and drew their swords. Argive swords were longer than Spartan swords, but this only encouraged false hopes of reaching the enemy. One after another Argive hoplite was killed trying to use his sword, and in so doing dropping his shield guard enough to allow Spartan hoplites to spike him fatally.

The killing had been going on for almost a quarter-hour, and what had been dry earth with sparse, scratchy grass had slowly turned into a morass as blood, urine, and shit soaked into it from the dead, dying, and wounded. Leonidas looked over his shoulder for Kyranios without really expecting to find him. If he'd been here, he would have already given the order. So he nodded once to the piper and ordered the advance.

At once the rear ranks lowered their heads, leaned forward, and pushed, their shields jammed into the backs of the men in front. They dug in their feet and started shoving forward as if they were pushing a wagon mired in the mud. The impetus from the back moved the front ranks forward without them having to exert a great deal of effort. Leonidas knew. He'd been there. The rear ranks carried them forward much as a wave lifts a ship onto a beach, while the front ranks concentrated on the grim business of hammering down the enemy with their spears.

The Argives were giving ground at last. Not a lot. They were resisting hard. But their front rankers were shouting again—this time with alarm. Leonidas saw a man at the outside edge of the Argive formation glance back and start to shout something—probably an order for the rear ranks to close up—but a spear pierced his throat, cutting off his words. His head, heavy with the helmet, flopped back, and then the body crumpled. The Spartan who had killed him stepped forward over the body, and the men from the middle and rear ranks, one after another, stabbed downward with their spear butts until the corpse was left behind in their wake as they continued forward, a lifeless, bloody rag.

They had advanced almost ten paces now, and Leonidas moved forward with the line, abreast of the middle ranks, the youngest five cohorts of active-service rankers. He looked left and right. Kyranios seemed to have disappeared into thin air. He noted, too, that the Pitanate Lochos was not recognizable as a body anymore, but the Limnate had clearly pinned down a large body of Argive troops before the woods. Then Leonidas realized that the Amyclaeon and Conouran regiments were also on the field, busy sealing off the flanks and back of the woods, where the bulk of the Argive army appeared to have fled.

Leonidas turned back to the task at hand. The Mesoan Lochos was slowly gaining momentum. Leonidas sensed more than saw that the Argive rear ranks were starting to break and run. "Keep up the pressure!" he called out once, and the piper repeated the order, condensed to "Harder!"

Even without orders, the Spartan phalanx sensed the change in the Argive resolve. It was picking up the pace. Soon the Argive rear ranks had thinned so much that the front ranks had lost support. The Argive front ranks started to buckle and go down, not from wounds but from the sheer weight of the Spartan wall of flesh. They screamed not in pain but in terror, knowing what would follow. The Spartan front ranks did not bother with Argives who had fallen; they left these to the middle rankers. The latter jabbed and stabbed into groins, intestines, and bowels as they dispatched the men already knocked down by the front ranks.

By now the Mesoan Lochos had advanced a hundred paces, leaving a carpet of bleeding, sometimes still writhing and whimpering, bodies behind them. For a split second Leonidas was horrified by the number of Spartans strewn behind—until he realized that the red that dominated the field came not from Spartan cloaks, but blood-soaked Argives.

A moment later, the Argive line broke.

"Hold!" Leonidas shouted instantly, halting the instinct to pursue before it could become more than a ripple in the line of bronze. He moved forward to the front rank, which stood absolutely still on his left. He could hear the rasping of hundreds of men gasping for breath. They were dripping sweat so profusely from their exposed limbs that it was a wonder he couldn't hear it like the trickle of a stream. Here and there the line swayed slightly, probably from men with wounds in their legs or feet.

He gave the order for the wounded to fall out and the rest to stand at ease. "Catch your breath!" he ordered verbally, not bothering about the pipes, now that the din of battle had paused in their immediate proximity. He prowled along each rank, making sure that his orders had been obeyed and that wounded men had relinquished their places to fit men. He ensured that the rear ranks adjusted for the losses forward, so that the depth of the files was roughly equal again. Only then did he return to the front rank and order "ready." The men dropped helmets and took up their shields and spears again.

The Argives were in headlong flight up the road. Many had tossed their shields—even their spears—aside. Some men were trying to tear off their armor as they ran. Leonidas shook his head in incomprehension and disapproval. He was confident that his phalanx would be able to overtake these men; and when they did, those in flight would be struck down and butchered like beasts, because they no longer had the means to defend themselves and die fighting. He did not understand how they could care so little about their honor.

What worried Leonidas more was that Kyranios was still nowhere to be seen. It was one thing to give orders in the engagement itself, but he felt the order to pursue ought to come from Kyranios—if not Cleomenes.

He looked around for the lochagos, and with shock noticed his horse grazing off to the side—riderless. Then he realized Kyranios was lying on the grass beside the horse, twitching hideously. Leonidas looked from his commander to the rock-still phalanx, and then up the road at the fleeing Argives. He could not wait much longer, or the Argives would indeed make good their escape. He didn't have a choice. He ordered the advance, and then ran back to Kyranios.

Kyranios had clearly had some kind of seizure. He was conscious, but his face was contorted. He tried to speak but his words were incomprehensible. His left hand and leg twitched, but evidently without responding to his will. With his right, he waved furiously at Leonidas. It was a gesture that might have meant "go away" or "fetch a surgeon," but Leonidas didn't think of that. He understood only "Forward!" or "Back to your post!"

Leonidas shouted back toward the helots, and gestured angrily for them to care for Kyranios. Why hadn't they noticed the commander fall off his horse? It must have happened close to the start of the engagement, Leonidas registered, somewhat ashamed. That was more than half an hour ago, he calculated. Were they all blind?

No, they had been transfixed by the killing.

He didn't have time to wait for the helots to arrive. The phalanx was advancing, as he had ordered, at double pace. They were starting to overtake the Argives, who had collapsed under the weight of their armor and were desperately trying to tear it off so they could run more easily. Leonidas hesitated only a moment; then he caught up the trailing reins of Kyranios' horse, vaulted onto its back, and cantered forward to catch up with his troops.

When he reached them, they had already overtaken the first of the Argives, the men who were wounded or simply unable to keep running. After that, the killing continued all the way up the road until they were within sight of Argos itself.

The men who were far enough ahead could be seen disappearing through a gate flanked by two tall towers. Most of the survivors, however, had abandoned their shields, spears, and armor. They would not be in a position to mount an effective defense. The walls, meanwhile, were lined with people, including women, many of whom already appeared to be screaming or keening in mourning.

There was no point in pursuing now. At the very least, they needed to rest, catch their breath, and regroup. Leonidas gave the order to halt and rest, jumping down from Kyranios' horse and letting it go free again.

The Spartan ranks sank down, exhausted, where they stood. Most men clasped their knees in their arms and dropped their heads on them, their shields still on their left arms, protecting themselves as they had been taught even in this moment of rest. Others, less disciplined or more exhausted, fell sideways onto the ground, their shields only partly protecting them. Their officers usually shouted at them and called them to order before Leonidas did.

Leonidas signaled for the company commanders to join him.

They, of course, had not sat down at all, and came with alacrity. "Kyranios has had a stroke," he told them simply.

They nodded.

"We can probably take Argos with this lochos alone."

They nodded again.

"Do you want to try, or do you want me to call for reinforcements?"

"Let's take the damn place, before they know what's hit them!" replied the commander of the Lycurgan Company.

Leonidas nodded, and wanted to start giving orders, but a horseman was galloping toward him at a pace that bode no good. They turned and waited.

"Leonidas!" The voice reached out to them like a thin wail, long before the rider was close enough to deliver a real message. "Leonidas!" It was not a messenger, not one of their light reconnaissance troops, but Arkesilos, the commander of the Limnate Lochos. He raised his arm and started waving furiously. "Leonidas! Come back!"

"What?"

Arkesilos reined harshly to a halt. "Your brother! He's slaughtering the surrendered Argives! He's butchering them! And now he's ordered the helots to set fire to the woods—to burn them all alive because they will not come out to be slaughtered!"

The officers of the Mesoan Lochos were staring at Arkesilos, uncomprehending. Behind them the rankers began to stir, look over their shoulders, or even get to their feet, trying to hear what was going on.

"Look!" Leonidas protested, pointing back at the city. "Argos is virtually undefended! We can take it easily. We can take it alone! Or if you bring forward your lochos, we'll have it faster and easier!"

"You don't understand!" Arkesilos countered. "Your brother has gone mad! He's butchering men who think they have been ransomed! He's defiling our victory with a bloodbath among the men who have surrendered! And the woods! It is where Argos found the steering oar for the *Argo*. Here Kastor and Polydeukes met with Herakles and Argos and sacrificed to Zeus before setting out for Thessaly! Come back, Leonidas. The city will be just as defenseless tomorrow! But I swear by the eyes of Athena, only you can save us from the vengeance of the Gods! Come quick!"

Leonidas did not resist any longer. What Arkesilos said about Argos was true. Since there was no one left to defend it, Argos could be taken as easily tomorrow as today. He grabbed Kyranios' horse and galloped back to the sacred woods beside Sepeia, which had been turned into a charnel house by his half brother.

The smoke and the screams met him long before he actually reached his brother. As Leonidas rode past the helots who ringed the wood holding burning torches, some of them called out to him, "Do we have to do this?" Even: "Can't you stop this?" They were terrified, caught between fear of their king and fear of the Gods.

Leonidas could understand their terror, because at close range he could see that the plane trees in this wood were truly ancient. Some of the trunks were so massive that more than one man could hide inside if he wanted. Furthermore, the leaves were not small and light like ordinary planes this time of year, but dark and broad. These were evergreen plane trees, which everyone knew were divine. His brother must indeed have gone mad to order the destruction of this wood! It could bring unfathomable revenge from the offended Gods.

The ancient trees, however, were already burning furiously, and the flames were fanned by a good breeze that was perversely not only whipping up the flames, but also twisting around like a cyclone. It was as if the Gods had maliciously turned against the men trapped inside and were intent on destroying them—or, perhaps, once the sacred woods had been defiled by blood, they were intent on its destruction, just as a man will destroy even something of great value if it has been contaminated by filth. When Leonidas saw how far the fire had already progressed, however, he realized no one would be able to stop the fire before it reached a natural barrier. He started praying to Kastor as he rode: "Forgive us. Forgive us. This is the work of one man, not the whole city. Forgive us." Never before had he felt it so important to commune with the Divine Twin. Kastor himself had come to this sacred wood and must treasure it. He must be furious with Sparta...

As Leonidas rode past the pickets who had orders to kill anyone who tried to get out, one of the officers recognized him and protested, "This is barbarous! The Gods will not forgive us!"

Kyranios' horse was starting to falter by the time Leonidas reached his brother. The Agiad king was completely soaked in blood—and surrounded by heaps of dismembered body parts from an indecipherable number of corpses. He was shaking violently and tears were running down his face, washing away some of the blood splattered on it. For a moment, Leonidas thought he had been seized with remorse for his brutality—and then he realized his brother was not crying, but laughing.

Cleomenes was laughing and shouting in delight, "Did you hear that? This is Argos! This is Argos!" He paused long enough to look up toward the clouds and shout: "Apollo! You joker! You tricked me! I was to destroy Argos, you said! I would destroy Argos! But you meant this Argos, didn't you? This pitiful wood dedicated to Argos!" He started laughing again, although his eyes were glazed with fury. "And I have destroyed it! I have destroyed Argos! I have destroyed Argos! Did you not hear? This wood is dedicated to Argos! I have destroyed Argos! The oracle was right! I have destroyed Argos." Cleomenes returned to laughing hysterically.

"You have insulted the Gods, brother, while the *city* of Argos lies untouched and unprotected," Leonidas countered, jumping down from his exhausted mount behind the barrier of butchered Argives.

Cleomenes went dead still. Then he turned and stared at Leonidas. The tears had smeared the blood on his face and washed some of it into his beard. "What did you say?" asked Cleomenes, staring blankly at Leonidas. His eyes were white in his filthy, bloody face, and Leonidas could see his chest heaving. The only sound was the crackling of the burning wood.

"While you are butchering and burning the already defeated, the city of Argos lies as unprotected as a bride to the north!" Leonidas pointed. "We need only march the rest of our troops north to take it."

Cleomenes stared at Leonidas and then said in a hoarse but apparently calm voice, "Who are you?"

"By all the Gods, Cleomenes! I'm your brother. Leonidas."

"Leonidas," Cleomenes repeated, as if the name meant nothing to him.

"We need to form up and march on Argos," Leonidas told him bluntly, thinking he had pierced the apparent fit of madness.

"No!" Cleomenes screamed, and the eyes were wide and wild again. "No! We cannot do that! We cannot do that! I have taken Argos *here*. *This* is Argos! The prophecy has been fulfilled! We will be destroyed if we advance further!"

"By whom and what?" Leonidas asked back sharply. "The women of Argos, perhaps? For their men lie here!" He gestured more widely now, beyond the heap of corpses around his brother to the broader field, paved with Argive dead or dying.

"The Gods!" Cleomenes screamed at him, in a voice so high and unearthly it made the hair stand up at the back of Leonidas' neck. "The Gods themselves will stop us!"

Leonidas kicked aside the body parts separating him from his brother, and walked straight up to Cleomenes until they were standing face to face and eye to eye. "You've gone mad," Leonidas told him softly.

They stared at one another. Leonidas was frightened, because the look in his brother's eye was inhuman.

"You think so?" Cleomenes asked softly, almost timidly. For a moment it seemed as if he were looking to Leonidas for guidance or reassurance or help. But before Leonidas could answer, Cleomenes' mind moved on. He announced abruptly and almost jubilantly, "We will consult the Gods! Yes! We will consult Hera!" Turning to shout over his shoulder at no one in particular, he ordered, "Bring my horse! We will consult Hera!"

They had passed a major temple to Hera on the road earlier in the day. At the time, they had skirted around it politely.

To Leonidas' horror, Cleomenes was giving furious orders to march back to the temple so he could offer sacrifice, and Leonidas was even more appalled to see Cleomenes' insane orders followed. He heard Niokles mutter under his breath, "Anything to get away from here!" Arkesilos and Diodoros had already hurried away to try to stop the slaughter and the burning. Only the usually wooden-headed Hyllus seemed to grasp the significance of what Cleomenes had just done. "Retreat?" he asked in amazement. "Retreat from victory? That's madness!"

But the pipes were wailing "reform/withdraw," and the Spartan units were dutifully breaking off whatever they had been doing and starting to fall in. Behind them the sacred woods burned out of control, and the corpses of Argos' young men lay littered in heaps as far as the eye could see. Leonidas found himself looking for Talthybiades and the other ephor. They ought to have been here stopping this! There was no going back. After invading and inflicting such heavy losses on the Argives, to withdraw was to risk terrible retribution—not to mention the likely reaction of the Assembly. Leonidas was reminded of the joke he had made to Gorgo about the consequences of a lost battle. This battle hadn't been lost, but the fruits of victory were on the brink of being thrown away.

Cleomenes' horse had been brought over, but the stallion was unnerved by the sight and smell of the slaughter, and especially by the blood still glistening on Cleomenes' arms and face. He reared and flailed with his hooves. Maybe, Leonidas thought, that would delay them long enough to make Cleomenes change his mind. He started after his brother, but before he reached him a second horse was brought up, and his brother successfully mounted and galloped away.

Leonidas reached the helots holding the still unnerved first stallion and shouted, "Give him to me!" The startled helots did not even protest, although this was one of the king's favorites from his own stables.

Leonidas galloped after his brother, while behind him the entire Spartan army started to retreat from the field they had so decisively won.

The temple to Hera was a large, modern temple surrounded by a double colonnade of solid Doric columns. The pediment depicted Hera, flanked by her daughters Hebe and Eileithyia, holding a pomegranate in her hand. The priests had spilled out of the building as the Spartan army marched north and were still crowding the porch. They could see the billowing smoke in the sky to the north, though not its source. At the sight of a mounted Spartan encrusted with dried blood riding toward them, they started chattering among themselves in confused but excited agitation. Surely this could only mean the Spartans had suffered a resounding defeat? But why the smoke?

Smoke suggested that Argos or Sepeia was on fire, and that suggested the Spartans had overrun the Argive army. Unable to make sense of the contradictory signs, they argued among themselves.

Cleomenes flung himself off his horse and stormed up the stairs. The younger priests parted before him—alarmed, offended, and frightened by the sight of him—but the head priest stepped directly into Cleomenes' path. He stretched out his arms to block his way. "Who are you to dare come here drenched in blood! Go cleanse yourself!"

"I AM KING CLEOMENES OF SPARTA!" Cleomenes roared.

"That does not make you any less filthy!" the priest replied.

Leonidas had arrived in time to hear this exchange. He dismounted and started up the steps; behind him Diodoros, Niokles, and Talthybiades were galloping up. Farther down the road, a company of Guardsmen were jogging as fast as they could to try to catch up with their king.

Cleomenes, meanwhile, was raging at the priest. "GET OUT OF MY WAY! I'VE COME TO SACRIFICE TO HERA!"

"You are a stranger and have no right to sacrifice here!" the priest told him proudly.

"I AM KING OF SPARTA! GET OUT OF MY WAY OR I'LL HAVE YOU THRASHED!"

"King or commoner, no Lacedaemonian has the right to enter here!"

Leonidas was still two steps away from his brother. He saw, but could not prevent, his brother knocking the priest aside with a sweeping thrust of his arm, uttering an inhuman roar of rage as he lunged forward. The priest lost his footing on the stairs and fell, tumbling down the marble steps to land with a groan of pain, sprawled at the foot, while Cleomenes charged headlong into the temple.

Leonidas looked from the priest to the temple, and opted to go back down the steps to see if the priest was badly hurt. He reached him at almost the same moment as Talthybiades and Diodoros.

"Your brother's mad!" Talthybiades snapped at Leonidas, as if he were to blame. "He's ordered the entire army to return to Sparta! He's throwing away the advantage we've won with this great victory!"

"Leo, try to talk sense to him," Diodoros urged, at the same time gesturing frantically for the other priests to come and see to their colleague.

Leonidas started up the steps again, but did not make the top step before Cleomenes re-emerged. His anger and even his madness appeared to have vanished entirely. His expression was normal, and he was even making embarrassed attempts to scratch the dried blood off his face and out of his beard. He looked at Leonidas with evident recognition, and then he flung his arm over his shoulder as if they were bosom friends and remarked as they descended the stairs together, "I'm sorry to disappoint you, Leo, but we must go home. Flames shot out of Hera's breast when I approached her, and you must see what that means. We have come far enough. She will not let us take the city of Argos. To try would be madness. It is time to go home. If we hurry, we can be there for Artemis Orthia," he added with a smile, as if offering a sweet to a child.

"You can't order the army home!" Talthybiades objected, overhearing this last remark.

Cleomenes looked at him with disdain and answered in a normal tone, "I can and I do. I am the king."

"If you take the army back to Sparta, I'll charge you with treason!" Talthybiades threatened.

Cleomenes shrugged.

Hyllus, the Guard commander, the second ephor, and Arkesilos arrived. Niokles told them what had transpired, while Talthybiades insisted in a low, threatening voice, "I'll see you deposed for this! You're mad and traitorous! I'll see Brotus put in your place!"

"Calm down, Talthybiades," Cleomenes urged, patting his arm patronizingly. "You're getting confused. It's Demaratus you want to bring down, not me."

While Talthybiades snapped for breath, Hyllus took up the refrain, "Treason is treason! You can't just order the army to go home with the job half done."

"I can and I do. All of you! Go back to your troops. I'm taking the army back to Lacedaemon as the Gods demand." Then he snapped his fingers at the Guard commander and gestured for him to follow, as he collected his horse and remounted.

The four lochagoi, the two ephors, and Leonidas were left at the foot of the temple steps. Diodoros gestured for them all to move out of hearing range of the Argive priests, who were still trying to calm their shaken leader after his fall down the steps. He was sputtering about being threatened with a "thrashing" and spitting insults at the "godless and brutal Lacedaemonians," as if Cleomenes were representative of the whole nation.

"If we pull back now, the Argives will claim victory!" Hyllus reminded his colleagues in horror.

"They've suffered the loss of more than five thousand men! They can't call that victory," Arkesilos countered.

"But they will!" Hyllus insisted. "If we retreat, they will say—rightly—that they remained in possession of the field and made us retreat!"

"Hyllus is right; but no matter what they call it, it will take them decades to recover from the casualties we inflicted," Niokles mediated between the other two.

"No defeat, no treaty, no end to attacks," Leonidas pointed out.

"With what could they attack? Ghosts and women?" Arkesilos asked, exasperated.

"Mercenaries," Leonidas answered. "Unless we can force them to acknowledge the defeat we inflicted or deny them the means to hire mercenaries, they will seek revenge for today's work before the solstice."

"We can't continue the campaign with Cleomenes in this state—even if we could convince him to change his mind," Diodoros countered, his eyes fixed on Leonidas.

"A thousand men could do a lot of damage—and we don't need a ruling king to deploy a single lochos."

"An active lochos, no," Talthybiades admonished in his best legal voice; "but we called up fifteen classes of reserves. To keep them in the field, we need the approval of all five ephors *and* a king in command." His words were accompanied by vigorous nodding from the other ephor.

"We could form a unit one thousand strong by pulling one active-duty pentekostus from each lochos," Diodoros pointed out.

"You won't get me to command such a force! I won't risk it after offending the Gods as we have done." Hyllus gestured vaguely toward the smoke-smudged sky behind them. "You heard what Cleomenes said! Hera forbids us from taking Argos! We must camp on the field overnight and send a herald to Argos demanding surrender. Then we must all go home."

"Surrender, after hearing and seeing us retreat?" Talthybiades scoffed, gesturing to the troops that were already marching past in good order. "The Argives will never do that!"

"An active-duty force need not attempt to take Argos," Leonidas countered; "only deliver the message that they are no longer defensible with their own strength, while destroying the source of the wealth with which they could hire mercenaries."

"I won't command it!" Hyllus again declared stubbornly.

Diodoros smiled faintly, but he let Arkesilos give the answer. "You don't have to. We have an Agiad prince to do that."

Hyllus' expression showed he had not even thought of such a thing; and Talthybiades frowned and seemed on the brink of protest, but then held his tongue. The others just looked at Leonidas for confirmation, and he nodded.

CHAPTER 22

THE PRICE OF HONOR

MYCENAE. AGAMEMNON'S CITY. IT CROWNED A hill that nestled against the backdrop of the majestic peaks of Mount Zara and Profitis Ilias. Deep ravines encased it, and the natural slopes leading up to the sheer walls were steep and treacherous. Mycenae, "rich in gold," was also a nearly impregnable citadel.

Of course, it was not Agamemnon's city. That had been burned and plundered and razed in the reign of Orestes' son Tisamenus. Somewhere nearby there must be ancient graves, perhaps still filled with the treasure of Troy. But the survivors of that final catastrophe had not been many; the descendants of Agamemnon's army had submitted to the invading Dorians and intermarried with them. This was a new city, built upon the ruins of Agamemnon's capital some three hundred years ago, and it was neither particularly large, nor rich.

Their intelligence suggested that the city consisted of no more than eight hundred citizens and held a total population of thirty-five hundred souls, including women, children, and slaves. The city was, according to the merchants they questioned, "allied" with Argos, but the alliance appeared to have been forced on them none too willingly fifteen or more Olympiads ago. The Tegean trader who was their principal informant insisted that the Mycenaeans were very proud of their individual identity and did not consider themselves Argives, although they were clearly within the Argolid and paid heavy tribute to Argos.

Leonidas knew that, but it was the other Mycenae that transfixed him. Agamemnon had commanded a united Greek force—a thousand ships filled with fighting men—and he had taken the army across the Aegean to defeat the leading power of Asia. The key to that success had been unity, based on the oath sworn at the Horse Grave above the Eurotas valley. Surely, unity could give them even greater strength in defense? United against Persia, Hellas could be made invincible. But how could you unite if you spent half your time destroying each other's crops, burning down mills, breaking bridges, and slaughtering livestock, as he had just spent the last month doing?

Leonidas had, from the start, given the order that they would take no slaves. Resistance was to be overwhelmed and anyone who fought them killed, but the women, children, aged, and infirm were sent back to Argos. The policy had two advantages. First, his troops were not distracted by guarding captives; and second, it increased the number of Argive mouths to be fed on dwindling supplies as the destruction of stores and crops started to bite. It was a rational policy, but hardly an inspiring one. Leonidas, no less than his troops, was tired of chopping down orchards, choking up irrigation ditches with debris, tearing down bridges, burning mills, and slaughtering more livestock than they could eat.

Combined with the devastating defeat Argos had suffered at Sepeia, Leonidas believed they would succeed in pacifying the Argive border for a generation. What came after that, he supposed, was a renewal of the fighting at a higher level of intensity. He might not live to see it, but his children would—unless they could come up with a more permanent solution. Kyranios had always said war was the failure of diplomacy...

Oliantus had served with Leonidas over a decade now, and he was the first to notice that Leonidas was brooding. "What are you planning, Leo?"

"I'm just thinking."

"You aren't listening to what we've been saying about the gates or the watch."

"I've listened enough to know we're not likely to take Mycenae without casualties. That's the damned thing about walls. We may scorn them, but they do serve a purpose."

The others, who had been discussing various means of attack, drawing figures in the dirt and moving pebbles representing units around in it, stopped and looked at Leonidas expectantly. To state anything this obvious was almost unworthy of a Spartan, and so the others waited to find out what he was really thinking. "I think we should offer to negotiate."

That stunned them for a moment, and then they all seemed to be talking at once. Their remarks and objections boiled down to: "What is there to negotiate?" Their orders were to weaken Argos' ability to wage war on Lacedaemon without attacking the city itself.

Leonidas walked away from the dirt sketch and stood leaning against a long-needled pine tree, gazing at the city backed up against Mount Zara. They would be attacking uphill without the support of archers or javelins. Even if they reached the walls without undue casualties, they would find it difficult to force the gates or scale the walls. Just two days ago, Leonidas had lost three men in a surprise encounter with mercenaries coming down from Arcadia. That put total losses to date at more than ten. Leonidas did not want more. "I think I'll go and talk to them."

"No, you won't," Oliantus countered instantly, straightening up from his crouch over the map in the dirt. "If you want to negotiate, you can send one of us," he told his commander and friend.

"I could," Leonidas agreed with a grin, "but then I wouldn't see the city and its defenses or its defenders for myself, would I? I'll go, but I'll take you with me, if you like."

———

They sent a herald first, of course, to announce their desire to parley; and after a very short time the herald returned with an olive branch. Leonidas removed his sword and handed it to Meander; then he set his helmet on his head, tipped back to show his face, and set out with a similarly unarmed Oliantus at his side. He designated the commander of the Heraklid Company, Pitanate Lochos—the debonair Dienekes—as his successor if he failed to return.

"Any orders, sir?" Dienekes asked.

"If they are so barbaric as to murder a man carrying the olive branch, take and raze the town to the ground, and then slaughter all the inhabitants, old and young."

"Of course, sir," came the almost insulted answer. That was obvious.

They were admitted through a small door in the wall beside the gate. Both Leonidas and Oliantus looked up, carefully and professionally estimating the height and width of the wall. They looked instinctively for weaknesses.

They were met at the other side by a troop of six fully armed hoplites with their helmets down over their faces. These men looked fit and determined, Leonidas noted; and although each man was self-equipped with armor and arms of his own choosing, there was nothing rusted or ill-kept in their appearance.

This escort led up a narrow street with a number of modest temples. Leonidas noted one to Eileithyia, depicted holding out her hands to a smiling infant. Leonidas saw Agiatis' features on the child, and he felt a sharp stab of homesickness. From inside came the keening of women, apparently in mourning or prayer for some young mother even now struggling in childbed.

They reached a modest agora, flanked by stoas on three sides that fronted small shops. On the fourth side, a large and elegant fountain house with a double row of columns housed an expansive room with deep marble basins fed from nine bronze spouts. It reminded the intruders that the Perseia Fountain provided this citadel with ample and perpetual supplies of water, making sieges more difficult. But there was no way of judging the state of their other supplies, as the shops were closed up and the agora deserted.

They turned a corner and passed an impressive temple evidently dedicated to Zeus. The pediment depicted Zeus handing a sword to Perseus. It was quite new, with an encircling colonnade, and the painted figures of the frieze and pediment stood out in sharp contrast to the dark blue of the background. That suggested considerable wealth, Leonidas noted.

At last they stopped before an old building with a narrow porch raised some five steps above the level of the street. They were taken up the steps and into a chamber with tiers of benches on three sides, evidently some kind of council chamber or assembly room.

Leonidas hadn't a clue what form of government this obscure, secondary city had, except that it was unlikely to be a monarchy. He presumed it was also less democratic than Athens, and that made it an oligarchy of some sort. At all events, he was facing ten old men.

"You wished to speak with us, Spartan?"

"Who are you?"

"The Governing Council of Mycenae. And you?"

"I am the commanding officer of the Lacedaemonian army surrounding this city. My orders are to subdue the Argolid and render it incapable of threatening us for another generation. Those orders could be interpreted to mean I should seize and raze Mycenae." Leonidas was watching the faces of the men opposite him very carefully. He had the impression he was not telling them anything they didn't already know. They, too, had spies.

"So why are you here, Spartan? Do you want us to surrender our freedom without a fight?" The man who said this was trembling slightly as he spoke. Leonidas considered him. He was not trembling from fear. Possibly it was just a frailty of age—or the power of his emotions. His eyes were milky with cataracts, but he sat very straight, wrapped in a soft woolen himation with a wide border of mythical beasts in rusts and greens.

"I know little of your city, but I was told you pay homage to Argos."

"Argos takes from us one-third of our olive-oil harvest, one-fourth of our wine, 100 head of cattle, 200 sheep, and 166 goats each year—and it led 116 of our finest young men to their deaths at Sepeia."

That did not sound like a declaration of loyalty.

"And what do you get in return?"

There was a long pause. The old man just sat with tears dripping slowly down his face, and finally one of the other men admitted, "Nothing." The man seemed to think about it and then added, "Nothing at all."

"You call that freedom?" Leonidas asked.

Another man spoke up, more hotly than the other two. "We still live by our own laws. We have our temples, our festivals and customs. We can sacrifice at the graves of our fathers. Our daughters go intact to their marriage beds, and our sons learn the use of spear and sword."

"That is true in Tegea, Corinth, and Elis as well."

"What does that have to do with anything?" the hot-headed man demanded; but the older man stirred himself and hushed his younger colleague. He focused his not entirely blind eyes hard on Leonidas while explaining to his impatient colleague, "Tegea, Corinth, and Elis are allies of Lacedaemon."

"We don't require tribute," Leonidas reminded him.

"Just obedience. To follow wherever your kings lead." Yet another member of the council spoke up.

"If a majority in the League Assembly approves," Leonidas reminded them. Leonidas was acutely aware that the changes in League leadership imposed upon his brother and characterized as "humiliating" by Leotychidas, Brotus, and others might prove decisive in avoiding bloodshed today. He pressed the point. "Your vote would be equal to ours."

The Mycenaeans exchanged glances and then put their heads together, to whisper among themselves. One cut the others short and asked the Spartans to step out into the street while they discussed the proposal.

On the porch, Oliantus murmured, "Are you sure you have authority to offer this?"

"Why shouldn't I?"

"Only the ephors can sign treaties, and the Assembly has to ratify."

"Do you think they would reject an application by Mycenae to join the League?"

"You *never* know what the Assembly will decide," Oliantus warned. "Especially not when Leotychidas and his clique start their whisper campaigns!"

The Mycenaeans, however, were finished with their internal discussion and called the Spartans back inside. The spokesman asked, "Are those your terms? That we become an ally of Lacedaemon?"

"That you break with Argos and join our allies, yes," Leonidas clarified.

The Mycenaeans again looked at one another, and then the spokesman asked, "What is your name, young man?"

"Does that matter?"

"It does. You seem very young to have so much authority, and you offer us something that seems quite unimaginable. We came here expecting demands of abject submission. We thought you would want us to hand over our daughters and humiliate ourselves in front of you. We thought you would take away our youths for your own pleasures and demand tribute that would leave us nothing at all but the naked walls of our homes."

"You were wrong." Leonidas insisted.

"But how can we know this is not just a trick—a way to make us let down our defenses and open our gates to your brutal troops?"

"I am Leonidas, son of Anaxandridas, brother of Cleomenes. I am a direct descendant of Herakles through my father and my mother both. My word is good. And I give it to you."

It frightened Leonidas a little to realize how much he enjoyed saying that—and it surprised him even more how effective it was.

———

The arrival of Demaratus, with the active Kastor Companies of each lochos, marked the end of Leonidas' independent command in the Argolid. He regretted that a little, because he had talked Tiryns as well as Mycenae into abandoning their traditional alliance with Argos and joining the Peloponnesian League. But it was almost two months since he had seen his wife and daughter, and he was ready to go home.

Demaratus invited Leonidas to dine with him. "You'll want to hear the news," he surmised.

Leonidas did, so he accepted. To his surprise, they dined alone, attended only by Demaratus' helots. There being no couches, they sat on folding stools next to a low table. "You know we put your brother on trial for treason because he failed to take Argos?" Demaratus opened, once the pleasantries about families had been perfunctorily exchanged.

"I know Leotychidas wanted to."

"Ah, yes. Leotychidas." Demaratus said the name with a twisted smile of hatred. "The unscrupulous are capricious."

"Meaning?"

"Your brother bought his loyalty back—though I don't know the price. The charges were brought by Orthryades, Lysimachos, and Talthybiades—backed stubbornly and none too cleverly by your other brother Brotus. Brotus tried to dig up the old issue of Cleomenes having no right to the throne in the first place. He claimed his madness was the Gods' way of telling us we had picked the wrong man. He was so convinced by his own arguments that he was already planning his move into the royal palace. I think his wife had even started packing."

Leonidas laughed shortly at Brotus' expense, remembering that his mother and Dorieus, too, had singularly failed to see that their view on Cleomenes' legitimacy was not shared by the rest of the polity. The three citizens were the real danger, not Brotus. Brotus was just their tool. The first two men were bitter malcontents, and the latter a man of driving but dubious ambition. "I gather my older brother was acquitted—or is Brotus now the Agiad king?"

Demaratus shrugged and narrowed his eyes at Leonidas. "Brotus would make as bad a king as Cleomenes."

Leonidas held his tongue—feeling it was disloyal to make disparaging remarks about his twin to the Eurypontid monarch, but not prepared to perjure himself by defending Brotus, either.

Demaratus understood him perfectly and sipped from the heavily watered wine. He nodded, apparently to himself, and then resumed the conversation. "Cleomenes was acquitted. He managed to convince the ephors that he had a clear and unambiguous sign from Hera that the attack on Argos was opposed by the Gods. They believed him."

Again, Leonidas thought silence was the only prudent response.

"You know," Demaratus remarked, sipping again without taking his eyes off Leonidas' face, "if you were anyone other than who you are, I might start to like you."

"Likewise." Demaratus laughed.

"Then let us pretend we are not who we are," Demaratus suggested.

Leonidas shrugged agreement; but he wasn't drinking even the light wine now, just waiting tensely to find out what this was all about.

"Cleomenes is a dangerous and unstable man. He has led us into one adventure after another—and he very likely *would* have gotten us embroiled in the futile Ionian revolt if it hadn't been for his daughter—your wife."

Leonidas acknowledged that with a nod. He was proud of Gorgo's role in the incident.

"He is unfit to be king in dangerous times."

Leonidas shifted uncomfortably. This was very definitely treason.

Demaratus appeared to sense his discomfort and changed the subject. "You've heard that the Persians are not content with defeating and punishing the Ionian rebels?"

"What more can they do?" Leonidas asked angrily, remembering the bay full of little corpses.

"They plan to punish Athens for providing support early in the rebellion," Demaratus explained. Leonidas stirred uneasily but said nothing, forcing Demaratus to continue. "If they send a fleet and army to take Attica, they will not stop there. The Persians are nothing if not greedy—and thorough."

"The Isthmus is eminently defensible."

"Indeed; but the army that lands in the Laconian Gulf will have already burnt our farms, slaughtered our livestock, and raped our women before they meet us at the Isthmus."

There it was again, the need for a fleet—a real fleet, not the handful of triremes Lacedaemon could launch now. Leonidas nodded, and asked, "So what do you think we should do?"

"Well, let me put it this way: the Persians can certainly overwhelm us if they *want* to. The key, therefore, is to convince them they do *not* want to. In short, to convince them that the conquest of Greece is more expensive and troublesome than it is worth. That will mean allying ourselves with Athens; but Cleomenes, with his history of interference in Athenian affairs, is not the best man to pursue such a policy."

"My brother is unpredictable. He might just decide to support Athens because it is what no one expects him to do."

Demaratus considered this with raised eyebrows and then conceded, "Perhaps," without sounding convinced. Then he went on: "And, of course, Athens itself might decide to submit to Persia. After all, there is nothing more fickle than the Athenian Assembly—a few more potters, tinkers, or cobblers bought by this speaker or the next, and their policy changes from black to white. Like a school of fish, one minute they're swimming one way and the next another—and all for no apparent reason!"

Leonidas laughed at the vivid and apt image.

Demaratus did not join him, but looked thoughtful. "You're a good man, Leonidas, and respect for you is growing. You are credited with the decision to keep at least one lochos in the field here, which is why the Council put your name forward to the Assembly as Kyranios' successor to the post of lochagos of the Mesoan Lochos." Leonidas nodded; he had received this news officially more than a month ago.

"Furthermore, bringing Mycenae and Tiryns into the League was greeted with genuine enthusiasm by the Assembly," Demaratus continued. "More and more people think you would be a better king than either of your brothers. But you have one serious flaw."

"Namely?"

"You lack ambition."

Not as much as you think, Leonidas noted mentally, but answered with, "Ambition did not bring my brothers either honor or glory."

"True. And Dorieus had enough ambition for the lot of you, didn't he?"

It seemed a rhetorical question, so Leonidas left it unanswered.

"Sometimes, Leonidas," Demaratus observed, scratching his beard thoughtfully, "we cannot escape our destiny, but sometimes we have a hand in shaping it. Your brothers have tried too hard to make the world dance to their tune, but you might be better advised to try a little harder. When the Gods give a man a gift, they are insulted if he discards it carelessly."

"What gift would that be?" Leonidas asked.

Demaratus tipped up his kothon and drank deeply, covering his face for a moment. When he finished, he tossed the dregs aside with a quick flick of his wrist and looked hard at Leonidas again. "I think you know exactly what I mean, and your pretense of being thick is wearing thin."

Leonidas looked down into the broad bowl of his own kylix. Demaratus traveled with the finest of Lacedaemonian pottery and the best Laconian white wine. Leonidas could see right through the white wine to the beautifully painted image of a smiling female sphinx with spread wings on a white field. She seemed to share his secret. Leonidas had no intention of letting Sparta fall into the hands of Brotus—much less the likes of Talthybiades, Lysimachos, and Orthryades. But until he had a son, he did not see how he could lay claim to a regency. No one was going to recognize Agiatis as heir to the Agiad throne any more than Gorgo herself.

"We could work together, Leonidas," Demaratus spoke, so softly not even the helots could hear. "For Lacedaemon's good, we *should* work together; because, I warn you, I cannot work with your elder brother much longer. If I must, I will find a way to bring him down."

"And have Brotus take his place?"

"The number of citizens in Sparta who do not want either of your brothers to command our army—particularly in time of crisis—is growing daily. You didn't become the youngest commander in the Spartan army without strong support in the Council, in the army, and in Assembly."

"That may be true, but if so, I won respect for being just what I am: a law-abiding Spartan Peer. I have not bribed or begged, threatened or flattered. Why should I change now?"

Demaratus looked at him hard, and Leonidas met his eyes. What Demaratus clearly wanted was for him to set his father-in-law aside and seize control of the Agiad throne in his own right. Were he a ruling king, and were the kings working together (rather than against one another, as was so common in the history of the two royal houses), they could together easily defeat the machinations of Leotychidas against Demaratus. But Leonidas did not feel it was his duty to save Demaratus from his cousin.

Demaratus shrugged, and looked around for a helot to refill his kylix. "Well, I guess you can lead a horse to water, but you can't make him drink." Then after a pause he added, with narrowed eyes, "Or are you even cleverer than I have been giving you credit for?"

Leonidas did not feel clever. He could see that beyond Leotychidas' determination to destroy Demaratus, the madness of one brother and the ambitions of the other were providing sinister individuals with a constellation of forces they could exploit for their own purposes. Cleomenes' madness was making even those most loyal to the Spartan constitution question whether Sparta could afford a madman at her helm.

Leonidas could see that Sparta was teetering on the edge of crisis, but he could not see what he could do to prevent it without breaking the law. Since he had been a child, obedience to Sparta's laws had defined him. As long as he had no son by Gorgo, Brotus was the heir to the Agiad throne, and in consequence any move against Cleomenes benefited only Brotus—not Sparta.

"What are you thinking, Little Leo?" Demaratus asked, bringing him out of his thoughts. The Eurypontid king was watching him with narrowed eyes over the lip of his kylix, and Leonidas was reminded of the humiliations Demaratus' father had subjected him to as a boy and of Demaratus' arrogance when he was younger.

Leonidas stood so he was looking down at Demaratus. "You do your case no good by calling me 'Little Leo,' son of Ariston. If you had made fewer enemies in your long life, you would not find yourself so threatened by the likes of Leotychidas."

Demaratus sprang to his feet. "I didn't invite you here to submit to impudent lectures from the likes of you!"

"Then I will leave you," Leonidas answered calmly, and stepped through the tent flap out into the balmy night.

The camp was still, the fires out. The men had stretched out to sleep under the clear sky, and the sentries paced on the periphery. A dog howled in the distance, and the wind rustled the needles of the pine trees on the slope behind them. Leonidas looked to the stars and found the constellations: the Bears, Andromeda, Cassiopeia, Leo…

He sighed. What was he going to do if his duty to protect Sparta conflicted with his duty to respect her laws? Was it still honorable to obey the law if the price was to surrender the city into the hands of the unscrupulous? But if he broke the law, didn't he become unscrupulous himself? Could he place the preservation of his individual honor above the fate of the city? Would it not be better to sacrifice his honor for the good of Sparta than the other way around?

Leonidas didn't have the answers tonight, but he hoped he would when the time came. With his right hand he grasped the edge of his himation and slung it over his left shoulder. Then he set out silently across the camp, unconsciously following his own star.

HISTORICAL NOTES

ALTHOUGH WE KNOW VERY LITTLE ABOUT Leonidas during the period of his life described in this second book of the trilogy, we know that he married Gorgo—a woman described even by non-Spartans as particularly clever. We also know he was later elected to lead a coalition of Greek forces against the Persians in 481. These two facts tell us significant things about what kind of man Leonidas was, and so provide hints about what was happening in this stage of his life, against the background of his society and historical developments generally.

Turning first to Leonidas' election to lead the coalition against Persia: this fact has far too often been interpreted as simply a tribute to Sparta's position as the leading military power of the age. Such an interpretation ignores the fact that just two years after Leonidas' death, the same coalition preferred Athenian leadership to that of Leonidas' successor Pausanias—and Pausanias had just led the coalition to a spectacular victory at Plataea! Sparta was no less powerful in 478 than she had been in 480, and her reputation in arms was greater. If simply being Spartan was all that mattered to the allies, the coalition would have either accepted Pausanias or asked Sparta to send another Spartan general to replace him; it did neither. Just as Pausanias was *not* elected in 478, Leonidas *was* elected in 480—not because he was Spartan, but because of who he was.

With respect to Gorgo, we know that Leonidas married her

before he became king. We also know that at his death Gorgo was still of childbearing age. But if Leonidas was, as Herodotus claims, born only "shortly" after his brother Dorieus, he would have been roughly sixty years old at Thermopylae. There are two reasons why I believe this is unlikely. First, his performance at Thermopylae, in the forefront of one of the most bitterly fought phalanx battles in history, is improbable for a man of sixty. Hoplite fighting was grueling, even if it lasted only a few hours on a single day. Second, it would mean that he married a woman young enough to be his daughter, which was not Spartan custom. Based on these facts, I have hypothesized that Leonidas could not have been much more than forty-five at Thermopylae: forty-five being the age after which Spartan reservists were no longer called up for front-line service. Likewise, I believe Herodotus intentionally underestimated Gorgo's age in his depiction of her encounter with Aristagoras in order to discredit Cleomenes, and because girls' ages were unimportant to other Greeks. By lowering the age conventionally given to Leonidas by a decade and increasing Gorgo's by half that, I have made the age difference between them consistent with their relationship as suggested by the evidence, and more compatible with Spartan custom.

Even with this adjustment, Leonidas would almost certainly have been married once before his marriage with Gorgo, because Leonidas would still have reached the age of thirty before Gorgo reached a marriageable age in Sparta. Bachelors over the age of thirty faced severe sanctions in Sparta—and Leonidas was, if nothing else, a law-abiding Spartan citizen. I have therefore hypothesized a first marriage and widowhood to make Leonidas free to marry Gorgo when she comes of age.

The key historical events incorporated into this novel are the scene between Gorgo, her father, and Aristagoras, and the Battle of Sepeia between Sparta and Argos. The fact that Mycenae and Tiryns escaped Argive dominance and were briefly independent members of the Peloponnesian League is another, often overlooked, consequence of the defeat of Argos at Sepeia. It reinforces Sparta's deserved reputation for sophisticated diplomacy, which left cities (except, notably, Messenia) their independence. While there is no historical evidence for Leonidas' playing a role either in the battle or in this diplomatic coup, I think the fact that he was later elected leader of all the Greeks opposed to Persia suggests he had a reputation, for both military competence and fair treatment of allies, that justified such trust. These events seemed a likely means for him to have earned that trust.

Cleomenes' campaigns against Athens and the successful Corinthian challenge to Sparta, which resulted in a significant change in the character of the Peloponnesian League, are also historical fact. The significance of the alteration of League voting rules can hardly be overstated. Equally important is that members of the League did not owe Sparta tribute. These are key features that made the Peloponnesian League less oppressive than Athens' Delian League would later be.

The Ionian revolt, the Athenian support for that uprising, and the defeat of the combined rebel fleet were also historical events. Although touched on only tangentially in this novel, these are the events that ultimately led to the Persian invasions of 490 and 480.

The main focus of this novel, however, has been character development and descriptions of society, rather than events. As in *A Boy of the Agoge* and my other novels set in Sparta, the Spartan society I describe is based on both research and common sense. I have drawn heavily on Conrad Stibbe and his depiction of archaic Sparta and on Thomas Figueira, who effectively refutes allegations that the Spartan population was already declining in the second half of the sixth century BC. Until the earthquake of 465, Spartiate population was increasing and causing significant social pressures and problems, such as those described in this novel.

Altogether, the depiction of Sparta in this novel differs from many stereotypes of Sparta not because I am ignorant of the usual allegations of pederasty, brutality, ignorance, humorlessness, and boorishness, but because analysis of the evidence decisively refutes these stereotypes and I consciously wanted to portray a Sparta that is closer to the historical Sparta based on the breadth of information available to us today. Let me address some of the most glaring misconceptions about Sparta common to many works of fiction and nonfiction alike.

Art and Culture: Even if Spartan sculpture and architecture never attained the heights known in Athens, Sparta was anything but a city without art, culture, or notable architecture. Sparta had a highly developed pottery industry that was not eclipsed by that of Athens until the fifth century. Its bronzeworks were coveted and exported throughout the known world, particularly in the sixth century BC. Its sculptors received commissions in Olympia and Delphi. Its dance and music were considered so superior that they attracted mass tourism, and artists from other parts of Greece competed for the honor of participating in Spartan musical festivals. The city itself was different from other Greek cities, but it was not just a collection of villages, nor was it lacking any of the features that characterized Greek cities—agora, theater, fountains, gymnasia, palaestra, temples, shrines, memorials —except walls. The Roman commentator Pausanias, who claims to have recorded only the "most significant sites," describes 100 shrines, 46 temples, and many other war memorials, graves, and statues in his description of Sparta in the second century AD. For a more detailed description of what Sparta was like in the age of Leonidas, see my articles *The Land of Leonidas* and *In Search of Sparta*.

Dress and Grooming: Some modern depictions of Spartans show them as shaggy, unkempt men with scrawny, chest-long beards and wild, tangled hair hanging around their shoulders. Other novelists have described them as stinking, filthy, and slovenly. These images contradict the historical record and existing archaeological evidence. Herodotus makes a great point of how the Spartans groomed themselves before Thermopylae. A statue fragment found in the heart of Sparta and dating from the early fifth century (commonly—or affectionately—referred to as Leonidas) shows a man with a clipped beard and neat hair. Earlier archaic artwork unanimously shows men with short beards and long, but very neat, "locks" of hair. Whether these locks were in fact braided or plaited in some way it is not possible to tell from the stylized nature of the evidence. However, it is physically impossible to keep long hair neat and in orderly strands when engaged in sports and other strenuous activities unless it is carefully confined in some way. Thus, practical modern experience suggests that Spartan men did braid their hair, something that is consistent with if not definitively proved by the archaeological evidence. Braiding has the added advantage of being something that can be done quickly and alone if necessary, or done elaborately with the help—as every Spartan would have had—of an attendant. This would have been a way for men to express individual taste and personality within the rigid limits of Sparta's code about not displaying wealth, and again consistent with remarks attributed to Lycurgus about long hair making an ugly man uglier and a handsome one handsomer.

As for Spartan women, there is no reason to believe that they, any more than women anywhere in the world in any period of history, were immune to the fundamental vice of vanity. On the contrary, contemporary plays depicting Spartan women (such as *Andromache* by Euripides) stress rather the reverse: that Spartan women were luxury-loving and excessively vain. Aristotle accuses Spartan women of pathological greed and portrays them as completely self-indulgent. More significantly, jewelry has been found in archaeological finds in Laconia. The fact that Sparta's lawgiver Lycurgus is credited with prohibiting the use of gold and silver as currency is not the same thing as prohibiting women from adorning themselves with these metals, much less with other decorative items. I have opted to show Sparta as a society in transition, where some women still wear jewelry, particularly the queens, but where a faction is becoming radicalized and scorns traditional forms of female adornment.

Illiteracy: Spartans could not have commanded the respect of the ancient world, engaged in complicated diplomatic maneuverings, or attracted the sons of intellectuals like Xenophon to their public school if they had been as illiterate and uneducated as some modern writers like to portray them. Clearly Spartans knew their laws very well, they could debate in international forums, and their sayings were considered so witty that they were collected by their contemporaries. Furthermore, Sparta is known to have entertained leading philosophers and to have had a high appreciation of poetry, as evidenced by her many contests and festivals for poetry in the form of lyrics. The abundant inscriptions and dedications found in Sparta are clear testimony to a literate society; one does not brag about one's achievements in stone if no one in your society can read! Likewise, Sparta sent written orders to its commanders, and anecdotal evidence suggests that mothers and sons exchanged letters.

Institutionalized Pederasty: There is absolutely no evidence of pederasty in Spartan society during the age of Leonidas or in the centuries before. Herodotus tells several tales of Spartan men showing loyalty to and affection for their wives, and of men being sexually attracted to other men's wives or young maidens, but tells not one tale of Spartan homosexual lovers. Xenophon, the only historian with firsthand experience of the agoge, states explicitly: "... [Lycurgus] ... laid down that in Sparta, lovers should refrain from molesting boys just as much as parents avoid having intercourse with their children or brothers with their sisters." It is hard to find a more definitive statement than this, and from the most credible source. To dismiss this evidence simply because it does not suit preconceived ideas is arrogant.

Xenophon goes on to add: "It does not surprise me, however, that some people do not believe this, since in many cities the laws do not oppose lusting after boys." And this is the crux of the matter. All of our written sources on Sparta come from those other cities, where pederasty was rampant. In short, the bulk of the written record on Sparta comes from men who could not imagine a world without pederasty. But then, neither could they imagine women who were educated, physically fit, and economically powerful who were not also licentious and lewd.

Modern readers ought to be more open-minded and admit that pederasty is not inherent in society—particularly not in a society where women are well integrated. My thesis is supported by another ancient authority, Aristotle, who blamed all of Sparta's ills (from his point of view) on the fact that the women were in control of things, a fact that he in turn attributed to the *lack* of homosexuality in Spartan society.

In this, Aristotle exhibits an astonishing appreciation of psychology, which modern research conclusively supports. We now know that male victims of child abuse grow up into misogynous men. The status of women in Athens fits this description perfectly, while the status of women in Sparta completely contradicts—indeed, refutes— the thesis that Spartan men were systematically subjected to sexual abuse by their elders.

Finally, I would like to call on the archaeological evidence. To date—in sharp contrast to the case of other Greek cities—no Spartan homoerotic artwork has been found. Since the Spartan legacy of artifacts is somewhat less plentiful than that of Athens, Corinth, or other cities, maybe something will still turn up; but until that happens, the evidence is against institutionalized pederasty in the agoge of the archaic and early classical periods—and against widespread homosexuality among adult Spartans as well.

Kryptea: The kryptea was a secret organization within a secretive society, and contemporary observers knew very little about it—meaning that we know even less. Allegedly it was composed of young Spartans who by night murdered innocent helots deemed dangerous to the Spartan state. In the late fifth century it was responsible for a couple of credibly recorded incidents in which helots were "disappeared." However, the origins of the organization—although attributed by Aristotle to Lycurgus—are unknown, and there is good reason to doubt that it was a fundamental feature of Spartan society throughout Spartan history. First, the murder of helots without any form of due process would have been disruptive to an economy based on helot labor, and many Spartiate landowners would have been outraged to have their best workers murdered. Second, it is not plausible that a population terrorized by the constant threat of arbitrary murder would have rendered the good service that Spartan helots did throughout the archaic period, and through Thermopylae itself.

In my earlier novel *Are They Singing in Sparta?*, I hypothesized that the kryptea was initially an irregular military unit used for conducting guerrilla operations during the Second Messenian War. I suggested that at that time it killed only helots who were in rebellion against the Spartan state, and none that were peacefully working on estates. I further suggested that after the conclusion of the Messenian war, the kryptea evolved into a kind of secret police charged with eliminating "traitors"—not on a whim but when ordered by someone in authority, whether ephors, kings, or Gerousia. It was this concept of the kryptea that I also employed in *Spartan Slave, Spartan Queen* and in *The Olympic Charioteer*.

However, Dr. Nic Fields recently noted that there is in fact no evidence that the kryptea existed prior to the helot revolt of 465. This is a very significant observation, as it suggests that the kryptea may in fact have been created as a *response* to that revolt. Such a theory would be completely consistent with the evidence of a stable society in which art and trade flourished throughout the archaic period, followed by a society in crisis and decay after the earthquake and revolt. The kryptea is an organization that fits well in a society that has become paranoid and xenophobic, but is incomprehensible in a stable, well-functioning society such as archaic Sparta. Thus, I have removed all reference to the kryptea from this novel.

Marriage Customs: Spartan marriage customs were viewed as peculiar even in ancient times—as was almost everything about Spartan women. Because all our sources on marriage are foreign, however, everything we are told about the alleged customs is highly suspect. In fact, almost everything said about Spartan marriage customs is contradicted somewhere else. For example, Lycurgus allegedly prohibited women from having dowries so that young men would select their brides for their virtues rather than their possessions; but we know for a fact that women inherited property and controlled vast fortunes, and that women (Lysander's daughters) lost prospective husbands because of inadequate dowries. It is impossible to legislate against greed. Another example is Plutarch's description on one page of how girls and women engaged in sports and danced nude "with the young men looking on," only to claim a few pages later that Spartan husbands often had children before they saw their wives by daylight—as if the girls who danced, raced, and swam nude in public weren't the same girls who became their wives.

Certainly, we know absolutely nothing about the reasons why Spartans apparently took their brides by stealth, rather than in a public festival as in most of the ancient world. Modern speculation about cross-dressing rituals and the need to accustom homosexual men to heterosexual sex are pure speculation and mostly nonsensical. (See note on institutionalized pederasty above.)

It is also important to keep in mind that despite the alleged ritual of a bridegroom coming for his bride by stealth, every reliable source on Sparta makes it clear that Spartan fathers, no less than fathers elsewhere, chose their daughters' husbands; and in the case of orphaned heiresses, the kings controlled the marriage. Furthermore, there is every indication that a marriage contract of some kind was made between the families of the bride and groom before the staged abduction. As far as can be determined today, the contract whether verbal or written, not the consummation, was what made a marriage legally binding.

Oppression of Helots: The status of helots in Sparta was significantly better than that of chattel slaves in the rest of Greece. Helots could not be bought and sold—chattel slaves could. Helots retained as much as 50 per cent of the fruits of their labor—chattel slaves, nothing. Helots had functioning family groups—chattel slaves were completely cut off from their families, and often did not know the names or locations of their parents, siblings, or children. Helots could marry and have children—chattel slaves were usually locked up in separate accommodations to prevent any intercourse between slaves, but could be sexually abused by their masters and their masters' friends at will. Any child born to a chattel slave was the master's property to expose (kill), sell, or retain for personal service. The better status of helots is underlined by the fact that 20,000 Athenian slaves ran away to join the Spartans in 413 BC, when a Spartan army was close enough to Athens to give them prospects of successfully escaping pursuit by their masters.

The prevalence of chattel slavery in the rest of the Greek world means that in all probability, the perioikoi and certainly travelers to Sparta would have had such slaves. A slave retained his or her unfree status unless explicitly emancipated; thus, human beings who had been sold as slaves in distant markets would still be slaves in Sparta. Ambiguous references in ancient sources suggest that Spartiates occasionally acquired these slaves. Since helot labor was predominantly agricultural, and helots could not be bought or sold outside of Lacedaemon, Spartiates may have purchased specialist labor abroad as needed; and they would, of course, have occasionally acquired slaves through capture or because parents sold their children into slavery—something that is still done in some parts of the world today.

It is also important for readers to distinguish (as ancient historians singularly fail to do) between the helots of Laconia and the helots of Messenia. The Laconian helots were probably not of Greek origin, and may have been the descendants of the original inhabitants, conquered by the Achaeans as early as 1200 BC. By the time of the Dorian invasion, they were already in a subordinate status and appear to have harbored no memories of an age of independence. These helots furthermore appear to have been, on the whole, completely reconciled to their status, and as such were reliable and trusted, albeit second-class, members of Spartan society. They provided the labor that kept the economy going and provided essential support troops for the army. The helots of Messenia, in contrast, had been conquered in the seventh or eighth century BC by the Spartans themselves. They retained a collective memory of being free, and this made them more resentful of their status as helots. The irony is that when other Greeks conquered other cities—as in Athens' victory over Melos in 416—it was common to slaughter the men and then carry off all the women and children as chattel slaves, sending out settlers to take over the conquered land. The Spartans' comparatively humane treatment of the Messenians, which enabled them to retain their identity, created a constant threat and earned them a modern reputation for brutality that ignores the alternative: Athens' method of outright slaughter, rape, pillage, and chattel slavery.

Finally, historical sources that describe the rounding up and killing of rebellious and potentially rebellious helots date from a period later than that of this novel, and they describe isolated incidents—not a continuous pattern, as modern writers too often impute. They occurred after a devastating earthquake that killed an estimated twenty thousand people—and after a significant revolt by the Messenian helots, who sought to exploit Sparta's weakness following the earthquake. The Spartan attitude toward helots after the traumatic effect of the double blow of earthquake and revolt is comparable to the impact of the terrorist attacks of September 11, 2001 upon the American psyche. Sparta's attitude toward its subject population turned radically intolerant following the shocks of 465-460 BC.

Xenophobia: Throughout the archaic and into the classical period, Sparta was not a xenophobic society. It welcomed poets, musicians, and philosophers from around the world, and these not only came to but often spent years in Sparta—as did, for example, the poets Alkman and Tyrtaios and the philosopher Pythagoras. Lesser-known foreigners came yearly as tourists to see Sparta's famous festivals, particularly the Gymnopaedia and the Hyacinthia. Meanwhile, Spartan athletes competed at the pan-Hellenic games in Olympia, Delphi, and Isthmia. Sparta maintained permanent representatives in Delphi, and sent envoys more than once to the court of the Persian king.

Furthermore, while Sparta itself was landlocked, Lacedaemon had ports that gave access to the Laconian and Messenian Gulfs and directly to both the Ionian and Aegean Seas. These ports facilitated trade with the rest of the ancient world, an activity that inherently led to contact and exchange. Sparta did not depend in the same way that Athens and Corinth did on imported materials (particularly grain), and its citizens did not live from trade. Nevertheless, Spartans were not inherently insular, paranoid, and xenophobic, as too many modern writers suggest. Spartans did not need to trade or become craftsmen themselves in order to enjoy and benefit from trade and manufacturing, because they could rely on the perioikoi to do the trading and manufacturing for them. The perioikoi, in turn, benefited significantly from a monopoly on trade and manufacturing in one of the largest and most fertile territories in Greece, which accounts for their loyalty to Sparta until Sparta's decadence and decline in the fourth century.

However, following the shock of the earthquake and helot revolt of the early fifth century, Sparta was drawn into a bitter war with Athens. The Peloponnesian War became a further drain on Sparta's dwindling manpower, and contributed to a "siege mentality" that had already been sparked by the double blow of the earthquake and the helot revolt. This was reflected in a variety of ways, from increased secrecy and xenophobia to declining production of exportable artifacts. In short, the long-drawn-out war between Sparta and Athens undermined the foundations of both societies. The Peloponnesian War turned *both* Sparta and Athens into brutal imperialist tyrannies, and a shortage of manpower in Sparta led to a sustained crisis that ultimately led to Sparta's military and moral defeat. By then, however, Sparta had long since ceased to be the nation Leonidas would have recognized.

For more information on Sparta, visit my website: Sparta Reconsidered, www.elysiumgates.com/~helena.

PRESUMED ORGANIZATION OF THE SPARTAN ARMY IN 480 BC

THE ORGANIZATION OF THE SPARTAN ARMY changed over time as the population of Sparta came under increasing demographic pressure. The best ancient sources—Xenophon, Thucydides, Aristotle, and Plutarch—describe the Spartan army at a significantly later period than covered in this book. Furthermore, they describe an army created after the traumatic impact of the earthquake and helot revolt of ca. 465 BC. Since all modern sources agree that the Spartan army underwent a major reform in the midfifth century BC following the shocks of the earthquake and revolt, the only ancient source that provides information about the Spartan army during the life of Leonidas is Herodotus.

Herodotus writes that a Spartan force 2000 strong arrived in Athens one day too late for the Battle of Marathon (after an impressive forced march). He tells us that King Demaratus gave the total number of Spartiates as 8000, and that the "full" Spartan army of 5 lochagoi and 5000 Spartiates fought at the battle of Plataea.

For the purposes of this trilogy on Leonidas, I have therefore relied heavily on Thomas Figueira in his article "Population Patterns in Late Archaic and Classical Sparta," published in *Transactions of the American Philological Association 116* (1986), pp. 165-213. Based on Figueira's excellent data, I have evolved a simple and logical structure for the Spartan army that contradicts no known facts and provides a consistent framework for the events described in this novel. Since the characters in the novel are presumed to understand every aspect of this organization, the terms are not described in detail in the text. Instead, they are provided below.

In accordance with Demaratus' statement to Xerxes in Herodotus, I assume that the total adult male population of Sparta was 8000, with an average of 200 men in each age cohort. The "active army," composed of the first 10 age cohorts of young men (those required to sleep in barracks), was, therefore, 2000 men strong. This is consistent with the size of the force sent to assist Athens in 490. A "full" call-up would be a call-up of 15 classes (age cohorts) of reserves to produce an army of 5000 men, all of whom would be expected to be fit enough to march long distances and fight effectively in a phalanx. This is consistent with the force sent to Plataea. The remaining 3000 adult male citizens are presumed to be over the age of 45 and fit only for garrison duty and home defense.

I further assume that in the age of Leonidas, the largest unit in the Spartan army was the lochos. While this term is used by ancient sources to refer to a variety of large fighting units from different cities, it is the term Herodotus uses for the Spartan units at Plataea. Also, later in the fifth century the Spartan army deploys mora, composed of two lochos each. I further assume that perioikoi units of this period were *not* yet integrated into the Spartan line, but served as independent auxiliary units—including scouts, cavalry, and naval units. This is consistent with Herodotus' statement that Cleomenes deployed a purely Spartiate army against Argos, and that the Spartan army at Plataea consisted of 5000 Spartiates and 5000 perioikoi. Based on this assumption, Sparta sent her full standing army to support Athens during the Marathon campaign—the only response that I believe would have been commensurate with the threat posed and the urgency of the Athenian request.

Based on our knowledge of hoplite warfare, I assume that the very smallest unit in the army would be a section of 8 men. This represents one complete file of hoplites at more or less minimum strength, or one man on the battle line backed by seven comrades in single file behind him. Again, this assumption matches references to a Spartan unit called an enomotia, which numbered between 25 and 40 men—that is, between 3 and 5 sections. Finally, although the existence of a unit called a pentekostus cannot be traced back to before the reform of the Spartan army in the midfifth century, the need for flexibility and control in a highly organized force such as the Spartan army suggests that in Leonidas' time there must have been some intermediate unit between the tiny enomotia and the thousand-strong lochos of Plataea. Since pentekostus means "fiftieth," I have postulated a unit called a pentekostus, or company, which is initially 100 men strong (one-fiftieth of the full army) and expands as reserves are called up.

The organization of Spartan society was designed to enable the rapid call-up and integration of older age cohorts into the army when needed. This could best be achieved if reservists were, to the extent possible, reintegrated into the same units in which they had served when on active service. Thus, the size of individual units and the composition of units would have adjusted marginally to accommodate reservists called up whenever the Spartan leadership felt the 2000-man standing army was insufficient to the task assigned. Where entire units needed to be added, these too would be created out of a mix of active and reserve troops—but by splitting out men from the active units and merging them with the older cohorts under, predominantly, reserve officers. With an estimated 200 men in each age cohort, it is unlikely that the Spartan leadership would have reactivated troops in increments smaller than 5 age cohorts at a time.

Taking all of the above factors into account, I have hypothesized the following organization of the Spartan army:

Active Army (all adult males 21-30 years old): **2000 Men (size of the Spartan force sent to aid Athens in 490—Marathon campaign)**

- 5 lochos of 400 men each, composed of 4 pentekostus (companies)
- 20 pentekostus of 100 men each, composed of 3 enomotiai
- 60 enomotiai of 32 men each, composed of 4 sections of 8 men each
- 240 sections of 8 men each

Army After a Call-Up of 5 Classes of Reserves (all adult males 21-35 years old): **3000 Men**

- 5 lochos of 600 men each, composed of 5 pentekostus
- 25 pentekostus of 120 men each, composed of 4 enomotiai
- 100 enomotiai of 30 men each, composed of 4 sections of 7-8 men
- 400 sections of 7-8 men each

(Note: Here the organizational structure is expanded by 1 pentekostus and by 1 enomotia per pentekostus—or a total of 5 pentekostus and 40 enomotiai—at the expense of a slightly shallower line depth.)

Army After a Call-Up of 10 Classes of Reserves (all adult males 21-40): **4000 Men**

- 5 lochos of 800 men each, composed of 5 pentekostus
- 25 pentekostus of 160 men each, composed of 5 enomotiai
- 125 enomotiai of 32 men each, composed of 4 sections
- 500 sections of 8 men each

(Note: Here the organization is expanded by 1 enomotia per pentekostus, and the depth is restored to the line at the section level.)

Army After a "Full" Call-Up of 15 Classes of Reserves (all adult males 21-45): **5000 Men (size of the Spartan army at Plataea)**

- 5 lochos of 1,000 men each, composed of 5 pentekostus
- 25 pentekostus of 200 men each, composed of 5 enomotiai

- 125 enomotiai of 40 men each, composed of 5 sections
- 625 sections of 8 men each

(Note: Here the organization is strengthened by adding 1 section per enomotia; alternatively the Spartans might have preferred to retain an organization of 4 sections per enomotia, but increase the depth of the line to 10, i.e., 4 sections of 10 men.)

In addition to these active units, 300 young men of active-service age (21-30) would have been selected for the elite unit commonly called the Hippeis. The term *hippeis* has often been translated as "knights" and implies cavalry. However, the Spartan unit was purely infantry, and it served as the honor guard to Sparta's kings. I have therefore preferred to refer to it consistently as "the Guard" throughout my works.

Based on the above organization, the strength of the Spartan officer corps would have ranged from 335 in the active army units to 775 in a full call-up. Specifically, 5 lochagoi, 20-25 company commanders, 60-125 enomotarchs, and 240-625 section leaders, plus the Guard commander, his 3 company commanders, 10 enomotarchs, and 30 section leaders. The above number, however, includes only the tactical commanders. In fact, the army would have required a corps of logistical specialists, at least for the larger units (pentekostus/company and lochos), and it would have been logical for the lochagoi to have tactical deputies as well. In addition, there would have to be surgeons, priests, and salpinx players, all with important roles consistent with officer-like status. Thus, including the Guard and officer corps, Sparta's active army would have numbered something closer to 2750 men, and the army after a full call-up of 15 age cohorts would have theoretically numbered somewhat over 6000. In reality, no society can consistently produce exactly 200 healthy young males each year; and there would have been losses, particularly in the older age cohorts, due to accidents, illness, and war casualties. All in all, the rounded figures used here provide a workable framework.

Looking at each unit individually, here are the key facts:

Section: A unit of 7-8 men (1 file in a phalanx), all drawn from the same tribe. They would be commanded by a section leader, who would be selected as the most competent of the men from the oldest 5 age cohorts in the unit, and would stand at the front of the unit in battle. The section leaders would retain their rank on retirement, and in a call-up they would assume command of additional sections as required. In units with mixed active and reserve troops, the section leader would stand at the front with the other active troops in descending order of age, followed by reservists in ascending age order.

Enomotia: A unit of 30-40 men, composed of 3-5 sections (depending on the number of reserve classes called up). All men would come from the same tribe. They would be commanded by an enomotarch, and would also have a deputy with responsibility for supplies and provisioning, and a flautist to keep pace. Although this term is often translated as "platoon," I have opted to retain throughout this novel the Spartan designations for both the unit and the commanding officer, as these are widely used in ancient literature. The enomotarch would be selected from the section leaders and would usually be on the brink of retirement. On reaching age 31, an enomotarch would have the option either to go off active duty, or to remain with the army and pursue a career as an officer. Those who opted to retire would be eligible to serve in the rank of enomotarch with reserve units reactivated in a crisis.

Pentekostus (or Company): a unit of between 100 and 200 men (depending on the number of reserves called up), composed of 3-5 enomotia plus the commander, a deputy/quartermaster with responsibility for supplies and provisions, a salpinx player and/or a priest, and a medic. Since the term pentekostus is quite a mouthful and it is not recorded during Leonidas' period, I have often elected to use the more neutral-sounding "company" and "company commander." The company commander would always be a man of full-citizen status and age, with the equivalent of a permanent commission.

Lochos: a unit of between 400 and 1000 men (depending on the call-up), consisting of 4-5 companies plus a staff including 1 commander, 1 tactical deputy, 1 quartermaster, and 2-4 surgeons, priests, heralds, and salpinx players. Since this unit is variously translated as battalion, regiment, or division, I have decided to stick to the Spartan terms lochos and lochagos for unit and commander, respectively. The commander would be a man of full-citizen status with the equivalent of a permanent commission.

We know that the ancient Greeks generally tried to keep kinsmen and men from the same villages or boroughs together in military units. The presumption was that men were more likely to help their neighbors, and less likely to run away in front of people they knew. Sparta had five villages that became boroughs, and we know that at least one of the lochagoi deployed at Plataea was named for one of these. Thus I have named the five lochagoi after Sparta's five boroughs:

- Pitanate
- Mesoan
- Conouran
- Limnate
- Amyclaeon

For convenience I have assumed that each lochos was divided into the following companies, with the Lycurgan Company the designation for the reserve units created only during a call-up of 5 age cohorts or more:

- (1st) Heraklid Company
- (2nd) Kastor Company
- (3rd) Polydeukes Company
- (4th) Menelaion Company
- (5th) Lycurgan Company

The assumption is that roughly 40 men from each lochos retired from active service each year, and were replaced by the young men who had just attained their citizenship. A call-up of one class of reserves thus meant adding 200 additional men to the army. A call-up of 5 classes would mean an additional 1,000 men (see above).

GLOSSARY OF
GREEK TERMS

Agoge   The Spartan public school, attended by all boys from the ages of seven through twenty and by girls for a shorter period—probably from seven until they had their first period. The agoge was infamous throughout Greece for its harshness, discipline, and austerity; however, not—as many modern historians would have us think—for the exclusion of literacy, the arts, or intellectual training from the curriculum. On the contrary, ancient commentators claimed that "devotion to the intellect is more characteristic of Sparta than love of physical exercise." Furthermore, although the children lived in barracks, they were also introduced to democracy early by being organized into herds, or packs, which then elected their leaders. Nor, as many modern sources suggest, were they completely cut off from their families. They probably went home at holidays (of which there were at least twelve), and would have been able to see parents in the city almost any day. Sparta was a small society, and the agoge was in the middle of it.

Andron   The chamber in a private house where symposia were held. It was often provided with permanent benches or shelves built against the walls for the guests to recline upon.

Aspis   The round shield used by Greek heavy infantry. Often also referred to as the *hoplon*.

Chiton   The basic undergarment worn by both men and women. It could be long or short, belted or unbelted, and bound at one or both shoulders. Slaves seem more likely to have worn it clasped only on one shoulder, and short chitons for mature men were also associated with unfree status.

Cithara   An ancient stringed instrument.

Eirene   A Spartan youth, aged twenty, on the brink of citizenship and serving as an instructor in the agoge.

Ephors   Executives of the Spartan government elected from among the citizen body for one year. Any citizen could be elected ephor, but no citizen could serve in this capacity for longer than one term.

Enomotia   A unit of between thirty-two and forty men in the Spartan army, commanded by an enomotarch.

Gerousia   The Council of Elders in Sparta. This body consisted of twenty-eight elected members and the two kings. The elected members had to have attained the age of sixty, and were then elected for life. Although this institution was highly praised by commentators from other parts of Greece, who saw in the Council of Elders a check upon the fickleness of the Assembly, the senility of some Council members and the "notorious" timidity of the Council were often a source of frustration among younger Spartans.

Helots   The rural population of Lacedaemon, descended from the original settlers of the area. Helots were not slaves. (See Historical Notes for more information.)

Hetaera   In Athens, an expensive whore, patronized by the very rich. Hetaerae were the only women allowed to take part in symposia. The majority of hetaera were slaves, pimped by their masters.

Himation   The long, rectangular wrap used by both men and women as an outer garment.

Hippagre-tai	Three men appointed each year by the ephors as company commanders in the royal Guard. Each of the three men selected one hundred men to serve in his company.
Hippeis	The "Knights" or Guards; a three-hundred-strong unit of young Spartiates (aged 21-30) chosen by the hippagretai. They served as the personal bodyguard of the Spartan kings when on campaign, and appear to have also fulfilled certain police functions inside Lacedaemon. Appointment to the Guard was very prestigious and was reversible. Since the appointments were made annually, Guardsmen had to maintain their reputation throughout the year to ensure reappointment. Presumably a change in commander might also result in a change in Guard composition.
Hoplite	A Greek heavy infantryman.
Hoplon	The full kit of a Greek heavy infantryman, including armor, greaves, aspis, spear, and sword. Often used interchangeably with aspis, however, to refer to the round shield alone.
Hydria	A pitcher for water.
Keleustes	The officer aboard a Greek warship who commanded the rowers–watching for problems, relaying orders, and the like. A very important position requiring a great deal of skill, these men were in some ways more "professional" than the captains, who were simply men drawn from the upper classes, often for their ability to finance the construction of a ship. They, along with the helmsmen and bowmen, were the "mates" or "officers" of ancient ships.
Kleros	The land allotment granted each Spartan citizen on maturity as a result of the Lycurgan reforms. A kleros was allegedly large enough to provide for a man and his immediate family; and according to tradition, there were originally six thousand of these allotments. Another three thousand were added in the next century as the population grew, but it is impossible for all kleros to have been equally productive, so that increasing inequalities of wealth were inevitable.

Kothon   A drinking vessel similar to a modern mug, distinctive to Sparta. In most of Greece, drinking cups had two handles; in Sparta, just one.

Krater   A large jar of pottery or bronze for mixing water and wine to the desired level of alcoholic content.

Kryptea   The Spartan "secret police," made up of young citizens who were tasked with keeping rebellious helots under control. It was probably not formed until after the period described in this novel. (See Historical Notes.)

Kylix   A drinking vessel with a low, shallow bowl on a short stem. These could be quite large, requiring two hands to hold, and were often passed around at a symposium.

Lacedae-mon The correct designation of the ancient Greek city-state of which Sparta was the capital. Lacedaemon consisted originally of only the Eurotas valley in the Peloponnese, Laconia. In the late eighth century BC the valley to the west, Messenia, was captured and remained part of Lacedaemon until the fourth century BC. There were a number of other cities and towns in Lacedaemon, but the bulk of these were inhabited by perioikoi rather than Spartiates. The Spartiates were concentrated in Sparta because of the requirement of attending the messes (syssitia) on a nightly basis.

Lochagos/Lochagoi The commander of a lochos; lochagoi is the plural form.

Lochos   The main subdivision of the Spartan army; variously compared to a battalion, regiment, or division. It had an estimated peacetime strength of four hundred men and a maximum strength (full call-up of fifteen classes of reserves) of one thousand men. (See appendix on the Presumed Organization of the Spartan Army in 480 BC.)

Mastigo-phoroi The assistants to the headmaster of the Spartan agoge, responsible for maintaining discipline among the boys attending the agoge. Also, the assistants to the judges at Olympia, who were responsible for maintaining order among the spectators.

Meleirene A Spartan youth, aged nineteen, about to become an eirene, and two years from citizenship.

Metoikoi/ Metics In Athens, free men living in the city but not enjoying citizenship status. They were subject to special taxes and in need of an Athenian patron in order to be registered. Anyone living in Athens more than a month without being registered was liable to be arrested and sold into slavery.

Mothakes In Sparta, youths from families too poor to pay the agoge fees, who were sponsored by other Spartiates. The status carried no stigma after attaining citizenship; and many famous Spartans, including Lysander, were mothakes.

Paidagogos In Athens, a man, usually a slave, responsible for looking after school-aged boys—essentially, escorting them daily to the grammar master, the singing master, and the palaestra or gymnasium.

Paidono- mos The headmaster of the Spartan agoge.

Palaestra A public place for exercise, particularly wrestling.

Penteconter A single-decked, fifty-oared Greek warship, predecessor of the trireme.

Penteko- stus A unit of 100 to 200 men in the Spartan army; similar to a company in the army today, and hence often referred to as such in this series of novels.

Peplos The most common garment worn by women in Sparta at this period. It was basically a single rectangular cloth, folded vertically in half and sewn up the open side. It was held up by clasps over one shoulder or—if a hole for the second arm was made in the folded side—by clasps at each shoulder. Spartan women continued to wear this garment after it was out of fashion elsewhere, and the fact that it was left open from the thigh down for greater ease of motion earned them the (derogatory) epithet of "thigh throwers."

Peristyle A courtyard surrounded on all sides by a colonnaded walkway.

Perioikoi   A non-citizen resident of Lacedaemon. Like the helots, the perioikoi were descendants of the non-Greek native population of the area prior to the Dorian invasion of the Peloponnese in roughly 900 BC. The perioikoi enjoyed free status and ran their own affairs in their own towns and cities, but had no independent state, military, or foreign policy. The perioikoi–like the metics in other Greek cities–were required to pay taxes to the Lacedaemonian authorities. They also provided auxiliary troops to the Spartan army. Since Spartiates were prohibited from pursuing any profession or trade other than arms, the perioikoi had a (very lucrative) monopoly on all trade and manufacturing in Lacedaemon.

Phouxir   The "fox time," an uncertain period during a Spartan youth's upbringing when he was required to live "off the land" and outside of society. I have chosen to place this period at the end of boyhood and before youth and to fix the duration at forty days. Some historians believe it lasted as long as a year. It was during–and only during–this period that stealing by the boys was tolerated by society. Otherwise, stealing was considered demeaning–although, obviously, a skill once learned could be used again if detection was avoided.

Pilos   A felt cap worn under the Greek battle helmet, or as a head covering against the cold; also worn by helot attendants without helmets.

Polemarch   A military commander.

Spartiate   A full Spartan citizen; that is, the legitimate son of a Spartan citizen, who has successfully completed the agoge, served as an eirene, and been admitted to the citizen body at the age of twenty-one.

Stade   The length of the Olympic stadium. It was used to measure distances in ancient Hellas.

Stoa An open, roofed area supported by columns. In its simplest form, it is little more than a portico built against a building. More elaborate buildings, such as Pausanias describes in his travel guide to Greece, might have several rows of pillars. They could be round or rectangular in shape; and Pausanias reports on several of these structures in Sparta, most built at a later date than those described in this novel.

Symposium A dinner or drinking party, popular in Athens. These could include intellectual discourse or be characterized by erotic entertainment and excessive drinking—or both.

Syssitia Spartan messes or dining clubs. Adult Spartiates were all required to join one of the many existing syssitia when they attained citizenship at age twenty-one. Thereafter, they were required to dine at these messes nightly unless excused for such things as military duty, athletic competition, or hunting. The existing members of each syssitia had to vote unanimously to admit an applicant. Recent research suggests that membership in the various syssitia may have been based on family ties or clan relationships, but this is not certain. They were not, however, merely military messes based on military units, and they were explicitly designed to encourage men of different age cohorts to interact. Each member was required to make set contributions in kind (grain, wine, oil, and so on) and was expected to make other gifts, particularly game, in accordance with his means. Failure to pay the fees was grounds for loss of citizenship, and failure to attend the meals without a valid excuse could result in fines or other sanctions.

Thetes The lowest class of Athenian citizens, who, although they were freemen, generally owned no land and could not afford hoplite panoply, let alone horses. They manned Athens' fleet of triremes, receiving pay for this service, and also made up the majority of the bodies voting in the Assembly or serving as jurors in trials. At the start of the Peloponnesian War there were an estimated sixty thousand thetes in Athens.

ALSO BY
HELENA P. SCHRADER

This is Sparta—as you've never seen it before

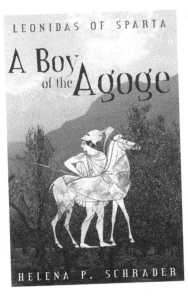

The smaller of twins, born long after two elder brothers, Leonidas was not raised as a prince, but rather had to endure the harsh upbringing of an ordinary Spartan youth. Barefoot, always a little hungry, and struggling to survive without disgrace, he never expected that one day he would be king or chosen to command the combined Greek forces fighting a Persian invasion. But these were formative years that would one day make him the most famous Spartan of them all: the hero of Thermopylae.

- Two cities at war;
- Two men with Olympic ambitions;
- And one slave–the finest charioteer in Greece.

This is the tale of one man's journey from tragedy to triumph–and the story of the founding of the first nonaggression pact in recorded history: the Peloponnesian League.

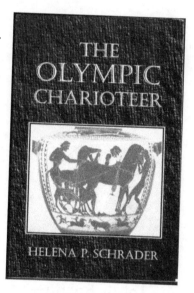

- A lame Athenian schoolmaster, sent to Sparta against his will—
- An ambitious Spartan officer, struggling to overcome the shame of his birth—
- And the widow of a hero, struggling to raise two young sons and a daughter in the midst of a vicious war—

These narrators tell the story of how the Spartans forged a revolutionary society under a radical new constitution after a period of unrest, and describe Sparta during the Second Messenian War.

Overnight, the beautiful Messenian princess Niobe and her disfigured slave Mika become captives of the dreaded Spartans. While Niobe's beauty attracts the attention of Prince Anaxilas, Mika is sent to work for an ordinary Spartan wife and her daughter, Kassia. Yet Niobe soon provokes the hostility of the Spartan queen, and Anaxilas turns his affections from Niobe to Kassia.

As the novel unfolds, the role of beauty and its impact on human interactions is explored, right up to the unexpected ending.

CPSIA information can be obtained
at www.ICGtesting.com
Printed in the USA
BVHW03s1618160318
510784BV00003B/280/P